Re

By Kal Spriggs

Published by Sutek Press

Kal

29 OCT 2016

Table of Contents

Part One

Deserter's Redemption
The Renegades, Book One
by Kal Spriggs

*Flames in microgravity had an indescribable beauty.
Mike watched the fire wash through the Noriko's bridge.
It crawled through the air like a living thing. It enveloped other
crewmen and turned them into shrieking sparks of fire. Like
some trapped and hungry predator, the fire came for him... came
to take his life.*

*Just before it reached him, he stepped backwards. He
fell, despite the lack of gravity. Then suddenly he hit the water.
Cold blackness enveloped him, and he could feel things slither
around him in the water...*

Mike let out a hoarse scream as he awoke. For a
moment, he thought his capture by the Chxor was an extension
of his nightmares; just one more horror among many, something
his mind must have fabricated. He wiped at the sweat that
soaked his face and felt the cool metal deck under his back.

The cold metal made him remember the tribunal, such as
it was, and the sentencing. The cold and emotionless Chxor had
sentenced him to a lifetime of prison labor. The steel prison that
held him and the other prisoners on Saragossa seemed more
difficult to picture. The Chxor had built the utilitarian structure
to process the conquered populace of the human world. *Well, the
populace and one random pilot in the wrong place at the wrong
time,* Mike thought with a sardonic smile. He could only vaguely
remember the prison after the tribunal and then how the other
prisoners had begun to fall...

They gassed us, he realized. It made sense. Mike figured
it would be easier to move potentially dangerous prisoners that
way, especially when the prisoners knew their final destination
would be one of the infamous Chxor work camps. Mike stared
up at the metal plating overhead and felt the thrum of a ship's
engines beneath him. The noise and vibration told him he was
aboard a ship.

If they had transported him by ship, his camp probably

3

lay off-world. He felt a sliver of hope that he would not work himself to death at a quarry or digging ditches. The Chxor death camps had obtained an almost mythical status of misery amongst the Colonial Republic. Not that he had ever expected to be sent to one, or even to encounter Chxor, not since his unorthodox departure from the Republic Liberation Fleet.

He ran a hand through his close-cropped jet black hair and rubbed at his eyes. His black eyes took a long moment to adjust to the dim light. Mike sat up and looked around the dingy compartment. The small cargo bay stretched ten meters long and three meters wide. The light came from a portable electric lantern. Mike lay at the middle of a line of figures that extended down the center of the bay.

He saw a hatch on each of the long walls of the hold. One door was clearly a pressure hatch to the exterior, complete with a green and red light to show whether or not the ship had a good seal, the other hatch presumably led deeper into the ship. Mike judged from the size of the bay that the door probably led to whatever passed for an engine room, and from there to the cockpit. It could not be a large ship, he figured, not with the noise from the machinery so close, and not with such a small cargo hold.

He stood up and went to look at the inner hatch. He saw no sign of the controls or any other means to open it. That did not surprise him, really. They would not put prisoners in an unsecured bay.

He glanced at the outer hatch. *Well, no means to escape it alive,* he corrected. The emergency release near the hatch would open it, but it would also vent them all into space- if the red light over the door indicated danger to the Chxor as it did to humans.

"I would stay away from that door," a deep voice growled from the corner.

Mike jumped into the air, startled. He spun around. He frantically searched for the source of the voice, but it took him a long moment to make out the dark form that loomed in the shadows of the corner. Initially, he felt a wave of relief because he thought he had gone mad.

The relief faded when he made out the shape. Panic replaced relief as the Wrethe emerged from the depths of the shadows. "Yes, human, fear me," the alien growled, his voice a deep baritone that Mike could feel in his chest. Like most Wrethe, thick hair covered his entire body. He stood tall, taller than most Wrethe that Mike had encountered, yet he had a lean look. His thick fur had the same dark color as empty space and almost seemed to absorb the light. Lean muscle rippled under his fur. He stood bipedal, with a long black tail that hung behind him. His jaws gaped in either a smile or a snarl in some terrible combination of hunger and humor. His jackal head pointed straight at Mike. The Wrethe's small dark eyes seemed little more than two inky pits of deeper darkness against his black fur. Anger and hunger lurked there, and a dreadful intelligence that saw Mike as merely food that could reason.

Mike felt his stomach twist and sweat break out on his forehead. The sudden, visceral realization that he shared the small space with a creature that could end his life struck him like a knife in the gut. Even so, Mike felt something force his spine ramrod straight; some instinct drove him to match the predatory stare and not retreat a single inch.

"You easily could have killed me before. You haven't -- so either you want something or you don't feel like killing. I've never heard of a Wrethe that didn't feel like killing, so that means you want something."

Mike's meager height didn't come near the Wrethe's two meters, but he stood as tall as he could anyway.

The Wrethe barked and his lips drew back in a snarl, "So you've got a bit of spine. Good. Perhaps you have some worth. We will see about the others."

"Since when does a human have to prove anything to a Wrethe?" Mike said. "As I remember, we've won all of the wars that your race started." He felt some of his confidence return with that knowledge. "No... you will have to prove your worth to me, especially if you want to escape."

"I can kill you if you try to leave me behind," the Wrethe

said, "Along with whatever stands in my way when I make my move. The question you should ask is what skills do you possess that will make *me* want to let you live?"

"If we go down this road, *dog*, you won't like where it leads," Mike sneered. He used the insulting slang intentionally. He saw the Wrethe's hackles go up at the word. *Good, so it knows enough about Humanity to hate the implication of the racial slur,* Mike thought. *That means he's worked with humans before, or fought them.* "I'm no physical match for you, but I refuse to play dominance games. I say we call a truce... You might as well acknowledge that the others won't follow a Wrethe, not without you having to watch your back for a knife and Wrethe or not, you have to sleep eventually."

"I'm listening," the Wrethe said, his deep baritone growl sounded slightly less hostile. Mike hoped that meant he had the Wrethe pondering more than just its hunger.

"We set up a deal right now... I do the talking, while you pretend to be just muscle. In return, I'll consult with you before we make decisions. You gain protection because the others will underestimate you, and you'll have my assistance," Mike said. He fought the urge to lick his lips as the Wrethe stepped closer.

"A good plan... but you don't seem to be one that I could manipulate from behind the scenes," the Wrethe said, "Why shouldn't I just kill you and propose that to a more... malleable subject?"

Mike felt sweat start to bead on his forehead. He forced himself to keep his voice level and meet the Wrethe's dark gaze. "You're smart enough to know that you don't know everything. You need someone who can talk fast, who can think on his feet, who can manipulate the emotions of others, and who would make a good partner. Frankly... *you* need *me*... partner."

"Partner..." the Wrethe seemed to chew on that word. The alien's lips drew back from his teeth, as if it disliked the taste in its mouth. Its fur rippled as if it felt uncomfortable. "Very well... *partner.* You have a deal. That is, until a better one comes along."

"Good to know," Mike answered as he held out his hand,

"I'm Mike."

The Wrethe stared down at his hand for a moment that seemed to stretch to infinity. Something uncomfortably close to hunger lurked in its eyes. Mike felt his heart race as the Wrethe stood in motionless contemplation. Finally, however, it extended its own hand to take his, and Mike saw with relief that its talons remained sheathed. "I am called Anubus by your kind."

"Fitting," Mike said, and tried to restrain an eye-roll. Just like a Wrethe to pick such a name, vicious and cruel. Mike had encountered a few that used names of human gods--or variations thereof--before. They seemed to get off on that sort of thing. Mike stepped back as he asked, "So, Anubus, do you have any skills besides taking people apart with your claws?"

"That's is both a survival trait and something I enjoy," Anubus answered. His bared teeth made it clear that he would demonstrate if given the opportunity. "I also know how to pilot a small vessel... though I don't know how to conduct Shadow Space navigation," Anubus said. "And as you noticed... I can be very stealthy."

Mike gave the Wrethe a nod, "Yeah, you can say that again."

"Excuse me?" Anubus said.

"Figure of speech, it means you made an understatement," Mike answered. "It is an archaic human phrase."

"Whatever," Anubus said as it shifted back into its corner. "I've kept watch since the Chxor gassed the rest of you. They transferred us from a Shadow Space transport to this vessel after a short jump. We've been under way for over twenty hours since then."

"The gas they used doesn't affect Wrethe?" Mike asked.

Anubus shrugged, "You ask a lot of questions, human. I remained awake. Now I am tired, so I will sleep... unless you wish me to renew my energy in another manner... perhaps by eating?"

"Is there food?" Mike asked

"For you... there's a bucket of gruel. For me... well,

7

there's plenty of meat available, but I'll restrain myself... for now."

"I appreciate that," Mike said wryly. "We might need these others."

"We'll see," Anubus muttered.

Mike didn't have long to wait before one of the other prisoners began to stir. The young woman did not seem troubled by the same nightmare that shocked Mike into awareness. The tall, blonde woman had a broad smile on her face with no sign of Mike's panic. When she opened her eyes and sat up, she looked as relaxed and at ease as if she had awakened in a luxurious hotel.

She looked over at Mike, "Hello!" Her bright blue eyes and broad smile made his heart flutter. He smiled in return, yet at the same time, it gave him considerable pause. Mike had dealt with his share of crazies in his life and her happiness under such dour circumstances suggested he add her to that list. She stood up, and looked over towards the corner.

"A Wrethe, how interesting!"

"Uh..." Mike immediately thought of Anubus's threat to eat him.

She turned back to Mike, and extended her hand, "I'm Ariadne Hutchins. Pleased to meet you." She wore a battered civilian ship's uniform, though someone had torn the ship's patch off the shoulder.

He started to extend his hand, "Mike Golemon." As the words left his mouth, he realized he had given her the name of a dead man....

***

"Spacer Second Class Mike Golemon, duty position helmsman," Mike identified himself as the hatch of the escape pod opened. He felt like nineteen years hadn't lasted nearly long enough as he stared into the barrels of the raised weapons. It took Mike a long moment to realize that they didn't wear RLF uniforms or even any uniform at all. The woman and two men

8

wore battered environmental suits, with multiple patches and what looked like custom repairs. They bore a mix of weapons, too. The three firearms aimed at him appeared pieced together from scrap, though the battered condition of their weapons did little to reassure Mike.

The woman snorted, "Well, crap; we have ourselves a survivor," She gave an exasperated sigh, "I figured you'd all have done the decent thing and died already. At least it's just the one, less effort to space him if he gives us trouble." She looked over at her companion, "Jessi, check the supplies and the power level, lets see what is worth taking."

Jessi nodded, "Aye, Captain."

"Excuse me?" Mike asked.

The woman glanced at him, "Shut up, kid, I'm doing business here." She spoke absently, almost as if she didn't consider Mike to be even worth the thought. She tapped the other man on the shoulder, "Roger, get back up to the bridge and scout out the debris cluster. See if there are other transponders, where there are transponders, there's power, and where there's power... we might find some good salvage."

The woman turned back to Mike, "Okay, Golemon, what ship was this, and did it carry any cargo?"

"Cargo?" Mike asked. "Am I a prisoner of war? Are you pirates?"

The woman gave a snort, "Nope, just salvagers." She had a rough face, one that had seen hardship and it showed in every line, seam, and gray hair.

Mike straightened up, "I'm not required to give you any more information: not to a scavenger like you, come to pick over the dead."

The woman stepped forward and seized Mike by the collar. "Listen up you self-righteous little prick! I just burned three hours of fuel to pick you up. Your pod's been out here, what? Three, maybe four weeks? You're low on food, air, and water, and if you had even one more person you'd both be dead. Whatever faction of the RLF you served abandoned you here -- left you and your fellow crew-mates to die."

Mike looked away at that. She had echoed the very thoughts that had run through his head over the past few days.

"Ah! You know I'm right, don't you?" She gave him a harsh smile. "Nothing to do out here but think, I bet, and you must have been able to hear those bastards in suits as they gasped out their last." She glanced at the pod's radio. "Did they damn you, with their last breath? Did they beg for help that never came? How many did you hear grow weak and then fade over the days, while you watched your own supplies dwindle?"

Mike shuddered as she brought back the memories, "What do you want?"

"It's not what I want," the woman said. She had a strange accent, one that suggested she came from a backwards world on the edge of space, "But what you need. You've seen that the RLF doesn't give a shit about their people. Ship with a pod like this, must have been a cruiser, maybe an armed merchantman... Ship like that would have escorts. They left you, abandoned you. You need someplace, a new start. You go back to them and they'll hang you for desertion as likely as they'll welcome you..." She gave him a hard smile, "Come to think of it, one man in a pod like this, they probably have reason."

Mike couldn't force himself to meet her eyes.

"You're alone now, with nothing and no one to have your back out here in the depths of space. You need friends, Golemon. Friends can help you get a new name, new identity. Friends can put you down on a world where they won't care what uniform you wore so long as you can pilot. You're a helmsman, right? That kind of skill could get you a place on almost any kind of ship," she leaned in close, "So, you aren't going to be Spacer Second Class Golemon, anymore are you? Golemon died with that ship out there. You want to be one of us, right? You want Captain Flynn to like you?" She waited for his nod, "Good lad! Now tell me, what was the ship's cargo?"

Mike told her everything he knew. Mike's shaken loyalty to the Shogun and the vision of a united and strong Colonial Republic didn't die, it just didn't matter, not any more. He told her because she was right, Mike Golemon had died with the RLF

Noriko.

It couldn't be any other way.

***

Mike snapped out of his reverie. He could see a slight frown on Ariadne's face, and Mike wondered how long he had remained motionless. He must look like some kind of idiot with his hand extended while he stood trapped in his memories. *I haven't thought of Captain Flynn in years*, Mike realized, *must be an aftereffect of the gas.* Mike gave her a practiced smile and clasped her extended hand. She had smooth hands, yet he felt a solid strength to her grip – one that suggested she had an iron will underneath her sunny exterior.

"Good to meet you Mike," Ariadne said. She held his hand for a moment, and cocked her head at him, "You're former military, aren't you?"

Mike felt an icy shock wash over him, "How would you--"

"The way you stand. You're uneasy... nervous... so your old habits surfaced, I think. You're almost at parade rest. Enlisted, right?"

"Yes..." Mike's eyes narrowed, "You seem to know an awful lot for a, what is it you do again, Miss Ariadne?" *Dammit, now that she mentioned it, I have reverted to military forms, next thing I know I'll call her ma'am,* he thought darkly. It must come from his use of his former name, nothing else made sense.

She gave him yet another sunny smile, "Oh, I'm a navigator and pilot. I'm not classically trained, though. I mostly go by intuition. I'm pretty good at that, if I do say so."

"Right," Mike stepped back. He had to hide a wince at the thought of what mistakes a self-trained navigator might make with Shadow Space. Clearly her attitude indicated some emotional instability. He could not think of anyone desperate enough to use an untrained navigator.

"You think I'm crazy?" Ariadne gave a laugh, "I get that a lot. I'm not insane though, I'm just psychic."

"A psychic?" Mike stared at her with wide eyes and open mouth. He would have been less surprised if she had claimed to be the Emperor of Nova Roma. His next thought was that she must be a liar or a con artist. He remembered the last man who claimed to be a psychic navigator, and how near that ship had come to destruction based on his input.

"Now we come to the tedium of explanations and arguments..." She shrugged. "How about I just demonstrate?" She held up a hand, as if she held something delicate. A flaming sphere five inches across suddenly leapt into existence. "Enough parlor tricks, for now?"

Mike licked his lips, "Uh..." He felt suddenly overwhelmed. So far he shared the compartment with a insane psychic and a homicidal Wrethe. Here he was, the least dangerous one in the room. "Sure." Mike focused hard to keep his voice level. He tried to ignore the acid burn of fear in his stomach.

"Good." Her smile held only good cheer, yet that gave Mike no sense of ease. "Now the Ghornath down at the end looks to be stirring. I shipped out with him from Vega. He's a good enough fellow, but he's got a bit of a temper."

"Of course," Mike said and he rubbed at his eyes. He had a nut-job psychic and a Wrethe, why not a three hundred kilo Ghornath with anger management issues?

"One thing, Mike... I recommend you don't steal anything or pick on anyone. He doesn't like thieves and he *hates* bullies," she said.

"Noted," Mike said. He sighed a bit as he walked away from Ariadne. *Why are things never easy?* he thought grimly.

The gas seemed to have affected the Ghornath in a similar fashion to Mike. He thrashed and shook violently as he began to wake. Finally the big alien gave a shout in his native tongue and sat up. A riot of colors flashed over his hide, before they settled on a deep red. He looked at Mike, and for a second his mirror-tinted eyes seemed to see someone or something he hated. His mouth opened in a shout, and his arms went forward.

Mike backpedaled as fast as he could. The big Ghornath

hesitated, then – a moment later, the red that had suffused his skin began to shift towards brown. Mike remembered then that he had heard the Ghornath tended to display emotions through their skin colors. "My apologies, human, for a moment, I thought myself... somewhere else." The big alien looked around. "Though whether this place is any better, I cannot say." The Ghornath looked over at Mike, "Where are we?"

"A small ship, headed towards one of the Chxor prison camps, probably a mining or salvage station," Mike said. "Though I don't know what star system." Mike looked the Ghornath over. He seemed big enough, yet something about him seemed young, almost naive. The eight-limbed alien had to almost squat in order to stand erect in the low cargo hold. Then again, at three meters height, he probably needed to hunch over in most places. The Ghornath wore a similar ship's uniform to Ariadne's though his bore rather more tears and... what looked suspiciously like bloodstains. Mike didn't notice any obvious wounds, though, and the big alien stood on his four legs without sign of injury. "I'm planning an escape, you want in?"

The big Ghornath gave a slow nod. "Yes. Though I might find it safer in Chxor custody." Mike saw the big alien flex his four arms as if to relieve stiffness.

"Safer?" Mike stared at the Ghornath. "We're headed for a death camp. You do realize that the Chxor will work us until we die of exhaustion or get killed in some horrific industrial accident, right?" Like the rest of the Ghornath race, his face reminded Mike vaguely of that of a cat, with the flattened nose and the shape of his lips. The long incisors went a good distance to reinforce the look as well. Mike remembered that spacer slang labeled them cats, just as Wrethe had obtained the moniker of dogs. With eight limbs, thick leathery hide, and eyes like two polished hematite stones, the Ghornath did not look like anything from Earth, much less like a house cat, to Mike: he looked alien.

"I grew up in a refugee camp, human," the Ghornath said. "I know something of the hazards of living in a place where few care about your survival." He shook his head, "But I refuse to let the Chxor break me of my will to live. I will help you to escape,

13

and we'll see where that takes us. I expect it will be a lot of fun."

"Fun? Right..." Mike shook his head. He looked over at the psychic, and saw her in conversation with a pair of men who had awoken while Mike spoke with with the Ghornath. "Alright, big fella, my name's Mike. Stick with me, and we'll get out of this alive."

"Of course," The Ghornath said and his belief in their ultimate victory came through in his voice. "I am Rastar. It is good to meet you, Mike."

Mike walked over towards Ariadne and the newly awakened men. Mike's studied the closer man as he approached. The tall, dark haired man had a sharp, chiseled jaw line and a confident smile that made Mike want to punch him in the face. He also stood balanced on his feet, as if ready to move instantly, yet he also seemed perfectly at ease. As Mike drew nearer, Ariadne looked up with her bright smile, "Mike, this is Crowe and this is Pixel." She pointed first at the handsome man, then at the other man who stood behind. "Crowe used to be a communications specialist aboard a freighter, while Pixel is an engineer."

"Ship's engineer?" Mike asked. He deliberately ignored the handsome man she'd introduced as Crowe. Something of Crowe's smirk suggested he caught the slight and took amusement from it.

The tall engineer shrugged, "I know a bit about it. I have graduate degrees in Aerospace and Power Engineering, and I paid my way on a couple freighters by lending a hand." He had a Colonial Republic accent, though Mike found it hard to place which system or even sector he might come from. He also wore a set of coveralls, with numerous oil stains. Mike frowned. He noticed that Pixel had not mentioned where he obtained his degrees. Plenty of people bought their degrees in the Colonial Republic. For that matter, Mike's 'official' pilot's license had come from a back room deal. "Okay, well we can certainly use the help. Anything you can do here?"

Pixel nodded over at the box in the corner. "I think that's the air scrubber. I might be able to scavenge some parts off of it."

"You know... if you break that, we suffocate," Mike said. "That's a bad way to die, friend."

"Oh, I won't break anything I can't fix," Pixel said with a smile. Mike studied him for a long moment. The tall, slender man seemed friendly enough, yet Mike didn't trust his quick offer to help. The engineer had a bit of unshaven scruff on his chin. Whether it was a deliberate attempt to grow a goatee or just a poor job with a razor, Mike couldn't guess which. His brown hair had an unkempt, scattered look. His blue eyes seemed level, though, and Mike felt akin to the humor and intelligence he saw there. Despite himself, Mike gave the other man a grin in return.

Pixel didn't seem to have any tools, and Mike didn't think he could get in much trouble without those at least. "Very well, give it a try."

Pixel moved off and Mike turned his attention to Crowe. The tall, handsome man looked down at him with a smug smile that made Mike's hands clench into fists. "Ship's communications, huh?"

Crowe smirked, "Yeah, and a few other skills. You know, things I've picked up here and there." He had such a tone of condescension that Mike had to bite back a retort.

Mike just gave the other man another of his practiced smiles and turned his attention to the remaining prisoners. Only two remained unconscious. The first was another human male and the second a diminutive Chxor. Mike had no idea what kind of crime a Chxor must have committed to end up with them, but he would not wager much, if anything, on the alien's survival. *Especially given the fact that I might just kill the damned thing myself,* Mike thought.

"Hey Mike, do you know where the rest of the food is? I only saw the one bowl," Rastar said from behind him. Mike turned and found Rastar had the bucket of food in one of his four arms, while another arm shoveled some kind of grain mush into his mouth.

"That was for all of us," Mike said with an exasperated sigh. "And we don't know how long it needs to last so we should

15

ration it."

Rastar looked down at the bucket, "Just this little bit? Are you sure? I mean, I need to eat a lot, you know."

"Yes, I'm sure," Mike said as he covered his eyes. He really did not want to hear the answer he expected to his next question. He asked anyway, "How much is left?"

"Uh..." Rastar passed over the bucket. Mike took it and looked in. He had no idea how full the Chxor had left it, but only about two or three cups of grain mush remained at the very bottom.

Mike sighed, "Well it didn't look very good anyway." He crinkled his nose at the smell, "What is this stuff anyway?"

"Mratha rice," Rastar said. "It grows just about anywhere, man. It keeps forever, too. Tastes like, uh, cardboard. We had to eat lots of it back at the refugee camps on Ghren."

"Right," Mike said. "Well... see if anyone else wants some."

"Sure!" Rastar said. The big alien looked at Ariadne and Crowe first, both of whom shook their heads. Then he walked towards where Anubus skulked in the corner.

Mike opened his mouth to stop him, but then shook his head. If his experience told him anything, then a conflict between the two big aliens would happen sooner rather than later. *Besides,* he thought, *my life would be much easier if the Ghornath managed to kill the Wrethe.* Not that he'd bet either way, he acknowledged. Rastar seemed too easygoing to be a real fighter.

Rastar walked right up to Anubus, "Hi there."

Anubus opened a single dark eye, "Go away."

"Hey, I just wanted to see if you wanted some food," Rastar extended his bucket.

The Wrethe did not move, but his deep voice growled, "I very much do... but I think you're too big to eat in just one sitting."

"Hey, man! That's not very polite! I'm just trying to be friendly," Rastar said.

16

"Do it somewhere else," Anubus said with a venomous snarl. "Or I'll rip your arm off and feed it to you." Mike waited... almost certain that the fight would begin at any moment. Mike glanced for someplace to withdraw. He felt somehow certain that this would become very ugly, very fast.

The Ghornath's hide shifted: first to a light shade of red, and then over towards green. His voice changed to an almost amused tone, "Hey, I get you man." Rastar slapped Anubus on the shoulder in a friendly fashion. "You just don't like being bothered. No problem, we'll talk later."

Mike shook his head as the Ghornath walked away. He glanced over at the others, none of whom seemed ready to hazard a guess on why the two aliens hadn't murdered one another. Mike started to turn his head when he noticed movement near the back of the bay. "What the..."

The little Chxor stood near Pixel. Mike shouted a warning, but Pixel just looked up with a confused expression. "Behind you, that Chxor!"

"Oh him?" Pixel asked. He hiked a thumb over his shoulder, "He offered to help." The tall engineer seemed confused.

"He offered to help?" Mike asked.

"Yeah, he seems alright," Pixel said.

The little Chxor looked around the tall engineer and gave a wave. Mike walked over, "Who are you and why are you here?" he snapped. He might have to tolerate a Wrethe and the overly relaxed Ghornath, but he would not accept a member of the race that had imprisoned him.

"Run!" the little Chxor squeaked.

"Run?" Mike asked.

"Yes, Run!" the Chxor responded.

"There's nowhere to run, so why don't you just answer my question, or are you saying you want to help us escape?"

"Escape, yes. Good idea." the Chxor said. "And we are not nowhere, we are here. Run is here." The little Chxor had the same gray skin and pale yellow eyes as the rest of his kind, but he seemed to lack their tan colored hair. Whether they'd shaved him or his bulbous head naturally had no hair Mike couldn't guess

"Stop speaking gibberish. Who are you?" Mike took a threatening step forward.

"Run!" The little Chxor hid behind Pixel.

"I think he means his name is Run," Ariadne said from behind them. Mike turned with a scowl, and she shrugged, "As amusing as I found it to watch you talk in circles initially, you started to grate on my nerves. There's no reason to threaten him, he looks pretty harmless."

"Yes, Run!" the Chxor shouted.

Mike took a deep breath and counted backwards from ten... in Mandarin. "Okay... his name is Run. He looks harmless, but that doesn't mean he's not a spy or that he won't turn informant on us to one of the guards."

"Not spy! Doctor!" Run said. He stepped out from behind Pixel. "I can help."

"A Chxor doctor?" Mike frowned. "I thought they didn't have doctors."

"I am a researcher – I seek ways to make people and inferior beings, better," Run said. "This is doctor, yes?"

"Make better, as in heal them?" Mike asked.

"Yes, and other things," Run said. "You will like, I promise."

"We'll see," Mike said. He looked over at Pixel, "You get to watch him."

"Watch him?" Pixel asked.

Mike closed his eyes and knew his expression would look pained. He wanted to explain to the engineer that just because the Chxor seemed nice enough, it didn't mean he wouldn't betray them at the drop of a hat. Then again, Mike didn't know if he trusted the engineer to watch anyone. *Come to think of it, I don't trust anyone in this room,* he thought. That realization put him back on an even keel once more. Since the destruction of the RLF *Noriko,* he had learned to put his trust in no one besides himself. This situation would prove no different. Trust would only mean that he would find disappointment in those he put his faith in, just like that last time.

Mike felt his tension ease as he returned to his normal mindset.

Almost as if on cue, a scream of terror erupted from behind him.

Mike spun, and he saw that all the attention in the compartment had gone to the final sleeper. The man screamed again from the floor, and then before anyone could move, he rolled backwards to his feet and spread his arms. He looked ready to fend off a wave of attackers. He stood still, eyes wide, and his head moved in quick, birdlike movements as he glanced from person to person in the room. "What's going on? Where am I?" The man wore black combat fatigues, but they'd clearly seen better days. One pant leg ended above the knee, and his right sleeve had similarly been torn off.

Mike held up his hands, "Calm down. We're on a Chxor prison transport, headed for one of their work camps." He took a slow step forward.

He heard Crowe mutter behind him, "Great way to convince someone to calm down. I hear Chxor prison camp and I just get all warm and fuzzy inside." Mike tuned out the other man's voice and concentrated on the panicked man.

His gaze flashed to Mike. Mike could see a rapid evaluation flash through his eyes. The stranger's hands clenched and unclenched in rapid movement. The way he moved reminded Mike of an animal show he'd watched once, about some small furry weasel that killed snakes back on Earth. "Don't come any closer. Who are you?" His words came quick, more like a rapid fire interrogation than a simple question. The tall man continued to scan the room.

Mike stopped, "I'm Mike. I'm not going to hurt you. I'm trying to set up an escape plan where we take this ship or we capture one when we get to the work camp." He noticed how the man shifted to keep the others in his peripheral vision. Military training, he guessed.

The other man stared at him for a long moment. Finally he dropped his hands, although Mike could tell he still seemed

19

on edge, "I like the sound of that."

"What's your name, soldier?" Mike asked

The other man stiffened, "I'm not a soldier... not anymore. I do... mercenary work now. I'm Eric, Eric Striker." He still didn't relax and his gaze flicked around the room. He stood around average height, with blond hair and blue eyes. Along with his accent, Mike placed him as from the Centauri Confederation; probably a descendent of the original German colony.

"Good to meet you, Eric," Mike said. He kept his distance though. The other man looked unstable enough that Mike did not want to provoke him. "You have military training... any shipboard skills?" Mercenary work covered a wide range of jobs too, from mall cops to paramilitary death squads.

"Give me any weapon, and I can use it," Eric said. The sheer arrogance in his voice gave Mike a spike of irrational anger. "But I'm a true artist with a scoped rifle."

Mike gave him a curt nod. *Great, just what we need, some sniper with a god complex...*

Mike looked around at the group. As he glanced at the others he felt a spurt of sudden envy. Why did he have to be the shortest man in the room? Even Ariadne stood a good four inches taller than him. Just another example of the universe's humor, Mike decided, along with his mostly Asian ancestry.

"Alright, we're all awake now; we've got three pilots, an engineer, a... navigator, someone to work communications, and some people good at breaking things. We've got a full crew, just about," Mike said. "Now we just need a plan to get out of here." He did not know why he did not reveal Ariadne as a psychic to the group, but he felt it best to keep that knowledge in reserve.

He did not know why he did not reveal Ariadne as a psychic to the group, but he felt it best to keep that knowledge in reserve.

"What about this door?" Crowe asked. He reached for the emergency release on the outer hatch.

"Stop!" Mike shouted. Crowe looked at him with puzzlement even as his hand continued its motion for the lever.

A black shadow moved faster than Mike's eyes could register and smashed into Crowe. He tumbled backwards with a cry of surprise. Anubus towered over the prone man and his deep voice spoke with calculated cruelty, "It would amuse me greatly to watch you expire from depressurization... but I might need you and the others."

"Idiot," Mike said. "If you had opened that you would have killed us all."

Crowe looked around at the others, "Oh. That's vacuum out there?"

"That's what the red light means, yes," Pixel said as he shook his head. "I thought you served aboard ship before, wouldn't you know better?

Crowe gave a cocky smile, "Oh, well... I guess the gas they used to knock us out must have muddled my head. I thought the light was green there for a moment."

Mike frowned in thought: in the moment that Anubus had hit him, something strange had flashed across Crowe's face. And as he stood up and looked around, Mike thought he saw a calculating look in his eyes, almost as if he were studying their reactions for some reason. Mike took the moment to study the other man. He wore a tattered ship's uniform of similar cut to the others. Clearly the Chxor had sorted them by their past careers, Mike noted. Yet the other man didn't have the normal pale complexion of most spacers. He stood tall, too, and without the slight hunch that living in tight confines gave most spacers. Despite his broad smile, his eyes seemed, cold, almost as cold and dark as those of Anubus, Mike realized. Mike had seen that kind of dark gaze in the mirror often enough to recognize the face of a man who had taken the lives of others.

"So our only way to take the ship is the inner door. We need to get it open," Mike said. "Does anyone have any ideas?"

"I can make an explosive," Eric said.

"What?" Mike froze in surprise. "Are you crazy? You could kill us all."

"Just a small one," Eric said, his Germanic accent thick. "Just a big enough bang to blast the lock off the door."

21

"The concussion could still kill us all," Mike said. Despite himself, he glanced over at the Chxor. "Run, what do you think?"

"Small bomb, we not die, I think," Run said. "But I stand behind the Ghornath."

"Thanks little guy, I appreciate the concern," Rastar said and to Mike he sounded totally sincere.

"I think he means he'll use you for cover," Ariadne informed him helpfully.

"Oh, well, he's small, I can understand that," Rastar said.

"Where will you get the materials for a bomb, anyway?" Mike asked.

"The chemicals in the air scrubber might work, and we can use the electric lantern as the casing, maybe even make a directional or shaped charge," Pixel said.

"Will that damage the air scrubber?" Mike asked. He had enough experience with suffocation to want to avoid it in the future.

"Well, we'll shut it off when we take it apart," Pixel said. "But I should be able to put it back together alright afterward."

"Do you even have any tools?" Mike asked. Pixel pulled a multi-tool out of his coveralls. "How did you smuggle that in... or do I even want to know?"

"Um, I had it in my inner pocket. I think they just didn't notice it," Pixel said. "It's my lucky multi-tool, too."

"Anyone else smuggle in anything useful?" Mike asked. He wondered why he had not thought of bribing the guards for something. *Oh yeah, I had nothing to offer, that's why*, he thought.

Ariadne produced a lighter. Mike raised an eyebrow, and he spoke in a low voice to her, "You can create fire with your mind, why do you need a lighter?"

"I like fire," Ariadne said.

"Anything else?" Mike asked of the others.

Crowe produced a shank, "I have a sheath on the inside of my thigh."

"You know how to use that?" Mike asked.

22

Crowe gave him an innocent expression, "You point it at someone and say bang, right? Oh wait, that's a gun, huh? I think I'm supposed to poke people with the pointy bit." Mike added that to the list of signs that suggested he needed to keep an eye on Crowe.

Mike looked over at the Wrethe. Anubus flexed his hands, and three inch claws emerged from inner sheaths. "I thought the Chxor would clip your claws or something."

"They did. They regrew. Another reason I'm hungry. Did I mention I get a bit irritable when I'm hungry?" Anubus asked.

"I offered you food," Rastar said helpfully.

"You *are* food," Anubus growled.

"Anyone else?" Mike interrupted.

"I have this!" Run said, triumphantly. He held up what looked like a small plastic pistol.

"What is that?" Rastar said.

"It makes people sleep," Run said.

"Nice," Eric said. "A tranquilizer pistol. Where'd you hide that?"

Run looked over at him. "I had it up my-"

"Alright," Mike interrupted, certain that the little Chxor would provide far too much information on the hiding spot for his pistol, "so we've got some weapons and tools, and something of a plan. Pixel, do you need any help with the air scrubber?"

"If Eric and Run will assist me, I think I can manage," he said. Mike wished he could read the engineer better. The man seemed confident enough, but if that was just a mask, he might well kill them all.

"We'll use less air if we don't move around. I suggest everyone rest up while they work, at least until Pixel gets the scrubber back online," Mike said. Even as he said it, he felt his stomach twist with anxiety. He hated having to be dependent upon other people's work, especially when he knew virtually nothing about the process. He fought down an urge to walk over and look over their shoulders. Instead he sat and leaned back against the cool metal bulkhead. He reviewed their resources, even as he pondered contingencies. If the air scrubber went out, they would have too many people breathing too little air. *Which of my fellow prisoners could I afford to do without?* he wondered. Even as he pondered that, he considered which ones might think of him as expendable. *Best not to get too comfortable with any of them.*

***

Mike's internal clock told him that four hours had passed by the time that Pixel and Eric went to stand in front of the inner hatch. Despite his own paranoia, he had slipped into a doze for much of the time. Even so, he awoke quickly. He rose and went to look over their shoulders. A reassuring hum emanated from the air scrubber in the corner.

"If we place it here," Pixel said. "We could cut through the power lock."

"I'm not sure how powerful this charge will be," Eric said. "I mean, the perchlorate purity is questionable at best..."

Mike consciously droned out the 'geek' talk. He looked at what remained of the lantern. They had rigged up the bulb from the lantern to a wire that led out of the air scrubber, he saw. The case looked no different, though a gray powder filled the clear plastic.

"The wall might be better," Pixel said after a moment of consideration. "If we cut the control lines for the door, the electronic lock may unlock as a safety measure."

"May?" Mike asked. "What do you know about this ship's systems, anyway?"

Pixel shrugged, "Well, most of the Chxor cargo ships are based off of copied human designs. We did so much more exploration before we found them. I imagine the safety protocols are similar."

"But can you find a control conduit from the far side of the wall?" Eric asked.

Pixel opened his mouth to answer but then he paused. After a moment he raised one hand as if he had an answer... and then shook his head. Finally he gave a shrug, "Maybe?"

"We only get one chance at this," Eric said. "Let the demolition expert handle this, alright?"

"Expert?" Mike asked. "I thought you were a sniper of some sort."

Eric twitched, "Well, yeah... but I know a lot about explosives too. I built this after all." He waved the improvised explosive device around. His too-quick motions made Mike uncomfortable, especially with a scratch-built bomb in his twitchy hands.

"Okay, fine," Pixel said. "Where do you want to put it?"

"Right here," Eric said, and pointed at the center of the door. "It should cut any mechanical lock, and then we can reach out to unlatch the hatch from the other side."

"Will it make that big a hole?" Mike asked.

"I'm almost entirely certain it will work," Eric said. Mike would have felt more confident but for the 'almost.'

"Go for it," Mike said. Mike backed to the far corner, grateful that at least he made a smaller target than the others. Well, except for Run, crouched down behind the big Ghornath.

Pixel and Eric came over a moment later. "I've run out these wires so that we can trigger it from a safe distance," Eric said. Pixel cleared his throat. "Alright, it was his idea," Eric rolled his eyes as he said it, as if to suggest he would have thought of that detail on his own.

"Will there be any fire?" Ariadne asked. If anything, she seemed unnaturally excited by the idea, Mike noted. *Great... a pyromaniac psychic,* Mike thought.

"There shouldn't be," Eric said. "Not if the charge works right."

"Oh," Ariadne sighed.

"Everyone get down, there may be some shrapnel and the concussion will be bad in this space," Eric said.

Mike knelt down. He grimaced as he covered his ears. He *really* hated this.

He saw Eric touch the wires in his hands. They waited a long moment. Mike withdrew his hands from his ears, "Well that was-"

The sharp detonation knocked Mike back on his ass. He felt the concussion drive through his body and shake his insides. His head rung and his vision seemed blurred.

A dense wave of smoke washed over the room, and a moment later, Mike saw a red glow of fire. He stumbled to his feet and headed towards the flame.

At the inner hatch he saw a large divot blown through the door, but only a couple inches wide. Blue-white sparks emanated from the hole, and the paint on the hatch had ignited. Mike saw Crowe run forward with the water bucket. "No, wait!"

Crowe skidded to a halt with the bucket ready to throw. "We have to put out the fire!"

Mike coughed against the dense black smoke. *Probably doing some terrible stuff to my lungs,* he thought. "It's an electrical fire. You could electrocute yourself or the rest of us. We need some other way to put it out."

A moment later, the air around him seemed to drop thirty degrees and the flames flickered and died. Mike stared with shock as the red edges of the hole cooled in seconds. He glanced over his shoulder and saw Ariadne with her eyes closed and a look of concentration on her face. He felt his jaw drop open, "How did you..."

She opened her eyes. For a moment, Mike could swear he saw the flames *behind* her eyes. "That was interesting." Her face had a look of intensity that made Mike shudder. Something just felt wrong about what she had done... even though she had saved their lives in the doing.

Mike looked back at the hole. A trail of sparks still sputtered from the severed power line. "Is the door safe to touch?" Mike asked.

Rastar the Ghornath walked up and reached out a hand. "It's cold... that's a pretty neat trick. I don't feel any shock or anything, I think the short is mostly grounded."

"If that was high voltage, you would be crispy right now," Pixel said.

Rastar shrugged, "It seemed safe enough. Besides, I'm

pretty tough."

"Electricity doesn't care how tough you are," Pixel said. "Enough amps and your heart stops." The engineer stared at Rastar for a long moment as if uncertain that the big alien really understood.

"I've got a very healthy constitution," Rastar said with a broad smile. He patted Pixel on the shoulder in a manner meant to reassure him.

"Back to the main issue," Mike said. "The short is in the area of the hole. And unless I'm mistaken, none of us could reach through such a small a hole safely anyway." He looked over his shoulder at Eric. "I thought you said this would work."

"It's not my fault," Eric said. "The stuff I had to work with... It's a measure of my skill that it worked at all." The mercenary gave a shrug, "It was a long shot anyway."

"What do we do if the crew heard that?" Crowe asked. "Maybe they'll come and investigate? Perhaps we can get one to open the door?"

"Other than the foul smell and the smoke, and the noise, I think this was a wonderful idea," Anubus said from his corner. "What will your next trick be?"

"Listen up you dog, I don't have to take that kind of thing from you," Eric snapped. "I don't see you doing anything besides standing there." The mercenary scowled at Anubus. His action seemed stupid to Mike, posturing that would merely provoke the Wrethe.

"Standing here, very calmly, not killing and eating you," Anubus said. He flexed his claws in a manner that suggested such restraint would not long continue.

Mike sighed. So much for his fellow prisoners' unity. His head hurt from the explosion and his ears still rung. "Look, it didn't work, whatever the reason. We need to focus on plan B."

"Plan B?" Ariadne asked.

"Yeah, we plan an escape from the camp," Mike said. "Which may well work better. We will have more people and more resources to work with."

27

"More chances for someone to rat us out," Crowe said with a grimace. "I suggest we stick together. The Chxor send all kinds to their work camps, and I'm sure there will be some who will try to alleviate their sentence through playing the informant."

"You seem to be a bit bitter about that," Mike said. He wondered at the source, if Crowe just had a thing against the Chxor and those humans who worked for them... or if he had more experience with prisons than he had let on.

Crowe shrugged, "I've reason." The dour scowl on his face made Mike smile. Perhaps it was just that something had removed the damned smirk off the other man's face. *Or maybe it's the thought that Crowe's fallen afoul of the law... it couldn't happen to a nicer fellow, I'm sure.*

"In any case," Mike said. "We need to hit the ground running once we get in. We need tools, allies and resources. Whatever we can get our hands on." He looked over at Pixel, "You take the lead on tools, anything you think we'll need, anything we can get access to, you tell us."

Pixel nodded. "I'll think about it."

"I could use a data slate," Crowe said. "I know a bit about hacking."

"You do?" Mike asked. He filed the information along with the other things he'd noticed about the 'communications specialist.' Crowe seemed to have more secrets than Mike and that made Mike very, very suspicious.

"Enough that I can cut through a Chxor system, I bet," Crowe said. "And I've got an implant to help out, if I can get access to their system with hard wire."

"A nanocomputer?" Pixel asked. "That's fascinating. How could you afford that, they're very expensive." The engineer frowned, "They're illegal in some places too, even the procedure to implant one."

"Oh, implants? Excellent, I must examine it!" Run said. The little alien rushed forward.

"You'd have to cut my head open to do that, you little twerp," Crowe said.

"Yes, when can I?"

"Over my dead body," Crowe snapped. He drew his shank again. "And if you get too close to me I'll make sure to open you up a bit."

"I find your behavior illogical and overly emotional," Run said his voice flat. "Examining your implant would be of great benefit to me in learning more about human anatomy and how cybernetics are implanted-"

"Later, alright?" Mike said. "Maybe when you have some equipment and a lab, huh?"

Run stared at Mike, "Promise?"

"I promise we can discuss it later," Mike said. He rolled his eyes. Why couldn't they have put him in a container with a criminal gang. He felt more like a babysitter than anything else. What he wouldn't do for a group of coldblooded killers who didn't like small talk.

***

Mike stepped out of the cargo bay, and into a large chamber. On the opposite side he saw another airlock. A conveyor belt ran right to the hatch and a pair of Chxor guards stood over a half dozen men who transferred heavy bars of steel from the belt to the cargo ship beyond the hatch. To his left and right he saw two other doors. One had a cluster of other prisoners around it as well as another pair of guards. The other had a conveyor belt that fed steel bars from elsewhere in the station.

A Chxor guard stepped in front of Mike, his weapon at the low ready. "Move along." He wore a drab set of body armor and Mike noticed patches of wire mesh over his vital areas. *Armor designed to protect against improvised weapons like knives,* he thought.

Mike headed towards the other prisoners. He glanced over his shoulder and saw the others follow him. *Lets see how long this partnership of ours lasts,* Mike wondered.

The prisoners formed into a line. He saw immediately

what had caused the holdup. The corridor beyond lay in microgravity, and the first prisoners to enter it had tumbled out of control. Mike would have found the scene comical, if not for the Chxor's weapons and their total lack of humor. It almost frightened a hysterical giggle out of him anyway when one of them began to push the most helpless prisoners down the hall.

When Mike reached the edge of the artificial gravity he made a smooth leap and drifted straight down the tube. At the far end he dropped lightly to his feet. To his disappointment the Chxor guard there did not seem impressed.

Mike gave a sigh. He joined the end of the line, and waited for his companions to arrive. Anubus and Ariadne managed the passage without difficulty. Eric tumbled through to the compartment and fell out of the air with a shout of dismay.

The others fell somewhere in between, though Pixel surprised Mike through his cautious movements. He obviously did not have microgravity experience, but he performed well enough despite that.

Ariadne moved up next to Mike, "That woman ahead of us is sick, she looks like she can barely stand."

Mike looked over at the woman. He saw the sick woman lean heavily on her companion. "Leave them be," Mike cautioned. "We don't want any attention. If we help them, we attract attention to them and to ourselves."

Ariadne frowned, "I can understand that, but I'm not sure that she'll make it to the front of the line, much less survive here without some medical attention."

"She'll have to," Mike said, and he nodded at where a line of Chxor guards waited to the side. "I don't think the Chxor care much about us, they'll care less about someone too weak to work."

Ariadne nodded. Even so, he saw her shift back in the line and speak with Run the Chxor. Mike guessed she hoped the self-proclaimed doctor would be able to help. Anubus moved up to stand behind Mike. For his size, he moved with abnormal quiet. He almost seemed like a living shadow more than a real person at times.

The line moved slowly. Mike took the time to glance around the room. At the front of the line he saw a cage, where a Chxor clerk took down information from the prisoners. Behind the Chxor clerk he saw an open door and some desks and other Chxor at work. To his left he saw processed prisoners cycled through an airlock with a green light above it. That boded ill for any escape attempt, he figured. If the compartment had an airlock, that meant the guards could vent it to space without any risk to themselves.

To his right, the Chxor guards stood and he saw another airlock beyond them, with a green light above it. He guessed it would be the station offices or perhaps the guards' living quarters. Off to the side, a corridor went down to another airlock, this one with a red light above the hatch. *Interesting,* he thought, *perhaps the Chxor crew shuttle docks there.*

The entire room had a crude, cheaply built appearance. The hatch welds looked rough, as if no one had bothered to grind them down. The hatch combings had sharp edges, and the lighting wiring lay exposed rather than behind panels or in a conduit. Dust and scuff marks also gave the area a dingy appearance, as though no one had bothered to clean it. He saw a couple lights burned out in one corner.

After he finished his study of the overall room, he turned his attention to the weapons and equipment of the Chxor guards. The nearest wore a riot gun; the pump action weapon would be ideal in a space station, he knew. The light pellets or flechettes would not penetrate the hull or damage essential equipment. He did not recognize the model, but it looked simple enough. Purely mechanical too, which gave him some hope. Many electronic guns had biometric safeties. Someone could work around that kind of thing eventually, but he didn't know how much time they would have.

The guards wore tactical armor, but it looked more worn than the room. They had body armor of the same color as the Chxor enforcers from Saragossa, Mike saw. The same muddy brown, with the odd purple highlights. On them, however, the muddy brown had faded almost to a tan color. One of them had a

31

large but neatly sewn patch of newer material on his chest, which made his armor look even more faded.

They did not have helmets, but all of them had emergency respirator masks on their belts. He also noticed several of them had grenades, though he doubted they were explosive or any type of plasma grenade, not aboard the station. More likely they had gas or riot grenades, he figured, or possibly some kind of flash or concussion grenades.

As he finished his evaluation of their equipment, the two women ahead of him reached the front of the line. He watched as they went forward.

"What is your prisoner code," the Chxor asked. His voice seemed even more robotic than most. His monotone had absolutely no inflection.

Both women gave their codes. Mike swallowed a curse and struggled to remember his. *Was it four nine five three eight or four nine three eight five...*

While the clerk typed the information into its datapad, Mike took the time to study the alien from up close. At first glance, like all Chxor, it bore a remarkably similar appearance to that of a human. It had two eyes, a nose and mouth, all roughly in the same location. Yet those features looked distorted on further inspection. Mike thought Chxor looked like a caricature of a human, with blocky heads, jug handle ears, and rubbery gray skin. "Do you have any skills with machinery, piloting, or metallurgy?" The clerk asked.

"No," the one woman said. Her friend swayed, and she reached out an arm to support her. "Look, my friend is sick, she needs medical attention."

"Is she unable to work?" the clerk asked.

"She can't function, not without help. Please, we just need some antibiotics. I think she's got food poisoning, please help her," the woman said.

The clerk looked over at the nearest guards. "This prisoner is unwell. I recommend removal so as to prevent contagion."

"Oh thank you..." The woman started.

The nearest guard stepped forward. Before Mike could move, the Chxor guard brought up his riot gun, worked the slide, and triggered a single round into the side of the sick woman's head. Mike stood frozen as blood, brains, and bits of bone exploded outwards.

The woman's friend let out a scream. A moment later she launched herself at the clerk. Her hands hammered the mesh as she screamed obscenities.

Mike stood frozen. He could not have moved if he wanted to, the sudden death for such a simple illness caught him entirely off guard.

The guard turned slightly and worked his slide again. The woman ceased her attack against the cage and turned to face the Chxor executioner. He triggered a single round into her chest. The woman dropped, to the floor, her chest and stomach ripped open. The copper smell of blood and stink of torn organs assaulted Mike's nose.

The woman moved, somehow still alive despite the terrible wound. She let out a cry somewhere between a whimper and a moan. The distinctive sound of the slide on his weapon cut through the otherwise total silence in the compartment. The guard triggered a second round into her head.

The guard turned to face Mike and Anubus. The Chxor's gray skin and yellow eyes showed no emotion. "Take the bodies towards the airlock," the Chxor guard said, his voice a monotone. He pointed at the airlock that Mike thought led into the administrative area of the station. Mike stepped forward, even as some part of his brain screamed at him to attack the alien guard. He tried to avoid the carnage, but despite his caution, he felt blood and other things squish beneath his boots. He grabbed a pair of legs by the feet, and started to drag the corpse. *Nothing I could have done,* he told himself. The thought gave him little solace.

Anubus grabbed the other by the arm and followed. The guard followed them to the airlock. Mike watched as the Chxor typed in a code. He did his best to memorize it, though he could not understand the Chxor numbers.

After the airlock opened, the Chxor gestured at a wheeled cart inside. Mike dragged the first woman over. It took an effort to get her lifted up and then to drop the corpse into the cart. He had seen his fair share of death, yet the casual execution of two people left him to feel cold. The Chxor, it seemed, did not value human life... not at all.

Behind him he heard a crunch. A glance over showed Anubus straightening up from the body of the second woman. Something red dripped from his jaws. Mike felt a wave of nausea. Evidently the Chxor were not the only ones with that opinion.

Anubus tossed the second body into the cart. Mike tried not to look for any missing pieces. He felt suddenly grateful for the fact that he had not eaten recently.

"Don't judge me," Anubus said. His voice sounded in a low growl. "She does not need the meat anymore." He gave a bark of his hideous laughter. "Besides, why do you think the Chxor have kept the bodies, instead of venting them out that other airlock? You don't give up free protein in space."

Mike shuddered at the thought that the Chxor might eat human dead. Then he frowned. "That doesn't make sense, the Chxor have a different physiology. They find most of our food toxic, right? We would not be much different. They're not like Wrethe, with your adaptive metabolism."

"Of course, human... but they have all these prisoners... it must save some money if they feed them their own dead, correct?" Anubus grinned.

Mike felt his stomach overturn. "You can't... that's horrible."

"Move back to the line, prisoners," the guard said.

Mike walked back in a daze. He saw the others had received cleaning supplies, but the mops just seemed to spread the blood rather than remove it. Mike took one of the towels and did his best to clean the blood off himself.

"Next," the clerk said.

Mike stepped forward. He felt sick to his stomach, ready to go into dry heaves, yet he felt certain that the Chxor would take this as some sign of disease and execute him on the spot. He swallowed a lot and tried to do multiplication tables to keep his mind occupied.

"Your prisoner code?" The clerk asked

Mike rattled off the five numbers without thought. They came to him automatically, as if such a mundane thing had come to the forefront of his brain as a result of the horrors.

"Do you have any skills with machinery, piloting, or metallurgy?" The clerk asked.

"I'm a trained pilot," Mike said. He kept his voice level and met the Chxor's eyes.

"You will be authorized to utilize the work sled. Be aware that the work sled will be destroyed if you attempt to leave the work area." The clerk made a note on his datapad. "Are you in good health and able to work?"

"Absolutely, I look forward to it," Mike said. He could not hide the sarcasm in his voice, nor did he really wish to do so.

"Excellent. The Empire welcomes such spirit," the clerk responded. He held out a neatly folded jumpsuit. "This suit will fit you. If you need any suit repairs, you may log that with Trustee Krain. You have four hours to recuperate from the trip before you start your first shift with Trustee Krain. He will instruct you on your duties and how to fill quota for the day. After your initial allotment, you will not receive your allotted food before you reach quota. You may go to the prisoner barracks now."

Mike took the suit and headed towards the indicated airlock, the one to the left, where the others had gone ahead.

He saw one of the guards pull down a lever. The airlock cycled open a moment later. *Controls on one side and the inner lock only I'd imagine, that will make things more difficult.*

He stepped into the airlock. A moment later, Anubus followed him. The guards cycled the airlock.

The corridor on the far side made the dingy processing room seem luxurious. Mike stepped out of the airlock and into the musty scent of too many unwashed bodies in a confined area. The foul stink suggested the Chxor had skimped on air scrubbers.

35

The handful of functional lights suggested they probably cut corners elsewhere as well.

Mike waited as the airlock cycled again, and then twice more. After the execution of the two women, he wanted as much companionship as he could get. He might not trust them, but at least they were human.

Run the Chxor walked up to him, "I had not realized the human body held so much fluids. How do you function like that? Do you slosh when you walk?"

Mostly human, anyway, he thought.

"I can't believe this," Ariadne said. "They just killed those two, with not a word of warning, and they didn't even do it as an example, they did it for no reason."

"We have to get out of here," Pixel said, his voice troubled. "I've got authorization for cutting tools and access to the smelter, wherever that is. What's the plan?"

As the others looked at him, Mike felt a sudden crush of pressure. They relied on him, they *trusted* him. That realization shocked him more than the deaths from minutes before. Total strangers – people who knew nothing about him – and they trusted him with their lives.

That trust cut both ways, he realized with a shock. That they trusted him meant that he had no choice but to include them in his plans, from the man-eater Wrethe to the Chxor outcast.

A part of him whispered that he should just cut them loose. Tell them now that they were on their own. Reject that responsibility and move on. He knew better than to trust in others. That road always led to pain and suffering – mostly his – but often enough those who had trusted him.

Yet, he couldn't. After the shock of the sudden death, he needed the comfort of companions. More, so long had passed since he had someone he could talk with, to share experiences with. He missed that, longed for it. It might end in failure... yet he had already lost so much.

How much lower can I go than a prisoner on a Chxor work station?

He knew there must be someplace worse, some position

worse off, yet he doubted he would find it any time soon and that assumed he even managed to survive to escape in the first place.

Besides, he thought, *I can always abandon them later if another option opens up.*

"Stick together," Mike said, his decision made, for the moment. "Find out everything we can. Priority is water, food, information, and tools."

The others nodded, all but Anubus. The big Wrethe had frozen and Mike saw his nostrils flare as he caught some scent.

"What is it?" Mike asked.

"There's another Wrethe here... and it staked its claim to this area. If we stay here long, I will have to kill it," Anubus said.

"Wait, Wrethe hate each other as much as they hate everyone else?" Crowe asked. "That's pretty funny. Didn't you guys invade human space a while back? I figure that takes some working together."

Anubus looked down at the man. "We follow a strong leader, especially when he has psychic abilities. Some Wrethe occasionally work for other races when they lack the intelligence to work on their own."

Mike declined to comment on Anubus's presence with the group. Instead he nodded, "I've seen an occasional Wrethe mercenary. They're real popular with gangs and other criminals."

"Okay, we'll be on the lookout for him," Ariadne said.

"Excuse me," a voice spoke from nearby. Mike spun, surprised that someone had approached without his notice. A man leaned against the wall nearby. He had a smirk on his face, "Mister Fontaine wants to talk with you."

"Mister Fontaine?" Mike asked. "Who's he?"

"He runs things, down here in the barracks. He can arrange things for you, if he likes," the man said. He gave them a more friendly smile. "And he's got a deal that might get you out of here."

"Oh?" Mike asked. "That's pretty convenient. Why is he here then?"

The other man's smile vanished. "Come or don't... but

37

take care not to say anything to offend him. He'll repay any insult."

"Very well," Mike glanced over his shoulder, "Lets go meet him."

"Not all of you," the man said. "Three of you are pilots, right? You can come. The rest of you... get lost."

"We all go or none of us," Ariadne said. Mike opened his mouth to deny that, yet he hesitated. She had a point, it would be too easy for this Fontaine to kidnap a pair of them. There was a strength in numbers, especially when Anubus warned of another Wrethe present.

The man hesitated. He looked them over, then gave a shrug. "Very well. But keep your pet Wrethe on a leash. If he starts anything, you'll all pay for it."

"I'll show you who the pet is..." Anubus muttered.

Mike shot him a glance, but the dark Wrethe met his look with one of barely controlled rage. He could not fault him that, not with the implied insult. For that matter, the emissary for this Fontaine had put him in a foul mood. "Okay, let's go meet Mister Fontaine."

***

The barracks room that Fontaine called home lay at the middle of the section of station. A pair of humans stood at the doorway. Mike did not see any obvious weapons, but both men looked tough enough to hold any unexpected company long enough for reinforcements from inside to ready themselves.

Their guide led them to the doorway, where he stopped and talked briefly with the larger of the pair. That guard stepped inside.

Mike turned to the other guard, "How you doing?"

The man stared at him with silent disinterest.

"Nice space suit you have, looks a little newer than mine," Mike said.

The guard just stared at him. Mike saw he had a tattoo, probably with smart ink, of a spider web or some strange symbol

38

on his neck. It glittered with iridescent colors.

"Hey, friend, you don't talk much, you can relax, you know, I don't bite." Mike grinned at the other man and slapped him on the shoulder. The guard didn't so much as flinch.

A hulking form stepped into the doorway. "I do."

Mike took a step back despite himself. He looked up at the large Wrethe, brown in color. He looked squat and more muscular than Anubus. A patchwork of long scars crossed his face and chest, some of them broad enough that Mike figured the Wrethe had lost two or three inches of skin. The fur in his scars had grown in at odd angles and some patches grew in lighter than the dark brown of the rest of him.

Even as it loomed over them, Mike saw its gaze go to Anubus. A growl, almost too deep for human ears to pick up, came from the Wrethe's throat.

"Ah, who are you, scar-face?" Mike asked. He didn't think any of them would survive the fight if the two Wrethe started it here.

The Wrethe stepped forward. He made no hostile move, he just got inside Mike's comfort zone. Way inside it, Mike realized, as he tried to backpedal. "I work for Mister Fontaine, that's all you need to know. Also, there are four pilots who came on the last transport. Mister Fontaine only needs one." The Wrethe turned away from Mike, and its gaze went to their escort. "Mister Fontaine told you to bring just the pilots. However, since you told them they could all come, that's put Mister Fontaine in a position where he has to honor your bargain, Ricky. You have Gerard's job now, understood?"

Their escort went pale, "The boss said to bring them..."

"And you did, which is why he didn't let me have you," the Wrethe growled. "Of course, if you fail Gerard's job, you won't have his protection anymore."

The Wrethe turned back to the group. "Follow me. And please, do something to piss off Mister Fontaine. I would love some fresh meat."

The Wrethe stepped through the doorway.

Mike followed. The barracks room beyond had a number

of blankets up to act as dividers, which formed a hallway that led to a larger area. As they past one, the curtain parted a bit and Mike saw a pair of scantily clad women. One of them had dark bruises along her arms and a black eye.

Mike grimaced and looked away. Either this Fontaine tolerated that sort of behavior from his men or did it himself. Whichever the case, Mike's expectations dropped sharply.

Three men sat in what looked like scavenged pilot seats in the area at the end of the corridor. A woman stood in front of them, but off to the side. She gave Mike and the others a quick glance before she returned her attention to the seated men. Mike recognized the seat from the one on the end as being from a Colonial Republic *Patriot* fighter. The center chair looked to have come from a larger ship, and the man who sat back in it looked like he claimed it more for the impressive size than for any preference of comfort. "Ah, welcome, my new friends." He was a small man, with an angular jaw, and dark brown eyes. He'd slicked his hair back somehow, and Mike thought it looked like he did it to cover a bald spot. That almost made Mike smile... until he met the man's gaze.

Mike felt cold all over as that gaze went over him. He remembered a man with a gaze like that. That kind of gaze came from someone without a soul, a person totally given to calculation of manipulation and personal benefit. Mike wondered if he would have to kill this man too.

"I take it you're Mister Fontaine?" Mike asked.

"Do you speak for these others, as well?" Fontaine asked. His gaze ranged across each of them. "Which of you are the pilots? The Wrethe, I know, and the woman, but who is the last?"

"That's me, I'm Mike Smith," Mike said.

"Ah, good," Fontaine said. He spoke with a distinct French accent, and a friendliness and joviality that set Mike's teeth on edge. "Let me explain things to you lovely people. I have made arrangements for a ship. In case you haven't figured it out, this is a salvage station. When the Trustees put you to work in a few hours, you'll see pieces of ships that we'll start to scavenge. We mine them for resources, which the Chxor then ship out when they have a worthy cargo. There's a thousand kilograms of osmium, a thousand of platinum, and four thousand of gold that the Chxor have stored up from our labor here. When I leave, I intend to bring that wealth."

"Why invite us?" the woman asked. Mike glanced over at her. She had a strange accent, and the darker cast to her skin suggested mixed heritage, not uncommon on some of the more remote colonies.

"Because my pilot suffered an unfortunate accident last week on his tug shift, and the only other pilots on the station are Chxor trustees," Fontaine said. "So this is your opportunity. I need at least one pilot, but I have room for a backup. You'll get a share of the wealth, and a very nice share that will make... yes?"

"What's the details?" Mike said. "How do you plan to escape, up the conveyor, into one of the ships?"

The seated man on Fontaine's left gave a laugh, "The conveyor is a certain route to death. That tunnel has the waste heat sinks for the station, average temperature is three hundred degrees Celsius. Last person that tried it came out a crispy skeleton."

Fontaine glanced at his assistant and gave a slight smile, "Thank you, Patrice, that will be quite enough. We wouldn't want to tell our new friends everything, now would we?"

The other man paled a bit, and Mike caught the implication. *Even his own men fear him,* Mike realized, *so not only is he a cold bastard, but perfectly capable of getting his hands dirty. He's not just propped up by his men's loyalty.*

"We need some details," Ariadne said from behind. She stepped forward to stand beside Mike, "What kind of ship, for one thing. A pilot won't be any good if she can't fly the ship you want her to fly." Mike shot her a suspicious glance. Had she decided to throw her lot in with Fontaine? Granted, it made sense to go with an established plan, but Mike did not trust the man, not with that cold look to his dark eyes. Especially not with how smoothly he talked.

When I talk like that, it means I don't care what I

promise, I'm lying to get what I want, especially when there's women or money involved, Mike thought. Come to think of it, he realized that Fontaine reminded him of himself. No wonder he hated the snake.

"The first ship will be a shuttle, the Chxor Warden's personal boat," Fontaine said slowly. Mike could see the other man's discomfort at the necessity to share such details. "The second will be a larger ship, with a Shadow Space drive. Are any of you navigators?"

Mike saw Ariadne open her mouth. "No," Mike interrupted. "We don't have a trained navigator." She looked over at him and frowned, but she gave a slight nod in agreement.

"I'm not certified, the female pilot said, "But I know how to put the coordinates in a computer, as long as you have a star map. And I'm in, I'm Cathy Motomi."

"Good," Fontaine said. "Glad to hear it. The rest of you have twelve hours to decide. After that, well... you'll be stuck here. And most people don't last over a year, especially without my protection."

"Would you have room for others?" Mike asked.

"Depends on their skills," Fontaine said. "I'll discuss that on a case-by-case basis. And frankly, it looks like Cathy here fits the best parameters. You'll have to convince me that I want you along."

"What happens if we threaten to tell the Chxor you're planning an escape?" Crowe asked. "I mean, that could get awkward for you right?" The big man had a smirk on his face, one that suggested he felt he'd found a solution to his problems.

Mike bit back a curse. *What was Crowe's problem? Didn't he realize that Fontaine had to have bribed at least some of the Chxor guards to get as far as he had?* Mike saw Fontaine raise his right hand, almost as if to give a signal, and then pause. Mike saw a faint glitter of color at his wrist, similar to the ones on the necks of the guards.

"I'm sure the Warden would find that very interesting, my friend," Fontaine said. "Which then leads to the question of whether I'd let you leave here alive at all, and if I did, which of the Chxor guards I'd have kill you. Or maybe I'd just arrange an accident for you in the Pit. Death by decompression is a terrible way to go. But at least that would not last long. If I let the Hun take you... well, my friend, that would last a very, very long time." The good humor in his voice made his threat that much more terrifying.

"The Hun?" Crowe asked. His face had gone pale and Mike saw him edge backwards, as if he thought to run. *Please don't,* Mike thought, *Fontaine's men will be on all of us then.*

"That's what I call my Wrethe friend here... he has terrible eating habits, he likes to play with his food before he eats it," Fontaine clucked in false disapproval. The Hun gave a wide, toothy, dog-like grin. Mike thought the temperature dropped a good twenty degrees with that smile. "A strong one like you might last a week or two. And the Hun doesn't like his meals reprocessed, like the rest of us. He likes his meat red and rare."

"We'll keep our mouths shut," Mike said. "Kid was stupid, just opened his mouth and put his foot in it. You don't need to worry about him or the rest of us. Either we'll work with you or we'll stay out of your way."

Fontaine's eyes snapped to Mike. "Good, Mike... Smith, was it? Rather bland name for you... but better than John, I suppose. Something I do wonder about, Asian fellow like you, how you got a name like Smith." Fontaine looked them all over again, and Mike saw his eyes linger on Crowe for a long moment. "You may go. Anyone who wants to talk with me, plead your case, can come by at your leisure. Cathy, you can stay, I'd like to discuss the details of our arrangement."

Mike didn't look over at the female pilot as he backed out. For one thing, he did not want to take his eyes off of Fontaine. For another, he figured that Fontaine would have her killed just as soon as she ceased to be vital for his survival. Better that she not seem human to Mike. He could not afford to pity her. She chose her fate.

After they stepped out into the hallway, Mike looked over at the others. "Let's find a set of bunks, shall we?" No one responded, but they followed him as he walked down the

43

corridor. He peered into two or three barracks rooms before he found an empty one. It lay at the end of the corridor, next to another airlock. Someone had painted 'The Pit' in lurid red paint across the hatch.

Mike threw his suit and helmet down on a bunk near the door. The others squeezed past him and chose their own bunks. The rectangular room looked more squeezed than the others he saw. The metal framed bunks each had a few millimeters thickness of foam and Mike did not see any blankets. A clatter and hum of machinery seemed to rattle at them through the deck plates, and suggested why this room sat empty.

Mike moved down to the end furthest from the door and gestured for everyone to come in. "Alright, in case anyone did not pick it up, Fontaine might have the best plan to get out, but he'll kill anyone who isn't one of his men. Those guards outside, they had gang tattoos, I didn't recognize them, but they matched one on Fontaine's wrist. He's got some serious criminal connections, I'd guess, and he's not going to cut some pilot or engineer in on it."

Ariadne nodded, "So I guessed. That's why I tried to find out more about his plan. We know it involves the Warden's shuttle, and another ship, maybe a smuggler's freighter he plans to meet with. He seemed to really want a pilot from that offer he made."

"Yeah, and a psychic navigator would have made his day." Mike frowned. "Glad you kept quiet on that?"

"I think that he noticed my hesitation," Ariadne said. "And I think he realized you hid something, which was why he threatened Crowe."

"Great, so you two got the psycho pissed at me," Crowe grimaced.

"No, you opening your mouth nearly got you and the rest of us dead," Mike said. "Fontaine was very close to having his goons come at us. When he lifted his hand, that signal would have brought his entire gang down on us."

"Oh," Crowe said. "I was just trying to find out what kind of resources he had, you know? Trying to figure out how connected he was." Crowe seemed so self assured once more that Mike wanted nothing more than to slap some sense into him.

"Regardless, we can't side with him," Anubus said. "I respect his acumen, but there's no way he'll take a second Wrethe. We'd have to fight it out for dominance, and I'm not sure I could take the Hun in a fair fight."

"Oh?" Mike asked. He felt surprise at the admission. Wrethe rarely, if ever, admitted to weakness, from his experience.

"I could kill the Hun, easily enough," Anubus said. "Actually I think it would be best, take out his strongest muscle. But I'm fast and sneaky, not pure muscle and toughness. I'd have to hit the Hun from behind and I'd have to kill it. Otherwise it would just challenge me later, when it knew it had the advantage."

"You Wrethe are psycho," Ariadne said. "How do a pair of you ever get together and make baby Wrethe?"

"We don't," Anubus said with a growl. "We self replicate and we control our genetic mutations to suit our needs and the survival of the species. And we remember mutations from other species we consume and other Wrethe we eat. So when I want to raise another army, I'll just plan a decade or two ahead."

"Wait, another army?" Pixel asked. "You've done that before? And how old are you?" The engineer looked fascinated. Mike found the idea disturbing himself. Particularly disturbing to think of Anubus with an army.

"Old enough," Anubus growled.

"Alright, back on subject," Mike said. "Anubus can't join him, Ariadne and I both realize we might as well sign our own death warrants. The rest of you..." He shrugged. "If you want to take your chances, go ahead, but I doubt you've any skills that he'll find worthwhile enough to bring you along and let you live afterward. He plans to rip the Chxor off for a couple hundred million of any currency you care to mention."

"So we're back to plan B... escape on our own," Eric said. "That's not much of a plan. Why don't we try to hijack his escape? Take his shuttle, catch his freighter." The mercenary grinned and his blue eyes almost seemed to glow with the thought of a fight.

"Uh, they've got goons, weapons and probably some Chxor guards on their side?" Pixel asked. He rubbed at his chin in thought. "We've got... precisely none of that."

"We've got a Wrethe, a big Ghornath, and me for fighting," Eric said. "Crowe said he knows how to use that shank of his. Plus we have psychic girl here, to do the whole fire thing. Plus we're together and no one knows our capabilities. Tactically we have an advantage, but that advantage goes away over time, especially if his escape goes down soon."

"If you're planning on taking down Fontaine, you should probably talk in a lower voice and watch your back," a voice said.

Mike's head snapped around. A man stood only a dozen feet behind Eric. He stood taller than any of the humans in the group, almost as tall as Anubus. "Who the hell are you?" Mike asked, even as he saw Crowe slip his shank out and slowly shift in the stranger's direction.

"I'm Simon," the man said. He shot a glance at Crowe. "And I'm no threat to you, though if he doesn't put that knife away I'll feed it to him."

"How do we know you aren't with Fontaine?" Mike asked suspiciously. As a matter of fact, the smartest thing for a man like Fontaine to do with a group of organized people new to his territory would be to send a mole.

"I'm something that Fontaine hates more than anything else," Simon said. "I'm a cop... well former cop. Worse, I was an honest cop."

"I didn't think those existed," Crowe said with a laugh, even as he put away his shank. "Sort of like Unicorns, Drop Bears, and Jesus Christ."

"I've seen a Unicorn before," Ariadne said. "And though I've never heard of a Drop Bear, I've a faith of my own that I'd prefer you not rag on others for theirs." She looked over at Simon, "I recognize that accent, you're from Centauri, or one of the Confederation's worlds. How'd you end up out here?"

He gave her a nod, "You're from Tau Ceti, right? Well, I suppose I can't hold that against you, I'm not too fond of the Confederation right now." He gave a grimace, "Well, I was involved in the Minister of Justice's investigation of some black government operation, around three months ago. Someone took out Minister Gunther with a high powered rifle right before we had our case all ready to go public. Right after that, my partner's car blew up, and what do you know, I'm suddenly the main suspect."

"So you end up on a Chxor prison station?" Mike asked. Out of the corner of his eyes he saw Eric move forward. He looked interested in the other man's story, or at least more than the others. Mike wondered about that, and why Eric had not spoken up about his own origins as a Centauri.

Simon shrugged, "There may have been a few other details in there, but why bore you? I took ship for the furthest planet I could, and my bad luck took me here." Simon gave a self depreciating grin. Mike studied the other man carefully. His tall, lean frame made him distinctive. His sharp features and stubbled jaw made him more so. He had an intensity about him that Mike liked. It suggested that this man was, above all else, a professional. Vastly different from the amateurs Mike had fallen in with.

"They accused you of bombing your partner, do you know bombs?" Eric asked.

Mike winced, *not this again*. He remembered the smoke and fire from Eric's last attempt. He did not want a repeat performance, especially not with a pair of them.

"Yeah, I spent a few years in police explosive ordinance disposal. We spend a lot more time than you'd expect building explosives, and learning about how to make them from scratch," Simon said. "Why do you ask?"

"I know a bit about explosives, mostly self taught, I was wondering if you could give me some pointers," Eric said.

"Yeah, sure," Simon nodded. "First one, one of the quickest ways I know to die is to be self taught with homemade explosives. Give up your hobby and leave it to the professionals... or do it somewhere far away from me. Because if I catch you anywhere near me with something like that I might well kill you myself."

Mike gave a snort, "You know, I think I like you. We could use a little common sense around here." Not that he really wanted a cop, even of the former type, around, but the man had already overheard enough that he could cause them problems. *Besides, if he prevents Eric from killing us all,* Mike thought, *he'll do more than I think I can manage on my own.*

"Good. You get any food yet?" Simon asked.

"Food would optimize my ability to function," Run said. Mike looked over at the little Chxor. He'd almost forgotten he existed. It seemed the little alien had an ability to blend in after all. "Are Chxor rations available?"

"We've heard... bad things about the food," Pixel said.

"Yeah, they reprocess our dead here. It's recycled protein, sterile and they put it through a biological process that makes it healthy enough. If you tell yourself that, you can choke down a few bites. They mix it in when rations get tight. But with the new shipment, if we time it right we can get just the grain mush."

"Mratha rice for everyone... hurray," Crowe said, his voice dry.

"You've... eaten?" Ariadne asked. Her face had gone green.

"I've been here long enough to do things I'm not proud of to survive," Simon said. "Eating the dead... well, that's not the worst. Pretty horrible, but not quite the worst."

"I don't want to know," Ariadne said. Mike saw her look away with a look of concentration on her face. He wondered at that, for she had spoken of her other mental abilities, but not any kind of mind reading. She almost looked as if she tried very hard *not* to look into his mind. Mike made a mental note to talk to her later, to see if she had abilities she had not wanted to share with the group.

"So what do you know about Fontaine's plan to escape?" Mike asked after a glance at the doorway to make certain they had some privacy.

"He's bribed the Warden and some of the Chxor guards. Pretty logical, on their perspective. This place is a dead end, punishment detail for all of them. I'd guess he has the schedules for supply ships as well as a way to escape the barracks when the time comes. I don't know more than that." Simon shrugged. "I will say that I'll be surprised if he doesn't have some kind of distraction planned, maybe even one that destroys the station after he's safely gone."

"Yeah..." Mike nodded. Something like that would cover Fontaine's tracks, much like his own distraction when he jumped ship back on Saragossa. For a moment, he felt a moment's pity for the crew of the ship, but he pushed that aside. They would have sided with the Captain... which meant they would have died anyway after they turned on Mike. "The Chxor won't know what happened if the station's destroyed and there are no witnesses. He might even abandon the Chxor Warden and the guards he's bribed."

Simon shrugged, "I don't know. I just know his type."

"Right," Mike nodded. He glanced around at the others. "We need to get more information and we need tools and weapons." He looked at Simon again. "The pit is where they haul in the salvage?"

Simon nodded.

"Once we get the opportunity, Pixel, I want you to get in there and see what tools you can get... and if there's anything we can salvage to make into weapons."

"Ariadne, you, Anubus and I will scope out these work sleds they mentioned. I doubt they've any legs on them, but we might be able to use them somehow," Mike said. He realized that he'd taken charge, but no one argued at the moment. *Count my blessings later,* he thought. "Rastar, and Eric, you two work with Simon, find out everything you can about the guards, how they're armed, and how they might react to whatever Fontaine has planned."

"Food, now?" Run asked.

"Yeah, let's get food... but someone needs to stand by

49

here to make sure no one messes with our suits," Mike said.

"I grabbed a bite earlier," Anubus said. "I'll wait here."

Mike felt his stomach overturn at the reminder. "Right." He wondered at Anubus's passivity at his orders until he glanced at the alien. The Wrethe's penetrating stare suggested it would have words with him when they had privacy.

He started to lead the way out, but Rastar the Ghornath put out a large arm and stepped in front of him. "Let me lead. If food is as precious as our new partner has suggested, it will be similar to the refugee camps I grew up in. I know how to handle this."

Mike frowned. They would go and get their food, probably under observation from the Chxor, how dangerous would it be? "Okay... sure."

Rastar led the way out of the compartment. Simon pointed the way back towards where they'd entered and then led the way into the room that lay nearest the airlock.

A cluster of people stood there, some in line, but most milled around. Some looked gaunt, on the edge of starvation. Many looked past that edge, and Mike looked away from the hollowness that lay in their eyes. Many of these people no longer lived, he realized. They'd found their own personal hell and while their bodies functioned, their souls had fled.

"Hold up there, big fella, you got to pay the toll before you get food," a man said. Mike saw the spider web tattoo on the side of his neck. *Right, of course Fontaine's men have a racket with the food,* he thought. After all, it wouldn't do for their boss to have to actually work.

"My friend, we just arrived," Rastar said. He had gone a light shade of pink, and he slapped the other man on the shoulder hard enough to stagger him. "What is this toll? Is it like a club membership?"

Mike saw the man reach inside his coveralls, but another man put a restraining hand on his shoulder. The other man spoke, "Sort of like that. You're the fellows that Mister Fontaine spoke with earlier, right?"

Mike spoke up, "Yeah, that's us."

"Well, then. Just for today, you don't have to pay, since you just got in. In the future, it's a ten percent by weight of your daily allotment... and it increases if you miss a day." The man said. "You can pay Armand here tomorrow morning. If you want a special deal, you talk to me, I'm Pierre"

"Does everyone pay, even the sick and weak?" Rastar asked. His skin shade had gone a deeper tone, almost red. Mike remembered then that Ghornath skin tones signaled their emotions. He also remembered this Ghornath had a temper. Mike wanted to say something, to interrupt, but he did not know if he might set the big alien off.

"Yeah, everyone pays... one way or another," Armand grinned evilly. "The woman there, she's pretty enough to pay her way on her back. You're not my type big guy, so you got to pay with food."

"I see," Rastar's skin had darkened, and Mike saw Pierre's eyes narrow as he put together the Ghornath's coloring and the topic of conversation. "What do we gain from this fee, then... your protection?" The Ghornath's deep voice had dropped an octave. Mike could almost feel it in his feet.

Mike grabbed Rastar's lower left limb, "Rastar, let's just go, alright." He did not want to start a riot, not with Fontaine's men, not right now when they didn't have any weapons.

"Yeah, maybe you should walk away... friend," Armand said.

"You are right." Rastar said. His skin darkened to a crimson, though, and Mike could feel the alien's muscles tense on his arm. "But if I did what I should do, then I would always wonder what this felt like."

Rastar's upper left arm came around in a huge fist. The blow caught Armand in the face and threw him back into the wall. A second later he surged forward at Pierre and the pair of men behind him.

Mike saw Pierre duck under one wild swing and saw him draw a shank out of his sleeve. He stabbed Rastar twice as he went by, but the Ghornath did not even slow. He snatched both the other goons, picked them up with two hands each, and slammed them together hard enough that they went limp in his hands.

Mike saw a half dozen more of Fontaine's men boil out of the crowd. He ducked under a wild swing from one and then let out a curse as another slashed a knife over the back of his hand.

He saw Crowe circle around behind that man, but before he could attack him, another tackled the bigger man. One of Fontaine's men leapt at Ariadne, but she dove to the side, and Mike saw him strike Eric instead.

The entire room dissolved into chaos. Rastar seemed to be at the middle of it, and his bellows of rage echoed off the walls as he threw men left and right. His four arms pummeled any of Fontaine's men too slow to escape him.

As a pair of armed men backed Mike against a wall, he shouted, "This is your idea of handling this?"

Rastar did not answer, but a body sailed through the air to knock both men over. Mike started to make a break for the exit. He skidded to a halt though as two Chxor guards piled out of the airlock, their riot guns at the low ready. Mike's forward momentum made him fall backwards and slide on his ass almost to their feet.

A speaker in the overhead crackled to life, "Cease your riot or you will be fired on."

One of the men, at this point Mike didn't know if he were just another prisoner or one of Fontaine's men, let out a shout and ran at the guards. The nearest guard triggered his riot gun. Mike heard the sharp crack and a whine as the flechettes went right over his head.

The man let out a scream and dropped to the deck. Almost everyone in the room froze, except for one of Fontaine's men in midair and Rastar the Ghornath.

The Ghornath turned to face the Chxor guards. Mike saw a dozen punctures in his hide, and a number of bruises. Yet his skin remained the red color of rage. He started to take a step towards the Chxor, "You bastards! You keep people like livestock, you exterminated ninety percent of my race..." Mid sentence he transitioned into his native tongue. Mike only

52

recognized any of it when it trailed into a series of obscenities.

In the chaos of Rastar's bellows and the moans of the injured, Mike barely heard a slight clink, almost like a silenced pistol or an air gun.

Rastar paused. He looked over his shoulder, "Hey you..." Then he toppled.

Another pair of Chxor guards had emerged from the airlock. "All prisoners will lie on the floor. Any who are too injured to work will be processed. Identify yourself if you can no longer work."

No one raised their hands. The Chxor gestured at a pair of prisoners near the door. "You will retrieve the dead." They looked down at Mike, "Get out of the way."

Mike edged back into the crowd. He glanced over his shoulder and saw Run the Chxor hidden beneath a metal table beyond where Rastar lay unconscious.

He looked over at Ariadne, who sat nearby. Mike could tell she had put things together too. "Maybe I misjudged the little bastard, good thing he had that tranquilizer gun," she said quietly enough to barely reach his ears.

"Yeah, pretty quick thinking on his part," Mike said. A firefight in the confines of the room would have left many bystanders injured. Bystanders like himself. "But I think this little incident gives us some important information."

"What, don't piss off Rastar?" Crowe asked, from Mike's other side. "I think I'll make an effort to remember that in the future, it might be hard, mind you, but I'll try."

Mike looked back at the four Chxor guards, who had withdrawn to the hallway to let the prisoners on cleanup detail work. "Well, *that*," he agreed. "But also what the Chxor reaction force is likely to do. Two guards through the airlock. Two more right after. How they're armed... and that this room, at least, is under observation."

"You think they have the barracks bugged?" Ariadne asked.

Mike frowned. "No. I don't think so. Probably just cameras to make sure we don't get up to any mischief like this."

Mike looked over at the guards. "And if we'd known that before, we could have used this to stage our escape. As it is... well, I just hope Fontaine doesn't kill us all as soon as they leave."

***

Fontaine's men seemed unwilling to take up where they left off before the interruption. Mike went to check Rastar's wounds first. The Ghornath seemed alright at first glance. His wide mouth lay open in a snore and a puddle of drool lay on the floor under his cat-like face. Mike noticed the small dart lodged in his back. He pulled it out and then walked over to where Run still cowered under a table.

"Good job there, it could have really gone bad with those guards," Mike said.

Run nodded, "I did well?" His big eyes stared up at Mike, and for a second, it almost seemed like the little Chxor felt some emotion. Th moment passed as the Chxor spoke, "Yes, it would be suboptimal if the big one resulted in our termination. I would not have the opportunity to conduct further research."

Mike grimaced, so much for emotion, "Yeah, suboptimal. How many of those darts do you have?"

Run peered up at him, "I have four more. Two which will work on humans, one which might work on a Wrethe, and one that works on Chxor physiology. I have to be careful not to get them confused, otherwise they could be lethal."

"Why is that a bad thing?" Mike asked. "I'm fine with you accidentally killing a Chxor guard with one."

"No, lethal to me, if I attempt to use them on the guards. They will have no effect on the guards," Run said. "That would be suboptimal. If I am terminated I will have no further opportunities-"

"To conduct your research, yeah, I can see that," Mike said. "Well don't get them mixed up." He passed the dart over, "You have any more that will work on Ghornath? Their physiology is similar to humans, we can eat a lot of the same things."

54

"I will have to test that. Can I shoot the Ghornath again when he wakes? I will be certain to take notes."

"No..." Mike said. "We might need him. Can you refill this dart, though?"

"If I have a proper lab, and my notes, and-"

"We'll see what we can do," Mike said. He saw Ariadne had moved over nearby. "You alright?" He kept his right hand clamped over the slash on the back of his left hand. A little blood still flowed, but the wound looked superficial.

She nodded. "A little bruised up. But Rastar took most of them on. I'm just surprised he didn't kill anyone."

"He didn't?" Mike asked. He remembered how the Ghornath had thrown men around. "That's pretty damned amazing. Though with how Fontaine will be after us now, I wish he'd thinned the numbers a bit." He glanced over at where Fontaine's men had clustered after the brawl. Several of them had marks from their encounter with the group. Yet nine of them remained of the ten from the fight. The Chxor guards had done the only killing.

He noticed the others of his group had begun to cluster around the unconscious Ghornath. "Everyone alright?" He looked around. Crowe sported a black eye, and Eric had a gash down one arm, but the others looked more or less unharmed.

"Uh... what happened?" Rastar's deep voice asked. "I feel like I drank an entire two liter." He sat up, and shook his big head.

"What's your poison?" Mike asked. He had heard that Ghornath could share human food supplies, he wondered if their taste ran to similar areas.

"Cola, preferably Coca Cola Classic," Rastar said. "It's the good stuff, made in Centauri..."

"Uh, that's just sugar, water and some carbonation," Pixel said. "That's not like alcohol. He wanted to know what you drink for fun."

"You humans are strange," Rastar said. He peered at Pixel, "Why are there two of you..."

Mike shook his head, "He's clearly suffering a bit from

55

the dart. Rastar, you started a fight with Fontaine's men, you put us in a bad situation with them. Fontaine will almost certainly have us killed now, or he'll look bad." He stared at the big alien, hopeful that he would understand.

Rastar's hide went through several colors, then settled on blue, "I'm sorry. I let my temper get the best of me. It's just... I cannot stand bullies and I hate those who prey upon the weak, as these scum did. As sorry as I am... I would do it again, because bullies like them deserve to be reminded that people can stand up to them."

"Well spoken, cat," a woman's voice said from nearby. "But even Fontaine's men aren't as bad as the Chxor."

Mike turned, "Will people stop doing that!"

"Doing what?" The woman asked. She stood shorter than Mike, with closely cropped red hair. She had a symbol of some sort painted on the left breast of her environmental suit. She also had a livid scar across her right cheek and bright green eyes. The determined jut of her jaw suggested she had a temper to match her hair.

"Sneaking up on us and interjecting on the conversation, is what I think he would say," Ariadne said. She rolled her eyes at the other woman. "And who are you?"

"I'm Mandy," the redhead said. "This is Miranda," she jerked a hand over her shoulder and pointed her thumb at a taller brunette who stood a few paces back. "I like how you stood up to Fontaine's men, we wanted to offer you a position with our resistance movement."

"What exactly is it you are resisting?" Mike asked. "I mean, you're on a prison station." The redhead flushed, and he saw her friend cover a smile.

"Just because we are here doesn't mean we can't do any good. I plan to seize the station, hold the Chxor Warden hostage until they send a ship to let us escape." Mandy scowled at them when no one seemed impressed. "What, you don't like that idea?"

"Uh... I could be wrong, but I've heard the Chxor don't really value their people like we do..." Pixel said. "It seems to me that getting someplace other than an unarmed and immobile station would have a better chance of not-dying."

"Right, because you've fought the Chxor for two decades," Mandy snapped.

"We could just ask Run," Pixel said. He pointed at the little Chxor.

"This plan is suboptimal," Run said helpfully. "The System Commander would order the destruction of the station. I do not like this plan." He cocked his head and peered at Mandy. "It appears that you have an infection of some kind. You have severe swelling in the chest. I should look at that-"

Mandy took a step back, "You've got a damned Chxor with you? Don't you know what that alien scum has done? How can you tolerate one of them in the same room as you..."

"He's useful," Mike said. "Which you don't seem to be right now. Look, you want off this station, then shut up and be helpful, instead of antagonizing the only people besides Fontaine with a plan, okay?"

Her mouth dropped open in shock. Mike suppressed a giggle at that. He hated idealists, they always either rode their theories down in flames or got beat up on until they turned sour and bitter. Either way, their high minded arrogance offended him.

"Look, we got off to a bad start, there," Miranda said and Mike saw her put a restraining hand on her companion. "How about we start over. You seem decent enough, maybe we can work together."

"If you hate the Chxor, I'll work with you," Rastar said.

"What resources do you have?" Mike asked. "Fontaine has weapons, and men to use them. What does your... organization bring to the table?" He hated to use that word, as he suspected the pair of them did not know even the basics of how to organize a tea party much less a resistance. Mike did, but he had no desire to help Barbie Resistance Fighter set up shop.

"Uh..." Mandy said. "We know people, here on the station. And we help people." She frowned. "There are some who will come when we tell them, but we're a free spirited bunch."

"Well tell them to get their free spirit asses ready," Mike said. "When it happens, it will happen quickly, just like this brawl did. We'll have to race Fontaine's men for the shuttle. If you get there late, we can't wait for you, understood?"

Mandy frowned and clearly the idea that someone might be left behind bothered her sensibilities. Miranda, on the other hand, gave him a calm nod. "We'll make sure we keep up."

"Good," Mike said. "Now who else on this station doesn't like Fontaine and would be up for escape?"

Simon spoke up, "There's a handful of Nova Roma marines I think, the survivors from their embassy. They're a protection detail for their ambassador, who's a clueless bitch, but they seem decent enough. There's also a Saragossan, Michael or something like that. Maybe a couple others."

Mike nodded, "Alright, go talk with them, tell them what's going on. Try to get them ready to move at a moment's notice." He glanced at the food dispensers. "I suppose we should eat while we can. I'm not sure how much time we'll have in the next few hours."

He went to the nearest machine, and typed in his prisoner code, then held his hand against the scanner for the biometrics check. A moment later, the machine instructed him to place a bowl in the dispenser. Ariadne passed him a bowl and a moment later he had himself a bowl of cold grain mush.

"Breakfast is served," Mike muttered. He peered at the Mratha rice, it looked edible, but something about it just seemed to depress him.

"Lunch and dinner, too," Simon said. "We're on short rations, that's what you have for the whole day."

"You're kidding, right?" Ariadne looked at the tiny amount that the machine had just given her. "How does anyone keep their strength here?"

"Mratha rice has a high caloric intake for small servings," Rastar said. He put his own bowl into the dispenser. Mike saw with a grimace that the Ghornath received roughly twice what he had. "And it contains enough nutrients to maintain health without use of supplements, for both Humans and Ghornath." He stared down at his bowl, and then he looked over at Mandy. "You know of some who have not made their quota, who need the food?"

Mandy gave a sharp nod, "Yes, there's a few people who're pretty hungry."

"Give them this, to share, as they need," Rastar said softly.

Mike stared at the big alien, "You sure about that?" His own stomach rumbled at the thought of food being given away, especially to this mythical resistance.

Rastar gave him a thumbs up and his skin turned a green shade, "I will not starve from missing a meal." He patted his stomach with his lower arms. "And besides, the menu may improve with time."

"Right," Mike looked down at the gray mush in his bowl. "Remind me to give my compliments to the chef."

***

Mike had just finished his bowl of mush when the speaker overhead crackled to life again. "All new arrivals report to the airlock for a brief by their assigned trustee."

Mike looked over at the others, "I've got Krain, who else?"

Ariadne nodded, "Me too."

"I've got Trustee Kranth, I think," Pixel said.

"Tralk," Crowe said. Mike saw Rastar and Eric nod at that. "I assume that Pixel told them he knows tools, and the pair of you will be told about the work sled they mentioned. What will we get?"

Run looked around at them. He still held his own bowl, which had some kind of black slime in it. "Tralk is a generic name typically used by a Chxor of the genetically inferior lower caste. He will instruct those with no skills on manual labor."

Mike had to cover his laughter with a cough.

Eric jerked his head around, "Hey, I got skills!"

59

"We will be used as brute labor until we die of exhaustion," Run said. "I find this suboptimal. We should escape soon so that I can continue my research."

"Working on it," Mike grunted. "The other Chxor don't value your research?"

"They do not understand that improvement of lesser races will improve things for all Chxor," Run said. "Improved slave species will make lower castes such as Tralk unnecessary, which will allow more castes to reach better jobs and to reproduce."

"Lesser races?" Ariadne asked. "You're calling us, lesser races?"

Run shrugged, "You are very emotional. This is suboptimal. Logic, not emotion will allow us to escape. Then I can continue my research and you can do whatever it is that unrestrained humans do in the absence of an authority figure."

"I can think of a few things you and I could do together," Crowe said to Ariadne. He gave her a leer and a wink.

Ariadne shot a glare at him, "In. Your. Dreams." She bit off each word. Crowe just gave her a smarmy grin. Mike restrained a sigh... *children*.

"I have not observed human reproduction," Run said. "Is it interesting? I understand that it can be done both for procreation and for entertainment purposes. I consider that wasteful, however. Would you mind if I recorded it?"

Mike grabbed Run by the collar and pulled him back behind him as Ariadne spun around, a look of rage on her face. "Alright... so back to work, everyone. Lets go meet our overseers who will no doubt instruct us on how to be good little slave worker drones."

He moved over towards the airlock. A small crowd of other recent arrivals waited. Two Chxor stepped through the airlock. They looked almost identical, even to the extent of their faded uniforms. The one at the lead spoke, "I am Trustee Krain, pilots will assemble near me."

Mike followed the Chxor down the corridor a short way. This Chxor looked much like the others he had seen. The same gray rubbery skin, the same block-shaped head, and the same wax-like features. The Chxor looked down at a datapad he held, then at the four assembled pilots. "Pilots may utilize the work sleds in order to meet their quota. Work sleds clock time worked as well as total haul of salvage. All salvage will be downloaded into the salvage bay for processing by other workers. Each work sled has a navigation computer with programmed flight paths. Any deviation from the flight path will result in destruction of the work sled. Any attempt to transit to another region of the station will result in destruction of the work sled."

"What is our quota?" Mike asked.

"A pilot quota consists of twenty metric tons of salvage per day. The Warden has selected this number to maximize total output and maintain an acceptable level of risk to pilots," Krain said. "You may supplement your quota with a standard worker's quota of seven hundred pounds of disassembled and sorted salvage on a percentage scale. In addition, theft of any salvaged materials to include but not limited to: weapons, computers, tools or valuables will be punished with immediate termination upon discovery."

"When do we start work?" Anubus growled.

"The auto-defense turret destroyed the primary work sled three work cycles ago. The station has not yet received the replacement. You will utilize the secondary work sled on an alternating schedule. Prisoner one five three nine four will begin the work schedule, and will have eight hours. The next prisoner will be..." Mike waited until he heard his own number rattled off. Apparently he had the last shift.

"Pending any further questions you may begin your work shift. The work sled will be retained for maintenance for four hours of every thirty six," Trustee Krain said. His monotone drawl almost made Mike want to fall asleep. That or stab the bastard just to hear something besides terminal boredom in his voice.

"You said acceptable level of risk," Cathy asked, "What level of risk is that?"

"After careful statistical analysis, we lose no more than one pilot to a terminal accident per eight hundred hours of work."

Ariadne spoke after a moment of silence, "So with eight hour shifts, one pilot will survive around one hundred days?"

"We operate on a thirty-six hour work cycle, and therefore do not measure it in human standard days. However, this is an approximate correlation to pilot losses," Krain said. "Do you have any further questions?"

"How do I get out of this chickenshit outfit?" Mike asked.

"Any further disrespect to myself as your overseer or the Chxor Empire will result in a penalty added to your daily quota," Krain said. "If I misunderstood your use of profanity involving a livestock animal, then inform me. Do you have any further questions?"

***

Mike and the others assembled in their barracks room.

"Alright, everyone knows what to look for and what their particular missions are?" he asked. Everyone nodded and most of them walked started to undress and slide into their ship's suits.

From decades of life in space, Mike tuned out the sights of the others. Spacers found little privacy aboard ship. He even managed to avoid any looks over at Ariadne, not that she lacked a fine figure...

"What an ass she's got," Crowe said from a few feet away. Despite his self control, Mike's gaze flicked over and caught a glimpse of bare flesh.

"What an ass you are," Ariadne said. Mike saw the air in front of Crowe's face flicker with flames. Crowe toppled back on his ass with a yelp of surprise. "And next time I'll put it in your too pretty hair."

Crowe scrambled backwards. "Fucking bitch!"

Mike stepped forward and stood over him. Crowe's eyes focused on his bare chest, then looked away. "She's part of this team. So are you. Act like a grown man or I'll see how hungry Anubus feels."

"Very," Anubus growled, "and don't taunt me like that."

Crowe glanced between Mike and the Wrethe. "You can't do that, you can't threaten me like that you fucking slant-eyed prick."

"Why not?" Mike said even as he ignored the racial slur. Somehow it didn't surprise him that Crowe would add racism to his repertoire. "You threatened Ariadne's privacy. I don't know what ships you served on, but I will not accept that kind of behavior."

"You aren't a captain, we don't have to listen to you," Crowe said. "This is a partnership."

"He's right there," Rastar said. "And I don't like those kinds of threats."

"The Ghornath has a point," Eric said. "You said that we're a crew, we work together, partners in this, right?" He glanced at the others, "Well I don't want to be in a crew where one member bullies the others into following his commands."

Mike ground his teeth. "Look, the little shit just eye-raped Ariadne, that kind of thing just is unacceptable. We can't have any kind of team with that kind of harassment."

"She handled it just fine," Eric said. "You did not need to get involved. You just have a desire to micromanage. Well, we either work together as a group, or we go our separate ways, I'm not letting you dictate what we do." Eric stepped forward and Mike grimaced at the other man's statement. A part of him wanted to tell him to go... yet Mike might need him.

"Things will work more smoothly with a commander, it makes things more organized," Simon said. "And I was under the impression that you had selected him for your spokesman. He certainly does most of the talking."

"Look," Mike said. "Forget I said anything. But the time we waste here in an argument is time we may need to escape."

"Agreed," Eric said. He walked over to Crowe and gave him a hand up. Then he slapped him across the face, "And don't be a shithead to your partners, or we'll return the favor." The mercenary gave a nod at Mike, then walked out of the compartment.

Crowe stood surprised, and Mike saw something flicker

over his face. He saw the other man's hand slip for his hidden shiv and then withdraw after a moment, empty handed. The glare he leveled at Ariadne a moment later suggested who he blamed for the encounter.

Probably best if he does not survive the escape, Mike thought.

Mike pulled his suit the rest of the way on. A moment later Ariadne walked over to him, also fully dressed.

"I've got first pilot shift," Ariadne said. "So if you want to come out and look the sled over, we can see if it's useful for any kind of escape."

"Sure thing," Mike said. He checked the seals on his suit and helmet one more time, and then hesitated, "You know how to check your suit, right?"

She gave a nod, "I've done a bit of vacuum work before. I got certified a while back."

"Good." Mike nodded. He glanced over at Anubus, who had donned his own ships suit. The Wrethe looked more angry than usual with his jackal head stuck out of the suit. "You coming?"

"I might as well," Anubus growled. "I heard I missed a fight with the gangster's men. Hopefully we will run across some on our way. I would like to kill something."

"Hey man, I find there's safer ways to let off steam, you know?" Rastar said. "I got some anger issues too, I just focus on some hobbies and it really seems to help."

"You are the one who started the brawl," Mike snapped.

"Yeah, but I didn't kill anyone, even that Pierre guy," Rastar said. "I'm pretty proud of that. I'm telling you Annie, a hobby or two really makes it easier to manage your negative emotions."

"Annie?" Anubus growled.

"Yeah, it's kind of like a nickname, almost a pet name and shows I can see past that gruff exterior of yours," Rastar said. "So, like I was saying, I got a few hobbies. I'm a real big fan of human sports. Surfing looks like a lot of fun, I watched a couple holovids of it and I think I could do it pretty well, you know, and whenever I'm really about to snap I try to think of myself out on the ocean-"

Anubus turned to Mike, "We should leave now."

Mike swallowed, suddenly overcome by the thought of surfing. He had a sudden vision of Saragossa's oceans and the things that swam through it. He pushed aside the flashback and wiped at the sweat that beaded his forehead. "Rastar, how about you go with Simon, eh? I think he mentioned he wanted to talk with some others about escape. Maybe you can back him up, huh?"

"Oh, sure," Rastar said. "Don't you want to hear more about surfing though? I understand back on Earth, there are these big fish things called sharks, and part of the fun with surfing is dodging these things as they attack you. There's this movie I saw called *Shark Surfer XI*, which I guess has some other movies before it-"

"Thanks," Mike gave Rastar a pained smile. "But we really need to get moving."

"Sure, man," Rastar gave him four thumbs up. "See you around."

The three pilots moved out out of their narrow barracks to the airlock marked as the Pit. Mike stepped inside and dogged his helmet. Ariadne followed him. Anubus joined them. His presence caused Mike's heart to race in the narrow confines of the airlock, especially with the additional bulk of the suit. Anubus stared down at him, and Mike's hands trembled a bit as he checked the seals on his helmet. He knew that he and Anubus had worked out a deal. Even so, his animal brain reminded him that he stood in a metal box with a hungry predator.

"Safer if we check each other's seals," Anubus said. "I can check yours."

"Thanks, thought the same thing," Mike said. "I feel so much safer with your claws that close to my vital organs."

"Oh, don't worry, human, I think my survival and yours are tied together at the moment." Anubus sealed his own helmet, and then did a pat-down of Mike. Mike did the same, and they both turned to face Ariadne. She stood frozen, helmet in hands, however. She had gone into a hundred mile stare. Mike waved a hand in front of her face. "Hello, anyone in there?"

She showed no response, but Mike saw her breath more rapidly, and then she let out a shout, "No, Mike, leave him be!" Mike reached and tapped her on the shoulder, but she did not seem to notice. He considered slapping her to break her out of her fit, but he hesitated as she spoke again, "Run, they're coming, no Anubus, don't do it, just run."

"What is she talking about?" Mike asked.

"She's... *Rhangar*," Anubus said, his voice muffled by his helmet. Yet Mike still heard something besides disdain in the Wrethe's gruff voice. Something that Mike thought sounded almost like awe. "She sees things of the past or things yet to be."

"What, like a..." Mike hesitated to say psychic, because, well, that was obvious.

"Your people once called them oracles," Anubus growled. "But they are few, most are charlatans, and the handful of others are mostly driven mad by what they see. My people have tried to make some, but it brings great danger. Too many possible futures will drive them mad."

"No!" Ariadne shouted. "Rastar!" A look of sorrow passed across her face. Mike saw tears flow down her face, and he felt suddenly uncomfortable, as if he had violated her privacy somehow. She blinked a moment later, and looked around. "Anubus... Mike... sorry about that."

"You get visions?" Mike asked.

"On occasion. Sometimes something will set them off," Ariadne said. She looked down and checked her suit seals, and Mike noticed her hands shook slightly as she did so, though whether from fear or some other emotion he couldn't tell. She settled her helmet on her head. "I saw... well, not the future, call it *a* future. What Anubus said about your lives being entwined set it off. I saw Anubus die, and you might have as well, Mike, I couldn't tell."

"What happened?" Mike asked.

"I don't know, exactly. Everything was confused. Sights and sounds seemed off, somehow, like from a damaged holovid.

We were at a spaceport... a world I've never seen, a planet with a twin and a green star... some kind of a shootout..." Ariadne sighed. "It fades so fast, there were details, Mike shot someone, then other people arrived, and Anubus..." she frowned, "you did something you shouldn't have. You died. I could feel Rastar die too, but I couldn't see him. And Mike, they had you pinned down."

"Well," Mike said. "The good news is we got off this damned station, so that's something anyway." He patted her on the shoulder, "And it's just a possible future, right?"

"Yes..." Ariadne said slowly. "But the worst part was not just that you three died, but that I realized that everyone else beside myself and Pixel had died as well."

"That sounds like one hell of a firefight," Mike said. "But I don't think we need to worry about it yet. Once we get off this station we can worry about twin planets around a green star, alright?"

Ariadne nodded behind her helmet. Mike toggled the airlock.

The airlock pumped down, and they stepped out into the Pit.

This section looked to be an open bay. Piles of twisted metal and larger pieces of ships lay in a tangle across the bay. Mike saw large bay doors in the overhead. A couple dozen or more prisoners worked across the bay, many with cutting tools that cast sparks across the bay.

Mike saw a trolley system that ran down the center of the bay. It led to an airlock at the far end of the compartment, this with a green light at the top. He saw a number of carts on the trolley. As he watched, a worker dragged a large metal plate across the room and lifted into one cart with a grunt. A moment later he typed his code into the side of the cart. *So that's how they log their quota,* he thought.

Not that he hoped to reside on the station long enough for it to really matter, but any knowledge might do him some good.

Anubus tapped him on the shoulder and pointed. Mike saw a small airlock along the outer wall of the station, off to their right. Ariadne had already started on her way towards it. He followed her as she wove her way across the bay.

She stopped at the airlock, then typed in her identity code. It opened a moment later, and she slipped inside. Mike followed her. The narrow airlock barely held them both. Mike put his helmet against hers, "You alright?" The contact allowed the vibration of his voice to reach her.

"I'm fine," she said, her voice sharp. "Let's just get to work."

The outer airlock opened, and they both froze. Mike had always found space a beautiful sight. Yet he never expected to find beauty in this place.

A vast blue gas giant hung above them, distant enough that it did not fill the entire sky, yet still close enough that Mike could watch vast storms sweep across its surface. A corona of gas hung in a halo around the planet, and the starlight caused it to fluoresce and glitter.

Closer lay a cloud of debris and ship wreckage. Mike could make out the hull of an ancient human colonization ship, massive beyond anything else ever built, as well as a cloud of smaller ships, and parts of smaller ships. They glittered and caught the multihued light from the gas giant, the halo, and the parent star. They looked like toys made out of jewels.

In human space, it might have become a tourist attraction.

Of course, the Chxor valued it only for the mineral wealth to be harvested off the wreckage. Mike wondered at the large cluster of ship debris. Had the Chxor towed every wreck in the system to this location? It made a certain level of sense, but only if they had other stations to do further salvage work. For that matter, he wondered how they had come to have so much wreckage in one system.

He followed Ariadne as she crawled up a loose scaffold towards what must be the work sled. It looked like nothing more than a steel frame with a seat, controls, and an engine. As they crawled closer, cautious in the lack of gravity, Mike saw a pair of magnetic grapnels on the front end. He hesitated to use ship's terminology with the tiny contraption, unwilling to give it that kind of distinction.

Ariadne tapped him on the shoulder and pointed. He followed her gesture and peered in confusion at a hexagonal shape. For a moment it looked like a hatch cover, until he saw a flare of an engine. He could barely make out the shape of a work sled as it pushed a large chunk of wreckage into the work bay of the other station.

The scale had thrown him off for a moment, then. It should not have, he knew. He had decades of experience in space, he should have recognized what must be a twin to their prison station, yet he rarely piloted with true line of sight. The feeling left him to suddenly feel very, very, tiny.

He pushed that feeling aside. He knew something of the vast scale of the universe, enough to mentally come to terms with the fact that he could never make any real impact against it. Emotionally, however, he realized that such thoughts did not matter. He could make a difference in his own life, and in the lives of others. That in itself mattered.

And his survival, as little as it might affect the universe as a whole, meant a great deal to him. Therefore, he did not give a damn about the scale.

He studied the distant station for a moment. The hollow hexagon looked similar to the old human wheel stations, fabricated to use centripetal force to generate gravity. Yet the station did not spin, there would be no need, not with artificial gravity, Mike knew.

He imagined it must be easy enough to construct in a modular fashion. Perhaps that was why the Chxor chose that form. And certainly it made sense from a security standpoint. The Chxor could limit their prisoners to three of the sides, and retain the other two for engineering, life support, their own barracks, and whatever other space they needed. Security would easily manage two access points. He could make out a narrow spoke that ran through the center to a hub. That, he imagined, would be where they'd docked with the station. A last security feature to prohibit unauthorized access to any cargo flights.

He could not make out the shape of a shuttle attached to

the other station, though he did see the flare of what he thought must be a cargo ship near their own station headed outbound or in a breaking maneuver.

He pointed at it, and thought he saw Ariadne nod. She pointed at the work sled, and Mike gave her a thumbs up signal. This was her shift. She had to get to work, if she wanted to make her quota.

Mike glanced at the chrono built into his suit and checked his air supply out of habit. The chrono said that the shift had started over an hour ago, which meant that he'd wasted a lot of Ariadne's time, between the discussion at the barracks, her vision, and their time spent gawking.

Well, if it becomes an issue, I can always give her some of my rations, assuming I make quota, he thought. He glanced back at the engine flare. It must be a fusion drive, he thought. He wasn't too surprised at that, those drives saw a lot of use in industrial settings like this, especially where time did not matter so much as reliability and cost. Other drives used more exotic fuels or burned more power. He doubted the Chxor cared whether a shipment of steel bars arrived in a day or a week. He traced its movement, and frowned. It hardly seemed to have moved, yet it had drawn noticeably larger. It must be a cargo flight on an approach vector.

Mike chewed on his lip in thought. He and the others seemed to have arrived in the scheduled flight. Trustee Krain had seemed to suggest that such flights occurred every few days or work cycles or whatever they called it.

Fontaine had said that they would move soon... and that they had a full shipment of precious metals, Mike thought. *Does he plan to hijack* that *ship?*

The thought bothered him, in more ways than one. He guessed they had only an hour at most before that ship would arrive. And with the timing, Fontaine's new pilot Cathy would have had time to rest up and prepare, maybe even preplot some Shadow Space jump if Fontaine had a navcomputer. It also that meant Ariadne would probably still be outside the station, away from help. And Mike would bet that the rest of his team would be scattered and tired after their own shifts.

So how would Fontaine have it go down, he wondered. A distraction, for certain, he thought. Not a riot, because that would require some of his people, and while he might sacrifice them, he would prefer to retain them for use in the capture of a ship or shuttle to escape.

That leaves sabotage of some kind, or a bomb, or both, he thought. The last made the most sense, a bomb, placed somewhere to draw attention and cause damage. Then he and his men would make their move.

He would have any Chxor on his payroll inform him of the target ship's estimated time of arrival. A backwards plan from the ETA would give him around thirty minutes from the time he triggered his little attack to work his way through the barracks and past any guards and then up the corridor to the hub. Mike would be willing to bet that the Chxor positioned the precious metals cargo before the ship docked. That would give Fontaine warning, even if he did not have some senior personnel corrupted amongst the Chxor such as the Warden that Simon mentioned.

Mike nodded; that plan made the most sense. A bomb somewhere in the foundry. The guards' attention would focus there, and Fontaine could slip out the other way, circle the station, and get to the bird.

He looked away from the ship on approach to gaze at Ariadne. She had strapped herself into the work sled. Mike saw her do some system checks, and then freeze. She sat very still for a long moment, before he saw her unstrap from the seat and look underneath it.

Mike crawled over, and as he came alongside her, he saw what looked like a metal can strapped to the fuel tanks under the seat. Ariadne turned to him, and she put her helmet against his. "I did a basic system diagnostic, just to be safe, and I found an error code. Someone added a prompt to power up an auxiliary system once the engine kicked on."

"And?" Mike asked.

"The wire leads down to that can," Ariadne said.

71

Mike glared at the can. It seemed rather innocuous at first, until he thought about how effective a bomb might be near the Pit, especially since Fontaine did not care about the prisoners in the bay. Mike didn't either, but he didn't think he could kill them as a quick distraction. The fuel tanks looked to be partitioned, which would mean fuel and oxygen ready to be mixed and burned. A bomb could mix and ignite the two. Mike didn't know what the effects of vacuum might be, but neither did he have a desire to turn it on and find out.

"But that means..." He thought through the changes to the plan he had projected. It seemed clumsier, but maybe Fontaine did not care about elegance, just about function. "Shit, we have to get back into the station, Fontaine plans to kick off his escape attempt right now." Yet he felt surprise that Fontaine's explosive expert had left such a crucial part of the escape plan to random chance. Why would they rely on someone else to start it?

As he thought that, he saw a red light start to flash on the control panel for the sled. He glanced at it, and saw a message flash across the screen: Remote Start-up Engaged.

"Move!" Mike shouted, even as he realized that she wouldn't hear him. Even so, he saw her start down the scaffold, headed towards the airlock. Mike suddenly cursed that he'd turned down Eric's offer to accompany them. The mercenary might have known how to disable the damned thing. Mike sure as hell wouldn't touch it.

They reached the airlock just as it opened and Anubus came out. He paused as he saw them scramble down the scaffolding towards him. Mike leapt past him and into the airlock. Ariadne followed a second later.

Anubus clearly realized something had gone wrong. He dove into the airlock as Mike punched the button to cycle it. The Wrethe's feet barely cleared the door as it closed. The inner door opened a moment later, and Mike broke into a run. He stumbled over Crowe and Pixel who both had their arms buried in the paneling of some ship wreckage. Mike grabbed Crowe by the shoulder and pushed him forward. Even as he ran, he waved to get others attention throughout the bay. He saw some of the prisoners pause at their work and some of them started to move in the indicated direction. Most either ignored him or focused too much on their work and did not see him.

Mike looked over his shoulder just in time to see the flash.

The wall behind him shattered. Splinters of steel flashed across the open bay. Most struck piles of salvage and created further shrapnel. Mike saw three prisoners simply vanish, swallowed by the wave of destruction. One of the ones who had begun to run behind him took a shard through the chest. It speared him, and he stumbled forward. Blood sprayed out from the horrific wound, and Mike forced himself to look away as the man convulsed.

Pieces of metal pelted him, and he felt something heavy strike his environmental pack hard enough to knock him off his feet. Yet somehow, nothing penetrated his suit.

He glanced over at Ariadne, who stood frozen. Her hand had clamped on the arm of her suit, yet Mike still saw a spray of air hiss out between her fingers. He could see the look of terror in her eyes as she realized that she was about to die, and in one of the worst ways possible.

Pixel appeared, seemingly out of nowhere. He pulled a paper carton off his belt and yanked a rubber pad out. Anubus moved up and pried Ariadne's fingers away just long enough for Pixel to put the seal in place.

Mike felt a wave of relief, even as he made note of Pixel's quick thinking. The engineer had impressed him. Before Pixel could do any more, they felt a shudder transmitted through the deck to their feet. The lights in the bay flickered and died. The artificial gravity began to fade moments later. Mike bit back a curse. He looked out the gaping hole that marked the former location of the work sled. The light from the gas giant cast strange shadows through the bay.

A moment later, Pixel lit up a work lamp. Mike pointed at the airlock that led to the barracks. If Mike understood Fontaine's original plan, the man would already have a lead on them. Worse, he might have already gained weapons from the guards. Mike should have taken the gang leader's brute force approach into consideration.

Especially after the work sled bomb. After all, what better distraction than multiple bombs?

***

Mike glanced around at the others. He saw Anubus turn his helmet to look at him. Mike pointed at the airlock. The Wrethe went still for a moment. Mike ground his teeth in frustration as he realized he would have to explain it to each of them. It seemed so obvious now.

Anubus seemed to get the idea, though. As the Wrethe ran for the barracks airlock, Mike turned to Eric. He tapped the former soldier on his shoulder. The man jumped in surprise and in the reduced gravity he soared almost two meters above the deck. He came down in an awkward, arm-splayed fall. Mike shook his head at the antics.

When Eric had enough control over himself to turn, Mike pointed at Anubus and the airlock. The other man seemed to understand and he began a series of cautious bounds after the Wrethe.

Mike reached for Pixel. He grabbed him by the arm and pulled him close so that he could touch helmets. He wished he had a set of radios. One thing to hopefully get from the guards. "Fontaine's making his break now. I saw a ship coming in, it may be the one that Fontaine plans to hijack."

"There's one already at dock," Pixel answered. "I talked with a pair of the foundry workers. They said they helped to load the precious metals shipment, but the Trustee said it exceeded the mass allowance, so the rest remained in the docking hub. That's why I came back to find you."

"Fontaine plans to take one of them," Mike said. "We have to beat him there." He glanced at Ariadne. The psychic leaned against the nose of a Marlin Three Eight Fighter. Mike knew she had to feel shaken by her brush with a gruesome death. "Give me a hand with her, will you?"

Pixel pulled back, and went to her right side. Mike took her left side, and they put her arms over their shoulders and headed for the airlock. Mike saw Eric cycle through it with Crowe. That surprised him, he had not seen the other man head over. The explosion must have confused him more than he thought.

They reached the airlock, and Mike caught movement out of the corner of his eye. He turned, as the airlock cycled, and passed Ariadne over to Pixel.

A cluster of other prisoners had drawn close. One held up his hands, either in question or a show that he held no weapons. Mike glanced back as the airlock opened. *What the hell, we can use more help*, he thought. He gestured for the others to follow, and then crowded into the airlock with Pixel and Ariadne. Pixel cycled the airlock as soon as he got inside.

After what seemed like an eternity, the inner door opened and they stepped into the barracks. Mike's hands went to his helmet, and he undogged the latches and pulled it off as he stepped forward.

Mike immediately tripped over a body as he stepped out. He sprawled out and barely caught himself from smacking face first into the floor. He glanced back at the body. He didn't recognize the man, nor could he guess who had broken his neck.

He glanced back down the corridor as something gave a deep bellow. A moment later a body soared out of one of the barracks rooms to slam into the wall. Mike winced at the audible sound as bones snapped. The Chxor left a smear of greenish blood down the wall.

A second Chxor backpedaled out of the room, followed a moment later by a red colored blur of limbs. Rastar caught the other Chxor as the guard triggered a round from his riot gun into him. Mike saw the blast cut a deep furrow down the alien's side.

Rastar caught the Chxor guard by the arms and swung him into the wall hard enough that Mike felt the impact through the deck plates.

The big Ghornath put two hands over the wound on his side. Mike stood and moved down the hall towards, him, "Are you going to be alright?"

Rastar gave him a thumbs up from one of his lower arms, even as his remaining arm reached for one of the riot guns. As he bent down, Mike saw the airlock cycle open, and another pair of guards step out. "Look out!" Mike shouted, even as he tried to duck away.

One of the Chxor raised his riot gun, but then an inky blot exploded out of the shadows behind him. Mike saw a spray of green blood as claws ripped into the Chxor. The second had time to chamber a round before a pair of suited figures tackled him.

Mike straightened from his crouch and started forward again. Rastar spun quicker than Mike expected for his bulk. The big alien snatched up a second riot gun from a downed guard. Mike saw the surviving Chxor guard throw one of his attackers away, and bring his riot gun around on the other.

"Clear!" Rastar shouted.

The remaining attacker looked up, saw him bear down on them, and leapt clear, even as Anubus ducked down.

Rastar fired both riot guns a heartbeat later. The two blasts cut the Chxor guard in half, and sprayed the interior of the airlock with body fluids and ruptured organs. Mike grimaced at the mess, though after what he had seen so far he felt no particular pity for the Chxor.

The airlock door started to close. "Get in the door!" Mike shouted.

He saw Anubus leap inside. Eric, the other attacker, grabbed at the fallen guard's riot gun and barely made it inside the hatch before it closed.

Mike ran up to the airlock. He glanced at Rastar, "Nice shot. Are you alright?"

"Thanks." Rastar held up the two pump action weapons. "They're pretty crude, but I'll hold onto them." He glanced down at the wound across his side. Mike looked at it too; it didn't look as bad now, though he saw a lot of red blood. "I'll be fine, man, I've got a pretty good constitution."

"Well, wherever Run went, we should have him look at you." Mike frowned. "Did you say you'll hold onto both weapons?" Mike asked. Granted it looked like the alien had hit with both, but still, it wasn't like he could use both of them at the same time on a regular basis. Mike realized he'd focused on an inane issue to keep his mind off of the wait. He did not know if Anubus and Eric faced the rest of the station's guards on the other side of the door, or if they found no resistance and decided to abandon them. *The Wrethe is a pilot,* Mike thought grimly, *he might well have killed Eric, or just offered him a deal.*

Rastar gave him a broad grin, "I could use four of them at once, if they weren't pump action. On two different targets."

"Really?" Rastar's boast seemed ridiculous to Mike. Sure, the alien might fire four guns at once, but how could he aim them all at one target, much less two?

"You should see me juggle," Rastar said.

"What happened back here, after the explosions?" Mike asked. The area did not seem to have lost power, at least.

"Area shook a bit, then a pair of Chxor guards came in and started shooting people. I let them know I did not like that, and you showed up," Rastar said. "One of them mentioned an escape."

"Maybe these were the ones working with Fontaine," Mike said. "Though I'm not sure why they came back here to kill prisoners..." Mike glanced down at the guard that Anubus had shredded. He saw the guard's utility belt had mostly survived the fight. Mike unclipped it and yanked it out from under the corpse. Underneath the gore, it looked to have a couple of grenades with unknown markings, a flashlight, and a combat knife.

"Good idea," Pixel said from behind him. The engineer poked at the corpse that Rastar's blast had shredded. He pulled the belt off, and then tugged a small pistol out of a holster on the Chxor's hip.

"You know how to use that?" Mike asked.

"Um," Pixel looked it over. He held it loosely, and lifted it up close by his face to look at it. Mike glanced past him just as he saw Pierre and two other gangsters slip out of the room behind Rastar.

77

Mike reached for the pistol. He missed though as Pixel leveled it at their attackers. He fired it, and the sound made Mike's ears ring, even as he heard the whine of the ricochet. A second later, Mike heard Rastar's riot guns fire simultaneously. After Rastar's skill, Mike almost expected to see Pierre smeared across the wall.

Instead, he saw Pierre frozen, hands raised. Two bloody smears marked where his accomplices had stood. Rastar had both riot guns pointed at Pierre's face.

"What have we here, waskally wabbit?" Rastar said.

"What?" Pierre asked.

"I have no idea," Mike said. "But he's got two guns pointed at your face. How about you tell me why the hell you're here, and where your boss is?"

Pierre seemed either unable or unwilling to pull his eyes away from the two muzzles in his face. "He'll kill me."

"Why do they always say that?" Mike asked. "We just killed your buddies, why do you think we won't kill you. I mean, we aren't the good guys, after all."

"You..."

The airlock cycled open. It stood empty, but for the splatter of the Chxor guard Rastar had shot earlier. Mike reached back and held out his hand. He waited a long moment. Finally, Pixel passed him the pistol with a sigh. Mike leveled it at Pierre. "Rastar, you go ahead, see if the others need help. Crowe, see if you can fit in there with him."

Crowe looked up from where he had begun to rifle through the pockets of the two dead goons. "But-"

"Do it, we're dead if we don't get a ship, so give them a hand," Mike said. "I'll have a talk with our friend here."

"And I've got your back," a deep voice said from behind him. Mike shot a quick glance back, and saw Simon. The former policeman had picked up the fourth riot gun, and held it at the low ready. Behind him, Mike saw a crowd of other prisoners. They seemed more nervous than anything else.

Mike looked back in time to see Pierre try to shift closer to the airlock. Mike centered the sights of his pistol with the man's left eye. "Look here, Frenchy," Mike said. "I don't know which colony you Euro-trash came from, but you have seriously started to annoy me. So here's the deal. Why are you here, why did these Chxor come here, and what's Fontaine's next move. You answer those three questions, and I'll leave you the use of your dick." Mike saw Rastar shade red a bit as the hatch sealed him away. *Right, he doesn't like bullies... Fuck it, let him take it out on the Chxor.*

Pierre licked his lips nervously. "Alright." He glanced at Mike, and then over at Ariadne, "Apparently one of the prisoners who got in with you has a big bounty back in human space. The Chxor Warden passed the message on to Fontaine. I heard the bounty might be worth almost as much as the loot we'll take from the metal shipment."

"So you were here for that, why the Chxor guards? They could have kept the airlock sealed, none of us would get out," Mike said.

"I think they were loyal to the Chief of Security," Pierre said. "They probably came here to kill Fontaine."

"Good, now where's your boss?"

"He planned to take the long way around, head through the guard barracks, engineering and life support, and the admin and supply section, take what he wanted and get to the hub."

"Alright, thanks, Pierre," Mike said. He had already thought through his options. He couldn't risk the chance that Pierre had a radio or some other way to communicate with Fontaine and he didn't know or trust the other prisoners enough to leave the man tied up. His finger started to tighten on the trigger.

Someone slapped his arm to the side as he fired. The bullet went into the cafeteria and clanged and whined around the room. Pierre let out a shout and bulled past him and into the crowd.

"Damn it, why'd you do that?" Mike said. He turned to find Simon. The former police officer had a hard look on his face.

"You don't kill prisoners, that's murder," Simon said.

79

"He would do the same," Mike ground out. "Worse, he'll go and tell his boss we're on the way, and that might well kill us all. We aren't cops, Simon, we're prisoners, in the middle of an escape attempt. You going to stop me from killing Chxor prisoners too, because it's wrong?"

"I'll stop you because there are certain rules you have to follow in life," Simon said. "You break the rules, you pay the price. Call it the law, call it karma, I don't care. It's the same with that idiot who talked about scratch built explosives. If you're going to cross those lines, you do it away from me."

"Understood," Mike said. "But you keep in mind that we are a team. Some of us got here not because the Chxor dislike humans, but probably because they did something heinous enough they'd end up someplace similar in human space."

"You talking about yourself?" Simon asked.

Mike looked away, "I think there are some more obvious ones, like the Wrethe."

Simon stepped back. "True enough. Alright, you've got your pasts. I can't say I don't care, but I'll try to keep that from getting in the way. But let's try to keep things as above the board as possible."

"Right, that's my number one priority in the middle of a *prison break*," Mike rolled his eyes. He looked over at Ariadne, "You feel up to whatever lies beyond the door?."

"Ready," she nodded. She still looked pale from her previous brush with death. Even so, she stood tall, and she didn't fidget or fret. Mike figured she would do alright. She looked over her shoulder at the crowd, and spoke in a loud voice. "We're busting out of here, who wants to go with us?"

The crowd of prisoners shifted, many seemed shocked at what had happened so far. From the back, Mike heard Run's voice, "Out of the way. Stupid humans. I need to get to front. I must escape in order to carry out my experiments. The universe needs me!"

Mike gave a snort as Run came forward. A moment later, a tall man stepped forward out of the crowd. "I'll come. I've got some unfinished business, and I don't want to die in this

80

hellhole." His accent sounded like those he heard on Saragossa. The stranger held out his hand, "Micheal Santangel."

Mike shifted his pistol to his left hand, and shook, "Mike Smith. Good to meet you." He saw some of the other prisoners step forward. "Honcho these others up. We'll cycle the airlock from the other side. Keep them coming."

"What if we want to stay?" A woman asked from the crowd. "The Chxor will just kill you all. There's no way you'll escape. We're safer here."

"Your funeral," Mike grunted. He looked over at Santangel, "If they don't want to come, leave them. We don't have time to fuck around." Right on cue, the hatch cycled open. "Alright, Ariadne, Pixel and Simon, lets squeeze in there."

"Run too!" the little Chxor said.

"I'm not sure we have the room..." Mike started, but the Chxor scurried into the airlock. "Whatever."

They squeezed in, and Mike hit the button to cycle the airlock from the inside.

The process seemed to take forever. Mike glanced up at the overhead. He mentally reviewed the events of the past few hours. He realized he had put himself in far greater risk than he liked. In fact, he realized he had risked himself, not just once, but several times, for people little more than strangers. What did he know about any of these people. *I just met Santangel, but I already plan on bringing him along if I can*, he thought. He never trusted anyone, he lived by that code, it brought safety, it brought security.

That came at a cost of loneliness, but he could tolerate survival in solitude. He figured the dead had plenty of company. *Like most of the human race,* he thought grimly.

He felt a sudden urge, to push straight to the ship, to ditch his companions and take off. The thought eased the tension in his chest. It made sense. What responsibility did he have to these others? None, he knew. He had not put them here, nor had he explicitly promised them he would wait for them. Sure, whoever could keep up, he could bring them, but he didn't really need any of them. Well, he had to admit, no one besides

Ariadne, and when it came down to it, he could probably force a Chxor to navigate or just go with whatever a navcomputer spewed out.

Time to go, he decided. Cut his losses, take the first opportunity and split. Just like he had aboard the *Noriko*. *Sometimes*, he knew, *the only person you could save was yourself.*

***

Alarms wailed, loud enough that Mike could hear them through his helmet. He stood next to the evacuation pod. It was rightfully the officers' pod, but most of the bridge officers were dead.

Only Ensign Inshi remained, and she had told him to ready the pod for the wounded. She'd sent him ahead with the key to open it, cut off of the Captain's suit.

Mike stood just inside the hatch. He watched as the corpsmen pulled the wounded down the corridor in microgravity. A part of him wished to go out and help.

The rest of him felt the hard metal of the release lever through his suit glove and wanted nothing more than to pull it. He recognized the various alarms. He had heard the klaxon that signaled fire aboard the ship. His suit sensors reported dangerously high hydrogen levels in the corridor. One of the fuel tanks must have leaked into the vessel's compartments.

Parts of the ship lay in vacuum, those wouldn't burn, but the crew would be trapped, probably exposed to radiation and debris that would kill them in only hours. The pod itself would only hold ten for a few days, but it would protect them from the hazards of space for that time, unlike their suits.

He stood firm, despite the fear he felt. Ensign Inshi had ordered him to this post, and he wouldn't leave it, or the wounded, not while he could save them.

He tried not to think about what Sensor Specialist Miushi had said about the convoy's departure. Surely they would return for them, and if not, the enemy would pick them up, this was a skirmish between factions of the Colonial Republic, not some pirates who didn't take prisoners.

There were laws of war, Mike knew, laws that both sides must follow.

Down the corridor he saw the Ensign, and he remembered how she had taken charge after the hit on the bridge. As before, she moved with a calm certainty, and the enlisted spacers followed her commands with speed. Mike Golemon felt his chest ease as she ordered two spacers to dog the hatch behind her. Clearly they would leave soon. The Ensign had things under control.

They would all make it out of this. Soon the rest of the convoy would pick them up and they would--

The fireball that blew through the hatch incinerated the two spacers and the Ensign. The fire that spread down the corridor seemed to move in slow motion. It seemed to dance from figure to figure, wreathing each in flames. Men and women danced in pain, limbs flailed, and people shrieked on their suit radios.

Yet the slow apparent motion proved deceptive. The corpsmen only a few meters away tried to rush. One of them cut the lanyard that tied him to one of the wounded and pushed off the other man, only to be wreathed in flames a heartbeat later.

Three men remained, only a couple meters from the hatch, the entire corridor behind them engulfed in flames.

Spacer Second Class Mike Golemon did the only thing he could do, he saved as many people as he could. He pulled the release lever. The hatch slammed down. The pod blasted out of its cradle, but not before Mike heard the screams of rage and panic from the men he left behind.

It was triage, he told himself, *save the ones you can.*
***

The airlock opened, and Mike stepped out of his memories and into what looked like a green-tinted abattoir. At least fifteen Chxor lay dead, scattered around the processing area. Most looked chewed by weapons fire, but Mike saw at least a couple torn apart by claw and blade.

Mike heard a shout, and looked over at where the mesh cage enclosed a door. Rastar stood there, and he waved at them. "Eric's down. Run, can you treat him?"

"Yes! I have assembled some tools. Hold him down, do not let him escape!"

The little Chxor scurried over, and Crowe and Ariadne followed. "What happened?" Simon asked. The other man stopped to pick up a pistol off a dead Chxor.

"Some kind of explosive on the door. Eric kicked it in and it blew up in his face," Anubus said. "I suggested we wait for Pixel, but he felt it worth the risk."

"I can pick locks," Crowe said, off hand. "What's in the room?"

Rastar's skin shifted color from a blue shade towards pink, and then red. "You do not seem concerned that one of our friends is hurt."

"You're letting a Chxor 'doctor' work on him," Crowe said. Mike saw him crouch and pick something off a guard. "So let's check out the room real quick, and see what they thought valuable enough to put a bomb on the door."

Mike went to the right, and glanced at the corridor that led to the hub. The others seemed to have forgotten Fontaine and his men, and that they must have gotten ahead of them. Certainly the gang had the time. And the lack of Chxor survivors suggested that their bribed allies had joined them.

Now was the time to go, he knew. The other ship must have docked, at this point. Fontaine might plan to take both, but Mike felt certain he could fight his way aboard one or the other ship. Maybe not as easy as with the others, but he could do it. And if he failed, it would be his own failure, not that of someone he trusted.

He would not be abandoned by the failure of someone he trusted, not again. Not like back aboard the *Noriko*. He remembered again the destruction of the ship. For a second he relived the last moments on the bridge, when the fire washed over the crew.

Worse, he remembered how things had only grown worse

84

afterward. He remembered how the handful of survivors waited for rescue that never came. How they had scavenged air tanks from the dead, and then from the gravely wounded, and finally, drawn lots for who would continue to breathe. Mike Golemon had died there, and Mike had not mourned his death. In ways, a rejection of those values that led him to join the Republic Liberation Fleet had given him purpose. He would live for himself, trust no one, and reject the people who had abandoned him to die.

Mike paused at the hatchway. He glanced back, just as gunfire erupted from the Chxor administration airlock. He saw the others crouch in the booth. The rattle of the submachinegun sounded distinct over the roar of his companion's riot guns as they tried to return fire.

Mike froze. He saw the Chxor step out of the airlock. He continued his suppressive fire even as two more Chxor stepped out and moved forward to flank the group pinned in the booth.

Mike glanced over at the airlock to the prisoner barracks. He saw that it had not yet cycled, they would find no help from there, not in time.

I should go, Mike thought, *I can't fight three of them, not with a pistol, not without any cover.* They had not yet seen him, but they would as soon as he opened fire. Under any other circumstances, he would never hesitate. He would chose to survive, to abandon the others, to get to the ship and escape.

Down the corridor behind him, he heard someone call out, "Alright, sounds like the Security Chief's men broke out of the armory. Time to go."

Mike turned towards the corridor, decision made. *Triage... save myself, it's the only thing I can do,* he thought.

Then he heard someone shout out in pain behind him.

Mike spun back around, "Aw shit." He felt his stomach twist in fear, yet his mind cleared of his emotional turmoil. He felt calm as he dropped into a shooting stance and brought his pistol up. The sights centered on the Chxor with the submachine gun.

Mike squeezed the trigger and then fired again. That

Chxor went down.

The other two spun to face him. Mike felt his stomach tense as he brought his pistol around. They had reacted too quickly, though. Mike saw the riot guns level in his direction. "This is really going to hurt."

A burst of fire exploded. The Chxor's very flesh seemed to erupt in flames, almost as if their bodies ignited from the inside out. Mike winced and looked away as the Chxor screamed in agony.

Chxor smelled like burnt rubber when they burned.

Beyond the sudden conflagration, Mike saw Ariadne stood clear from the cover. Her blonde hair whipped, as if caught in a gust of wind, and she had one gloved hand pointed at the guards who still burned.

In the silence that followed, Mike heard Crowe say, "Alright, I *really* want to take this time to apologize for whatever I did wrong earlier. It won't happen again, I promise."

***

"They're buttoning up the ships, we have to get up there," Mike said a moment later. Anubus and Rastar both emerged from the shelter of the cage. Chxor blood soaked Anubus's fur. Bits of tissue clung to his extended talons and he had a shred of cloth stuck in his teeth.

Rastar looked like he had taken at least a couple hits from the surprise attack. Mike saw blood run from several holes in his legs, but the Ghornath kept up with Anubus as the two raced towards the hub.

"Get him off of me!" Eric shouted from behind the counter.

"Do not let him escape," Run said, his high pitched voice calm. "It will make this operation much harder."

Mike hesitated. He looked between the two fighters as they leapt down the microgravity in the corridor and where the others worked on Eric. Now that he had chosen to support the others, he felt lost. What was best for the group, as opposed to best for himself?

Mike grimaced; either way, they needed a pilot to take charge of whatever ship they captured and someone to think ahead rather than charge blindly. He dove into the corridor, just as Anubus and Rastar landed at the far end.

He saw gunfire spray across the Hub. Anubus gave a grunt of pain and stumbled, but Rastar's two riot guns barked, both in separate directions. The gunfire cut off. Rastar used his upper arms to work the slide and then fired both weapons a second time.

Anubus ran forward and cleared the hatch.

Mike landed lightly on his feet, only to slip in a patch of blood. He immediately saw a pair of downed Chxor guards. His eyes went to where Anubus had pinned a third Chxor against the wall. This one wore a brown uniform, rather than the armor that the guards wore.

"Who do we have here?" Mike asked. He glanced at both airlocks. One had gone shut, and the light above it changed from green to amber as Mike watched. A moment later the amber light went out and changed to red.

Mike scowled. The ship there had undocked. "Rastar, get aboard that other ship there, kill anyone who's a threat, and make sure it doesn't leave."

The Ghornath rushed past him, even as Mike walked more calmly to stand next to Anubus. "I don't think they'll leave without you, though, will they?"

Anubus glanced over at Mike. "Think he's worth much?"

"His life isn't worth much, not unless he helps us out," Mike said.

"This is not logical," the Warden said. He had a thicker accent than the guards, and if anything, his monotone voice seemed even blander than that of the guards. "You should allow me to leave. Without a ship to escape the system, you will be caught and executed. I am a Chxor and therefore can hide amongst the populace. There is no need for all of us to die."

"All of us?" Mike asked, and his eyes narrowed. "What do you mean, all of us?"

"You will die, of course, for insurrection against the

Chxor Empire," the Warden said. "Allow me to leave. If you have offspring I will see to it that they receive payment."

"Very kind of you," Mike said. "But I don't think I've got any rug-rats and the Wrethe here doesn't have any parenting instincts, as far as I know. How about you tell us what Fontaine's plan is, and what he paid you?"

The Warden showed little expression, "Your behavior defies logical reason. Your lack of genetic offspring shows some restraint that I wish the rest of your race would follow, however." His pale yellow eyes went between Anubus and Mike. "I insist that you let me go. You gain nothing from my demise at the hands of the Empire."

"Revenge is something, and you may not live long enough for your buddies to kill you," Mike growled. "I never hated the Chxor, but since I hit Saragossa you have done your best to make me, and you've done a damned fine job at that at least."

"Hatred and revenge are wastes of resources, emotions that have a profound effect on reason…"

Mike placed the pistol against the Warden's forehead. He copied the Warden's monotone, "Continue your lecture, as you can tell, I am *very* interested." He thumbed off the safety, grateful for the archaic mechanical feature rather than a more complex biometric safety. It both allowed him to use the damned thing and made a sufficiently impressive click when pressed against the Chxor's forehead. "Tell me what Fontaine's plan was, and why you worked with him, especially when your buddies will kill you for this."

"He kept the other prisoners in line, and maintained peak efficiency," the Warden said. "In addition, he boosted recovery of quality equipment over and above scrap metal, which showed a substantial profit increase on my behalf."

"You're emotionless corporate drones?" Mike asked, "Why am I not surprised?"

"No we do not have an economic system like humans. Free market systems have too great of waste, and do not always reward those they should. We maintain a command market, and we have no currency. All Chxor work for the Empire." The Warden seemed proud of that.

"You know, that might have brought a tear to my eyes, except I don't really give a damn," Mike grimaced. "So that Frenchy bastard kept your other slaves in line and boosted productivity, so you allowed him to stage his escape? I don't see how that would not make you look bad."

"Security is not my area of responsibility," the Warden said. "By directive twelve seventeen forty seven of Penal Station Regulations, I am responsible for the maintenance of tools and the station, scheduling supply and salvage shipments-"

"Oh, shut up," Anubus growled. "So someone else holds the bag, the security chief or guard captain or whoever?"

"Yes, Chief of Security Kras had responsibility for security. Any violation of station security would reflect upon him, rather than me," the Warden answered. "To further shift blame, I scheduled my leave to coincide with the breakout. Fontaine would make the Chief of Security look bad, I would salvage the situation, and therefore receive a better evaluation and promotion."

"How did you plan to salvage this?" Mike waved the pistol in a circle.

"Well, that is obvious. During my leave, I filed a memorandum that I suspected Chief of Security Kras had become suborned, and that a group of prisoners planned an escape. I knew that Fontaine planned to link up with another ship, so I requested a Fleet detachment to investigate. They should arrive shortly."

"You double-crossing little shit," Mike snarled. He did not know how the Chxor Empire's space fleet would react, especially with how their forces must be stretched thin with their conquests, yet he did not doubt that they would manage *some* reaction. He glanced over at Anubus, "Get down to the others and tell them we need to get moving *now.*"

The Wrethe leveled his gaze on Mike, and his dark eyes seemed to flicker with suppressed emotion. Mike saw the muscles on the Wrethe's body tense, and the fur rise along its body. "You seem eager for me to leave. Do you perhaps think to depart without me?"

Mike let go of the Warden and turned to face Anubus. "No. For one thing, we've got what I bet is a short legged fusion drive cargo boat, not even worthy of the title ship. There's no way I can get out of the system with just that. For another, I'll need the others, especially Pixel for his engineering skills and probably Crowe for his communications skills. I don't particularly need you... but the quickest way to get them is to have you get them, and frankly, I don't trust you alone with the ship."

Anubus stepped forward. He loomed over Mike for a moment, "You shouldn't. I'm half tempted to kill you and leave. But your point about needing the others is well taken. I will get them, but we need to revisit the way you order the rest of us around. We are neither your followers nor your servants."

Before Mike could respond, the Wrethe took off in a lope. Mike let out a deep breath, and felt his legs tremble a bit. Something about the Wrethe just had that effect on him.

"I have secured the ship," Rastar said from behind him.

Mike jumped several feet into the air. He spun around, "Christ on... How do you move so quietly?"

"I have stood here since you threatened the Warden," Rastar said, though his hide showed green. Mike figured that meant humor. He made a mental note to have a discussion with the Ghornath at a later time regarding his sense of humor, amongst other things. "I searched the ship. The Chxor pilot will no longer be an issue, and I managed to avoid too much of a mess."

"I would have liked a Chxor to talk me through the controls," Mike said.

"He saw me and reached for a button on the panel. I did not want to risk him disabling the ship or calling for help," Rastar said.

"That's good," Mike grunted. "How big is it?"

"There are two cargo holds, the same size as those we awoke in," Rastar said. "One contains several heavy crates, which I didn't open, and what looks like Chxor food, which I think it best none of us try," Rastar gave a slight smirk. "Though I imagine that Run will be pleased with the results."

"I'm sure," Mike said. He hoped the little Chxor really knew medicine, and not just how Chxor bodies worked. Despite their external physical similarities, Mike somehow doubted that they shared much in common internally.

"There is a corridor that runs almost the length of the ship, and connects the cockpit with the engine room. I am not familiar with Chxor writing or much in regards to ships, so I cannot tell you much more."

"Alright, as soon as some others get here, I'll go check it out."

"You read Chxor?" Rastar asked.

"I know ships, how hard can it be?"

***

A few minutes later, Crowe and Pixel came out of the corridor, carrying Eric between them. The former soldier looked pale, and a broad stain of blood covered the side of his suit. He seemed conscious though. "How is he?" Mike asked.

Run landed in the hub chamber, "The test subject will live. I successfully removed the shrapnel from his wound. I recommend rest and time to heal. Also, once he has fully healed, a vivisection will allow me to further study how human bodies react to damage and heal."

"You're not coming near me with a knife again," Eric said. He looked over at Mike, "The little bastard just pulled out a knife and started cutting. No pain killers, nothing!"

Mike looked over at Crowe, who gave him a nod. Crowe actually looked green, and he swallowed carefully before he spoke, "Run kept talking about the details, organs and bones and..." the man lost his battle with nausea and left Pixel to support Eric. He ran over to the side and started to heave.

"Oh, is this some waste removal system natural to humans?" Run asked. The little Chxor tapped his fingers together as he peered at Crowe.

91

"You should ask him," Mike said helpfully.

"Very interesting, I must take notes," the little Chxor scurried away.

Mike saw others leap down the corridor. He turned to Eric and Pixel. "Lets get Eric aboard. Pixel, I need you to look at the ship's engine and drive. Find out what we have to work with. I'm going to check out the cockpit." He glanced at Rastar, "Get everyone loaded, and send Ariadne up to the cockpit when she gets here."

He and Pixel got Eric inside and propped him against the pile of crates just inside the hatch of the ship. The cargo hold looked almost identical to the one they had arrived inside, except the inner hatch lay open. Mike led the way inside. He glanced down the corridor. The ship had rougher edges than the station. It seemed designed for the shorter-statured Chxor rather than humans, with a ceiling that made even Mike feel vaguely claustrophobic. The corridor lighting also had a greenish tint that made him feel vaguely as if he were underwater.

That in turn made sweat break out on his forehead. *This is ridiculous, we're in space, a couple million miles from the nearest water... and that's probably frozen comet remainders orbiting the gas giant out there.* The thought did not seem to help much, but he forced himself down the hall anyway.

Mike saw that both hatches at either end of the corridor lay open, along with the hatch to the second cargo bay. It looked empty. He saw a tangle of machinery beyond the open hatch at one end. Before he could say anything, Pixel gave him a broad smile and started in that direction. The engineer looked perversely happy to see machinery.

Mike glanced the other way and saw the back of a pilot's chair, seat restraints neatly folded on the back. He couldn't help a broad smile of his own. "Well, I never thought I'd fly again, it's not the same, not at all," he said to himself as he walked forward. Flying meant freedom, self control... what could an engineer see in machinery?

Mike found the Chxor pilot's body near the controls. As Rastar had said, he prevented too much of a mess. Mike still had to wipe away green blood from the main control panel. The rest of the flechettes from the riot gun had also shredded the copilot's seat, but Rastar had angled the shot to miss any of the controls.

He bit back a curse as he stared at the Chxor glyphs. Like most ships, it didn't have an actual control yoke. Buttons controlled thrust, vectors and the details of the ship. Unfortunately, Mike didn't know what the buttons meant. He tapped at one screen, and angry purple glyphs flashed up on the main heads up display. A Chxor voice spoke harsh words that Mike thought probably signaled something bad.

Mike leaned around and shouted down the corridor. "Have someone send Run down here, I need his help!"

He tapped at some other controls experimentally. Most seemed locked down, however. Probably a good idea, he acknowledged, when the ship lay docked with a station.

A moment later, Ariadne and Run stepped into the narrow compartment. Run immediately looked at the mess of the pilot. "I think that you have probably come to overestimate my skills," Run said. "This is understandable, due to my various talents. However, I must state that there is nothing I can do for this Chxor."

"I don't care about him," Mike said. He pointed at the control panel. "I need you to translate these."

"Oh," Run said. He squeezed up beside Mike and started pointing and reading.

Mike lost him after thirty seconds. "Alright, wait. Does anyone have a marker or something?"

"I've kept up alright," Ariadne said. "I'm cheating though, I'm picking the meaning for symbols out of his head."

"You can do that?" Mike and Run asked at the same time.

Mike and Run looked at each other, startled at the echo. Mike looked back at Ariadne, "I thought you just did... you know, stuff with fire, and navigation."

"Mind reading is not my strongest suit and I don't tend to tell anyone. Most people aren't very comfortable around telepaths," Ariadne said quietly. "You know the slang for us?"

"Mind freaks, right?" Mike asked soberly. He had heard

93

and even used the term before himself. It seemed rather... derogatory, now that he thought about it from her perspective.

She nodded, "No one trusts a telepath, not when we can mess with other people's minds. None of you seemed too put out by my other abilities. And... well, no one asked so I didn't make a big deal out of it."

"Okay," Mike said. He tapped the buttons he remembered that he figured would unlock the console. Ariadne reached over his shoulder and tapped another button, and the console went live. "So..." Mike said. "Have you messed with my mind at all?"

She didn't answer for a long moment. "I really don't like to do that. It just feels wrong, somehow. But yeah, I did, once."

Mike felt a wave of relief. He looked back at his decision to put the safety of the others above his own, when the Chxor guards had them all pinned down. "The Chxor with the submachine gun, you made me shoot at him, right?"

She looked at him with surprise, "Of course not. Truth to tell, I froze at first. I couldn't see you or them, and my abilities are weak enough that I need line of sight. No, when we first met, I nudged you a bit so that you'd be more open to me, so that I could decide whether or not to trust you."

Mike felt shock roll over him. He had leapt at the chance to blame his selfless act on someone else. *That's not the man I am, not any more, not after...* but he shut those thoughts away. Maybe he had changed. Maybe the sights of what the Chxor did to people gave him back some concern for his fellow man. Or maybe not, maybe he just identified with the dregs of society grouped together by circumstance. Either way... "Run, go see if Pixel needs any help with the engines."

"No need," Pixel said from the corridor. Mike looked over his shoulder. The engineer wrinkled his nose at the Chxor corpse. "You should do something about that, before he stinks up the place."

"Engines are up?" Mike asked.

"Oh yeah, fusion reactor is hot, fusion drive is ready, and the thrusters are online, so we can get clear of the station, I even found a datapad linked to the ship's engineering console." Pixel said. "The engine's pretty simple, actually, everything's in a logical place, too, well designed, if unimaginative. I can see a lot of shortcuts they took to decrease build time, but they could have made it much better and still kept build times low if-"

"Very interesting," Mike said. "How about you go see how loading is coming along. Also, what kind of sensors and comms does this thing have?"

"Uh, I saw a diagram on here..." Pixel frowned as he pulled out the datapad. "I think just some simple radar, and a basic high definition video telescope, same kind you see on cheap freighters where the captains cut overhead and skimp on sensors. I think it's just got high frequency radio."

"Okay, I can work that, at least, and it won't let anyone else know we're live, not like pinging them with radar," Mike said. He turned to Run, "What buttons for sensors?"

The more technical terms of ship systems seemed to limit Run's grasp of English. But after a short time, they worked through the necessary sequences to bring up first the video telescope, and then the radio.

That was when they got their first bad surprise. As the radio came up, a deep voice spoke in Chxor. Mike looked at Run, who started to paraphrase, "...Security Kras. Warden Hral has subverted some members of security to lead a mutiny in conspiracy with workers aboard the station. Under authorization code five seven three four nine seven five I request all available military assistance and request the destruction of any ships which attempt to leave the station. This is a recording. I will attempt to regain control over the administration section. I repeat, this is Chief of Security Kras..."

Mike waved Run to stop as he began to repeat himself. He switched the volume down. "That's bad. If the Warden's little betrayal didn't have any Chxor military force on the way, that certainly will." He typed in commands on the sensor console. It took a moment to work through the unfamiliar controls and his own limited knowledge of sensors. When he finished, Mike looked at Ariadne, "How close to loaded are we?"

"Around twenty others have decided to come, the rest don't think we have a chance," She said. "I... I thought about manipulating some of them, but I'm not sure I could control that many, and some of them are just so broken..."

Mike grimaced, "If they want to stay here, they've already given up. I won't try to kidnap them to bring them with us, not with how tight things are already." He mentally reviewed the size of the bay. "How are we for food and water?"

"Crowe found some human ration bars in the administration area. They're expired, but it's better than nothing," Ariadne said. "I'm not sure about water."

"The ship has a potable water tank, looks like five thousand liters," Pixel said. He peered at his datapad. "There's no link from there to the cargo bays, but there's a faucet in the bathroom off the engine room."

"Head," Mike corrected automatically.

"What?" Pixel asked. "Yeah, I need to watch my head here, the ceilings are pretty low. I should to do something about the lighting too."

"No, the bathroom is called a head. And it's not a ceiling, it's an overhead. The floor is the deck," Mike said patiently.

"Oh, right, jargon," Pixel said. "What was it you typed in the sensors a second ago? It looked like a monitoring program of some sort, sort of like what engineers use to check engineering software."

"Something like that," Mike said. "Just a simple sweep with the video telescope. It's mounted forward, so between the bulk of the station and our fixed position, we'll only get a fraction of the sky, but if something's out there..."

A harsh buzzer sounded, and an image popped up on the screen. Mike peered at it for a long moment. He looked at Run, "It found something, what does it say?"

Run had gone completely still. His big eyes went wide. Mike saw his body tremble. "Hey, what does it say?" He reached out to shake the little Chxor, but got no response. He glanced over at Ariadne, who had gone pale as well. "Can you do your..." he waved his hands around his head... "You know?"

96

"It's not magic," Ariadne snapped. "But yeah, I did. He's so shaken because he thinks we're all going to die. It turns out that Run has a very heightened survival instinct-"

"Run hide!" Run shouted. The little Chxor bolted out of the cockpit, and scrambled down the hallway and into the engine room.

"...and from what he understands, we're pretty much screwed," Ariadne said. "That message indicates that six ships have come within visual identification range. Four of them are ten-class Chxor cruisers."

"Cruisers?" Mike asked. He felt his stomach drop. Four cruisers... they effectively possessed no weapons, the riot guns wouldn't so much as scratch a fighter. He didn't know how the Chxor armed their ships, but four cruisers sounded bad. "What about the other two... support ships?"

Ariadne gave him a grim smile, "No, the identification codes on their transponders report them as five-class dreadnoughts."

***

Mike felt sweat bead his face, "Well, I guess I should have just taken the ship and abandoned the rest of you when I had the chance."

"What?" Pixel asked.

Mike smiled, "I joke." After all, with how he had needed Run to translate controls, he would not have gone far anyway. Well, not unless he captured the pilot alive, or dragged the Warden in to do the work. After all, he could have disposed of either of them at his leisure. "Well, anyway, we're not totally screwed."

"Why is Run hiding in the bathroom?" Simon said from the corridor. "We've got a lot of people on board. Some of us have a dire need to relieve ourselves."

"We have two Chxor dreadnoughts coming up on us, and the Chief of Security and Warden both tried to screw each other and told half the Chxor fleet about a planned mutiny in the process," Mike said.

"Oh," Simon said. He seemed to think the entire thing through for a moment. "Well... at least I don't need to pee anymore."

Mike snorted, "Yeah, I would shit myself, but that mush they gave us stopped me up pretty well." He gave a sigh, "But anyway, we may have a chance. It looks like only those ships, and they're coming in at an angle that puts the bulk of the station between us and them. The only reason we even saw their approach is because the nose of this boat sticks out a little bit around the docking hub, and that's where they installed the telescope."

"There could be more of them coming from directions we can't see, though," Pixel said. "I mean, you said yourself before that we can only see a part of the sky."

"Yeah, but if we think about all the stuff we don't know, and all the things that the universe could do to screw us over, we'd never get anything done, we'd be paralyzed by fear," Mike said. "Besides, why would they need to send more than a pair of dreadnoughts to put down a riot on a station?"

"Why would they send two dreadnoughts in the first place?" Ariadne said. "I mean, my grasp of military vessels is pretty weak, but those are big ships, right?"

"Yeah, you can say that," Pixel said. "If I use those cruisers for scale... they're over two thousand meters long."

"Big enough," Mike said. "But maybe that's just what they had nearby, or maybe some admiral or someone thinks it's good training. I don't know why they sent those two ships-"

"The Chxor only have two types of military ships," Eric said. He shakily leaned against the hatch combing. "Five-class dreadnoughts and ten-class cruisers. They use mass production of those two classes to sustain a massive fleet."

"And you know that how?" Mike asked

"You shouldn't be up," Ariadne said, her voice harsh. "You need to rest, heal up." She seemed very motherly all of the sudden. She reminded Mike of his older sister for a moment. That thought seemed absurd on the face of it. His tiny, Asian, sister had no resemblance to the tall blonde woman. Mike hadn't thought of her in years, he realized.

"I can rest later," Eric said. "I did some time as a weapons officer in the Centauri Confederation Fleet. I got a bit of experience identifying enemy ships, and I studied them a bit... before I joined the Centauri Commandos."

"You were a Commando?" Mike asked, surprised. Military he expected, but the Centauri Commandos retained an almost mythical status amongst those who knew about them. The successors of the Amalgamated Worlds Special Forces, the Centauri Commandos had the best training and equipment, many had extensive training in a number of fields of fighting, from counter-terrorism to insurrection.

"For a while, before I got recruited for..." Eric paused and shook his head, "Sorry, must be going a bit loopy from blood loss."

Mike frowned though; someone had recruited him *from* the Commandos?

"Anyway, the Chxor dreadnoughts are the only ships in their fleet with any real offensive firepower. The cruisers just have some light interceptor weapons, pop guns really. Good enough to kill us, I bet, though. The rest of them are defenses, jammers, defense screens, and electronic warfare systems. The dreadnoughts are the dangerous ones, the cruisers just screen them."

"Alright, well, we still don't have any weapons, so we'll focus on escape," Mike said. "And I have a plan. We pull out, use our maneuver thrusters to get clear of the station and drop into the debris cloud. Put something big and solid between us and their sensors, and then light off the main drive."

"The thrusters burn a lot of fuel," Pixel said. "We might burn ourselves dry to get behind the gas giant."

"Yeah, well, we'll cross that bridge when we come to it," Mike said. He didn't want to die in a cold ship, but it might well beat whatever fate the Chxor reserved for rebellious prisoners.

"I have an idea," Pixel said. The engineer tapped at his screen for a moment. "Look, if I make some simple modifications to the engine, I can get a sort of pulse drive effect."

"A what?" Simon asked.

"He means the engine will give a massive pulse of thrust, and then go quiet, right?" Mike asked.

"Exactly. We'll only be detectable for a few seconds," Pixel said. "It puts a lot of strain on the drive, but we don't really care if we add a few thousand hours of strain on the magnetic plasma guide rods, right? I mean, it's not like we'll keep this ship; we're going to have to get one with a Shadow Space drive soon or we're dead."

"Right," Mike said. "If this ship blows up a few minutes after we're clear of it, I could care less."

"Really?" Pixel said. "Hey, you know..."

"How long would you need to make the modifications, and how long will the burn last?" Mike asked even as he brought up the thruster controls. He glanced at Ariadne, who gave him a nod to show he'd brought up the right ones. *Next time we get a choice, we do not take a Chxor ship,* he thought. He hated that he had to rely so heavily on someone else to do something he normally would have found simple.

"Uh..." Pixel tapped at his datapad. He frowned and stared at it for a moment, then rotated it upside down and tapped at it some more.

Mike looked at Simon, "All aboard?"

"Roger," Simon nodded. "We've got around twenty others, besides our little group. Should I have everyone brace themselves?"

Mike frowned. Normally he would have engaged the the inertial dampeners before he brought up even the maneuver thrusters. Yet once they separated, they would have to rely on internal power and internal fuel. He glanced at the fuel gauges, which at least showed a bar graph of the hydrogen level in the fuel tanks. The maneuver thrusters would drain a lot of fuel, just as Pixel had said. Inertial dampeners and artificial gravity would drain more. "Yeah, tell them to secure everything they can. Tie it down, tie themselves down. Whatever they can do. They have three minutes and then I cut artificial gravity and we move."

Simon nodded, "I think I saw some straps by the crates

and there may be some rope in the engine room. I'll get it done."

"Take the former pilot with you, would you?" Mike asked

Simon shook his head, "Would it have killed you to take him prisoner?"

Mike gave him a level glare, "I didn't kill him. Rastar did, after he went for a switch." Mike glanced at the switch in question. From what Run had said, that control would have shut power down to the controls. Mike felt he could stay silent on that, however, as Simon gave him a glare and grabbed the corpse by the feet.

Mike gave him a sixty second count and then flipped the switches that closed the outer hatch. He kept the umbilical that shared air and power with the station for the moment. He doubted that the ship's designers had planned for thirty passengers when they designed the life support. The longer they breathed station air, the longer they'd have air aboard the ship.

Finally Pixel looked up, "I could be wrong, but I think I can get us around ten gravities acceleration for twenty seconds. We'll only be able to do it once, though; after that the engines shouldn't run at higher than normal load. We can't trust their magnetic guide rods under that strain more than once." Pixel frowned, "I can do all of it from here, most of it is just setting up the process in the system. But once I hit execute, we'll be locked in."

"Understood," Mike said. He looked at Ariadne, "You good for normal space navigation too?"

She nodded, and she typed in a series of commands into the navigation computer. A system map appeared on the heads up display. Mike opened his mouth to make a suggestion, but she just closed her eyes and typed in further commands. Mike frowned, she didn't even seem to check the numbers she typed in. He'd known some pretty hot shot navigators, especially from when his more recent work aboard smuggler ships, but he had never known one to plot a course on the fly without even the use of a calculator.

She typed in the last command, and a curved line appeared on the screen. Mike frowned at the course, it seemed to take them out and around the gas giant in a maneuver designed to use its gravity well to throw them deeper into the system at a higher velocity. Also, it curved past two planets before it cycled past the star and then towards the outer system again.

"Those two planets are both in the life bearing belt," Mike said. "Can we break and try for orbit over either of them with this course?"

"Yes, but we'll give away our position. I tried to align our course to match a probable shipping lane between the two, we may get lucky and come across a freighter we can hijack."

Mike snorted, "Right, that's pretty damned unlikely. But thanks for thinking of it." He glanced at the timer. "Alright, strap in to a seat if you're staying here. Otherwise find someplace to hang on." He saw Ariadne take a seat in the rather messy copilot seat in front of him. He heard Pixel take a seat, and out of the corner of his eye, saw Eric lower himself to the floor and brace against the hatch combing.

Mike cut the artificial gravity first, and then the umbilical to the station. A moment later he brought up the thrusters. He used light taps, just enough to get them clear of the station itself, before he swung around and increased the burn.

The thrusters put out seven hundred thousand newtons of force, enough to accelerate the ship at almost four gravities of acceleration. They also drained the fuel tank at a rate that made Mike wince. He kept an eye on the fuel even as he worried about the signature the vessel would made as they vented superheated hydrogen plasma at a prodigious rate.

It put out a serious thermal signature, he knew. He could see the high visual signature as well, as florescent gas flared out in a bright trail. But not nearly as much as the fusion drive. *That* would put out measurable radio and x-ray and even a little gamma radiation as well, and a much higher energy signature. He somehow doubted that the Chxor would overlook that.

"Why is the acceleration throwing us forward?" Pixel asked. His voice sounded slightly strained from the acceleration.

"I'm using our forward thrusters," Mike grunted,

"Because normally those are bigger to assist in braking on boats like this. Also, it lets me gain a visual of the station, and the ships headed there."

He saw Ariadne type in a command on her console, and the radio went live again. A Chxor voice spoke. Ariadne reached back and touched Mike's knee. For a moment, he heard the Chxor words and then he heard the human translation, only in his head. The thought of what she did made him shiver. She considered her psychic abilities weak. Mike really did not want to meet up with one of the powerful psychics, or worse, one of the infamous Shadow Lords.

"Penal Station 2214, this is Ship's Commander Krakkan. I notice gas venting in your vicinity and note a debris cloud near your salvage bay. I notice that the emergency message recording has ceased its transmission. My sensors also show your defense turret offline. If Chief of Security Kras is available, have him communicate on this frequency. If he is not, put Warden Hral on."

A long period of silence passed. "This is Warden Hral. I regret to inform you that Chief of Security Kras was killed by the prisoners aboard the station. It seems likely that he had formed an alliance with them and they subsequently betrayed him."

"What a bastard," Mike muttered. He could understand the Warden's survival instinct, but his betrayal of his own kind, and his lack of loyalty to those who served and protected him, left Mike feeling nothing but disgust.

Ship's Commander Krakkan answered after a moment. "Warden Hral. Chief of Security Kras' death represents an unfortunate loss. However, I find it fortunate that I can speak with you directly. This maximizes efficiency, as I can directly inform you that for your treasonous activities, System Commander Hran has ordered your death."

If Mike didn't know better, he might have sworn the other Chxor actually sounded the slightest bit happy about that, almost as if he gloated about it a bit.

Mike shook his head; the thought seemed ridiculous, after what he had seen of the Chxor so far. If they had emotions, the crazy bastards suppressed them. No Chxor, especially not one ranked high enough to command a dreadnought, would show emotion.

"Ship's Commander Krakkan," Warden Hral spoke after a moment. "I request that you put aside any philosophical differences that we may have and look at the opportunity presented here. The station has a full load of precious metals and-"

"The logical thing for you to do is to surrender, Hral," Krakkan said. "You have betrayed the Empire, so you will face a tribunal. You will almost certainly be granted a quick execution, rather than sentence to a work camp. Your genetic offspring will not be purged if you follow the System Commander's orders."

"You will have to fight your way aboard," Warden Hral said. "This will result in a loss of your personnel. In addition, a result of violence will reflect poorly on your own career."

"Not particularly, Hral." Ship's Commander Krakkan said. "And System Commander Vren has authorized use of munitions if I felt them necessary. In the interests of efficiency, and to preserve the forces under my command, I will authorize use of a single mark three fusion warhead. Ship's Commander Krakkan out."

Mike stared at the station ahead of them. "Shit." They had put a good distance between them at this point. He didn't know if it would be enough. He cut the thrusters as they cleared the shadow of the station. "Pixel, you ready?"

"Um, almost?"

"You have thirty seconds," Mike said, a moment after the sensors caught a flare as something separated from the lead dreadnought.

The camera tracked the shape as it flew, and Mike threw up a countdown. He felt confident the warhead would detonate almost in contact with the station. He didn't know what bad blood lay between the two Chxor, but it looked like it had killed all the prisoners left aboard along with the Warden.

As Mike watched the timer countdown, he nudged the thrusters and spun the boat around. He tapped in the commands

104

to bring up the drive even as Pixel looked up, before the engineer could open his mouth, Mike slammed his hand on the initiate button for the drive. Mike just hoped he did it in time.

The world went white and then Mike's world faded to black.

***

Mike opened his eyes and groaned.

His groan turned into a yelp of surprise as something big and angular passed the cockpit window close enough for Mike to see the pockmarks on the surface.

He shook his head, and then felt his muscles tense as something else swept past before he could fully react.

"Ugh, are we dead?" Eric asked.

"No," Mike said. He flinched as they flashed past another chunk of debris. "Not yet anyway. Ten gravities of acceleration knocked us all out though." He checked the plotted course. Ariadne had put them dead through the middle of the debris cloud. *Of course,* he thought, *how else to use the gas giant as a slingshot.*

"Oh, good... I'm going to pass out now," Eric said.

Mike unstrapped the seat restraints. He saw Ariadne massage her temples, and Pixel seemed to stir as Mike stood from his seat.

He turned away from the sight of their flight through the debris cloud. He couldn't face that, not after their remarkable survival. He had to trust in Ariadne's course, and hope that she knew her job as well as he knew his. Just as he'd trusted in Pixel to bring the engines up and to set up the drive for its pulse. Just as he had trusted Eric, Rastar, and even Anubus to manage the fighting, and Run to save Eric's life.

Mike had given a lot of trust, more than he had since... since the destruction of the RLF *Noriko,* he had to admit. More, he had rediscovered hope. He found hope again when he had no real reason to, hope that with the help of these others, many of them strangers, that they would escape.

And so they had. And Mike realized that he'd gained

something more than his freedom when they broke out of Penal Station 2214. Mike had learned how to live again. Maybe, just maybe, Mike Golemon hadn't died after all. Soon they would have to make plans. Soon they would have to find some way to extend their freedom and survival. But not right now.

Right now, Mike figured they had all earned a break.

He looked over at Pixel, "Great job," then at Ariadne, "You too. We all did good." He gave a broad smile. "Today was a good day."

"We nearly died, multiple times. We've got a murderous Wrethe aboard, we're low on food supplies, and we've got a Chxor who views us as his own personal lab rats," Eric said. "Good day... are you insane?"

"We're alive," Mike said. "It's not much... but that's enough for now."

###

Research Notes
The Renegades
by Kal Spriggs

Expeditionary Laboratory Research Notes of Senior Scientist Rhxun

Disclaimer: All of the current experiments and research have been conducted in field conditions without the support of a full laboratory and the equipment necessary for detailed investigation. However, slight modifications to standard procedural analysis can be made to accommodate such a situation. In the interest of proper scientific procedures and maintenance of excellent research, a highly skilled and extremely knowledgeable researcher has exhaustively gone over all findings and applied his particular skills to the issues. Fortunately, as this key researcher is also the primary researcher, all findings are doubly investigated, both in initial research and by a scientist supremely skilled in his fields of expertise, which includes all sciences, particularly those areas of biology, genetics, life sciences, molecular biology, xenology, organic chemistry, and medical science.

Field Notes

Field Notes Disclaimer:

Initial field notes were recorded on scrounged cellulose fiber materials which the humans seem to use after defecation for cleaning purposes. This material proved flimsy and did not retain the recorded information very well. Of particular note, despite their inferior intelligence, the humans noticed the disappearance of this material, which possibly contaminated the research procedure.

Field Notes Overview:

The field notes cover the initial time period with observations of alien humans and their symbiotic companions. The initial time period covers the first 216 hours spent in observation or one full Chxor weekly cycle. During this time, particular note was made of the dominant male and dominant female of the human species, as well as their superstitions, emotional outbursts, and other inferior behavior.

First Thirty Six Hours:

Introductions with the humans has proceeded apace. I have flawlessly integrated myself into their band and I believe they see me as one of their own. After careful observation of their introductory rituals, I gave them my name. A peculiar trait I have noticed is their leader seems to ask for the name multiple times, perhaps as some ritualistic tendency. This seems very inefficient. I, nevertheless, conducted this ritual, as the male showed signs aggressive behavior which might have escalated without my flawless ability to adapt to their primitive society.

The humans proved remarkably ingenious in their attempts to escape the prison transport. In this, I cannot blame them, because labor aboard a penal station is the same as a termination sentence. They initially created a primitive explosive which they attempted to breach the door. Unfortunately, this proved hazardous to our continued survival. As a note, I must add a respirator to my future kit of expedition gear.

I observed the psychic abilities from the single female of the species. It was a very interesting display, the female seemed able to control fire with only the power of her mind. As these abilities are unknown amongst the superior Chxor, I will need to conduct proper research upon humans and other lesser species which display these abilities. The humans seem to think that these emanations come from their brains. This seems unlikely given the overly emotional nature of such species, surely too much brainpower is in use to allow additional activity as psychic emanations.

Arrival to the station allowed me to observe how one human band meets and greets another. I stayed unobtrusive during this time so as to properly observe the process and not interfere. The two bands interacted with much emotional posturing and outbursts. This new band of humans wore decorative marks of unique coloring. I believe such to be sign that they are inducted into the same tribe and have been so for some time. I hope that as this band of humans I have joined does not follow suit, as such colorful displays could be seen as signs of emotional affections once I return to civilized space. I shall have to look into markings that will appear permanent but removable.

The human dominant male, who calls itself 'Mike' seemed especially aggressive after the interaction with this other tribe. He initially instigated a strange threatening posture towards the one known as Crowe. This was followed later when he assigned the emotional Ghornath to lead the way to their feeding grounds aboard the station.

This was an excellent example of how the human emotions work against the concepts of logic and efficiency. The smaller human band initiated hostilities with the larger, well-armed, band, much like the human tribal nations have done against the Chxor Empire. Such tactical errors could only be the result of their highly emotional states or primitive cultural imperatives that the Chxor have outgrown. Luckily Chxor guards arrived and interceded before the human internecine warfare could get out of hand. The Ghornath, showing his highly illogical state, seemed bound to continue his aggression, this time against the prison station's guards. Unfortunately, I had to act in order to preserve my lone Ghornath subject. I used my dart pistol to pacify the large primitive. This also served to cement my own position in the band. More importantly, the loss of the singular Ghornath in the human band would be suboptimal to my cultural and xenothropology research.

Of particular interest is that after the human band's aggressive display, several other humans approached the dominant male. They seemed attracted by his group's fierceness, despite their more limited numbers. I think this must be some part of the human psyche, an attraction to their fellow inferiors who struggle against a superior foe. Why this is a survival instinct among such an oddly successful species I am not certain. From a genetic standpoint, it seems like an answer to why the species is a failure. They have bred the desire to fight superior opponents. This will, I believe, lead to their inevitable extinction. Certainly their resistance to proper subjugation by the Chxor is a sign of serious cultural imperatives that I find tantamount to species suicide.

I was surprised when the dominant male, Mike, asked my advice on tactical behavior. While certainly my advanced intellect and logical behavior make me a crucial adviser to his primitive strategy, I had not expected so sophisticated a response as to the creature eliciting advice in regards to Chxor culture and behavior. I realize that I have underestimated the human male, somewhat. I will have to revisit some of my initial assumptions. It seems that humans are not entirely driven by hormonal and emotional responses.

During the aftermath of the small battle, I took time to replenish some of my medical supplies. Most of it had to be field expedient types. In particular, various crude human knives and weapons I appropriated after the small skirmish between my band and the larger. Fortunately, the larger band seemed distracted by the threat of the smaller band and did not notice my acquisitions. Given time and access to chemicals I can also replenish my drug supply.

Following an explosion elsewhere in the station, my band of humans attacked the Chxor guards. I am not sure as to the source of the explosion, however I suspect my band found some means to use that event as a distraction. The Wrethe, a violent and dangerous species, proved his loyalty to the band through his attacks on the Chxor guards. I suspect that the Wrethe, Anubus, feels kinship and company to the other violent members of the band. Certainly some of the humans seemed to revel in the combat. In particular, the actions of the one known as Eric impressed me. He seemed very energetic and active in battle. His reactions, also, seemed particularly fast, even for a human. This suggests that he might be the product of some kind of warrior caste of humans. Although, his low pain threshold and illogical attempts to escape my field surgery after his injury suggest why he no longer in serves in this capacity. The tactical acumen of the dominant male also impressed me. Mike managed to catch a team of Chxor guards which included the station's chief of security in a crossfire. This required him to use his wounded members as bait for the guard's attack. How Mike realized the guards would attack and positioned himself to their flank is unknown, but is an interesting datum. His logic in the use of a wounded member of the band as bait impressed me and I see potential in him, particularly if I am given the opportunity to continue my earlier experiments with him as a subject.

It was unfortunate that I could not intervene to prevent the deaths of the low caste Chxor guards. However, as they are very low in caste and the prison duty is a punishment for some other infraction. Therefore, I doubt their loss will significantly impact the Empire as a whole. Indeed, it is most unlikely that the Chxor aboard this station have had or will have ever earned breeding status, therefore their genetic lines are probably inferior in any case. There is, of course, the added issue that my survival required these other Chxor to die. The logical thing, therefore, was to allow their termination.

I encountered a traitor to the Chxor Empire not long after this battle. The Chxor Warden had apparently worked with the human prisoners aboard the station. In exchange for precious metals, the Warden passed messages and allowed the human 'Fontaine' to conduct illegal activities aboard the station. While precious metals function as an illegal form of barter amongst the Empire, I find it illogical as to why the Warden would betray the Empire for such a reason. Certainly it brought his destruction as a result. The Empire learned of his treasonous activities and the insurrection aboard the station and dispatched several five-class dreadnoughts. The arrival of that much force would certainly have meant the destruction of the station. Fortunately, the humans secured a simple, in-system transport freighter and managed to escape the station. I had to preserve my crucial knowledge and experience for the benefit of all Chxor, so therefore I strategically positioned myself in the most armored portion of the transport.

The rations aboard the ship are highly efficient and designed for maximum nutrition and long term preservation. This will allow me food for some time, though I will have to monitor their levels carefully and be prepared to engage alternative food sources.

Preliminary Findings

The inferior species such as humans, Ghornath, and Wrethe are extremely emotionally compromised, driven by illogical mental processes, and often behave at a sub-sentient instinctive level. While they do, sometimes, show some limited capabilities at logical behavior, this is often overridden by their primitive natures.

The peculiar mixed nature of the group has an interesting dynamic. They do not behave as tribally as I had originally estimated. In fact, they seem to welcome new members into their band. They have already invested a human called 'Simon' which they chose due to his obvious structure-oriented mentality. He is clearly more evolved than most of them and has an almost acceptable appreciation for efficiency and order.

Part Two

113

The Gentle One
The Renegades, Book Two
by Kal Spriggs

The blue green clouds of the gas giant whipped past the cockpit close enough to touch. Ariadne stared out at the massive shape which filled the entire view. She could see the ripple of clouds and the eddy of currents. They flashed past the crackle of a lightning storm, there and gone in only a few seconds. Ariadne marveled at the beauty even as a part of her hungered to touch the energy of the storm.

"You think you could have brought us any closer?" Mike asked, "I could almost go outside and run my fingers through the clouds."

Ariadne smiled, "I wouldn't say that so loud, some of our friends might want to try it." She bit back a giggle at the thought of Rastar out on the hull trying to catch clouds as they swept past.

The pilot snorted, but when he spoke, Ariadne could hear his serious tone again. "You feel comfortable enough with... them to call them friends?"

Ariadne heard the hesitation in his voice, "I trust all of you. We stuck together through that mess on the station, why should I not?"

Mike looked back up at the passing planet. "For a mind reader, you sure do have an over-inflated opinion of people. You don't know if they're worthy of that trust. None of us had any choice but to work together-"

"That's nonsense, and you know it," Ariadne said. "We had plenty of choices! We could have given up like those poor people back there, some of us could have sided with Fontaine, and some of us could have gone it on our own." She ignored his comment about her psychic abilities, even as she shot a glance at the closed hatch behind her. None of the others knew about her ability to read minds. They thought her skills limited to pyrokenetics and navigation. She preferred it that way, people rarely trusted someone who could read or tamper with their thoughts. *I don't even trust* myself *sometimes...*

"None of that would have worked, not like this," Mike growled. "Working as a group is in our best interests, yes, for now. It won't be long before that is no longer the case."

"I understand that," Ariadne said. "But I think the bonds we have built so far will keep us together, despite our differences. And it is our different backgrounds and skills that make this team work."

"So we're a team now?" Mike said. He looked back at her, "Just be careful. You let them inside your guard and they can hurt you."

"Are you worried that I'll be hurt?" Ariadne asked.

Mike looked back and his dark eyes met her gaze. "Yeah, actually. As much as I hate to admit it. Once the survival high passed, I actually feel pretty darned good about our little band of misfits. That doesn't mean, however, that I trust some of them as far as I could throw Rastar."

Ariadne chuckled at the thought of the diminutive Mike even lifting the four armed and four legged alien. Rastar must weigh in at three hundred kilos, she knew, and he stood three meters tall. "Right, well, I'll be careful." She took one last gaze at the beauty of the storm-ridden planet. "But I should go back and see how our other passengers are doing."

"You mean the other escaped prisoners, right?" Mike said. "I'd be doubly careful with them. They didn't do a damned thing to earn their freedom... nothing besides following our lead."

"Not everyone has the abilities and skill to do what they want," Ariadne said. "It's up to those of us with such abilities to help out the ones who can't help themselves."

"Some of them would kill you for a Colonial Drachma," Mike grunted. "The Chxor didn't send just anyone to that prison station, they sent the ones who they thought might be the biggest risks, the most dangerous prisoners. Some of them might be decent enough people, but I imagine that a few of them would get locked up in human space too."

Ariadne sighed, "We've come full circle again. Right now it's in their interest to work with us. I think that if we show them we trust them now, they'll continue to work with us in the future. If we keep them locked in the cargo hold, we'll be no better than the Chxor."

Mike didn't answer her, and Ariadne gave him a nod of victory as she stepped out of the narrow cockpit. She paused to pull the heavy hatch closed behind her and gave Mike an encouraging smile as it slipped closed. *He worries too much,* she thought.

She almost ran into Anubus as she turned around. She felt her heart race as the big alien edged into her personal space. The Wrethe's black fur seemed to absorb the light. His jackal-like head peered down at her, his dark eyes unreadable. His smell, more than anything, reminded her of a weapon. He smelled like a steel blade to her, like the well-oiled sword her foster father had kept in his study.

"Hello," Ariadne forced some cheer into her voice. It wasn't that she didn't think he had merits, but of all the crew, he was the only one she *knew* viewed her and the others as prey capable of reason. Tasty prey, at that.

"Ariadne," Anubus growled. "I came to see you. Do you have a moment to talk?" He glanced down the hallway, almost as if nervous they would be overheard. His unusual attitude made Ariadne tense. Anubus was dangerous enough and if he wanted privacy...

"Yes, I suppose so. Do you want to go somewhere or..." She frowned at the hesitation in his voice. She restrained her desire to open her mind to read his thoughts. For one, she did not want to see the world through his eyes. For another, she had tried to read aliens before, and the way their minds functioned made her head ache, especially those of the Chxor. Her little foray into Run's mind earlier had given her a headache for a few hours. She didn't know what she might find in Anubus's mind, but she felt pretty certain she would not enjoy it. Humanity knew little about the origins of the Wrethe, but they had come to understand their psychotic level of aggression well enough.

Ariadne had once heard Wrethe described as violent sociopaths and that description seemed apt enough from her own experience. From what she'd seen so far, Anubus seemed only a few heartbeats away from murder.

"With the hatch closed, this is the most privacy we will find on this tiny craft," Anubus said. The Wrethe hesitated, and if he were human, she would have thought he had paused to build up courage to speak. As it was, she wondered what might worry a Wrethe. "I found your abilities very impressive, back on the station. You are a very dangerous human."

Ariadne grimaced, "You're talking about... what I did to those Chxor guards who attacked us?"

"Exactly," the Wrethe gave a sharp nod. His jaws moved up and down in front of her face in a motion very similar to a lunge. Only the solid metal hatch at her back prevented Ariadne from taking a step back. She couldn't help the jolt of adrenaline as those teeth looked ready to rip her throat out.

"Well, thanks, I guess," Ariadne said, even as she tried to push back the memory of the Chxor engulfed in flames and control her own fear of Anubus. She felt a trickle of sweat run down her back. It itched terribly. She smelled something else then, it almost smelled like burning hair. *Aw crap, get yourself under control,* she thought, *you are not going to lose it right now.*

Despite her focus on control, the temperature in the corridor started to heat up.

"It is rare that a Wrethe finds someone as deadly as itself among the lesser species such as your own," Anubus said. Ariadne held back a semi-hysterical giggle at his backhanded compliment. *Anubus must find his status as a superior being so troublesome,* she thought. "When that is the case, we often must test ourselves against them, to find their place. This often results in death, of course."

Ariadne felt her heart drop. Sweat broke out on her forehead and she almost let her power slip, even as she had a mental image of Anubus engulfed in flames. She restrained a semi-hysterical giggle as she thought, *very pretty flames...*

"But obviously, your abilities and mine differ," Anubus

said. "Yours are those of the mind, and mine are those of stealth and physical strength. Therefore, I think we have an even match, but it is easy to see who would win under different circumstances. So I do not wish to fight you."

"What?" Anubus's words came as she stood on precipice of her fear. She had almost stepped over the edge and given into her desire to light him up like a furry match. His words came as sufficient shock that she felt like he had doused her with a bucket of cold water. That gave her the break to lock down her powers again. She mentally stepped away from that abyss... reminded yet again at how close she stood to a transition into a terrible killer. She wiped at sweat on her forehead and saw he had cocked his head at her, almost as if he thought *she* thought it too bad they couldn't fight. "Well that's good, I mean. I don't want to fight you. We gain nothing from it, and we can work together. Our abilities actually complement one another, in a way."

"I suppose," Anubus said. He pulled his head in, almost as her words made him uncomfortable. "But what I wanted to ask, was if you could... teach me."

"Uh..." Ariadne swallowed. How exactly did she explain to him that he needed psychic abilities in the first place?

"I see your confusion," the Wrethe said. "I possess some minor psychic abilities, which I have not trained with much due to... personal reasons. I wonder if you could assist me."

"What?" Ariadne said, "I didn't realize the Wrethe had any psychics."

Anubus gave her a broad grin, "It is not something that my species advertises. Many of us focus on our physical strengths, often at the cost of any inherited mental abilities. Individual Wrethe on occasion choose to sire offspring with psychic abilities to assist them, but inevitably, when they reach adulthood, there will be conflict."

"Is that your story?" Ariadne asked, "Did your... parents produce you to help them?" The thought intrigued her, that Anubus might have a similar story to hers. She remembered her foster family fondly, but she had always wondered about her true parents, even as her brother had asked her questions about them.

119

"I killed the one who bred me," Anubus said. "We self-reproduce, and use additional genetic material we gain from other species we consume to introduce genetic variation. He intended me to be his healer as a juvenile."

Ariadne blinked at that. *So much for any similarity of background*, she thought.

Anubus continued to speak, "I possess what humans call Psi Beta abilities, I can intuitively manipulate anatomy, heal myself and others, and... do some other things."

"Wow, I never met someone with those skills," Ariadne said. She had read about them, when she researched her own abilities, but the few books she found on the subject suggested it a rare area of natural talent. She thought it fascinating that the dangerous Wrethe had skills that could heal. "Have you tried to help out Eric, yet? Run did some good work on him, but if you could speed his healing, that would be great."

"Why would I do that?" Anubus stared at her with his dark eyes.

"Uh, because it would be a nice thing to do?" Ariadne said.

"He will heal on his own," Anubus grunted. "I will not expose my abilities to others, not without benefit to myself. That idea is ridiculous. Besides, Eric is an idiot."

"...Okay," Ariadne said. She wished she could think of a way to politely decline to help him. Truthfully the thought of a pyrokenetic Wrethe made her *very* uneasy. "Well, I suppose I can work with you. I recommend we do it later though, if you don't mind. There's no real room to work here, and if you find success, it might be dangerous in the close confines."

"Of course," Anubus said. "I prefer to do it someplace we can find solitude as well."

"Good, well, I'm going to go check on the others, care to join me?" Ariadne forced herself to ask. She somehow doubted the others would feel very talkative with a two meter tall werewolf from space following her around, but she felt it polite to ask.

"No, I prefer solitude," Anubus said. "I also would prefer

120

to avoid unnecessary confrontation and preserve my energy for seizure of a ship for escape."

"Alright," Ariadne said. "I guess sometime-"

"Anubus, my man!" A deep voice boomed. "There you are, I wondered where you got off to!"

The overly loud voice startled Ariadne. She turned to face the speaker, then had to crane her neck to look up at him as he came closer. The three meter tall Ghornath had to hunch over to fit in the low corridor, but his leathery hide had tinted green, which if Ariadne remembered right, that meant he felt happy, or at least friendly. She had also learned that when he turned red, bad things started to happen.

"Rastar," Anubus growled.

"Hey man, I wanted to let you know that I think we worked really good together, and you know, I think you're a pretty good... well, friend I guess," Rastar said. He held out one of his four hands to shake. "What do you say to being partners?"

"I say get your hand out of my face before I feed it to you," Anubus growled.

"Hey, no need to be so hostile, Annie," Rastar said. "I know your tough guy outside is just an act, you know, because other people, especially humans don't trust us big guys. But it doesn't have to be like that between us, you know?"

"I want you to know that your pathetic attempt to pretend friendship has not deceived me in the slightest," Anubus growled. "As a matter of fact, I find it insulting that you think me so easily swayed. I will not let your act slow me in the slightest when you move against me." Ariadne bit her lip at that, she really hoped Anubus did not think that the rest of them plotted his demise.

"Uh, dude, that's really not a healthy attitude," Rastar said. "I mean, we should be allies, friends even. Two big aliens against the rest of the universe, you know?" Despite her nervousness, Ariadne nodded as Rastar echoed some of her own sentiment.

Ariadne saw Anubus's lips twitch and saw his sheathed claws extend and retract. Clearly Anubus found Rastar infuriating. She didn't think the eruption of a fight to the death between the two of them would leave much left of the ship. "Hey Rastar!" She said cheerfully.

"Oh," Rastar looked over Anubus's shoulder, "I didn't see you there, Ariadne. How are you?" He shaded slightly yellow, "Uh, I hope you realize the whole thing about humans judging other races was meant as politely as possible."

"I understand what you meant," Ariadne said with a smile. She saw Anubus had stopped twitching. She hoped that the Wrethe physiology mimicked Humans in that regard. She said a silent prayer that Anubus had himself under control. "Honestly, as a psychic I find myself as the target of some prejudice myself."

"Really?" Rastar asked. "I had heard something of the sort, but it seems silly to me. The Ghornath have few psychics, but those often become mediators and judges amongst my kind. You may have heard that the Ghornath have a slight reputation for impulsiveness at times?"

Ariadne blinked at him, uncertain if he had made a joke or not. Ghornath had a reputation for extreme impulsiveness and many had temper issues to boot. In that last respect, Rastar seemed a perfect example at least.

Evidently Rastar took her silence as assent, "Yeah, well, the handful of psychics among my race act to moderate that, especially among our young. Many psychics become teachers. I never got the opportunity to have a psychic teacher, but I have a lot of respect for your kind. Fortunately I have excellent control over my impulses, and I rarely completely lose my temper."

"Um, I almost hate to bring this up," Ariadne said. She gnawed on her lip, "But you kind of exploded back on the station and nearly got us all killed because of a brawl that you started." She remembered the fight vividly, if only because she had very nearly cut loose with her own powers until the Chxor guards showed up. She wasn't sure whether Fontaine's criminals deserved to live or die, but she didn't want to be their killer.

Rastar nodded, "Yeah, but if you'll remember, I managed to avoid killing anyone." He somehow managed to say it like he had carefully bludgeoned thugs and thrown men across the room with caution, Ariadne noted.

"But they nearly killed us!" Ariadne said. She remembered how the Chxor guards had arrived and broken up the impending riot with aggressive force. "And the guards would have killed you if not for Run tranquilizing you with his little dart gun."

"Well, you know," Rastar said with a broad shrug, "Sometimes you have to take the good with the bad."

Ariadne stared at him with shock. She felt too stunned to speak.

"She does mention something that bothered me," Anubus said. Ariadne looked at the Wrethe, who had cocked his jackal's head as he studied the Ghornath. "You received several stab wounds during that brawl. You seem remarkably healthy now."

Ariadne frowned, "You know? He's right. I remember when you fought that first group of Chxor guards one of them caught your side with a riot gun shot. You also took a couple of bullet hits when that Chxor Chief of Security had us pinned down, but you don't even look wounded now."

"Also, when Eric triggered the explosive on the door to the administration offices, you stood near him," Anubus said. "You took some shrapnel to the leg, yet you seem to walk without issue now. How do you explain your rapid healing?"

Rastar looked between them. A flicker of colors washed across his body. He seemed pale when he answered, "Well, you know, Ghornath have a good metabolism, and I'm pretty young, I think I just heal quickly."

"From *bullet* wounds?" Anubus asked, and Ariadne could hear the incredulity in his voice. "And shrapnel... I can't believe that your race is *that* tough. Maybe if you were a Wrethe, or if you were the product of some sort of genetic tinkering or prototype cybernetics."

Rastar went a bit pale for a moment and then he shaded green, "Hey man, you know, maybe you and I just share some pretty similar qualities. I mean, we're both pretty tough..."

Anubus growled. "I can see you will continue to play the

imbecile. Do not think I will not find out your secret and take it from you." He edged past the Ghornath, "And leave me be or I will see if I can find it in your entrails."

"See you later, Annie," Rastar said as the Wrethe stalked away in disgust.

"You know that if you push him to far you'll have a fight on your hands," Ariadne said nervously. She didn't know which of the big aliens would win, but she did not want to be in the area when it happened. Especially if Rastar lost his temper in the process.

"Oh, him?" Rastar said. "Nah, Anubus is a big softie, I bet he likes kittens and drinks hot chocolate." He shaded a deeper tone of green, "Say, do you know anything about the food situation? I'm pretty hungry."

"You gave away your rations back on the station," Ariadne said. She had thought it a pretty noble act at the time, though she wondered if it came of his impulsive nature or if he truly had felt for the other prisoners. Either way, it spoke well of his generosity.

"Yeah..." Rastar's hide darkened to blue. "I wish we could have saved more of them. I know how it feels to give up hope, especially in a place like that."

Ariadne sighed, "Me too. I grew up in a foster family, they were nice enough, but before them there were a series of orphanages... My brother and I had our experience of bad places." Granted none as bad as the Chxor Penal Station, but rough enough for a child. "You grew up in refugee camps?"

"Yeah, the Vega system and one on Tannis as well," Rastar said softly. "You were orphaned, too?"

"War orphan, at least my papers said that," Ariadne nodded. "The Centauri Civil War, or Tau Ceti Separatist War, depending on which side talks about it." She smiled then in memory of her adoptive parents, "My brother and I got lucky, we got a good adoptive family. A really nice older couple, they raised us like we were their own." She remembered then that she had not sent them a message in weeks now, she hoped that they did not worry too much about her.

Rastar rested a hand on her shoulder, "I had not realized we shared that bond. My family died on Ghornath Prime when Nova Roma invaded. My father actually served in the Fleet, he was a sensors officer. My mother served as a military nurse." He sighed, "I don't even have a picture of them, but it is good to know that they served my race well."

Ariadne patted the Ghornath's big hand, she felt a little awkward at his touch. He had a strange smell, she realized, sort of like cinnamon and mint combined. His skin felt like smooth leather, warm and textured. "Well, my brother and I never learned the identity of our parents. It's something that we both did a lot of research about. It's rough not knowing... even when you have adoptive parents who love you, you still want to know where you came from." Ariadne closed her eyes, "Especially when you develop psychic powers at a young age."

"Ah," Rastar said. "Well, though our circumstances vary, I think that we share a common bond in this." His hide went back to its normal brown color. "What happened with your brother?"

Ariadne looked away, his presence suddenly felt invasive. "I don't know, stuff happened back on Tau Ceti. We both had to run, and I lost him."

"I'm sorry," Rastar said. "I take it you search for him still? Well in that case, I insist that I will help you. Whatever help you need, I will be there. Family is important, and if I had a brother, I have no doubt you would help me to find him and welcome him as a friend as well."

Ariadne felt a headache come on as she imagined two of Rastar in the same place at the same time. *I think that the universe might well implode at that level of potential destruction,* she thought. "Um, thanks. I'll let you know if I need your help. In the meantime, I'm going to go check on the others." She frowned as she searched for some way to deflect his helpful nature. "Hey, you know, Mike mentioned he felt drowsy and might want some company to keep him awake, maybe you should see how he's doing in the cockpit?"

She felt a moment of guilt about her escape, but then she

remembered that Mike had said he didn't trust most of their companions because he did not know them. Well, she'd give him a better opportunity to get to know Rastar. Not that she didn't like him, she admitted. He just seemed to take up a lot of space and time.

"Hey, sure, I'd be glad to help," Rastar said.

"Well, I'll just get out of your way..." Ariadne squeezed past him and continued down the corridor. She stopped when she heard the cockpit hatch close behind Rastar. Her hand dipped into her pocket and pulled out the small metal lighter she had put there. She pulled it out and stared at it for a long moment. The dented and scratched surface seemed so familiar, along with the inscription on the side: Aut Inventiem Viam Aut Faciam. The set of initials on the bottom, the only thing she knew about her father: BTM.

She shot a glance up and down the corridor, then pulled the top off of the lighter and pulled the inside out. She tipped the case up and caught the small glittering object that she had hidden in the base of the casing. Ariadne gave a slight smile at the small silver crucifix on the gold chain in her hand. Everything she had from her parents... and far more than some people had, she knew. Her mother's faith, and her father's motto.

Ariadne had sought to embrace them both, as a child. Yet her faith had faltered numerous times, especially after she went on the run, and then after brother's disappearance. As much as she believed in people, she found it hard to believe in a god that made good people do bad things. Yet, as she looked down at the silver cross, she felt... peaceful. She almost felt that if she gave in, if she looked for his will, she might find her way through these dangers.

Ariadne shook her head. She would put her trust in her new friends. She tucked the crucifix back in the bottom of the lighter, and then put it back together. She fought a sudden urge to light it and stare at the flame, as she had as a child. The flame had come to represent her missing father to that lost child, but Ariadne didn't need that -- not now. She took a deep breath and continued down the hallway. She didn't need symbols and she did not need faith, she had friends, they had a plan, they would come through safe and sound.

Ariadne continued down the short corridor. She stopped and peered into the port cargo hold. Most of the prisoners had ended up in that one, almost all of them strangers. She felt an urge to step in and introduce herself, but most of them had gone to sleep, some wrapped in blankets, but most just passed out on the metal deck plates.

She felt a twist of sorrow at their discomfort. She remembered the thin pallets back on the station in the prison barracks. The things had smelled stale, but still she wished they had time to bring some, they would improve conditions over the cold metal deck. She made note to ask Pixel if he had found anything in the engine compartment they could use for padding at least.

She looked in the starboard cargo bay. The pile of crates remained in the center of the hold, strapped down and secured in a manner that looked very professional. She saw the man who performed that job a moment later. He had one crate open and made notes on a datapad as she watched. She saw Run stood nearby, and she guessed that Simon used him for translation of the Chxor glyphs.

"What's the haul?" Ariadne said.

"Well, that depends," Simon said. He pointed at the corner, "Those two heavy crates are proper pirate booty, around three hundred kilos of gold bars. Though Anubus seems to have staked his claim to them."

"What?" Ariadne said. "Three hundred kilograms!?"

"Yeah, it looks like the Warden had a backup plan in case he couldn't talk his way into being the hero," Simon said. She remembered how Mike had told them of the Warden's plan to allow the human criminal Fontaine to stage an escape attempt to make the station's Chief of Security look bad. The Warden's overall plan seemed to be to increase his chances of promotion when he foiled the escape attempt. Ariadne didn't follow exactly how a breakout attempt on the station, even a foiled one, would make the Warden look better. *Then again,* she thought, *I'm a human and not a Chxor.*

Either way, it had not worked out well for the Warden when the Chxor Fleet showed up and nuked the station. Fontaine seemed have escaped on another ship and a stockpile of precious metals along with his gang. And the rest of them had made it aboard this cargo boat.

"That's got to be worth..." Ariadne tried to do the conversion from grams to ounces, and then to remember how much an ounce of gold might be worth.

"You're from Tau Ceti, so around sixty seven point two million Separatist Dollars, as of the time I got captured," Simon said, as he turned his datapad to face her. "Or around seventy five point three million Confederation Dollars. Or one hundred and twenty five point three four million Colonial Republic Drachma..."

"Okay, I get the picture," Ariadne said. She shook her head, "So we're rich?"

"Doesn't do us much good right now," Simon said. "We can't eat gold. We can't breathe gold, and short of dumping it out the airlock to use as a projectile, we can't use it as a weapon right now either."

"Still..." Ariadne said. "It's *gold.*"

"I thought you females went for diamonds," Simon grunted.

"Diamonds aren't rare," Crowe said from the doorway. "Their price is artificially maintained, especially now that we can manufacture them to spec. Most jewelers make a huge overhead off of diamond sales. And resale value is essentially nonexistent. Gold, on the other hand, is a relatively rare metal, which is why it has so much worth."

"Good to know," Simon said. "I didn't know that about resale value. You have much opportunity to try to sell used diamonds?" His voice took an overly casual tone, but Ariadne could see the calculation behind his eyes as he stared at Crowe.

Crowe gave him a slight smile, "Mister Policeman, are you asking me if I stole some jewelry?"

"I'm not a cop anymore," Simon answered. "However, it

would clear up some questions I had about your skills, particularly with how easily you hacked the Chxor station systems. I think it took you around two minutes, including the time it took to plug in the datapad."

Crowe shrugged, "What can I say? I've got some serious skills."

Ariadne restrained a sigh, time for a change of subject. "So, what's in these other crates?"

"Well, in box one, we have..." Simon swept out a hand, "Chxor rations. Box number two contains... More Chxor rations. And box number three..."

"Let me guess, more Chxor rations?" Ariadne said helpfully.

"Yep," Simon answered. "The other boxes have the same labels, but I'm still going through it, just to see what all is here."

"We can't eat their food, can we?" Ariadne asked. "I mean, we've got different proteins and stuff, right? I've heard that some species can eat similar foods, like the Ghornath..."

"Yeah, the Ghornath are able to eat our stuff," Crowe said. "Stupid Rastar found my stash of ration bars."

"Stash?" Simon said. "I thought we agreed not to hoard the food supplies, but to take a bar as needed," Simon said. "We have enough food for a full week if we share supplies."

"Yeah, well, maybe I don't want to share," Crowe said. "And didn't you hear what I said? Rastar went and took all of mine!"

"Hey," Ariadne said. "I'm sure Rastar just plans on dispensing them. He's got a low opinion of letting people go hungry... and for good reason."

"Yeah, you would take his side, wouldn't you, mind freak?" Crowe said. "You're no better than one of the aliens."

"Walk away," Simon said. "Before you start to *really* annoy me."

Crowe looked at Simon and then gave Ariadne a nasty look. "Oh... I see how it is. Well, then. I'll leave you two some privacy. I'm certain that the little Chxor there will find it *interesting*, especially if you let him take notes."

Ariadne felt her face flush. She opened her mouth to deny his allegation. But he left before she could find the right words. She looked over at Simon, and saw he had gone still. He didn't meet her eyes when he spoke, "Sorry about that. He's a piece of scum, I shouldn't have let him get to me."

Run looked between them, "Is this some human emotional ritual? I must note that I have no interest in psychological functions. I find your biological functions of interest." He looked between Simon and Ariadne. "Or is this your reproductive rituals? I understand that humans put much value on emotional bonds with regards to mating. We Chxor fortunately are above such petty necessities and procreate only to produce superior genetic lines after we have earned our right to reproduce."

Desperate to change the subject to something that didn't involve further embarrassment, Ariadne addressed the little alien. "Run, is there any way that humans can eat these Chxor rations?"

He shook his head, "This experiment would not work for very long. Humans and Chxor have different proteins as you said before. Also, we make use of different chemical compounds, many of which each species finds toxic to the other. I am aware of several experiments where Chxor tried to survive on humans, none of which found success."

"Human rations," Ariadne automatically corrected.

"No, they had no need to ration them, they had a surplus available," Run answered.

Ariadne frowned, "No, I mean you meant to say that Chxor tried to survive on human rations."

"I did?" Run asked.

"Of course," Ariadne said patiently, "Otherwise it sounds like the Chxor ate humans."

"Right," Run said.

"Glad we cleared that up," Ariadne laughed. The little alien seemed so odd sometimes. She felt certain he was different from other Chxor though, if only because he viewed humans as something to study rather than exterminate.

"Um..." Simon frowned at Run. "I'm not really sure we

did."

Ariadne shrugged, confused by his cryptic statement, "Well, anyway, we know that Run will have plenty of food, even if the rest of us can't eat this stuff. We still have about a weeks worth of ration bars, at one bar a day, right?"

Simon stared at Run with pursed lips. He blinked a bit, almost as if caught off guard by the track of her conversation. "Yeah. One week. Your course puts us near the first of the inhabitable planets in a day, and the other one in five, right?"

"Yeah, It's actually a moon of this gas giant. It should take around a day, but if we have to do braking maneuvers, then that will draw out the time somewhat." Ariadne said. "It depends on how extreme maneuvers we can manage, but I think another day at the most."

"Alright," Simon said, "Then we'll be fine for food until after we have a ride out of the system or we get caught and killed. Either way, it's not a huge issue."

"But the trip elsewhere could take several months," Ariadne said. "It depends on what system this is. They gassed us, for transport, so I'm not sure where we are. If we're deep in the Chxor Empire... well, it could take weeks or even months to get back to civilization."

"I can only plan for something if I know the full parameters," Simon answered. "We don't have a ship capable of escape yet. We might get lucky and find a human freighter or even a smuggler. In that case, we trade some gold for a ride out, and we don't worry about food."

"What if we don't find a ship like that?" Ariadne asked.

"Then we starve to death or Anubus kills and eats us to survive," Simon said.

***

Ariadne left Simon to his inventory and went aft towards the engine compartment.

She felt somewhat hesitant as she stopped outside the open hatch. She didn't really understand the machinery there and a small part of her worried that just her presence might throw

131

things into chaos and perhaps destroy the ship. It seemed a silly idea, she fully realized. *Then again, if I lose my self-control, who knows what might happen,* she thought.

She straightened her shoulders though and stepped inside, despite her fears. She would not let some vague fears limit her interaction with her companions. "Hello?" She asked. She stared around the tiny compartment, surprised that she didn't see Pixel. The tall, gawky engineer normally stood out. Certainly she did not see anywhere where the brown haired engineer might hide in the tiny space not occupied by the fusion reactor or its support machinery.

His head popped out of an open panel in the floor several feet away, "Oh, hey, how ya doing?"

Ariadne nearly jumped out of her skin. She didn't know how he had fit through the hole, much less how his entire body fit underneath, but for a moment, it looked like his disembodied head floated there in front of her. "Uh, what are you doing down there?" She finally managed to ask.

"Oh, just checking out the magnetic plasma guide rods. We put a lot of strain on them with that pulse burn. I just want to make sure they'll hold up to normal work when we need to do maneuvers so that they don't fail on us," Pixel said. "Want to help?"

"Uh... sure?" Ariadne said.

"Pass me that gauge there, please?" Pixel said. Ariadne looked at the pile of tools nearby. She vaguely recognized wrenches and a hammer, but the rest looked arcane in the extreme. "It's the black thing that looks kind of like a pistol, only with a big screen on it."

"Oh," Ariadne picked it up and passed it down to him.

"Thanks. Getting in and out of here something of a pain," Pixel said. He dove down into the mess of piping and wire conduits below the deck plates. He spoke a moment later, his voice muffled, "You have no idea how often I wished I had telekinesis, if only so that when I got stuck in a job like this I could just call over that one tool I always seem to forget."

Ariadne smiled, "Well, you have no idea how often I

wished I had some technical expertise, if only to fix stuff when it breaks."

"Hah, that's funny, I hadn't thought of it that way," Pixel said. "You know, I could teach you some things, if you're interested. Just simple stuff, how to start the plant, how to read the gauges, that sort of thing."

"That sounds like fun," Ariadne said. She always liked to learn new things. She had no real interest in the fusion reactor or the fusion drive. But still, she thought it might be useful to know a bit about it. "When can we start?"

"Well, I've been at this for... oh, jeez, like six hours now. So I think I'll take a break. After I get some sleep maybe?" Pixel said. She heard a clank as he worked on something out of sight, then he gave a grunt, "Well, that should do it... let see here...." Ariadne waited patiently. She didn't mind the silence, it gave her time to zone out. "Huh, that's interesting." The dry tone of his voice managed to impart special emphasis upon the word *interesting*.

"Good news, I hope?" Ariadne asked.

"Nope... just interesting. Apparently the Chxor designed the rods with less of a margin for crazy stuff like we did. We actually exceeded the safety margin by... well quite a bit. The guide rods peaked out at almost five hundred degrees centigrade, and I think that it's a good thing we only did that pulse for twenty seconds."

"What does all that mean?" Ariadne asked.

Pixel's head popped back up from the open panel. "We nearly lost magnetic containment on the fusion drive," he said.

"Uh... isn't that a bad thing?" Ariadne asked.

"Oh yeah, but we would never have noticed," Pixel said. "I bet the Chxor would sure find a second fusion explosion after the station very confusing, though."

"So can we still make maneuvers?" Ariadne asked.

"We should be fine, just no fancy stuff like we pulled. If we planned to use this boat any longer than we do, I would recommend maintenance, but..." he shrugged. "Honestly, I mostly checked out of curiosity." He lifted his shoulders out of the hole and held up a bag of tools, "Could you hold this?"

Ariadne caught the bag. Pixel braced himself on the edges of the panel and squeezed out. Close up, she could smell him. He smelled like a strange mix of warm bread and motor oil. Though she didn't know how, his scent reminded her a bit of her brother. "Phew, thanks, I would hate to have had to crawl out and then right back in just to get that gauge..." his eyes went distant. "Oh darn."

"You left it down there?" Ariadne asked.

He nodded sheepishly, "Yeah. Well, no help for it..."

Ariadne looked down in the hole. She held up one hand to stop him. She saw the gauge, the black tool lay on a shelf formed by two pipes that ran together. She narrowed her eyes in concentration. She reached out with her mind and lifted the small object up out of the hole. She caught it by the pistol grip, and gave Pixel a broad smile as she passed it over.

"You're pretty useful to have around," Pixel said. "And not just for roasting bad guys."

Ariadne grimaced, "Thanks."

"You didn't like what you did?" Pixel asked.

"No," Ariadne answered. "I am strongest with pyrokenetics, more so than my other abilities. When I first manifested my abilities, that came first."

"I don't see the problem," Pixel said

"Imagine a teenager with hormonal issues who can light people on fire with her brain if she loses her temper," Ariadne said. "Luckily I got it locked down for the most part. My little brother helped me a lot with that. But there for a while... what with my other abilities, I could have become one hell of a little monster."

"Oh," Pixel said. He seemed to think that over. "Well, at least you didn't kill anyone, right?"

"Not then," Ariadne said softly.

"Oh?" Pixel asked.

"I... got careless, went the other way, tried to help some people and got caught doing it," Ariadne said. She looked down at her feet. "My brother and I had to go on the run. We came across some pretty rough sorts, and some of them just would not stop pushing. One of them attacked my brother... and I lost it. Worse than with those Chxor, actually."

"You saved your brother, though, that's important," Pixel said. "And at least no one innocent got killed. Shoot, I don't think you got it in you to hurt someone who doesn't have it coming."

"Thanks," Ariadne smiled. She cleared her throat, "Anyway, so what brings a university trained engineer way out here?"

Pixel looked away, "Well... I guess you could say I trusted the wrong people. They asked my advice on what I thought was a joke or prank of some kind. They put their own little spin on it though, and people died. I could have stayed back on New Glasgow and faced some serious prison time. I ran instead, and here I am."

"I'm sorry," Ariadne said. "The people who used your work, did you know them?"

"One of them I considered a friend," Pixel said. He sighed, "We had a difference in opinion over some things... I thought it just something that we discussed an argument we both used to stimulate thought. I guess he felt a lot more serious about it."

"Did you ever talk to him, afterward?" Ariadne asked. "Maybe it was a misunderstanding?"

Pixel looked over at her, and for a second, she thought she saw a look of anger flash across his face. The moment passed, however, and he gave her a sad smile, "No... I think I know pretty well that he knew exactly what he wanted to do. And as far as I know, he did not survive, so I've no way to ask him anyway."

"Gosh, that's got to be hard to live with," Ariadne said. "Thanks for sharing, though, I feel like I know you better now."

"What a bunch of sappy bullshit," Eric said from behind her.

"What?" Ariadne turned around.

The former soldier stood in the hatchway. His face had

135

twisted in derision. "So he just says that a buddy of his betrayed him and died in the process and you say thanks for sharing? Right. Don't even pretend to give a damn, save your breath," Eric said.

"Excuse me," Ariadne said, suddenly uncomfortable.

"Whatever," Eric rolled his eyes.

"What's your problem?" Pixel said. "And who invited you to this conversation anyway?"

"I found Crowe lurking outside listening in," Eric said. "I came over to warn you two that he eavesdropped out here for a while. But then I hear the emotional crap psychic chick shoveled and I had to interrupt."

"Crowe is out there?" Ariadne asked. She felt a sudden dread, she'd seen his eyes on her, and how he always managed to say something nasty to her when he thought he could get away with it. She did not want him to know about her past, or worse, to find out the details she had *not* shared with Pixel.

"Not anymore," Eric said. Like I said, I chased him off." He looked over at Pixel, "And my problem is her bleeding heart. People die every day, and worse things happen to people than that. She grew up in Tau Ceti space... and her nation has any number of atrocities to pay for. If she wants to make things better, maybe she'd make a better impression if she didn't seem to wear her home like a badge of courage."

"What?" Ariadne asked. "I don't know what you mean." She frowned. "I mean, sure, I'm from Tau Ceti, but its not like I joined the military or participated in any fighting."

"You supported the Separatists," Eric said. "Just in passively allowing their civil war to continue. If you really cared you would have taken up arms against them."

"What?" Ariadne said. "Look, I'm not a fighter or soldier, or anything like that. Honestly, even if I was, I don't know which side I would pick: the Separatists or the Confederation. There's not a lot to choose from between the pair of them."

"It's not about one side or the other," Eric snapped. "It's a choice, one you clearly never made. In the Centauri

Confederation we have all kinds of hard choices to make. Some people sacrificed a lot more than their lives to ending the civil war."

"What do you mean?" Ariadne asked. "You mentioned earlier you joined their military, one of their special units, right, their Commandos?" She frowned at that. She had limited knowledge of the military of the Separatists, much less the Confederation. Even so, she remembered dark rumors about what the Confederation military did on occupied worlds.

"I mean, your inability to pick a side is an insult to someone who paid real sacrifices to the civil war," Eric said. "And I find your pretense at cheer and friendliness grating."

"Well, excuse me," Ariadne snapped back. "I never served, no. But I'm a war orphan. Do you know what it means to never know your parents, to grow up in orphanage after orphanage, to live with foster families who treat you like an unwelcome guest? I went through that because of your damned civil war. And I tell you honestly... whatever you sacrificed for a war that continues to orphan kids like my brother and I... I'm sorry, but I don't think it was worth it."

Eric looked away. "Sorry," he grunted. "Didn't know about your family." He stood silent, and for a moment, Ariadne studied him. He stood above average height, with blonde hair and blue eyes, he looked every inch the soldier. Yet he had the twitch reflexes of a hyperactive mongoose. He also boasted to skills with various types of firearms. He had a strange smell, too, one that she picked up when he grew angry. He had an almost animal musk, not overpowering, but certainly noticeable. She saw the muscles along his jaw flex as his anger returned, "Still, why do you care about Pixel and his past, or anyone else for that matter?"

"Because I do," Ariadne said. "We are partners now. And the more we know about one another, the better I think we will work together."

"Familiarity breeds contempt," Eric said. He recited the phrase as if from some book he had memorized. "And I really doubt that your new buddy here gave you the full story. I sure as hell don't feel like telling a complete stranger my dirty little secrets." He cocked his head at her, "What I can't figure out is if you're just so naive that you really trust everyone... or if you're just a manipulative bitch."

Ariadne ground her teeth together, "Shut up, alright? Why do you have to be such an ass? I think we need to work together. We need each other, and we need to trust one another. I think we've already shown that we can be a good team, I just want to show that to everyone."

"Right..." Eric shook his head and spoke with a tone of complete derision, "Well, I apologize. You really are *that* naive." He looked over at Pixel, "Good luck pal, I'm done trying to talk sense into her for the day."

"Why does everyone treat me like I'm a child?" Ariadne felt her cheeks flush with a mixture of embarrassment and anger. She hated that Eric had got under her skin. She also hated that she felt her control slipping. She felt sweat start to bead her forehead.

"Maybe because you act like one?" Eric snapped. Ariadne felt the temperature of the compartment raise a couple degrees.

"Hey guys, that's enough," Pixel interrupted. "I don't think this argument will really solve anything, and it just seems to have made you both angry. Let's leave it at a difference in opinions, shall we?"

"Sure," Eric muttered. "But keep your touchy-feely attitude away from me. I don't mind you when you're in a killing mood, but right now I want to strangle you." He turned and walked out.

Ariadne closed her eyes and concentrated. She took deep breaths, in and out, and thought back on happier times. Slowly she felt her calm start to return.

She heard Pixel sniff, "Hey, do you smell burning hair?"

Ariadne's eyes snapped open, "Uh, nope. Hey, I'm going to go get a ration bar to eat, see you later!" She could feel his puzzled eyes on her back as she hurried out of the compartment.

***

Her problems had started in middle school.

As a foster child, she had confidence issues aplenty. She and her brother had transferred from home to orphanage to home often enough that she had plenty of worries, especially as a young teenager. Those worries had compounded anger issues and a bitter attitude about the hand that life dealt her. To top it all off, she found out one day in the girls restroom that when she gave into the anger, she could make things catch on fire with her mind.

Thankfully for her sanity, she had never gone beyond malicious pranks before she and Paul ended up in the home of Tony and Amanda Hutchins. The aged couple had a history of taking in the roughest of orphans. They also had showed her something that she never would have expected to find. They showed her love and affection, not because of who she was or what she might do, but because she was a child and needed it.

Amanda Hutchins went from some batty old lady to a role model in about a week. In a month, Ariadne had rebuilt herself. She found that she lived happier when she cared about others. The remarks from insecure girls who wanted to establish their place in society no longer mattered. If anything, Ariadne had felt pity for them, and in that process, reduced what they said to something inconsequential.

She and her brother had thrived under the elderly couple's care. No one would have recognized the cheerful, pretty young girl she became after only six months. She still remembered the words that had transformed her life. "When all else fails, put your faith in people. They may disappoint you at times, but then again, they may surprise you."

And then one day it had all gone terribly wrong and it was Ariadne's fault.

Ariadne had found that as much as she cared for her friends, sometimes she saw them do things that hurt themselves or others. She had just developed her telepathic abilities. At the time, it had seemed such an obvious solution. She had her gift, her friends *needed* her help, even if they didn't realize it. With her powers, she had the responsibility to help them, didn't she?

It had started with such a small thing. She'd nudged one friend just a bit, just enough to get her to admit her feelings to the boy she liked.

And within a month Ariadne and her brother went on the run, desperate to preserve their freedom and their lives. Their adoptive family had given them what help they could, but even they could not protect her and Paul from the danger she had brought upon them.

Ariadne revisited all those memories as she fled the engine compartment. She regretted her childhood arrogance, when she looked back. But she couldn't regret her compassion that drove her desire to help others.

"Interesting group of refugees we have here, eh there freaky lady?"

Ariadne looked up. She saw she walked past Crowe in the corridor without noticing him. That startled her, because normally she prided herself on her situational awareness. She forced herself to put away her distrust of him and to regain her calm. "Crowe, how are you?"

He stood close enough that she could smell his stale sweat and the other, deeper smell she associated with him. He almost smelled reptilian, like a snake, a dry, sandy smell that made her stomach roil. "Not bad," he said. "I had not realized you were from Tau Ceti too... I grew up on Cetus."

"Oh?" Ariadne smiled. "I hadn't realized we had that in common. You don't have much of an accent. I figured you from the Colonial Republic actually."

"Nope, grew up in Sternhaven, the capital itself, actually," Crowe said. "Though I traveled a lot once I got old enough."

"Oh, were your parents traders?" Ariadne asked.

Something flashed in his eyes, too quick for Ariadne to catch what emotion her words had provoked. "No... my father worked as a laborer. He took me with him when he went to find work."

"That's nice," Ariadne said.

"Not really," Crowe snapped, "He was an idiot who never amounted to anything. He never understood why I left home and never looked back. I've made quite a bit of money in my travels. I wiped the dust of that planet off my boots and never regretted it."

"Ah," Ariadne said. She frowned, "You seem pretty proud of your job for a sensor tech." He sounded just like the insecure girls back from middle school, lots of big talk to hide his own insecurities. She felt a moment of guilt that she couldn't find it in her to pity him.

Crowe gave her a crooked smile, and he leaned close to her. "Can you keep a secret?"

"I guess..." Ariadne said as she edged back.

"I wasn't a sensor tech. I know sensors, and communications, sure, but I picked that up in my real craft. I'm something of an artist, you see..." Crowe's smile grew broader, "I'm a professional thief."

Ariadne stared at him, "Really?" She couldn't help the flat tone of her voice. She had little respect for someone who stole from those who worked for what they had.

He frowned at her lack of awe. "Yes, really, and I'm very good. As a matter of fact, I'm the best. I've stolen from politicians, rich corporate types, military men, even crime bosses. I'm something of a legend... in the right circles."

"Oh, really?" Ariadne couldn't help but arch an eyebrow at that. "It seems more likely that you would be on the run if people knew who you were and who you stole from. I mean, it can't be that smart to steal from criminals. The police need evidence, I would think a criminal would just kill you and dump the body... maybe torture you to find out where you sold their stuff."

Crowe ground his teeth. It made him look like a child who had his toy taken away. "That's none of your business. And just so you know: if you steal the right things, they can be valuable enough to pay for whatever kind of protection you need."

"Oh," Ariadne nodded. She had suddenly developed a

headache. "Well, that's very interesting, Crowe. I think I'll leave that sort of thing to you, though. I don't have the... mindset to take things from people who earned them."

"Well, maybe not, but I got an offer for you," Crowe said. "I heard that you have some precognitive abilities."

"Who told you that?" she asked. She didn't suffer from her visions of possible futures often. The only time she remembered doing so around anyone of her fellow escapees had happened with Mike and Anubus as the only ones present.

"I might have overheard it..." Crowe said, his eyes shifty. "But I wondered, what triggers it? Is it something you can do consciously or is there some kind of reaction or what?"

"It's something that just happens sometimes," Ariadne said cautiously. "Sometimes seeing something or hearing something can trigger it, other times, it just happens."

"Oh, can you tell me if this triggers anything?" Crowe asked. He held up a green and black object.

Suddenly Ariadne stood on a flat plain, its surface melted into black glass. A raging firestorm swept all around, her, but she stood at the center of it unharmed. A star hung red and sullen on the horizon and alien ships swept through the shattered skies above her.

You should not be here, a voice spoke in her mind.

Ariadne spun, and she found herself face to face with a young man. He had brown eyes and shoulder-length brown hair. The flames licked around him but he stood in an area untouched by flame.

"Who are you?" Ariadne asked.

I am the one who must witness... he said in her mind. *And this you must not see... or you will become trapped here like me.*

"Can I help you?" She asked. "For that matter, can I help myself? How do I leave this place... what is this place?"

There is no escape, this is where the last of our race dies, the final defense has fallen... his mental words faded for a moment. *This is Earth... after the Balor defeated us.*

***

Ariadne awoke to find a ring of concerned faces above her.

Her back hurt. Come to think of it her, head hurt, "What happened?"

"You gave a shout," Eric said. "We all came to see what happened. You seemed to be stuck in some sort of trance. When it ended you fell to the deck and then you woke up."

"Did I say anything?" Ariadne asked.

"Something about someone," Mike said. "Someone was trapped. What happened, another vision?"

"Yeah, I was talking with Crowe..." She sat up, "That bastard! He showed me something, and that set it off. Where'd he go?"

"Crowe's been with me the whole time," one of the female passengers said. Her thick accent added a further level of oddity to the moment.

"Who are you?" Ariadne asked blearily.

"Elena Ludmilla Lakar," the woman responded, her accent marked. "And as I said, Crowe and I were together."

What? But I had a whole conversation with him!" Ariadne said. "He told me about his childhood on Cetus."

"Crowe is from the Anvil system," Eric said patiently. "I talked with him about it before."

"But..." Ariadne shook her head. The encounter had seemed so real. It couldn't be a product of her imagination. Crowe had triggered her vision, even if he hadn't realized what he was doing – and she doubted that – he must know something about the object he showed her.

She couldn't picture it, when she thought back. The single glimpse she had of it, she thought it looked angular and glossy, with black and green colors in a strange pattern across its surface...

She shook her head, "Never mind. I'm alright. Someone give me a hand up?"

Mike and Pixel both offered their hands. They lifted her to her feet and she wobbled a bit. "I think I'm done for the day,"

Ariadne said. Her head still hurt, and she thought she'd bruised herself pretty bad when she fell to the deck. She glanced around the corridor one last time and, for just a second, she saw the black glass plain under a sundered sky.

Just a possible future, she thought, *and probably not one I can affect at all, so no need to worry about it.*

***

Ariadne went back to the cockpit. Mike allowed her to take the pilot's seat to get some rest, while he sat in the copilot seat and monitored the sensors.

Ariadne's mind seemed too active to sleep though. She stared out at the face of the gas giant as they soared past. They had just finished their slingshot maneuver, and the blue-green surface drew away steadily. She gazed at it as they coasted away, and she thought about what the others had said.

Did she trust people too easily, as Mike cautioned? Or worse yet, had Eric driven to the truth when he said that she pretended to care in order to manipulate others? She did not want to think either of them were right. She trusted people, yes, but only because she could see their potential. *We can be a great team,* she thought.

Yet something cautioned her that even she could not be fully trusted. Twice in just the past few hours she had come close to losing her hard-earned control. She had nearly given in to her anger with Eric, and worse, nearly allowed fear to crack her control in the presence of Anubus.

Had her control stood at such a close margin all along? She wondered if her vaunted self control came only from the fact that she had never really suffered any challenges to it. She remembered well enough the few times she had let loose with everything she had. Those times, with few exceptions, she thought she had no choice. Now she had to wonder if she made excuses for her actions after the fact.

I can't do this to myself, she thought, *I will just start second guessing every action I've ever taken.* She closed her eyes and tried to stop her mind, to seek some inner calm. Yet when she closed her eyes, she saw the face of the first man she had ever killed... the first man she ever fell for.

* * *

"Ariadne."

She drifted in that state between sleep and full awareness. She knew the voice that called would only try to wake her for something important. Even so, she did not want to open her eyes, to face the world that seemed so much more complicated.

"Ariadne."

She forced her eyes open. Mike looked back at her from the copilot seat. "Hey, sorry to wake you, but we need you."

She blinked at him blearily. She rubbed at her eyes, "Sorry, how long did I sleep?"

"How long did you lie there until you fell asleep?" Mike asked. "I could tell you had trouble. For that matter, I'm not sure I could get any sleep after what we've been through."

Ariadne gave him a smile. She glanced at the ship's chrono. "A few hours. Plenty." She refused to let her worries drag her down. She would maintain her positive outlook on life, if only because to do otherwise would seem petty. "Though I think the Chxor need some notes on how to make a seat comfortable."

"Try one that got shredded by a riot gun," Mike grunted.

Ariadne turned a bit green at the reminder. The Chxor pilot had reacted to Rastar's arrival with an attempt to hit some switches. Just what he intended, either surrender or to destroy the cargo boat, they didn't know. But Rastar had killed him without hesitation.

Ariadne couldn't say she blamed him. But she still felt nausea at the thought of gruesome death in the small cockpit. "So what's so important," she asked. "We find someone willing to help us?"

"Not willing, per se," Mike said. "While you slept, I had Crowe rig up a sensor sweep with passive video telescope. We've picked up a few ships, some of them on similar orbits actually. I wanted to get your feedback on which ones you think

145

we can match orbits with."

"Right," Ariadne pulled up the data. She frowned as she forgot which keys to hit. "I think I'm more tired than I realize. Is Run available?"

"I thought it best to keep him occupied elsewhere for the moment," Mike said. "He seemed very insistent that he be afforded the opportunity to open up your head and take a look at the insides."

"Ah," Ariadne said. "Well, he means well, at least." She could very well imagine that the little Chxor thought he could somehow grant psychic powers to all those who needed them or perhaps 'cure' humanity of it. She doubted either way that he thought of what others might want, but at least he had the intention of doing his work for others benefit.

"Well intentioned or not, I thought you'd rather not wake up dead," Mike said. "I can call him in, now, if you really need his help."

"No..." Ariadne said. "I think I got it." She tapped a couple more buttons and the highlighted ships appeared on the heads up display, along with their projected vectors and a map of other objects on their path.

Ariadne closed her eyes. She found it difficult to explain her mental process and all it entailed.. She called it navigation, but that merely described the outcome. In reality, she didn't understand the math for orbital mechanics, much less the differential equations necessary for even the most simple Shadow Space navigation. What she did seemed linked to her ability to sense the world around her, and to 'feel' the various effects of gravity, the ship's drive, and even solar wind on the ship's orbit. She then could adjust that, tweak it a bit, until those various pressures put the ship where she wanted it to go. She'd read once that the old Amalgamated Worlds government had called her skill cognitive navigation.

To her it seemed more about a feel or sense than any real thought. She didn't know *how* she did what she did, but she knew when it felt *right*.

She worked for an hour, and she managed to plot courses

for over a dozen of the ships before she finally transmitted the data to Mike. "There you are. Most of those we can delay any maneuvers for a day or so at least. There's one or two we need to maneuver in the next few hours. The rest of them, I don't think we could match, though we'll pass pretty close to a couple of those contacts."

Mike gave a snort, "Yeah, I noticed." He hit a button and one ship lit up. It was one with a course that crossed theirs at almost a right angle. The difference in velocities meant they would have only a few tenths of a second to see it with the naked eye as it flashed past. "We had a discussion earlier with one of the prisoners who wondered why we didn't harpoon that one as it passes by and just reel ourselves in."

"Harpoon..." Ariadne shook her head. "But... there's so much wrong with that idea that I'm not even sure where to start."

"It took us a while to explain it to him," Mike said. "The worst part was that anyone who even vaguely understood physics started laughing. I would have felt sorry for the guy, except he got so angry and thought we deliberately picked on him."

"Thankfully we don't have any kind of harpoon gun or I'm sure someone would want to try it, anyway," Ariadne said. She giggled at the idea of someone out on the hull, like some space version of Ahab with the passing ship his white whale.

"Oh, you missed that. That's what spawned the whole thing, Eric found a harpoon rifle in a storage locker in the engine compartment. Who knows why the Chxor had that... but he's broken it out and worked over the entire thing like it is his personal baby."

"Good for him," Ariadne said.

"Sure, you say that now," Mike said. "He's developed an unhealthy relationship with that thing. He's even named it already."

"Oh, dear," Ariadne said. Eric already seemed to have difficulty with other people. She didn't want to think how much less he would make an attempt at talk when he had his attention locked on a weapon. She wondered if she should talk with him about it.

147

"Yeah. Well anyway, we'll try to refine data on these ships to pick a likely target. Any suggestions?" Mike asked.

"You mean did I have any impending visions of doom if we go after one ship in particular?" Ariadne gave him a head shake and a smile to show she had not taken offense, "Nope. But I will say that I added notes to the ships that we can approach from aft, where their own drives might mask any maneuvers we do to match vectors. There's three of them that I think we can do that with minimal effort."

"Good to know," Mike said. "I'll look at those a bit more carefully then. Have you had a chance to grab your ration bar for the day?"

"No?" Ariadne glanced at the chrono again. "Not today. Where would I get mine?"

"Rastar and Simon have them under guard, after Rastar found Crowe with a hoard of them," Mike said. "Though I can't imagine why he might want to... I thought Mratha rice mush tasted bad."

"I'm sure we'll get used to them," Ariadne said helpfully. "And we should be grateful for what we have, you know?"

"You haven't tried them yet," Mike said.

"Okay, well, I'll do that while you and Crowe get us some more information," Ariadne said. She thought the ration bars could not be as bad as he had suggested. Granted, she found the Mratha rice bland and tasteless, but it at least seemed filling. And Rastar had mentioned that it held most of the vitamins and minerals they needed for survival, so it would prevent any deficiencies there.

She felt certain the ration bars would have the same qualities.

Ariadne went down the corridor and paused outside the hatch for the cargo hold at the sound of raised voices. "I insist that you provide me with access to better rations," a woman said. "Not even the abominable Mratha rice proved so unpalatable. I am an Ambassador to Nova Roma, I am entitled to whatever you have, as a diplomat and a noblewoman."

"Lady, unless your Emperor shows up with a ship and

some food, we haven't got anything to give," Simon snapped. "If you don't want to eat it, then fine, don't eat."

"My father will hear of this. He is a powerful figure in Nova Roma, my family has connections..."

"Ambassador, you will have a hard time telling anyone about this if you starve to death," another man said. "Let's go back and rest. I'm sure you'll want to add this to your official complaints." The man's voice had a tone of resignation that made Ariadne's heart ache. Clearly he put up with the majority of her tantrums.

A moment later, a tall, dark-haired woman swept through the hatch. A pair of men in the ragged remains of military uniforms followed her out. The younger one looked Ariadne over with a quick, mechanical precision. Ariadne wondered at that, but she let them pass without any questions. She stepped into the cargo hold after they passed and then walked towards where Rastar and Simon stood. Rastar had his arms crossed, and a crimson flush suffused his skin.

"Hi, guys, what's for dinner?" She asked brightly.

Simon gave her a slight smile, "Well, we have a special on out of date ration bars. You might even say we're giving them away." He reached into a brown plastic bag at his feet, then lifted out a shiny black object and held it out. "Truth to tell, starvation doesn't seem so bad after you bite into one."

"They can't be that bad," Ariadne said. She took it in one hand. It seemed heavy for its size, a solid weight, almost half a kilo. She stared at the shiny exterior with confusion. She had thought it wrapped in some kind of plastic package. She didn't see any way to open it though. She looked up with a frown. "How do I get it out of the wrapper?"

Rastar's color had faded back towards the brown that signified calm. "That's the outside of the bar. They're compressed to save space."

"Really?" Ariadne asked. "Well that seems... efficient. How do I eat it, just bite it?"

"Not unless you want to break a tooth," Simon answered. He held up a slip of paper, "It comes with directions. Break off a

149

piece, preferably with something metal and heavy. Then put the piece in water and let it soak for three hours. We have some bowls here, and you can get water from the head in the engine compartment. Then you should be able to chew it."

"You read the directions?" Ariadne asked.

"Yeah, it was the first thing he did when he opened them up," Rastar said. "The rest of us had the things out trying to figure out what the joke was. I thought they had swapped the label on the box with hockey pucks, it's a sport I read about once, which involves men beating one another with sticks on ice."

Ariadne made a mental note to avoid that sport. "Good thing you decided to read the directions."

Simon shrugged, "I always read the directions. It saves time, and it prevents mistakes. If there's a manual, someone smarter than me probably wrote it for a reason."

"That makes sense," Ariadne said. "And I think you probably saved me a chipped tooth." She saw the pile of bowls and took one. "So how does this taste?"

"Like bleached boot leather," Rastar said helpfully.

"I imagine it would be flavored for humans," Ariadne said. "Maybe it just doesn't taste good to you because of that."

"No," Simon said. "He actually seems to like them better than most of the rest of us." He glanced over at the end of the room, "Except for Anubus; he loves the things."

"What?" Ariadne said. She felt a sudden surge of hope, "Maybe he likes them because then he doesn't get hungry enough to think of us as food." *Maybe we can convince him to switch over to these rather than view us as a food source.*

"I like them because they have a high density, similar to that of bone," Anubus said. "One of these makes an acceptable substitute for bone so that I can clean and sharpen my teeth. Preventive medicine of a sort, so that I can bite into something a bit more tasty."

So much for that, she thought.

"I meant to ask you," Simon said to Ariadne. "I heard you picked up a pistol. I wondered if I could get it. I'm pretty good with one and I seem to be the only one in the group without a weapon of some kind."

"But..." Ariadne pulled the pistol out from the holster she'd strapped on her suit's webbing. "What do I use then? That would leave me without a weapon."

Simon stared at her for a long moment, "You set people on fire with your brain."

"Oh, yeah, I guess you're right," Ariadne hesitated, "It's just nice to have it on hand, like another tool, you know?" She sighed, and passed the pistol over to Simon.

He took it gingerly, and angled the barrel away. He flipped a switch on the side. "You had it on fire, you know?" He ejected the magazine and worked the slide. Ariadne saw him catch a round that ejected with smooth practice. "And loaded. Tell me you at least checked it after you picked it up?"

Ariadne shrugged, "I made sure it had a magazine in it and grabbed another one later."

He shook his head, "I hereby forbid you to touch a weapon until I certify you on a weapons safety class. You and Pixel both. I have no desire to be shot in the back by people who don't know the basics of firearms."

Ariadne gave him a smile, "That sounds like it would be pretty useful. Let me know when you want to teach the class, I'll make sure everyone attends."

Simon frowned, "I will have to come up with a curriculum and some reading material, as well as a manual. Give me a day or three."

Ariadne's smile faded a bit at the thought of a manual. She didn't mind if someone else did the reading and summed it up for her. Reading through technical manuals really did not appeal to her. Particularly if Simon felt so precise about the requirement to read it, "Well... I'll just go set my ration bar to soak."

She left the cargo hold and used the ship's head and then filled her bowl with water. It took her several blows against the hatch frame to break off a medium sized piece of the ration bar. The edge looked sharp enough to use as a knife. She dubiously put her 'breakfast' into the bowl, pocketed the rest of the bar, and returned to the cockpit and set her bowl of water with the ration bar in it on the floor out of the way. She saw Mike and Crowe, their heads together as they read data on the tiny sensor screen. "Hi, guys, what's the good news?"

Crowe looked back at her, "Oh... you." He seemed nervous. Ariadne restrained a sigh. She really hoped that Mike had not told Crowe about her telepathic abilities.

"We've narrowed down our selection to three or four ships," Mike said. "Most of the traffic we can intercept consists of fusion drive ships, and most of them are small boats like this one or not much bigger." He brought up the sensor display on the heads up display. Ariadne stared at the HUD for a long moment until she picked out both the four ships he'd chosen and the courses she plotted.

He highlighted two of the ships, "These two are freighters, but they're on courses that suggest they arrived from out system, which in turn suggests they have Shadow Space drives." He lit up another, "This one looks like a courier ship of some sort, or maybe a customs cutter. Hard to tell, but either way it might have a Shadow Space drive."

"And that last one?" Ariadne asked.

"It's a freighter on a course from this other planet," Mike said, and he zoomed out until a planet on the other side of the primary fit into the map. "It's another world in the inhabitable zone, and looks like a nice piece of real estate, actually. Just in where I figure it would have pretty moderate seasons. Maybe not a resort world, but nice enough."

"Three inhabitable worlds in one system," Ariadne shook her head, "This is a pretty nice star system, and one heck of a prize for anyone to colonize. Do we know which system we're in yet?"

"I meant to ask Run," Mike said. Then he frowned... "Now that you mention it, I haven't seen him in a while. That bothers me."

"I'm sure the other prisoners wouldn't hurt him," Ariadne said. "I mean, look at how helpful he has proven himself!"

"Uh... I'm more worried about what he might have done

to one of our passengers," Mike responded. He looked over at Crowe, "Can you ask Eric or Rastar to come up here? And if you see Run around, send him up too." To Ariadne's surprise Crowe left quickly and without any comment.

"Do we really need Eric to track down Run, I mean, I'm sure that he's probably just asleep or..." Ariadne trailed off as Mike gave her a level stare. "What?"

"You need to develop a sense for danger. Whenever things get the quietest is when someone or something is up to the greatest mischief." Mike said. "*Especially* someone like Run."

"What's the worst that can happen?" Ariadne said.

"LET ME GO, I MUST CONTINUE MY EXPERIMENTS!" Run's shrill voice cut through the silence like a power drill through butter. Ariadne nearly leapt out of her seat. She looked over her shoulder just in time to see Eric carry Run up to the hatch. "Found him," Crowe said from behind him.

"Your behavior is illogical and overly emotional. I promise that you will suffer no lasting ill effects as long as you survive the operation," Run said, his voice lower but no less shrill.

"That last part just makes me feel all warm and fuzzy," Eric said. He looked over at Mike, "He's your problem now. I woke up to find he'd crept over and got his 'tools' out." Eric hiked a thumb over his shoulder to point at a heavy bag that Crowe held up. "I swear he's got a rusty saw blade in there, along with needles, some jars and vials of chemicals, and who knows what else."

Mike put a hand over his eyes, "Thanks for not killing him, I appreciate the restraint."

"Like I said, he's your problem now," Eric said. "And from now on, I say we just kill any Chxor we come across. Or we institute a no more than one Chxor on the crew policy. Maybe we can get an upgrade, get one who's less of a hassle."

"I am the pinnacle of Chxor genetic engineering!" Run said. "My genius is unsurpassed, as is my vision of improvement! You will not find another Chxor as competent, intelligent, and knowledgeable as I am!" His shrill voice seemed to bore through Ariadne's head.

"You seem a little short to be the pinnacle of anything," Eric said. "In any case, you guys can watch him, I'm going to go get some sleep."

Crowe stayed in the hatch and Ariadne saw him peer in the bag for a long moment, "Hey, where'd he manage to get a staple gun?"

"GIVE ME MY TOOLS!" Run shouted.

"I thought that Chxor did not get emotional," Ariadne said to the little Chxor. "Why are you shouting?"

He looked over at her, and spoke in a calm, level, voice, "I find that humans seem to respond better to a loud, authoritative voice." Run turned back to Crowe, "GIVE ME MY TOOLS NOW!"

Ariadne stood and snatched the bag out of Crowe's hands. She held it out to Run, "You get these, but you have to behave. No experimentation on unwilling people, understand?"

"I WILL AGREE TO NO SUCH-"

Ariadne reached out to his mind. She felt a moment of disorientation as she connected. His thoughts, the way he saw the world, seemed so alien. She felt as if she dove into a reef. The muted colors of the cockpit panels seemed so much brighter. The drab ship suits the humans wore seemed garish and flashy. His mind seemed a thing of right angles and progressions. She found what she wanted quickly enough, his desire to experiment, a massive foundation of his very being. She could no more change that about him than change him into a human, but she could nudge it a little. "If you received consent from people, you would probably gain better feedback, and you would have fewer interruptions with your work," Ariadne said, just as she nudged him slightly.

"Agreement from my subjects would improve my data collection," Run said. "Your argument meets logical parameters. I will accept such terms." The little alien tapped his fingers together in thought. "This will require some planning and preparation."

"Well, you can get around to that after you tell us what

you know about this star system," Mike said. "Three inhabitable worlds, plus the gas giant in the inner system. That must be pretty unique right?" Ariadne nodded. Surely the Chxor doctor would know where they were.

Run peered at the display, "It could be Logan or Krandel."

"Logan or Krandel?" Mike asked. "You have more than one star system with three inhabitable worlds?"

"That question seems illogical to ask," Run said "Of course we have more than one system that meets such parameters. I know of four such systems we have colonized, but two of them lie much more distant from Human space and the Beneficiary Council has decreed that no humans are allowed there, not even as slave labor."

"Four systems with more than two inhabitable worlds," Ariadne said. "Wow that's a pretty impressive set of colonies.

"Oh, no, you misunderstand, which hardly surprises me with your emotional mindset," Run said. "We have over a dozen systems with more than two inhabitable worlds. Laran has five worlds, while Garan has four, both lie near human space, the other worlds do not."

"Five inhabitable worlds?" Mike asked. "That's... how do they even fit in orbit?"

"I am not a physicist," Run said. "I do not know this information. I have, however, studied the biospheres of many of these worlds, including the subject species of those worlds, extensively."

"Subject species? As in sentient?" Ariadne asked. "You Chxor have enslaved others?"

"Yes, though we find few as mentally and emotionally unstable as your own race," Run said.

"Thanks," Mike said. "Well then, do you happen to recognize any of these ships? Do any of them have Shadow Space drives?"

Run stared at the screen, "This is outside my area of knowledge."

"Care to hazard a guess?" Ariadne asked.

155

"Guesses are illogical leaps in thinking and often lead to easily avoidable mistakes," Run said. "I do not guess. I state a hypothesis after careful study."

"Care to make a hypothesis?" Ariadne said and she could not keep a note of irritation out of her voice.

"No," Run said. "I must return to my research. I will obtain a list of volunteers for my further experimentation." He snatched the bag out of Ariadne's hands and scurried away."

"Well, that was useful," Mike said. He frowned, "Though the thought that they have that many worlds to colonize scares me, frankly. I thought the Chxor Empire didn't have more than a handful of systems."

"Well, I mean, it sounds like they have expanded out away from human space," Ariadne said. It seemed to her that signified a preference of the Chxor to open up new worlds, rather than conquer human ones. "And there are limits to natural expansion."

"Those are mostly limits of population and distance," Mike said. "The Chxor have expanded their border with human space since we first discovered them. I would bet that they have something of a population boom too. Something else to worry about anyway."

Ariadne frowned, "Well, I think it more important to select our next ride than those kinds of worries right now. Should we call the others in, talk it over and make a decision?"

Mike shook his head, "I would rather make one and just tell them later, once we have already committed everyone and they can't change it. Otherwise we'll have an argument, some chaos, and Anubus will probably threaten to eat anyone who disagrees with him."

"It's not that bad," Ariadne said. She did privately agree with his assessment of Anubus, however. "And they have a say in this too. We're a team, remember."

"Right..." She didn't need to be a mind reader to tell Mike had rolled his eyes. "Well, if you want them all to see this, you can rotate them through. We'll discuss it in the mostly empty bay."

"What about the other escapees?" Ariadne asked, "Should they get a vote too?"

"They got their vote," Mike growled, "They voted to come with us, that's the only vote they get right now. No battle is ever won by committee, and this whole team thing feels too much like rule by committee already."

***

After an hour, the group managed to rotate everyone through the cockpit to look at the meager data from the sensors. They sat on the crates in the cargo hold, all except for Rastar who sat on the floor and Anubus who crouched in the corner.

"Very well," Simon said, his voice calm and precise, "It seems we have four viable ships, correct?"

"Yeah," Mike answered. "Two larger freighters, one ship that might be a courier or cutter, and a smaller fusion drive freighter, that last one will be the easiest to intercept."

"But least likely to have a Shadow Space drive," Ariadne felt necessary to add.

"Right," Pixel said. "I have to say the sheer amount of traffic in this system is very impressive, it's far over what I saw in most systems in my travels."

"Yeah, those crazy Chxor sure are productive," Eric said. "If they didn't work humans to death to achieve their productivity, I might not want to kill them all."

"It's not just humans who have suffered," Rastar said. Ariadne had noticed that his hide had shifted towards red, "The Chxor have exterminated over ninety percent of my people, and conquered my home-world. Trust me, you have nothing near the rage I feel at them."

"Why don't we just focus on the task at hand?" Anubus growled. "We pick a ship, capture it, and then get somewhere that we can go our separate ways. I keep the gold and you all keep whatever ship we take."

"Wait, you keep the gold?" Mike said. "That doesn't seem fair."

"I'll throw in a guarantee that I won't kill and eat you

unless you try to touch any of it," Anubus said. "With the qualification that I retain the right to do so at any time if you piss me off."

"Anubus, buddy," Rastar said. "I know you mean well, but that kind of behavior is just the kind of thing I won't tolerate. We worked together to escape the station, and to capture this ship and that gold. I know that if you value our friendship, you'll agree to an even split with the group."

"Friends are for those too weak to stand on their own," Anubus growled.

"Let's worry about the gold later, alright?" Ariadne said. "I mean, I'm sure we can work out a deal on that. I mean, there's no need to fight about it."

"Not yet," Anubus growled.

"Okay..." Ariadne said, grateful for even the token agreement, "So we've got these four ships. We've all spent time looking at the imagery we managed to get of them. None of us recognized the classes, but we have some pretty good assumptions to make plans from, I think."

"Sure," Eric said. "Which means that we'll get our plans torpedoed as soon as we get close enough to see how badly we misjudged our targets." He looked over at Mike, "I think it more likely that the fast one you pointed out is a customs cutter, especially with its current course. That looks like a patrol of sorts."

"If it is, it will have weapons," Mike said. "Maybe not much, but I bet enough to smash us."

"And if it is designed for system patrols, it probably doesn't have a Shadow Space drive," Pixel said. He frowned, "So should we just write it off?"

"It would be nice to capture something with guns," Eric said. Ariadne saw Mike nod in agreement.

"What, so we can shoot it out with a Chxor dreadnought?" Crowe asked. "I'd rather get something small and fast and get out of here."

"Well," Mike said, "That leaves the other three. The two freighters are both pretty damned big. Probably a crew in the hundreds." He looked over at Rastar and then at Anubus, "How many Chxor can you guys handle?"

"Not that many," Eric said. "No offense to you two, but all it takes is time for one crewman to decide he'd rather die a hero and sabotage or destroy the ship. I don't think we could operate on a larger ship, especially not with the small number of weapons we have."

"So the last ship, the small intrasystem freighter?" Ariadne asked.

"But it probably doesn't have a Shadow Space drive," Pixel said. "And if that's the case, how is that an improvement?"

"We get a bigger ship and one that the Chxor traffic control expects, rather than a cargo boat probably reported destroyed already," Mike said. "For that matter, we gain whatever cargo it carries, some of which may be valuable, and the rest could be useful."

"Good point," Pixel said. "That ship looks big enough to have a machine shop, maybe I can make some things."

"So we go with the small intrasystem freighter?" Ariadne asked. She smiled at the nods of agreement on everyone's faces. "See, how well things work out when we discuss the issue and find a solution?"

"Sure," Eric said. "We get threatened by Anubus, bullied by Rastar, and I get to listen to your drivel. I feel so much better about myself now." He looked over at Mike, "We done here?"

***

Ariadne sat in the copilot seat in the cockpit as they began their final maneuvers. As they drew closer to the target ship, they had made out more details. The ship appeared larger until a closer inspection revealed it as some kind of containerized transport. Racks of containers covered the relatively small inner ship.

It seemed an interesting idea to Ariadne. Pixel had found it fascinating, and he had spent the past few days with his datapad as he went over different designs for similar ships. Ariadne did not really understand his interest, but it kept him

159

happy and she thought that a good enough result.

"Perfect course, by the way," Mike said from behind her. "We're coming up from directly behind them, and it doesn't seem that they have any sensors to aft."

"Thanks," Ariadne smiled happily. She felt good to use her skills. The knowledge that she helped the team made her feel even better.

Mike adjusted the thrusters a bit as they came closer. Ariadne could see the other ship out of the canopy now, and it grew at what seemed like a glacial crawl. She knew the course, knew that their plan required a gradual approach to avoid detection. Even so, she felt nervous as she waited.

She worried about Eric, out on the hull. Granted, he annoyed her, and his bitter and sarcastic attitude kept her at bay, but she realized he must have his reasons for his behavior. And besides, for all his bitter talk, he had volunteered to go out on the hull to do the most dangerous task.

I think that really shows he wants to be a team player, Ariadne thought. She smiled at that, glad that she had not misjudged him and the others. When it came down to it, they worked together, despite any minor differences of opinion.

"You're smiling again," Mike said. "I know you're naturally cheerful, but can you stop that? It bugs me, I keep trying to figure out what you're so happy about."

"Thanks, Mike," Ariadne said. "I was just thinking about Eric and how he volunteered to lead the boarding operation. I told you we all worked well together."

"Right," Mike said. "Sure we do. You think he's doing that because he really cares about the rest of us?"

"Of course, why else would he put himself at risk like this, I mean, he's going across to the other ship on a bit of metal cable!" Ariadne said.

"Don't forget his little love affair with that harpoon gun of his," Mike said. "I think he just really wants a chance to shoot the damned thing. More than that, I think he really wants an opportunity to kill something. Same thing with Anubus, or did you think he volunteered out of the goodness of his heart, too?"

"Well..." Ariadne said, "maybe not him."

They had drawn close enough now that the freighter hung only a few hundred meters away. It seemed close enough to touch to Ariadne, yet she suddenly saw the scale of it when she made out an airlock on the port side, projected out from the racks of containers. "It's pretty big, something over a hundred meters long and about fifty meters wide, right?"

"Yeah, plus or minus," Mike said. "Pixel drew up a rough interior sketch earlier, based off of some modeling he did on his datapad. I think he said a crew of ten or so." She could hear the worry in his voice, and she realized that worry lay partially with the risk to their companions, and partially in the lack of control he had over the situation once they began the boarding. "I hope Crowe's little hacking program works with their communications."

"It will," Crowe said from behind them. Ariadne repressed a start of surprise, but only just. She had not heard the hatch open behind them, nor had she heard Crowe slip into the cockpit. She repressed an urge to shoot him a glare.

"Will people stop *doing* that," Mike snapped.

"Doing what?" Crowe asked.

"Sneaking up behind me when I'm talking and then interrupting me and scaring the crap out of me," Mike said. "Doesn't anyone know how to knock?"

"Sorry, didn't realize that you and pyrogirl here needed some private time," Crowe said. Ariadne could see the smirk on his face in her mind. She felt her cheeks flush in embarrassment. She wondered why his opinion and comments bothered her so much.

"Did you come up just to annoy me while I do some delicate piloting or did you have some actual meaningful purpose?" Mike said.

"Oh, Anubus wanted me to tell you that Eric is about to take the shot," Crowe said.

"Right," Mike said.

They waited. A moment later, Ariadne saw a shadow swing out over the canopy of the cockpit. She held back a gasp as she saw Eric climb hand over hand across the gap. A deeper shadow followed behind him, and Ariadne recognized Anubus's suit a moment later.

"Are we sure we're outside their proximity alarms?" Crowe asked.

"Should be," Mike said. "Those are normally infrared sensors that pick up a ship or shuttle about to dock, and our course is still behind them enough I think we're clear of that. Granted, I'll bring us in after they secure the bridge. This whole thing depends on surprise."

"Why is that?" Crowe asked, just as Ariadne saw Simon go up the cable hand over hand.

"Because if they can maneuver at all, they can avoid letting us dock," Ariadne said. "Just a little bit of thrust or even some spin would make it difficult, and if they mix things up, they could make it too dangerous to try."

"So why do pirates have such luck in movies?" Crowe said.

"Because they have a ship with guns?" Ariadne asked. "I don't know, I don't watch a lot of movies. I'm more of a people person." A larger shadow went up the line next, and Ariadne recognized what had to be Rastar. He had volunteered to take the last position, he said he felt certain he could grab someone if they slipped, and still retain the ability to climb.

Of course, if they fell and drifted away from the cable and out of his reach, then he would not have the opportunity to save them. They would drift through the void, lost forever to the cold airless emptiness of space. Ariadne felt her heart in her throat as she thought of one of her new friends exposed to that kind of death. "They'll make it, right?"

Mike did not look away from the controls. "I give it a fifty fifty chance that we lose someone during this. Boarding an unfamiliar ship is dangerous, and we don't have any safety equipment or any real medical gear. Plus none of them speak Chxor, so..."

Ariadne looked at him, horrified by his calm detachment in the face of that terrible possibility. "We'll get through this,

162

they'll be fine," she said. She raised her chin. "As a matter of fact, I'll bet you that we all get out of this system without losing one person."

"Yeah, right," Crowe said. "I got dibs on the stuff from whoever dies." He went silent. A moment later, when he spoke, he sounded almost too casual, "Hey, you know, I'm going to check and make sure everything is secured back there. Wouldn't want anything loose flying around if you have to make any maneuvers." Ariadne didn't say a thing as he left, but she forced her irritation aside. She would not let the one bad apple turn her sour.

Mike didn't look up from his controls. "Tell you what, I bet you that you'll regret that some of them don't die here eventually, how about that?"

"Mike, now I know you're just trying to get under my skin," Ariadne said. "You're doing it to keep my mind off my worry, which I appreciate. But, no... you're wrong. We're a team. I've become friends with these people, I don't want any of them to get hurt."

"Not even Anubus?" Mike asked.

Ariadne hesitated, then she gave a nod and because Mike seemed focused on his controls, she answered him out loud, "Yeah, even him. It's not his fault he's a Wrethe, and I think if I work with him long enough he might--"

"Not be an alien killing machine?" Mike finished for her. "I won't hold my breath. Not because I don't think you'll try your hardest, but because I've seen his type, alien or human, before. Anubus cares about his own survival above anything else. He might open up a little bit, but when the chips are down, he'll choose himself over anyone else." Mike let her stew on that for a moment, "And how about Crowe, you think he's a swell guy underneath it all?"

Ariadne kept quiet at that. Anubus had his upbringing and his alien nature as an excuse for his attitude. Eric, she had seen the pain in his eyes, someone or something had hurt him. She didn't know what lay at the cause of it, but she could feel his emotional wounds. Crowe... he was just an asshole. Useful, but

Ariadne had come to believe that he hurt other people because he liked to... and that he might be a true sociopath.

Mike did not speak further; he seemed to understand her silence.

They sat quietly for long minutes while Ariadne stared at the freighter and tried not to worry. She wished she could do something... "I'm an idiot."

"Yeah, but what does that have to do with the price of tea in China?" Mike asked.

"I can help, I can scout out what's happening there with my mental powers," Ariadne said. Why had she not thought to do so? Granted, it held risk, but her friends had already put themselves at risk, why should she not follow suit?"

"Uh, you can do that?" Mike asked

"Yes, I can try to focus on the other ship. It's difficult, not my strong point at all. But maybe I can see where their crew is and what they're doing," Ariadne said. "I just have to be careful not to join with one of the Chxor or if I do... well I need to avoid any kind of backlash from what they might feel or do. Oh and I don't want to overstress myself, especially because this is something I haven't really experimented with."

"What happens if you do that?" Mike asked.

"Um, well, If I overstress myself I could pass out, or if I really push too much I suppose I could fry my brain," Ariadne said, "Or if I get some kind of feedback, well, I'm not sure. Once I... had a connection with someone I killed and it nearly killed me."

"I don't think this is such a good idea," Mike cautioned.

"Well, they might need my help," Ariadne took a deep breath, "But don't tell anyone I risked myself, please, I still don't want them to know about my telepathic abilities."

"Right, so if you keel over dead I should just tell them you had an aneurism?" Mike asked

"Yep," Ariadne said. "Oh, and please don't let Run cut my brain up, that would be gross."

"Yeah, it would be a real mess," Mike said. "When are you starting?"

Ariadne didn't answer. She closed her eyes and focused. When she really felt calm, she opened her mind to the world around her. It felt similar to when she used her abilities to navigate, except she could actually see things, and she consciously noticed things. It seemed more difficult, and she could only sense a small area around her. She could sense everything around her, the bloodstains in the seat, the small insect that had made some sort of nest under the console. She could count Mike's heart beats, which seemed to happen in slow motion. She could vaguely feel movement throughout the rest of the ship, but could feel no details. Slowly, she tried to expand that area of sensation, but it refused stubbornly.

Then she tried to move it. It shifted, almost without resistance and she slid it up out of the ship towards the other vessel. Darkness and silence immediately surrounded her. For a moment she panicked as she lost even the sound of her own heartbeat. The world simply vanished into complete darkness of the void.

Yet in that moment of panic, she felt something else. She could feel the energy of the void, the slight hum of vacuum's energy, and beneath the surface of reality itself, she could taste something else. Without the interference of everything else... she could feel the fabric of Shadow Space.

Ariadne felt a moment of awe as she touched that boundary with her mind. She had never approached her sense of Shadow Space from this method before. It had always seemed a thing of intuition; something she unconsciously processed. To feel it like she did now, it seemed so much more than the realm of shadows that most considered it. She felt a sudden urge to dive deeper, to open her mind to that barrier and to taste the alien energy of that other universe.

Then she remembered her friends. Her desire to help them overrode her curiosity. She slid her consciousness further outward and then she felt the steel of a container at the edge of her senses. As she moved further, she found that her sphere of senses had contracted over the distance. More, she found that the details had faded.

Ariadne continued along the container until she reached where she felt the hull of the ship. Her mind sank through the steel, and then through the insulation, conduits, and wiring. They proved no barrier as she sank her mind deeper into the freighter. Finally, she came to what felt like a galley. She could sense a stove top and a meal heater. She also felt several Chxor. She could hear their conversation, and she could sense the edges of their minds, fuzzy with distance, but open and inviting.

A moment later, she felt a familiar mind sweep into the room.

She sensed Rastar enter, and then the reaction of the Chxor crew. Most went still, their minds frozen by the impossible intruder. One reacted quickly enough, however, to dive to the side.

She could hear and feel Rastar fire. The shots seemed muffled, as did the Chxor's scream of agony. Ariadne sensed the other Chxor freeze, either frightened or aware that they would die if they challenged their attacker.

The situation seemed well in hand, so Ariadne sent her mind towards the aft of the ship. She could sense the hum and energy of the ship's fusion reactor. As she approached it, she could feel the footsteps of two others. Her mind caught up to them, unfettered by the speed at which they ran. Her senses had grown less detailed, but the black shadow that raced down the corridor could only be Anubus. The other seemed to be another Chxor. She could feel both their hearts race as Anubus continued his pursuit.

The Chxor heartbeat picked up as he reached a closed hatch. Ariadne could hear his hands as they scrabbled to open the hatch. They rose to a crescendo as Anubus closed the gap. Ariadne felt Anubus's lunge, and his mind seemed to blaze for a moment as his jaws closed on the back of the Chxor's neck.

Ariadne tore her mind away, terrified that Anubus's mind would draw her in. She went forward instead. Her awareness seemed to move slower now though, and she felt the details fade even more. Her bubble had contracted still further, she sensed details only a few meters in radius now.

Her mind found Eric and Simon as they pushed towards the bridge of the ship. They stopped outside a hatch, and Ariadne pushed her mind through. She sensed only one Chxor, his mind a still thing of order, like some clockwork machine.

Simon opened the hatch and Eric swept in, riot gun at the ready. The captain stood still, motionless and calm as Eric and Simon approached. Yet something was wrong. Ariadne could feel it, something about the Chxor captain's calm put her on edge.

Even as she realized that, she felt her awareness start to fade entirely. She could taste the edges of his mind, though, and in a last push of effort, she dove into it.

She almost recoiled from what she found there. Inside the layers of angular logic and hard, emotionless decisions, she sensed a creature devoted to hate. The Chxor captain might not even realize it, but he built his life on that hate. A hate devoid of any kind of pity and long buried so deep that he could not know he held it. Hate drove every action in his life, however, a burning hate for those who gave into the emotions that he had long denied himself. A hate that fed on pain and cruelty to whatever other races came within his reach... and on whatever Chxor he found lacked a proper pattern of behavior.

Yet as she recoiled, she could sense his thoughts. She could taste his satisfaction, that even in his demise he would manage eliminate his killers. *They will have time to see their death and give into emotions such as despair before they die, the pathetic lesser creatures they are,* he thought.

His hand darted for the switch on the console. The switch which would initiate the program he had activated when he heard the first gunshot. The switch that would drop the radiation containment on the reactor and flood the ship with lethal radiation. It was the logical solution to the pirates who threatened him and the ship. The ship would continue to its rendezvous in orbit over Logan Two, the pirates would die from the radiation surge, and the majority of cargo would remain intact, along with the ship after a cleaning procedure.

"No!" Ariadne shouted. Her mind wrestled with that of

the captain and for a moment, just a second, she had the strength, even over the distance, to hold his hand still.

In that moment, she shared his consciousness. She sensed him recoil from the emotions he felt from her, even as a part of him railed at what his society had denied him. She also saw through his eyes as Eric brought up his weapon. She and the Captain both stared down the barrel of the riot gun. "Eric, wait-" she spoke with the Chxor captain's voice.

Eric squeezed the trigger.

Ariadne threw her mind away from the Chxor. She had become too deeply meshed with his mind though. She felt his mind vanish and the chaos of destruction nearly pulled her with it. Her thoughts shattered and she felt herself scream as thousands of metal darts screamed through the brain that she shared.

Then her world disappeared into blessed, painless darkness.

***

Ariadne came into awareness slowly. Her brain felt fuzzy, as if she had stuffed it with cotton. The inside of her head seemed to itch, as well. And she smelled something... it almost smelled like formaldehyde...

She sat up sharply, "Run, you will not put my brain in a jar!"

The little Chxor stood at the end of the table. He had a jar in hand and Ariadne could hear the liquid inside slosh. He peered at her, "I think that she is delusional. Clearly I could not fit her entire brain in this jar, only the pieces I find interesting after thorough investigation..."

Ariadne looked over at Mike, "I thought I asked you not to let him cut my head open?"

Mike shrugged, "He seemed pretty insistent. I told him to wait and see if you woke up. He has very patiently waited the entire time."

"Well, except for when he offered to put you down like a wounded animal," Eric said.

"Oh?" Ariadne looked down at Run. "Really?"

"Euthanasia is a viable method to reduce unnecessary pain, and would retain your brain for scientific research relatively intact," Run informed her. "My personal preference for research has nothing to do with this matter."

"Right..." Ariadne said. "I thought we agreed you would not conduct research on anyone without their permission."

"When a being ceases to function it no longer has an identity or the ability to reason," Run informed her. "Therefore it can neither give assent or deny the option-"

"Freaky mind reader chick woke up?" Crowe stuck his head in the galley for a moment. "Just as well, she has nothing worth stealing."

Ariadne felt her heart stop. She looked over at Mike, "You told them."

"Ah, here we go," Mike said with a sigh. "I can honestly say I didn't say a damned thing. You gave your secret away with the little trick with the Chxor Captain."

"Which freaked me the hell out," Eric said. "Especially after Mike docked and we figured out what you did. Thanks for that, by the way," he said, "If he had finished his work, everyone aboard the ship would have died. You would have been safe enough, but you saved us." Ariadne heard the discomfort in his voice as he spoke.

"I didn't do anything you wouldn't have done, if you had the chance," Ariadne said.

Eric didn't answer her, he looked away, almost as if he felt guilty or uncomfortable. Ariadne gave him a smile anyway, "Hey, don't worry about it, okay?" She looked around, "Where's everyone else?" She shifted her feet off the table and then stood. Her sense of balance felt off, and for a moment, the room spun around her.

"Rastar went to help transfer the refugees. Anubus has gone to oversee the transfer of 'his' gold,"Mike said. "I think Simon has started an inventory of the ship, and Pixel should have finished clearing out the remains of the trap that the Captain emplaced." The pilot grimaced, "Though I understand he's made

169

a copy of it to study."

"You never know when something like that will be useful," Pixel said from the hatchway. "Hey there, Ariadne, glad to see you're better. Neat trick there earlier, wish I could have seen it."

"Thanks," Ariadne said. "Honestly, I've never tried anything like that before, I'm just surprised it worked."

"So, if you wanted to, could you push your mind out and set someone on fire from a distance?" Pixel asked. "You could be a great assassin, no one would ever figure it out."

"Except for a policeman who happens to notice lots of smoldering corpses," Simon said as he stepped into the galley. "Granted, it might be a little less suspicious than some other assassinations, but not much less."

"I wouldn't do something like that anyway," Ariadne shuddered. "I could feel him die, and I think I very nearly went with him as he did. I'd prefer not to repeat that." She looked over at Mike, eager to change the subject, "So what's the news, did we get lucky and does the ship have a Shadow Space drive after all?"

"Nope," Mike said. "But what little we've managed to translate suggests it has a scheduled cargo run to the industrial hub for the star system, and that we can expect enough shipping in the area that we can probably find a good one to hijack."

"Well, I'm sure this will work out," Ariadne said.

Eric shot her a glare, and she saw his face flush, "What's wrong with you? You nearly died only a few hours ago, and now you're certain we'll all be okay? Well, things don't always turn out that way."

Ariadne gave him a smile, "Well, I didn't die, and that's reason enough for me to be happy. On top of that I managed to save the lives of my friends, which includes you."

Eric scowled at her, "Right, whatever." He looked over at Pixel, "Hey, you want to help me out with that project I mentioned earlier?"

Pixel shot a glance over at Simon, then chewed his lip, "Uh, sure."

Ariadne looked between the pair of them. She wondered what project the former soldier and the engineer might have planned together. She figured she would drop in on them later, when she felt more certain she could walk without falling over. "Seems like there's a bit more room on this ship, at least."

"Until everyone else is aboard," Mike grunted. "There's a single crew bay, with bunks for about fifteen, and a small storage area we cleaned out where we'll put the rest of the others. Our little team gets to share the officer's quarters. Two sets of bunks and we'll throw some padding in there so the rest of us can sleep on the floor."

"What are we doing with the old boat?" Ariadne asked.

"Oh, I wondered if you could plot me a course," Mike said. "It's a bit tighter than the other ones, but I noticed something off the ship's data logs, and I think that we can get a little bit of use out of the old girl." He seemed inordinately happy about whatever he had planned.

Ariadne wondered at that, but she gave him a nod, "Sure, I'll take a look at it. She took a step and the room swung slightly, "Later, though, I think. I should probably lie down."

"You may suffer from brain damage. Euthanasia is still an option," Run said. "This would prevent you from living a pain filled life as a mentally deficient. Also it would allow me to study your brain for science."

"Thanks, I'll keep that in mind," Ariadne gave him a polite smile. "But right now I think I just need some rest." She looked over at Mike, "I believe you mentioned some bunks?"

"I'll show you the way," Simon said. "It's on the way to the bridge, and I wanted to look over the cargo manifests again."

"Thanks," Ariadne gave him a smile. She followed him out of the room, careful to take small steps. She had to pause when she reached the corridor. She felt exhausted, mentally and physically. "Who carried me over?" she asked.

"Oh, I did," Simon said. He seemed suddenly uncomfortable. "I was going to put you in the captain's quarters, but the others wanted you out where they could see you and make sure you were alright. Also, no one trusted Run with you somewhere out of sight."

"I'm sure he wouldn't do anything to me," Ariadne said. She started walking again, though she kept one arm on the bulkhead to support her.

"If you say so," Simon answered. He led the way past two other hatchways, "These two are both equipment and support machinery. Life support on the right and sensors and communications on the left."

"Port and starboard," Ariadne corrected.

"Right, shipboard terminology, I'll have to pick that up," Simon nodded. "Technical terms are pretty useful to know. You spend much time aboard ships?"

"Not really," Ariadne said. "I sort of stumbled upon my navigation abilities after I got my pilot training..." she shot him a quick glance, "Well, I got my pilot training working for a smuggler from Tannis. He needed a shuttle pilot and he offered to pay me for it, which seemed better than remaining a penniless drifter at that point."

Simon raised an eyebrow at that, but refrained from comment.

"I noticed that if I concentrated, I could, well... feel a course, so I tried it, did a little experimentation. Got a job on another smuggler ship as their navigator. That paid well enough that I got a nice savings put together. Then I a spacer I knew mentioned meeting a psychic who matched my brother's description in the Cortona system. So I took my severance, bought a ticket, and rode as a passenger on the only cargo ship headed that way out of the Vega system."

"And got captured by the Chxor, along with Rastar." Simon finished her story. "Bad luck for you, but good luck for the rest of us, I suppose," He gave her a nod, "Especially for those of us whose lives you saved today. I have to admit a certain level of... discomfort with psychics. But I appreciate the risk you took and that you saved us."

"Thanks," Ariadne said.

"This is the Captain's quarters," Simon pointed. "I believe that Anubus and Rastar have claimed portions of the

172

floor. Crowe took one of the bottom bunks, but the other should be open." She noted a change in his tone when he spoke next, "Let me know if you need anything."

"Well, thanks," Ariadne said and gave him a smile. She fought the urge to give him a kiss on the cheek. "Maybe after I get some rest I can give you a hand with the inventory." She received a polite smile in return. He seemed very reserved and that bothered her for some reason. She almost reached out with her mind, to either sense his emotions or to read his thoughts to find the source of his discomfort. She quashed that urge, it felt wrong to violate his privacy, for one thing, and for another, she didn't know if she had enough mental capacity to read a book much less someone's mind right then.

She watched Simon walk away and then stepped into the cramped cabin. She flopped down on the lower bunk, grateful for the foam pad. As she closed her eyes, she made note that she should talk with him, find out what bothered him. *Later*, Ariadne thought, as her mind dropped into an exhausted sleep, *much later.*

***

Ariadne awoke sometime later. She felt better, though her stomach reminded her that some time had passed since she last ate. "Well, at least the ration bars will probably taste better with how hungry I am," she said out loud.

She sat up from the bunk, and noticed that some helpful soul had put a ration bar to soak next to her bunk, along with a glass of water. She chewed on the ration bar for a long moment. It took a lot of chewing before it seemed ready to go down. "Well, maybe not," she sighed.

The water tasted delicious, however.

Her stomach reminded of its place, Ariadne stood and stretched. She noticed the still form of Rastar, curled up into a ball of limbs near the far corner. She looked over at a snore, and saw that Crowe lay sprawled across the other lower bunk, his head tossed back, mouth agape. She wrinkled her nose at the smell of body odor, and then sniffed at herself. *Time to see if*

173

they have a shower, and maybe some soap, she thought. She really wanted a bath, with a long soak in scalding water and lots of bubbles.

She noticed a door at the back of the cabin. She shot a suspicious glance at Crowe, then moved over and opened the door. A narrow head lay beyond, and she breathed a sigh of relief to see what could only be a shower, though she thought it unlikely that someone much bigger than her would manage to fit inside. The other facilities looked rather rudimentary, but Ariadne had used pit latrines on rugged frontier worlds before. She made sure to lock the door behind her before she made quick use of the facilities and then hopped into the shower.

Not that she expected anyone to barge in, but she wanted to relax a bit, and the privacy gave her that opportunity.

She found that the Chxor shower had a thirty second timer, which if she read the indicator correctly, would issue only two sets of water: one to lather and one last to rinse. She made use of the shower, and then reluctantly pulled her old clothes back on. She made a note to try and find a laundry machine or something. Most human ships had something, so hopefully the Chxor vessel would as well.

Her skin itched from the Chxor soap, and she noticed a strange, almost chemical smell on her skin afterward. Still, she felt far less grimy, and that made her feel better.

She slipped out of the head and then across the cabin and out the hatch.

Ariadne turned and headed towards the bow of the ship, where she'd seen Simon head to the bridge. She stepped through a hatchway at the end of the corridor and found a cramped bridge. It seemed quiet and the lighting had dimmed. She looked around, and then saw Mike seated in the captain's chair, his feet up on the console in front of him. He had a metal mug in one hand, and he gave her a wave with the other. "Feeling better?"

"Yes, much," Ariadne said. She worked her fingers through her damp hair. She wondered if the Chxor used combs or brushes. She would have to look. "What's happening?"

"Not much. It's 'night' shift right now, most everyone is asleep or finding some way to keep busy. The orbit for this ship will take us to Logan Two in three days, so we've got some time." He looked over at a screen, "Say… remember that course I wanted you to plot? I've got the data here, if you could take a look at it."

"Sure," Ariadne said. She pulled up the coordinates and checked the date and time stamp. Some helpful soul had worked a translation program into the ship's computer, and Ariadne wondered if it was Pixel or Crowe. Either way, she felt grateful that she could actually read the information rather than working through Run. "You want our old ship to go through these coordinates at that time," she frowned. "But you don't care about velocity? I could have it brake there, though that might be difficult to manage..."

"Nope, I want it to go through there pretty fast," Mike said. "We've had time to look at the sensor logs... and well, look at this," he brought up a set of video imagery on the main screen. Ariadne gave a gasp after her brain realized what she saw.

The screen showed a brown and green planet. It would have seemed unremarkable, except for the silver metal ring that encircled it and the metal spokes that ran from the surface to the inner face of the ring. "That's some kind of ring habitat... isn't it?"

"Got it in one," Mike said. "And each of those cables has attached elevators. The scale is hard to pick out, exactly, but I've seen some of their dreadnoughts dock with that thing. It's massive, a bigger construct than anything humans have built, including Earth's old space elevators."

Ariadne counted the spokes she could see, she stopped at fifteen, "Yeah, this is incredible." She frowned, "What do you want me to plot a course to it for?"

Mike gave her a slight smile, "Not a course to it... a collision course. I want our old little boat to plow right through the junction of a spoke and the ring."

"What?" Ariadne stared at him. "But that could kill thousands, tens of thousands of civilians!"

"Yeah..." Mike nodded, "It could also give us the chance to escape in the confusion. Also, don't forget: this is the race that tried to kill us, sentenced us to death as slave labor, and plots the extermination of the human race."

Ariadne looked away, "You're asking me to participate in what amounts to terrorism."

Mike sighed, "Look, don't do it if you don't want to. But I'll tell you this: I picked that spot because the records show military ships docking and undocking from there, and almost no civilian traffic. More important, if you don't do this... I'll have to give it a try, and I'll have to use this clunky Chxor piece of crap computer and a lot of guesswork."

"You're saying you might kill a bunch of civilians if I don't help?" Ariadne hated the whine that she heard in her voice, yet Mike's option made her stomach roil.

"No, I'll probably miss the ring entirely," Mike answered. "But there's a significant chance that I could hit some other part of the station, or worse, hit the planet. Think of that kind of mess," he said.

"You promise this is a military target?" Ariadne asked.

"As far as I can tell, yeah," Mike said. He shrugged, then, "Honestly, the way their society is, they make no distinction between military and civilian. For that matter, we've translated some of their news articles they had for the crew." He pulled up a set of articles on his screen, "The one about their new 'riot prevention' nerve gas Pacifix Three scares the crap out of me, personally."

"What?" Ariadne looked at the article. Some remained untranslated, but the pictures of bodies scattered in piles told her enough. She looked away, "They tested that on people?"

"Doesn't say where," Mike said. "But there's also an article in there about the recent conquest of a Nova Roma system, Danar, I think."

"Jesus," Ariadne said. She forced herself to look at the pictures, to see the scattered bodies as those of people. She looked up and suddenly she didn't care too much about any Chxor who happened to be in the wrong place at the wrong time.

"Okay, give me a few minutes. Someone will have to input the course, by the way."

"Pixel already created a program," Mike said. "It will load whatever course corrections you give it at the appropriate time."

"Great," Ariadne sat down at the navigation console. It took her only a few minutes to come up with the course. "I made some modifications to your plan," she said.

"Oh?"

"If they're anything like us, they probably have the area around the planet seeded with sensors. They also probably have defenses to stop this sort of thing, right?"

Mike gave her a nod.

"Well, I set it up so that it looks like it will coast well clear of the planet, but if Pixel can get it to do one last pulse burn, it will alter course from only a few minutes out, and I also set up as much of a dodging course as I could. Honestly, I don't know how likely it will be to get in there."

"Well, even if it just draws their attention and they destroy it, that means they won't be looking at us," Mike said. "And even a little bit of confusion could be a big help."

Ariadne nodded, even as she transmitted her course to his console. "I'm going to go walk around a bit. Want me to get you anything?"

"A nice red steak would be good right about now," Mike said.

"I'll see if I can find one," Ariadne said with a laugh.

She heard Mike mutter, "Good luck with that." as she stepped off the bridge.

***

Ariadne walked into the galley and did a double-take.

The galley table lay strewn with boxes, bottles, wires, and what looked like pieces of plumbing. More junk lay strewn across the floor, some bags of powders torn open, and some bottles and vials tipped so they dribbled their contents into the mix. Eric Striker stood over it, and as she watched, he sprinkled

177

a white powder into a bowl and stirred it into the sludge within. Pixel stood nearby with a box of what looked like mothballs, he also had his ship's suit sealed up and his helmet on..

"What's up?" she asked. Whatever Eric and Pixel were up to, it looked interesting at least.

Eric looked up. "Making something for any Chxor we run across," he looked down at her feet. His face went pale, "Ariadne, don't move."

"What?" She asked.

"By your left foot, there's a small black object, it looks sort of like a cigar," Eric said. Ariadne noticed sweat beaded his brow, "I need you to very carefully pick it up and hand it to Pixel."

"Sure thing," Ariadne reached down and picked it up. It felt heavy for such a small object. She wondered what might be in it. She walked across the galley and handed it to Pixel. "Here you are. What was that about?"

Pixel glanced at Eric, his voice sounded muffled from the closed helmet, "Uh, nothing to worry about... say, could you do me a favor?"

"Sure," Ariadne said.

"Well, I'd really appreciate it if you don't do any of the fire thing in this room. Well, on the ship at all with some of the fumes he's probably making. Also, well it might be best if you leave the room, just in case," Pixel almost sounded worried, but Ariadne found it difficult to tell what with the helmet and all.

Ariadne looked over at Eric, who didn't meet her eyes, "Uh, and if you see Simon, I'd appreciate it if you didn't mention this."

"Mention what?" Ariadne asked. "What are you guys doing?"

Eric gave her a nod and a smile, "Exactly, just like that."

Ariadne looked back and forth between the two of them, Eric with his bowl of mysterious sludge and Pixel who had very carefully set the strange object down in a foam-lined box. "You guys are weird. So where's everyone else?"

"Simon started an inventory of some of the ship's

engineering equipment," Eric said. "That's why we have time to do this. He's pretty thorough, so I think we'll finish up before he gets back." He gave a shrug, "Anubus is camped out on top of the crates of gold. I'm not sure where Run went."

"Well..." Ariadne looked around at the mess. "Be sure you guys clean up after yourselves."

"Yeah, whatever," Eric said, even as he lifted up the bowl. She saw Pixel pick up a metal pipe with one end sealed off and the other open. "Oh, and please shut the hatch on your way out."

Ariadne shook her head as she left the galley. She slipped through the hatch and then nearly ran into another woman. "Oh, excuse me!" Ariadne said. She looked the other woman over. She was blonde and tall, with a lean build and a sharply angular face.

"My fault," the other woman gave her a smile. Something about her cold dark eyes set Ariadne on edge though. "I should have watched where I was going." She had a thick eastern European accent, one that clicked in Ariadne's memory.

"Hey, aren't you Elena?" Ariadne asked, "You were talking with Crowe on the other boat, right? I meant to ask what about..."

"My name is Elena Ludmilla Lakar," the woman nodded. Her eyes narrowed a bit, "Not that it's any of your business, but I had an arrangement with Crowe. He let me know of your escape attempt so that I could tag along."

"Oh, well, I'm glad you made it out with us," Ariadne said with a slight smile. "You're going to talk with him now?" She did her best to keep any negative feelings she had for Crowe from bleeding over to the other woman.

"No, actually." Elena said. "I wanted to speak with your leader. Mike is his name, correct?"

"Oh, yeah, we don't actually have a leader, we're a team, but we just make the decisions as a group for now," Ariadne said. "But Mike acts as our spokesperson a lot, and he's come up with a lot of plans, so if you've any useful skills, he's the one to talk with."

"Right," Elena said. "Where do I find him?"

"He's on the bridge," Ariadne said. "If you want, I could walk you up there?"

"No, I will find my way," Elena said sharply. She gave Ariadne a single nod and stepped past her and into the galley. Ariadne glanced back at her, then shook her head. Something bothered her about the other woman. She just seemed dangerous, for some reason. Ariadne fought a sudden urge to follow after the woman and make certain she didn't cause trouble with Mike.

Ariadne shook her head again. Mike could handle himself. Ariadne felt pretty certain she had just imagined the other woman's attitude. And who was Ariadne to judge Elena for her deal with Crowe? Ariadne would bet she would have taken any way off the labor station, and Crowe's deal, whatever it involved, must have seemed a godsend.

Ariadne continued down the corridor. She passed an open hatch, from which she heard snoring. She shook her head at that. Most of their passengers seemed to want to catch up on their sleep, not that Ariadne could blame them for that.

She found a hatch at the end of the corridor labeled with the Chxor marking for engineering. She thought it was engineering, at least, either that or possibly a kennel. Since the latter seemed unlikely, she undogged the hatch and stepped inside.

She found a similar scene to that of the galley. Simon and Run had tools spread out over the work bench and across much of the free deck space. The scene differed, however, in the precisely straight rows, each tool and item lay evenly spaced across the bench. The scene looked eerily well ordered. Even more so as Run read off an item, and Simon added it to his list on his datapad.

"Uh, what's up?" Ariadne asked. She felt like an intruder at the sight of their perfectly organized world.

"We have begun to inventory the ship," Run said. "This human has a very logical approach to this process. We have already inventoried all medical equipment."

"I see," Ariadne looked at Simon and raised an eyebrow, "I hadn't realized the ship had medical equipment."

Simon looked down at Run, "Neither did I. All we inventoried before this are some ratchet straps and a set of drills and power tools."

"Yes, essential medical equipment," Run said. "I will need those for operation procedures, especially the straps. This will prevent patients from escape."

"You could use painkillers," Ariadne said. "Then they would not experience pain and try to escape."

"I'm a little hung up on the idea of him using a metal-cutting saw on a person," Simon said. "Especially if I'm that person. What kind of certification do you have as a medical professional?" He asked Run. "I mean, Chxor have some kind of licensing system, right?"

Run stared at him for a long moment, "All Chxor receive qualification training for their assigned professions. I am certified for my profession. Next question?"

"Why'd you get thrown in jail?" Ariadne asked.

"A simple misunderstanding," Run said. "One that I have addressed and insured will not happen again. I have even added it to my notes."

"Misunderstanding?" Simon asked. He glanced at Ariadne, "They sent you to what amounts to a death camp. The Chxor don't seem to value life much, but if you are a trained doctor, I would imagine that they would not waste such a resource without what seemed like a good reason."

Run looked up at Simon for a moment, and Ariadne resisted a sudden urge to poke inside the Chxor's mind and see why he took such care in his words. The Chxor had shown no such caution with regards to any other conversation before. Finally, the little Chxor spoke, and Ariadne realized that he actually sounded miserable, his high pitched voice almost hoarse, "I made a mistake with an experiment. A minor mistake, one that I should not have received my punishment. I did not take into account signal interference with relation to a mechanical implant in a biological."

"What does that matter?" Simon asked.

"I pushed it into mass production and implanted the entire biological population on Khreta Seven and during a solar flare the signal became interrupted on that planet. This resulted in interference with much of the populace." Run shrugged. "The event received the attention of the Benevolence Council, and they decreed that I must work off my debt to the Chxor race."

"What kind of interference?" Simon asked.

"You know, he seems pretty unhappy about this," Ariadne said. "Let's just let him get back to work. I'm sure he's sorry, right Run?"

The little Chxor looked up at her, "Sorrow is a human emotion generated as a result of their acknowledgment that they are incapable of perfection. Logically, it is yet another emotion that no Chxor will feel, as we are the pinnacle of both genetic maturity and we continue the improvement of our species through genetic engineering and bio-mechanical implantation." He paused, "I regret that my experiment wasted both time and resources, and that it resulted in my possible termination. However, I acknowledge that science needs me, therefore I will do my best to survive and continue my efforts."

Ariadne gave Simon a smile, "See, he's sorry."

He rubbed his head, "You give me a headache." He waved at Run, "Alright little guy, continue, we stopped at adjustable wrench, flex, magnetic coupling. Next item?" As Run went back to the orderly piles, Simon looked over at Ariadne, "You clearly found the shower after you got some sleep. Did you get the ration bar I left for you?"

"I did," Ariadne smiled. "Thanks. It was an excellent gift."

"I don't know that I'd go that far," Simon grunted. "I would not have believed it before, but those bars make Mratha rice sound good right now."

"Well, I appreciate it anyway," Ariadne said. She noticed him shrug uncomfortably. "What's the problem?"

Simon scratched at his forehead. He glanced at her and then gave an apologetic shrug. "Look, I didn't want to bring it up... but there's something you should know about me. I'm pretty sure you won't like it, but I think it's best to get it out there and clear the air."

"You're not a closet serial killer or something, right?" Ariadne asked.

He snorted, "No."

"You aren't a Xenophile and secretly plan to make Hurnath babies with Rastar?" Ariadne said.

Simon coughed in surprise. "No!"

"This is genetically impossible," Run said. "Despite the similarity of the two species, they do not even share the same cell structure." He looked up, "Though the experimentation would provide an interesting combination, particularly the lower intelligence of humans and the strength of the Ghornath."

Ariadne ignored Run's interjection, "You aren't secretly planning to conquer the known universe?"

"...no," Simon answered, "though I would like to keep the option open."

"And you haven't tried to kill me in my sleep..." Ariadne smiled, "Other than giving me a ration bar, which falls under homicide by bad food, which I'll put under the slightly questionable but understandable category." She held up her hands, "So what's the terrible secret you need to get off your chest?"

Simon cleared his throat, "Well, you know I said I was a cop, right?"

"Yeah, some kind of investigator, right?" Ariadne asked.

"Yeah, the Confederation Security Bureau, CSB," Simon said. "We guard government officials and conduct investigations on security threats to the Confederation. We do a lot of counter-terrorism and threat reduction." He sighed, "Some of that includes elimination of rogue psychics."

"Elimination?" Ariadne asked.

Simon met her eyes, "Yeah, elimination. Most of the ones they send us after have hit the monster category. They stopped being people. Most of them had some history of violence before they developed their powers. There weren't many cases like that, but a few, some pretty terrible."

"Oh," Ariadne said. She took a deep breath, "Yeah, I can understand that. I've only met a handful of psychics. Before all this... well, I mostly kept my abilities to myself." She hesitated, "What do you classify as a monster?"

"Someone who kills indiscriminately or for the pleasure of it," Simon answered. "Not just a psychic, either, anyone who does that goes into the monster category for me. Those are the people who belong either behind bars or in the ground."

Ariadne nodded slowly, "Okay, I think we can agree to that," She gave him a sad smile, "Honestly, I've had too little contact with most psychics to consider myself part of any 'community' so if you think confessing to killing some nut jobs who hurt people for kicks will scare me away, you need not worry."

He nodded, "Well, that's not all. Security work runs in my family. My dad and both my grandfathers worked security. My dad in the CSB as well... and back when they worked primarily as the government enforcers, especially against the Separatist movement."

"Secret police?" Ariadne asked.

He shrugged, "He never talked about it much. But I gather he worked more the protection side of things. That's what pulled me into the service... well that and my grandfathers' stories. They were partners, back in the day."

"With CSB?" Ariadne gave him a broad smile.

"No..." Simon took a deep breath, "With ESPSec."

Ariadne felt her heart stop. "Oh." She had heard legends about ESPSec, the abbreviation for ESP Security. Under the reign of Amalgamated Worlds they had served as the enforcers for the strict laws against psychics, and towards the end of Amalgamated Worlds rule, their enforcement had made them little more than executioners.

Ariadne figured that their earlier years where they stuffed people into 'containment' camps back on Earth didn't amount to much better. Those years of containment had ended in the largest prison escape in human history, when fifteen million psychics and their families escaped the camps and hijacked the Agathan Fleet. Where those psychics went with the most advanced fleet Amalgamated Worlds ever built remained a mystery. One she wondered about at times when she ran into psychic prejudice and wished she could go somewhere she belonged.

"I see," Ariadne said.

"They both got into it for good reasons," Simon looked down at his feet, "But I won't say they weren't a product of their times. They hated psychics, especially mind readers. And they were not saints. Hell, Grandpa Zhu worked at the San Antonio Camp as a guard for seven years. He was there during the prison break, actually met one of the Agathan's leaders. Story about it scared the hell out of me as a boy."

"So how would they feel about you calling me a friend?" Ariadne asked.

"They probably would think you did something to my head, and one or the other would try to kill you," Simon said softly. "They could be mean old bastards sometimes. But their stories got me interested in protecting other people. And... well, after my father died, they raised me. I can't say that their hatred for psychics didn't effect me, but I'm aware of their background. I think I have it mostly in hand."

"Yeah, you haven't tried to kill me," Ariadne said. "Well, other than the ration bar, but I'll forgive you for that." She took a deep breath, "So, got that off your chest, nothing more to worry about, right?"

He nodded slowly, "If you're willing to leave it at that, so am I."

Ariadne nodded, "Whatever our grandparents might have done to one another, it's in the past, and I for one, think that's a good thing." She stuck out her hand to shake.

Simon took her hand in his own and shook it. "I like to think I would react with as little anger to hear that your grandparents might have killed mine. But thanks, I appreciate it."

Ariadne smiled, "I try not to throw tantrums about things I can't change. You didn't pick your grandfathers' jobs, they lived their lives. And I never knew my parents, much less my grandparents. For all I know, they could have been in ESPSec too!"

"Well, if you're interested," Simon asked, "I could do some research, once we get back to civilized space. I might be able to track down some details on your family, maybe give you some closure on that."

Ariadne shook her head, "I'm more interested in finding my brother. My parents and presumably whatever family they had, died in the war. My family is the man and woman who adopted me and my little brother. The rest doesn't really matter to me." The cool weight of the lighter in her pocket proved her words to be a lie. Yet her family and whatever history they had seemed like something private, some aspect of her life she did not wish to share. *Not even with the cute guy who seems at least a little interested in me.*

"Okay," Simon frowned. "I don't really understand that attitude, but I'll accept it. If you need any help tracking your brother down, I would be glad to help with that. How did you get separated, anyway?"

"We had to run," Ariadne said as her smile faded. "Someone I trusted outed us as psychics and some things got blamed on us." She shrugged, "Well, blamed on me really. A girl I knew, she had some emotional trouble and committed suicide. Her family blamed me, they said I had messed with her head," Ariadne looked down at the floor. "So... I ran. And my brother came with me, tagged along like he always did. We went to the Epsilon Erandi system, and then the Altair system. We found a place there, and I found some work... waiting tables actually." She shrugged, "I met a guy, he seemed pretty nice, but he had some rough friends. They tried to get my brother and I to help them rob the place I worked at. I said no, they threatened Paul..."

"So you ran again?" Simon asked.

"No, I told Paul to run and I fought them," Ariadne said. "First, I tried to just scare them off, but they came at us with knives and worse. I killed one of them." Ariadne felt tears well

186

up in her eyes, "Paul got to the spaceport, I tracked him that far. But, I couldn't stay. The people I fought went to the cops, gave them my information. So, I boarded the first ship out of Separatist space."

"Sorry," Simon gave her a nod, "But it sounds like you did what you could. I'll get some more information from you when we get somewhere I can use it. I'll need a description, his name and any aliases he uses, and I'd like to take a blood sample so I have someplace to start."

"All that?" Ariadne asked.

"Well... of course," he nodded. "I will start a full database search and contact some people I know who do that sort of thing. It will probably take a few weeks, but I imagine I can at least locate what system he's in. Otherwise we might as well wander aimlessly looking for him."

Ariadne felt her ears and the back of her neck burn with embarrassment, "Well, that's sort of what I did. Just asked questions at whatever port I made."

She could feel Simon stare at her, "Well, that's a technique, I suppose." The tone of his voice suggested he didn't exactly know what else to say.

Run looked over at them, "Your discussion has exceeded allocated break time by approximately one hundred and seventeen seconds. We must continue our inventory or I will be forced to use a commanding voice."

"That's not a commanding voice," Simon said. "That's a shrill childish shrieking. The only reason anyone listens to anything you say is to shut you up."

"Your argument is illogical as you admit that my commanding voice has the desired effect," Run said. "NOW WE WILL CONTINUE THE INVENTORY."

Ariadne rolled her eyes, "I'll let you two get back to it."

*　*　*

"So we put the blasting cap in like so..." Eric said as he slid the cigar-like tube down into the top of the pipe that Pixel held.

187

"Blasting cap?" Ariadne asked from the hatchway, headed back towards the front of the ship. "You guys are making explosives?" The galley seemed a terrible place to do it, particularly with its location at the center of the ship.

Eric looked up, "Well, yeah, what else did you think we were doing?"

Ariadne gave a shrug, "It's a galley, I dunno... cooking?"

"Less talk please," Pixel said from behind his helmet. "We need to cap this before it becomes unstable."

"Oh, right," Eric grabbed a pipe cap and went to put it on.

"No!" Pixel shouted, "Wipe the threads! Wipe the threads!" Eric froze mid motion.

Ariadne looked between them, "Is this safe?"

"Totally safe," Eric said. He set the pipe cap down and reached for a rag from the pile.

"Not that one," Pixel said. "That one is soaked in ether, it might ignite on contact with the residue on the threads."

"Oh! Right..." Eric said. He looked over at Ariadne as he grabbed a dish towel. "Totally safe. You might want to close that hatch, though. And probably don't step in any of the stuff on the floor, some of it might eat through your suit."

"Okay, I'm just going to leave you guys to it," Ariadne said. "I'll be on the bridge with Mike."

"Oh, sure," Eric said, as he gently wiped the threads of the pipe bomb. "Oh, and if Mike asks what we're doing..."

"Let me guess, I don't know?" Ariadne asked with a sigh.

"No, he wanted an update," Pixel said. "Let him know we should be done soon, and I'll be up to do some modeling of his scans soon-ish."

"Soon-ish?" Ariadne asked.

"Well, I think some of the nitric acid ate a hole in my suit. It smells like lemons inside here, and I'm getting slightly light headed," Pixel said. "So I'm going to have to rinse my suit and probably do a full decontamination, just in case. And cleaning this place will be interesting."

Eric shrugged, "Why not just mop?"

"Because mopping will mix this mess into a slurry rather

similar to what we just put inside that pipe," Pixel said, and Ariadne heard a note of exasperation in his muffled voice. "Not to mention that some of this stuff becomes highly reactive in water. So..."

Ariadne tuned out his chemistry lesson as she walked carefully around their mess and then out the hatch. Not that she didn't find their work to be of interest, but she didn't feel like a lecture right at the moment. Besides that, her method of cleaning would probably be similar to Eric.

She had just cracked the hatch to the bridge when she heard Elena's voice, "As you can see, I could be a valuable addition to your team." Ariadne felt a moment of guilt as she listened in, but she quashed that. *It's not like I'm reading their minds,* she thought, *just listening in to a conversation.*

"You could," Mike answered. "That's a pretty interesting skill set. But our little group has worked well together, mostly because we work *together*. I'll run your suggestions past the rest of them, as well as your request to be a member of our team." Ariadne could see Mike and Elena through the opening. Mike sat in the pilot's seat, but he had rotated it to face Elena, who stood with her hands on her hips. His eyes flicked to the hatch and he gave Ariadne the slightest nod.

"Have I not been very *persuasive?*" Elena put a hefty weight on that last word, and Ariadne frowned slightly. She did not like the emphasis, nor how the other woman seemed interested in weaseling her way into the group.

"You have," Mike said. "And I will definitely take that and your other..." he coughed, "offers into consideration. But, like I said, I need to talk to the others. There's no rush, we've got some time. And as far as what you said about Anubus, well, I'll think that over too."

"Are you sure?" Elena said, and Ariadne saw her walk forward to rest her hand on Mike's shoulder. "I am sure that we can come to a private arrangement. And you could present it to the others as a done deal..."

Ariadne chose that moment to open the hatch. She made sure to let it slam against the wall, "Hey, Mike, how's it going?"

Ariadne could not restrain her smile as she saw Elena jump back and tuck her hands behind her back.

Mike looked over at Ariadne and he gave her a wink, "Not too bad, Elena here wanted to offer her services. She has quite the skill set, actually: a little bit of guns, some expertise in hacking and communications. With her background, she might be a a good addition to the team."

"Oh, really?" Ariadne asked. "That's pretty impressive. What did you do before you got captured by the Chxor and stuck on the station?" She saw the other woman grimace slightly at the reminder that she'd needed their help to escape.

"I was a retrieval specialist," Elena said. Ariadne had heard some 'corporate' terms for things before, but something about the phrase had sounded sinister.

"She was a bounty hunter," Mike corrected, and Ariadne gave him a nod.

"You make it sound more dangerous than it was," Elena smirked, "I mostly retrieved lost husbands for their divorce hearings or the occasional parole violator. I operated out of Tanis, yes, but I was not one of their registered mercenaries."

"You ever collect on the head bounties?" Mike asked.

"I am not a killer for hire or an assassin," Elena said. "Though I have, on occasion, ended up with a dead bounty rather than a live one. It is a risk I face in my job, and sometimes people don't come with a smile when I show up," she nodded at Ariadne, "I can see that bothers you. But some of us do not have the ability to control people with our minds. If I had that skill set, I think I would have brought back all of my bounties alive. I do not like to kill."

Ariadne smiled at the admission, "I can understand that. And I imagine it's hard for a girl in your line of work." Maybe she had misjudged the other woman. Her attempt at seduction with Mike might just be the product of her career and Ariadne could understand a woman using all the weapons at her disposal in her line of work.

Still, it was not something to encourage, "But I hope that you understand that our team works on trust. We have to be able

190

to trust everyone, so the way you work might not mesh with how we do business. We like everything out in the open."

"Right..." Elena gave her a cold smile. "I'll keep that in mind. Well, thank you for your time, Mike. Good talking with you again... what's your name again?"

"Ariadne," she gave the other woman a polite smile.

"Yes, I'll try to remember that," Elena Ludmilla Lakar gave her a nod and then swept past her.

Ariadne waited for the hatch to close before she flopped into the navigator's seat. Then she winced as one of the supports jabbed her through the thin padding. *Chxor need to learn how to pad a seat properly,* she thought. "So, little miss bounty hunter wants to join the team?"

"Something finally sinks through the cheerful shield, huh?" Mike asked.

"Cheerful shield?"

"Yeah, you're almost always bubbly... it's good to know someone can get under your skin," Mike grinned. He snorted at her scowl. "Hey, don't blame me, I just observed her in action. She might be good to have around just for that reason."

"Right," Ariadne shook her head, "Did she mention her arrangement with Crowe? He's the one who told her about our escape plan."

Mike frowned, "No. And that suddenly bothers me. She might have mentioned that she and Crowe talked at least. That she didn't... well either she knows that Crowe and I don't necessarily get along or..." He frowned, "Well there's a few possibilities, some of them pretty trivial, some sinister. So what are the others up to?"

"Rastar and Crowe haven't moved from sleep," Ariadne said. "Eric and Pixel might well blow up the galley, and Simon and Run are engaged in their inventory."

"Good, Rastar can't get in trouble when he's asleep, and we may need some explosives," Mike grunted, "Simon may well have time to do his complete inventory. This ship's lower velocity means we'll hit orbit around the planet in three more days."

191

"Okay," Ariadne did the math, "So we should be on scene for an hour or two before the cargo boat goes in on its run. Let's just hope we don't dock with that ring."

"From what I understand about the ship and the way they load and unload it, I doubt it," Mike said. "You saw the containers strapped on outside?" She nodded. "Well that's done to allow cargo shuttles to grab the containers. I've seen similar designs on ships that do frontier work. This way, it doesn't require much in the way of a support structure from a spaceport. All they need is a cargo shuttle with the right attachments and someplace to set down."

"They seem to have pretty good industry here," Ariadne said. "Why would they need a ship like this? The planet we're headed towards looks very developed."

"The other planet, maybe not," Mike said. "The little bit of the log that Run translated suggests that the other planet is mostly agriculture, lots of farms and such. So most of the cargo is food... of one sort or another."

"Too bad we can't eat it," Ariadne said.

"I wouldn't think some of it would be what we'd like," Mike grimaced. "Among the load is a container labeled 'agents of disorder'. When I asked Run for a clarification... he said they were Chxor who rebelled."

"Wait, in a container?"

"Frozen. And already 'processed' Run said. For eating."

She wrinkled her nose in disgust. "That's gross," Ariadne said. "So the Chxor cannibalize their own dead?"

"It appears so," Mike grimaced. "The more I learn about them, the less and less I want anything to do with them. Except maybe to play pirate and steal their ships and equipment."

Ariadne smiled, "Mike Golemon, pirate of the space-ways?"

He gave her a nod, but she saw his face turn serious, "Something I'd ask, by the way, Ariadne. I don't give my full name to others for a variety of reasons. I'd appreciate it if you don't spread it around."

"Oh?" Ariadne asked, suddenly interested.

"I... well, I joined the Colonial Republic Liberation Fleet a long time back," he grimaced again. "It ended badly. I don't want to go into the details, but if someone looked up my records, there would be some questions raised, including how I survived. I'd rather not go into that, so I just travel under a name of convenience, and avoid areas of Colonial space where they do biometrics scans."

"Understandable," Ariadne said. "I'd prefer to avoid official inquiry into my past for a similar reason." She shrugged, "So what would you prefer I call you?"

"I keep it simple," He grinned, "Mike Smith, or Mike Johnson."

"I have to ask..." Ariadne said. "You're, well, you're clearly of Asian ancestry, why the Caucasian name?"

"You think I don't blend in with you 'round eyes'?" Mike grinned. "It's complicated. I'll leave it like that. Not real interesting. My family came from North America before they went out to the colonies. Their name got Americanized, that's mostly it.

"Oh," Ariadne said. "Well, I guess that works. I seem to be the only one on the team with a non-interesting family past. Even Rastar's family fought in the Ghornath war with Nova Roma."

"You're a war orphan, right?" Mike said. "I'm sure there's a story there. Maybe your parents had a role there."

Ariadne shrugged, "Military orphans got special treatment in the Separatist orphanages. My brother and I just got the impression that our parents were normal people." she looked around, eager to change the subject to a less depressing topic. "So, I guess Anubus has claimed the gold?"

"For the moment," Mike grimaced. "We may have a fight on our hands later over that."

"I'm sure we can work it out," Ariadne said calmly. "I mean, the whole team worked to capture the ship, it's only fair that we share it out evenly."

"I doubt he'll see it that way," Mike said. "But I'll let you give it a try, maybe you can... you know," Mike wiggled his fingers.

"I'm not going to mess with someone's head over some money," Ariadne said with a smile. "Besides, like I said, I bet we can talk him around. He seems pretty reasonable."

"Sure..." Mike shook his head. "You do know how unreasonable *humans* get about gold right? Can you imagine how nasty a Wrethe might get if he thinks we're out to rob him?"

Adrian frowned. "Well, it's not much of an issue right now. Besides, how unreasonable can he be?"

***

"Human, if you touch that crate, they'll hear your screams back at the station," Anubus growled.

Ariadne saw Pixel look up from his work in the corner, "Sound doesn't propagate through vacuum. Also, the Chxor blew the station up. So they can't hear anything."

"That won't matter," Anubus growled. Ariadne saw him flex his sheathed claws.

"Look, not that you don't terrify me and all," Pixel said. "But I have to finish this up. We might need to vent this compartment if the Chxor send a boarding party to inspect the ship. If we can kill them with something simple like this, it will save people like you from taking a couple of bullets."

"I have my eye on you… and the rest of them. I know you want my gold."

Pixel gave another sigh. "I'll keep that in mind."

Ariadne walked up, "How's it going, Pixel? Mike said we're almost done braking. He's received a message for the orbit they want, as well."

"I should finish up soon," Pixel said.

"Anubus, are you ready?" Ariadne asked. "We may have some fighting."

"I am very ready to kill something," Anubus growled, "Especially if they threaten my gold."

"Right," Ariadne smiled politely. "I'll let Mike know."

Ariadne walked out of the small cargo bay that attached to the airlock. She made her way to the bridge quickly enough,

194

but then found her way blocked by a crowd in the corridor outside.

"Excuse me," Ariadne said politely.

The man nearest her glanced back and then returned his attention to the front, "Anyone got any news? I promise a thousand Republic Drachma to any man who can tell me if there's a freighter headed for Colonial space."

"I need to get by," Ariadne said. Her normal smile faded slightly. The man in front of her shifted slightly to block her progress.

No one in the crowd looked back at her.

"Everybody MOVE!" shouted someone in a deep bellow behind her.

The crowd flattened to the sides of the corridor. Ariadne glanced back and saw Rastar stood above her, his four arms crossed over his chest and a flush of red anger on his hide.

"Thank you, Rastar," Ariadne said sweetly.

"Not a problem," Rastar said. "I hate rude people." He glanced down at the human who had ignored her and then blocked her. "They really make me angry. You wouldn't like that, would you?"

"You don't want to hurt me," the man blustered. Ariadne saw that he had somehow found some oil or something for his dark hair, he wore it slicked back. "I'm a lawyer, and I'm worth a lot of money."

"Of course you are," Rastar said. He waved a hand forward for Ariadne, "After you."

She walked past the others, many of whom seemed to only see Rastar as she led the way onto the bridge. She found Eric stationed at the hatch, a grimace on his face. "Sorry about the crowd," he scowled at one of the men who tried to edge after Rastar. "Mike had me kick them all off the bridge."

"Well, they just want some more information, I suppose," Ariadne said. "I can't blame them for that. Any news?"

Eric shrugged, "I work with weapons, and this tub hasn't got any. Crowe, Mike, and Simon are pouring over the sensor feed. Go ask them." He looked up at Rastar, "Oh, and Mike said he wouldn't mind your input either."

Ariadne stepped through the hatch. She saw that Crowe had sprawled out over the communications console and had his feet propped up on the navigator's seat. Mike sat in the captain's seat while Simon had tucked himself into the sensor area. "Pixel says he's nearly done. Anubus is ready for a fight. What's the news up here?"

Mike looked up, "Well, good and bad."

"Mostly bad," Crowe said.

Mike ignored the interruption. "There's lots of traffic, some of it definitely equipped with Shadow Space drives."

"But we don't know which ships," Crowe said. "And they're all Chxor ships, so we'll have to figure out how to work their tech."

"Isn't Chxor drive technology based off of ours?" Ariadne asked. "I sort of remember something about that, from school."

"Yeah," Mike grunted. "They developed pretty high tech back on their homeworld, but they never did space travel before we showed up and showed it to them."

Simon spoke from his console, "Big mistake there."

"So if it's based off of what we gave them, then it can't be too hard to figure out, right?" Ariadne asked.

"Sure, if you can read Chxor and if we can even find where their bridge is," Crowe said. "For that matter, if we can even identify a ship with a drive that's not a military ship full of armed Chxor."

Mike sighed, "Yeah, there is that."

"With all the traffic here, you haven't seen one ship we can board?" Rastar asked.

"We've seen dozens, just most of them are too big for a handful to operate, or too small to have a drive. Or we spot something that looks promising and it pulls out of orbit or docks with that damned ring," Crowe snapped. "Which I don't think I need to mention why going aboard that thing would be a bad idea?"

"You seem to be in a wonderful mood," Ariadne said with a smile. "Relax, I'm sure something will present itself."

"Look, little miss sunshine, I hate to piss on your parade-"

"Enough," Mike snapped. "We get nothing from arguing with each other."

"I'll show you what we're working with," Simon said. "Maybe we just need a fresh set of eyes."

The imagery showed up on the main screen a moment later. The sheer scale of the massive orbital ring took Ariadne's breath away. Then she saw the thousands of ships that hung in orbit above the planet. The majority had movement to and from the ring, though others seemed stationary.

"What kind of orbit did their traffic control stick us in?" Ariadne asked.

"High orbit," Mike said. "Well away from the ring. They also said the cargo shuttles will begin approach in three hours... and that a personnel shuttle will arrive to take the crew to the station sometime after that."

"Oh, good, so we'll have transportation at least," Ariadne said. "We can use that to go where we need." She nodded, clearly things would work out for the best, at least once they figured out the whole ship thing.

Crowe snapped, "You say that like-"

"Freeze the frame," Rastar said, his voice intent. "That ship there, in the shadow of the ring. Can you zoom on it?"

Ariadne looked back up at the screen, she barely saw the tiny ship. Against the scale of the ring it seemed hardly a speck. Simon spoke, "This is from a recording, but I can get the video telescope to zoom in, as long as that area hasn't rotated around the planet yet." Simon glanced at his datapad, and then tapped commands on the sensor console in a precise order. The screen cleared, and then a moment later, showed a larger version of the ship, as well as a section of the vast ring above it.

"That is not a Chxor ship," Mike said, suddenly. "I'm not sure what it is, but it's not Chxor."

"It is a Ghornath ship," Rastar said. "Unless I am mistaken, it is a Berganyr class Corvette. I can't quite make out the name on the hull. My mother served as a nurse aboard one of those in the defense of Ghornath Prime."

"It's capable of making Shadow Space?" Mike asked.

"Yes..." Rastar nodded. "It will also be fast, and well armed for its size. They were the newest ships my people created before the fall of my homeworld."

"How did it get here?" Simon asked. "I thought the Ghornath hated the Chxor?"

"We do," Rastar nodded. "But perhaps they captured the ship or someone else did and the Chxor purchased it. Either way, it may be easier to take than another ship."

"Yeah, but none of the rest of us read Ghornath," Crowe said. "So that doesn't make things easier."

"The bridge will be located near the rear, and probably the upper part of the ship." Rastar said. "The engine room located near the center."

Mike frowned. "Yeah, I can see what looks like view-ports on that part near the rear, the projection up above the rest. And I can see what looks like a pair of turrets on the port side. So it's got some weapons at least."

"If we have to fight our way out of here," Simon spoke up, "We're probably not going to make it." He looked uneasy at the thought of shooting his way out. Ariadne wondered if Mike had mentioned his plan with the cargo boat.

"No, but we've got a long way to go before we get back to any kind of civilized space," Mike answered. "I would rather have the option than not. Besides, we've got the element of surprise; we might do some serious damage before they kill us."

"I think we can avoid the last part," Ariadne said. "And with Rastar to translate, I bet we can get that ship up quickly enough." She looked over at Rastar, "Plus, the Ghornath eat food that is mostly compatible with humans, so we have a food supply available."

Mike nodded, "Good point." He looked around at the others, "Alright, so we make for that one?"

No one argued. "Very well. Ariadne, I'd like you to work out a couple of courses from where our orbit will be. One as a rapid sprint and the other with as much dodging and jinking as you can manage."

Ariadne nodded slowly, "Sure, but I'll need some parameters of the shuttle. And I'll be more accurate as we get closer to our orbit."

"I know, just start thinking about it," Mike said. He looked up at Rastar, "Big guy, I'd like you and Eric and Anubus, I suppose, to set down and talk over everything you can think about as far as that ship and the layout."

Rastar gave him a thumbs up, "Not a problem, man. I just want to lead the way. The Chxor don't deserve that piece of my people's history. They stole it... and I'm going to take it back." Ariadne saw the big alien's skin turn a dark red. "And any of them that get in the way will be very, very sorry."

***

Ariadne tapped her foot impatiently as she stood with the others near the airlock.

"Stop that," Anubus growled

"I can't," Ariadne said. "I get fidgety when I'm nervous."

"Stop that or I'll take your leg off," Anubus growled.

"That doesn't help," Ariadne noted. "And besides, I won't be able to help out if I'm on the floor screaming in agony. And I imagine that would be a lot more annoying." She gave him a smile.

"Why is she here, anyway?" Crowe asked. "I know she can do that fire thing, but I thought we wanted the shuttle intact?"

"We do," Eric said. "But she can pilot it and she'll navigate it as well. So it is best to have her in place quickly." He looked over at Crowe, "You on the other hand, are here to catch any stray bullets that might hit her."

Crowe shot Ariadne a glance, "Good luck with that."

"Where's Rastar?" Anubus glanced around. "He better not have chosen now to make a play for the gold. I don't need that kind of distraction."

"Hey buddy, your gold is fine, I'm just, uh, a little stuck," Rastar called from behind them.

199

"Stuck?" Eric asked, and turned to face down the corridor. Just then, Ariadne saw the airlock hatch turn amber.

"They've docked," Mike's voice crackled through the speaker near the airlock hatch.

"Shit," Eric turned back to face the airlock, just as the light turned green and the hatch swung open. A pair of Chxor guards stood in the airlock, and behind them Ariadne saw four or five more, their weapons slung. As per plan, the Chxor had opened both airlocks, the better to allow the entire 'crew' to embark quickly.

They had expected a couple guards, they had not expected a mostly full shuttle of Chxor. The shuttle had no seats and it looked to be standing room only.

Eric fired his riot gun at the nearest of the two guards, who had not yet reacted to the sight of a Wrethe and four humans in the passageway. Simon fired his pistol as well.

Ariadne realized it wouldn't be enough. As she did, her eyes dropped to the pipe bomb that hung from Eric's utility belt. She reached out with her mind and tugged it free, then sent it end over end through the airlock. It struck one of the Chxor guards in the head, hard enough to drop him to the deck.

Ariadne stepped past Anubus, who halted his lunge forward at the sight of so many Chxor. Her hand caught the airlock hatch and she slammed it closed even as she reached out with her mind and ignited the area around the bomb.

The airlock hatch muffled the blast to a dull thud.

Eric moved up to peer through the porthole. He shot her a glance, "Good job, you saved our asses there." His voice held a measure of respect, for once. Ariadne gave him a smile in return.

Her smile died after he opened the hatch. Green blood spattered the inside of the airlock, and pain-filled cries from the Chxor in the shuttle made Ariadne's heart twist. "Oh god..." She had to look away from the sight.

Eric gave a shout, "Perfect! And look, no damage to the shuttle!"

Simon looked over at him, his eyes narrow, "Where did

that come from?"

Anubus pushed past them both, he prodded at a dead Chxor, "You humans make combat much less personal at times."

A Chxor guard tried to raise his weapon at the Wrethe. A single backhanded swing swatted him up against the wall. Anubus stalked further into the shuttle.

"Guys? What's going on? Can someone help?" Rastar called from back down the corridor.

Crowe scowled, "I'll help him get unstuck, otherwise we'll be here all day."

Ariadne took a deep breath and looked back at the shuttle. The stench of Chxor blood assaulted her, and she felt her eyes water up. *I will not cry*, she thought, *I did it to save my friends, there's nothing wrong with what I did.*

She took a step into the airlock, and did her best to ignore the squelch of fluids beneath her feet.

Simon put his hand on her shoulder, "Hey, it'll be alright. Quick thinking back there, Eric's right on that."

Ariadne nodded, but she kept her eyes up as she walked through the shuttle. She saw Anubus emerge from the pilot's cockpit, he dragged a Chxor out. The Chxor pilot tried to struggle against his grip, but Anubus held him off the ground with little effort. "I thought a live pilot might be of more use this time."

"Right, I'll let you know if I need him," Ariadne said. She started to step forward when she heard a gunshot behind her. She spun around and dropped into a crouch. Eric looked up from where he'd just shot a wounded guard.

"What?" he asked.

"A little warning maybe?" Anubus asked.

"Sorry," Eric said. He turned to another wounded Chxor guard and chambered a round.

"Wait, he's wounded, he can't hurt you!" Ariadne said.

Eric gave a shrug, "Not right now, no, but he doesn't serve any purpose alive, and the bastard would kill any of us in a heartbeat."

Simon walked forward, "You will not execute that

201

prisoner-"

Eric fired, and Chxor blood spattered across a previously clean section of wall.

"What's wrong with you?" Ariadne all but screamed.

"What's wrong with you?" Eric asked. "It's not like I killed the rest of them. Shit, only the ones at the door were armed, after all."

"What?" Ariadne asked. She looked -actually looked- at some of the bodies that lay strewn around the compartment. She felt her stomach drop as she saw he was right. She had killed civilians. "Oh, Christ." She covered her eyes with her hands.

"We don't have time for this," Anubus growled.

Simon put his hands on her shoulders, "Look, Ariadne, don't fall apart on us now. We need you to plot a course."

Ariadne let him lead her towards the cockpit. Just as she took a seat at the controls she heard another shot. She hunched over the console and tried to shut the rest of the world out. For a long moment, she simply could not force her brain to function. She felt completely lost; she had done something terrible in a moment of reaction.

Or had she? *I remember seeing the weapons of the guards,* she thought, *did I see the others did not have weapons, did I want to kill them all?* The thought shattered her self control. She stared at the console for a long moment, and she remembered. She remembered the words of Victor on the day she had killed him.

"You pretend to care, because you think it makes you a better person, but deep down inside, you're just as much of a sewer as the rest of us."

***

She had stood there in the empty warehouse. She had not known why he wanted to meet with her and her brother here. At the time, she had some half imagined dream that he wanted to leave the planet behind, to go to some frontier world and start anew.

But he hadn't. She remembered how he had arrived with

his friends, the rough group that always seemed to get Victor in trouble. And then when she refused his initial request to help them rob the restaurant, he had thrown those words in her face, "You pretend to care, because you think it makes you a better person, but deep down inside, you're just as much a sewer as the rest of us."

Ariadne shook her head, "No, I refuse to do something like that. They took me in, gave me a job, they almost treat me like family..."

"They hired you because they know you're a fugitive and they can pay you less," Victor snarled. "They know you've got trouble in your past and that you won't cause trouble. Hell, I've seen the way that Andrews looks at you. Give him half a chance and he'll rape you in the pantry while his wife's away."

"No," Ariadne said. "You're saying that stuff to make me do what you want. Leave this be, alright, Victor? Look, I really like you..."

"Oh, don't give me that shit," Victor said, and his normally pleasant face twisted in anger. "We have something special, and you know it. Or do you think that I share my hard earned money with just anyone? You're better than this place, and with your abilities... we can do so much better. Think of how much money we could take from those who don't deserve it!"

"Victor..." Ariadne shook her head, "I've already seen what happens if I abuse my abilities, when my friend... when she died..." She shook her head, "I won't toy with people, not for something as petty as money."

"You will," Victor said, and he glanced over at Karl. The biggest man in the group moved forward. "And I hate to force you to do this, but it's for your own good. If you won't do it because it's the right thing to do, you'll do it because otherwise I'll have to hurt Paul."

"No!" Ariadne shouted as the big man walked towards her brother. Without thought, she lashed out with her mind, and saw Karl stagger and clutch at his head.

"Ariadne," Victor said, his voice calm. "Don't do that. If

you attack my guys again... well I'll have to take it out on your brother..."

The calculated cruelty in his voice reverberated in her memory. That shock she had felt that she had not seen it in him, that she had made herself blind to his flaws. She had lived in willful ignorance and in that moment, someone would have to pay for that mistake.

Ariadne looked at her brother and saw the fear in his eyes. She looked at Victor and saw the slight smile on his face, the smile she had always thought meant he cared for her, and only now realized he had felt some other emotion when he looked at her.

"No," Ariadne said. "If you send anyone after my brother or I... you will be the one to pay the price." She forced confidence into her words, even as she met his gaze. All of her fear and uncertainty washed away, replaced by anger at his cruelty. She felt the sweat bead her brow, smelled the slight scent of burning hair that suggested her control had begun to slip.

"Nice try, Ariadne, but we both know you've got that soft center, you won't hurt anyone, it's not in your nature," Victor said. He turned to his men, "Grab the kid, and if she does anything else, rough him up a bit." He drew a gun from an inner pocket and aimed it at her, "And just in case you try any mental tricks... well I'd hate to lose you, but..." He shrugged, that slight smirk still on his face.

Ariadne saw them draw knives. She saw Paul's eyes flit from them to the doorway behind. "Run, Paul," Ariadne said.

And then she reached out with her mind. She felt Victor, as she had before, only now she saw him as he was: a piece of organic matter ready to give in to entropy. Even as she melded with his mind to hold him still she reached out with her anger. His betrayal, his cruelty, and his horrible smirk all boiled the furnace of rage inside her. She poured that through her mind and into his body.

She held him immobile as his flesh erupted into flames. She held his mind trapped, and experienced every second of his agony as he burned from the outside in. And as she did it, she

204

saw why she did what she did. She saw that his threats to her brother had crossed the line, he could threaten her all he wanted and she would have ignored it... but he threatened her family, and for that, she would make an example of him that *no one* would ever forget.

It might have taken five seconds or five years, afterward she had no idea how long it took Victor to die. His goons had fled, terrified by what they saw or just driven away by the inferno that the warehouse became. The old building had ignited from Victor's flames, and that fire spread to the whole section of rotting warehouses. She later learned that the fire burned for days.

Ariadne walked out of the flames untouched.

***

Ariadne snapped back to the present.

What she had done to the Chxor aboard the shuttle sickened her... yet she felt her head clear. She had done worse before. What she wondered now, was if what she'd done happened because the Chxor threatened her friends. *They can be violent and sometimes not the best people... but my friends nonetheless,* she thought.

Was that why her inner monster had awoken? Had she felt that the Chxor needed an example to be made? Ariadne didn't know the answer. In the end, she could not be the judge of that, not without some time to put it behind her and reflect.

Even as she thought that, she remembered her purpose. She had to plot their course, and do it quickly. She opened her mind to the world around her again. Her hands went to the console as she tapped in coordinates and commands. The use of her powers for something so unrelated to violence put her in an almost trance state, and she felt some of her tension ease.

As she typed in the last commands, she heard the hatch behind her open. "What a mess you lot made back there. Good thing we won't reuse this shuttle." Mike sounded cheerful. *He's definitely made for the pirate life,* she thought.

"We won't?" Ariadne asked.

"Nah, the Ghornath corvette doesn't have a docking clamp or any hard point large enough for this beast. And I don't want to spend time trying to jury-rig something. We're crunched for time as it is," Mike said. "How does it look for the course? We ready to go?" He took a seat in the copilot seat.

Ariadne nodded, "We're ready."

"Good, everyone should be loaded, along with all the stuff that we're bringing from this ship. It's pretty crowded back there, and I know some of the passengers wish we could have vented the compartment or at least rinsed it to clean it off a bit."

Ariadne went green with sudden nausea, "Yeah."

"Hey, no worries, they can live with a little mess, especially that arrogant bitch of an ambassador," Mike said. "And we dragged the bodies out, so it's just a little gore." He glanced at the control panel. "Alright, it looks like Simon has shut the airlock. Time for us to move. Bird is yours."

"Right," Ariadne said. She flipped the switches that released them from the side of the cargo ship. She brought them up under the shadow of one of the cargo shuttles. Her hands flickered over the controls, and she let her instinct guide her as much as her senses of the world around her.

Mike flipped on the intercom, "This is your pilot speaking, we'll be flying through hostile Chxor space with the likelihood of meeting a fiery death if they spot us." He paused, "Oh, and has anyone seen Run? We may need him to talk to their traffic control."

The cockpit door opened and Run stepped in. "I would not suggest doing anything that results in our termination. I would not finish my experimentation if I am terminated. This would be suboptimal."

"Right, suboptimal," Mike said. "Well, just stand by there to talk on the radio if and when they see us," he passed over a headset.

Mike glanced at the shuttle chrono. "We have around thirty minutes before the cargo boat comes barreling through. I wish we'd timed this better."

"I'm sure this will go just fine," Ariadne said. And as she

did, she believed it. She couldn't say why, but she had the feeling they would all make it through alright. She gave him a smile, "I've got faith in the team."

Mike gave her a nod, "Well, you should, I suppose. Pixel thought up another neat little trick, it should take some attention off of us when the time comes. Come to think of it..." Mike flicked on the intercom again, "Pixel to the cockpit please."

"You called?" Pixel asked.

"Just need you standing by for when we need your distraction," Mike said.

"Oh, right..." Pixel squeezed over to where he could look over Ariadne's shoulder. "Just let me know when."

Ariadne focused on the pilot's controls. She had Mike's skill to compare herself against, and she knew that if he had the time to go over the course she plotted, he probably could manage to fly the shuttle better. But she knew that she would do for the moment. As long as she didn't hit the cargo shuttle they shadowed.

The course change came up, and Ariadne fired the shuttle's maneuver thrusters. They swept out of the shadow of the cargo shuttle. Just a moment later, the radio squawked. A stream of Chxor words came out of the radio. "What are they saying?" Ariadne asked.

Run cocked his head. "They want to know who we are and why we just now appeared on sensors." He glanced at Mike, "I will answer them in a manner that they will accept."

He spoke into the radio for a moment, then looked up. "I told them that we are personnel shuttle thirteen seventy six, and that we experienced an accident on-board that damaged our controls and communications."

The radio squawked again. The stream of Chxor words might have sounded more aggressive, though with the monotone voice they used, Ariadne found it difficult to tell.

Run answered. He seemed to pick his words with more caution than normal. Ariadne took that as a good sign. She glanced at her sensor feed and felt a wave of relief as she saw they had drawn perceptibly closer to the corvette.

"The traffic controller put his manager on," Run said a moment later. "He is very rude. He accused me of lying due to the fact that we have made several maneuvers and are currently in contact with them."

"Uh," Pixel said, "You are lying though."

"Yes, it is very rude of him to make note of this," Run said. "I think that he will probably request that we be targeted and destroyed. I find this a suboptimal result."

"Yeah, me too," Mike said. "Shit, something just hit us with active radar... Pixel, I think it's time for your distraction."

Out of the corner of her eye, Ariadne saw Pixel draw what looked like a bastardized radio out of his pocket. Pixel extended the antenna and he flipped off the top, and revealed a button. "Here goes." he mashed the button.

Ariadne glanced at the sensors as she flew. She didn't notice anything.

"Uh, Pixel, any time now, bud," Mike said.

Pixel looked down at his remote. "That should have done it." He shook the control a bit and hit the button a couple more times. "Huh, that's odd."

"They've got us targeted," Mike said, "Ariadne go into evasive-"

A bright flash erupted to their rear. The boil of light burned out their sensors on the aft end of the shuttle. Half the indicator lights on the panels went red or amber a moment later, and a puff of smoke erupted from the radio box.

"Oh, there it goes," Pixel said. "Must have been a delay as the safeties disengaged."

Ariadne fought to keep the shuttle on course. Her adjustments grew a little frantic as it seemed that a number of systems had either restarted or gone completely offline. "Was that a nuke?"

Mike gave a long whistle, "Yeah, you could say that. That was one hell of an EMP signature on that thing, good job buddy."

"Where did he get a nuke?" Ariadne demanded. "And who thought it a good idea to set it off anywhere near us? We've lost half the shuttle's systems, there's no way we could dodge anything right now."

"We had the ship's fusion plant," Pixel said. "And I made some modifications to the Chxor captain's little sabotage program, so it created a high energy radiation burst, which then caused the plant to lose containment." Ariadne tried to parse that while she piloted the shuttle. She thought she understood most of it.

"I thought EMP didn't work well in space?" Ariadne asked.

"It doesn't, but a high burst of radiation can cause a similar effect, basically induce currents that fry electronics. I used the Chxor stuff we had encountered before as an example to choose the frequency," Pixel sounded inordinately smug. Then again, it sounded complex enough that Ariadne figured he had a right to be impressed.

"Won't that fry the ship we want to capture too?" Ariadne asked. She felt pretty certain that Pixel would have thought that through. Still, it didn't hurt to ask.

"It might," Pixel said. "But the Ghornath have a very different technology base. The same frequencies should cause minimal damage at most."

"Alright, well, I'm seeing a lot of ships in trouble out there," Mike said gleefully. "And a couple that look to have some nasty collisions if they don't get things fixed soon. I think we're the least of anyone's worries right now."

"You can say that again," Ariadne said. "You guys realize that the boat will start its sprint mode in the middle of all this chaos, right?"

Mike gave her a smirk, "I was just thinking that. Maybe our little gift will make it to the Chxor after all."

Ariadne felt a sudden sweat break out on her forehead. She might well be responsible for thousands of deaths, if not tens or hundreds of thousands. A part of her wondered if her own life and those of her friends might be worth such a scale of destruction.

Yet the Chxor would exterminate her race. *How to*

balance that calculus, I really *don't know... but I know which side I want to win.*

She wanted to bury her head in her hands and maybe cry a bit. Instead she focused on her job and nursed the damaged shuttle towards the Ghornath ship that awaited them.

***

"Okay, final approach," Ariadne said a few moments later.

She brought the shuttle up and around to the midships airlock. She felt the shuttle lag a bit as they came in the last bit, but she managed to adjust as it came down to the last few meters. She felt a slight impact as the shuttle struck against the side of the ship.

"Hey, watch the paint," Mike said with a chuckle, "We want to keep this ship."

"Right," Ariadne said. She stood from the seat, "Let's go."

She followed the others out of the cockpit. The majority of the passengers still waited in the compartment, but she saw the airlock hatch open and caught a glimpse of Simon as he followed the others into the other ship.

Mike paused to draw his pistol, "Ready?"

Ariadne gave him a slight smile, "Sure."

Mike led the way off the shuttle. They entered the airlock, which had both doors wide open for rapid access. Mike glanced back at Pixel, "Get everyone to move the gear over. If they're not going to help fight they can help carry. Oh, and take whoever you need to get the engine up, you should find Anubus and Simon down there somewhere."

Pixel gave him a nod, and Mike and Ariadne continued deeper in.

The size of the corridor made Ariadne pause. The ceiling stood over three meters above the deck. The wide corridors also made Ariadne feel like a small child. The control panel for the airlock sat at head height for her. She shook her head, "Right, well, at least Rastar will be comfortable here."

210

Mike gave her a nod, "Seems roomy enough."

They continued down the corridor until they came to an intersection. Ariadne looked away from a green mess that looked to have run into Anubus. "Aft to the bridge?"

Mike nodded. They walked down the corridor a short distance, "I'm really surprised we haven't seen any Chxor guards, I mean, I figured there would be at least a few aboard the ship." Ariadne said

Mike nodded, but before he could answer, a hatch in front of them opened and a pair of Chxor stepped out into the corridor. The two Chxor wore brown uniforms with unfamiliar symbols embroidered on their shoulders. Each also wore a holstered pistol.

"Oh, right," Mike said. He brought his pistol up and fired, and the lead Chxor gave a shout of pain. The other one drew his pistol and returned fire.

A dozen more Chxor seemed to boil out of that room and another further down the hallway. Ariadne dove for cover and she saw Mike dive into an open hatchway to the side. "Sorry," she shouted, "I'm pretty sure this one is my fault."

"Yeah," Mike said, as he leaned around the doorway and fired a single shot. "You really need to watch what you say."

Ariadne felt her control start to slip. Yet so soon after the killing on the shuttle, her stomach turned at the thought that she must kill once again.

Mike gave a shout of pain, and Ariadne saw him drop his pistol and clutch at his shoulder. Ariadne felt a spike of rage boil up inside. *Hurt* my *friends will they?* she thought. She did not bother to peek around the hatch frame. She reached out with her mind, found the largest cluster of Chxor, and she unleashed her inner monster.

The hallway flared bright with the explosion of flame. She heard Chxor scream in pain. She tasted the sharp burn of bile in the back of her throat as she smelled Chxor burning. Yet she had missed some, for she heard bullets continue down the hallway.

Ariadne shook her head, suddenly weakened by the

exertion. As she shook her head to clear it, a pair of Chxor surged into the hatchway, pistols drawn. She tried to focus, to push some energy at them, but her mind felt too sluggish. She had used too much over the past few hours.

As their guns came up, Ariadne closed her eyes. *Where have my friends gone,* she thought desperately, *surely they won't not fail me?* Just as she thought that, she heard two loud shots as someone fired a pair of riot guns. Ariadne opened her eyes to see the two Chxor guards down. Rastar stood over them, "Hey guys, sorry if I'm late."

"No, you have perfect timing," Mike said.

"Agreed," Ariadne said.

"Oh good. Thanks for saving some for me," Rastar said. "Oh, we secured the bridge. There's some bigwig female Chxor up there, that Crowe suggested we could use as a hostage or something. Eric and I both voted to kill her, but we agreed to leave her alive until everyone else weighs in."

"Great," Mike said. "Lead the way, big guy."

Rastar turned around and led the way forward. Ariadne picked up a pistol, as they passed one of the fallen guards, and then a second one. Rastar led the way up a steep set of stairs and then up a second set to an armored hatch. He tapped a button on the panel next to it, and the hatch slid open. "Lots of automation on this thing," Rastar said.

"So it appears," Mike said.

The bridge impressed Ariadne. After the Chxor ships, the bridge looked open and spacious. Also the consoles looked light and compact, the screens seemed larger and she could see a high detailed sensor scan of the area up on the main display.

Eric stood near a Chxor female. She wore a brown uniform with five white pips on her collar. She also had her hands in the air, though she did not seem nervous. Then again, she didn't seem to display any emotion. Ariadne considered reaching out to read the Chxor's mind, but she felt too tired and worn out from use of her powers for the day. *Best to save the energy I've got for something we really need,* she thought.

"I booted up the navigation computer," Eric said, "But

that's about all I could manage."

"Okay, I'll take a look at it," Ariadne said.

"Eric, take a look at the weapons, let me know what we have," Mike said.

"You tell me the nicest things sometimes," Eric responded. Ariadne saw him move over to another console. She tuned him out though as she brought up the navigation computer's star map. It took her a few minutes to make sense of what she saw.

"We have a couple problems," Ariadne said, even as she started to reach out with her senses.

"Oh?" Mike asked.

"Someone erased the original star map on here. The Chxor put a basic one in, but it only seems to list Chxor worlds for the most part," Ariadne frowned as she concentrated.

"Can you read it?" Mike asked.

"They use some of the human numbers and names for some systems," Ariadne answered, "Also they use the same coordinate system for Shadow Space. So no problem there. It's just that we've only got a limited selection of destinations. Our first option is to head south towards Ghornath Prime and try to work our way towards Tannis."

"Not recommended," Mike said. "That's a long way to a friendly port, and there're plenty of human pirates to worry about down that way."

"And that's where the Chxor captured the ship I was on, so we'd have to worry about them as well," Ariadne responded. "Our second choice is to try for the closest human system: Malta." She tapped a command and brought the system up on the main screen, even as she continued with her jump calculations. "Problem with that is that it's a heavily fortified system. Even the basic Chxor markers annotate it as a large military presence. And the Chxor and Nova Roma are at war... we could wind up right in the middle of a battle."

"Yeah, let's avoid that," Mike said.

"I dunno, it sounds like fun," Eric said. He looked up with an eager grin, "Now that we have a way to shoot back, anyway."

"Get the weapons up and we can see about that," Mike answered. "So what other options do we have?"

"There's a system called 443C98 that's to our galactic north," Ariadne said. "The Chxor map shows they have claimed it, but it also notes two jumps to nearby systems they don't claim, both headed towards Nova Roma space. If I remember right, there's a couple of independent colonies up that way too. We might come across a freighter or even a military patrol, maybe get some help."

"That sounds like our best option, get on it," Mike said. "How long will it take?"

"I've already done the rough calculations for entry, I'll have our course plotted soon," Ariadne said. After his approval of her chosen course, she reached deeper and felt for Shadow Space. After her previous experience, it seemed ridiculously easy to reach out and sense it. For a moment, she let the currents and flow of it sweep her away. She found something hypnotic about it, now that she consciously sensed it.

She focused on the coordinates from the computer. That gave her a destination in Shadow Space, a place where her universe and the other one lined up. As she sent her mind into that other place, she felt a shock as she sensed depths she had never before seen. Her previous navigation had gone by sense and instinct as much as by any real skill. Now that she focused, she could see other paths that would lead to that destination, some of them might well shave hours or even days off the jump.

Yet she also sensed other destinations, places that normal navigators could never reach, places that normal people could never see. She suddenly realized how the Shadow Lords, the infamous psychic pirates who lived in Shadow Space, had become so powerful. With a psychic navigator, they could hide wherever they wanted, or they could pounce on ships as they transited through Shadow Space. The possibilities stunned her, and for a moment, Ariadne forgot her purpose.

She regained it a moment later, and she pulled back from her suddenly expanded senses long enough to type commands into the navigation computer. She went with the simplest of the routes, but even so, the computer spat angry lines of warnings, many highlighted in red or purple. Ariadne tapped the ignore button a few times. Her work done, she slowly, carefully, drew her consciousness away from Shadow Space. As she did, she felt something, almost an echo of her own mind, react to her presence. But she pulled back too quickly to get more than a glimpse of that other mind.

Ariadne shook her head, completely exhausted. "We're good. As soon as the engines come up we can go."

"Weapons look good," Eric said at almost the same time. "We've got five twin pulse laser turrets for missile or fighter interception and a chase mounted 'pulse cannon,' whatever that is, for a main gun. There's some lockouts that I'll be around in a second and I'll bring them online.

Mike looked over at Rastar, "Intercom?"

Rastar tapped at a console near the central couch. Mike nodded in thanks, "Pixel, how we looking as far as engines?"

"Good. I've got the fusion plant coming on line, drive will be up in around a minute after that. Plant is mostly automated, I'm just flipping switches. Luckily everything is on standby."

"Hey, Pixel, weapons are going live," Eric said.

Pixel sounded nervous when he spoke. "Wait, you probably don't want to do that, there's some kind of warning down here, and I noticed some damage..."

"Nah, I don't see anything up here," Eric said. "Going to full power on the main gun, then we can take a few shots and see what happens!"

Ariadne felt the deck hum beneath her feet. A moment later the ship shuddered and Ariadne heard a muffled explosion. The lights on the bridge flickered for a moment. Everyone in the room looked over at Eric. He looked at the red lights that flashed on his console. "Uh, Pixel, what was that?"

They received no response.

"Pixel, you alright?" Mike asked.

A moment later, they heard someone cough over the

215

intercom, "Yeah, but the engine room is a mess. The capacitors for the mount must have taken some damage sometime. I think they all just exploded. I can't believe no one had them locked out, that's a huge safety risk."

Mike looked at Eric. When he spoke, Ariadne could hear the anger masked behind his words, "They did have them locked out. Eric worked around them. Are we still good to go?"

"Yeah... let me check. I don't think it damaged anything else."

They sat in silence for a long moment. Ariadne glanced at the chrono. It showed Ghornath time, though, so she didn't know how much time had passed, "How long for the cargo boat to do its maneuver, anyone know?"

Mike looked over at her. He frowned, "I'm not sure." He looked over at Rastar, "Can you open a channel to the shuttle?"

Rastar nodded, "I think so..." He flipped another switch.

"Hello?" Mike asked.

"This is Simon, we're getting everyone off the shuttle, not much time to talk," Simon sounded either angry or impatient, Ariadne thought. Or possibly both.

"Hey, just check the chrono in the cockpit and-" Mike broke off as a bright flare lit up on the sensors. "Never mind."

Crowe brought up the cargo boat on the main screen. It juked 'up' towards the planet and its orbital ring. Ariadne followed its course, and she bit her lip as she saw no reaction to its maneuver.

Had no one seen it?

A moment after she wondered that she saw fire erupt from one of the orbital defense platforms. She had expected direct hits, yet it seemed that Pixel's earlier distraction seemed to have degraded the platform's sensors, both shots went wide, and one smashed a parked freighter into splinters.

"That's some heavy firepower," Eric said soberly. "I'd rather that not be aimed at us."

"Me too," Mike said.

Ariadne bit her lip as the cargo boat went into final maneuvers. She winced as it missed a drifting freighter by what

216

seemed like a hair.

And then it went into final burn, right before it struck the orbital ring.

The flash of the impact darkened the screen for a moment. As it cleared, Ariadne gave a gasp of shock. A wave of debris poured out from a massive wound in the ring. As she watched, the cloud of shrapnel smashed into a chain of parked ships, and pinpricks of explosions flashed out of the center of the cloud.

"There's some big chunks headed our way," Crowe said nervously. "And I think the ring just... wobbled."

"What do you mean, 'wobbled'?" Mike asked.

Crowe pulled up a broader view of the ring. And Ariadne saw it, a shudder that seemed to pass all along the ring... and she also saw several of the spokes snap off from the ring. "Oh my god," Ariadne said softly, "The whole thing might come down."

"Surely they designed this thing to take damage... right?" Crowe asked.

"I don't know," Mike said. "But we won't be here to see it, one way or another." Mike tapped at his screen and brought the focus over to the cloud of debris headed their way. "Pixel, we need to go now. Are we ready?"

Pixel sounded nervous, "I think so. But there's some weird messages that keep flashing here. I'm almost certain we can make the jump, I'm just not sure what will happen if we can't."

"We'll be dead," Mike said. "We good to hit the switch?"

Ariadne's hand went to the navigation console even as she watched the tidal wave of debris sweep down towards them. *I caused that*, she thought, *not someone else... I did it.* A part of her thought that it would only be fair if she died here as a result. Yet she had her friends to think about, people like Rastar and Mike who had risked their lives for her.

"Simon, everyone off the shuttle?"

"We're clear, and I cut the Chxor pilot loose and told him to fly if he wanted to survive."

"You let him go?" Eric asked.

"Yep, and we can talk about it later," Simon said.

Ariadne saw the light come up on her panel. Mike turned and she saw his mouth open but she hit the switch to activate the Shadow Space drive before he could say anything.

The ship's engines rose into a sharp whine, and the ship seemed to lurch.

The wave of destruction vanished.

They hung suspended in a gray emptiness. For just a moment, Ariadne felt her hands tremble with reaction. She wondered how close she had come to killing them all.

"Good job," Mike said.

Ariadne gave a slight sigh, and she pushed all her doubts and worries and guilt to the back of her mind. She would have to face them, she knew, but for now, she would do what she always did. For now, she would take pleasure in the little things. She gave Mike a cheerful smile, "Well, I told you we'd get out of it alright."

###

Runner
The Renegades
by Kal Spriggs

"Senior Scientist Rhxun, you are allowed three juhn to explain your failures," Tier Three Investigator Ghren said to the diminutive Chxor who stood across from his desk. Ghren had risen through the military police force of the Chxor Empire, and his squat, muscular body showed it, particularly in the livid scar that ran down the side of his face. The other Chxor's gray skin and yellow eyes looked healthy and fit, and his perfectly trimmed dull tan hair suggested a dogmatic dedication to regulations, as any Tier Three Investigator should. His heavy frame showed his genetic heritage as one of the Ruhl line. Ghren's genetic forebears had probably served as muscular enforcers for the Benevolence Council for generations, Rhxun knew. Clearly, Ghren saw little threat in Rhxun's own slight frame and scientific disposition. This meant that Rhxun stood in his pale green lab suit and had been allowed to continue his research without constant oversight. It also meant that Ghren had dispensed with the optional guards, due both to Rhxun's rank, as well as the relative inequity between them should Rhxun be so crass as to resort to physical altercation. The very idea seemed preposterous, even to Rhxun. "You are afforded this only due to your previous contributions to the Chxor Empire. You may begin."

Scientist Rhxun did not need to collect his thoughts. Like the thoughtful, concise and methodical Chxor he was, he had determined exactly what course to take. "Tier Three Investigator Ghren, I will explain the circumstances in precision and with sufficient information as to draw the correct conclusions. My experimentation on Klar Three was extremely thoroughly researched and in no way did I fail to take all circumstances into consideration. The failure occurred as a result of Planetary Governor Hlaar, who failed to ensure that I had full access to the planetary conditions, and who sabotaged the entire program deliberately--"

"I have already investigated your accusations of Planetary Governor Hlaar, his judgment is already decided," Tier Three Investigator Ghren interrupted.

"Yes, Tier Three Investigator," Rhxun answered, by his count, he had another two juhn to make his statement. A lesser being, such as a human, might have grown nervous, but Rhxun was a Chxor and above such pointless emotions. Not even the slightest sign of discomfort touched his own pale yellow eyes and he met the gaze of Ghren with calm certainty. "To continue, I was not given crucial information about Klar Three's atmospheric and space conditions. In the interest of efficiency, in order to maximize production, I implemented the implant design based upon faulty parameters given to me by Planetary Governor Hlaar."

"This does not address why you implemented administration of the implants to the entire planetary population against his orders. Nor does it explain why you circumvented necessary testing procedures in the process. These procedures are in place to prevent such failures," Tier Three Investigator Ghren stated.

"I do not have time to go into the technical explanation of the science that backed my decision," Rhxun stated. "Planetary Governor Hlaar lacked the intelligence to understand the science behind my decisions." *It would not be diplomatic to explain to the Tier Three Investigator that he lacks the intelligence to properly understand,* he thought. Though he would like to think that a Tier Three Investigator would have the impartiality to admit his limitations, Rhxun had already encountered many of his fellow Chxor who seemed unable to admit that they had nowhere near his own mental capabilities. "However, I will state that I established and followed a highly comprehensive standardized operation procedure for my laboratory as well as the implantation facility which I ensured all Chxor followed rigorously. This seven hundred page document was issued to all personnel and I required they follow it to the letter. Technical Assistant Khlain can verify this."

"Technical Assistant Khlain was sentenced to the hard labor camps for his negligence in this event, and has already been shipped to a processing facility," Tier Three Investigator Ghren answered. If Rhxun had the limitation of emotions, he would have felt dismay at the loss of his primary assistant. Then again, he had found Khlain's constant whining about 'proper regulations' a waste of time. *If Khlain had simply gone along with the project,* Rhxun thought, *perhaps he would have proven of actual use and discovered the additional information which would have facilitated the project.* "This concludes your investigation. In consultation with the Benevolence Council and after careful and procedural investigation, I have determined the following about this event."

Ghren paused as he pulled up his notes: "On 5674-Juhnar, Medical Scientist Rhxun, violated standard methodology and protocols with his current experimentation. He disobeyed direct orders from the Planetary Governor, violated Chxor Medical Procedures seventeen, forty-two, one-nineteen, and seven-thirteen through eight-forty-five."

"Also, technically, nine-fourteen," Rhxun added.

"As well as nine-fourteen," Ghren amended. "Due to his inability to follow proper procedures regarding medical methodology, he implanted three quarters of the population, four million of the Than sub-caste with implants designed to limit free will and induce loyalty protocols to the Chxor Empire in general and to Senior Scientist Rhxun in specific. His implants utilized wireless signals to maintain overall control of the population and possessed minimal electromagnetic shielding."

"Four million, three hundred thousand, four hundred and seven of the Than sub-caste," Rhxun corrected automatically. "With an additional one hundred and twenty test subjects who survive at the shielded testing facility."

"Correct, four million, three hundred thousand, four hundred and seven," Ghren stated with undue force. Apparently he did not appreciate the reminder that his inferior intelligence did not allow him to retain data as well as Rhxun. *Well, it isn't as if I didn't expect as much,* Rhxun thought. The Tier Three

Investigator continued, "When a stellar flare erupted, it caused massive radio frequency interference across a broad spectrum, this interference proved particularly hazardous to the population implanted by Senior Scientist Rhxun. The result was initial extreme pain, followed by violent aggression. Final results appear to be the destruction of higher level brain functions and feral behavior. This subsequently resulted in the termination of the entire test population as well as some three million – "

"Two million, nine hundred thousand, nine hundred and thirty," Rhxun interrupted.

" – of the rest of the population. This number included seven District Administrators as well as the Assistant Planetary Governor, Police Commander, Deputy Fleet Commander, and Investigator Krell who had been dispatched to investigate Planetary Governor Hraal's statement regarding insurrectionist activity in regards to Senior Scientist Rhxun's research." Tier Three Investigator Ghren paused. "I therefore find that the proper punishment is to strip Senior Scientist Rhxun of his rank and sentence him to immediate termination."

"I understand how you have come to this decision," Rhxun shook his head. "And I believe you have done your best at the limits of your intelligence and understanding. Am I correct in my estimation that you have followed procedure fifteen of the investigation protocols and have waited to file your official findings pending my sentencing?"

"Of course," Ghren said. The tone of his voice suggested that any other option would not follow the proper regulations. A loyalty to regulation and bureaucracy that Rhxun agreed with and appreciated immensely.

"Excellent," Rhxun said. He drew his dart pistol and fired once. The small dart struck Ghren in the side of his thick neck, just above the collar of his brown uniform.

Ghren stared at him in shock for a moment. Then the convulsions began. Rhxun walked calmly around the desk and deleted the Tier Three Investigator's notes. He then pulled the dart out of the dead Chxor's neck and carefully dropped it down the incinerator chute behind the desk. A moment later he tapped the intercom button. "Excuse me. It seems that Tier Three Investigator Ghren has undergone a seizure. I would suggest that a body disposal team be dispatched."

***

Little had changed of the office after the three months since his last interview, save that Tier Four Investigator Thrun sat behind the desk, he had two armed guards posted behind Rhxun, and Rhxun wore manacles at wrist and ankle. The guards had searched him thoroughly, though they had allowed him to wear his normal lab suit. Rhxun had expected this, but he still found it ridiculous that they considered he might repeat his previous termination of Tier Three Investigator Ghren. *Do they think me to be of such low intelligence,* he thought, *that I would attempt the same result?*

Tier Four Investigator Thrun looked much similar to Ghren, and Rhxun supposed that the two had come from similar military lines. Thrun looked a little older but seemed to possess the same heavy frame and absolute dedication to regulation. If anything, his brown uniform looked more severe. "Senior Scientist Rhxun," the Tier Four Investigator began. "After thorough investigation into both the failure of your experimentation and the termination of Tier Four Investigator Ghren, I have come to the following conclusions – "

"Am I not allowed a statement of defense according to paragraph five of investigation procedure fifteen?"

"You are, unless the accumulation of evidence indicates that your statement of defense would be of little value," Thrun stated flatly. "Which in this case, the termination of Tier Three Investigator Ghren would indicate that your statement would be of little use. It is most likely that you would merely repeat your previous arguments, would it not?"

"I would," Rhxun stated, "And from your statement, I would interpolate that you have reached a similar conclusion?"

"Yes. In addition, I find your manipulation of regulations to ensure a Tier Four Investigator must be dispatched resolve this investigation is a blatant case of abuse of your position to – "

223

The Tier Four Investigator broke off. One hand went to his throat and Rhxun could see the Chxor's throat muscles tense, as if the other Chxor tried to force words out against some pressure.

"I am left with little option, then," Rhxun stated, "as you have proven as limited in both intelligence and personal bias to understand my devotion to research and my importance to science. Therefore, I will have to hope your replacement proves to be senior in not only rank, but also intelligence." Rhxun raised his foot off of the crushed glass vial. He saw both the two armed guards collapse to the ground. Both of them clawed at their throats as the neurotoxin paralyzed their lungs.

Tier Four Investigator Thrun's hand flailed towards the alarm, but Rhxun stepped forward and caught it. The Tier Four Investigator had little strength and Rhxun easily held his hand away from the button. "Now, Tier Four Investigator, that would be a waste of personnel. Any response team would die of the gas I released unless they received the proper antidote before hand. Seeing as I tailored this agent specifically for this occasion, I find this problematic at best."

Senior Scientist Rhxun waited until the neurotoxin did its work and then dropped the limp arm. He shook his head slightly at the typed notes of the Tier Four Investigator. "A note about my unprofessional use of materials and research? This shows very little understanding of the science. I will have to conclude that I must try once again with your superiors."

***

Once again Rhxun waited the result of the investigation.

This time, however, he stood stripped naked, and in a quarantine inspection airlock. On the other side of the inspection glass stood a squat female Chxor in the uniform of a Tier Eight Investigator. This confused Rhxun slightly, as he had not expected such a senior ranking investigator. Then again, he had expected that his reason and logic would eventually penetrate one of the previous investigators. *Perhaps I ask too much,* he thought, *after all, the investigators tend to be such limited castes, far inferior to me in intellect and resourcefulness.*

Still, the Tier Eight Investigator showed both intelligence and foresight in his preparation for Rhxun's statement of defense and sentencing. At least that suggested that his fellow Chxor had some capability to learn from the mistakes of her predecessors.

She did not look particularly intelligent, Rhxun noted. She stood silently on the far side of the inspection window. Her hair had an odd trim, almost out of regulation. Her block-like head looked narrower than the Chxor normal, and her eyes had a darker color than the normal pale yellow. She looked... vaguely predatory, Rhxun realized. In fact, he noted that as she stared at him, he felt some of his otherwise suppressed primitive body functions awaken. In particular, he felt his heart beat increase, a sign that his body recognized danger. This caused Rhxun a brief moment of reflection, for it seemed illogical that he would lose control of his mental balance so easily. Still, something about her dark yellow eyes made his normal calm very hard to contain. He rationally knew that many of the Abaner genetic lines had darker eye color, yet this did little to reassure him. *The Abaner are an inferior line, drawn to intuitive thought patterns and almost... emotional behavior,* he thought.

Rhxun awaited her prepared statement. He had little else to do. Yet her calm gaze did not break, nor did she relieve the silence. In fact, the silence seemed to grow. To pass the time, Rhxun ran through a review of his statement. This new Investigator's silent gaze gave him the strangest mental pattern, one where he felt some slight uncertainty. *No, not her gaze, merely the extra time, I must use it,* he thought. Yet even as he reassured himself, he wondered why he needed such reassurance.

He studied her uniform, and noted seven small, gold pips above her name-tag, which read Khlen. Each of those, according to regulation, represented a commendation from the Benevolence Council. Rhxun had not heard of any military commander who possessed more than three. His mentor had possessed two for his research in genetic engineering. "You present an interesting problem, Rhxun," Investigator Khlen said.

Rhxun felt his uncertainty grow. This did not follow the standard procedure. She had neither asked him a question nor had she made a statement in regards to the investigation. *Perhaps,* he wondered, *this is a test of some kind?* "Do you know what cases I normally investigate, Rhxun?"

Rhxun felt his uncertainty grow at her neglect to use his official title. Unless he had been sentenced, then he retained his title and rank and all Chxor would honor that. Had this odd Tier Eight Investigator bypassed the normal procedure and sentenced him before his statement? Rhxun realized that she still stared at him and realized that she expected an answer to her odd question. "No, Tier Eight Investigator, I do not." He made sure to use her entire title, a reminder to use his own.

"Normally I only investigate very senior levels of subversion and treason within the Chxor Empire. Cases that involve Fleet Commanders and System Governors." She stared at him for a longer moment. "These cases often require intricate knowledge of both the official and unofficial policies and politics well beyond the normal knowledge of rules and regulations most Investigators possess." Rhxun waited. He had little interest in policies beyond those of his own field of research. He had far less interest in the politics of the Chxor Empire, beyond the current desire for expansion which had yielded his rapid promotion and backed his current research. He did not see why this Investigator had chosen such an odd course of dialog. *Perhaps,* he thought, *she suffered from some brain damage?* It would explain her odd gaze, he decided.

"Your elimination of Ghren and Thrun has attracted my attention, which prompted me to conduct a more thorough investigation of you," Khlen said. "This began with your production lot. You were from the Urn Creche in the Urgal system. Your lot was Seven-thirteen Flen Twelve. You and your fellow reproduction were an experiment in genetic engineering by Senior Scientist Gurn. All other subjects were eliminated due to mental instability and physical defects. You are literally unique." She continued to stare at him. Rhxun felt his uncertainty grow as she peered at him. None of the other Investigators he had encountered had gone that far back into his past.

"Senior Scientist Gurn personally instructed you from when the creche released you. You trained under him while he further developed his genetic engineering knowledge... right up until his termination in a lab accident." She paused. The silence grew long again.

Rhxun realized she expected some statement. "Yes, I acted as his assistant," he said. "The investigation of the accident was very thorough. It is very unfortunate that the aggressive human subjects got loose and attacked him. His dedication to science was commendable."

"I'm sure," the Tier Eight Investigator said. "Though I find some of the evidence of the accident rather slim. In fact, the accidental deletion of the lab security records is particularly odd, do you not agree, Rhxun?"

Rhxun felt an odd hollow sensation in his bowels. He suddenly felt the need to utilize the organic waste facilities, though he somehow doubted that the Investigator would allow him the option. "Yes, this might be odd, however, I would point out that the human test subjects had access to the entire facility for several hours. They could easily have accessed the records–"

"The records, written in Chxor and secured by pass-code known only to security staff and key research personnel?"

Rhxun felt the hollow sensation in his lower intestines shift. "It is not unthinkable that they would seek to access it and bypass such safeguards during their escape."

"Not unthinkable that they could, I agree," Khlen said. "But rather odd that they felt it necessary. Certainly even humans must know it would be obvious that they had escaped and terminated the lab personnel present."

Rhxun felt his left cheek begin to twitch. "Perhaps they wished to create confusion as to their escape attempt and gain themselves more time." He must suffer from some vitamin deficiency, he thought, to cause the involuntary muscle spasm. "Though it can be pointless to attempt extrapolation of the reasoning behind emotionally-driven human actions."

"Perhaps." The Tier Eight Investigator answered. "Though I did find interesting notes in Senior Scientist Gurn's

227

personal records. He seemed to disapprove of your professional standards and felt that overall you put too much trust in your own judgment."

"I think my actions so far have proven that decision incorrect," Rhxun said.

"Interesting," Khlen stated. She continued to stare at him. Rhxun suddenly realized that he had seen such a gaze before... when he stood outside a specimen cage and stared at one of his test subject. The twitch in his cheek redoubled in pace and his stomach seemed to twist. "I also found it interesting that the escaped human test subjects managed to seize a courier vessel docked with the labs and escape the star system. Their timing for escape could not have been better... not without help from a Chxor."

Tier Eight Investigator Khlen let him stand in silence for a long moment, "After Senior Scientist Gurn's demise, you went to work at the research labs on Thran as a Technical Assistant. You developed a series of strength enhancement drugs originally intended for labor castes. You also implemented production of these drugs before full completion of the testing procedures. The drugs also boosted aggression as a side effect, which earned your full promotion to Scientist when you developed it into a battle drug for use in riot dispersal."

Rhxun nodded, "This has proven to be of obvious benefit–"

"The drug side effects also include long term addiction, mental instability, and hallucinogenic properties if improper dosages are administered," Khlen interrupted. "These side effects were noted by Scientist Vxor before general distribution, though he suffered an unfortunate accident before he could publish those notes."

"Yes," Rhxun said, "He fell into the biological reprocessing equipment during his inspection of the facility."

"Yes... and the two menials on duty both were both long term test subjects of your drug Xenaltropine, the most addictive of the drug series you developed," Khlen said. Rhxun felt his stomach twist again. Clearly his food had not agreed with him, normally he had much better control over his bodily functions. "Your following assignment took you to Xarkhun, where you joined a team to develop a means to harness the local populace as a servant race into the Chxor Empire."

Rhxun felt an unfortunate realization that he knew where this line of discussion would go. Even so, he attempted to guide it towards his success, "Yes, and there I developed an essential translation implant that we imbedded into the Xark diplomats. This allowed the Chxor diplomats to explain our purpose and brought the Xark into the Chxor Empire without bloodshed. The Xark have since been one of our preeminent servant races and their militaristic capabilities have proven exceptional in conquest of other lesser races."

"Indeed," Khlen said. "In fact, every senior diplomat report noted your essential contribution to the mission. The entire expedition met with unparalleled success, except for the termination of Scientist Hruun. He was working on a similar device, only designed to be held rather than implanted, and his research was almost completed when..." Khlen glanced down at her datapad. "Well, it looks like he *also* suffered an unfortunate accident."

"Yes..." Rhxun trailed off. He realized that his knowledge of the incident might look suspicious.

"Indeed, he seemed to have suffered from a failure in the environmental systems within his quarters. He suffocated overnight. An unfortunate loss, I'm sure." The Tier Eight Investigator stared at Rhxun for a long moment. "But his termination meant that you had time to complete your work and draw the accolades of the diplomats, who did not care how the translation occurred, only that it did so." Khlen cocked her head slightly, as if she needed some slightly different view to consider Rhxun from. "This secured your promotion to Senior Scientist and then your assignment here, where you were allowed to look into loyalty implantation to improve productivity."

Rhxun chose to remain quiet.

"So, you understand now why I find you to be an interesting problem?" She seemed to take his further silence as assent. "On the one hand, you have proven valuable to the Chxor Empire. On the other, you have proven extremely dangerous to those in your way. If not for this setback, I would expect that to eventually include the Benevolence Council. This in turn, would suggest subversive if not treasonous intent. The punishment for such actions, of course, is immediate termination." Khlen glanced down at the large red button to her left. "Very easy to conduct from this location, of course."

"I have never had subversive intentions – "

"No, but you also have little more than contempt for the intelligence of anyone besides yourself. You possess a dangerous quality of self confidence, which were I to use an emotional label, I could call arrogance. You believe in yourself, to a degree that I would label fanaticism, and anyone that violates your faith becomes an obstacle you must eliminate."

"Those who cannot understand my importance–"

"Yes, this behavior is the issue I have identified," Khlen said. "The obvious solution is to vent you out the airlock. Of course, this then leads to your extremely capable intellect. You have, to date, eliminated three Scientists and three Investigators through a mixture of guile and calculation. I cannot entirely rule out some method which you might have devised that could kill me should I conclude your termination to be necessary."

"According to Investigation Procedure Fifteen, Paragraph nine, an Investigator will come to all decisions in a manner impartial to the consequences to themselves–"

"I am aware of that section," Khlen said. "I am also aware that I have already filed a termination order of my own should I suffer an unfortunate accident. It begins with: 'For High Crimes and Treason against an emissary of the Benevolence Council.' But I would find that to be unfortunate. You are a valuable resource and your experiments have proven to be of some use."

Rhxun took a moment to consider that. "A wise precaution. I appreciate your honesty and appreciation of my abilities. However, I would like to assert that as long as you understand my importance to science, we will have no issues. As soon as I am allowed to go back to work and continue my vital research–"

"Do not misunderstand me, Rhxun," Khlen interrupted. "I think that ordering your termination is a hazard. I also think that your intelligence could be an asset to the Chxor Empire. I did not once say that you could or would return to your laboratory or your research. You are too dangerous... and sooner or later some accident like this was bound to happen."

Rhxun considered that for a long moment. "I do not understand your proposal, then. If I am not to be terminated and I am not to be reinstated, what does this leave me?"

"This leaves you with one option, an option that I am certain an intelligent and capable person such as yourself can make the best of. If you are sentenced to labor at a minimal security prison facility I would propose that you would then escape. Due to your previous encounters with humans, you would probably make your way to human space, correct?"

Rhxun considered this for a long moment. "This would be the next best place to conduct research. I would have many opportunities for new fields of study there. This theory, however, has the inherent assumption that I would escape."

"Are you saying that you would not be intelligent enough to escape?" The Tier Eight Investigator asked.

Rhxun felt his facial muscle twitch begin to ease. "Of course not. It will be simple. More difficult will be conducting my research in such limited conditions."

"Very well," Khlen said. She tapped a command on the console in front of her. A moment later, the light above the airlock turned green. "I have made preparations for your next sequence of experiments, then. You may board this prison transport. It will take you to a prison station."

Rhxun cocked his head in thought. "I do find this acceptable. However, I am curious what benefit you see in this for the Chxor Empire. I will be unable to return if I escape, and I will likely cause some damage to the Chxor Empire when I do. How does this benefit the Benevolence Council?"

"Senior Scientist Rhxun... I personally think that

someone made a grave error in judgment when they allowed you to reach adulthood. I think that your sense of self importance and arrogance has no checks... that your experimentation – if left unchecked – will sow chaos and disorder wherever you go. I hope you escape and that your travels take you far from the Chxor Empire, because wherever you go, I am certain you will cause destruction, disorder, and chaos. Also, if you go to human space, your special brand of insanity will damage the humans rather than your own race."

Rhxun shook his head, "I see that I am still not understood. However, I appreciate your honesty and your faith in my intelligence. I promise you that I will return, and that my contributions to science will change the Chxor Empire for the better."

"As a Tier Eight Investigator, I hereby strip Senior Scientist Rhxun of all authority and rank. I furthermore decree that his sentence is labor at a prison facility until he has paid his debt in full to the Chxor Empire. Sentence to begin immediately."

Rhxun started for the hatch.

"One last thing, Prisoner Rhxun," Khlen said. "Was I correct when I stated that you had some measure of defense should I chose your termination?"

Rhxun paused. In reality, he knew he owed the Investigator little. Still, he felt she must perform some essential services to the Chxor Empire. Certainly, she had presented him with a course of action that, while not the ideal, did offer some interesting new fields of research. *And there is the termination order if she should die,* he thought, *though it depends on how she backed those up.* He turned around, "You will want to dose yourself with the antidote to the accentia toxin. In the meantime, please strive to keep your thoughts calm and do not perform any strenuous activities." Rhxun turned back and stepped aboard the prison transport.

###

Part Three

Declaration
The Renegades, Book Three
by Kal Spriggs

Pixel stretched his stiff shoulder muscles and considered his reflection in the mirror. His light brown hair stuck up in tufts and his bushy brown eyebrows jutted out. His glasses had taken a beating and he made mental note that he needed to either replace them or to apply a lot more electrical tape. His battered coveralls seemed to have more patches than they did original material and a pair of welding goggles hung around his neck.

I should definitely grow a goatee, he thought, *it will really pull together my whole evil scientist look.* Who knew, perhaps it might alter his face enough that no one would recognize him from his wanted poster. He felt a surge of bitterness at that thought. One more reminder, he knew, of why he should stick to machines and leave people alone.

He stepped back from the sink and looked around the oversized bathroom. He felt certain it had some appropriate nautical or spacer term, but he didn't really care about that at the moment. What Pixel cared about was the scale. The entire ship seemed designed to make him feel like a child. The sink went up to his shoulders and he could only see his entire face in the mirror above it when he stood on his tiptoes. His gaze went to the Ghornath toilet and he shook his head, "This is ridiculous."

Someone had put a stool in place to allow humans to climb to an adequate height to use it, at least. Still, Pixel felt like Alice in Wonderland or possibly a kindergartner who had walked into a high school by mistake.

He went to the door, then waved his hand across the controls. The hatch slid open, and Pixel immediately forgot his previous bemusement. He pulled out his datapad as he stepped out and began a quick sketch of the hatch. The engineer made a note to check the ship's manuals and see how the mechanism worked. After days and weeks spent aboard Chxor ships, a hands-free hatch seemed marvelous. Especially since most

Colonial Republic ships he'd been aboard had similar muscle powered tech for things like doors, when they didn't have some kind of clunky hydraulic system or worse.

He shuddered as he remembered the spring loaded system aboard the freighter he caught out of Lithia. Each hatch had slammed open and shut like a blunt guillotine. The captain and crew had disabled about half of them, but that in itself made for a multitude of safety issues. The ship's chief engineer had horror stories about those hatches, Pixel remembered, stories that made the hair on the back of his neck rise even now.

I do not believe in ghosts, Pixel thought, *much less doors infused with malignant spirits of dead colonists.* Even so he patted one of the automated doors as he walked past. Pixel loved well designed machinery. He just wished he had someone else who appreciated the same things to share it all with.

He pulled up the ship schematic on his datapad and nodded to himself. He had yet to become familiar with the ship. Some might consider it small for a military ship, but the Ghornath corvette still stretched over a hundred meters in length and had four levels. It would take him a of couple days to get to know the details of the corridors.

Longer than that, he estimated, to get to know the machinery and systems. Pixel glanced at the countdown on the side of his screen. It would take four days to travel to 443C98. From the Chxor star map and what little remained of the Ghornath records, the system had no planets of note, just a couple cold gas giants and some barren rocks. They should have a longer journey from there to Nova Roma space, or whatever independent colony they could reach.

Pixel turned right at the next intersection and waved his hand in front of the door control. It slid open and he stepped into the slightly louder engine room. His eyes went immediately to the control booth. Unlike most human designs, the booth lay at the center of the room. It was an open platform that looked out on the entire room. Ladders connected it to the various areas. *The Ghornath made excellent use of space*, Pixel thought to himself, even as his brain sought to make sense of the ladders

236

and catwalks that seemed to hang from the ceiling as well as several of the walls. He didn't know how they managed to keep the different gravitational fields in balance, yet their engineers clearly saw one more method to trim space requirements and improve access to the systems of the ship.

Pixel approved of that. In particular, he liked how the design forced him to think about the best way to examine each section of the room. That in turn made him want to consider how and where he should begin his survey of the entire plant.

He stood there for a long moment, lost in thought, when he heard someone clear their throat behind him. Pixel turned around and found Eric Striker stood just inside the door. The tall, lean former soldier looked nervous. Pixel might have felt surprise at Eric's presence, but he didn't. "What's up?"

Eric gave him a nervous smile, "Hey, uh, I was going to do some work, and I wondered..."

Pixel gave him a nod, "Yeah, some more explosives, right?" He had enjoyed their previous work together... but not so much the results.

Eric nodded, "Yeah, and you helped out a lot last time. I think we make a good team, in that regard." The former soldier's twitchy stance reminded Pixel of a wind-up toy, jerky, almost uncontrolled movement. His personality seemed just as out of control, which on the one hand, Pixel liked the energy and enthusiasm of the other man, on the other...

"What happened back on the shuttle?" Pixel asked.

"Oh, with the bomb?" Eric shrugged, "Ariadne thought the Chxor were a danger so she triggered it. Probably a good move. There were enough of them that if they had attacked, we couldn't have stopped them." He didn't seem particularly broken up over the death of the Chxor civilians. Then again, Pixel found it hard to weep over them either, not after what he had seen in Chxor captivity.

"Actually, I meant that I heard you shot the wounded," Pixel said.

"Oh, that?" Eric snorted, "One of them tried to shoot Anubus in the back. After that, I felt it best to make sure of the rest of them. Not that I would cry any tears over the Wrethe, but I didn't want someone else to get hurt."

"You could have tied them up or just checked them for weapons and dragged them aboard the ship," Pixel said. He studied the other man's face and he wished suddenly that people came with display panels.

"Yeah, but you blew that ship up anyway, so it doesn't matter if I killed them then or later," Eric said.

Pixel shrugged at the reminder, "Yeah..."

Still, it felt wrong to him that Eric had killed the wounded Chxor. Pixel would have expected that behavior from Anubus or even Rastar maybe, but not from Eric. *No...* he thought, *Rastar has that moral code of his, he **probably** wouldn't hurt the wounded.* "Well, I've got a lot of work to do down here, I need to figure out this engine and all its systems, check the maintenance logs, and just figure out what I can. I'm not sure when I'll be free."

"I can understand that," Eric said. He turned to leave, "Oh, Simon wanted a team meeting in about fifteen minutes, up on the bridge."

"Yeah?" Pixel glanced at the chrono on his datapad, "Sure thing. What's it about?"

"Dunno, maybe about that female Chxor officer we took prisoner when we captured the ship?" Eric shrugged. "She's exceeded my two living Chxor rule, so I say we space her or Run. Depending on the info she has, I'd suggest Run."

"You know the little guy saved you, right?" Pixel asked.

"He had Rastar hold me down while he cut shrapnel out of me with a shiv," Eric said. "And, he tried to cut me open later to see how well I healed. And, for that matter, he wants to open Ariadne's head and put her brain in a jar. And, if that isn't enough... he's a damned Chxor!"

Pixel stared at the other man for a long moment, "With how you talk to Ariadne, I'd almost think you'd prefer he do that."

Eric looked away, "For all that she annoys me... no, not really. She means well, and I realize she cares about us. She just drives me nuts. I've had some bad shit go on in my life. I've come to realize that you can't rely on others; you got to look out for yourself and then your team. She goes on the way she has been, she's going to end up dead." Eric met Pixel's gaze, "I've buried enough friends that I don't want to be there for her death either. So, I try to get her to grow up and worry about herself."

"Maybe you shouldn't worry about fixing her," Pixel said, and from Eric's scowl, the advice was not well taken. "But I'm an engineer, not a psychologist, so what do I know?" Pixel rolled his eyes. He looked down at the chrono again, "Well, I'm going to head up there, probably swing by the galley to get something to eat. You up for it?"

"Nah, I need to find Crowe still," Eric said. He turned around and stepped out of the engine room. Eric gave one last wave over his shoulder as the door slid closed behind him.

Pixel brought up the ship's schematic again, and then gave a nod, "Two rights and a left and then up the stairs..."

***

Pixel stepped onto the bridge a few minutes later than he intended, but he held a pastrami and rye sandwich in one hand and a mug of hot apple cider in the other. "Hey guys."

"Wait... we have real food now?" Mike asked. The short Asian had an expression of pure lust on his face.

Pixel tried to talk around a mouthful. He gave up after he nearly spat mustard and pastrami on the conference table. He swallowed and took a sip of cider to wash the rest down. He tried again, "Yeah, loads of food. Some of it pretty random though."

"We should inventory it all before we just go through it," Simon said. "We could waste a lot of it if we just open stuff."

"Hey, that's a good idea," Pixel nodded. He stuffed the rest of the sandwich in his mouth.

Simon frowned and stared at him. Pixel wondered if Simon wanted a sandwich of his own. Maybe he should have brought some for the others. *Nah, then I'd be really late,* he thought.

"Well," Mike said, "We can decide that during this committee, right?" Pixel caught the sarcastic edge in his voice. Then again, Pixel thought it sounded more like a sarcastic hammer or perhaps a mallet. Then again, with some of the team, it might not be enough to penetrate.

"Excellent, I think that we should establish twice daily meetings to go over our agenda for the day and to review what we have accomplished," Run the Chxor said. Apparently, sarcasm was not common among the Chxor. "In addition, I require a room set aside for my research, as well as three volunteers for vivisection."

"Noted," Simon said dryly. "And on the subject of meetings, the reason I asked everyone in here is that we have something of a conundrum. We agreed to operate as a team, and to discuss our goals and plans ahead of time. Yet several team members have taken it upon themselves to make some pretty profound decisions on their own. These are decisions that affect the team and much more than that."

"I agree, " Eric said. "Like the decision to head to 443C98, I figured we would just run towards the nearest human space. There's no reason we have to take the long way back, right?"

"I made that decision based off information from Ariadne," Mike said. The short Asian pilot looked around at the group and Pixel saw his eyes narrow as he considered their reactions. "We didn't have a lot of time and it seemed like the best option at the time."

"That's the problem," Simon shook his head, "You made the call, without asking anyone else. I can accept a chain of command if we establish one, but I don't accept an individual making the choice for a group, not when he's self-appointed." Simon looked over at Ariadne, "Truth be told, if our navigator made the call on her own, it would make sense. But you said it yourself: she suggested it and you made the decision."

"Well, really *I* made the decision," Ariadne said. She gave everyone a smile, "It really was the best option, I think. Especially given the dangers of jumping into a military system without any kind of knowledge of how we might be received or the very long route back to Colonial space."

"I think they both made the right decisions," Rastar said. The big Ghornath had taken a seat in one of the Ghornath couches and he seemed absurdly comfortable. Pixel made note that once he had the chance, he should see if there were some way to adjust the couches for human physiology.

"You would," Anubus growled. The big Wrethe lurked in the back of the room. His deep voice and sinister emphasis startled Pixel. He had almost forgotten about the jackal headed alien. "You follow Mike's lead like a stray puppy."

"Hey, man, that's not nice," Rastar said. "I just think–"

"Let's not start bickering," Mike interrupted. "Clearly, mister by-the-book has an agenda he wants to push, so let's move past the bullshit and we can see what he wants."

Simon gave him a sharp nod, "Personally, I agree with your decision. But I think we need an established chain of command. I think that we need to select a captain."

"A captain for the ship or a captain for the team?" Eric asked. He clearly seemed excited by the idea. Perhaps it was just his military training, Pixel thought.

"Why do we need a captain?" Pixel said. He thought the last thing they needed was someone to tell them all what to do. If anything, he would rather just do his own thing and let them know about it later. The thought that any of the rest of them had the capability to judge his own efforts in science and engineering almost made him laugh. He rubbed his chin, yes, he should probably grow that goatee and work on his laugh. He tapped a note on his datapad.

"I think we need a leader for the team," Simon looked around at them all. "We spend too much time in discussion and, in the end, the individuals tend to do what they want regardless."

"I agree," Mike said with a nod. "In fact... well, Simon might use my decision as a negative example, but I agree with him. A self appointed individual shouldn't make the decisions. We need a charter or contract, and we all need to agree to abide by it, no matter who gets selected as captain."

"We know who will get that choice," Anubus growled. "There can be only one obvious selection."

"I agree," Simon nodded. "And I think we all have the same person in mind. Still, we all agree to abide by the decision?" He looked around and met everyone's gazes.

Pixel frowned when Simon looked at him, "I'm not good on this whole leader thing. I mean, what's the limits? Do we have any way to appoint a new captain if the old one does something we disagree with?"

"Of course a good leader does something you disagree with," Eric said. "Military leaders have to make the best of bad decisions, some of which will lead to the death of their people. We can't have a democracy, or we'll have an election every day. If we select a captain, we do it until the captain can no longer serve."

"That sounds more like a king than a captain," Ariadne said. "And though we have weapons and now a warship, I must note that we are not military. In fact, if our goal is to form some sort of militia, I think we should rethink that. I mean, we can do so much good if--"

"A general election, among our team?" Eric cut her off.

"Yes." Simon nodded. He glanced at Mike, "And I thought that the captain would select officers, an XO, and so on and so forth."

Mike nodded, "Makes sense."

"But what about..." Pixel trailed off as the others stared at him. He wanted to tell them all the problems he saw, but he found his confidence fail, "Never mind."

"So we vote verbally?" Eric asked.

"Of course," Mike nodded. "And I assume just a simple majority of votes selects the captain, right?"

"Yeah, but I feel pretty certain we know who this will go to," Crowe said. "There's one obvious leader in the group, but let's get the showmanship over with."

Pixel looked around at the others. Each of them seemed certain they knew who would win, yet he felt no certainty himself. For that matter, given the choice of who he would elect

242

as what amounted to the reigning tyrant, Pixel couldn't say which choice he felt the least bad about.

Eric killed the Chxor prisoners and he caused the primary weapon mount to explode within five minutes of when he came on board, Pixel remembered. Mike had a tendency to micromanage, to the point that drove Pixel almost insane as he had to stop and explain every detail of his engineering efforts. Simon did not seem to know anything at all about ships beyond a basic knowledge of how to use sensors and communications. Rastar seemed like a decent enough fellow, but he knew less than Simon about ship operations. Anubus would probably kill them all...

"Alright, let's put this to the vote," Simon nodded. "I'll start it off. I think we all agree that the crew and ship needs order and rules." Pixel saw Mike and Eric both nod. "Therefore, I vote for myself. I have the experience in organization to get things straight."

"You're kidding, right?" Eric asked.

"What?" Simon looked at him sharply, "Of course I'm not kidding, I'm the obvious choice in that regard."

"Maybe not as obvious as you thought," Pixel said lightly. He flushed as Simon and Eric both glared at him. "Hey, I'm just saying. Don't we have a vote to continue?"

"We do," Anubus growled. "And I for one say that the obvious choice is the strongest and most powerful of the group. I vote for me, and I dare any of the rest of you to challenge me."

"You do know that command by threat just means someone will try to kill you, right?" Mike asked. The pilot voiced one of the comments that Pixel had refrained from voicing earlier.

"Someone will try anyway... best to get it out of the way," Anubus growled.

Rastar slapped Anubus on the back, "Hey, Annie, come on man, you know we love ya." The big alien managed to get his hand back before Anubus's jaws snapped closed, but not by much. Rastar gave a slightly nervous chuckle, "I think that the obvious captain for a Ghornath ship is a Ghornath of course. I mean, this ship rightfully belongs to my people and any of them we encounter will want to make sure that they are properly represented. So I say I am the obvious choice."

"Right, well, I vote for the one person in the room with enough military experience to matter," Eric said. "I was a senior NCO and I know the fundamentals of tactics. I vote for me."

"Ground tactics," Crowe said. "Which is not the same thing as space tactics. And you blew up the main gun when you tried to power it up. Pixel even warned you not to mess with it. I think we can safely say that you lack the right credentials." Crowe looked around at the group, "I can't believe no one has realized me as the obvious choice. I haven't failed at any task yet, and I've the ability to plan ahead far better than any of the rest of you. You'd be lost without me at the helm. I vote for me."

"This is crazy," Mike said. "We get no where if everyone votes for themselves." He glanced around. "To break this stupid deadlock, I vote for Ariadne. She's a skilled navigator and we can all agree that she has concern for the crew."

"No way!" Ariadne shook her head, "You will not saddle me with that job." She looked around at the others frantically. "Look, I respect your feelings about this, but I'm the wrong person for that job. I vote for Mike."

"Your behavior is illogical," Run said. The little Chxor shook his head. "Your self interest blinds you to the fundamental choices you have received. To go with an emotional and inferior species is to limit yourself to mere mediocrity. The obvious choice is the one member of the crew whose intelligence, logic, and superior reasoning skills have made the difference for our continued survival. Therefore I say that I should be the ship's commander. I will of course accept the rest of you changing your votes to my favor at this time."

"Good luck with that," Eric said. "I will change my vote though, I vote we space the little twerp."

"Noted," Simon said, "but we'll table that particular discussion." He looked over at Pixel. "Well, you're the deciding vote, it appears. Whoever you vote for, as long as it's not

244

yourself, will be the captain."

Pixel looked around at the others. He felt sweat break out all over his body. "Yeah..." He took a deep breath. "I don't think this whole captain thing is a good idea. But if we have to go down this road, I think a deadlock is the best thing, it forces everyone to really think about this. So I'll abstain, in the interest of forcing some thought into this."

"Really?" Crowe shook his head. "That's what this comes to?" He looked around, "I can't believe that no one else voted for me. Look at everything I've done for you guys!"

"Um, what *have* you done for us?" Ariadne asked.

Crowe scowled at her, "A lot, freaky mind girl, that's what. Or would you like to try to program a translation into the ship's computer yourself?"

"Well... since we have a deadlock, can we decide on the other stuff we need done in the meantime?" Pixel asked. "If we're just going to set here and bicker, I've got some work to do."

"Right," Simon said. "I think it best if we do a complete inventory of the ship."

"We should talk to the other prisoners, learn if any of them have useful skills that'll help out, and most of them have nothing else to do besides help," Ariadne said. "I'm sure they can be a big help. And that will make them part of our crew, build up morale, and..."

"And, if any of them are dangerous, give them full access to the ship," Eric said.

"Which is why we'll interview them," Mike answered. "Ariadne and I can handle that, unless anyone objects?"

"I will inventory the armory," Rastar said.

"There's an armory?" Eric asked. "Where?"

Pixel brought up the schematic on his data pad, "Second deck, near the elevator to the bridge."

"I'm there already," Eric grinned, "let's wrap this up."

"Right, any other business?" Mike asked.

"When do we have the next election?" Simon seemed resigned more than anything else, Pixel thought. The former policeman's shoulders slumped a bit as everyone looked to go off in their own direction. Pixel didn't understand that. As an engineer, he knew machinery worked best when designed and controlled, but from his experience, people worked the opposite way most times. Or maybe that was just how he worked, either way, he didn't see the problem with the current plan. Hopefully he could show that to the others.

"We've got three more days," Mike said, "Before it really becomes an issue. I suggest tomorrow night. That gives us long enough to organize and establish a chain of command afterward, and some time for people to state their case before hand."

"Right, great, political parties," Eric grimaced.

"This election will be won by the person who understands the motivations and interests of the other crew," Run said. "Clearly that will be myself."

"You just asked for volunteers for vivisection," Eric noted.

Run nodded, "And as captain, I would require none of *you* to volunteer."

"Your generosity warms my heart," Mike said. "How can you lose?"

***

Pixel decided to stop by the galley again before he returned to the engine room. He found a group had gathered there. He saw no sign of the bread or the pastrami he had left out. He looked around the galley and gave a sigh at the mess that some of the passengers had made. He saw a dozen boxes and bags torn open. He also saw a pile of trash next to the recycler, which made him shake his head. He didn't mind clutter, but that kind of slovenly mess made him angry. The ship seemed so clean. Why couldn't the others keep things clean?

Pixel turned around to find Simon and Run. Simon turned an interesting shade of red when he saw the mess. Pixel decided that discretion would be the better part of valor and slipped past him before the other man exploded. Not that he didn't want to watch, Pixel just felt no desire to get caught up in that level of drama. Besides, Pixel had work to do.

Pixel pulled up the schematics on his datapad and as he stepped out of the galley, chose a different route back to the engine room. He highlighted a couple areas where auxiliary systems machinery sat tucked away. *I should probably check those out on my way through*, he decided. He took the stairs down and then opened a small hatch and took a narrow ladder down to the lowest deck. Pixel stopped at the first area. He toggled open the engine space and stepped inside. He gave a low whistle, "Oh, man."

He had not had the opportunity to get with Rastar yet to translate the Ghornath text. So until he opened the door, he had no idea what he might find, beyond engineering systems. And his expectation had proven false, to an extent. This was not, strictly speaking, an engineering system. It was a sensor system, unless he missed his guess. He saw the twin beryllium spheres suspended in the electrode solution in the crystoplast tank. He gently caressed the outside of the casing. Clumsy human hands could come no closer the delicate piece of machinery. The two superdense cores inside the beryllium would react to minute changes in gravitational force, fine enough that in conjunction with others scattered around the ship they could triangulate the location of planets, astral bodies and even other vessels.

Pixel remembered the theory from his classes in applied gravitational astrophysics but for most of the Colonial Republic, such tech remained just that: a theory. He thought about how difficult just the creation of the superdense cores would be. It required gravity induction forging according to everything he had read. That required tremendous levels of power and better control of gravitational forces than anything he had ever seen outside a lab. "Very cool." Pixel made a note on his data pad. He would have to come back and check this out later. He couldn't help but think, *Jack would find this fascinating.*

But Jack had betrayed him. More than that, his best friend had died in the process. Pixel lowered his datapad. He felt suddenly far less interested in this new toy. What fun was it without someone to share it with? Why could he not get along with people as easily as he did machinery?

Pixel stepped out of the compartment. He tapped in commands on his datapad and walked towards the next compartment. Yet even as he did so, he wondered why he bothered. His pursuit of science seemed so empty without someone to discuss it with. As much as he loved to figure out new technology or how to apply old technology in new ways, he didn't feel free to do that. Part of that lay with the others. Mike seemed eager enough to see some of that, but only in ways that directly applied to their escape. Eric seemed fascinated only with weapons. Anubus didn't seem to understand or care about anything besides power and the ability to kill. Simon seemed far too driven by his rules. Crowe... had a wealth of knowledge about computers, communications, and sensors but he seemed to view that knowledge as a weapon or tool.

Of the others, he thought that Ariadne and Rastar would indulge him in his studies, but neither seemed particularly interested in them. Oddly enough, only Run struck him as someone who would share his passion for research and experimentation. Pixel still felt too nervous around the Chxor to even talk with him.

Pixel sighed as he walked up to the next compartment. *Having no one to share this with really takes a lot of the fun out of it,* he thought as he toggled the hatch open. His eyes lit up as he saw the banks of capacitors in that room, "Oh, cool."

***

Pixel had managed to bury himself head first into what he thought was the control panel for the ship's defense screen when he felt someone tap him on the back. He started and he yelped as his hand slipped and rubbed against an open circuit. He pulled himself carefully out of the controls and then rubbed at his forearm gingerly.

"I have work for you to do," Run said from behind him.

"I have lots of work for me to do already," Pixel said.

"This must be a priority. I insist that you do it, and if you reject my logical demands, I will be forced to use my command voice," Run said.

248

The little Chxor stood calmly and Pixel could only shake his head. "You know, asking politely might get you further than demands."

Run held out his hand, and Pixel recognized the dart gun. "I need this made better. I need to be able to shoot multiple darts."

"Oh, cool," Pixel said, his disagreement suddenly forgotten. He gingerly took the tiny gun and examined it. "Compressed air to fire, huh? You must be running low on that. And on darts." He pulled two pins out of the side and then opened it up and examined it. "Wow, this is actually pretty well designed! Who did this for you?"

Run nodded, "I put it together in my lab as a security measure. Mechanical parts are not my primary interest or area of study, but I find the ability to make such simple things useful. It allows me to make tools. It saves me time from having to explain what I want from lesser minds."

Pixel found himself nodding, "I can see that, actually. And having multiple skill sets is useful. So... what do you want me to do? I assume if you just wanted the air tank refilled or more darts you could do that yourself."

"This is an accurate assumption," Run nodded. "It is good to discuss this with someone whose intellect somewhat approaches my own." He pulled out a real pistol and held it out. Pixel took it even more carefully than he took the dart gun. He felt more than a little nervous about guns. "I would like to integrate features from this design into the other. A storage place for additional darts and a means to fire multiple times without reloading."

"Ah, a magazine and semi-automatic fire," Pixel nodded. "I like that, it sounds like an interesting build." He looked down at the dart gun, "I can do that." His mind ranged over the possibilities, but then he cocked his head, "How about a deal?"

"A deal?" Run asked.

"Yeah, I make this for you but in return you give me some of your knock-out solution for Wrethe, Humans, Ghornath, and Chxor," Pixel said. He didn't think he'd go with a dart gun like Run's, in fact, he felt an idea had begun to percolate.

"You assume that I will manufacture more of my pacification drugs," Run said. The Chxor contemplated him for a long moment in silence. His pale yellow eyes and gray skin made him look distinctly alien, despite his outwardly similar physiology. "That is a valid assumption. I do not see the purpose, however, of making Chxor drugs."

Pixel thought that one through. He thought very carefully of how to talk around the fact that he might need to tranquilize Run. "We are still in Chxor space and we have at least one Chxor prisoner aboard." Pixel suddenly wondered where the others had put the Chxor officer and if they had captured any of her guards alive as well. "Therefore, I will have use for it."

"Agreed," Run nodded. "I will accept this mutually beneficial arrangement. When can I pick up my new pacification device?" He seemed to hesitate, "It took me two weeks to construct this one, and I understand that your inferior brain may take longer to make the necessary improvements...."

Pixel shrugged, "This afternoon, I think."

Pixel's offhand reply seemed to paralyze Run. It took the little Chxor a long moment to speak, "Clearly, your brain works better at mechanical problems than I thought. Perhaps your intelligence is greater than expected. I must assume this is due to your ability to ignore such things as emotions and to reject the illogical hormonal behavior common in other humans."

Pixel shrugged, "Nope, I get emotional at times and I have plenty of hormones." He tried not to think about what had happened to his last girlfriend. Suddenly he didn't want to talk with Run anymore. "Hey, I've got to finish up this examination here, but I'll bring it by along with a design sketch and you can tell me what you think later today."

"This is acceptable," Run nodded. "Also, I will have a document for you to sign. I find your intelligence to be an anomaly and I would like your permission to examine your brain."

"Sorry, little guy, I think I need my brain. Some other time, maybe," Pixel said with a smile.

"This is understandable," Run gave him a nod and walked away.

Pixel tucked both the tranquilizer gun and the pistol away in his pockets. He tapped a reminder into his datapad, and then frowned as a scrawl of Chxor glyphs appeared on the screen. He really needed to get a human standard operating system. He had heard good things about a Linux kernel...

Pixel glanced at the defense screen console and then at the list of other things he wanted to check out. The one that really seemed significant was the fusion reactor output. Either some of the ship's damaged systems drained more power than they should, or the reactor did not put out the right level of power in the first place. Either way, Pixel felt he needed to find out the cause. Though Eric had destroyed the capacitors for the primary weapon, the secondary weapons still functioned. The lighter secondary weapons primary purpose lay in fighter or missile interception. The ship's other systems, to include the defense screen, drained too much power to make even those secondary weapons operational.

Pixel glanced at the schematics for the reactor and then made yet another note to have Rastar translate what he could when he got the opportunity. In the meantime, Pixel closed the panel for the defense screen and tucked his datapad in the oversized pocket on his hip. *Time for me to see what this baby has under her skirt,* Pixel thought. With how the Ghornath sized the ship for their access, he always seemed to have plenty of room to get inside the guts of the equipment and get his hands dirty. He rubbed his hands together in anticipation and got to work.

***

Pixel wiped at the grease on his hands as he stepped into the galley. He should have cleaned up at the workshop sink in the engine room, he knew. But he hadn't put a stool in there yet, so he couldn't reach the faucet without the need to balance on the edge of the sink. *Sometimes there are penalties to oversized ships*, he figured.

"Stop right there," Simon said.

"What?" Pixel asked.

"We've instituted a daily cooking cycle. Unless you're on the list, you pick up food in the lounge," Simon said. The former policeman looked sternly at Pixel.

"We have a lounge?" Pixel asked

Simon's gaze dropped to Pixel's hands, "You need to wash up too. How *did* you get so dirty?"

"Yeah, um, working?" Pixel said. He looked around, "Where's the lounge anyway?"

"Down the corridor another five meters, on the left side," Simon said.

"Starboard side," Pixel corrected. Not that he cared, but Simon seemed so precise about everything else, he might as well use the right terms if he wanted to boss people around aboard a ship.

"Right, starboard," Simon nodded.

"Yeah... *not* right, starboard," Pixel shook his head, "Left is starboard, right is port, unless you face aft, then right is starboard and left is port."

Simon didn't respond. Pixel thought he saw his eyelid twitch.

Just then Eric stepped into the galley followed by Rastar, "So then there I was, no shit, right in the middle of a swarm of those Seppie bastards with no ammo and bare assed naked except for my-"

"The galley is off limits unless you have kitchen duty," Simon snapped.

"Hey man, we're just here to get a snack, lots of work to do down in the armory," Rastar said. Pixel looked up at the big alien and then suddenly wished he had not. The glare and clash of colors on his shirt almost induced an epileptic fit. *Some of those colors shouldn't be legal,* he thought, *much less allowed on the same shirt.*

"Is that a Hawaiian shirt?" Simon asked. His mouth went agape at the rape of his visual cortex.

Rastar stuck his chest out and spread his four arms, as if

252

particularly proud of it, "Ain't it cool, man? I found a whole closet full of them in the bunk room. Dunno what happened to the crew, but some of them had some good taste, huh?"

"Are you serious?" Simon said. "Who the hell makes Ghornath sized and shaped Hawaiian shirts?"

Eric looked at Rastar, "Dunno, but I wish I could get some new clothes. There's a laundry near the cabins, but this suit I've worn still smells like sweat after three times through. I think Rastar really lucked out with his find."

"You do?" Pixel asked.

"Yeah," Eric nodded, "I mean, you can conceal all kinds of weapons under a Hawaiian print, it breaks up your shape pretty well, excellent for concealed carry."

"I think I want to puke," Simon said.

"Hey, man, no need to be jealous," Rastar said and slapped Simon on the shoulder, "I'm sure we can find some your size when we get to civilized space." Rastar continued past the stunned man and opened the nearest refrigerator. "Ah, excellent, someone stocked some Coca Cola! I'll just take two, since I'm on duty...."

"I'll take one, too," Eric said.

Rastar gave a snort, "Lightweight. Alright, what else do we have here?"

"I said earlier that unless you're assigned to kitchen duty you get your meals in the lounge, and the next meal starts in an hour," Simon said. His glare might have worked better if he hadn't had to squint and look to the side against Rastar's shirt, Pixel noted.

"Sure thing, man, we'll be out of your hair in a second," Rastar waved one hand while his other three pilfered through the refrigerator.

"Way to come up with some pointless bullshit," Eric grunted around a mouthful of something brown and crunchy, "Besides, who are you to make that decision? We've got plenty of food now, right? No need to ration."

"We would have plenty of food, except the other escapees tore this place apart and spoiled about half of it for long term storage, so we have to eat it all-" Simon broke off, "Rastar, did you just stick an entire jar of mayonnaise in your pocket?"

Rastar looked up, "Yeah, goes great with the pickle and anchovies toppings for the pizza. Really pulls it all together. Say, do you mind if I take the rest of this flour?"

"Where are you going to cook a pizza, if not in the galley?" Pixel asked.

"There's a camp stove down in the Armory, I figured I'd just cook it down there while I worked," Rastar said. He snagged a six pack of Coca Cola bottles, "And... some for the road. See you guys later!"

Simon stared at the mess that the pair had left of the previously ordered refrigerator. Something about the set of his shoulders suggested the stance of a broken man to Pixel. "Who's got cooking detail, anyway?" Pixel asked cheerfully.

Just then, Run the Chxor stepped out of the back of the galley. He carried two trays covered with a mix of food. The smell that came off them resembled nothing so much as scorched rubber. "I have prepared food for my experimental subjects. I will require time to take notes and observe their eating habits before I can clean my laboratory."

Simon looked at Run and then shook his head, "Right, whatever." He looked over at Pixel. "This is why we need a captain. Those two just destroyed a good hour's worth of work."

"Do you think that organizing food is the best use of your abilities?" Pixel asked.

Simon gave him a glare, "Someone has to do it. As far as I know, Ariadne and Mike haven't interviewed anyone they trust with food yet."

Pixel tried very hard and quite unsuccessfully to contain his smile, "So, you put Run to cooking?"

"I am very well versed in the nutritional requirements of humans," Run said. "I carefully meted out those requirements from a variety of foods available and then processed them together and heated them to neutralize any bacteria, viruses, and other contaminants." He looked down at the blackened bars, "They are very healthy, I assure you."

Pixel gave a sigh, "Run, one of those illogical things about humans... we like to eat things that taste good – health is a secondary factor."

"Taste..." Run nodded. "I will add this factor to the others. What is a good paradigm for taste factors?"

"Try a cookbook," Pixel said. "You can't go wrong if you work your way through a cookbook." He stepped around Simon and then pulled a box of cereal bars off the top shelf of the pantry. "In the meantime, I'll munch on these, thanks guys."

"Where you going?" Simon asked.

"Armory, I think," Pixel said. "I need to drop off a pistol and then I wanted to check out some of the power drain that I saw from there."

"I'll join you," Simon said. "I want to check this pistol in and see if I can get something more reliable. The Chxor don't seem too high tech regarding small arms." The other man followed him out of the galley.

Pixel led the way down the corridor. He liked Simon better when the former cop didn't try to boss anyone around, "Their mechanical stuff seems to work just fine. And it's easier to produce in mass from an engineering standpoint. I had a friend who was something of a weapon historian, he said that his favorite firearms came from the twentieth century. He claimed everything since then is derivative."

"Your friend sounds like a smart man," Simon said as they went down a ladder. "Maybe you can introduce me to him when we get back. I'm something of a weapon collector... well, I was. I had an original magnum forty four... and a few replicas of some other classic pistols."

"Unfortunately, Jack wound up dead," Pixel said softly. "I think you two wouldn't have got along anyway; he was something of a firebrand."

"My condolences, friend," Simon put his hand on Pixel's shoulder and he cleared his throat. Simon drew and held up his pistol, "I just don't like the small caliber round on this one, truth to tell, and the weird slide mechanism. Damn thing cut me open a couple times already. Plus, the grip feels wrong, somehow."

Pixel nodded, "Yeah, well, Chxor designs, so they probably didn't bother too much with ergonomics or anything like that. They just don't seem to consider things like comfort and ease of use. Also, the Chxor hands are shaped different than ours – one less knuckle so they hold things different."

"I hadn't noticed," Simon said. "But that makes sense."

They turned a corner and stopped in front of a heavily armored hatch. Pixel waved his hand over the control and it slid open.

Rastar and Eric looked up. They both stood over a bench, which lay covered with weapons, pieces of weapons, and ammunition. Pixel gave a long whistle.

"What is that?" Simon pointed at something that looked vaguely like a metal spider the size of a polar bear. It hung from a rack in the corner, and Pixel saw that numerous cables and wires led into it.

"It's a Wrostact Mark Seven Ghornath Power Armor," Rastar said, as he set down a case of ammunition. "And I think it's missing some pieces." Pixel saw the big Ghornath shift colors to a slightly pale tan, "Pixel, I know you are very busy, however...."

"You want to know if I can take a look at it?" Pixel asked. "Sure, when I get time. In exchange, I need you to come down to the engine room and do some translating sometime in the next couple days, deal?" After he saw Rastar nod, he pointed at the cables attached to the suit, "I noticed a big power drain in here, is it from that?"

"Uh, that's probably from these: we just plugged them in to charge," Eric said. He pointed at a rack of weapons. Each of them seemed too big for a normal person, though when Pixel looked at Rastar he thought they seemed the right size. They all had thick black boxes with indicator lights instead of magazines and Pixel felt a start of surprise as he realized what that meant.

"Are those energy weapons? Like laser guns and that sort of thing?" Pixel's voice nearly broke with excitement. *I want to take them apart right now,* he thought. Energy weapons were still extremely rare throughout human space. Lightweight and reliable was still out o reach, and most such weapons were both extremely expensive and extremely temperamental.

Rastar flushed green, "Indeed, quality Ghornath manufacture. The two medium sized weapons are pulse guns, the smallest is a pistol, and the largest is a pulse rifle." He reached out and stroked the weapons with one hand, "They are priceless, as the Nova Romans destroyed the Koman Defense Factory during their invasion. Most of the engineers and experts who designed these weapons died during the raid."

"Wow," Pixel said. *I* really *want to take them apart now,* he thought.

"Those will be confiscated on the first civilized world we come to," Simon said. "There's no way they'd let civilians have them."

"Only if we tell someone," Eric said. He got up and pulled the pulse rifle off the rack. He flipped a switch and a hologram flickered into existence above the top. "It's got holographic sights, and Rastar says the manufacturer guarantees a factory zero out to a kilometer... and that is *without* a scope. A kilometer! Can you imagine what *I* could do with this?"

"What's that writing painted on the side?" Pixel asked. It looked like someone had used a paint pen or something.

"Oh... uh, I sort of named her," Eric said, he sounded embarrassed. "Lorretta, after a girl I knew." He cleared his throat, clearly embarrassed, and walked the weapon back over to the rack.

"Someone who meant a lot to you clearly," Pixel said. He felt a spurt of envy that the other man had someone special like that in his life. He wondered, *why did women always go for the jerks?*

Eric sneered, "No, she was a bitch who destroyed my life." He slammed the rifle down into the rack with a bit more force than strictly necessary. *Well, maybe I don't envy him after all,* Pixel thought.

"Oh, well that's nice," Rastar said. "Anyway, we'd just finished the weapons inventory and started on an inventory of ammunition while my pizza cooked and Eric's – what is it you're making again, man?"

"Pork loin medallions in a rosette sauce," Eric said. "With some mushrooms stuffed with cheese." He shrugged, "The mushrooms are flash frozen, so they will be a little chewy, but beggars can't be choosers." He went over to the camp stove, and opened the lid. "I didn't realize anyone else would come down or I would have prepared more."

Pixel looked over at Simon and whispered *sotto voce*, "Maybe you should ask him if he would mind kitchen duties?"

Simon scowled at Pixel. A moment later Pixel heard him mutter, "Maybe I should."

***

Pixel left the others in conversation and wandered over to look at the Ghornath power armor. He almost tripped over something else that lay at its feet. When he looked down he jumped back with a shout of surprise.

"Oh, he found Randy," Eric said.

"Who the hell is Randy, and why's he hiding in the armory?" Simon asked.

Pixel took a calming breath and shook his head. "Randy is a suit of human power armor." He looked down at the mangled suit. The human power armor looked, at first glance, like a metal man, though the torso, arms, and legs looked thicker – mostly from the extra armor and the requirement to put someone's body inside, Pixel would guess. Someone, presumably the previous crew, had scrawled 'Randy' across the suit's chest in red paint. An explosion or some other damage had completely mangled the legs of the suit. They ended in a tangle of wires and pieces of metal that hung from the frame. Most disturbingly was the smiley face painted on the front of the helmet where a human's face would be.. and the rather large hole blasted through its forehead.

"I looked it over when I checked out my Power Armor," Rastar said. "It looks like they cannibalized it pretty thoroughly already. It would take a lot of work to get it up, I think."

"That's a Nova Roma Marines unit symbol painted on the

shoulder," Eric said. "I think it's one of their recon units, but I'm not sure."

"Well, this guy didn't make it home," Pixel said. "Maybe we can turn it over to the Nova Romans if we hit one of their systems. There might be a reward for turning it in." *And with how mangled it is, they probably wouldn't notice if I took it apart and put it back together before we turn it in,* he thought.

"As long as they don't think we did it," Eric said.

"Yeah, I'm sure they track where they send their people," Simon said. "I mean, what kind of military doesn't know where they send several hundred thousand dollars of equipment and a soldier?"

"Marine," Eric corrected automatically. "But yeah, they should."

Pixel frowned, "Well, I totally forgot, but meant to drop this off earlier," he pulled the pistol out of his pocket. "Where do you want it?"

"We've piled up all the Chxor stuff in the corner there," Rastar said. "Most of it's pretty crappy quality, but we can use some of it, like the riot guns, until we run out of ammo."

"I'd like to teach a firearms safety class to the team members who need it," Simon said as he set his pistol down in the pile. "We can use the Chxor stuff for that." He looked at the bench, "I wanted to get a better pistol. Any recommendations?"

Eric waved his hand down the table, "You're a former cop, so you probably want a black powder muzzle loader or a revolver. But we've got a bunch of nine millimeter human stuff, that looks like it was made by Liberty Arms out of Tau Ceti."

"What's that?" Pixel asked, and pointed up at a plaque above the hatch.

Everyone except Rastar looked up. The Ghornath spoke in a low voice, "It is a trophy, taken from a Nova Roman officer that the crew captured. The writing on the plaque says where they executed him and lists his crimes against my people."

"It looks like a replica of a forty five automatic. Maybe a nineteen eleven," Simon said. "Chrome plated and pearl handle grips... a bit flashy for my tastes... does it work?"

"I do not know," Rastar said. He reached up without a look and then passed the weapon to Simon. "But you may keep it." His hide had shaded faintly blue.

"You sure?" Simon asked. "I mean, I know you like guns and all..."

"I would not use it, even if I had not found weapons more to my liking," Rastar said. Pixel saw his hide turn a deep shade of blue, almost purple. "Among the crimes listed, the plaque notes that Colonel Cassius executed the child Emperor of Ghornath Prime with the weapon, as well as his younger sister Princess Hycar. The weapon is bad luck, cursed by the blood of the royals whose lives it took."

"Oh," Simon said. "Well, I don't believe in luck. But if it bothers you, I'll leave the weapon here."

"No," Rastar said. He patted Simon on the shoulder, "I consider you a friend, like the others. And as a friend to me, I think you could also be a friend to my people. I would be honored if you could redeem this weapon, especially as it is a nineteen eleven. This is the weapon that your cowboys back on Earth used, before you went to space, right?"

"Thanks, Rastar," Simon said. "I don't have any cowboys in my lineage, but I appreciate the gift."

Pixel frowned, his grasp on history wasn't the best, but he thought Rastar might have his times mixed up. But it didn't matter that much, so he let it pass. "Well, I suppose I'll just take one of the pistols."

The others went quiet.

Rastar shaded back towards a mellow brown, "Hey, Pixel, um, man, I hate to say this..."

"What?" Pixel asked.

"You really don't know how to use a firearm," Simon said bluntly.

"No clue, whatsoever," Eric nodded.

"Yeah, man, that one time you shot, you managed to wing me," Rastar said.

"That was an accident on the station, that guy was going to attack Mike," Pixel looked around at the others, who didn't seem swayed by his logic, "Well, how do I get better if I don't practice?"

"We'll get to that, in the meantime, I think we're all safer if you leave it here, for now," Simon said. "I promise we'll do a class sometime soon."

"What if I need a weapon?" Pixel asked. "In case you haven't noticed, I seem to be the only one on the team who can't either shoot, rip people apart with my bare hands, light people on fire with my brain, or some mixture of the three," Pixel said. "I really feel like I'm the soft chewy center on this team."

"Right., right..." Rastar nodded. "Don't worry, man, we'll protect you."

Who protects me from you guys? Pixel thought, with the recent memory of when Rastar lost his temper and started a riot. "Yeah, fine. But I want that class soon."

"Right after we have the election," Simon said.

"Who are you planning on voting for, anyway?" Eric asked.

"Someone who can manage to bring some order to the chaos," Simon answered. "What about you?" He looked around at the others, as if to show that his question applied to them all.

Eric shrugged, "Rastar and I both have the same guy in mind, actually, now that we've talked about it." He glanced over at Pixel, "What do you think, Pixel?"

Pixel shrugged, "Honestly... I still think a captain is a bad idea. The last thing we need is someone to micromanage us or get in the way of good ideas."

"I got to agree with you there," Eric said. "But at the same time, I think we need someone to give us a goal to work towards, especially now that we're looking good on escape."

"I guess," Pixel shrugged, "Well, now that I got rid of that pistol and I know what the power drain came from, I need to go check out some other systems."

"Why the worry about power?" Simon asked.

"Well," Pixel rubbed at his chin as he thought about how much to say without inducing a panic over the whole matter. He really needed to grow out a goatee, he decided. It would probably make him look more authoritative. "The reactor took some damage during either the capture by the Chxor or before that. It's nothing major, we just get about two thirds the power from the reactor that we should."

"Oh," Eric said. "But will that affect weapons or guns?"

"Yeah," Pixel nodded. "One or the other. Its something we can work around, but I'd rather do the repairs sooner than later. I don't want to go into details," *mostly because you three wouldn't understand them and I'd waste the rest of the day explaining them,* he mentally added. "But the repairs should only take three or four days if I can get together the supplies and the labor to help."

"Alright," Simon nodded, "Well, keep us informed, would you? And any help you need, just let us know." Pixel gave him a smile as he walked out of the armory, even as he remembered the last time someone said those words to him.

And he tried not to think of how many people had died in the aftermath.

***

"My man, Kev-O! How's it going?" Travis asked. Though he worked as a graduate student in applied wave theory, he still looked and sounded like a jock to Kevin. Loud and with a braying laugh that grated on his nerves. Luckily they had the whole floor to themselves, the week after finals, the lab might as well be a graveyard. No one would hear the big blonde man's laugh and come to see what they had going on so late at night.

"Almost done here," Kevin said. "Where's Jack? I'll need those codes he acquired to finish this."

"Right here, Kevin," Jack said as he stepped into the lab. His friend might serve as Kevin's polar opposite. Where Kevin had long brown hair in a ponytail, Jack had his hair shaved down to his scalp. Where Kevin stood over two meters in height, Jack barely topped a meter and a half. Where as Kevin wore his patched coveralls and had a pair of glasses perched on his nose, Jack wore a pair of steel toed leather combat boots and a metal studded leather jacket. "How goes the hard work?"

"Not all that hard, just compiling the commands and checking the whole thing over. This last bit is real tricky, you know?"

"Yeah, one wrong bit of commands and the whole reactor could go up, that's why we needed you for this little prank," Jack said. "But keep us informed, would you? And any help you need, just let us know."

"Sure thing. Truth to tell, I finished the last bit of my work on it a few minutes ago. I just had to double check everything and I needed those access codes from you," Kevin said. "If you don't mind, I'd actually like you to look it over before we go down to set up. I just want to be sure it's perfect, you know? I'd hate to have an accident with a fusion reactor downtown."

Travis looked shocked, his eyes went wide and he looked over at Jack. "You think-" Something about his expression made Kevin feel suddenly uncertain. He almost looked surprised that Kevin had suggested the possibility...

Jack gave a giggle, "Yeah, that would look pretty bad right when you go up to defend your PhD thesis, 'Oh, I kind of blew up the whole city.' No worries, Kevin, I got your back. And I'll take it down there, I know you got a bunch of work to do still on your thesis, I don't mind taking it down there, you've done enough already."

Kevin nodded slowly, "Yeah, well, I kind of want to see this through, and just make sure about the commands and the parameters on the reactor..."

"Kevin, you know me," Jack gave him a broad smile, "This was my idea, don't worry about it, I'll double check everything." Jack held out his hand.

Kevin hesitated, "You promise you'll double check?" Not that he didn't trust Jack. After all, the whole thing came from one of their discussions; a prank that would outdo anything anyone else had ever done in the history of the campus. To hijack an entire fusion reactor for a light show... well, that would sure as heck impress anyone who had the eyes to see it.

And if it also highlighted the idiocy of certain

government officials who had nominal responsibility for the reactor's security... well, all to the better. After all, those same government officials had just cut the research budget by over fifty million drachma.

"Alright," Kevin passed over the terminal he had spent the past ten hours on. "But I need this back, afterward. I've got some of my thesis stuff on it."

"I promise, you don't need to worry about that," Jack said. "This is the big time, buddy, go to work, but be sure you get outside to watch the light show... I think even you will be impressed."

***

Pixel snapped out of his memories as he stopped in front of the lounge door. He waved his hand to open it and stepped into the room. He froze a step inside the door. The plush carpets, leather couches, and the huge aquarium that occupied the forward bulkhead all surprised him. What caught his immediate attention, however, was the woman he nearly ran over.

She stood much shorter than him, shorter even than Ariadne, he thought. Yet she had more mass than the slender psychic. Quite a bit more mass, he estimated. Most of it in two places that drew his eyes like magnets. Pixel realized that his mouth had dropped open. He managed to mumble, "Excuse me," and step to the side. *Way to be smooth,* he thought to himself.

He felt himself flush, but it took a lot of effort to drag his gaze off her chest and to her face. "Uh, hi?"

She sighed. Now that he looked at her face, he saw that she had red hair, blue eyes, and freckles. She also had a look of resignation on her face. "Hello, I'm Mandy. You're Pixel, right, the engineer?"

"Yeah..." Pixel nodded. He tried to think of something smart or scientific to say, but the only words that came to mind included disproportionate, buoyancy, and floatation. He figured he should keep those thoughts to himself.

"We meant to talk to you earlier," another woman spoke.

"I'm Miranda, by the way. Mike said you were occupied."

Pixel pulled his eyes away from Mandy. The raven-haired woman stood behind Mandy, and slightly to the side. She stood at least fifteen centimeters taller than her companion. She had a considerably more *proportionate* figure than her companion as well, which Pixel thought a good thing, if only for his sanity. "Yeah..." Pixel shook his head, "Yeah, I mean, I was down in the engine room, checking out the systems. I just took a break for food, and then I got side-tracked at the armory..." He held out his box of cereal bars, "Want some?"

They both looked over their shoulder. Pixel recognized the two platters with the charred 'food' that Run had produced. "Uh, the little Chxor said that anyone who didn't eat his cooking would get volunteered for experimentation."

"He's joking," Pixel said, "I think. He doesn't have the authority to make that call, anyway."

"Chxor don't joke," Mandy said, and the sharp hatred in her voice made Pixel wince. "Ever. And I still don't know why you've kept that pet one around."

"He's useful," Pixel said. "He's saved a couple people's lives, at least." *Well, two if you count tranquilizing Rastar before the Chxor guards would have shot him in that riot,* he amended. Granted, Eric seemed more angry than grateful over his medical treatment, but he'd come through alright. "Plus he translated for Mike and Ariadne to pilot us out of there."

"Well, don't expect any gratitude from me," Miranda snapped. "His entire race shares responsibility for the atrocities they've committed on a dozen worlds."

Pixel made a mistake and looked back at Mandy after she spoke. His gaze dropped somewhere south of her face. He couldn't help it, and he desperately wondered if they had become large enough to have their own gravity well... He pulled his gaze up and met her eyes finally, "Yeah, did you just want to talk to me about Run? I've got a lot of stuff to do."

"I'm sure," Mandy scowled. "But no, that's not all. I understand that Elena has signed on with your team."

"Who?" Pixel asked.

"Elena Ludmilla Lakar," Mandy said patiently. "Bounty hunter, blonde, blue-eyed, two meters tall, we called her the ice queen because, well, never mind." She sighed again. Pixel wished she would stop with the sighing, it made his gaze drop again. She seemed to have very healthy lungs, among other things. "Anyway, I wanted to talk with you because you seem like a decent enough sort, and Ariadne's busy."

"Busy?" Pixel asked. He forced his brain to work, "Oh, yeah, she's interviewing the other passengers."

"Yeah, and there's a long line. We wanted to offer our services," Mandy said.

Pixel suddenly wondered if it were possible to die of embarrassment. "Yeah... services?"

"What she meant," Miranda said sharply, "Is that we both have skills that would help you. We fought the Chxor before both on Saragossa and other worlds. We've worked as revolutionaries and insurgents. But your team seems to have done more damage to the Chxor in the past few days than entire planets have over the past ten years. So we want to sign on."

Pixel forced himself to focus, "What skills do you bring?"

"Well, I'm mostly combat oriented," Mandy said. "And I've got pretty good people skills. Most people just can't say no to me. Miranda is a mechanic and she's pretty good with thread and needle for sewing people up. I've got a scar on my chest..."

Pixel closed his eyes. He ran through his calculations on the reactor power output and hoped that she did not lift up her shirt to show the scar. Well, actually, he hoped she did. *I really need to get out more,* he thought. "Yeah... well, I'll let the others know you're interested."

"We'd really like to talk with Ariadne," Mandy said. "Could you get her to swing by and talk with us? We're staying down in the cargo hold, right now."

"Of course," Pixel nodded. Honestly, he didn't trust anyone but a female to talk with Mandy. Or perhaps Anubus or Rastar, neither of them would be affected by her attributes, he imagined. "Well, I'll talk to you later."

"Sure," Mandy said. "And thanks for the cereal bars."

Pixel waved at them as he walked past. He did not entirely trust himself to look back. He definitely needed to get out more, he decided. He hadn't felt so flustered since his freshman year in high school. Thank god he had buckled down and graduated right after that, he didn't want to think about what three more years there would have been like.

Pixel stopped and stared at the aquarium for a moment to collect his thoughts. He rested one hand against the glass and peered into the tank. The soft blue colors calmed him, right up until the three meter long predator stirred from the bottom of the tank. Pixel gave out a shout of surprise and jumped back as the eel's jaws slammed against the glass of the tank right where his hand had rested.

"What is *that*?" Pixel said.

"It's an Arcavian Fighting Eel," Crowe said from his seat on a couch nearby. "Beautiful isn't it? Can you believe they're illegal on over thirty worlds?"

Pixel shook his hand, suddenly grateful that he hadn't decided to let his fingers trail in the water. "Yes. I can. That thing scared the crap out of me." He watched as the eel went through a dozen colors, some of them brighter than Rastar's Hawaiian shirt. It finally settled on a mottled blue that made it seem almost invisible in the water.

"Yeah, they're vicious predators," Crowe said. "But the fights are why they're illegal. The fights are amazing to watch, way more complex than dog fights or the like. They put two in a tank, and you won't believe the shit they do. It starts with them stalking each other, shifting colors and patterns...that can go on for hours or even days before one feels it has the advantage and attacks. Then the blood really flies..."

"You seem very interested in that," Pixel said. "I don't see the enjoyment of two animals killing each other for someone else's pleasure."

"Oh, I just like to see predators at work," Crowe said.

Pixel stepped away from the aquarium, suddenly certain that if he wanted to find peace, he'd need to search elsewhere.

"What's the matter?" Crowe called out after him, "Scared of what you see in there?"

His words echoed those of Jack, and Pixel felt his memories return even as he stepped out of the lounge. He had definitely chosen the wrong place to try and forget.

***

"I'm telling you, there's only one way to break through the public's apathy," Jack said. "We've got to show them the cost that comes with their lack of involvement."

"Yeah," Kevin rolled his eyes, "You're talking violence. Terrorism, really. Scare them into doing... what exactly, getting involved in politics? That sounds sort of counterproductive. Especially since the people doing the violence are the ones that you want them to vote for."

"Sure, in theory," Jack said. The shorter man rolled his head around and Kevin heard his neck crackle and pop. "But what if they didn't know who did it... or what if it seemed like the people in power let it happen or even arranged it themselves? We could have a change over night, planet wide, if that violence got enough attention."

"You're talking a lot of people dying," Kevin said. He shook his head, "I can't agree that this whole thing is worth it. I mean, we've had elections before, the people in power are the ones that our planet chose. You and I know they're idiots, but the people seem to want idiots in charge."

"That's because only fifteen percent of the population bothered to vote," Jack snarled. "Worse than that, there were no real candidates, the guys who get elected are just the public face. Everyone knows the bureaucrats have the reins now. That's the other reason no one votes."

"Yeah, but that won't change," Kevin said. "Not without something that would really need to shake things up, and I don't think the shake up would be worth it. You and I both ran simulations on that, and I didn't look afterward because I knew how bad it would get."

"What's the matter?" Jack said. "Afraid of what you see in

268

there?"

"Frankly, yeah," Kevin said. "The simulations we worked deliberately went for decapitation strikes, Jack, but they still would kill millions easily."

"That's what happens when intelligent people think about terrorism," Jack said softly, "Numbers like millions and tens of millions become easy to bring up. Who ever thought that a revolution could be gamed in a university lab by a couple of engineering students?"

"Well, it's all just a game, anyway," Kevin said. "I mean, neither of us could do something like that anyway."

"Yeah," Jack said, and something about the set of his shoulders suggested that he hadn't given up the argument. "But I bet someone else would, and I really don't trust anyone else to do it right, you know?"

"You stubborn idiot, come on, let's get back to work, say have you talked with Bridget lately?" Kevin asked.

"Yeah, that's over," Jack said. "She got a little too clingy, and after that whole deal with her parents, well, I broke up with her."

"Shit," Kevin said. He rarely swore, but he meant it, Jack had seemed far happier than normal when he and Bridget hit it off. He felt a little nervous his friend might slide towards one of his morose depressions, yet Jack gave him a smile instead.

"Hey, let's finish up this work, and you can tell me about your night with Christyne."

***

Pixel stepped onto the bridge just as Mike, Anubus, and Ariadne and a tall blonde woman stepped out of the lift. "Oh, hey guys, how's the lift working?"

"Good, why?" Mike asked.

"Oh, I thought I cut power to it, so I'm just surprised to see it works," Pixel said. "Now I have to find out what I did cut power to..." he frowned. *I really need to get Rastar to translate those schematics,* he thought, *some of this guess work might cause issues later on.*

269

"Okay," Ariadne said. "Well, let us know if it was anything critical please?"

"Sure," Pixel nodded. "Oh, hey, Mandy and Miranda wanted to talk with you. I think they want to join our team. They mentioned someone else..."

"Elena?" Mike asked and hiked his thumb over his shoulder at the tall blonde woman.

"I guess," Pixel gave Elena a nod. "How are you?"

She gave him a crisp nod, "I am well." She pronounced her words with a strong Eastern European accent, which Pixel figured placed her from Centauri or somewhere in the Confederation. "Mike has said I will be an associate member, until the team accepts me to full membership. You are engineer, yes?"

"Sure am," Pixel said with a smile. Something about her cold blue eyes chilled him. It might just be that he knew she was a bounty hunter, he thought. He looked at Mike, "What are you guys up to?"

"Mike forgot about the Chxor prisoner," Anubus growled.

"I didn't forget," Mike said. "We just had other stuff going on. And its not like she had anywhere to go."

"Uh, where is she?" Pixel asked.

Mike pointed at the supply closet hatch. "It locks from the outside. So I put her in there to cool off. So, shall we see what the prisoner has to say?"

Pixel shrugged, "Go for it, I'm going to check out some of the power usage here on the bridge." He paused, "That reminds me, I'd like to talk with you about that when you finish up with her."

"We should call Rastar," Ariadne said. "He'll want to be here."

"Good idea, he's pretty intimidating, especially with those riot guns of his," Mike said.

"What am I?" Anubus growled and flexed his claws.

"You're absolutely terrifying," Pixel said.

"You say the nicest things," Anubus growled. "When the others turn against me, I'll let you live." From someone else,

Pixel would have considered it a joke. From the deadpan growl of the Wrethe and the way his dark eyes glared at Mike and Ariadne, Pixel figured it a fifty-fifty shot that he really thought that way.

"Run would be useful," Anubus growled. "In case she doesn't understand English or a more civilized tongue."

"What do Wrethe speak anyway?" Ariadne asked.

"Whatever we want," Anubus growled.

"I'll be over here," Pixel said, as he pulled out tools. He just hoped that things did not devolve into violence as they tended to do around Anubus and Rastar. If for no other reason than the fact that Pixel didn't want to have to clean blood out of the panels he had open.

He had just traced out the conduit he had cut power to, and realized it went to the waste water system, when Rastar and Run arrived on the bridge. He glanced up as Run walked over, "Here is my end of the bargain. We are even now." The little Chxor passed him four vials.

"Thanks," Pixel said. He put the panel cover back on, and started to tighten it down by hand, but he let his attention drift to the interrogation.

Run walked back over to the group. Pixel saw Mike wave at Anubus to open the closet hatch.

A moment later, the female Chxor officer stepped out. Her brown uniform looked positively garish for other Chxor, with a number of marks along the sleeves and four white pips on the collar to denote her rank.

"I assume that you have decided to interrogate me?" she asked. Pixel's eyes widened as she spoke with clear, unaccented English. Better, in fact, than that of Elena. "Force will not be necessary. It is only logical that I tell you what I know in order to preserve my life."

"No loyalty to the Chxor Empire?" Mike asked.

"For my capture, they would sentence me to death, along with any genetic offspring of mine that survived your attack on Logan Two." She looked around at the group. "What is it you wish to know? I am Fleet Commander Krann, commander of

271

Fleet Two One Four."

"How many ships in your fleet?"

"Most were docked at the Logan Two Orbital Ring, however prior to that, I commanded sixty four dreadnoughts and two hundred and fifty six cruisers," Krann said.

"Two hundred and fifty cruisers?" Mike said, and Pixel didn't need to look over to see the shock on his face. "Sixty dreadnoughts? Was this a major offensive fleet?"

"No, this was the system defense fleet for the Logan system. It is the standard size for a Chxor fleet. Much like the one we sent to capture Danar from Nova Roma." Krann looked around the room. "In fact, it was my fleet which captured this ship, after it dropped out of shadow within our defensive perimeter. I personally brought the vessel back to Logan Two for scrapping."

"What happened to the crew?" Rastar asked.

"After we discovered that they had wiped the navigation data and erased their files, we processed them," Krann said. "The remains were used for fertilizer on Logan Three."

"You bitch," Rastar went dark red. "You just killed them without even a thought of what they'd gone through..."

"Rastar, that's enough," Mike said. Mike took a deep breath, "Why did you have them killed?"

"They had military training and from my previous experience with Ghornath, I knew they would be more trouble than they were worth as labor on a prison station or camp," Krann said. Her monotone almost seemed to have an edge of something, though, Pixel noted. Not quite smugness, but close, he thought. Her yellow eyes seemed bland enough, but something about her voice made him wish he could open her up as easily as a machine and look inside.

"Alright," Mike said and Pixel saw the other man had clenched his fists. Evidently he didn't like that she killed prisoners out of hand, either. "So why do we need you alive?"

"I know Chxor pass codes, both those for their military ships and their freighters, to include a handful of licensed human civilian ships. I know their patrol and convoy schedules. I know

272

military tactics, both for space combat and ground combat. I can act as your adviser in regards to these areas."

"What's your military experience?" Mike asked

"I participated in the pacification of Ghornath Prime, and acted as a field commander for the fifth pacification battalion-"

"You massacred Ghornath civilians!" Rastar shouted.

"Rastar, buddy, calm down." Mike said.

Pixel winced though when he saw that Rastar's hide had gone bright red, "No! I will not stand by while this Nakarta Shothu brags about her Grath noctu Mrabra!" Rastar took a step forward and brought his arms up, ready to smash the Chxor officer.

"Rastar!" Ariadne shouted. Pixel saw the big Ghornath shake his head, almost as if a fly buzzed around his ears. But he continued forward.

Over the enraged Ghornath's bellows, Pixel heard a distinctive ping. He looked over to see that Run had fired his new tranquilizer gun.

The big Ghornath paused. He looked down and pulled the dart out of his back. "You little Pthara Mragath! I Hrath Nranta Morbus!" The Ghornath changed direction and started towards Run. He brushed past Mike and didn't seem to notice as he knocked him over. Ariadne scrambled out of his way.

Pixel saw Run look down at his dart gun. The little Chxor lifted it up and fired again. The dart struck Rastar directly in the neck. The big alien didn't so much as slow as he went after Run.

Pixel started to come to his feet, not sure what he might do, but certain that he had to stop Rastar's attack on Run somehow.

Run looked down at his dart gun. He held it up to his face, and shook it and then turned it over once, as he peered at it in confusion. He seemed entirely oblivious to Rastar for the moment.

After one last shake, Run aimed his dart gun at Rastar. He fired five more darts in quick succession as Rastar charged him.

The drug finally had some effect on Rastar. The big alien stumbled. Then collapsed in an avalanche of muscle and bone. Pixel winced as Rastar's head bounced off the deck plates with an audible thud. Run walked forward and prodded him with his toe. "I may need to adjust the dosage for further use against him."

"Good job, Run," Mike said, as he picked himself off the floor.

Pixel looked at Krann then, and he thought he saw the slightest expression of satisfaction on her face. He felt a cold fear then, had she manipulated that outburst, had she planned to get Rastar angry in the hopes that he might hurt someone? *Is she that aware of others emotions that she can manipulate us*, Pixel thought. That last idea scared him, for the Chxor's only weakness so far had seemed to lie in their blindness to human emotion and reactions.

They already have the numbers and if they learn tactics that manipulate us, there's no way that humanity can beat them, Pixel thought grimly.

Yet the moment passed and when Fleet Commander Krann turned her head to meet his gaze, Pixel saw no more than the standard Chxor. If anything she seemed slightly puzzled by the outburst, for all that Pixel could read her.

Mike rubbed at his face. "Right, well, I think we're done for the moment. We'll decide whether or not to... what's the word you used, 'process,' right? We'll decide whether or not to process you once we get a bit of time to think about it," Mike said.

"If we process her, I request I be allowed to keep the remains to supplement my rations," Run said. "It is important that I get sufficient protein in my diet to maintain a healthy metabolism."

Mike nodded, "Of course. You can make her into puppy chow for all I care. After we decide, of course."

"Your threats are illogical," Krann said. "As is making a committee decision. My talents and the value of my information is obvious. You will want to retain me alive for those reasons. I will, however, wait your official decision. I assume I will be remanded to the closet in the meantime?"

"Yeah," Mike said. He tossed her a plastic pouch with Chxor glyphs on it. "Run said this is the most tasteless and nasty glop in his rations. Enjoy. And don't say we never gave you nothing."

She stepped back and Mike shut the hatch. He turned to face the pile of Ghornath on the floor. "What do we do with him? Will he be alright, Run?"

"I am not certain," Run said. "I might have given him too much of a dose of the pacification drug. There is the slight chance that his heart will stop and that he will die." Run looked up. "If that is the case, I request--"

"You're not cutting up Rastar," Ariadne said sharply.

"But Rastar will be deceased, therefore no longer Rastar, so I will merely dissect a Ghornath corpse which no longer has an identity-"

"No." Ariadne said.

"This is why I should receive more votes to become captain," Run said. "Then I will not be limited by your minimal understanding of science."

"Enough," Mike rubbed at his head again. "And don't resort to your 'command voice.' I don't think I could take that, you'd end up in the closet with Krann."

Rastar groaned.

Run scooted back a meter. "Very well. It appears that Rastar will awaken soon. As I have expended the entirety of my Ghornath darts on him, I will leave in the interests of maintenance of the peace," Run looked around. "Especially as he will likely notice the darts in him, and may suffer memory loss as to their origin."

"You don't want to explain why you had to shoot him, have him get mad and pound you, without being able to shoot him again?" Mike asked.

"This is an accurate statement," Run said. He stood on tip-toes and worked the door control, then scurried off the bridge.

Pixel stood up and went over to Rastar. He saw the big alien's eyes come open slowly. "Hey big guy, how you doing?"

"I feel very bad," Rastar's deep voice sounded gruff. His

hide had gone a deep, dark blue. "I dreamed... I dreamed of the refugee camps and of the stories from before. Of the genocide of Ghornath Prime..." His mirror eyes stared up at Pixel. "Have you ever wished that you could go back in time and change just one thing?"

Pixel looked down at the deck. "Every day of my life."

***

"Alright, everyone," Mike said. "I think we should move this downstairs. I hear that this ship has a lounge, let's meet there."

Anubus gave a deep throated growl, "I agreed to help interrogate the prisoner. Now I'm going to go back and see how much gold people stole from me while my back was turned."

"I'm sure your gold is fine," Ariadne said. "And really, remember, it's all our gold-"

"If you hear screaming, I will have found the thieves," Anubus growled as he stalked out.

Mike sighed, "Everyone needs a hobby, I suppose. Anyone else?"

Rastar shook his head, "I think I will go lie down. Let me know if you need me."

Pixel patted him on the shoulder. "You do that, big guy. I'll see you later."

Pixel followed the others off of the bridge. He saw Ariadne and Mike hesitate at the next deck down. "I know the way," Pixel said. He led the way down the corridor and then into the lounge. A strong smell of something spicy brought his attention towards a platter of food. *Hopefully that's a result of Simon and Eric working something out,* he thought.

He turned back to face Mike just as the other man swept his gaze around the room. The pilot froze then, and Pixel saw sweat bead his forehead.

"Mike, you okay?" Pixel asked.

Mike swallowed convulsively, "What is that?" He pointed at the floor to ceiling aquarium that took up the forward bulkhead. Pixel had a sudden thought that he should check out

276

how the crew had secured it to the wall and to check the tensile rating of the cystoplast

"Oh, cool, there's a fish tank," Ariadne said cheerfully. "I had a pet fish once." She walked up to the tank. "Doesn't look like there's anything in it though."

"Yeah, I wouldn't get too close--" Pixel started to say.

Ariadne tapped on the glass.

The Arcavian Fighting Eel exploded into motion. Its jaws snapped shut on the other side of the tank, and it flashed through a hundred colors as it tried to get at her through the glass. "Ooh, what a pretty fish," Ariadne said.

Pixel started to tell her it was an Arcavian Fighting Eel, but he froze though at a distinctive click behind him. He looked back to see that Mike had drawn his pistol and had it aimed roughly in the direction of the tank. Pixel considered it only roughly because Mike's hand shook too much to really consider it aimed at anything besides the entire compartment. "Uh, Mike?" Pixel asked.

Mike didn't answer, his eyes remained fixed on the eel.

Pixel walked slowly out of the line of fire and then moved to stand next to the Asian pilot. "Mike, can you hear me? Mike?"

"What?" Mike snapped.

"Yeah... Mike, you realize you have your gun aimed at an aquarium, right?" Pixel asked.

Mike looked down at his hand. "Shit." It seemed to take him a big effort to bring his arm down. Then Pixel saw his hands tremble as he tried to find his pistol holster while he kept his gaze on the eel. "What is *that*, and why is it in the lounge?" Mike said. A sheen of sweat covered his face and his voice sounded rough to Pixel.

"It's an Arcavian Fighting Eel," Pixel said helpfully.

"Ooh, sounds fierce for such a pretty thing. I think I'll call her Rainbow," Ariadne said. She still hadn't taken her gaze off of the eel. Pixel wondered if she knew how close she'd come to having bullet's fill the air around her.

Probably not, he thought.

"Why is it still on the ship?" Mike snapped. "I want that thing vented out an airlock, the damned aquarium too."

"Uh, it's really valuable, I think," Pixel said.

"It's a fish," Mike said. "Unless its made out of gold, I doubt its worth that much."

"You are *not* killing Rainbow," Ariadne said. The psychic turned around and Pixel saw a determined look on her face.

"You did not just name the fish," Mike said.

"Eel," Pixel corrected helpfully.

"Whatever," Mike growled. "That thing is dangerous and I don't want it on-board."

"Good thing you're not in charge then, right?" Ariadne asked. "If you don't like it, leave the lounge."

"I didn't say I was afraid of it!" Mike said.

"Uh, neither did she, actually," Pixel said.

Mike looked at the two of them. Pixel saw him clench his jaw. "Fine. Leave the stupid fish."

"Eel," Ariadne corrected. "And she has a name: Rainbow."

"Well, Rainbow better behave or her name will be sushi," Mike growled. He resolutely turned his back on the tank and walked over to the food. "Who the hell cooked? This actually smells pretty good." Despite his light words, Pixel thought the other man still looked jumpy.

"Oh, tonight it's oriental pepper steak, white rice, and a salad," Eric said from the doorway.

Pixel turned and saw the former soldier had two platters in his hands. Pixel hurried over to take one. Eric gave him a sharp nod and then walked over to set the tray down on the table. "We only have flash frozen vegetables for the salad, so I made a vinegar sauce to season it a bit."

"You can cook?" Ariadne asked. "I thought you were alpha male, hear me grunt, cave man style?" The psychic lifted the lid off a tray and stared at the food.

"I picked it up in the military, actually," Eric said with a shrug. "Military food quality leaves something to be desired. If

278

I wanted something that tasted good, I had to cook it myself."

Ariadne stared at him, "You can cook?"

"Eat up," Eric said. "Simon let the others know that food's available. Also, he had Crowe modify the galley control panels to limit access. But Run and Simon both volunteered to take the first week of kitchen clean up. We have to eat up a lot of this stuff because those idiots tore some stuff open. But I'll do meals while we've got stuff for it. After this though... well, some of the stored rations I can work with, but then we're down to ration bars again."

"You can cook?" Ariadne still stared at Eric.

"Evidently something besides violence busts through your cheerful shield," Eric said. "Yes, I cook. Well enough that at one time I wanted to start up a restaurant." His smile faded, "That didn't work out so well."

"Well," Mike said, as he loaded up a plate, "You're now the official chef of the *Gebnar* now."

"The what?" Pixel asked.

"The ship is the *Gebnar*," Ariadne said. "Rastar told me it means Fierce Toad."

"Clearly it loses something in translation," Mike said.

"Are you sure that he wasn't joking?"" Pixel frowned. "Which reminds me, I really need to get Rastar to translate some of the ship's manuals." He pulled out his datapad and grimaced as it flashed purple Chxor glyphs at him. "And I need a datapad I can read."

"I think Crowe found one," Eric said. "He used it to reprogram the controls on the galley, anyway." The man had taken a seat on one of the couches and he stared at the aquarium for a long moment. "Hey, where'd that fish come from?"

"It's an eel," Mike, Ariadne, and Pixel all said at the same time.

"Oh," Eric said. "It's pretty cool looking."

Mike grunted and turned to face Pixel. He managed to do it without bringing the tank into his line of view, Pixel noted. "You mentioned earlier you wanted to tell me something about the ship's power? Is there some kind of problem?"

Pixel nodded, "Right, thanks for the reminder. The reactor took some damage when the Chxor captured it, or possibly before that, I'm not real certain."

"Crowe's trying to salvage something from the main computer, the Ghornath crew wiped it pretty thoroughly before the Chxor boarded," Mike said.

"Oh, well, that might tell me *how* it happened, but it doesn't change *what* happened," Pixel said. "It looks like some sort of power surge fried some of the conductive filaments in the reactor coils. It's something I could probably fix in a week or so, less time with some helping hands. But we'd need to shut down the reactor. And I'd need around..." Pixel glanced at his datapad, "Two hundred meters of thin conductive wire."

"Do you want to scavenge that from elsewhere on the ship?" Mike frowned. He seemed calmer as he thought about the problem, Pixel thought. He didn't know why the eel and the aquarium bothered Mike, but he doubted he'd get a real answer if he just asked.

"No, I can make the wire out of any conductive metal with the ship's tools, though it will take some time. The problem is that I'll need more material for a less conductive metal like iron and less for something like copper," Pixel said.

"Alright, well, I'd suggest you work on what you can for now. After we choose a captain, you can probably make your case to whoever it is and we can go from there."

"Right, I just thought you should know," Pixel said. "By the way, are you really sure about this whole captain thing? I mean, things have worked well so far..."

Mike nodded, "Totally certain. We did well before because we had one goal to work towards. Now... well now we will have nine individuals who want to do their own thing. That kind of chaos can get us all killed."

Pixel sighed. He understood Mike's argument, yet he disagreed on principle. Pixel wondered how he could convince the others, how he could make them see that their strength lay in their different talents, and that one person in charge of them would limit their abilities.

But he didn't want to start an argument, and with how tense Mike seemed around the aquarium, Pixel figured the wrong word might trigger that. "Well, thanks for the talk. I'm going to head down to finish up some work." He looked over at Eric, "Thanks for the food."

Eric gave him a nod.

As Pixel walked out of the ship's lounge, his mind struggled more with the philosophical problem than any of the matters with the ship, though. How could he change the others opinions, how could he show them that they didn't need a captain?

And why did he feel so uneasy about his own position?

***

Pixel woke up early the next morning and slipped out of the officers cabin he shared with the others. The Ghornath 'beds' were what amounted to super-sized beanbag chairs or nests. Pixel found it remarkably comfortable, but his mind had remained abuzz with thoughts that prevented much sleep.

When he got to the engine room, he decided to see what he could do about the bank of charred capacitors that ran along the central column of the ship. Each of the capacitors weighed around twenty kilograms, but some had fused together and others had shattered. Worse, either end of the capacitor bank had direct ties into the ship's power, so the damage meant a number of direct shorts to the hull.

Pixel had cut the two connections to the main power bus and had just started to pull out the first of the damaged capacitors when Eric spoke from behind him. "Pixel, I wanted to get your help on something."

Pixel grunted as he pulled the twenty kilo capacitor out and dropped it on the portable work bench he'd already positioned. "What?" He couldn't help but snap. The lack of sleep had affected him more than he thought or maybe it was just the work.

"Uh, remember I wanted to do some more explosives? Well, Simon and I worked out a deal, that he'd help me out if I'd do some cooking. Which works out, really, but I wanted to know if you could make me some casings for grenades."

"I'm kind of busy here," Pixel said, and gestured at the bank of capacitors.

"You've got to pull all of those?" Eric asked. "Wow... that looks like a major job."

"It is," Pixel said.

"Wow, I hadn't realized the ship took this much damage from before," Eric said.

"It didn't," Pixel said. "Remember when you bypassed the lockouts and tried to power up the main gun? This is the capacitor bank you blew out."

"Oh," Eric looked at the twenty kilo capacitor, "So I take it you probably won't get to the grenade casings today?"

Pixel shook his head. He reminded himself that Eric meant well, "No, probably not today."

"Well, I'll let the others know you need help down here if none of them are busy," Eric said as he turned around and walked out.

"Right," Pixel moved to the next capacitor. He thought about the situation a bit as he worked. His anger at Eric faded a bit as he went into problem solution mode. He didn't think Eric even realized that Pixel might be angry with him for his creation of more work. For that matter, he felt certain that Eric thought his request for grenade casings just as important as any other job Pixel might have to do.

Anger with Eric over that attitude would do him no good, Pixel knew. Just as anger with Mike and Simon for their desire for a ship's captain would do no good. Pixel needed to think through the issue and find a solution. Really, he wished the others would spend more time with that. He felt certain that if he could only convince them to think for themselves, rather than to react, they would see his point.

But they all seemed stubbornly set on the need for a captain, as if someone to tell them what to do would absolve them of the requirement to think for themselves.

Pixel slammed a melted capacitor down on the work

bench harder than he needed to and it shattered into several chunks. Pixel waved a hand in front of his face and coughed at the cloud of dust.

"Hey Pixel," Ariadne said cheerfully behind him.

Pixel sighed, "Hi, Ariadne, what can I do for you?" He didn't bother to turn around.

"I'm here to help, actually," Ariadne said. "And I brought more help."

"Really?" Pixel turned. He saw Mandy and Miranda behind her, as well as three men he vaguely remembered amongst the other escaped prisoners.

"Yep!" Ariadne said cheerfully, "Mandy and I are unskilled labor. But Miranda has some mechanical skills, and Feofil, Anastasiy, and Matvei all worked aboard a Centauri freighter before."

Pixel stared at them for a long moment. Finally he shrugged, "That works, I guess. Well, I'm pulling the damaged capacitors out of the bank. I already marked them, so any of them with an orange or red mark pull out and then stack them. Damaged ones on this bench and the destroyed ones over there," Pixel waved at a pile of capacitors.

They went into motion and Pixel stood back and let them work for a moment. It felt strange, almost like an invasion of his privacy, at first. Pixel realized that he had grown too solitary. He really needed to get out more. He joined them as they worked and after a moment, he found he enjoyed working with a group again.

"So, I take it you had a chance to talk with Mandy and Miranda?" Pixel asked quietly.

"Oh, yeah, they're both pretty helpful," Ariadne said with a smile. Yet for a moment, she almost looked guilty, as if she had some kind of secret. "I figure we need more girls on the team anyway, too much testosterone and... well whatever it is that Wrethe, Chxor and Ghornath males produce."

Pixel frowned at that, though he couldn't disagree. Then again, Wrethe didn't have a sex, so her statement seemed somewhat inaccurate. "Same deal as with Elena?" Pixel asked,

"Sort of provisional members until the group signs off of them?"

"Yeah. But I'm not sure how long they'll stay with us," Ariadne said softly. "Mandy seems kind of flighty sometimes."

Pixel stopped his work and stared at her. She seemed serious enough. "How's Rainbow?"

"Oh, she's good. I fed her the scraps from dinner."

Pixel thought this the best chance to try his idea, "You know, depending on who they elect tyrant, I mean captain, they might want to get rid of your new pet, or even just sell it."

"Yeah," Ariadne nodded. "Truthfully, I'm not big on the whole idea of electing a captain. But the others seem pretty set on it. Though it would make decisions quicker. And someone with some authority to tell some of the other escapees what to do would be nice."

Pixel chewed on his lip in thought. He wasn't sure whether to consider her admission a victory or defeat. "So what will you do during the election?"

She shot him a look, "I've already chosen who I'll vote for. I picked the person least likely to micromanage, I think."

"Huh," Pixel frowned at that. The only person he could think of in that regard might be Rastar. "Well that works I guess." He decided he'd have to change tactics come the meeting later in the day. He would need to think up a new tactic first, though.

"Hey, Pixel, what's this thing?" Ariadne asked. She pointed at a panel of glowing indicator lights next to the capacitor bank.

I really need to get Rastar down here to translate those manuals, Pixel thought yet again. "I'm not entirely certain, I haven't traced that one out yet."

"Oh," Ariadne said. "Well, I'm sure you'll have time."

Pixel snorted, "Maybe not. Everyone keeps bringing more work for me. Eric just came by, and I'm sure that others will have stuff for me to do soon enough."

"At least you haven't had to spend the past day interviewing people. Some of them were very unpleasant," Ariadne said, "Present company excepted of course."

"Oh?" Pixel asked.

"She's got to be talking about the Nova Roman Ambassador, she's *such* a bitch," Mandy said.

Miranda spoke up from further away, "Lady Alara Vibius. Some rich-bitch daughter of some noble. Very full of herself. The marines with her seem pretty decent though. I feel sorry for them, stuck waiting on that ambassador, I bet they want to kill her. I know I would if I had to protect her sorry ass all day."

"They support the Nova Roma expansionist tendencies," Mandy snapped. "They're just as culpable as she is for pushing that crap. I'm glad the Chxor are fighting them, it takes some pressure off the rest of the colonies."

"Well, what happens when Nova Roma falls?" Pixel asked. "I mean, I don't know much about the strategy of war, but they've got the most solid military I've heard about, the biggest shipyards, all of that. If the Chxor beat them and no one else steps in, won't the Chxor just move on and capture the rest of human space?"

Mandy frowned. "Well, I suppose. But that will take some time and give the rest of us time to prepare to fight them, anyway. Don't get me wrong. I hate the Chxor, but the Nova Romans are not much better. They've conquered dozens of colonies in the past ten years alone."

"Well, I don't really know much about them," Ariadne said. "But if their choice of ambassador to the Chxor is any sign..."

"Maybe they sent her there to annoy them?" Pixel suggested.

Mandy paused, "You know, inflicting her on the Chxor would be one hell of a bit of psychological warfare. I mean, if they viewed her as expendable..." She shook her head, "Nah, the arrogant bitch seems too well connected. I'll just chock it up to incompetence."

Pixel let the conversation drop. He had heard plenty of negative commentary from people about the Nova Romans. Even so, he wondered what they had accomplished in the positive. Surely they must have done something right if they had

285

men such as the pair of Marines who guarded their ambassador. Men who stayed loyal despite the hell they must have gone through on the prison station and in whatever fight killed their fellow Marines.

Pixel figured that he should probably talk with them or some of the other Nova Roma passengers, when he got the chance. Sometime after he took care of the long list of other things he had to do, of course.

***

Pixel had called the work off just before lunch. They had already removed the damaged and destroyed capacitors at that point. He gave the three experienced space hands some directions on how he wanted the area cleaned, and then told them to work on it later. As the others walked out, Pixel paged through the inventory of spare parts on the main engineering console.

He recognized the symbols for the capacitors or at least he thought he did. The ship didn't have a full set of spares, but they might have enough, he hoped, that if he could repair some of the damaged capacitors they could get the weapon operational.

"Engineer Pixel, I have come to a decision," Run's high pitched voice spoke from behind him.

Pixel turned around and raised an eyebrow. "Oh?"

"Yes, I have decided after much review that you possess an intellect that somewhat approaches my own. This is a rare honor, as I have only encountered a handful of sentient beings so capable. I therefore offer you this rare opportunity to become my research associate."

"What would that entail?" Pixel asked suspiciously.

"You would help me on whatever research I conduct which requires your knowledge of mechanical or other areas of physical engineering," Run said. "In return, my knowledge of chemistry, biological processes, and my own vast intelligence would be at your service when necessary." He said it with such benevolence in his voice that Pixel barely kept a smile off his face. *I somehow doubt he'll be very eager to drop whatever project he's working on and help me out whenever I ask,* Pixel thought dryly, *still...* After his work with a group earlier, he felt suddenly reminded of how he had missed that feeling when engaged in research and design.

"Alright," Pixel said. "I can work with that, glad to know you consider me your equal."

Run blinked at him, "While I value your intelligence, you remain inferior in many ways to myself. However, do not let this fact depress you, as I have yet to find my equal. Indeed, among the crew, you are the only one I find capable of intelligent conversation."

Pixel scratched his head. The little Chxor seemed to expect some kind of response to that. "Yeah... Thanks?"

"Your thanks are not necessary, this is merely a statement of fact." Run raised his chin, "In addition, I require a sample of your genetic material to study. I find your remarkable intelligence in an inferior species to be very interesting, and I would like to determine whether it has a chemical, genetic, or some other cause."

"Will it cause me excruciating pain or to die?" Pixel asked cautiously.

Run stood in thought for a rather long moment. "No, I do not think so. I just need a small blood sample."

Pixel stuck out his arm. "Get it over with."

Run pulled out a needle and a small vial. He jabbed him once and then tucked the needle and vial into a pouch on his belt. "I appreciate your assistance in this research. Also, I have another offer for your consideration. I believe I have found a solution for the issue that faces both of us upon the selection of a ship's captain," Run said. "I am certain you will agree that several of the options for command lack the interest and dedication to research and science that you and I both share."

"That's a safe bet," Pixel nodded.

"Yet we still need a strong hand to guide the others, to ensure that they put their full effort into our pursuit of the sciences," Run said. The little Chxor stood very straight, almost as if he felt taller as he spoke. Pixel decided not to mention that he disagreed with him there. He really didn't mind what the others did, as long as he could do what he wanted. "So obviously, I should be selected as captain, and both of us will find the resources and freedom to pursue our goals."

Pixel frowned. On the one hand, Run might well be the worst possible choice as captain. He could very well see that some of the group might have serious (and valid) concerns about putting Run in charge. For one thing, his lack of anything resembling empathy would be an issue, Pixel felt certain. On the other hand, he thought that Run would keep his bargain. Pixel would have total freedom to conduct his research... no one would interfere in that.

Well, nothing besides limits on funds, materials, and whatever issues come up with him as captain, which are sure to be a pretty big distraction, Pixel acknowledged.

Then again, Pixel realized that those issues might well cause the others to come around to his own perspective. Run could easily serve as an example of how things could go wrong with someone in charge, rather than their operation as a group of free-minded individuals.

"You know, that doesn't sound like a bad idea," Pixel said slowly. "But just two votes is unlikely to win you the election."

"I have taken this into consideration. I believe I have worked out other such mutually beneficial arrangements for the remainder of votes I will need," Run said. He did not elaborate further, and Pixel wondered what the little alien had promised others for their acceptance. He could not picture Eric or Rastar voting for Run. Or Mike for that matter. Really, he found it difficult to picture *anyone* else might select Run as the captain.

"Yeah, well, either way, I guess good luck," Pixel said. "I'm going to get some lunch, care to join me?"

"No, I must get your sample to my lab. Also I found that human eating habits seem rather repetitive. I had hoped them to be more interesting." Run frowned. "In addition, if you see Ariadne or the human with the swollen chest, inform them that I await an answer to my request to observe their reproduction methods."

Pixel made a note on his datapad to not admit that he'd seen Run if Mandy or Ariadne asked.

Run stepped out of the engine room, and after he closed down the console, Pixel followed him out. He considered further exploration of the ship on his way to lunch, but his stomach rumbled to remind him that he had skipped breakfast. He took the direct route and ran into an older man as he stepped out of the stairwell onto the second deck.

"Excuse me," Pixel said.

"Oh, this is entirely my fault," the man said, and Pixel recognized his accent immediately. There were only a handful of french colonies all of them lay near his own home system. "Pardon me, but are you the engineer?" The old man had dark black hair in a comb-over that seemed to start south of his ear. He also wore the remains of a plaid jacket.

"Yes," Pixel said, and tried to smile. The fake smile felt wooden on his face.

"I wanted to speak with you, in regards to your degree. I had heard you graduated from Lithia System University?"

"Yes..." Pixel frowned, "Where did you hear that?" He tried to remember if he had shared that information with anyone. He couldn't remember if he had even told anyone about his home system.

"Well, you see, I recognized your accent, and I knew that there's only one real engineering school in that system," the old man said. "I had a number of colleagues from Lithia, you see, and in my line of work, I learn to recognize accents, it saves so much time at conferences."

"You're a professor?" Pixel felt his heart drop. Did this man know who he was?

"Oh, yes, I am Professor of Xenoarchaeology Bastien Jascinthe of Loire," the old man nodded. He adjusted his bow-tie. "And my main concern was what field of engineering you studied? I was on a dig in the Garan system when the Chxor captured me. I have managed to preserve my notes from my dig there and I wanted an engineer's evaluation of the structural integrity of the dig location. You see, as soon as we get back to human space, I plan to launch another expedition there, and I want to make certain the dig location remains intact."

Pixel frowned, "Do you think it's wise to go back to the location the Chxor captured you?"

"My dear boy, the site lies near a Chxor industrial center, I feel certain if I don't move quickly they will damage or destroy it. I had nearly excavated what I believe was the control room for the alien facility. If I don't get some solid results, my grant will expire. And I think there may be intact devices there. The site could be worth millions!"

"Huh," Pixel frowned. "Yeah, I guess I can look at it."

"Excellent," Bastien passed over a data chip. "This is just the structural overlay of the tunnels and the previous excavation on the site. My partner had a copy as well, but I'm not certain if he survived. He made an escape attempt when the Chxor first captured us."

"Huh," Pixel said. "Well, I'll check it out."

"Thank you," The professor cocked his head, "I am curious, were you on Origin when the terrorist attack destroyed the capital? I understand the university survived."

"Yeah," Pixel said, his voice suddenly harsh. "I was there at the time. I left not long afterward."

"Ah, terrible business, no? I had a number of colleagues who died at an xenoarch conference downtown."

"My condolences," Pixel said.

"It worked out for me, there was less competition for research grants for years. And I never had to see that unmitigated ass Jean again or his harridan of a wife. So some good came of it, at least. I understand they never caught the terrorists responsible, can you imagine?" Bastien shook his head. "That kind of thing would *never* happen on Loire."

"Yeah..." Pixel said. "Well, I'm headed to lunch. I'll let you know what I can about the dig site when I get around to it." He walked past the other man and down the corridor before the professor could make any response.

He made it to the lounge without further incident, but even the smell of good food did not make him feel better. He clenched his hands as he leaned against the wall. He didn't know how he felt. He felt angry, but his anger at Bastien Jascinthe had tangled with his anger at himself. He felt fear, too, fear of discovery, fear that his friends might hate him if they learned the truth. And he felt... tired. Tired of the judgment that had hung over his head for so long.

"Hey there Pixel, how's life?" Crowe asked.

Pixel looked up, surprised that he hadn't seen the other man when he came into the lounge. "You're pretty sneaky sometimes," Pixel said.

Crowe gave him a smirk, "Something I've picked up. Sometimes it's useful to remain unseen."

"I guess," Pixel said. He did not feel up to conversation, especially not with Crowe.

"Hey, I heard you had some issues with your datapad," Crowe said.

Pixel closed his eyes, "Yeah, it keeps displaying Chxor gibberish now and again."

"Well, I found a Sunto-Crispin 5909," Crowe held up the datapad, "It's a pretty nice one, I might be willing to give you it..."

"What do you want?" Pixel asked, resigned to have to deal with the other man.

"Well, not to add more to your plate, but I've got my components assembled for a computer build. Not just a datapad, but something with some serious processing power. I can handle the software, but I wanted you to put it together. I'm not as good at hardware."

"You want it to plug into your neural jack?" Pixel asked, interested despite himself.

"Yes, and I've got a Shintaru wireless modem off a security terminal back on the prison station, found it down in the Pit, stuck in some scrap," Crowe nudged a plastic carton with his foot. "Its all in there. As a token, you can have the datapad now, but I'd like this stuff soon, I still have to finish my work with the ship's data restoration and some other stuff."

"Any luck with that?" Pixel asked, even as he walked

over to look down at the carton of parts.

Crowe snorted, "I might get pieces of the ship's log. A few other things, but the navigation data got overwritten fifteen times by their scramble program. There's nothing I can get out of that. Not sure what else I can get, really, but it's something to do."

"Right," Pixel leaned over to root through the box a bit. Some of the parts looked damaged, which meant he'd have a lot of work to get anything functional. Even so, the idea seemed interesting enough. He already thought about how he could use the machine shop tools to repair or salvage parts off the different boards.

He straightened up, "I'll see what I can do. It'll take a lot of work, though."

"So I expect," Crowe smirked. "Let me know when you finish. Oh and the smoked crab is excellent, I highly recommend it."

***

Pixel showed up a few minutes late to the election. The others did not seem particularly unhappy about it. Mike had the Chxor officer Krann out of the closet and Eric continued to speak as Pixel stepped onto the bridge, "...before, I still say we keep just one Chxor at a time. We don't need Chxor pass codes or patrol schedules if we're headed out of Chxor space. We just kill her now, before she finds some way to screw us later."

"I agree with Eric," Rastar said. "And more, she is a war criminal who committed atrocities against my people. When we kill her, I request the honor of doing so."

"We'll keep that in mind," Mike said. He looked over at Pixel, "Now that we're all here, I think we can start our little election."

"What about the others who are up here?" Crowe asked sharply. "They don't get a vote, do they? I mean, one emotional female is bad enough, but three more exceeds my limit of listening to women."

"Your concern touches," Mandy snapped.

"I'd like to do some touching, all right," Crowe smirked. "But I'm busy doing grown up things. Maybe later?"

"Quiet," Anubus growled. "I find this constant bickering tries my patience. You do not want to exceed my *very* limited patience."

"Anubus," Crowe said, "you don't scare me."

Anubus leaned forward. "Try me," He drew his lips back in a snarl, "...please."

"Hey, guys, remember about the vote?" Ariadne said cheerfully. "How about we get started?"

"I agree, we should initiate the vote and select me as commander of the ship," Run said.

Pixel saw the Chxor prisoner's eyes narrow at that. Evidently she had not realized that they valued Run as a full member of the crew.

"I'll start," Anubus growled. "I vote for Run."

Everyone stared at him in shock. "Why is that?" Mike asked.

"He bribed me, why else?" Anubus said.

"Alright, well, I'll go next," Pixel said. "I vote for Run as well."

The room had gone quiet enough that Pixel had to seriously fight the urge to let out his evil laughter he had practiced... or even just a mad cackle.

Run stepped forward, "I vote for myself as well, and will graciously accept victory-"

"Vote's not over yet," Eric snapped. "And I still think we should space you." Eric looked around at the group. "I think we need someone who's a thinker, and someone we all trust to think for the crew and ship." Pixel tried not to roll his eyes. Surely Eric didn't plan to vote for himself again, did he? "So Rastar and I have talked it over for a bit. I vote for Pixel. He's one hell of a guy, and I think he'll do a great job."

Pixel stared at him. "What?!"

Rastar stood up, "I agree. Pixel has constantly applied critical thought to problems as they arise and he has always acted in the good interest of the crew. I vote for Pixel."

"But I don't want to be captain!" Pixel said. "Hell, I don't even *want* a captain."

Crowe waved a hand, "Doesn't matter, you're stuck with it if they select you. He looked around at the group, "Well, this might seem crazy, but I'll explain myself before I make this vote." He took a deep breath, "We need someone with lots of experience, someone who knows this area of space. We need someone who can think logically and not get emotionally involved, and who doesn't have a stake in this. Therefore, I vote for Krann the Chxor."

"Are you insane?" Rastar surged to his feet. "I will not accept this! This is an insult and an outrage--"

"Sit down," Anubus growled, "Before I make you sit down."

"Quiet, both of you," Mike said. "Crowe's vote is his to cast how he wants." He shook his his head, almost as if bothered by a thought. "As is mine. I think that Crowe made a good point. I vote for Krann, she's got a lot of experience I think we could benefit from."

Pixel stared at Mike, somehow certain that this must be part of some strange prank.

Yet Simon stepped forward, as if nothing unusual had come from Mike. He nodded gravely, "I believe that we have too much chaos, too many voices. I think we need someone who knows how to institute a bit of order. I vote for Krann as well."

Pixel felt his stomach drop as he realized that their Chxor prisoner had three votes, and so did Run. For that matter, two of the crew had voted for *him*, which confused him enough. All eyes in the room went to Ariadne.

"Wow, that's no pressure or anything," Ariadne said. "I'm the deciding vote..." She shook her head, "Well, I talked with Rastar before this, and I agree with the points he made. I vote for Pixel as captain."

"This is unacceptable," Run said. Pixel looked over just in time to see Run draw his dart gun and fire.

Pixel swatted at the dart in his neck. He stared at Run in shock, "But... I voted for *you*..."

The world went black.

***

Pixel came to propped on one of the Ghornath couches on the bridge. His head throbbed and his right eye stubbornly refused to focus. "Ugh, what happened?"

"Run shot you and the other Chxor, and then claimed victory as Captain," Eric said.

"What happened after that?" Pixel asked. He looked around blearily, but he saw no sign of the little Chxor. His head hurt terribly and he felt like his tongue was two or three times its normal size.

"I took his gun and threw him off the bridge," Mike said. "I won't tolerate that behavior."

"So where do we stand?" Pixel asked, as he managed to stand up. The room spun around him slightly but he shook his head to clear it.

"We've got a deadlock... again," Mike said. "This is why we need... he shook his head, as if he'd lost his train of thought. "This is why we need... Krann as captain," he said. Pixel stared at him, and his gaze went to Simon and Crowe as well. Simon seemed confused for a moment, but then he nodded. Crowe looked suddenly uncomfortable. It was almost as if they didn't know what was going on or as if they were machines that had received directions that countermanded one another...

Pixel's eyes widened and he looked over at Ariadne. She had her eyes narrowed as she looked between the three who'd voted for Krann. She felt his gaze and looked over. She seemed to understand the questioning look he gave her or maybe she just read his mind. She gave him a nod.

"I think we'll take a break, here," Ariadne said cheerfully. "Pixel, I wanted to talk with you about some of that capacitor fluid we changed earlier today."

"Capacitor... fluid?" Pixel asked.

"Yes," Ariadne's smile grew brittle. "Remember, the capacitor lubricant that you thought Rastar and Anubus might know how to find?"

295

Pixel looked at both the two big aliens. "I did?"

"Yes," Ariadne said, "You did. We should talk about that. Now."

"Oh... sure," Pixel said. "Anubus, Rastar, let's go talk about capacitor... lubricant."

He led them off the bridge and a moment later Ariadne joined them. "We need someplace we can't be overheard," she said quietly.

Anubus nodded, "This way," he growled.

He led them down a corridor, and then down a narrow stairwell. That stairwell opened up on a small room whose design Pixel couldn't guess. It had an interesting shape, though and he brought up his new datapad absently as he tried to figure out the purpose from the schematics.

"Okay," Ariadne said. "Sorry about the capacitor fluid thing, Pixel, I had to think of an excuse to get you all where I could talk to you."

Ariadne looked around at them, "I hate to suggest this, but did our friends seem, a bit odd during the vote?"

"They voted for that genocidal Mokta Rhagu," Rastar said, his hide tinged red. "I do not understand how they can consider themselves my friends and still do this."

Pixel spoke, "It almost looked like they were confused... like someone messed with their minds."

"Exactly," Ariadne nodded. "And I felt it happen, at least the second time with Mike. Someone in that room used their abilities to bend Mike and Simon around to vote for Krann." She met their gazes, "And I swear to you it wasn't me. For one thing, she creeps me out."

"I felt it too," Anubus growled.

"You're a psychic?" Pixel asked. He suddenly felt even more terrified of the Wrethe.

"Only a little," he growled. "Enough in some areas that I could sense something happen." He glared at Pixel, "If you tell anyone else, I might have to kill you."

"Hey man, we need to work together on this," Rastar said. "And Pixel's a good guy, he won't share your secret."

"Why just those two?" Pixel asked. "Why not all of us?"

"It takes attention and focus to bend someone's mind like that," Ariadne said. "I don't think I could manage it, not against more than one person at a time, that's for sure." She frowned, "And truthfully... well, Mike has a mind that would be more open to that kind of thing than most of the rest of you. Rastar's an alien and he hates the Chxor, so I doubt that he'd bend to that kind of control."

She looked over at Pixel, "Your mind is pretty resistant, just the way you think. So I think you're safe enough. Simon... he's very order and logic oriented, if they went after him that way, they could do it pretty easily."

"So someone attacked Mike's mind and Simon and Crowe," Rastar said. "To do what, try to get the Chxor Krann selected as captain?" He shook his head, and his hide turned a yellow color. "This makes no sense. What purpose does this serve?"

"That I don't know," Ariadne said. "It could be that Krann is the psychic..."

"That's very unlikely," Rastar said. "My people have never heard of a Chxor psychic."

"Well, *someone* did it," Ariadne said. "And that makes as much sense as anything else right now. Whoever it was, they might try again. We have to keep our eyes open for this kind of thing."

"So we have a rogue psychic aboard," Pixel said. "That's bad."

"It was probably someone in the room," Anubus growled. "Possibly one of the new humans who wanted to join the crew. They might seek to incite division so that they can take the position of those we kill in the subsequent fighting."

"Man, that's pretty coldblooded," Rastar said. "I mean, come on man, you know we couldn't kill any of our friends!"

"I have no friends," Anubus growled. "Only enemies who have yet to reveal their true nature."

"Could it be someone else, doing it by remote, like you managed?" Pixel asked.

297

Ariadne nodded slowly, "Yes... for that matter, there could be a Shadowlord vessel trailing us right now, trying to drive us insane before they board. But unfortunately, I think Anubis is right."

"Of course I am," Anubus growled. "We should kill the others in the room, just to eliminate the threat."

"No!" Pixel said. "Some of them are good people."

"That doesn't matter to me," Anubus growled. "They're still a threat because our enemy hides among them. Killing them will end the threat or drive our enemy into the open."

"We aren't killing anyone," Ariadne said. "And anyway, the psychic tipped his or her hand, already. We know about this threat, so we need to keep our eyes open and stay alert."

"How do we do that, without tipping off a mind reader?" Pixel asked. "I mean, you said he or she can't mess with our heads, or not easily, but that doesn't mean they can't read our thoughts and realize what we're up to, right?"

"Yes," Ariadne said. "For that matter, he or she might already know that we realized what happened. But that's a risk we will have to take. If you are around someone we've identified as the possible psychic, try to think of something that requires a lot of attention. I can shield my mind and those of people nearby, but if your brain is fully occupied, they won't find our suspicions in our surface thoughts." Pixel saw Ariadne chew on her lips nervously. Finally she let out a deep breath. "Look, I know it wasn't Mandy or Miranda."

"Why?" Pixel asked.

"Because the reason they wanted to talk to me is that they're both psychics," she said after a long pause. "And they asked me to keep it quiet. But neither of them are very powerful, not nearly as powerful as this would require. And neither of their abilities lie in telepathy."

"How do you know?" Anubus growled, "Perhaps they deceived you. Perhaps they plotted–"

"I checked them out, pretty thoroughly after I learned they hid that from us. And it is far easier to hide psychic abilities in the first place than to mask what ones you have when you've revealed them, or at least that's the feeling I get from them," Ariadne said. "And for that matter, they hate the Chxor as much as Rastar."

Pixel rubbed at his eyes, "Well that still leaves Elena and our Chxor prisoner..."

"And Crowe," Ariadne said softly.

"Crowe?" Rastar asked, "But he seemed just as confused as the others."

"Yes, but I never sensed anyone tamper with his mind." Ariadne said. "As far as I can tell, he made that vote on his own."

Pixel rubbed at his chin. He really needed to grow a beard or something to give him the appropriate somber look when he found himself struck by eloquence, "Well... shit."

***

Pixel cornered Run in the lounge, "Run, I need to talk with you."

"If you have an irrational grudge against me for my attack on you, I assure you that it is misplaced," Run said. "I only attempted to follow through on my plan to--"

"Oh, that?" Pixel shrugged, "Water under the bridge. No I had a question for you."

"Water under the bridge..." Run muttered to himself. "I see." He looked up, "Of course I offer my assistance to whatever line of research you pursue."

"Great," Pixel said. He glanced around the lounge, and made certain to keep his voice low. "I want to know if the Chxor have any psychics."

"No," Run said.

"No you don't know or no there aren't any?"

The little Chxor shook his head, "No Chxor has ever manifested psychic powers. Some of the greatest minds in science, barring myself, have researched that extensively. All attempts at induction of psychic abilities to include genetic manipulation and biomechanical augmentation have failed."

"You're saying that you're aware of every attempt, and

299

that your people have tested your entire population, that's got to be in the tens if not hundreds of billions, right?"

"The population of the Chxor Empire passed thirty trillion as of the last census, approximately three of your months ago," Run said. He seemed almost offended at the insinuation that his people might not have complete knowledge. "Among the various tests that all Chxor receive is a test for psychic potential. This includes a magnetic resonance scan of the brain and a quantum reaction test. No Chxor has ever shown anything near the level of even a latent psychic in over seven thousand years of our recorded examinations."

"Not even one, huh?" Pixel asked. "Well, so much for that idea."

"Although, negative data does not disprove something, I must conclude that my race has no capabilities for psychic potential," Run said. "Which is why I need to examine the brain tissue of human psychics, to see if their hormonal imbalances and emotional irrationality somehow ties into their abilities."

"Yeah," Pixel nodded, "That actually makes sense..." He looked up as Crowe stepped into the lounge. The other man looked around the room and then noticed Pixel and Run. He walked over, and something about his walk and his clenched fists suggested anger. Pixel tried to focus on the sketch he had drawn up of the computer for Crowe, even as he hoped that the other man was not the psychic they hunted.

"You voted for a captain without me?" Crowe demanded.

"I'm sorry, what?" Pixel stared at the other man without comprehension.

"I think that you suffer from mental instability," Run said. "You clearly suffer from delusions. You were present at the vote."

"I was not," Crowe said. "One of the passengers passed me a message from Mike, that he wanted me to check out something in the communications array up near the bow. By the time I finished that, I ran into Eric coming back from the vote. Cranky bastard almost ran me over in the corridor, and then called me a Chxor lover!"

Pixel's mind raced. "Who passed you the message?" Pixel asked

Crowe opened his mouth, and then he froze, "That's funny, I'm normally pretty good with names and faces. Uh, a man, medium height... brown hair I think?"

Pixel closed his eyes, "Shit."

"I do not follow this conversation," Run said. "I must assume that it somehow links to human humor. If you have no further questions of me, I will speak with you later, Pixel."

"Yeah, sure," Pixel waited for Run to get out of earshot. "Crowe, I need you to come with me and talk with Ariadne. This is important, I can't say more."

Crowe frowned, "Uh, I'm not real comfortable around the mind freak. And she doesn't like me much as it is..."

"Trust me, you'll want to talk with her," Pixel said.

He led Crowe down the corridors to where they had met earlier. He found the others back already. "Ariadne, I brought Crowe, you need to hear his story."

Crowe seemed shocked to see Rastar and Anubus present, "What is this, a meeting of the outcasts? You guys planning a mutiny or something?"

"No," Ariadne said. "But we felt it best to discuss something in private. What story is it?"

Pixel waited as Crowe repeated his story, including his inability to identify the man he'd spoken with. "So now I'm really confused. Especially since Run said I voted."

"You did, or at least we thought you did," Ariadne said. "The person we thought was you voted for Krann the Chxor."

"What?" Crowe seemed stunned, "That's ridiculous!"

"I agree," Anubus growled, "Which is why we suspect a psychic tampered with minds."

"But I wasn't even there?"

"Is it possible for a psychic to... do that?" Pixel asked.

Anubus answered, "Yes... I know of one way at least."

Ariadne nodded too, "It could be a couple of methods, some pretty subtle." Yet Pixel saw her stare at Crowe for a long moment. "It would be very difficult to maintain that and to mess

301

with Mike and Simon at the same time."

"Hey, I was down in the commo room for almost forty minutes, you can check the hatch logs, if you want," Crowe said. "I'm just pissed someone impersonated me. I mean, you'd think you guys would know me better than to think I'd vote for a damned Chxor!"

"You would?" Pixel asked.

"I mean, yeah!" Crowe said. "I hate the Chxor, and I'd be more likely to vote for the eight limbed freak or the freaky pyro girl, or even the damned Wrethe here over Krann."

"We will note that for future reference," Anubus growled.

"What's our plan?" Crowe asked. "I mean, it could be anyone on the ship right?"

Pixel opened his mouth to explain the situation, but Ariadne spoke quickly, "It could. We are trying to narrow the range of suspects. Keep an eye out, and if you think you noticed some suspicious behavior, let us know right away. Don't try to take the psychic on your own."

Crowe nodded. "Right. Well, I guess I should probably go talk with Mike, mention the communications work I did. Should I bring this up with him?"

"No," Anubus growled. "We think him particularly susceptible to this type of attack. We would prefer he not know information that someone else could use against us."

"Right," Crowe said. "Well, talk with you later." He brushed past Pixel and headed for the bridge.

"Well, we know it wasn't him, at least," Pixel said.

"No," Anubus growled, "We know that if it was him, he wanted to alleviate suspicion and to see what we knew."

"What?" Pixel asked. "That's pretty paranoid," Pixel looked around at Rastar and Ariadne, "Right?"

"It is," Ariadne said quietly. "But we have to welcome that level of paranoia. Right now, our main suspects are Crowe, Krann, and Elena. And while Crowe's story might check out... I don't trust him."

"But what about this mystery man he talked with?" Pixel asked.

"A good way to cause us to run in circles, man," Rastar said. "They're right, it could be his best bet to find out who suspects him." For once, Rastar's voice seemed serious and thoughtful.

"Well, that means I led him right to us," Pixel said. "Shit, I'm sorry guys."

"No need to be sorry," Ariadne said. "You did what you thought best. And honestly, if he's our target and already suspected you, then he could have read your mind and found out as much as we told him. We didn't give him the details of our suspicions, so keep those to yourself."

"Could you..." Pixel shrugged, "You know, read his mind?"

"I thought about it," Ariadne nodded. "But I'm not very skilled at that and if he is our psychic, it would tip our hand. He could play possum and if he's skilled enough, throw just enough confusion into his thoughts to fool me." She shrugged, "I'm better at the whole lighting things on fire than this kind of thing." She looked down, "Also, it feels... wrong, somehow to invade his privacy, even if I think he's a dirtbag."

"I guess I can understand that," Pixel said. He shrugged then, "I've got good news and bad news from Run. He says there are no such thing as Chxor psychics. I guess they've gone extensive testing over the past seven thousand years. Magnetic resonance scans and something he called a... quantum reaction test."

"Huh," Ariadne said. "Seven thousand years? That's a long time. But humans find ways around tests all the time, so I think we should at least entertain the possibility that Krann might be a psychic."

"I will keep an eye on her," Rastar said. "Any time Mike interrogates her, I will insist on my presence, that will ensure someone resistant will be present."

"Right," Ariadne nodded. "That leaves Crowe and Elena as prime suspects." She glanced at Anubus, "Can you shadow him? See what he's up to?"

"I would rather just kill him," Anubus growled. "But I

don't mind stalking my prey first."

"Okay..." Ariadne turned to Pixel, "That leaves Elena to you."

"To me?" Pixel asked. "What can I do?"

"Talk with her, find out what you can about her, and maybe we'll get lucky and she'll slip up," Ariadne said. "If it *is* her." The blonde psychic bit her lip in thought.

"What will you do?" Anubus growled, "We all will be very occupied. And you could have easily engineered the entire event."

"What?" Ariadne said. She looked completely surprised.

"Hey man, that's pretty paranoid," Rastar said. "She's done nothing but help the entire time."

"It is a possibility," Anubus growled. "One I will not discount out of something as ephemeral as 'friendship' that you espouse."

"Hey Annie, I think you can relax about her," Rastar said. "I mean, if she were the psychic who messed with the others, don't you think she'd have them vote for her? And Mike already voted for her before, so she wouldn't need to even tamper with him."

For once, Anubus ignored the nickname Rastar had given him, and his dark eyes glared at Ariadne, "Unless the election is not her goal, but maybe she intends to sow chaos, get us to distrust one another. Note how she has painted Crowe as the most likely traitor, and how he and she have hated one another from the first."

"I don't hate Crowe," Ariadne said. "I don't hate anyone. And for all that I don't like him, he's still a member of the team." She looked at the other three. "I'm not going to set here and argue this with you. But I will tell you that I'm going to be wandering the ship with my psychic senses open to search for this other psychic. I'll have Mandy and Miranda with me as back up, as well."

"Right," Pixel said. "That makes sense. You're like our troubleshooter."

"A quick reaction force, or mobile reserve," Rastar said,

"This makes sense."

Anubus growled. But Pixel saw the big Wrethe give a single, grudging nod.

"Well, at least you have the easiest task," Pixel said to Rastar, "It's not like Krann will get out of that closet on her own."

"She might," Ariadne said. "She should be able to push her awareness out like me. If she has telekinesis as well as telepathy, she could then activate the door control from the outside at any time. For that matter, if she can mentally twist someone to vote for her as captain, she could command someone to open the door for her."

"Oh," Pixel said. Then he frowned, "Hey, then why didn't you do any of that back when we first woke up on the cargo boat that dropped us at the station? Wouldn't that have worked there?"

Anubus looked over at her, "Yes, that would have gotten us free right away, why did you not do that?"

Ariadne looked back and forth between them, "Uh... well," She smiled weakly, "I just thought of it, actually, as I thought about how dangerous it would be to keep a psychic contained. I never thought to try it myself..."

"You're kidding, right?" Anubus growled. "I take back what I said before, you're too stupid to engineer that level of manipulation."

"Well, I guess we can try that in the future then, at least," Pixel said. He pulled out his datapad and made a note that he needed to set down with Ariadne and find out as much as he could about her capabilities. The fresh example of her rather chaotic approach made him think a more scientific approach might reveal some things she had not thought to try. As he did so, a note about Rastar popped up. "Oh, Rastar, while you're up on the bridge with nothing else to do, would you mind translating some of the ship's manuals for me? I can set down with you later and go over them."

"We have a rogue psychic on the loose and you want him to translate manuals?" Anubus growled. "How have humans managed to be so successful when your priorities are so skewed."

Pixel shrugged, "I call it 'multitasking.' You should try it sometime."

"I do that," Anubus said, "When I concentrate very hard on not killing everyone in the room and still find time to make small talk."

Rastar gave a laugh and slapped Anubus on the back, "Oh, Annie, you have the best jokes sometimes." Pixel saw Anubus's claws flex out of their sheaths. He really hoped that Anubus continued to multitask.

"Rastar, you'll hear me make a joke someday," Anubus growled. "It might be the last thing you ever hear. Right after I rip--"

"Okay," Ariadne said brightly, "I think we're done here. Thank you everyone for meeting, and we'll meet again tomorrow night, right before the vote, agreed?"

Anubus drew his lips back over his teeth, but he gave her a nod, and Rastar one last glare before he stalked out of the small compartment. Ariadne gave a relieved sigh, nodded at Pixel and Rastar and stepped out. Pixel pulled a datachip out of his pocket, "These are some copies I made earlier. Do you mind looking at them?"

"No problem, man," Rastar said, and he gave Pixel two thumbs up with his upper limbs while he took the chips in his lower hands. "But I'm not real educated on some of the technical stuff, so there may be some issues."

"Well, something's better than nothing," Pixel said. "And I've had a couple accidents over the past few days when I tried adjusting some things through trial and error." He tapped a note on his datapad to check with Rastar in the morning to see what he had managed to translate.

"No worries, man," Rastar said. "At least it's not your fault about the sewage that sprayed the whole galley while Simon and Eric cleaned up after dinner last night. What a mess! I think they'll kill whoever was behind that." Rastar's hide had gone green with humor, "But it was funny to see them afterward."

"Yeah..." Pixel said. He suddenly remembered he had neglected to restore power to the waste water system in the galley. "Good thing that wasn't me. I had absolutely nothing to do with that." He cleared his throat, "They didn't happen to mention if they had any suspects... did they?"

***

The small cargo hold lay on the lowest deck, close to the forward airlock. Pixel stepped inside and found a gypsy camp of sorts. Someone had hung up sheets, blankets, and curtains to divide the hold into separate rooms for privacy. Pixel looked around with confusion, right up until a man stuck his head out of one slit. "Looking for someone in particular?"

"Uh, yeah, Elena," Pixel said.

"Oh," the man stepped out and extended his hand, "I'm Micheal Santangel."

"Hi, there," Pixel said, and shook. The other man had long thin fingers, but a firm grip. "I remember you, you took charge of some of the other prisoners on the station, right? Mike had you get them to the ship."

"Yes," Santangel nodded. "I did that task. Though I wish we could have left the Nova Romans behind." He had an unfamiliar accent, one that almost rolled the r's and made his enunciation sound energetic.

"Uh, you're another one who doesn't like them, huh?" Pixel asked.

"He has more reason than most," another man said from nearby. Pixel looked over to see a man in the rags of a military uniform step out of another draped area. "He's a Saragossan, so he's probably bitter about what we did to his planet. I'm Staff Sergeant Carmine Santander, by the way, one of those hated Nova Romans, and my family came from Saragossa, so I have a unique perspective, I think."

Michael Santangel gave a dignified sigh, "Hello Sergeant."

"Saragossa?" Pixel asked. "Isn't that a Chxor occupied system? Why should they hate the Nova Romans?"

307

Santangel looked at the marine and raised one eyebrow, "Might I tell my story, or would you like to institute your propaganda first?"

"Go for it," the sergeant seemed more resigned than anything else. "He's got to be the only one who hasn't heard the story on the ship. And I'd hate to rob you of the chance to make a good first impression."

"My gratitude," Santangel gave a graceful bow to the Nova Roman Marine. He looked over at Pixel, "It's a simple story, really. Twenty years ago, Saragossa was an independent world, with six or seven minor systems tied in alliances and a powerful military and merchant marine."

"Sounds like it was a nice place," Pixel said.

"I found it so, as a child," Santangel said.

"You were a son of one of the Five Families," the Nova Roma Marine said. "Those of us who had to leave due to limited social advancement might disagree." He held up his hands at Santangel's glare, "Sorry, I won't interrupt again."

"As I was saying, we had a powerful military. Strong enough, at the time, that we presented a tough target to the Chxor and we looked like a good ally against other nations, such as the Colonial Republic or Nova Roma." Santangel shot a glance at the sergeant, "And I will admit we used that to our advantage, and played several sides against each other to strengthen our own position. But we saw the advance of the Chxor, so we sought an alliance with the largest organized body in human space."

"The Nova Romans," Pixel nodded. "What happened?"

"We received intelligence that the Chxor planned an attack on the Tibur system. We passed it along, certain that our allies would want every bit of support from us that we could muster." Santangel pursed his lips. "Instead, they betrayed us, their allies, much as they betrayed their previous allies, the Ghornath." Santangel said, and his face twisted in a grimace, "They launched a surprise attack against our fixed defenses, and then destroyed most of our space and ground infrastructure. They threw our entire planet into chaos, just weeks before the Chxor planned to launch their attack."

Pixel looked over at the Nova Roman Marine, who gave a shrug.

"He won't deny it," Santangel said. "He can't. Millions of my people starved to death, the food from the fields unable to reach them in the cities. The Chxor learned of our weakness and swept in. By that time... we welcomed them. They immediately began repairs to infrastructure, instituted ration dispersal... they saved almost two thirds of our population." He gave a sigh, "And they killed another million or so of my people, the leaders who had survived the attacks and the chaos, doctors, teachers, the sick and wounded... just as they do on every world they captured. Yet my people still valued them, because they saved far more than they killed. Indeed, many of my people are loyal subjects to the Chxor."

"Not you?" Pixel asked.

"I was, as the sergeant mentioned, a son of the Five Families... the wealthy and elite, the men who owned much of the businesses and served as the politicians and leaders for Saragossa," Santangel gave a shrug. "I survived their purge of the Families due to some luck, but the fact remains that I have something of a blood debt that I will continue to bleed the Chxor over. I lost my older brother, my father, my two sisters..." He trailed off, and he smiled, "Then of course, there is the personal loss of my profession. I was in training to be a police inspector, the Nova Romans betrayal cut my school years short, and the Chxor occupation ended it for good."

"Why did you do it?" Pixel asked of the sergeant.

"Well, I don't speak for Nova Roma," Sergeant Santander said. "But from a military standpoint... the Chxor went in an entirely different direction after that. Saragossa's fall opened up a new front, caused them to threaten Colonial Republic worlds in addition to Nova Roma. It makes sense in that it bought us time... and it got us more allies than we could have gotten from Saragossa."

"And it killed millions of my people, and sentenced the rest to Chxor occupation," Santangel said.

"Yes," the sergeant said. "And you know... it's

unfortunate. I regret that the decision was made, but I'm not the man who made it. You'd have to ask the strategy makers if it bought us enough time or not, and if they used that time as well as they should have."

Pixel recognized what must be an argument that the two had repeated many times. The Saragossan's voice rose, "You absolve yourself of responsibility--"

"Hey, I'm just here to find Elena Ludmilla Lakar, is she around?" Pixel interrupted.

"No," both men said at once. Then they glared at one another.

"Great, I'll just see myself out." Pixel said.

"Wait, please," Michael Santangel said. His voice sounded pained. Pixel wondered if it came from the requirement to ask or merely for the interruption to his favorite argument.

"What?" Pixel asked. On the one hand, he felt for the other man's loss. On the other... the aristocrat represented a lot of what Pixel hated about his own world. The elite who had held all the power, and controlled the money and positions of authority.

"I had heard that some, such as the bounty hunter, have joined your ranks. I wish to put forward a request of my own," Santangel said. "Short of a liberation of Saragossa, I have no home. I would like to join your crew. I have my skills as a policeman, but I am also knowledgeable about security systems. I could be a useful addition to the crew."

"Alright..." Pixel nodded slowly, "I'll pass that along." He didn't know why all these others seemed so eager to join up, especially with the whole election of a captain. But he wouldn't turn down the help, even in the form of an exiled, penniless nobleman.

"My thanks," the Saragossan gave him a bow. "I will be here if you have any news."

"Right," Pixel nodded. He felt suddenly awkward, but he was an engineer, he had not gone to school on how to deal with rich folks. "Well, nice to meet you both, and thanks for the history lesson."

Pixel backed out of the hold and then glanced down at his datapad. *If I were a possibly psychic bounty hunter with some mysterious goal, where would I go,* he thought.

"Hello, Pixel, what brings you down here?" Simon asked.

"Oh, hi," Pixel said, as he turned to find Simon had just come out of the stairwell, "Looking for Elena, actually, had a question for her."

"What about?" Simon asked.

"Uh," Pixel's mind went blank. He had not really thought that far he realized. "Um, she mentioned she knew weapons pretty well, and since you all said I'm pretty hopeless, I wondered if she could give me some tips."

Simon frowned, "Well, that's fortunate."

"Oh?" Pixel asked.

"Yes, she just volunteered to help me with the weapons safety class. Eric and I just gave her access to the Armory."

"Oh?" Pixel asked. In conjunction with the suspicion that she was the rogue psychic, that might be a very bad thing indeed.

"Yeah, Crowe helped us to set up a security lockout of the Armory hatch, so only a couple people on the ship have access. Rastar, Eric, and now Elena and I." Simon gave him a smile, "Just some security precautions Eric and I thought up."

"Yeah... good idea," Pixel wondered if Simon would notice if he buried his head in his hands and had a panic attack. Had Elena orchestrated that, and if so, did she plan to take over the ship with Eric and Simon as her mind-controlled pawns?

Or had Anubus's paranoia just rubbed off on him?

"Yeah, it just came to us, Eric and I, and then Crowe showed up right after that..." Simon gave a broad smile. "And it's so efficient!"

"Crowe was right there, huh?" Pixel smiled weakly, "Wow, what are the odds, right?" What were the odds that two of their suspects had their role in the whole thing. A sudden suspicion hit him.

"Yeah... by any chance did you talk with Krann at all before you thought this up?"

"No," Simon said. "Though now that you mention it, I

311

feel kind of silly for voting for her. I mean, she probably would make things more orderly around here, but, well, she is a Chxor, you know? I'm not sure if we could trust her."

"Yeah, there is that," Pixel said. Evidently the effects of the mental compulsion had faded at least somewhat. Pixel brought up his datapad and made a note to ask Ariadne about how long she thought the others might be affected. "Well, you said Elena is at the Armory, right?"

"With Eric," Simon nodded, "They're cleaning some of the Chxor weapons, for the class."

"Right, probably a good idea," Pixel said. He felt like a broken record. A sudden thought hit him, "Oh, there's a Saragossan, Michael Santangel, one of our passengers, he wants to join up. He was in training to be a police inspector, before the Chxor took over Saragossa, I guess. You might want to talk to him."

"Sure," Simon nodded, "Thanks for passing that on."

Pixel took the stairs up and then made his way to the armory.

He found the reinforced hatch open, and Eric and Elena both seated at the bench. "Hey there," Pixel said as he approached. He tried not to think of how jumpy Eric could be, or of what he might do if a rogue psychic pushed him just right.

"Oh, hey Pixel," Eric said. He set down the pistol he'd just assembled. "Hey, do you mind hanging out with Elena here? I need to check on lunch, and I don't want to leave just one person here alone."

"Sure!" Pixel said brightly, *I'd like nothing better than to be alone in a room filled with weapons with a possibly hostile rogue psychic.* Then he remembered to concentrate on something other than his suspicions. He felt wrung out already. Pixel wiped his sweaty hands on his coveralls as Eric pushed past him and headed towards the galley. He realized that he should probably say something to Elena. "So, how's it going?" Pixel asked.

"I am well," Elena said, her accent sharp. "I find that your group treats me well. I am surprised, as in my profession, most men constantly test women or simply disregard them as inconsequential."

"Oh?" Pixel asked. He felt sudden inspiration, "That must be rough, did you have any special talents that helped you to do well?"

"Persistence," Elena said. "I do not give up, not when I see my goal. This surprised those who underestimated me." She cocked her head, "You are from the Lithia system, da?"

Pixel frowned and concentrated hard on the power issues that he had tried to solve, so far without real success, "Uh, yeah, where did you hear that?"

"Professor Windbag from Loire," Elena said. "He is one of those men who think they are smarter than everyone and must brag about it, no? Particularly to a pretty young woman."

Pixel shrugged. "He does like to talk."

"Yes, he mentioned you graduated from university there," the bounty hunter said, and she had a faint smile on her face. "This reminded me of something I read once, about the terrorist attack there, you know of this?"

"Yeah," Pixel said. He wiped his sweaty palms on his coveralls again. "I know of it. I was there, at the university when it happened." He met her eyes, "I still have nightmares about it," he said truthfully.

She shrugged, "People die, I do not let this bother me." She licked her lips, and her smile became something that sent a shiver of fear up Pixel's spine. "But what I remembered, then, was a wanted poster I saw once. I did not pay much attention, as the poster just noted persons of interest, no rewards for their return, da?"

"Oh?" Pixel asked. He wondered if she might shoot him in the back if he broke into a run.

"Da. No reward, so I did not care, though I think that someone suspected of carrying out the attack might want to alter his appearance some... Though he looked much fiercer in that photo, more fanatical."

"Yeah..." Pixel said. He had no idea what to say. Either she really didn't care or she just waited to drop the hammer.

313

Either way, no reason to deny it further. "Well, they used my university ID photo for that... I had just finished a four hour presentation where my professors dragged me over the coals, I was pretty ticked at the time."

"Ah," she smiled, and her smile seemed much more natural. "That is understandable. I must tell you sometime about how I had to pass my licensing exams on Centauri Prime. You would find the story amusing, I am sure."

Pixel couldn't manage a smile back at her, his stomach felt twisted into a knot, "Well–"

"Hey guys, food looks good," Eric said as he came out of the corridor. "And no sign of another burst pipe like yesterday, thank goodness." He looked between Elena and Pixel. "I miss something?"

"No," Elena gave Pixel a broad smile, "Pixel told me some about his time as a student, and some of why he left Lithia." She looked over at Eric, "He is quite talented, no? Very accomplished, even infamous, I might say."

"Really?" Eric looked over at Pixel, "That's cool, I hadn't realized engineers got famous."

"Yeah..." Pixel managed a nod, though he felt like his face had frozen.

"I have finished with these weapons," Elena said. "I will take break. I will return tomorrow, Eric, to finish. I hope you will make it to our weapons instruction class, Pixel. You would not wish to disappoint me, no?"

"No..." Pixel tried not to think how she could ruin his life with the others if she told what she knew. He tried not to think of how easily she could insinuate to the appropriate authorities how his actions in the escape might signify his involvement in what happened on Origin.

She gave him a predatory smile and walked out.

Eric gave a low whistle, "I hate to see her go, but I love watching her walk away." He slapped Pixel on the shoulder, "You dog you, she was coming on to you, I think."

"What?" Pixel asked, shocked out of his frantic thoughts.

"I know, I'm surprised too, especially with me here," Eric

said. "But some girls go for that nerd look, I guess. Might have something to do with nerds getting paid better than grunts like me, of course." He gave a sigh, "And here I hoped my cooking might swing some ladies my way."

"Uh, we don't get paid," Pixel said. "The only thing we have close to currency is the gold that Anubus claimed."

"You know? You're absolutely right, she must not be interested in you, then," Eric nodded. "She's trying to make me jealous, play hard to get. Well... two can play at that game." Eric rubbed his hands together in anticipation. "Oh, this will be great."

"What?" Pixel said.

Eric shot him a look, "Now don't go telling her, but I'll have a talk with Ariadne, I'm sure she'll help me out. It's for a good cause." The former soldier gave a decisive nod.

Pixel felt so wrung out that he forgot to be diplomatic. "Eric... you treat Ariadne like crap, why would she help you get laid?"

"Well, I treat her that way so that she learns to look out for herself," Eric said reasonably. "I'm sure she won't hold it against me. And this is more than just sex..." Eric waved his hand after the departed Elena, "This is a challenge, she's thrown the gauntlet, my friend, and I have to accept."

Pixel felt bereft of words. He wondered if perhaps Run were right, about him or if Eric might just be a bad example to compare himself against as far as critical reasoning skills. He brought up his datapad and made a note to have Run compare his own hormone levels against those of Eric. Maybe there would be some correlation...

"You alright, Pixel?" Eric asked. "I hope I didn't hurt your feelings with the whole nerd thing."

"Nope," Pixel said. "Not a problem. Truthfully, I haven't had a girlfriend in a while.. and that ended messily."

"Oh?" Eric asked. "I heard about that terrorist attack on Lithia, it happened around the same time as I moved from the Centauri Commandos to... well never mind." He shrugged, "You lose your girl in that?"

315

"No," Pixel said. "We'd broken up by then. This was before that. Christyne... well, she was a little immature, and rather emotional... we had a misunderstanding, it was very public." He remembered the argument they'd had about the flash bulb prototype, how she had insisted he bring it to impress her family, and then demanded a demonstration with her and her mother.

"Oh," Eric stripped down a pistol, "Sounds like fun."

"She got flashed, she overreacted," Pixel shrugged.

"What?" Eric dropped a spring. "You flashed her?"

"Yeah..." Pixel said. "She asked for it, though I'm not sure why she wanted me to do it in the restaurant. I think she just wanted the attention, but she got more than she expected."

Eric dropped the other pieces of the pistol to the bench. Pixel heard several bounce to the floor. "Wait. Just so I'm straight here, you gave your girlfriend public nudity after she asked for it, and she got upset?"

"What are you talking about?" Pixel asked. "I designed a prototype flash bulb for instant tanning. I designed it to work through clothing, one quick flash and you get a nice golden tan. It was based on some of my undergrad work, actually."

"Oh, so no public nudity then," Eric sighed. "This story just got way more lame."

"Well, I didn't say that..." Pixel hedged.

"What? But you said that you hit her with this tanning death ray... where's the nudity? Did she loose her mind and tear off her clothes, because that would totally make the story much better," Eric said.

"No!" Pixel said. "God, you're pretty juvenile sometimes." He sighed, "But yes, she did end up naked."

"YES!" Eric did a fist pump. Parts of the pistol bounced off the ceiling.

"It wasn't my fault." Pixel said.

"Of course not," Eric said. "Women take their clothes off all the time, and then they blame it on alcohol or the heat of the moment or hormones or drugs you might have slipped them, these things happen," Eric said with a leer.

"It was a prototype. I'd tested it with some clothing, and it had no effect on my coveralls. Not on the clothing of some of the women who volunteered at the lab, either. But Christyne wore some kind of long chain woven carbon material for her dress and her bra and panties used the same stuff."

"So your tanning death ray did what, make it hot so she had to pull it all off?"

Pixel raised an eyebrow, Eric seemed very interested in the story, "...No. They hit the perfect wavelength that they broke the carbon to carbon bonds and caused her clothing to disintegrate. And gave her a perfect tan all over." Pixel shrugged. "Oh, and she had some weird shampoo or something because it reacted too and turned her hair platinum blonde."

"YES!" Eric did another fist pump. "You have to make me one of those."

"The odds against it working like that again..."

"Don't tell me the odds!" Eric said. "You can't tell me that story and then say it won't work." He shook his head, "So your girlfriend was suddenly a naked blonde in a restaurant, what's the problem? Some girls like that kind of attention."

"Well... she asked me to do that to impress her parents. She had just graduated business school," Pixel admitted. "It was also the first time I met them."

"Oh," Eric said. "Well, could be worse, I mean, her mother could have been wearing that same stuff, right?"

Pixel kept his mouth shut. Though, come to think of it, the other restaurant patrons had seemed very impressed and appreciative. *Very* appreciative, he received a standing applause, even.

"Well, anyway, that's a pretty interesting story," Eric said. "I hadn't realized you had crazy stories like that."

"Oh, I should tell you about the time my friend Jack and I..." Pixel trailed off. "Never mind."

"Yeah, save it for another time," Eric said. He glanced around, "Did you happen to see where that spring pin went?"

***

On his way back down to the engine room he ran into Mike.

"Pixel, just the man I wanted to see," Mike said.

"Oh?" Pixel asked.

"Yeah, I worked out this charter, for team, plus anyone else who wants to join up," Mike said. "I wondered if you could look it over."

"Me?" Pixel asked. "I mean, sure, but I'm an engineer, not a lawyer."

"Right, but you're a thinker, which is more important right now," Mike said. "Plus, most of the crew listens to you, so if you think it makes sense, they'll accept it with less argument."

Pixel stared at him for a long moment, "You really want this captain thing to go through, don't you?" Up until now, he had genuinely thought that the others wanted a leader to remove their need to think for themselves. Now he wondered at his own assumption.

"Yeah," Mike nodded. "It's important, especially in a crisis, to have one person in charge. I know you're against it, but this isn't a lab or design firm somewhere. We're on the knife edge of survival, you know?" Mike pulled a datachip out of his pocket, "But anyway, even if you don't want a captain, I'd like your opinion on the fairness, on how you think the shares break down, that sort of thing."

Pixel took the chip, "I'll look at it. I suppose you want feedback before the meeting tomorrow night?"

Mike nodded, "Sooner the better so I can make changes and get it to everyone else."

"I'll get it to you by tomorrow morning," Pixel said. Whatever his personal feelings about the idea, Mike had laid out a pretty good reason for him to at least look it over and give his opinion.

"Thanks, I appreciate it." Mike said. "Hopefully, even if this one ends up with another deadlock, we'll at least accomplish this much, you know?" Mike glanced over his shoulder. "And to tell you the truth, I'm just worried that when we're in a life and death situation we'll have something similar happen. Or worse, everyone will run off in their own direction and someone will get killed."

"I can understand that," Pixel said. "Oh, Eric is making steak for lunch tomorrow, I thought you'd be interested in that."

"Excellent," Mike grinned, "I'll be there." His grin faded, "Wait, food in the lounge, right?"

Pixel managed to keep his face solemn, "Yeah, is that a problem?"

"I'm not so hungry any more..." Mike said.

***

"So this Vlarblir acts as a conduit for the Kra," Rastar said.

"The same Kra that the gravity field maintains in a state of flux?" Pixel asked.

"No that is the Kro," Rastar said.

"Oh, right," Pixel made a note on his datapad. "I think I've got it, now."

"I hope so," Rastar said. "As I am very confused."

"You've done fine," Pixel said. "And the important part is that I understand. You're translating, not trying to learn the systems yourself." He frowned then, "Though I wish you knew a bit more of the technical terminology. I think that the Kro are exotic matter particles the ships drive uses. But I'm not sure of the polarity... It's all very fascinating, especially since this is totally at odds with a lot of the theory I received."

"That is good?" Rastar asked. "I would think you would find that aggravating? Does not the Confederation have similar drives?"

"Oh, they do, except they run off of human tech, and the data I've seen on that suggests they use an entirely different method to generate forward momentum," Pixel said. "I'm trying to learn the theory of how your drives work at the same time as I learn the basics of how to conduct maintenance on them. Which feels like I tried to drink from a fire-hose nozzle on full blast."

"Oh," Rastar nodded, "That sounds difficult."

"But I like difficult," Pixel said. "So it's actually kind of

319

fun." He paused, "What do you do for fun, Rastar?"

"Oh, various things," Rastar said. "I have found a number of human holovid recordings as well as some Ghornath ones. I watch those, sometimes. I drink a coke now and then to relax. I talk about weapons and tactics with Eric, though he seems inordinately fascinated with long range combat. And at times I set and remember my childhood, and make note of the honor I must regain for my family name."

"Well, that's an interesting set of hobbies," Pixel said. "Though I think I'll stick with taking things apart to see how they work." He watched as Rastar translated the manuals on the consoles. Now that he saw a Ghornath at work, the oddly-shaped, dual keyboards made sense, as did the multiple monitors at each work station. Rastar seemed to read and work at both screens and an upper and lower arm typed as a pair on each set of keyboards. "You multitask very well," Pixel noted.

Rastar answered without a pause in his work, "I can do this all day, man. Though thinking about some of these words forces me to pause. I have very good coordination between my limbs, something which has proven useful before, though most often in combat."

"Were you a member of the Ghornath resistance?" Pixel asked.

"No," Rastar's hide shifted blue. "You know, man, I really considered it. Then I figured that kind of anger would just bring me down, you know, man?"

"How did you get your military training?"

"I worked as a bouncer on Narobi, that got me bodyguard gig, and then for a while I got work as a registered mercenary out of Tanis," Rastar paused in his typing. "Some pretty good dudes in that work, but one job went bad right from the start, and then I had to split. Dropped the contract and caught a ship headed away from the Confederation. Things got pretty hectic there for a while, and even Chxor space seemed like a safer spot than where I was."

"Sorry to hear that," Pixel said. "But it all worked out for the best, right?"

320

Rastar looked down, "You know, man, I hope it does, but somehow I worry that my past will catch up to me when I get back to human space."

"Well, I don't know much about mercenary work or the people that hire them," Pixel said. "But you've got to figure that they assume that something like that comes with the business, right?"

Rastar gave him a nod, "I hope so, man. But they seemed pretty unhappy with me at the time." He looked back at the console, "I've finished the next section on the engines, do you want to look it over?"

"Definitely," Pixel nodded. "Though if you slipped another line in there about the flux capacitor requiring cheeseburgers as fuel, I might try to strangle you."

"Man, I have no idea what you're talking about," Rastar held up his four hands to show his innocence. The green color of his hide belied his words. "I'm telling you, that's what it said in the manual."

"Right, along with the reference to Hawaiian shirts being required safety equipment," Pixel said. He shook his head at the big alien, "You do realize I need to try to train other people how to help me down there with these translated manuals?"

"Yeah, man," Rastar nodded. "And this way you can make sure they're paying attention, right?"

Pixel opened his mouth, and then paused. He could think of a few classes where he might have paid more attention if the professors had put a bit of random humor into their textbooks. For that matter, it made a good way to check to see if someone had actually read the manual, they would have questions about the things that just didn't make sense. "Actually, Rastar, you might be on to something."

"I know," Rastar said. "I am pretty awesome. Hey, before we start this next part, let's get some lunch. Eric mentioned steaks for lunch."

"You like steaks?" Pixel asked. He'd seen the big alien eat a variety of odd foods, some of which included a bizarre mix of human and Ghornath rations.

"Oh, yeah," Rastar gave him a nod. "Especially with the right condiments. Let's go."

Pixel looked down at his datapad. He felt reluctant to leave off his work, but he'd skipped breakfast to give Mike his notes on the charter. His stomach rumbled at the reminder. *Not like these files will go anywhere,* he thought, *besides I could probably use a break before I get Kra and Kro mixed up again.* He tried not to think how disastrous *that* could be. But he had to admit, the explosion would look extremely impressive.

Pixel tucked his datapad into his hip pocket and followed Rastar off the bridge. As he walked the corridors behind the big alien, he brought out his datapad again and made a note to ask Run about the Ghornath's eyes. Ghornath seemed to have a mirrored surface to their eyes but they seemed able to focus on multiple things at once. That made some of their display screens a headache for Pixel, but it also seemed an impressive feat. Pixel wondered if he could design a set of smart glasses to mimic their eyes. Pixel didn't know how the display would function, but it might well enable similar multitasking for him.

They came up towards the lounge just as Run pushed a pallet out of the galley. Pixel frowned at the sight of Run dressed in his full jump suit, complete with helmet. He pushed the fifteen cases of Coca Cola into the corridor, and then froze at the sight of them. Rastar's hide went through several shades before he seemed to settle on a dull red. "Where are you going with that?" Rastar demanded.

Run looked up, "I need to dispose of this hazardous material."

"Hazardous?" Pixel asked.

"Dispose?" Rastar's deep voice dropped to an ominous growl. "You will put that back in the galley. You will not threaten the Cokes."

"This material does not belong in the galley," Run said. "Your own addiction does not mean I need to tolerate..." Run trailed off as Rastar walked slowly forward. The big Ghornath reached down and pulled a glass bottle out of the top case. He popped the cap off with one hand, and then stared down at Run.

322

"This behavior is illogical," Run said even as he took several steps backwards.

"I think this pallet would look great in my quarters, Run," Rastar took a sip from his bottle. His hide had shifted green, "Unless you would like some."

"Of course I would not want any of this material..." Run trailed off as Rastar took a step forward and extended the bottle.

"What's going on?" Pixel asked. He looked between the two aliens, suddenly confused. He knew that the two aliens would handle different chemicals in odd fashions, yet he couldn't help but think that the two of them were arguing over cokes. While Pixel liked it as much as anyone else, he didn't think it worth fighting over. He certainly didn't know why Run seemed to want to get rid of it.

"Nothing to worry about, dude," Rastar said. "Run just wanted to move these someplace safe, like next to my bed in the cabin, right Run?"

"You understand that this is not over," Run said.

"You shot me with your little tranquilizer gun," Rastar said genially, "Consider us even."

"Guys, what's this about?" Pixel asked.

"A mere discussion regarding the disposal of this manufactured poison," Run said. "But I have no logical counter to Rastar's threats, for now." The little Chxor turned the pallet around and pushed it away towards the cabins.

"I'm really confused," Pixel said.

"No worries, man," Rastar said. "Hey, want a coke?"

***

Pixel sipped at his coke and considered a second steak as he relaxed in the lounge.

He watched as Rastar squeezed peanut butter onto his third steak. While Pixel thought it rather unusual, the sounds that Eric made as Rastar did so served as entertaining background. *Granted, Eric makes a damned good steak,* he thought.

Most of the team had assembled for the meal, and even Mike had made an appearance in the lounge, though he kept his back to the tank and he seemed a bit jumpy to Pixel.

Pixel frowned as he remembered the charter that Mike had drawn up. The other man had shown a great deal of thought in regards to what the others would find fair. It also addressed a number of issues that Pixel had not even thought of, which both surprised and embarrassed him. Pixel had no problem with the admission that with the exception of Run and possibly Ariadne, he was the most intelligent person aboard the ship. More than that, he had the most education, as far as he knew, only Simon had finished college. Yet they continued to surprise him by how they thought of things that never occurred to him.

Pixel frowned as his mind returned to the main engineering issue. The fusion coils he needed to replace would require approximately twelve hundred meters of conductive filaments. He knew that some way must exist for him to produce that without scavenging the ship. He had already analyzed the on hand stock of copper and even iron and come up short.

"Crowe, if I see you near my gold again..." Anubus growled.

Pixel tuned the threat out as soon as he realized the Wrethe had returned to his normal topic of conversation. Did Anubus really believe they had some plot to take his gold or did he simply amuse himself with his threats? Pixel could care less about those gold bars.

Now where will I find... Pixel's thought trailed off. "Yeah... that could work." He glanced over at Anubus. *How will I convince him to give up* that *much of his gold, even for such a good cause?*

He figured he should do the calculations, both to see how much he would need and what kind of issues the use of gold rather than copper might cause in the fusion reactor. For all he knew it might even boost efficiency. Best to do those calculations and then once they chose a captain, to deliver those to him or her, and then let *them* talk Anubus around.

That brought his thoughts around to the pending election. If the previous two served as any judge, Pixel felt certain this one would turn into another deadlock. Though he worried about the psychic tampering in the last one, he feared that regardless of the selection they would face issues.

Yet he no longer felt bothered by who would eventually win or even if he could convince them of his own belief that they didn't need a captain. The revelation of his own blindness and hubris disturbed him. He had grown arrogant, he had to admit. He had assumed that because he was smarter than the others, then it must follow that he knew better than them.

And as he listened to their laughter and talk, he realized that he had fallen into the same trap that he and Jack had back on Lithia. They had tried to change society based upon the assumption that they knew better. That they'd done so from a desire to give people greater freedoms and improve their lives made no difference. Pixel had somehow come full circle, he realized, and had almost reached the point where he fell into Jack's side of the argument. He had derailed the initial election with his refusal to vote. The last one he had made a bargain to intentionally twist the election result to one that he had hoped would show the others the danger of a tyrannical leader.

Yet he had never considered whether they might have chosen the correct action from the start. Certainly a captain would limit his own freedoms, yet a good captain would also protect them from each other, enforce the peace, and in times of crisis would indeed allow them to act in a quick fashion. That last, which seemed so trivial before, took on a more profound importance now.

Pixel had never wanted to serve in the military. He did not, he knew, have the right mindset for it, even if he had found some nation or cause which inspired that selfless dedication. Pixel had his own flaws, and he knew that a level of selfishness was one. Yet he found himself aboard a warship, in hostile alien space, far from safety. The crew consisted of dangerous people, some of them quite able to kill without remorse or hesitation.

Yet he had never felt as part of a team as he did now. He watched Mike's eyes dart nervously to the fish tank and Ariadne laugh and smile at everyone, and even Anubus, who sat in the corner and stared at them all with suspicion. They had become friends and companions. People, some of them entirely alien, who shared in some of the most terrifying events of Pixel's life. He valued them all enough that he cared desperately about what they thought of him. He wanted their approval and he wanted their friendship.

And he realized, he wanted their security. Pixel might risk his own safety on the odds that the group would have time for discussion or that they would not require instant reaction to a threat. He could not bear the thought that his friends might die, that Ariadne would never laugh again, or that Eric would never cook another meal for Rastar to ravage with some terrible mixture of ingredients, not when something so simple as the loss of some personal freedom might prevent it.

Pixel had thought to convince the others of the importance of their own freedoms. Instead, he had discovered that in some circumstances, at least, on the edge of survival, he would give up some of those freedoms to protect those he had come to love.

***

"Well, since we have everyone here," Ariadne said, "And since everyone's in a good mood with great food, why don't we knock out this election now?"

Eric gave a bow, "My thanks, and you'll note I managed not to call you an idiot for the entire meal."

"Thanks, I appreciate that!" Ariadne said cheerfully.

"I did not benefit from any meal," Run said. "Therefore I think you owe me something in order to gain my good will."

Eric glared at Run, "You cut on me with a dull shiv without painkillers and *I* owe *you*?"

Run stared at him, "The water has passed under that bridge." Pixel snorted some coke out of his nose. The painful burn allowed him to keep a solemn look on his face when Eric shot a glare in his direction.

"What the hell is that supposed to mean?" Eric asked. Pixel tapped a note on his datapad to give Run some more phrases to use inappropriately.

"The situation is in the past and you would be illogical to feel any ill will--"

"How about this vote," Ariadne interrupted with a smile. "While we're all still in a good mood from Eric's cooking."

"So we do this entire farce again," Anubus growled. "Good plan to sate my hunger. The meat slows my blood and makes it less likely I'll murder my competition. I'll take your forethought into consideration, Eric."

"Thanks," Eric said. "That's the nicest thing you've ever said to me, or anyone really, I appreciate that."

"That probably means he'll kill you if he thinks you're about to move against him," Simon said.

"No way," Rastar bellowed, "Annie would never..." he paused to belch, "...hurt one of us, we're like family to him!" The big alien swayed a bit, and Pixel noted a pile of empty coke bottles on the table near him. His fixation with the carbonated beverage suddenly took on a different light to Pixel.

"Let's get this over with," Crowe said. "Before I vomit from a mixture of Ariadne's niceness and Rastar's shirt."

Pixel took a deep breath and looked around at the group. "Alright, before we kick this election off... I just want to say one thing." He gathered his thoughts. "Most of you know that I've been against the idea of having a captain from the beginning. I am very much an Individual, with a capital I. You may not know or understand why, but I've had experience before with people telling me what was allowed and what wasn't. On Lithia... well, when I grew up, the bureaucracy ran everything. Their rules limited what we could eat, what we could watch on holo, where we could go, and who could go to college. I hated that control, I still hate it."

He met the eyes of his companions. "More than that, I fear it. When Simon first proposed the selection of a captain, I feared we would have one person who would try to command our every action and deed. I feared a tyrant, and I think that fear somewhat justified."

"Yet I've grown to know all of you, and though I might fear what some of you might do with that power, I also know that you are friends and I've seen several of you try to do your best for the group." Pixel typed in a command on his datapad. The lounge holovid flashed up a copy of Mike's charter. "Mike asked me to look at his proposed Charter. We've all seen it already, but what struck me is not what he wrote, what struck me is that *he* wrote it. That he cared enough about all of us to codify something that was fair to us all. He didn't try to write it up to his advantage or to put him in a better position. He didn't write it to give him or the elected captain uncontested power. He wrote it because he thought it would make the ship run smoother, and make things easier for all of us."

Pixel took a deep breath, "After reading it and after thinking, really thinking about this, I came to one conclusion. We do need a captain. More than that, we need someone who thinks of the others, who has experience in space, and who already acts as our spokesman. Therefore, I nominate Mike as our Captain."

No one else spoke for a moment, then Ariadne stepped forward, "I agree, I think Mike's a perfect choice as our leader. He helped to make us into a team from when we first woke up in that cargo boat. From then on, we've worked together, all because of him. I say Mike should be our captain." She had a sunny smile on her face and she gave Pixel a nod.

Pixel looked around at the others. Rastar stepped forward, "I agree, Mike has treated me with respect and has shown great honor. I think he will make a fine Captain."

Eric nodded, "He's got some military experience. A squid, but still something useful. I vote for Mike."

"Me too," Simon spoke up.

Crowe didn't speak, Run looked bored, and Anubus glared around the room. Pixel felt uncertain whether the Wrethe felt suspicion at the sudden surge of votes for Mike or angry no one had stepped forward to nominate him. Possibly both, Pixel decided.

Mike stood. Pixel saw his shoulders slump, "I *really* don't want this job, guys."

"I know," Pixel said. "But you're stuck with it, for now."

"I can't think of a more miserable job," Mike said, "Than trying to herd this group of... unique individuals. If I'm going to do this... well the charter is only the start. We need an agreement, from everyone here, that this is not just a temporary thing. When we hit civilized space, we stick together. Otherwise, you can take this job and blow it out the airlock." Mike glared at them all. "It is too damned much work otherwise."

Pixel felt his tension ease a bit. He had spoken out, he had changed the outcome, and perhaps they got an imperfect result, but they got a man that Pixel knew would do his best for them. That mattered more to him than he had realized, and he knew as he looked back at his idealistic arguments with Jack, that he had taken a step that Jack would never have managed.

Pixel had chosen to do the responsible thing, to sacrifice what he wanted for the sake of the group, and that felt pretty good just then. Pixel gave Mike a crooked smile, "Sure thing boss, where do we sign?"

###

Dishonored
The Renegades
by Kal Spriggs

The other cubs saw me as prey. This is understandable. I had no parents. Indeed, their parents rejected me for the failures of my father. I didn't know or understand this, at that age. All I knew, then, was that I must run. I ran like a Dronthir, with long bounds and leaps, as it flees the pursuing Koon.

I raced through the alleys and corridors of the shanty town. My skin flushed with *lur* and fear. I was small, less than a meter in height, which gave me the ability to dodge under and around obstacles which my pursuers needed to climb over or shift. I ran, my four legs moving me in long bounds, the sharp garbage reek of the refugee camp burned in my nostrils.

As with all pursuits, this one ended suddenly. I dove for a familiar hiding spot. The narrow crevasse where I had hidden from such beatings before. This time, however, I had grown too broad. I got halfway in before my midshoulders stuck. Before I could try to squirm deeper, my pursuers seized my rearfeet and pulled me out.

The five of them took no time to gloat. They were bigger than me, two nearly full grown. They hated me, with the rage that only comes with youth and *kava*. They didn't understand *why* I was somehow responsible for the misery of the camp, only that their parents said I shared in that dishonor. The impacts of their fists drove me into the ground. Twenty fists beat me, twenty legs stomped on me.

I screamed when they broke my forelegs. I howled when they ground my face into the mud. The sharp stones within cut into my face. When they worked out their anger, they left me, crippled and battered, long after Ghren's star had set.

No one came for me.

I dragged myself to my hide. It was not the first time they or others had caught me, or even beaten me. Nor, in fact, was it the worst beating I had received. There were adults of my people, broken ones driven mad by loss and pain, who had done worse. Still, it hurt. I felt my broken bones grind against one another as a crawled. My entire body throbbed and my vision blurred from the blows I had taken to my head.

In my hide, I did what I had done before. I put a length of bone between my jaws, set the bones in my legs, swallowed down some Mratha rice, curled into a ball, and went to sleep. It is fortunate that young Ghornath heal so quickly, because otherwise I would never have survived.

I crawled out of my hide a week later: hungry, gaunt, and limping. I was out of Mratha rice, out of drinking water, and I smelled like a drowned Aalat. I kept to the edges of the refugee camp, injured as I still was. Only when I was able to run again would I dare to walk inside, where my attackers would be.

I found edge of the camp, in the reeking garbage pits, I found my goal. The refugees sometimes hunted the local animals. Often, they would discard the bone and offal in the garbage pits. Sometimes they wouldn't clean the carcass entirely. I found a recent carcass and took the leg from near-Dronthir. The bone had little meat on it, but there were enough scraps for me to gnaw on and gain some sustenance. Plus I cracked open the bone and sucked out the marrow. What can I say? I was nearly feral, at that point.

The faint sounds of conversation nearly made me flee. Although I knew language, it was something I rarely, if ever, shared. Still, I knew I couldn't flee, not in my current state, so instead, I waited and listened.

"Remember, retain the sight. Hold the weapon gently, just enough force to keep it still, not enough to make your muscles tremble," the deep voice spoke. It was an old voice, one that sounded weary, yet still strong.

The younger voice that spoke was not familiar, which meant this other Ghornath had not participated in my beatings. I knew *those* voices by heart. "It is hard to do it with two, Grathir."

The voices came from behind the embankment that held

the garbage pit. A glance that way showed where I could sneak through the brush to observe and yet stay hidden. "Yes, it is a matter of muscle memory," Grathir said. "We will practice this every day, the aiming and the firing, with two hands."

I crept up the embankment, until I could see them both. I recognized the elder, though I had not known his name. He wore the faded tatters of a uniform. His rearlegs ended in stumps, which someone had set into a wheeled cart so that he could at least pull himself around. I had seen him before, though I had avoided him most of all. He was *Chigathi*, most honored, and I knew that I was not worthy to even be seen by him.

The young cub with him was one I did not recognize. She was young, perhaps as young as I. She held two stocks of wood, each carved to resemble a gun. For a moment, I did not understand it.

Then as she went through the motions to aim and fire the toy weapons at a target, I began to understand. Much as I practiced stealth, even when I knew no one watched, she practiced firing and aiming. She practiced for hours, under the hot star and the mid morning heat. Grathir coached her through holding the weapons, firing, and then loading and cleaning procedures. I watched and listened until the two finished and went away.

The feral part of me saw little opportunity, but some part of my soul awakened. I was tired of skulking through the garbage pits. I was tired of living off of scraps… I wanted more, wanted to challenge myself. I crept back down to the garbage pit and picked out four sections of wood. The *chigathi* taught the female cub the use of two weapons. I had four arms, I would learn the use of *four* weapons.

In my youth, I had some vague mental impression that I would acquire four guns, and with those, I would return the pain and agony upon my tormenters. As I said, I was feral. I did not understand the complexities. But I would come to learn those… and of honor.

***

"Grathir, when will I use a real weapon?" the female cub asked. Grathir had called her Chuni, now and then, but I still labeled her as *Ulla*, which meant soft. An ironic term, I know, for none who lived in the refugee camps were soft. Still, the feral part of me hated her, for she had not experienced the terror of pursuit. She had Grathir to talk to her, to guide her.

I had no one.

Grathir's hide fluoresced with *rew* and sadness. "You may use a real weapon only when necessary. When Leader Turak and his freedom fighters come to recruit, you may receive a weapon. There is also the mercenary recruiters, if Turak will not take you."

"But…" I could see her hide turn *rew* as well. "Grathir, I would not wish to leave you."

"You must," Grathir's voice was strong. His hide suffused with *yir*. "You must become strong, become a leader to our people. More importantly, you must lead with *Chiga*. You must gain the experience in battle which all our people will honor."

His words seemed odd to me. From what I had seen, *Chiga* was granted by my people with birth. I was born Xurok, dishonored. I had that beaten into me from when I was young enough to understand the words.

"I know, Grathir," Chuni responded. "But I do not want to leave you."

They discussed their plans for her often, but many times they came back to this. As Chuni grew, it became more and more likely that one of the mercenaries or freedom fighters would take her on. Her training, too, had grown, and Grathir led her through tactics and even discussed strategy, honor, and philosophy with her. I picked up these last things as I was able, though I cannot say that I understand them fully, even now.

Some part of me felt shame that I listened in where I was not invited. Still, I continued, when I was able. I missed some sessions, over the months and years, either due to beatings or the necessity to find food. But I also practiced. I learned and I had begun to grow and develop myself. I was now two meters in height, though I still retained my ability to hide and to move stealthily. More, I had practiced constantly with my four arms, to the point where the training exercises were second nature.

Grathir gave a chuff of exasperation, "Chuni, I will—"

He broke off and looked up. A moment later, I heard the whine as well. A ship was landing. It was sleek and slender, the barrels of weapons jutted from the tip. I bit back a whine of fear and crouched lower in the brush. I did not recognize this ship, but I had seen ones like it before.

The predatory craft dropped down to the north end of the camp, where the supply ships sometimes dropped food and other supplies. There were shouts and a few screams from there The side doors on the small craft opened and Humans dropped out. They wore a motley mix of garb, most with some type of body armor strapped on over it. I recognized them as scavengers, men who looted the best of whatever pitiful goods the camp contained.

Four of the men, however, came towards us.

"Chuni, go and hide," Grathir said.

"Grathir, I can't leave you," Chuni said.

The *Chigathi* turned a sullen shade of red, and I could see the *ral* fluoresce under his hide. "Chuni…"

Perhaps it was my years of being prey or perhaps the old *Chigathi*'s tactical knowledge worked its way into his lessons. Either way, I saw that it was too late. The men who approached had already cut them off from the camp. The female cub could not reach the camp before they could intercept her.

"What have we got here?" one of the men laughed. "Ghornath playing at being soldiers? You wouldn't want us to think you're dangerous, now. We protect your camp, after all."

"You're pirates," Grathir grunted. "You take what you want. We will not oppose you. I just am playing with my granddaughter."

"She's female?" one of the pirates laughed. "God, you are an ugly bunch. Good thing for you, too. It's been a while, but it hasn't been *that* long."

I felt my fists clench and *ral* suffuse my hide. Rape was

one of the worst crimes, punishable by death in the most painful manner among my people. Not even one of my tormenters had threatened that to even a lowly *Xurok* such as myself.

Evidently, Grathir viewed the dishonorable in even graver terms, "She is but a child, how could you even joke at such a--"

"My men will say whatever they please, cripple," the man in the lead said. He wore a black shirt and black pants, and carried a shotgun. Unlike the others, he wore no body armor. "They will do as they please, as well. If you offend me, I will end you. If your pathetic excuse for a camp causes me issues... I'll wipe it off the face of this shitty planet, understood?"

Grathir seemed at a loss for words. He looked driven almost to the point of *noman kar*, blood-rage, but he somehow, ever so slowly, pulled himself back. "I understand. I apologize. We don't want any trouble." His voice was tight, controlled.

"Good," the man said. His head jerked around at the sound of gunfire. He gave a chuckle, "Sounds like some of my men needed to make an example. Good thing they did it first, I wouldn't want to have to drag your corpse up there."

He looked over at his men, "Search them."

"We haven't anything," Grathir said.

"We'll determine that," the pirate boss said.

Two pirates stepped forward and searched Grathir first. They kicked at the wheels of his cart, as if he might have hidden some wealth inside it. Then they patted his harness down. One of them pulled out a cluster of his medals, then threw them to the ground.

The feral part of me had taken over, and I had started to creep down the hill towards the pirates. I was still small for my age, only two meters in height, but I had put on mass and muscle. In the past years I had begun to hunt some of the creatures in the area of the camp for food with a javelin. I knew how to stalk prey.

The two men moved on to Chuni. One of them patted down her harness, then gave a whoop. "Look here, nothing of value, eh?" He held up a ring, a large red stone central on it.

"That looks nice," the pirate captain said. "We'll be

335

keeping it."

"You *can't*," Grathir snapped.

"I warned you already about telling *me* what I can't do," the pirate captain brought his shotgun up.

I had drawn within a dozen meters at that point. I don't know why I threw. Some part of me had come to like these two, the old veteran and the young girl he protected and taught. The feral part of me hated these humans, who stole the pathetic treasures we still kept.

The javelin struck the pirate in the torso. He gaped at it, the three foot shaft jutted from his chest. The three men with him stood in shock as well. I ran at the captain and the man closest to him. The captain had fallen to the ground, but his guard started to bring his shotgun up. I bowled into him, a hundred and fifty kilograms of angry young Ghornath. I was caught up in *kava,* with nothing but the hunt on my mind. I grabbed at his weapon and wrenched it from his hands, even as my forelegs drove him down and smashed him against the ground. I brought the weapon up, aimed at the two men who had begun to rush back to their boss. The words of Grathir went through my mind, even as my muscles followed the training which he had meant for someone else. My finger found the trigger and I fired.

The noise and light came as a shock. I stared towards the two men and I saw the comical expressions of shock on their near-chouma faces. One of the men stumbled and fell to his knees. His hands went to his abdomen. The other fumbled with his weapon, tried to raise it. I aimed my stolen weapon at him and fired once. He still stood so I fired again. The pirate stumbled backward and lay still.

There was silence for a long moment and I lowered the weapon.

"Who are you?" I heard Grathir's voice.

I almost bolted, but I knew that I had been seen, people would talk, and it was best to show respect to one of the *Chigathi.* I lowered my head submissively, I am *Xurok*, honored one," I said.

336

He wheeled his cart forward and I could see that Chuni had moved to the two dead pirates, where she pulled weapons off of them. "*Xurok…*" Grathir mused, as he studied the scene. "What is your name, cub?"

I dropped lower. I dreaded this, most of all. There were a handful of *Xurok* in the camp. However, even they looked upon me with disgust when I revealed my name. I felt the *lur* make my hide pale with shame. "I am Rastar Bastaff Antor."

Grathir did not answer for a long moment, "You came aboard the ship *Benrath Zul?*"

It took me a moment to speak, "I did."

"Your mother was Atcari Bastaff. She was a skilled healer," Grathir said. "I was told that her cub had died."

I couldn't meet his gaze. "I was… left at the garbage pits." I had been beaten and discarded. It was not a memory that I wished to revisit, not with the smell of the human's blood in my nostrils.

I heard a tinny voice and looked down. The dead pirate captain wore a radio, clasped to his belt. From it I heard the voice repeat, "Captain, any trouble over there?" I heard an echo of the voice from a radio that Chuni held.

Chuni stepped forward and passed the radio to Grathir. She did not meet my gaze and her coloring was *rul*. Grathir adjusted the radio and then spoke into it. His voice sounded heavily distorted with static from the radio at my feet. "Local scavengers," he said. "Had to chase some of them off. We're headed over, found some good stuff, have the crew come out, we'll need their help to load it."

"Be a good thing to get something worthwhile," the voice answered. "I'll let them know. We had to kill a couple of the cats. Jash was drunk and pissed on one of their little shrines so we had to make a few examples after that."

I could see *rul* fluoresce through Grathir's hide. Still, when he spoke, his voice was even, "Well, Jash gets to carry the heavy boxes. I'll meet you at the ship." He lowered the radio and I could see rage that lurked in him. I cowered back against that rage, for I had received it before from others. I did not think to defend myself, not even with the weapon I held. I was *Xurok*, he was *Chigathi*, should he wish to take my life, it was his.

He noticed my stance and he gave a grunt, "Rastar, you have done well."

My head came up in surprise.

He noticed the *kul* that went through my hide. "Do not fear, Rastar. You have done well. *Very* well," he said. "Had you not intervened, Chuni and I would be dead." He grunted, "It is the second time I owe my life to a Bastaff."

I didn't understand his words, then, but I understood his meaning, "*Chigathi*, I am but—"

"You killed the four of them," Grathir said. "Do not underestimate your value. You might be seen as *Xurok*... but *Chiga* can be earned. The time has come to earn more," he pointed at the distant ship. "They will attack the camp, if we do not kill them all."

He took the rifle that Chuni handed to him. "We will not have much time. They will grow suspicious as time passes. We must attack them while they are outside their ship." He looked over at Chuni, "You must go with Rastar. Attack them from up close. I will signal the attack and will snipe their leaders."

Chuni looked between Grathir and I. "Yes, Grathir."

Grathir looked back at me, "Guard Chuni, she is... crucial. Promise me you will protect her?"

"I swear," I said. I did not realize how painful that oath would later prove.

I knelt and pulled weapons and ammunition off of the two dead pirates at my feet. I held their larger shotguns with my lower arms while I clutched their submachine guns in my upper arms. I fumbled a bit as I reloaded, but soon enough I had figured the weapons out. I took off at a ground-eating lope, Chuni caught up with me. We ran in silence, but I could tell she was curious about me.

I could see *lir* flush her hide and she opened her mouth to ask a question. I picked up the pace so that I had no breath to speak and she matched my pace. Best to keep our minds on the coming fight, I thought.

338

I felt odd. I had been prey so long, only recently had I hunted even the weakest of creatures near the camp. Now I had taken the lives of humans. It gave me a sense of power and yet at the same time an ache. I did not want to take more lives... yet I saw, for myself, an opportunity. There were *Xurok*, I knew, who died in heroic deeds. These *Xurok* were considered cleansed. Their crimes and dishonor forgotten.

Could I but die in battle, I knew, I might erase my father's failures.

At this point, I knew the hidden ways of the camp well. I led Chuni into a drainage ditch, heavily overhung by Tranzi Bush, which allowed us to move rapidly and stay out of sight. I heard her grunt in disgust at the smell, but I didn't care. The refuse of the camp drained here, but I had used it as a shelter before.

At last, we reached the north end of the camp. I pushed up the embankment and slowly crept through the fragrant Tranzi Bush. It's long, needle-like thorns broke off against my hide. Each bush extended long, vine-like creepers, heavily laden with thorns, which would spread everywhere and strangle out other plants. It also reeked, a full scent of corruption and rot. The Tranzi's grew wherever they could and, if allowed, would overgrow the camp in a matter of weeks. The Tranzi Bush was normally brought with whatever aide workers came to the camp.

I hated the Tranzi's, but they provided good concealment as Chuni and I crept towards the open field. Two dozen pirates stood in clusters as they talked. Two of them stood near the open hatches to their ship. The others stood near the boxes of supplies we had last received. I felt *lur* suffuse my hide when I saw that they had dumped the bags of Mratha rice on the ground. The Mratha rice was the refugees main supply of food. Even I managed to get some small handfuls to sustain me. Ghornath would go hungry at the waste and destruction.

I could see a cluster of Ghornath to the side. They stood with slumped shoulders and drooped ears. I recognized the faces of some who had pursued me before. They had looked so fierce as they bullied me then... yet now, I could see, they were broken, hopeless. My faint ideas of revenge seemed so petty now.

The human pirates on guard at the ship both dropped, followed a moment later by a pair of shots. I surged out of the Tranzi Bush, all four weapons aimed.

Humans, I know now, have eyes designed as predators. They focus on one object at a time, with precision. Ghornath have eyes that can focus on everything in their field of vision at the same time. We have some problems with different distances and perspective, but we are more able to work at multiple actions at the same time. Almost all Ghornath can intuitively accomplish two different, even unrelated tasks with each set of limbs.

In the past few years, under Grathir's unknowing tutelage, I had developed myself to the point that I used all four limbs at the same time, each armed with a weapon. I opened fire with my four weapons. I focused on the pirates nearest the Ghornath, so that they would not have the chance to harm more of my people.

Behind me I heard Chuni open fire. She seemed to notice my focus and fired on the pirates to the other side.

Imagine a crossfire of six weapons, all of them firing in controlled bursts, all of them controlled by two people who have clear fields of fire. Next, imagine two dozen men, most of them relaxed and thinking themselves safe. Our ambush tore through the pirates like a Koon through a pack of Dronthir. Pirates staggered and screamed. One of them brought up a weapon, aimed at either myself or Chuni, but I cut him down even as I fired at three others. My shotguns ran out of ammunition and I dropped them and picked up two weapons from downed pirates.

The firefight ended with eerie suddenness. The last of the pirates grasped at his wounds and tried to crawl towards the ship. He jerked and lay still and a moment later single shot echoed from Grathir.

I lowered my weapons. I looked over and saw Chuni had gone pale as *kul* saturated her hide. The shock she felt showed in how she stood, as well. Still, she gave me a nod, and I felt a sudden connection with her. I felt a surge of confidence. I had accomplished something, I had made a difference.

340

The Ghornath on the edge of the camp came forward. They seemed hesitant, yet as they approached, one of them gave a shout. "The *Xurok*, he risked the entire camp!"

I lowered the weapons, "No, I-"

"Get him!" Two of my normal tormenter's charged forward and the others pursued.

I did what I knew to do. I ran.

***

It was several weeks before I dared to return to the camp. In the time since, the pirate craft had disappeared. Either Turak and his freedom fighters had taken it or the refugees had hidden it. I found myself drawn to the spot where I had watched Chuni and Grathir train. In the starlit night, the spot was empty. Even the pirate's bodies were gone, though dark spots remained where they had bled and died.

I had fought. I had killed. I had gained *Chiga,* yet I was still *Xurok*. I could never be anything but *Xurok*… for my father's failures would always overshadow anything I could do.

I curled up, tired and sad and so filled with *awel,* that my hide turned as yellow as a Pitri flower I wanted so much for things to have been different, for the connection I felt with Chuni to grow into friendship, for Grathir to be the mentor I had pretended he was, for the refugees to see me as a hero, and not as the source of their suffering.

Grathir found me. So lost in my own aches I was, that I did not hear the creak of his cart as he approached. "Rastar Bastaff Antor."

I looked up. I felt the *kul* flood my hide white with surprise. "My apologies, *Chigathi*, I…" I wasn't even certain what I apologized for, only that I must.

"Chuni has gone," Grathir said, his old voice worn. "Gone with Leader Turok. To fight Nova Roma and the Chxor, to gain honor. I asked that you protect her, yet you were gone, when you could have gone with them."

"I apologize," I said. My body ached with the idea that I had failed this great warrior.

341

"You needn't," Grathir growled. "It is I who should apologize to you." He lowered his forelegs in an awkward bow, the cart that held his rear section creaked alarmingly.

I darted to my feet, *"Chigathi*, you need not bow to *me!"*

He straightened, "I must, for I am in your debt of honor, twice and more." He gazed up at the stars, "I had hoped you would return here, in time. I must explain." He paused, and his hide took on the blue tone of *rew.* "You have no doubt heard that I was one of the Royal Guard?"

I could not speak, for I felt emotion choke me. I barely managed to nod.

"I was a Leader among them, entrusted with the protection of Princess Hycar," he said. "When the Nova Roma Empire attacked, my team protected her as we withdrew. We took much fire, for they knew the importance of our leadership to us." I could only nod at this. Many of the refugees had felt adrift at the loss of the Emperor and his young sister. Legend said that they were descended from the *Nogathi*, the Blessed. Certainly their dynasty had ruled Ghornathi Har since before we had a recorded history.

The aged warrior took a moment to speak, "What most here know is that I was gravely wounded and evacuated along with what remained of my family and that the Nova Romans captured Princess Hycar and executed her." When he spoke, his voice was low, "They do not know that I had no surviving family. The princess stayed by my side while a decoy, my own granddaughter, was captured and executed."

My eyes widened with shock, "Then Chuni-"

"Is the rightful Empress, yes," Grathir said. "Something which I have told no one… no one save you and her. She bears her mother's signet ring, a mark of her bloodline. She is the *only* surviving heir and I swore to defend her as long as I could."

"But…" I wanted to ask why Grathir hadn't revealed her identity to the others in the camp, but I knew that quickly enough. She would not be safe, not until she proved herself. Just as some Ghornath had hesitated to protect the young Emperor, others would hesitate to defend his sister. She must be proven in battle, a hero who the others would honor. Then she would command not just their loyalty, but their hearts. "Why tell me?" I asked finally.

"Because, you fought in battle with her. More, you impressed her. She begged from me the story of your mother... and your father," Grathir answered. "When Leader Turok arrived, she insisted I find you, to try to talk you into joining them."

I shook my head, "He... would not have me." I did not mention, then, that it was Turok who had cast me out to die as a young cub. Those in the camp looked well upon the veteran, but I would not set him against Turok.

"I did not think so," Grathir said. "There are others who fight for our people. Some in obvious ways, such as Turok, others from the shadows. War with Nova Roma has drained our people, turned many of them to hate. We must become strong again, build again. I know of some who try to build a better day for our people." He sighed. "In truth, it was your mother, Rastar, who saved my life, who made it so that I lived long enough to instruct the princess in combat. I owe her for that. Indeed, I promised her that I would look after her cub and I failed in that, for when I arrived here, I heard that you were dead and did not ask questions."

I could not answer, I felt unworthy, "Grathir, my father..."

"Made a mistake. A simple one. I know, I have reviewed the tapes myself, filled with rage over the events. Our entire race blames your father, but we might as well blame ourselves."

I thought of the recording and how my punishers had held me so that I must watch it, over and over as they beat me. I thought of the distracted look upon my father's face as he gave the order to check again in regards to the suspected ships. Those ships led the Nova Roma surprise attack which gutted our system defenses and took the lives of over half a million of my people... to include my own father. His order had alerted those attacking ships that they'd been discovered and given them the opportunity to launch their munitions. This was what the survivors of my

343

race not just believed, but *knew*. I was the son of the man who had killed his race.

"Rastar Bastaff Antor," Grathir said. "You listen to me. You saved the life of the rightful Empress. You slew pirates who would have killed thousands of unarmed Ghornath. You have no honor debt to repay… not to me, not to our people."

"They will not believe that," I said.

"Then show them that you are a warrior. I saw much promise and potential in that fight. You will be an unparalleled warrior, Rastar. You come from great families and you will redeem your name and gain much *Chiga* in battle… I have seen it."

How does one argue with a statement like that? I wonder to this day if the old warrior was gifted with some measure of prescience… or if he was just trying to encourage me.

"There is a human mercenary ship which will return in a week. I have already spoken to their commander… He needs muscle, but you must become more than that. Become a leader, learn tactics and strategy, study human culture… we will need allies among them to fight the Chxor."

I nodded. I felt dazed from the revelations and the honors this old warrior bestowed upon me. "What do I do?"

"Grow strong, gain *Chiga*, and then, when she needs you, help her," Grathir said.

***

The icy, windswept planet of Howell had little of apparent value. The small human colony there had issues with a Centauri mining conglomerate. I hired on mostly because I didn't like bullies. They couldn't afford to pay much, but they were kind, they cooked good food, and they kept me stocked with coca cola. The other mercenaries they had weren't nearly at my level, though there was one, Antonov, who I liked. It had been four years since I left behind Ghren. I sent most of my pay to Grathir, who now and then would send me a message about 'Chuni.' She had been promoted to Leader and had her own team. She asked about me. I had written her one letter, where I told her that my services and honor were hers, should she ask. I did not receive a reply.

Antonov interrupted my latest round of reading old mail and cleaning my weapons. He and I had worked together several times before. He had, in fact, been with the first mercenary who had recruited me from Ghren. Antonov had a passion for holovids and he introduced me to them.

They are fascinating, a vision into history and entertainment at once. I've learned much about Earth, particularly their vibrant and violent past. Their ancient Romans are, by far, more bloody and cruel than the Nova Romans. They seem to have been plagued by all manner of terrible monsters, which they have slain with a mix of human ingenuity and superior firepower. In particular, there are a manner of beasts, which Antonov called 'kaiju' which seem to attack large cities. These beasts are towering constructs of flesh, which I am told, resist all manner of conventional weapons.

It is little wonder, then, that humans moved to other planets and systems. Even Howell seems a much nicer place than one which is so filled with predators.

Antonov kicked in the door and then came to huddle over the stove. "My friends, it is colder than my wife's heart out there," he said, his accent thick.

"Which one?" Riley asked, a cocky smile on his face.

"Both of them," Antonov said with a laugh.

Riley joined in. I didn't like Riley, he was stocky and blonde, with blue eyes. Riley was one of those mercenaries who reminded me of the pirates I'd killed back on Ghren. He seemed to think that a gun gave him power and authority. Still, Antonov had said he was good in a fight and that he would work well on the team, so I put up with him.

The other five members of our team were less experienced. Three of them had the looks of bouncers who wanted to make more money, big tough men. None nearly as big as me, of course. The other two were just normal men, down on their luck, who took a job as a hired gun with calm reluctance. Don't get me wrong, I started out as little better than a bouncer, myself. But I became something more, I'd earned my mercenary charter from Tanis, from hard work and real combat.

The locals had hired us all from Irkut. It wasn't much better than Howell, but my last contract there had fallen through after the man who hired me as a bodyguard tried to rape a hotel maid. Antonov said I should have just killed him, but it seemed wrong to take his money and then kill him, so I'd just broken his arms and legs.

The maid had helped Antonov and I to escape, at least.

"Well, I've got some news," Antonov said. "This little garrison duty is getting a little rougher. Locals said they spotted some armed men out near Huval's crest. We should go and check it out, make sure the corporate types aren't making a move."

Riley grimaced, "I don't know if we're getting paid enough to go out in that."

I stood up. I wore body armor sized to my frame, and carried four submachine guns and four fully automatic snub shotguns slung to my tactical armor. "They're paying us what they can. Let's check it out. It's better we see them out there rather than in here with us," I said. I didn't want to be here if they attacked. The building had windows, but the others kept them closed against the wind and weather. Any attacker could slip up next to the building without us realizing it. That was why Antonov and I did foot patrols around the compound.

"Right," Riley grimaced. He glanced at the others, "Bruce and Ken, you coming?"

Those two stood. Ken Salazar was a former bouncer, tough, but lazy. I didn't like him, but he seemed to know how to handle his rifle at least. Bruce was one of the normal types, tall and thin. He had a smirk on his face, now, one that made me suddenly uneasy.

I led the way out, followed by Antonov. As he came up next to me, I said, "Something's up with Bruce."

Antonov glanced back. "You think he might have sold us out?"

I shrugged uncomfortably, even as I tightened down my cold weather gear against the wind. "I don't know."

Antonov patted me on the shoulder, "Don't worry, I'll keep an eye on him."

I gave him a grateful nod and a thumbs up. "Let's go," I said.

Riley and Ken Salazar led the way. It was several kilometers to Huval's Crest, the hill that overlooked the compound. We made it quickly enough. Despite any misgivings I felt about them, they moved cautiously and quietly as we went up the slope.

"How many?" I asked. I felt a prick of unease as I studied the slope.

"What?" Antonov asked, he looked distracted, his eyes on Bruce as the other man followed us. He also glanced at the distant compound, almost as if nervous about the men still there on guard.

"How many armed men did the local see?" I asked. I studied the rocks above us and *kul* made my hide go pale. "There's no way he could have come up this way without being seen by someone up there. We're dangerously exposed."

"Yeah, tell me about it," Antonov said. He looked over his shoulder at the distant compound again. His voice sounded distracted.

"You keep looking back there," I asked, "Why?"

"Well, you know, I just want to be sure..." He trailed off as the rumbles of explosions reached us. I crouched and looked back in time to see the last structures of the compound erupt in a chain of explosions.

At the same time, Bruce opened fire from below us. I drew my weapons and fired before I even really knew what had happened. The rounds cut the other man down. Behind me I heard more fire and I ducked to the side and took shelter behind a boulder. "They betrayed us! Antonov, I'll cover you!"

"Sorry friend," I heard. I turned my head to see that Antonov had his grenade launcher aimed at me. "They offered a lot of money... and I knew you wouldn't take it."

He fired. The grenade detonated at my rearfeet. In the flash of high explosives, I saw Antonov's smiling face burned

347

into my mind.

***

I awoke, and for a moment my past and present merged. I couldn't tell if I was a cub again, beaten by my enemies and left for dead or if I was a mercenary betrayed by my companions. I could tell I was badly injured. The blast had shredded my rearlegs, bone and flesh dangled down, connected by strings of tissue. My intestines had spilled into the dirt. I tried to crawl, but the pain was too much.

Antonov and Riley had stripped me of anything of value. My guns, my money, even my holovid player was gone. My body armor was twisted and torn. I felt the cold and blood loss had begun to drag me towards a final sleep, for my body felt cold and sluggish. The pain began to grow somewhat distant.

I regretted that I had failed the people of this world. I had failed them, and they had died because Antonov was greedy and I hadn't seen it. I regretted that I had failed Grathir and Princess Hycar. I could not serve them, not if I were dead on some meaningless rock. I did not regret my death, only that I had failed.

Then I saw the light. It came from a shuttle. The shuttle drew closer, and I saw a team, in bulky black body armor, rappel down. One of them drew near, "Ghornath, fits the description of the merc."

"Gods," another said, "He's still alive."

"Wow," the first said, as he came closer, "I'd heard you cats were tough, but... hey, can you hear me?"

"Yes," I said, my voice faint, even to myself.

The team leader spoke into his radio, "Command, this is Lancer Five, we have a survivor here. Looks like the Ghornath might make it. Can we get a recovery team down here?"

I didn't hear the response. My world faded. Some part of me watched as the Centauri Commando team recovered Bruce's corpse. Their medic team arrived not long after, and two of them went to work on me, even as the shuttle lowered a harness. "Hang in there, tough bastard."

348

I awoke in a hospital. I had no real experience in human hospitals, but the sterile metal surfaces and bright lights matched what I had seen in holovids. I still felt somewhat disconnected, either from my wounds or medication, I couldn't tell which.

"Mr. Antor," a woman's cool, cultured voice spoke. I could barely see her silhouette against the lights.

"I am Rastar," I said.

"Rastar, then," she responded. "You are gravely injured. I am told you are a mercenary, that you protected the people on Howell?"

"I failed them," I said. "I failed everyone."

"Rastar, you fought well. You are very tough. My people have little experience with aliens, most of your kind populate the far reaches of human space. We conduct some research, here, research which might help you."

"Help me?" I asked, puzzled.

"Your legs, your back, they are very badly mauled. We could save only a limited amount of the tissue, your body will not recover, I'm afraid. You will have limited use of your front legs. No use to your rear legs, we had to amputate to just below the hip," her voice contained no emotion. "Your lower set of arms also took severe burns, along with much of your body. I'm afraid that we have to keep your body cleansed to prevent necrosis of your tissue as well as secondary infection."

I couldn't answer. What she had described would make me a cripple. I might as well be dead. In fact, it would be better if I were dead. Then at least, I would not be a burden. "What can you do?" I finally managed to ask.

"We have a number of experimental procedures," she said. "For one, cybernetics are an option, as are some experimental procedures. We'll examine your case very thoroughly and we'll apply whatever resources we feel are appropriate."

"What do you want from me?" I asked.

"We will employ you as security for our facilities," she

answered. "Your exact duties will be laid out by someone more familiar with those aspects. Your contract will last as long as we need to study the repairs. In return, we'll get you functioning and pay you for your services."

This was my chance, I saw. I could have a second opportunity, to serve my people and to regain my *Chiga*. I would not fail, I would take whatever recovery, suffer through their studies, and then, when I had my opportunity, I would once again become the warrior that Grathir had charged me to become. "Do it."

***

I was not quite sure, even now, how things had gone so completely and utterly wrong. How could I have underestimated the humans? Had I not seen how untrustworthy their powerful elite could be, in the destruction of my home-world's defenses and the looting of my system? Had I not been betrayed by Antonov, my first human friend?

Still, as I stepped into the offices of the ship's Captain, I tried my best to keep my emotions in check.

The portly human behind the desk looked me up and down, "Ship's security? You got any experience in that?"

"Yes," I said, truthfully. "I've served as private security aboard several ships." Granted, at the time, they put me in powered armor and had me guard top secret cargoes, all the while they monitored my every move. Even so, I thought I could manage aboard the aging freighter, even armed with only a pair of pistols and garbed in just a utility uniform.

Captain Phillips grunted noncommittally. "I can't pay much. We're doing a quick run to the Crow system I just need someone who can keep stowaways off and make sure my crew doesn't jump ship with my cargo."

I gave him thumbs up, "I can do that." It would be nice to have a relatively relaxing trip. Hopefully it would be a long journey through shadow space to a distant world, far from the Centauri Confederation and the shadowy group who had first recruited me and then betrayed me, yet again. I hoped that I had outrun the bounties and bounty-hunters that would pursue me.

Some part of me wondered how I would manage to do as Grathir had asked. I had not dared to contact him, for fear that it would draw the attention of those who pursued me. I wondered if Princess Hycar would hear of the bounties on me, if she would take that as a sign of my failure.

"Very well, our navigator, Ariadne is off duty, she just signed on yesterday. She'll get with you and show you around," Captain Phillips said. Rastar turned and headed for the hatch, his head low so it didn't scrape the ceiling. Human ships almost always made him feel claustrophobic. "Oh, one last thing. We're skirting the edge of Chxor space. We shouldn't have any issues with them, not unless we get unlucky enough to stumble into one of their patrols. On the off chance that happens, let me do the talking, understood?"

I felt some *rul* fill my hide with red. "If they board, they will take the ship."

"Leave that to me," Captain Phillips said.

***

"I repeat, all personnel report to the crew lounge," Captain Phillips sounded terrified. I stood behind him, next to the murdered Purser who had attempted to bribe the Chxor inspection team. My hands twitched, eager for the fight. Still, there were too many to fight. If they had jumped away, as the navigator had suggested, they could have escaped. Rastar saw the human woman had a pinched look on her face, that mingled regret, anger, and sadness. He felt the same. The Terrathi Voyager had stumbled across just a single Chxor patrol craft in its brief stop at the Saragossa system. Only by the worst of luck had they been within range of the other vessel.

Only by Captain Phillips' fear had they not jumped out before the other ship could board. I felt the *kava* begin to build in me again. Still, the Chxor inspectors had locked down our navigation board upon arrival to the bridge. They'd also ordered Captain Phillips to transfer a list of passengers, crew and the cargo manifest.

That was when the purser tried to bribe them. Captain Phillips had lost what little bearing he had after the Chxor calmly executed the officer. I just didn't see anything I could do at that point. They had the bridge, they had the ship targeted, and they seemed to have no compunction about killing anyone who caused trouble.

It looked like my best chance at fighting another day was to remain calm. I glanced at the navigator, who looked worried, and I gave her a thumbs up. She gave me a slight smile in return. *Well,* I thought, *at least not all humans lack a sense of humor.*

I would survive this, as I had survived so much else. I would become the warrior that my people needed… and along the way, I would have the opportunity to kill some Chxor. Also, importantly, the Chxor would not track human bounties or allow human bounty hunters in their space. I would have some time for my pursuers to lose interest, and perhaps for the whole misunderstanding to blow over. I felt *yir* suffuse my hide, and for the first time in a long time, I felt suddenly happy.

###

Part Four

Ghost Story
The Renegades, Book Four
by Kal Spriggs

Eric had a very peculiar talent set in that he made for a very talented chef and an absolutely perfect killer. While the former meant he had taken over the ship's galley, the later meant he got to do less fun things sometimes, such as his current task.

He gave a sigh as Pixel assembled his pistol and managed to 'flag' everyone in the room. "Pixel, keep the damned muzzle down unless you plan to shoot someone with it," Eric repeated for what felt like the twentieth time.

With a new private, he would have dragged them outside and gone for a more physical method of instruction. He did not have that option with the crew of escaped prisoners. For one thing, they wouldn't accept those tactics. For another, most of them had some experience with weapons. To Eric, that just meant they had more time to develop bad habits. Mandy and Miranda both had some bad habits, but Mike, their recently elected captain, served as a case in point.

"Captain,I appreciate you assembling the weapon, but I would suggest you keep your finger out of the trigger well unless you intend to fire," Elena said. She managed it with more tact than Eric could have mustered just then, which he appreciated.

"That's what the safety is for," Mike shrugged.

"There is only one safety, that is your trigger finger," Eric said. He gnashed his teeth as he saw Ariadne smile in the back of the room. "Pay attention, Ariadne, or do us all a favor and blow your fucking brains out now and get it over with."

She looked hurt at that and Eric cursed silently at that. He should not have lost his temper with her, not when she at least, had listened and followed all his directions, unlike some people, to include their new captain.

She just reminded him too much of Ivanna Stravinsky, one of his medics from his time as a squad leader in the Centauri Commandos. Ariadne had the same cheerful attitude, the same positive outlook. Eric feared she'd end up dead the same way too. Ivanna had cared too much about people, and that cost her life when she went to treat a wounded Seppie terrorist and took a round through her throat.

Eric held her when she died. She choked on her own blood as she tried to talk him through treatment. He had seen Ivanna's weakness and not acted on it, he would not make the same mistake with Ariadne.

"Well guys," Rastar said, his voice calm, "We've gone through the fundamentals of safety as well as a field strip of the pistols." Eric glanced over at the big alien and felt some of his anger ease. Rastar seemed particularly safety conscious, especially for someone who had learned his trade through mercenary work. His easygoing attitude also made his corrections carry more weight with the others.

When they bothered to listen.

"So when do we get to shoot stuff?" Crowe asked impatiently.

"You don't," Simon said. "There's nowhere on the ship safe to put up a range. When we find an appropriate location we can set one up, but until then, you get to dry fire and practice weapons maintenance. These Liberty Arms HQ7's are pretty simple. Case-less ammo still leaves a residue though, which can lead to barrel fouling. So a daily cleaning cycle is a good habit to get into. It should take you fifteen minutes to disassemble, wipe everything down and then reassemble your weapon. Once a week you should do a full strip and cleaning. I've posted a schedule on the outside of the door, you should all initial by your name each day on the board after you do your cleaning."

"What a waste of time," Crowe said, "I mean, we don't even get to shoot these things yet, why bother to clean them?"

"It builds good habits, which is important because a lot of you have bad habits we need to break. Especially you," Eric said. "If you continue hold that pistol like you've seen in the holovids you won't hit a thing."

Run the Chxor spoke up, "I have a question."

Eric looked over at the little alien. As much as he hated

Chxor, he had to admit that the little bastard had followed every direction. "Yes?"

"What methods would you recommend for your fellow humans to prevent hormonal imbalances from hindering their actions in combat? I have seen some of the others fire when they had excessive levels of adrenaline and I felt it unsafe to remain in the same room." Run looked over at the engineer, "This includes those less familiar with firearms."

Eric snorted despite himself, "That's actually a good point." He suddenly remembered his last mission with the Commandos, and how he had taken his wounds on that mission. "It's a serious matter, and even a well trained shooter can make a mistake if he loses track of the situation." Eric opened the top of his suit and turned to the side. "I got these scars from a teammate, a new sergeant who had just joined our team. His first mission out he put two in my side and killed one of his own soldiers when he got turned around in the firefight." *My fault,* he thought, *I should have made certain he knew our team procedures, Ivan would have survived then.* No one spoke for a moment, and Eric nodded as his graphic lesson of the dangers of friendly fire seemed to sink in.

"What were those other scars, the ones that looked like straight lines?" Ariadne asked.

Eric closed his eyes. He could see the clean lines that the laser scalpels had left from memory. Even if he didn't have the nightmares to remind him about them, he felt the dull ache from those every day of his life. "Something else. I'll save that story for another day."

He took a deep breath, eager to return the subject to one that wouldn't stir his own nightmares, "I recommend practice and rehearsals. I think it obvious that our main offensive team consists of Rastar, myself, and Anubus. We have done some discussion of tactics, but we haven't worked together as much as we should. But all of us should practice together, and rehearse various situations aboard the ship, like a deranged passenger," despite himself, Eric glanced over at Rastar, "or an enemy seizing some part of the ship, such as the engine room or bridge."

"Those last two seem a little far fetched," Mike said.

"Agreed," Eric said, "But drills like that build team cohesion and allow us to know the abilities of our fellow crew. I for one would be clueless in the engine room without Pixel to guide me."

"I can see that," Mike nodded. "When we get some time, we'll institute some drills. I'd like to see you draw up a rehearsal plan, first though. Set down with me and we'll talk about shipboard duties for that." Mike looked around at them all, "That's a good segue to something I wanted to bring up. I've talked with you all about billets and positions on the crew. I'll post the actual duty roster later today, but this is our core group. So I wanted to tell you all in person."

Great idea, do it when everyone has a gun in their hands, Eric thought, *just in case they* really *want to take exception to their new job.*

"Ariadne is our navigation officer, of course," Mike said, "But I've also made her our executive officer, which means if I become incapacitated, she's in charge."

Eric frowned at that. The psychic certainly knew how to react in a crisis, but he didn't think she could manage people from a position of authority in the day to day operations. She wanted people to like her too much. And every XO he ever had in the military was an asshole. It came with the job, as the enforcers of the commander's orders and the people who screened ninety percent of the bullshit.

"Eric, you're our best expert on ships weapons, so I've assigned you as the weapons officer, with the secondary task as part of our mobile reaction force for shipboard combat," Mike continued. He looked at Eric as if he expected some comment. Eric just gave him a shrug, he could do either task. "You're also assigned as our chef extraordinaire."

Everyone gave a cheer at that, and Eric couldn't restrain a sheepish grin, "Thanks guys, I'm glad you like the food."

Mike slapped him on the back and Eric winced as the Captain managed to put his finger in the trigger well of his pistol *again*. "Well, I like to eat well. Keep that up."

Mike turned to Rastar, "I've assigned you as our Master of Arms, to keep peace aboard the ship and as the team leader for our mobile reaction force." Mike looked around at the rest of them, "I had my doubts, but believe me, Rastar has a very *colorful* record of experience. I think he'll do fine... as long as he keeps his temper."

"Hey man, not a problem, I'm, like, totally cool," Rastar gave Mike four thumbs up. Eric had mixed feelings about that, but he felt pretty certain that Rastar wouldn't kill anyone that didn't deserve it if he *did* lose his temper, so he let it pass. Besides, Rastar had become something of a friend, so Eric didn't want to call him on his impulse issues in front of the others.

"Simon, you're going to be our sensors officer, and another member of our mobile reaction team. Which means that if we have a situation aboard ship, we will be down sensors and weapons," Mike said. "Which is why Pixel of course, has engineering as our Engineering Officer. With him there, and Ariadne and myself on the bridge, I think we can at least run away effectively enough."

Eric nodded at that. Tactically, they had no business to attack anyone if they had a fight on-board already. With Ariadne's abilities, as long as the engine stayed up they could at least escape into shadow space.

"Anubus isn't here, but I've already informed him that he'll serve as our auxiliary pilot and once we get a shuttle or fighter, he'll serve as our pilot for that," Mike said. "Of course, his main duty will be with the mobile reaction team." The last could have gone unsaid, Eric knew. Most Wrethe seemed physically intimidating. Eric found Anubus flat out terrifying, not only for the stealth with which he moved but also for his raw physical strength and the savage retractable claws that tipped each of his three fingers. *Lets see, then there's his rampant paranoia and his whole thing about eating people...*

"I suppose I'm stuck with communications?" Crowe asked

Mike nodded, "Yes, though Pixel has mentioned he'd like your help with some system security upgrades he wanted to run.

The Chxor cracked just about everything open and he rightly feels there's not enough control on who can access what in the system."

Eric frowned at that, the part about security sounded out of character for the engineer. He had to wonder if Mike had suggested the idea to Pixel.

Then again, he agreed with the idea himself.

"Elena, Miranda and Mandy, you're all on our provisional list, so you don't have any hard duty assignments yet," Mike said. "Elena, I'd like you to continue to assist myself with crew interviews and other tasks. Miranda continue to help Pixel in the engine room. Mandy... well I've noticed that Pixel is a long way away from any help if he needs it." Mike said. Eric nodded at that, the armory and bridge lay close together at the stern of the vessel, while the engine room lay closer to the front of the vessel. "I want you down there as manual labor, but keep a weapon handy. You and Miranda back him up if there's a need."

Mike looked around at them all, then he paused, "Oh, right Run."

"I will continue my experimentation?"

"Uh, well, you're our acting ship's doctor, and please help out with any other tasks from people who need your unique skill set," Mike said.

"I will also cross train in languages and other skill sets," Run said. "I have begun to learn Russian from Elena Ludmilla Lakar. I will study with Engineer Pixel to figure out engineering. When I have finished I will study sensors, weapons, and communications."

Mike nodded, "Good job, Run."

Eric grimaced at the thought of the little monster seated with him for hours at time while he went over the various aspect of weapons systems. Still, at least he followed directions.

Mike holstered his pistol and Eric gave a silent sigh of relief. "Alright, well, I understand that Eric has prepared quite a meal for us for our last dinner before we emerge in 443C98. So let's not waste any more time."

Rastar slapped Eric on the back hard enough to stagger

him. "Yes, let's eat!"

***

Eric arrived at the lounge well after the others. He had wanted to do a last functions check of his new rifle. Maybe in this new star system he would get the chance to use it. Something about the lethal perfection of the laser rifle just gave him a warm glow in his stomach.

Eric smiled as he saw the crowd of people gathered for his food. Up until a few days ago, he had heard that some of the escaped prisoners still ate the horrid ration bars rather than come up to the lounge. It looked like his cinnamon and saffron chicken breast had drawn the rest of the holdouts.

Eric walked up to serve himself, and as he did, an unfamiliar woman stepped in his path. "I understand that you are the ship's cook?" Her voice sounded like pure sex, and Eric caught a whiff of what smelled like flowers.

Eric looked her over. She stood short for a woman, with curly dark hair, large brown eyes, and a remarkably narrow waist for her curves. Eric realized he'd let his gaze linger a little too long when she cleared her throat. Best to clarify that while he could cook, he had more talents than that, "I cooked the meal, I'm also the ship's weapons officer."

"Very well," She nodded, she had a grace and poise that both attracted and oddly repulsed him. She reminded him of one of the high end prostitutes one of his commanding officers trafficked with. "I am Ambassador Alara Vibius. I must commend you for your skill, however will require my meals delivered to my quarters from now on."

Eric said the first thing that came to mind, "Are you fucking with me?"

"Excuse me?" She demanded.

"No, I don't excuse you. I'm not your servant, I don't care who you are. I've got enough to do that I don't have time to deliver your meals," Eric snapped. "For that matter, you look healthy enough to walk your happy ass down here to partake."

He hadn't realized his voice had risen until a stocky man

361

in the remains of a uniform stepped between him and the Ambassador. Eric gave him a quick once-over, and evaluated him as an experienced noncomissioned officer, but way out of his league compared to Eric. Even so, Eric took a step back and gave the other man a nod. He had no intention to further escalate things.

Evidently the Ambassador had no prior experience to such treatment. She stared at Eric with a look of shock. Eric gave her a nod, and walked around them towards the food. *I really need to learn to watch my mouth, but she blindsided me with that,* he thought. Then again, she deserved it, so he didn't feel bad about it. He did feel irritation from the stares of some of the other passengers, however.

He stepped up to the buffet table and helped himself. He had expected the weapons safety class to run long, so he had enlisted the help of Michael Santangel to set things up. The former noble from Saragossa had done a fine job, and if he felt the job beneath his talent set, well, he had kept his mouth shut about it at least.

No sooner had Eric thought of the man than he appeared at his side, "Nice job with the bitch."

"What?" Eric looked back over his shoulder, even as he started to load down his plate with food. Ambassador Alara stood where she stood where he had dressed her down. "Yeah, well, she pushed the wrong buttons." Eric gazed at her for a bit longer than necessary and when he looked forward he gave Santangel a grin, "I'd like to push some of her buttons, if you know what I mean."

The other man coughed on some of his spiced potato au grait, and Eric patted him on the back, "Yeah, that's a bit spicy, can catch you off guard if you don't expect it."

"Ah, no, it was not the food that surprised me," Santangel said. "I am surprised by your attraction for the Ambassador, is all. She is arrogant, insufferable, and unbearably rude..." Santangel trailed off, and Eric saw a look of realization come across his face. "Oh, my."

"What, did I miss something?" Eric asked. The other

man suddenly looked uncomfortable. "Anyway, to answer your question, she's a bitch, but she's got a nice body, and frankly, it's been a while. Besides, it's not like I want to hear her talk. Well, scream my name a bit maybe, but that's not really talk."

"Right," Micheal Santangel said. "If you would excuse me, I think the Captain has signaled he wished to speak with me." Eric saw that the other man had flushed. Probably couldn't handle his spicy food, Eric figured.

"Yeah, sure," Eric nodded even as he finished loading his plate with chicken. He saw Pixel stood only a few meters away. The engineer looked tired, and Eric briefly considered that he could probably use a break from all his engineering work.

He stepped closer, "Pixel, made any progress on those grenade casings?"

Pixel looked over at him, "Uh, I've been pretty busy."

"Right, I figured something like that would be a break from the rest of your work, and all the other stuff people have loaded you down with," Eric said. "I mean, it's for something fun, explosives and all that, and useful too."

"Yeah..." Pixel shook his head, "Well, I appreciate your intention, but I've had a lot to do."

"I can understand that," Eric nodded. "Which reminds me, any progress on the weapons mount for the main gun or the capacitor damage? We could really use that."

"There's a lot of work to do there," Pixel said. "The Ghornath seemed low on supplies, what without having a base and all that. So with the capacitors I scavenged and the handful of replacements they had, the system still won't work, it's around fifteen percent power, not enough to even generate a beam."

Eric sighed, "Look, Pixel, I understand you might have other priorities..."

"You're the one who destroyed the mount and the capacitors for the weapon!" Pixel snapped. "You do realize that with that one action you've added hundreds of man hours of work, right? That's with the assumption that I can even fix it."

"Well," Eric shrugged, "Maybe it was my fault, but as an engineer, I figure you had some way to stop the damage before it happened. Isn't there some kind of engineer override or something?"

Pixel grimaced, "Yeah, there sure is. There's a big red button on the fusion reactor control terminal. That overrides everything."

"Really?" Eric asked. "How's that work?

"Yeah, it automatically detects any potential engineering problems and prevents further damage to the ship's systems." Pixel nodded. "And it's powered by magic fairy dust and unicorn tears." Eric felt his ears burn at the bite in Pixel's voice. "The only thing that big red button does is scram the reactor, cut power to the entire ship and shut down the reactor instantly. I could have done that to stop you, but we would have sat dead in space for hours while we brought all the systems back online."

"Oh," Eric said. "Probably a good thing you didn't do that in the middle of our escape."

Pixel rolled his eyes, "You think?" He drank the last of his cup and set down his empty plate. "If you'll excuse me, I need to go get some work done."

Eric watched the engineer walk away and shrugged a bit. Clearly Pixel needed to get some more sleep, the engineer had gotten cranky with his work load. Eric saw Rastar next to the jello bowl, and walked in that direction. Rastar still wore one of his Ghornath sized Hawaiian shirts, this one an electric lime green with bright purple flowers. "Hey big guy, how's it- Oh, tell me you didn't just put some horseradish in your jello?"

"Hey man," Rastar said. As Eric watched, he scooped a big spoonful of jello and horseradish into his mouth. Eric felt his stomach twist. "Great spread, man. Though I can't touch that potato stuff, I think some of those spices are toxic for me."

Eric closed his eyes. He made a mental note to find out which ones in particular. When he cooked, he put together complex meals from the eclectic supplies of the ship's previous crew. That the alien Ghornath had very different tastes than most humans and found a variety of human foodstuffs not only unpalatable but also toxic made cooking for the crew of escaped prisoners something of a challenge.

That the crew included a Ghornath, a Wrethe, and a Chxor, as well as a variety of humans from different colonies and walks of life made it more of a challenge. The Ghornath seemed able to eat most human foods, as evidenced by the former Ghornath privateer crew's eclectic mix of foodstuffs. They also seemed to react to various foods and spices in completely different fashions. Anubus could metabolize just about anything organic. Eric had seen him consume Chxor and their rations both and had heard from Mike that the Wrethe had grabbed a bite off of a dead human prisoner back before they made their escape from the prison station. The Chxor couldn't eat anything that humans could. So that made it easy enough for Eric. He just didn't bother to prepare anything for the little bastard. Nor did he bother with their single prisoner, Fleet Commander Krann. They had a variety of Chxor foodstuffs taken from the two previous ships that the pair could consume, or not, as they wanted.

If it were up to Eric, he would shoot Krann and possibly Run. He didn't like the Chxor species. For one thing, they seemed far to assured of their genetic and intellectual superiority. For another, they seemed bent on a war of conquest and extermination against the various human colonies. Eric could have tolerated either one, but both together just offended his sensibilities. *Well, that and the fact that Run seemed happy enough to cut on me with a dull prison shank to get the shrapnel out,* he thought. That memory made him rub at his side and the still sensitive scar.

"Well, I'll leave you to it," Eric said. He turned away and almost ran into Ariadne.

"Hi Eric, great job with the food!" Ariadne said.

Something about her cheerful attitude put him on the defensive. Somehow when she said it he felt uncertain. Where he had smiled and nodded at the comments from others, he barely managed a noncommittal grunt as a response.

"How do you think the class went?" Ariadne asked.

"Well enough," Eric said. He thought about Ariadne's performance, and he figured some positive comment would not hurt, "And you didn't fuck up." *Aw, crap, that sounds real great,* he thought darkly. "I mean, good job not fucking anything up." That probably didn't improve things, he had to admit.

Ariadne stared at him for a long moment, and when she spoke, she sounded more subdued, "Well, thanks for the food." She walked off without another comment.

"Dude, that was a little harsh," Rastar said from behind him.

Eric grunted, "Yeah, I meant to tell her she did a good job. I'm not so good on the positive reinforcement end of things." From what his experience, pain taught better anyway, the brain would forget, the body and heart remembered.

"Really, man, you should probably practice," Rastar said. "I practice interaction all the time, and I'm always watching holovids to learn more..."

"Well, that's different, you're an alien," Eric said. "Trust me, I'm human, she'll understand what I meant." If all else failed, she was a mind reader, for all he knew, she was in his head already.

Rastar's voice sounded dubious, "If you say so..."

"Eat your horseradish jello," Eric snapped. He stalked away from his friend, suddenly angry. He knew he had some issues with his interpersonal skills. The last thing he needed was a three hundred kilogram eight armed alien to whisper suggestions in his ear. Still, he should work on it, he knew. He saw Simon seated at a couch near the aquarium and Eric nodded to himself. The two of them had come to a sort of truce after Eric volunteered to take charge of the galley, but they still had a bit of tension. Where better to practice his conversation skills?

He took a seat next to the former policeman. "How's life?"

Simon didn't look away from the tank, "I'm trying to spot that damned Arcavian Fighting Eel."

"What, Rainbow?" Eric asked. Ariadne's name for the creature seemed wildly inappropriate. That meant the name had stuck over all other suggestions, of course. Eric didn't care for the name, except it seemed to drive Mike nuts. That meant that he used it as often as he could within earshot of Mike. Out of the corner of his eye, he saw Mike twitch slightly. *Weird how he doesn't like the thing, I figure it's a fish and he's Asian, if nothing else he'd want to roll it up in rice and eat it.*

"Yeah," Simon peered at the tank. "Damned thing is impossible to see until it attacks."

"Why not tap on the tank?" Eric asked and leaned forward.

"No!" Simon said. "It's almost a game for me and it passes the time."

"Right," Eric shrugged. "So what did you think about the class?"

"I think my suggestion of a precise curriculum and a manual for them to read would have made it run much more smoothly," Simon answered. "And the way you interrupted Elena and I whenever you disagreed probably confused the others."

"I meant what did you think about the students," Eric said sharply. He wanted to apologize, yet the other man's focus on his own mistakes put his back up. "And some of those things you taught might work fine for a police job where you might never have to fire your weapon, but we're on the razor edge of survival here, we may not have time to go by the book."

"What I meant," Simon said, his voice cold, "was you should have discussed your differences with us ahead of time. And Rastar, as Master of Arms, had the final say on what to teach, so we should have worked it out with him ahead of time. The four of us have different techniques, we should settle on a standard operational procedure, and train the others to work off of that."

"Oh," Eric said. "Well that makes sense."

"That's why I suggested it, but you and Rastar never answered the query I sent to the armory console," Simon said. "And I didn't have time earlier to come down and ask questions."

"Oh, truth to tell, Rastar just turns on holovids on that thing and I didn't realize it did much more than that," Eric said. "Well, next time we should do that. So what do you think about the students?" Eric thought he had done pretty well so far, they had avoided a real argument.

"I think that Mike's got too many bad habits, most of them from his prior service. Navy types always scare me, they're military so they think they know everything about weapons, but they handle sidearms less than most small town cops, and most of them have minimal training experience." Simon shrugged. "And every time he puts his finger in the trigger well I want to duck."

"Yeah, me too," Eric laughed. "I swear, I thought he was going to shoot me at least three or four times. Elena seemed to manage him pretty well, though."

"Yes," Simon nodded. "But she bothers me."

"What the whole bounty hunter thing?" Eric asked. "Actually I find that kind of hot." He glanced over at the tall blonde woman where she stood in conversation with Mike. She seemed to feel his eyes on her, and her blue eyed gaze flicked in his direction. She met his look with a raised eyebrow and returned to her conversation.

"Why am I not surprised?" Simon said. "Though yes, the bounty hunter past disturbs me, mercenaries and bounty hunters work crosses the law a bit too much for my tastes. That's not what bothers me, mostly though. Something about how she seems to know so much about us irritates me."

"What's your problem with mercenaries?" Eric asked. He had suggested to the others that he had worked as a mercenary after he left the military. It stretched the truth a bit, but it made for less questions. While his work had not strictly been mercenary work, he *did* get paid for rather similar, though far less legal, work.

"Some of them are little better than hired guns, and others are bandits with a permit," Simon said. "And the worst of them are just thugs or assassins."

Eric went cold at those words. "You seem pretty down on that."

"I'm out of work because one assassin killed my boss and another killed my partner and framed me for it," Simon answered, his voice cold. "Whether they were mercenaries, thugs, or just some criminal scum, I distrust those who take money to kill, even if they have a permit for it. And bounty hunters and mercenaries do that as a part of their job description."

Eric looked over at Simon, and he did not trust himself to speak. The cop had his own point of view, and nothing Eric could say would change that. Still, something about his sanctimonious attitude, the way he seemed to suggest himself as morally superior to those driven to such work shot a spike of anger down Eric's spine.

"So, what does that make the secret police? I mean, a lot of you acted as enforcers and government bag men," Eric said. "You ever throw a bag over some guy's head in front of his family? I bet that kind of thing makes for *great* law enforcement." He did not bother to hide his sarcasm.

"I worked with Confederation Security Bureau, thanks," Simon said. "We didn't do that sort of thing. I worked security and government investigation, remember? You seem a little bitter, one of your mercenary buddies get a late night visit after they take the wrong job?"

Eric looked away from Simon, even as he remembered a dark night twenty years ago. He leaned forward and tapped on the aquarium. "Hey look there's Rainbow. Good talking with you Simon." He treasured the look of surprise and anger on Simon's face as the eel exploded into motion and snapped and thrashed against the glass.

I probably could have handled that better, Eric thought as he walked away. Yet as he remembered what had happened to him and his family, he just felt a sullen anger. Anger at the destruction of his family and anger at what they did to him after ten years of loyal service.

***

As a child, he had not understood the source of the fear on his father's voice as the men pounded on the front door. Neither had he understood why his mother cried as she bundled him into his coat. "Son, when they come, you need to go out the

369

back door. Go to Uncle Striker's house."

"Papa, what's going on?" Eric would not cry. He was ten years old, his father had said to be brave, so he would not let himself cry.

"Eric, no time for questions. Be strong, and know that we love you," his father said as he led him to the back door of their apartment. The service access at the back of the kitchen should have required a special key to unlock, but his father tugged it open without effort. He ducked his head in the low door, "Alright. In you go my brave little man." The impacts on the door had stopped, but the quiet seemed ominous somehow. An adult Eric would later realize that the secret police outside had emplaced a breaching charge on the door. "And remember, go to Uncle Striker's house."

Eric nodded, "Yes, Papa, I will. When will you and Mama join me?"

His mother's crying rose at that, and Eric saw tears well up in his father's eyes. "Soon, my son. I love you, now be a good boy and go."

Eric stepped into the narrow passageway, and his father closed the access door behind him. Eric knew that he should go, now, but he waited, instead. He knew that his papa meant to meet the men who seemed so angry at him. He knew that his mama would not send him away unless she feared something bad. Something like when their neighbors had disappeared, even little Kyle. He pressed his face up against the mesh grate and peered into the kitchen.

A loud concussion threw him back. He sneezed as dust filled the air. A moment later he heard shouts in his parent's apartment. Then he heard his mama scream. Eric pressed his face up against the mesh and he could see his papa. Two men had him by the arms and one kicked him hard, behind the knee.

Eric wanted to shout at them, to tell them to stop, but he held his tongue. Papa had said to be quiet and to go. Papa had said to be brave, so he couldn't cry. Eric saw a police man step forward and draw a black bag down over his father's head. The others dragged his father out of sight.

He heard his mama cry out again and then he heard what sounded like a blow. Her cries stopped, and Eric felt rage curl his fists closed. He felt hot tears well down his face. He wanted to kill these men. He wanted to scream and shout as he shot them for hurting his mama. But he couldn't. He had told Papa that he would go to Uncle Striker's home. He told his Papa he would be quiet, and brave.

Eric stepped back from the grate. He knew the way, though the access tunnels were off limits, his papa had showed him where to go in the massive apartment tower. His papa had sent him on errands throughout the access corridors often two or three times a day over the past few years. Only years later would he realize that his father had used him to pass messages in whatever resistance group he had joined.

Eric followed the route out of memory. His small feet followed the dark corridors while his mind ranged over what he saw. Over and over he saw the expression on his father's face as that black bag came down over his head.

Eric's papa always looked brave. He had served in the Centauri Marines. He had fought the Seppies and he had the medals to prove his bravery.

Yet the last sight Eric had of his papa's face had showed fear. Fear for his family, fear for himself, and most of all, fear of that black bag, of the knowledge that once it went over his head, his life would end.

***

"Thirty seconds until normal space emergence," Ariadne said. "Wow, this is exciting."

Eric rolled his eyes, yet he felt his heart begin to race. His eyes flicked over the Ghornath weapons console. He wished he had more time to familiarize himself with the systems. For that matter, he wished that Crowe's translation program had worked.

"Weapons hot," Eric said as he tapped the buttons to activate the turrets. "What we've got of them anyway." The five turrets provided the Ghornath corvette with a complete range of

371

fire. The problem was that Pixel had found that damage had cut the links from the main console to the weapons on the port side. Which meant without someone at the actual weapon positions to fire them manually, they could not fire. With a full crew, they would have personnel for that. Unfortunately, they didn't have a full crew, much less a trained crew. So for now, a couple of the spacers that Ariadne and Mike had certified had taken position at those weapons consoles.

None of which changed the fact that the turrets mounted light pulse lasers, the equivalent of the point defense guns that most human ships mounted. They put out a mass of interceptor fire, designed to destroy missiles and fighters. They might damage another corvette or even a destroyer. They would have no effect at all on anything larger.

Of course, the main weapon would have served much better for that task. But it too had taken damage and Eric had further damaged it when he powered it up without knowledge of that damage. *Lets face it, I screwed up,* he thought grimly, *I tend to get sloppy when I rush, slow is smooth, smooth is fast, I must remember my training.*

He let out a breath as they emerged from shadow space. The gray emptiness which seemed haunted by barely seen motion vanished, replaced by the stars of normal space. A red giant hung sullenly off their port bow on the main screen. Eric's gaze went immediately to where Simon worked at the sensors. Rastar stood over his shoulder and pointed at various controls.

Eric gritted his teeth. He hated the wait. A ship lay at its most vulnerable on emergence from shadow space. They needed sensors up to get a picture of what lay around them, yet they would appear as a beacon to anyone who waited. And if some hostile lurked with their ship dark and their passive sensors ready, it would take a minor miracle to see them upon initial entry.

Eric tried not to think of all the possible threats, to include a pirate vessel with a stealth hull,\ or a Centauri commerce raider with a stealth field. Either of those would mean the destruction of their ship, particularly with a sensors technician unfamiliar with the Ghornath systems.

He knew the odds lay against any of that. Space, even in a star system, held a massive volume, the odds that they had emerged within range of a hostile vessel remained miniscule. Yet Eric did not let his guard down. He had seen too many good troops die when they or their commanders relaxed or trusted in the odds. Worse, he had too many ghosts who reminded him of the times *he* had not prepared for the remote contingencies.

Simon finally looked up, "Immediate area looks clear." He brought up a schematic of the system, "Some minor debris in the inner system, nothing you could call a planet. Two gas giants with some debris rings, nothing else of any real note." He didn't need to say that they would not see something smaller than a planet outside their sensor range. The tiny ship had excellent sensors for it size, but they did not have the resolution that a larger ship would have.

"I've got something," Crowe said from the communications console. "It's pretty weak, but its open signal..." he trailed off. "Wow, you will want to hear this."

Before Mike could tell him what to do, Crowe had already brought it up on the bridge intercom. Eric repressed a grimace, but he caught Mike's eyes and saw the other man give a shrug. A good military commo tech would have sent it to the captain to review first. Still, Mike would probably talk to the man later, and as much as Eric wanted to chew Crowe's ass, he also wanted to hear the broadcast.

The speakers brought in the signal, though the voice sounded tinny, "...mayday mayday. This is the freighter *Sao Martino* out of Saragossa. Our power plant has taken damage and we have lost power. We are on a mission of mercy for Saragossa. We request assistance. Mayday, mayday, mayday..." Crowe cut the signal.

"It just repeats after that, some kind of automated message. Very weak, I don't think a normal radio jockey would pick this up, we barely did with a military transceiver," Crowe said.

Ariadne frowned, "Those poor people, we need to go help

373

them."

"That's not a crew decision, that's one for the captain," Eric snapped. She had to learn her job as the executive officer lay in enforcement of the Captain's orders. Even so, he felt a little bad for yelling at her. He privately agreed that they should investigate. If nothing else, it might be a pirate trap and he would get a chance to kill someone.

"Any time stamp on the recording?" Mike asked. "I don't want to check out whatever it is and find the crew's been rescued and the ship salvaged for a decade."

"Nope," Crowe shrugged, "Just the base message, from the weak signal, I'd bet its operating on battery power only."

"It must be a trap," Anubus growled.

"It could be," Mike nodded. "But if so, I'm a bit confused. The signal's pretty weak, Crowe says a normal freighter couldn't pick it up."

"Well, they could if I was at the console," Crowe said. "But anyone else wouldn't stand a chance."

"Skilled and modest too," Simon drawled from the sensors console. "Captain, I've located the ship. The Chxor database has no match, but it looks like a freighter hull. And it seems to have no power. The hull looks cold too, which means either most of the ship is in vacuum or the ship hasn't had power for weeks at least."

"Good work," Mike nodded. "I'm inclined to investigate. If nothing else, I think we might find a better star-map aboard the other ship, which will get us to civilized space." He glanced at Ariadne, "Any psychic tingling?"

She smiled, "Not really. I'm sure things will work out though, and I'd like to rescue those people." She looked happy. Eric had no doubt that she wanted to do good by some poor bastards stranded in space.

Eric rolled his eyes. He doubted they would find any people to rescue. The way the universe worked, the people who sent that message either died or they sent it because they hoped to lure someone in to kill. Not that he would mind saving some innocent civilians. He just found that if he went into a situation ready for the worst, then, when things went wrong, it would not catch him off guard. People died when he failed to plan for the worst... and not the right people.

"Alright, plot us a course," Mike said. "Simon, I want you to scan the immediate area. If this is pirate bait, the pirates will wait until after we power down the engines and send personnel aboard. They won't be far though, probably within two or three hundred thousand kilometers, close enough that they can pounce before we have time to do anything and perfect range for a cheap shot."

Eric nodded, though he thought that some raiders might pick a spot even further out than that. Then again, with Simon at the sensors and with the various abilities available to a raider, it would take more than a little luck to spot anything outside that range with passive sensors. And Eric knew they did not want to go with active sensors, not yet anyway. Those would make them light up like a star to anyone with the sensors to see them.

"Course plotted," Ariadne said. "I brought us in slow, to give us more time to check it out. But I hope they can hold on until we get there."

"Right, good job, I'm bringing up the drives now," Mike said.

Eric tapped his jaw impatiently. Their corvette had the acceleration that they could have covered the distance at a sprint. Yet the course made sense, even if he wanted to get on with it. He ran the three turrets under his control through a full readiness check. He briefly considered a request for a test fire, but with how Pixel had complained about the power requirements, he figured Mike would deny that.

Besides, that would show their presence even more than an active sensors sweep.

Mike brought the drive up, and the distance began to close. Eric glanced at the scans from Simon, even as he waited for something to happen. Anything to happen, he privately admitted.

"Captain, can we get a better resolution of the ship?" Eric asked. "We might be able to notice damage and if weapons fire or something else caused it."

"Good point," Mike said. He glanced over at Simon, "Can you do it?"

"Sure," Simon nodded. "I think I've got the sensors on a rotational scan of the area. I can use one of the telescopic video lenses for a closeup of the ship." He tapped at his console for a moment. "Yeah, the Ghornath build some pretty good ships. I'm getting some decent video, a little grainy at this distance."

"The shipyard that built this ship no longer exists," Rastar said softly. "The Nova Romans looted the Hovranta Yard during their raid, and the Chxor destroyed it when they conquered the system." Eric saw his friend had gone a dark blue that seemed to represent his melancholy over what had happened to his race.

Eric wanted to reassure his friend, "That sucks, but don't let the bastards get you down." Eric cursed his word choice a moment later. He hoped that Rastar understood what he meant. *I've got to work on this whole teamwork thing,* he thought, *I've been a loner for too long now.* But that came from what had happened to him at the Blackthorn labs. He had nowhere to turn and no one to trust after that.

"Wow," Simon said, "You'll want to see this for sure, Captain." He tapped a command on his console, and Eric saw Mike lean over the pilot's console to stare at the imagery.

"Can you get better resolution?" Mike asked

"Yeah, but it's about to rotate to the other side. The whole ship, well, you can see, it's got a bit of spin on it," Simon said. "Probably from whatever caused that."

"Yeah," Mike tapped a control and the image appeared on the main screen.

The squat, ugly ship appeared on the screen. It had a boxy, flattened appearance, Eric thought, but it looked familiar. He couldn't remember if he'd seen that model of freighter before or not, but it did look familiar. What did not look familiar was the gaping hole that rose on the back end of the vessel's top.

"Looks like something blew that section out," Crowe said. "Granted, I'm no expert on weapons or bombs, but the edges flare outwards."

"Yeah," Eric nodded, "And you can see from the way the girders peel back..." he trailed off as the ship rotated the damaged section out of sight, "Well, you could see. I think that damage occurred from the inside."

"Well, we can see the ass end now," Mike said. "And its got a fusion drive, which means a fusion reactor. So what interests me is how it blew out like that." He paused, then flipped a button, "Pixel, I forgot to bring you in the loop on this. We've got a ship-"

"No worries, I've tied in the engineering console into the bridge network. As soon as you turned on the main screen I saw it. I also have the intercom set to my panel so I can listen in, just in case you need me," Pixel said.

"Oh," Mike said. He seemed surprised that Pixel had paid attention, much less that he had set up what Eric considered a potential security breach to monitor the activity on the bridge.

"But to answer your question, I can think of several ways that you could have problems with the fusion reactor and not lose the entire ship. Some of them are pretty complex, but most of them shouldn't happen, so I would guess either really bad luck or sabotage."

"Really?" Mike frowned, "Well, that doesn't rule out pirates, then. They might have taken the ship and then either the crew or the pirates damaged it. Alright, we'll continue in. Any contacts yet, Simon?"

Eric looked up eagerly as Simon didn't respond for a moment.

"Nothing, Captain," Simon said. "I just ran through the scans, if there's anything nearby, they're either cold as space or they've got some good systems."

"Right," Mike took a deep breath. "We are about to make our final course change, before we do, I want you to go full active with sensors, give me a complete scan of everything nearby, and then hit the immediate area around that ship with a complete sweep."

Simon nodded, "Affirmative."

Eric tapped on his chin even as he wanted to run another

readiness test on the turrets.

The active sensor scan went without incident. Eric waited, his fingers ready to feed the weapons target data and open fire, yet nothing appeared. The more lengthy sweep of the immediate area around the damaged freighter seemed to take an eternity, yet at the end of it, nothing beyond a couple minor pieces of debris appeared on the screen.

"Alright, I'm going to bring us in," Mike said. He tapped the commands in and the Ghornath ship flipped over and began to decelerate. Eric frowned down at his weapons console. Perhaps Ariadne was right, he privately admitted. Perhaps they would come alongside the ship and be welcomed by a grateful crew.

Probably not, he thought, *but if that happens, she'll be insufferable.*

They drew closer to the other ship, and the hole swung back into view. "Got a potential docking port," Simon said, and a flashing carat appeared on the display of the ship. Eric saw it then, a standard docking port. "There's also cargo bays along the sides, but we don't have a dock that would work. It looks like one of them might be open, but it's hard to tell with the shadows."

"Yeah, the number three bay, there," Eric highlighted the cargo door. The knife edge shadows made it difficult to judge if the cargo door lay open or not. "Maybe someone tried to get a shuttle or something off before they lost power?"

"Small ships like that don't normally run with an on-board shuttle," Mike said. "And you can see from the pitting along the edges of the thing that it has seen a good bit of atmospheric work. I've flown more ungainly craft on smuggling runs before."

"Oh?" Ariadne asked. "I'd hate to try to plot an orbit for something like that, much less land it on thrusters." Eric nodded. The fusion drive would be useless for atmospheric work. He figured it would take one hell of a pilot, and one suicidal captain, to land that boxy craft, much less do it more than once.

"Thrusters?" Simon asked, "Why not use the main

drive?"

"The backwash from a fusion drive in atmosphere..." Mike trailed off. "Well, just the heat transfer through the atmosphere would probably melt your guide rods, then you'd have plasma splash back. You'd vaporize parts of the hull."

"That doesn't even consider the atmospheric effects," Ariadne said. "You would generate a massive movement of heat in the atmosphere, huge currents generated from the thrust. You'd level a city from takeoff."

Pixel spoke from the intercom, "And the charged particles would probably fry all electronics in a good distance. You might not effect your own ship, but anything below you will get hit by a huge electrical potential. Lightning storm effects... it would be a great way to really screw a section of planet over."

"Oh," Simon said. "Well... let's avoid that."

"We don't have a fusion drive, silly," Ariadne said. "We've got a nifty Ghornath reaction-less drive. I'll let Pixel explain how it works, I just navigate."

Eric looked up as Mike gave a chuckle, "And I don't do either of those tasks, I just pilot. But I can match speeds and vectors well enough. I've got us in position. Anyone got any reason I shouldn't bring us into dock?"

"This is an obvious trap," Anubus growled.

"You've said that twice, but I have yet to hear why you think it's a trap," Crowe said. "Not that I'm arguing, I'm just interested to hear your reasoning."

"We have come up on them, close enough that any survivors would see us from the bridge," Anubus growled. "We've yet to see any sign of survivors. If I were to set this trap, I would wait until we docked, trigger some method to disable the ship and then take us over at leisure. I would not need to wait nearby, but well out of our sensor range." Anubus paused, "A well resourced pirate might have several such ships as bait in various nearby star systems, which he would then check his traps over time for whatever prey gets caught."

"You seem pretty well versed on pirate tactics," Eric said. He gazed at Anubus with a thoughtful expression. Most Wrethe

379

in human space had two possible methods of employment, mercenary work and pirating. Anubus had not yet spoken about his past, but Eric wondered if the Wrethe would care for one over the other given the preference. He did not seem like the type to take orders, even for money.

"I am well versed on a number of tactics," Anubus growled. "But this is an ambush, it is what I know. The most dangerous way to fight is to never let your enemies know you're there before they die."

Mike looked back at the Wrethe. Their Captain seemed conflicted, and Eric had to agree with the sentiment. Anubus had presented a very good case, yet they had no evidence, besides a total lack of response from the freighter. *And that means they're probably all dead on there, pirate trap or not,* Eric thought.

"Those people need help," Ariadne said. "And we need the star-map they'll have in their navigation computer, or we might as well wait here until someone else comes through."

Eric grimaced. She had hit the main point there. They had no further coordinates from this system onward. They had to get a more complete set of navigation charts or at least something besides the basic Chxor one that they found aboard when they hijacked the ship from Chxor custody.

"Right," Mike nodded. He looked at Anubus, "Any thoughts on how they might disable the ship? There's a lot of ways I can think of, but most of them would cause a lot of damage to our ship."

"I don't know," Anubus growled. "I can't say what options they have. Something simple is best, though, or something easy to repair. Damage the engines, capture the bridge, or just electrical shock to damage the ship's systems."

"Well, the ship doesn't have any electrical charge beyond a minor static one, but nothing our ship can't take," Pixel said. "And we've got plenty of guns to prevent a hijack of our bridge. I'm not sure how they could damage our engines, at least not without permanently disabling the ship."

Mike frowned, but he nodded. "I'm bringing us in. Port side dock. Rastar, you're our master of arms, so I want you down there ready for anything." He glanced at Eric, "I know you want to man the guns, but I think we could use you down there too."

"Right," Eric said. He felt a twinge of unease to step away from the weapons console. Yet then he thought of the Ghornath laser rifle in the armory. That gave him a sudden surge of hope. Maybe he would get the chance to use it. Or if not it, then the nine millimeter Freedom Arms TEK-15 submachine gun that he had selected. It took him a lot of arguments to convince Rastar to give that one up, but the big Ghornath already had four, one for each arm. He just wanted a spare. Granted, Rastar already had two Freedom Arms Rager Twelves and two of the Chxor pump action riot guns. The fully automatic Ragers fired packets of angular pellets, designed for close combat and ship boarding.

Rastar could unleash hell at close range and a part of Eric felt glad that the big alien only had two of the Freedom Arms Ragers. At least that would limit his fire somewhat. A particularly important fact to Eric given Rastar's volatile temper.

Not that he thought the big guy would turn a weapon on him. But he might spray an area and not realize friendlies lay in the line of fire. Eric didn't hold that against him, too much. He liked Rastar, but he saw the Ghornath as a skilled amateur. The young alien had nowhere near the experience in combat and nothing of Eric's own professional military training.

Eric took the lift off the bridge and down to the second deck. The armory lay across the corridor from the elevator. Rastar already had the door open and had drawn his weapons out of the racks. The eight weapons that dangled off of Rastar made him look somewhat ridiculous. Eric gave him a smile though, and stepped past him to pull down his own TEK-15 and grab the Ghornath laser rifle down. "Ready?"

Rastar nodded. He kept his helmet off for now. Eric felt grateful for that. The helmets made talk difficult, and they had yet to find radios anywhere on the ship. That was high on Eric's search priority for when they went aboard.

Rastar sealed up the armory again and Eric led the way to the intersection of the main corridor and the branch that ran from the port and starboard airlocks. They walked down the corridor and Eric held up a hand as they passed the turret work stations. He stuck his head in the narrow room, "Hey, Matvei and Anastasei, you can head back to the engine room and help out Pixel. We can't fire these turrets with how we're docked." They slipped past him without response. He wondered at that, until he looked back at Rastar. *Well, ridiculous and scary aren't too far apart from one another,* he thought with a smile, *just a matter of perspective.*

The port airlock lay just down the corridor and as they came up to it Eric pressed the intercom switch, "Captain, we're in position."

"Roger, docking now," Mike said.

He brought them in smooth and Eric gave a slight nod as he barely heard the faint clunk as they made contact. Mike knew how to pilot, whatever his other faults. Now to see if Anubus was right...

Just as he thought that, a dull thud passed through the deck plates to his feet. Eric looked up sharply, even as Rastar seemed to sprout weapons from his four arms. Eric looked at the control panel, but beyond some flashing purple and red letters, he couldn't make sense of the Ghornath writing. "Rastar, what does this say?"

The big alien kept his four weapons trained on the airlock hatch. His mirror like eyes didn't seem to move, but he spoke a moment later. "Something disabled the docking clamps after they engaged the other ship. I'm not sure how or what kind of damage."

"Shit," Eric said. He tapped the intercom, "Mike, we've got a problem. Looks like Anubus was right, something has disabled our docking clamps, we are locked onto the other ship."

"Pixel?" Mike asked

He didn't answer for a moment, "Yeah, uh, something fried the circuitry. Possibly the motors too. There's a mechanical crank on third deck we can use to open those. I can go down there-"

"No," Mike interrupted. "Send one of the space hands

we've got, tell them what to do. How long will it take?"

"Well, I'm not sure, those things aren't designed to disengage quickly, they're designed to lock down in an emergency. I'd guess fifteen minutes at the soonest, probably closer to thirty," Pixel said. Eric bit back a curse. That would give whoever it was plenty of time to draw close.

"Alright, change of plans," Mike said. "Rastar, I'm sending Ariadne and Anubus down. You, Eric and Ariadne will move to the *Sao Martino*'s bridge. Anubus will provide security on our side of the airlock. Primary mission is to get us a star-map Eric, I know you'd rather be on weapons, but I can man those, since we can't go anywhere right now."

Eric nodded before he realized that Mike couldn't see them, "We're standing by, make sure Ariadne brings her angry side, we might need it."

"She's already in the lift, tell her yourself," Mike said. His humor in the situation made Eric frown. It reminded him too much of another man he had trusted... only to find the humor at his own expense. He knew Mike thought for their safety, but at the same time, he flashed back on the last time he had given that level of trust. What did he really know about Mike?

***

He first heard about Blackthorn on, of all things, a rescue mission. The briefer had mentioned their call sign. The counterintelligence team called the major out mid brief for a huddle. When he returned, he informed them that even the name 'Blackthorn' was classified as Secret Compartmentalized Information, with pass phrase authorization.

Essentially, they had not heard the word Blackthorn. If someone asked them about it directly, they still had not heard of Blackthorn. If someone gave them the pass phrase, they could admit to having heard the call-sign in a brief.

None of that seemed particularly odd at the time, the Centauri Commandos dealt in layers of the black. Most of their missions had SCI level security. A pass phrase just meant their mission probably oriented on the rescue of some Parliament

Member's mistress or something equally public sensitive.

"Your objective is to secure Blackthorn Five at this location where he and his escort have holed up in their safe-house due to a conflict with local gangs," Major Neubauer continued. "Your insertion will take place from high altitude release, with inertial damper arrival. Lethal ammunition is fully authorized. Intel estimates enemy activity limited to mostly gang level violence, but this is a hostile world, so expect that to escalate once you are observed. Priority of effort is the security of Blackthorn Five and retrieval to landing zone alpha or beta, with secondary effort the destruction of all classified materials at their compound to prevent spillage when the locals overrun."

Sergeant Schill spoke up, "What about the objective's security detachment?"

"Their mission coincides with yours," Major Neubauer said. He glanced at the counterintelligence team and then shrugged. "They're MoJ security, plainclothes. If it comes down to it, your priorities are the survival of the objective, destruction of classified materials, members of your team, and lastly the security detachment."

Eric had tuned out as soon as they said the security detachment were cops. He respected them for their jobs, but between their survival and that of his team, they didn't have a hope in hell. "Understood, sir. Ready for deployment."

The mission went without a hitch, right up until they fell out of the sky and the inertial dampers kicked in fifty meters above the rooftop and brought them to a gentle landing. Then the entire world seemed to open up. He lost Meyerdahl and Krebinsk to enemy fire. Enemy jamming blocked their long range communications, which meant they couldn't call for aerial support. They made it down into the building, only to run into an ambush two levels down that killed his point man Timovich.

He pushed through, and they killed most of the Seppies who got in their way, and then passed through the perimeter and into the 'safe' area of the building.

"Sergeant Striker, good to see you," Lieutenant Colonel Andreysiak said with a broad smile. He didn't duck or flinch at the crack of small arms fire that ripped through the corridor only a meter away. "Welcome to the party." The light colonel wore tactical armor and had a slung SKL-15 assault rifle which, other than an attachment or two, looked identical to Eric's.

"Thank you, sir," Eric said. "We were told minor gang violence, we didn't expect their militia and law enforcement on scene. What happened?"

"Apparently the local crime boss didn't like his payment, and figured he'd turn us over to buy himself some leniency with the locals," Andreysiak said. "They arrived just before you made your drop. Is there a problem, staff sergeant?"

"Negative, sir," Eric responded. "Once we confirm destruction of the classified documents my squad will lead the breakout along axis corridor three, and we'll move to the building vent shafts for rappel to the seventeenth floor. The landing pad on the north side is designated LZ Alpha. If we cannot secure that location we will move to LZ Beta, which is located-"

"Change of plans," Blackthorn Five said. "I have a team with classified mission essential package located off site. The package in their possession cannot be destroyed and must be retrieved." Lieutenant Colonel Andreysiak paused and glanced down at his wrist computer and rattled off a grid coordinate. He smiled the whole time, as if he recognized the absurdity of the situation.

"That's not in my orders, sir," Eric said. On his team net, Sergeant Schill reported the enemy had brought up heavy weapons.

"Well, consider it an addition," Andreysiak said. "We will move to the team's location and conduct retrieval, then we withdraw to my prepared extraction location."

"Sir," Eric took a deep breath, "Without authorization from higher-"

"Override code is Seven Seven Juliet Seven Juliet," Andreysiak said.

Eric closed his eyes and thumbed on his team net. "Change of mission. Complete destruction of classified materials. We have a secondary retrieval mission, our primary

385

objective will accompany us. Jenkins, prepare to move to the vent shafts, we will utilize inertial dampers to move to the ground floor and push to the final grid, 42 SMZ 54789 31234 and retrieve the package. We will then withdraw to a LZ specified by the primary. Any questions?"

He had good people, they might swear and bitch in the privacy of their own minds, but they didn't waste time doing it on the net. They trusted him, and Eric hated himself for what he'd ordered them to do. This kind of harebrained mission would get too many of them killed.

"Classified material destroyed," Jenkins drawled. The earth-born sergeant always sounded odd on the net, but his 'cowboy' attitude never failed to get the job done. "Ready for the breakout."

He glanced at their primary, who gave him a nod and his well humored smile. Something about his smile seemed off, almost like he laughed at Eric and his team. For just a moment, he considered the option to disregard Andreysiak's orders. The other man wore the rank of a Centauri Army Lieutenant Colonel, but that in the world of black operations, that meant little. Besides, as the commander on the ground, Eric had the final say. He might face a court-martial, but he could probably just pull for a letter of reprimand. He had enough of those that one more wouldn't hurt his career any more.

But whatever Andreysiak's real rank, his title as Blackthorn Five was classified. His very call sign had higher clearance than his team's identities. Whatever the man's mission here, it had to have profound importance and maximum secrecy. Eric had to decide between the potential deaths of his squad and the impact of a failure of Andreysiak's mission on the Confederation.

"Execute," Eric said.

***

Ariadne's arrival brought Eric out of his memories. "Hey guys, ready to go save some people?"

His decision still haunted him, and her good cheer and

optimism for a moment incited instant rage. "Are you ready to kill the pirates who plan on killing us?" Eric said. "If you really believe there's anyone over there to save you're either an idiot or Run slipped you something special in your breakfast." He bit back an apology as he saw the hurt on her face. *She needs to learn that just because she thinks things will work out, that the universe won't follow her plans,* he thought sourly. He remembered Ivanna's death, yet again, he would not allow Ariadne to make those same mistakes.

They piled into the airlock and Eric ran a functions check on his suit and then his weapons, even as Rastar and Ariadne checked theirs. Eric tapped Ariadne on the shoulder and had her turn so he could check hers then. She hadn't missed anything, and Eric gave her a nod, even as Rastar began to check Eric's own suit. Their checks complete, Eric hit the switch to cycle the airlock.

Eric grimaced as the airlock cycled to reveal a dark compartment with a tangle of floating debris and a bloated corpse, its face distorted from explosive decompression. From the way he lay tangled in an environmental suit, he had not quite managed to get it all the way on before the damage to the engine area.

He saw Rastar ahead of him, already halfway down the compartment. The flashlights he'd strapped to his helmet and his weapons swept the compartment and cast crazy shadows. Ariadne hung motionless next to Eric in the airlock. She seemed to stare at the dead man. He nudged her, and she gave Eric a nod before she pushed off. He figured if the corpse bothered her then she would check her suit more carefully in the future. A good safety lesson there, he thought. He made a note to try to get Simon or someone else to get a picture for that purpose.

Eric sighed at the lack of gravity. Rastar seemed to handle himself well and Eric imagined that the extra set of limbs helped in that regard. Ariadne seemed to drift without any issue. He saw her shift direction mid-flight to avoid a tangle of detritus. *Of course,* he thought, *she's a psychic so she cheated.*

Eric pushed off and he immediately veered into a

bulkhead. He managed to catch himself and when he looked forward he didn't think either of his companions had noticed. Eric's microgravity training lay years in the past and he knew he had gone rusty in that area. He more cautiously pulled himself along the bulkhead and made good progress. He swept the compartment with his sub-gun, and peered into the deeper shadows of the compartment.

This area seemed to be some kind of auxiliary storage area or perhaps the crew's cargo share. Eric seemed to remember that cargo ships sometimes paid their crew with spare cargo space for their own trading. He would have to ask Mike or Crowe, the pair had more experience on merchant ships than the others. That kind of information had not seemed important before, but it might prove more applicable in the near future.

Rastar paused at a set of hatches at the far end of the room. He traced two of his flashlights across the stenciled letters on the hatches. The right side said cargo hold and engineering. The left said lift. Before Eric could catch up, the big alien tried the lift access hatch, and then pulled the emergency release lever to the side and slid the hatch open along its track.

The bottom of the ship's lift hung a meter above the floor. The cage lay open, without a door, clearly designed for freight as well as personnel. Rastar squeezed up into it, and a moment later he disappeared above. Eric grimaced at the big alien's quick movement. Rastar technically had command of their little team. However, Eric hated that his friend had left him behind and had even drawn ahead of Ariadne.

They did not want to get spread out.

Eric glanced at his suit's chrono and grimaced. He wished the Chxor had not removed the radios from the suits before they issued them out. They had a thirty minute count before Mike planned to disengage from the freighter. Eric doubted Mike could leave the system without Ariadne, but he might well put some serious distance between them if some other threat materialized. Eric had no intention to spend the rest of his life on this airless hulk.

Ariadne floated up into the lift and out of sight.

A moment later, Eric reached the lift and pulled himself up. He saw that the top of the car opened up to the sides, which was how Rastar had managed to move further up the shaft.

He saw the big alien had stopped at the top of the lift. Rastar braced his four legs against the sides of the lift shaft and pulled on the door with his left set of arms. His right arms held two weapons ready. Eric approved of that caution.

The door came open and Rastar moved through. Ariadne drifted through a moment later. Eric felt suddenly uneasy, and then remembered the mission on Altaria Three, where his team had gotten separated on a recon mission in the planet's tunnels. The rebels had attacked them from behind to cut them off. Only he and Piotr had made it out of those tunnels alive.

Eric kept his weapon trained on the lower door they'd come in. He would not make the same mistake. He wished yet again for a radio, this time to caution Rastar. He would have to get Pixel to cobble something together, and soon.

Coming in here without communications was a mistake, he thought, *a mistake that will get someone killed if I'm not careful.*

He reached the top door. Eric saw Ariadne just ahead of him. The upper deck seemed oval shaped, and the corridor curved around to the right. The bridge should lie close by, he knew. Eric pulled himself down the corridor, careful to give himself a good field of fire at any hostiles that might emerge from the elevator.

He glanced back to see Rastar and Ariadne paused outside a strange construction of plastic panels and what looked like a hatch torn from somewhere else. Ariadne moved back next to Eric and put her helmet against his, "Looks like someone survived to rig up a makeshift airlock to the bridge. Rastar is too big to fit in it, though. You and I can go in, one at a time."

"I'll go first," Eric said. Just in case they found a hostile or a trap on the other side.

"Don't shoot anyone, they may be hurt or panicked."

Eric chuckled, her concern seemed comical, given the mounting evidence that no one remained alive, "They're probably dead."

She pulled her helmet back. Her face looked angry behind her helmet.

Eric frowned suddenly and sniffed at the inside of his helmet, did he smell burning hair? He wondered if he had an issue with his environmental pack. He would have to check it as soon as they got back aboard their ship.

Eric pushed past her and tapped Rastar on the shoulder and then signaled him to cover their rear. The big alien gave him a thumbs up and spun around to point his weapons back down the corridor. Eric slipped past him and then worked the hatch. The door seemed crooked on the salvaged frame, but Eric got it open, finally. He barely fit inside the tiny space inside and when Ariadne joined him, they filled the entire space. He felt uncomfortable so close to her that he could feel her press against him. Not that she wasn't attractive, Eric felt painfully aware of that suddenly.

No, something about Ariadne made him protective of her, even from himself. She deserved someone perfect for her. All Eric had to offer would be a night or two of sex.

That thought led down a rabbit hole that he did not want to explore while in such close proximity. Particularly because she wouldn't need her skills as a mind reader to notice where his thoughts were headed if he did not get out of the room's confines quickly. He found a set of air bottles strapped to the wall. From the pressure, they would probably only work the airlock thrice or at most four more times.

That would have to be enough for now, Eric knew. If they had more time, they could bring over more air bottles from their ship.

Eric opened a valve and a moment later his suit showed the pressure rise. It seemed to take forever, but the pressure finally balanced out near standard atmospheric pressure and Eric cut off the flow. He worked the wheel on the bridge hatch, and then grunted as he pushed on it. It felt jammed, and for a moment, he got nowhere. Then it lurched open and he heard a hiss as the pressure equalized between the two chambers.

The hatch swung wide, propelled by Eric's shove, and he swung with it, drawn along by inertia. It slammed against the wall and started to bounce back. Eric grabbed hold of a handhold in time to prevent its return swing. It felt for a moment like he had jerked his shoulder out of its socket.

Eric glanced around the bridge. It looked pretty basic. A couple crash seats, some simple control panels, and hatch out the back. Eric frowned at that. That hatch must lead to another airlock behind the bridge projection. They hadn't seen that when they came in, probably because of the angle, and the spin of the ship, he guessed. He peered through the small porthole on it and he could make out stars. The other door must lay open to space.

He looked over to see Ariadne open up her helmet. "You idiot, we don't know if there's some kind of poison or something in the air. Maybe plague."

She shrugged, "It stinks, but I'm still alive so far."

Eric grimaced. Truth to tell, in the dark bridge, his tinted helmet made it hard to see. He pulled his own off a moment later, and then wrinkled his nose at the stink. "That's not just stale air, that's..."

"Rotting blood," Ariadne pointed at a broad set of black stains across the deck. Eric looked again and noticed a cooler lashed down against the bulkhead there. And a bloody combat knife with bits stuck to the blade hung from a cable tied off to the cooler. "I think I might be sick."

Eric opened his mouth to console her, but instead he said, "Be sick in the corner away from the consoles, we don't know which one is important yet." *Great move, jackass,* he thought.

He pulled himself over to the one console with lights. "I think this is the communications console," he said. He found a cable spliced into the panel and traced it down to a heavy box. "Probably the battery power that keeps it live."

"Where did the survivors go?" Ariadne asked. Her voice sounded shaky, but Eric had to give her props for keeping her breakfast down.

"If I had to guess..." Eric said, "The last of them went

nuts trapped in here. One of them killed the others, and then when he realized what he'd done, he took a walk out yonder airlock, probably without a suit." Eric didn't have much sympathy for whoever it was. That cooler and the gore around it suggested just how sick that bastard had gone.

"That's..."

"Horrible, yeah," Eric shrugged, the galaxy had more than its fair share of horrible events. "Hey, help me get this radio to work so I can talk with Mike. He needs to know what we've found just to make a better decision on what we do next."

"Sure," Ariadne looked the console over. "I think this is the recording." She flipped a switch. "And here, this should be transmit..." She pulled out a headset. "Simon, this is Ariadne, can you read me?"

Eric rolled his eyes, "Are you serious, have you never heard of radio discipline? That's an open net, anyone could be listening."

Ariadne ignored him, "Hey Simon, yeah good to hear your voice too. We're on the bridge, looks like someone survived a while, but... well we think the last survivor killed the others up here and then... what was that? Yeah, you probably don't want to know."

Eric waited impatiently, "Tell him no sign of pirate activity, yet, but we need to search the ship to be sure. Ask him if there's any threats outside. I can get down to the ship to man the weapons right away if he needs me-"

Ariadne held up a hand impatiently, "Yes. Sure thing. Are you sure about that?"

"Is he sure about what?" Eric asked. Had Mike decided to pull them out? *Really need Pixel to get on personal radios,* he thought, *I hate not knowing what is happening.* He couldn't even tap his foot impatiently in microgravity, when he tried, it started to send him in a spin.

"We'll do that, I'll let them both know," Ariadne looked over, "Mike says that there's no sign of any hostiles so far. Simon has scanned the entire area around us, and done active sweeps of the area as well. Nothing yet."

"So...not a trap?" Eric asked. He almost felt let down.

"Looks like we can relax," Ariadne smiled. "He sent Crowe over, along with Mandy and Miranda. Also, when Simon finishes his last sweep, he'll relieve Anubus at the airlock and he'll join us. Mike wants the ship searched. Anything we can use we'll take. Priority is food, weapons, parts, and then whatever else we need. I'll help Crowe out up here if he needs it, then join you in searching the ship."

Eric nodded, but he couldn't shake the impression that they had missed something. Something important, or at least something that he should not have missed. He worried about everything that could go wrong with the crew scattered all over the ship without radios. "We need to stay in groups, at least two people..."

Ariadne nodded. "Of course. I don't want to wander this spooky place by myself."

"Also, let Mike know that we'll need a couple more air tanks for the makeshift airlock in here." Eric glanced at the rear airlock. He could suggest that they use it to move up without the passage through the ship's interior, but they had no means to recover anyone who drifted off the hull.

He waited while Ariadne passed that information along. "Alright, I'll go out and join Rastar. I'll send Crowe in when he gets here and then we'll start a search of the ship. Ask Crowe to get the ships log up first." He paused, because he realized that he had taken charge. He felt a sudden surge of pity for Ariadne, stuck between Mike on the radio and himself. "Any suggestions?"

"Be careful," Ariadne said. "Even if there's no one on the ship, there could be hazards from cargo or just damage to the ship. We don't want to lose anyone, so just use caution."

"Right," Eric nodded. "I'll pass that along too." He thought suddenly of Rastar, alone in the corridor. He hoped his impulsive friend had not gone to find trouble while he waited.

"Shit, I need to tell Rastar that Crowe is on his way up, I wouldn't want him to shoot him," Eric pushed off to the hatch.

"Right, that would be... uh, really terrible," Ariadne said

with something less than total sincerity.

Eric gave her a smirk as he pulled the hatch closed. At least someone got through her cheerful nature sometimes. He would have to tell Crowe to ease off a bit, though who knew if the other man would listen.

Yet the last thing he saw as the hatch closed was the blood and the bloody knife. That blood and the callus disassembly of people chilled him. For a moment, he didn't see the bridge or Ariadne.

He saw the 'package' that Andreysiak had wanted retrieved.

***

Eric lost Simulak and Miku in the tunnels below the building. Most of Andreysiak's security team died in the same firefight. Eric led the counterattack and rolled the enemy back, but by then the damage was done. They lost immediate pursuit after the first kilometer, but Eric knew it would only take a few minutes for the enemy to widen their search area and localize them again.

The lack of resistance meant that they moved fast. They came back out to street level as they drew within a hundred meters of the target. Andreysiak had pointed at a parked van, which lay parked off the street just past a police barricade.

"Jenkins, take down the police, everyone else, establish a perimeter," Eric said over his squad net. "Colonel Andreysiak, you and your security team are up."

"Yee-haw!" Jenkins shouted over the net. His CKY pistol made little noise with its integral suppressor and had minimal visual signature. Both police at the barricade dropped before they had time to call for help. With any luck, the squad jammers would prevent any panic signals from the dead men's equipment which monitored their life-signs.

Two more security men piled out of the front doors of the van at Andreysiak's signal and moved to the back. More out of random curiosity than anything else, Eric positioned himself where he could see the contents of the van. Which was why he had to bite back a swear when they dragged the bloody woman out. Seams of scar tissue ran along her arms and legs and parallel to her spine. They had her secured to a gurney and Eric saw bloody welts around her wrists and ankles where she'd fought those restraints.

"What the hell is this?" Eric asked.

"This is none of your business, Sergeant Striker," Andreysiak said. "Leave it be."

Eric looked back at the woman, and for a moment, he met her gaze. Her eyes seemed to open as two twin pits of hell. *What the hell is Blackthorn,* he thought, *and how can I make these bastards pay for what they did to her?*

For a second, he considered a quick order to take down Andreysiak and the remainder of his security team. Without direct supervision, his command would have no way to verify what had happened. Certainly, he trusted his people to keep their mouths shut. The story could go easy enough, 'ran into an ambush when we proceeded to a secondary site on Blackthorn Five's orders.'

But Eric knew they would have a long push to get to LZ Bravo. How many of his people would die along the way? He would save more of them at this point if he went along with Andreysiak's plan, so long as the bastard had some means for extraction as he had stated.

It all made so much sense at the time, but when he looked back, Eric figured the prisoner showed exactly what level of trust he should have given Andreysiak.

***

Eric hung from the top of the lift shaft as Rastar moved into the second deck of the crew quarters. Mandy and Miranda had gone towards engineering already, laden down with tools and cables.

Eric followed Rastar into the corridor beyond. They found another pair of dead crew, these two cold and still in an emergency atmospheric pack. The oversized plastic bag had a small re-breather attached, but evidently the pair had died before help could reach them.

Or maybe the pack malfunctioned. The bag still had pressure, but they might have suffocated within minutes if the re-breather had failed to siphon out the toxins. Either way, both had died. Eric forced himself to pull his eyes away. That kind of death made him feel sick to his stomach. He could face death by violence, but a lingering death like that...

Rastar tapped him on the shoulder and pointed ahead. They passed a couple of rooms, the hatches open wide. Eric wondered at that. He had not thought even a tramp freighter like this would get so sloppy with safety to leave so many hatches open. A quick glance inside the first pair showed what looked like officers cabins, narrow, but a single bunk with more room than a space-hand might have.

They came up to the far end, and Rastar pointed at the open hatch first. Eric nodded, and Rastar led the way in while Eric covered him. A moment later, Rastar signaled the all clear.

Eric followed him in. The room clearly had more space than the others on the level. A large bed took up a good deal of the floor space, and dressers and actual furnishings occupied a lot as well. An open safe lay empty on the wall of the room, and a mauled body in an environmental suit drifted near it, a pistol clenched in one hand. The name-tag on her breast read 'Maria.'

Eric frowned at that and played his flashlight over the body. He saw the extended pistol first, a Samsonov PRK nine millimeter. The pistol looked locked back, either empty or jammed. What he saw of what had happened to the woman's body made him hiss in shock though. Three parallel gashes had opened up her suit and her flesh from sternum to her throat. The horrific wound had caused her to bleed out, hopefully before decompression killed her. Either way, Eric could see her face twisted in pain behind her helmet visor. This woman had died after the ship had lost pressure, and she had died fighting.

And from the wounds: a Wrethe had killed her.

Rastar touched his helmet to Eric's. "Dude, we have a problem."

***

They ran into Ariadne as she came out of the bridge. Eric pulled her to the side and put his helmet against hers, "We have issues, there was a Wrethe aboard. I'm pretty certain that last survivor, the one who killed the others, was a Wrethe."

"But why would a freighter have a Wrethe crewman?" Ariadne asked.

"It shouldn't. Which means we've missed something," Eric said. "I've got to talk with Mike, and Crowe needs to get that ship's log up."

He pushed past her and cycled the makeshift airlock.

The door seemed heavier than before and it took three or four hard pushes, braced against the bulkhead to get it open. He found Crowe on the other side, "What's the problem? I heard you banging on the hatch."

Eric tugged his helmet off, "One of the crew died from what looks like a claw attack, I'd guess Wrethe from the looks. Which means we've got a problem."

"A Wrethe?" Crowe went pale. "Here, are you sure? I mean I would think we'd have seen one of them around here." Crowe glanced around the bridge and for a moment, Eric thought the other man's eyes lingered on the rear airlock hatch.

Eric glanced at that hatch, but he saw no sign of anything on the inside, it still lay open to space on the outside. "Maybe... or maybe it's playing with us or its a sneaky one like Anubus," Eric grimaced. "We need him over here. He'll know how the bastard will think. And we need to know what happened with the ship. I need you to get the ship's log up."

"I've got a battery pack for it, but it'll still take some time," Crowe said. "It might be easier for me to pull drives out and plug them into my new computer," Crowe waved at a canister that floated nearby. "Pixel just finished it last night."

"Whatever you need to do, get it done," he looked over at a partially disassembled panel, "What's that mess?"

Crowe bounced over to it and gave a laugh, "It's my labor to get the star-maps out. Those things are expensive, so the folks that map them tend to bind them to the hardware. I'll have to

397

disassemble the entire panel to get the memory drive out, and then I may not be able to copy it. We might have to do a hardware installation on our ship..."

"Huh, well do you need help up here?" Eric asked, even as he pulled on the headset for the radio.

"Nope," Crowe said quickly. "Just time. Give me that and we'll be good."

"That I don't know if we have..." Eric muttered. He toggled the transmission switch. *Shit, we haven't got call signs yet,* he thought. So much for his criticism of Ariadne. "Mike this is Eric, open net, but we've got some potential problems."

Mike answered a moment later. "Go."

"We found one of the crew, killed by what looks like a Wrethe, after the ship lost pressure. We haven't seen any sign of a dead Wrethe, so far, which suggests there might be a live one somewhere aboard."

"That's bad," Mike said. He seemed distracted, Eric thought. "Keep me informed."

Just that, Eric thought, *keep me informed?* He had a sudden urge to go over and yell at their new Captain, yet he restrained himself. He bet that one or more of their crew might have caused a distraction aboard. And truthfully, Eric had little evidence of the threat beyond the conviction that something just felt wrong about the situation. They needed the star-maps and any supplies they could get. They couldn't pull clear until they got the star-maps at least.

"Right, will do, and stay frosty over there," Eric said. He pulled the headset off and looked at Crowe, "Mike says to keep working."

"Right," Crowe grinned. "I'll try to get the logs up."

"Pull the star-map first," Eric said. "We need those more than anything else right now."

"Sure thing," Crowe grimaced. "But that'll take me a lot of time, so try to keep other interruptions to a minimum."

"Well, if a Wrethe comes up here and starts gutting you, try to scream loud enough for us to hear, alright?" Eric said. "Oh, and leave Ariadne alone, she's under enough strain as it is, she doesn't need your shit."

Crowe's face went still. "I'll do what I want. And if that was some kind of threat, let me tell you this soldier boy, I don't take threats well."

Eric smiled, "Crowe, I don't care what you take well. I don't threaten or bluster. But if you become a threat to the safety of our ship or my friends, I'll kill you. No muss, no fuss. I'll eliminate you and then I'll go prepare a nice meal and everyone will wonder what happened over a nice dinner of pit ham and candied yams."

Crowe didn't like what he saw in Eric's eyes and Eric felt a surge of satisfaction as the other man looked away. On the one hand, he felt bad for intimidating Crowe. On the other... Well, Crowe needed the reminder that others on the ship had their methods of dealing with him if he crossed the line.

Could I have handled that better, he thought, *but this will have to do.*

"Let me know if Mike calls over," Eric said. "I've got to check with Mandy and Miranda and see what they've found in the engine room, and if that changes our plans at all."

"Sure," Crowe said sullenly.

Eric gave him a wave as he headed back out the makeshift airlock. As the door closed, he noticed that the combat knife from the cooler had disappeared.

***

He and Rastar met up with Anubus near the airlock.

The sudden reminder of the danger of the Wrethe made Eric hesitate to draw within arms reach of the alien. Yet he forced himself to move up and put his helmet in contact with that of Anubus. A moment later, Rastar joined him in the huddle. "We have a problem. We found a crewman killed by a claw attack, sometime after the ship lost pressure. I think it was a Wrethe."

"Excellent," Anubus growled. "There is no chance that a Wrethe would travel aboard this hulk. There must be another ship."

"You're sure?" Eric asked. "Simon searched the entire area. There's nowhere nearby that it could hide, not without some serious stealth capabilities. If this Wrethe had that level of tech, why would he bother with this tramp freighter?"

"Then Simon missed something," Anubus growled. "Or this ship's cargo is more valuable than the outward appearance suggests. Therefore it drew a better class of pirate."

Rastar spoke up, "Dude, I think Annie's on to something there. I'll check with the girls in the engine room. Ariadne and you two check the cargo holds. See if there's anything we can use, but also find out if there's some cargo valuable enough for a well equipped pirate."

"Roger," Eric said.

"I will of course, have first pick of any loot," Anubus said. "I insist."

"Big talk for a guy wearing gloves," Eric said. "Kind of hard for you to get your claws out with those on, at least without breathing vacuum." He regretted the words as they came out, yet Anubus's almost constant demands for more than his fair share just hit him the wrong way.

"I don't need claws to take you apart, human," Anubus answered with a growl. He said human, but from him the word sounded like *food.*

"Guys, fight later, we need to work together," Rastar said.

Eric pulled back without another word. He knew he would say the wrong thing, like he always did, if he tried to talk again. *I can screw up even the most simple conversations,* he thought. Eric led the way towards the cargo bays.

The narrow corridor seemed too small for cargo, until Eric remembered the outer bay doors. The crew probably only used the inner areas for access and maintenance he figured. The cargo bay access doors were evenly spaced down the hallway. Bay one lay closest and Eric waited for Ariadne and Anubus to draw up. He signaled Anubus to lead the way, while he braced himself and covered him.

Anubus hesitated a bit. He went up to the ceiling and worked the hatch with his long arms. As he threw the door open,

Eric brought up his weapon, ready to fire.

Something flashed past the hatchway there and gone before it registered. It looked like a man, but in full motion arms flailing. Another figure flashed directly towards them and Eric triggered a burst from his TEK-15.

Anubus signaled him to cease fire.

Eric saw the form recoil, but he saw no blood. A moment later, Ariadne brought her lamp up.

"Shit," Eric said to himself.

Well, I definitely ruined that set of coveralls, he thought. His burst had chewed a hole through the center of the coveralls. As Anubus crawled into the bay, and Ariadne followed, Eric could see more and more. It looked like someone had dumped an entire store's worth of clothing. Most of it drifted slowly through the room, all but those articles hit by Eric's fire.

He saw Ariadne scoop a pair of boots out of the air and examine the tag. She tucked them under her arm. Eric shook his head, *what was with women and shoes?*

Then again, he needed something besides his environmental suit to wear. He saw a variety drifting through the bay, everything from tuxedos to plaid skirts. Eric would have to check it out later, when they didn't have to worry about a homicidal Wrethe on the loose.

Anubus ripped a crate open and the top barely missed Ariadne.

Alright, when I don't have to worry about a second *homicidal Wrethe.*

More clothing spilled out into the microgravity and Anubus moved on to another crate. Eric caught his arm as he went past. The Wrethe jerked away, but it got his attention enough for Eric to point to where Ariadne waited near the hatch. She had a clipboard off of the wall and she waved it at them both.

Eric approached and they huddled to confer. "Manifest for this bay says clothing, shoes, boots and that sort of thing. All donations from Nova Roma for the people of Saragossa."

"Nothing valuable then," Anubus growled.

"Hey, these are some nice boots," Ariadne said. "Maybe a little worse the wear, but nice. And I see a couple sets of other stuff that might fit, when we come back through."

"Your focus on our mission inspires me," Anubus growled. "Let us move on."

Eric let the big alien lead the way. The door for bay two opened without issue. Anubus did a quick sweep through the bay while Ariadne looked the manifest over. She shook her head and they moved on.

The third bay's inner door lay partially open. Eric glanced through it, and he could make out stars through the gap. He reached through and fished around until he found the bay's manifest. He tried not to think about what might happen if an angry Wrethe grabbed his arm while he made himself so vulnerable.

Eric glanced over the manifest, but it just listed more donations. These were electronic viewers and simple game platforms for entertainment purposes. He chucked the clipboard back through the door in disgust, what a waste of time.

He led the way forward towards the last door, but as he drew near, he slowed. This door had a large box with an electronic display on it. As they drew nearer, Eric could see that the box had magnetic clamps that attached it to both the bulkhead and the hatch itself.

As he came within a couple meters, a bright red light flashed on the top of the box, and the display lit up.

He looked over at the others. Someone had added this and it still had power. Perhaps they had found the mysterious valuable cargo.

The display flashed a loading screen and then text appeared. Eric peered at it:

Warning, I am a Defenseworks Portable Security Lock, Mk II . If you are approaching due to your interest in my design, please contact Defenseworks in the Tannis system to order your own version today! If you are attempting unlawful entry, be warned, I am designed to respond with immediate and

overwhelming force to ensure the security of my owner and his
property!

Eric looked over at the others. His initial urge was to ignore it and try to get past it.

Still, he'd seen some of Defenseworks weapons and equipment before. They made their money from innovative designs, and Eric somehow doubted they would put a message like that in as a bluff.

Yet if this unknown pirate Wrethe had put it there, that meant the important cargo probably lay inside. They needed someone with technical expertise which meant Miranda or Pixel, and probably someone with some experience in security. Which would mean Simon.

Eric just hoped they had long enough to work through it.

***

Eric found his patience long expired when Simon had suggested they get Crowe to look at it as well. The suggestion seemed good enough, except Crowe had just finished extraction of the star-map and had pulled the data drives for the ship's log. He passed the entire pile over to Ariadne, who along with Mandy and Miranda headed back to their ship.

Crowe spent some time in the corridor, just outside of the lock's sensor perimeter. He moved up and waved the others in for a huddle. "Good thing you called me. I've got some experience with these things. They're nasty, especially if you don't know what you're up against. First warning you get a ten thousand volt shock. There is no second warning. The lock detonates an explosive charge to explosively weld the door shut, and the detonation normally kills whoever didn't take the hint."

"Shit," Eric said. "So what do we do?"

"Like I said, good thing you called me," Crowe said. "It has a wireless signal that the owner sends from the controller. Most of the time it's a five twelve encryption at a variable frequency."

"I'm getting tired of your technical talk," Anubus

growled. "Something valuable is in that bay, can you open it... or are you useless to me?"

"Oh, I can open it," Crowe said. "Most people don't ever change the factory settings from these things, which means they leave the manufacturer's default override code in place." Crowe held up his new computer. "And luckily this baby has a security port, so..."

Crowe tapped on the screen for a moment. Out of the corner of his eye Eric saw the red light on the top of the lock flash to green. "Hey, good job, Crowe, thanks for not screwing us over this time." He realized he'd put his foot in his mouth. "Uh, I meant you did a good job."

"Whatever, Twitch," Crowe grunted.

Anubus led the way up to the hatch. He pulled the lock off with a grunt, and then passed it back to Crowe. Eric took up a position to cover him, and saw Simon do the same further down the corridor.

Anubus worked the hatch and jerked to the side.

Eric suddenly felt glad they didn't have radios. Otherwise the others would have heard his panicked yelp as the turret with three rotary multibarrels rotated to face him. The barrels spun up as he watched.

Eric froze.

That's really overkill, he thought. The bores of those barrels looked thirty millimeters, designed to tear up missiles or other small craft. He really did not want to think of what one of those rounds would do to him. The weapon hung from the nose of a ship of some kind. Heavy armored plates hung off the brutal looking craft. The heavily armored cockpit sat up high on the nose of the craft. Eric saw some glyphs or writing in red paint along the side, though he couldn't quite make out the details, what with the barrels of the apocalypse in his face. The craft filled most of the bay, and Eric figured it the size of a cargo shuttle or bomber.

Anubus waved him to move to the side of the hatch, out of sight of the ship. Eric moved slowly, partially afraid that the ship's pilot watched him.

They gathered in another huddle. "What the hell is that thing?" Eric asked.

"It is a Prowler," Anubus growled, and even through the muffle of the helmet Eric could hear the longing on the Wrethe's voice. "It is a Wrethe warship, the ship of an experienced killer. The writing along the side names it the 'Red Hunter.' We've found proof of the pirate."

"So this was a trap," Eric said. "Shit."

"Who's on security for our ship, again?" Crowe asked.

"We need to get back there, now!" Eric shouted. He pushed off from the huddle, and bounded down the hallway. A moment later, Rastar flew past him, propelled by eight limbs, with a grace that seemed impossible with his bulk and size. *That's totally not fair,* Eric thought.

The entire group piled into the airlock, and Eric gave silent thanks for the oversized Ghornath airlocks. It seemed to take forever for the airlock to cycle. As it did, Eric tried to review areas the Wrethe pirate could have already boarded or might yet board. The aft airlock and the starboard airlock both seemed likely routes. They needed to get people there, and they needed to sweep the ship, he knew.

The airlock finally opened and Rastar led the way out. Mandy and Miranda stood with Ariadne just on the other side. "Oh, hi guys, any luck with the lock?" Ariadne asked.

"Yes," Eric said, even as Rastar went to the intercom. "There's a Wrethe ship of some kind, Anubus recognized the type."

"We have a Wrethe pirate on board our ship already," Anubus growled. "It will be experienced at this and will have already put its plan into motion."

"That's bad," Miranda said. "I just finished talking with Pixel. The other ship suffered its damage from sabotage. Someone cross-polarized the fusion reactors magnetic coils. They detonated like bombs, ripped the entire engine room apart and opened the compartment to space."

"Oh," Eric said. "We definitely want to avoid that."

"Why doesn't Mike answer?" Rastar said. "Who is up

there with him? Should not Elena be present?"

Crowe looked up, "No... Mike told me he sent Elena down to guard Pixel in the engine room."

Eric felt his stomach drop. He pushed past Rastar and hit the intercom for the engine room. "Pixel, buddy, what's going on, talk to us." Out of the corner of his eye he saw Rastar and Anubus run for the bridge lift.

"Uh, well, I mentioned earlier that I set it up so I could listen in on the bridge, right?" Pixel asked.

"Yes..." Eric frowned.

"Well I also installed a camera, just so I could see who was talking and all that," Pixel said. Eric frowned, that sounded more like a security precaution... a good one for that matter. "Well, here's the feed. As far as I can tell, no Wrethe on the bridge, but Mike just opened up the closet and let Krann out, and gave her a pistol."

"His pistol?" Eric demanded. He had no idea why Mike might have armed their Chxor prisoner, not unless the other man either thought he faced a fight for his life or he planned to betray them all to the Chxor. Eric really hoped it wasn't the latter. It would suck to have to kill Mike.

"No, looked like a Chxor pistol." Pixel said. "And then he locked down the bridge. And Krann has accessed the navigation computer."

"Pixel, send Elena back aft to help out. We'll need to storm the bridge," Eric closed his eyes. "This could get very messy..." He heard Elena in the background as she said she'd head their way immediately.

"Eric," Ariadne spoke from behind him, "I don't think Mike realizes what's going on."

"What?" Eric said. "The bastard must have betrayed us, he's armed Krann, maybe she made him a better offer-"

"No," Ariadne said, her voice calm. "We believe there's a rogue psychic aboard the ship, and if it's Krann, like we suspect, well, she's just controlled him."

"That's impossible," Eric said. "For one thing, Chxor don't have any psychics, everyone knows that. For another, how would you know about a rogue psychic and the rest of us wouldn't?"

"She's right," Pixel said. "We suspected Krann before, but we heard Chxor didn't have psychics. She may not be it, maybe she's under control too. Either way, Mike's not behind this. We can't hold his actions against him."

"Whatever," Eric snapped. "It's obvious that Mike has betrayed us. You're too trusting, Ariadne. You've let your emotions override your-"

"Shut up, Eric," Ariadne said. "You're letting your own fears take over. Focus on the problem. We have a Wrethe pirate aboard and the bridge is under the control of the rogue psychic."

"Yeah guys, and..." Pixel trailed off. "Hey, did you send someone down here? I just heard the rear hatch open, and Elena left from the upper hatch."

Eric felt his blood go cold. "Pixel, get out of there now." He had screwed up yet again, just like on York, when he pulled his team out to save the others and caused the left flank to crumble... *Why can't I do anything right...* "The Wrethe pirate targeted the engine room on the other ship, you're at risk. I'm headed your way now..."

Mandy shook her head, "No, we need the bridge. Miranda and I know the engine room, we'll go support him."

Pixel spoke, his voice low, "I don't see anyone here, but I'm getting out of here."

Eric took a deep breath. "Right, you two go, I'll head for the bridge."

He and Ariadne ran for the bridge lift. They found Rastar and Anubus outside it, and the Wrethe pounded on the lift's hatch in frustration. "Locked down. We need to take the stairs, but the hatch for that is locked down too."

"Crowe!" Eric called out. "We need your skills."

Before the other man could respond, the shipboard intercom went live. "Hello crew of the *Gebnar*. You have a very nice ship. I am very tempted to claim it for my own, but I would find it difficult to operate on my own," the high pitched voice that came from the speakers had a sort of gloating malevolence about it that set Eric's teeth on edge. "I will explain the situation. I offered the same bargain to the crew of the *Sao Martino*. Turn over all valuables and weapons. If you do not comply within one hour, the program I uploaded into your engineering computer will cause the destruction of the ship's reactor and probably the deaths of most of the crew. In addition, I will then hunt you down one by one until you are all dead."

Eric stepped over to the nearest intercom switch, "Look you bastard, you go ahead and make your threats, because we'll find you and kill you and our engineer will fix whatever it is you did before it will have any effect."

The Wrethe chuckled, "I like that sort of spirit. Your engineer, however, seems to have problems of his own. I think you'll want to get someone down here to look at him. He seems to have problems breathing. Still alive last I checked, but not looking well at all."

"You son of a--"

Ariadne pushed him to the side, "Look, I'm sure we can come to an arrangement. However, if you let Pixel die, I'll guarantee that we'll kill you. We may well kill ourselves to do it, but we'll kill you. Let's talk bargains here," Ariadne said. "We have three hundred kilograms of gold. That kind of thing takes a long time to move, more than an hour."

"Where did you lot get that kind of treasure?" the Wrethe said.

"Who am I talking with?" Ariadne asked calmly.

The high pitched voice gave a hyena like laugh, "Spine among you all. You may call me Ghost, the fear that it evokes in some I find gratifying."

"Okay, Ghost," Ariadne said. "Let us get our engineer out of there, get him patched up, and give us time to move the gold--"

Anubus reached over her shoulder to flip off the intercom switch. "You aren't giving it my gold," Anubus growled

"He's right," Eric snapped, "That Wrethe will just kill us when it has finished toying with us first."

Ariadne looked back at the pair of them and she rolled

her eyes, "Oh, really, you think I *want* to give it the gold?" Eric could see that her face had gone hard, and her eyes seemed to smolder. Eric winced as he thought he saw flames flicker in her eyes. "I'm trying to delay, and to get Pixel out of there before he bleeds to death."

Oh, good, she's angry now, that means she's actually thinking instead of her fluff head crap, he thought. "Oh, I hadn't expected that kind of thing from you, good plan," Eric said.

"Thanks *so* much for the vote of confidence," Ariadne rolled her eyes again. "Now get with Crowe and find a way to take the bridge back. "I'll try to get Pixel out of there alive."

For a moment she reminded him of his first platoon commander back when he was just a private in the Centauri Commandos. Eric gave her a sharp salute, "Yes, ma'am."

Behind him Rastar snapped off a technically improper but very impressive four-limbed salute of his own, and even Anubus seemed impressed by her change in attitude.

"Dude, she's totally perfect as the XO," Rastar said loudly as they hurried away. Eric heard him sniff loudly, "Say, does anyone smell burning hair?"

***

It took Eric longer than it should have to find Crowe. He finally found Crowe and Elena in close conversation in the lounge. "What the fuck are you doing here? We need you to unlock the bridge," Eric said.

Both of them looked up at him in surprise. "Eric," Crowe smiled thinly, "How are you?"

"I'd be better if we had killed this damned Wrethe and stormed the bridge already, and put a bullet through that damned Chxor's brain," Eric replied. He looked over at Elena, "Oh, and I know you must feel bad about leaving Pixel unprotected. You don't need to blame yourself over that, it's my fault entirely."

"What?" Elena asked. "Oh, yes, I feel terrible about Pixel." She wiped at her eyes and Eric felt his heart twist. He hated it when he made beautiful women cry. "Do you think he will be okay?"

"We don't know how bad this Ghost hurt him," Eric said. "Ariadne will try to get us in there to get him out. In the meantime, we need to secure the bridge. We can't accomplish anything if we don't control those two essential areas of the ship."

Crowe glanced over at Elena, "Are you sure about this?"

"Of course I'm sure, Mike's clearly lost it. Either this psychic controls him or Krann offered him a better deal for our betrayal. He gave Krann a weapon, for god's sake," Eric shook his head. "And just looking at the tactics, we need the bridge before we go after Ghost. We can control the automated doors from there, as well as other stuff." Eric waved a hand at that. He didn't really know what other controls there were aboard the bridge, but he doubted that they wanted someone hostile in control.

"Look, Eric, I know you're a real focused guy..." Crowe said.

"Crowe has just discussed potential contingencies with me," Elena said. "Such as the fact that your 'friend' Ariadne had a conspiracy with Anubus, Rastar and Pixel. She had them all convinced that a rogue psychic tampered with the election for captain and that it was either Crowe, Krann or myself."

"What?" Eric frowned. Now that he thought about it, Mike's actions, particularly his votes for Ariadne and Krann had seemed rather suspicious.

"What I'm afraid of," Crowe said, "is that *she* is the rogue psychic."

"That's ridiculous," Eric said. He looked between their faces. Both of them looked serious and he felt a twinge of doubt, "Isn't it?"

"Think about it," Crowe said, his voice low but intense, "Mike voted for her in the first election. Then in the second one he voted for Krann, so did Simon, who we've both seen spend more time than usual around Ariadne." Eric frowned as he thought back. It seemed unlikely, to say the least. "And Elena told me about a psychic she had to hunt down, one that used Chxor bodyguards because their minds are more easily influenced. And think about the other candidate: Run. Both of them she could have controlled more easily than you could access a computer."

"That seems a little far-fetched," Eric said. Even so, some of Ariadne's actions took on a far more sinister cast when he stopped to think about them. "And besides that, *you* voted for Krann the one time. And Mike voted for Ariadne in the first election, if she hadn't voted for him, she would have become captain."

Elena shook her head, "That's the thing, Eric." Her sharply accented voice seemed to put particular weight on her words. "Crowe was not present at the second election," She saw Eric's look of consternation and shook her head, "Trust me, I remember too, or I thought I remembered at least. But then Crowe told me his story, how he got a message from Mike to check out something with the communications systems near the bow. And when he got back, the meeting was over. More than that, I checked the door logs and the access times for the system. He was there, not at the election."

"I would sooner have voted for Anubus than that damned Chxor," Crowe said.

"That's crazy, that would mean either someone impersonated him or..." Eric trailed off. He felt his blood run cold. *I can't have misjudged her, not that badly,* he thought, *she's a fluff head and she cares too much about people, she's soft...right?*

"Exactly. Someone must have implanted his presence on our minds. And who's the one person we *know* is a psychic?" Elena's cold blue eyes stared into Eric's, and he had to look away from that gaze. "What's more likely, that we have two psychics aboard or that we have one rogue psychic who has manipulated us all from the beginning? Psychics are rare, Ariadne as much as told us she hasn't encountered any others besides her brother in her entire life, yet now we must believe that there is a second one aboard this ship?"

Eric shook his head, "But how... no, that doesn't make sense, why would she have Krann and Mike fortify the bridge?

411

For that matter, Krann has accessed the navigation computer."

"I don't know," Crowe said. "But she seems damned eager for us to storm the bridge. Which is why I say we delay. We pressure her and find out what she wants. We leverage what Ghost is doing, use this disruption to her plans to crack her."

Eric took a step backwards, "Now you can't be serious. Every moment we delay gives Ghost more time to escape. Worse, whatever... whatever the goals of the rogue psychic -whoever it is- we know that Ghost intends to kill us."

"Do we?" Elena asked. "Remember, Ariadne has messed with our minds before. How much of what we heard is real? Perhaps--"

"You're talking about a Wrethe that killed an entire freighter already, then hunted down and ate the survivors," Eric snapped. "Chopped some of them up for later and put them in a cooler for that matter."

"You are right," Elena nodded. "We should not let paranoia drive us too much. However, we need to find out Ariadne's goals. And we need to stop her."

Eric raised one eyebrow, "Really, stop a psychic with mind altering powers? How do you recommend we do that, exactly, ask her nicely?"

"There's one certain way," Crowe said softly. "We kill her."

"No. No way," Eric said. He closed his eyes and he saw Ivanna again, as she choked to death on her own blood. "That's off the table."

"It's the only way," Crowe said. "Nothing else will work. Unless you think we can trust her after what she's already done?"

"No," Eric shook his head. "We don't know anything yet. This is all supposition. Rampant paranoia. I will not kill her without some kind of proof." Yet as he said that, he realized that he had just admitted that under the right circumstances he *would* kill Ariadne.

"Which is why we need to delay her, prevent our attack on the bridge for as long as possible. Put pressure on her,"

Elena's thick accent seemed to bore into Eric's head. He met her gaze again, and her blue eyes seemed almost to glow with intensity. "I do not want her to die, either. She has seemed nothing but kind to me. Yet if she is the source of this attack, if she has manipulated us all along..."

"She'll have to die," Eric whispered. He buried his face in his hands. "I'll do it, but we have to be sure. Absolutely sure, not just suspicions."

Elena and Crowe both nodded, yet their reasonable agreement made Eric's heart sink further.

"Of course," Crowe said softly, "We will make sure of it."

***

"Mister Striker," a cultured woman's voice spoke from behind Eric.

He turned to find the Nova Roma Ambassador behind him, flanked by her pair of marine guards. She looked as confident as before, and her dark eyes met Eric's gaze without hesitation.

"What?" Eric asked impatiently.

"I had heard this pirate has threatened to kill us all," Alara Vibius said, "Is this true?" The sharp edge on her voice immediately put Eric's back up.

"A Wrethe has seized the engine room," Eric said as patiently as he could manage. "So get out of my way while we try to deal with it." He decided not to mention the other chaos aboard, if only out of spite. The woman could learn to ask more nicely if she wanted to know more.

"What exactly does that mean?" She demanded. "Do you have some sort of plan? Have you tried to negotiate with it?"

"Yes, we have a plan. And we're pretty sure it plans to kill us regardless of what we do for it, so we're trying to delay it while we prepare a response." Eric paused, then shrugged, "Ariadne is talking with it right now."

"Well, perhaps someone competent could discus things with this pirate," the Ambassador said, her voice showed exactly what she thought of an amateur engaged in such discussions.

"If we find someone for that, I'll let you know," Eric said as he turned away. He did not trust the woman, especially not with Pixel's life. The engineer needed help, and fast, and Eric had a low opinion of bureaucrats that normally manned such posts, and an even lower one for this privileged and spoiled woman in particular.

"Mister Striker... Eric, please wait," she said behind him. The slight catch in her voice stopped him, and when he turned, he saw tears in the corner of her eyes.

Eric told himself not to believe that, but as much as he hated himself for it, he felt immediate sympathy for her. *Damn me, but she's pretty when she's not trying to be a bitch*, he thought.

"Yes?" *Come to think of it, she looks beautiful enough when she is a complete bitch.*

"Please, this is my life on the line as well," Alara said. "I know I can be difficult... but this is my job, this is what I do. Allow me to help, please don't send me back down to that damned cargo hold like a child sent to her room." Something about the way she stood, the almost fragile set of determination on her face, and the openness that she showed, now of all times penetrated Eric in a way her abrasive arrogance had not.

"Very well," Eric said. "But we have an injured man in there, our engineer. We need him alive and well. That's the main priority, no matter what else we agree to, we need to get Pixel out of the engine room alive, understood?"

"Of course," she nodded.

"Alright, follow me. I'd recommend you keep your bodyguards close in case this goes bad. Your ship suit as well, because we may end up in vacuum soon enough," Eric said. He led them up the stair well and then down the corridor to where Ariadne waited with Rastar and Anubus.

Lines marked Ariadne's normally happy face. She looked worried, but a part of Eric wondered how much worry came from the danger to their friends and how much came from how her plan had unraveled. *That is... if she has a plan,* Eric thought, *assuming Crowe and Elena aren't just paranoid.*

"The Ambassador here has offered to negotiate with Ghost," Eric said. He cocked his head, "You know, might not be a bad idea to bring them in on those drills that we had planned." Eric paused, "Though,I don't think even I would think to do a drill to fight two different enemies in charge of the bridge *and* the engine room at the same time."

"Yeah, seriously, this is ridiculous," Ariadne nodded, but the worry on her face did not decrease. "We need to get Pixel out of there, Eric, I don't know how much longer he can last." She wiped at her eyes, "I sent my mind out... he's hurt pretty bad. Ghost punched its claws into his chest--" Ariadne choked back a sob. "He's unconscious."

Eric turned to Alara, "You're on."

She stepped up to the terminal without a word. Rastar pressed down the call button, and Alara Vibius spoke, "I am Alara Aurelia Caelia Vibius, daughter of Duke Vibius, whom am I speaking with?"

The Wrethe gave its hyena's laugh, "That's quite a mouthful. I do so love the Nova Roman fetish with names. I go by Ghost."

"Well, Mister Ghost, we have something of a standoff," she said. "You may have realized it, but we have a number of capable marines and troops aboard this ship. You might well destroy it, and possibly kill us, but I doubt that you will get off this ship alive if you do not give us some sign that you bargain in good faith."

"You think your threats concern me?" Ghost demanded.

"Not threats, observations," Alara said, her voice cold. "I acknowledge that you must have several capabilities at both combat and tactics to act as a pirate with any level of success. However, we have aboard a contingent of Nova Roma Marines, who have much experience with pirates. Besides that I have auxiliaries with military training from the Confederation and the Colonial Republic. Whatever your talents, you cannot face a unified military force by yourself and survive."

"So, you are their leader... or their treasure they protect,

415

then?" Ghost said. "How interesting. How much, I wonder, would Nova Roma offer for you in ransom?"

"Nova Roma does not negotiate with kidnappers," Alara said. "And in truth, your actions are already close enough that I wonder if we should not simply storm the engine room and take our chances." Eric nodded at that, though he saw Ariadne frown. Eric knew well enough that any nation or organization that showed that they would pay out to kidnappers or terrorists in turn drew those types in the future. If they killed those who sought such blackmail, regardless of the hostages, they often lost fewer people in the long run.

"Very well," Ghost said. "Yet I fail to see where this conversation has headed. I will not leave here empty handed, and you seem to imply that you will not give me what I want. So why don't I just activate my program and kill you all?"

"Give us a show of good faith," Alara said. "Let us get our wounded man out. We will send two men in to get him--"

"One man, unarmed," Ghost said. "And in return, you will start to move the gold aboard my ship." The high pitched growl sounded very intent.

Eric spoke, "We can't get aboard your ship, the turret-"

"I will deactivate some of my security systems by remote, as well as open the cargo compartment. If you attempt to access any other part of my ship, I will know. I will not allow that. If you attempt to attach anything, beacon, bomb or whatever to my ship, I will know. I will not allow that. Any attempt by the one you send in to retrieve your engineer to attack me or affect the ship's systems in any way, I will know and I will not allow. Am I understood?"

"Agreed," Alara said, her voice haughty. "We will send one man down to retrieve him."

Ariadne turned to Rastar, "Get Run ready. I'll go in--"

"No, I'll get him," Eric said. He didn't want to go in there unarmed. However, if Ariadne was the rogue psychic, then the last thing he wanted was her anywhere near the Wrethe. She might well warp Ghost over to her side, and then they would really be screwed. Or she might take it in her head to kill the

Wrethe, but without complete knowledge of what Ghost had done to their systems, that might well make it worse.

Particularly if Ghost had a dead man switch.

"Okay," Ariadne gave him a nod. "Be careful and get him quickly. He grows weaker as we speak." The concern on her face seemed completely legitimate. Everything about her seemed that way, yet Crowe's insinuations made too much sense.

I hope we are both wrong, he thought. He gave Ariadne a smile that felt wooden, "Don't worry about Pixel, I'll get him out of there alive."

***

Eric hurried down the corridors and stopped outside the engine room hatch. Ariadne had said that Pixel lay only a few meters inside the aft access hatch. She had also warned him that Ghost stood nearby and that something about the Wrethe's suit seemed 'odd.'

Eric activated the hatch and as it opened, he raised his hands. "I have no weapons. I am here to retrieve my friend." He glanced over his shoulder. Rastar and Anubus both waited down the corridor. Mandy and Miranda had taken up positions at the forward access hatch. Eric really hoped that they would not have intervene. If they did, Eric would probably need as much attention as Pixel.

"You may enter," Ghost said. The Wrethe's strange high pitched rasp held more menace in person. Eric clenched his jaw, suddenly angry. He hated the bastard, and he decided then and there that when they killed the Wrethe, *he* would get to finish it off.

Eric stepped forward and swept his gaze around as much as he could. He spotted a garish clash of red against the whites and blues of the engine room. Pixel lay sprawled in a puddle of blood, and he lay still enough that for a moment, Eric worried the engineer had already died.

But as he came up, he checked his pulse and found a beat, faint, but still there. And he saw Pixel's chest raise as he took a breath. "Hang in there, buddy," Eric said, even as he slipped one arm under his shoulders and other other under his knees to pick the other man up. He heard Pixel give a moan of pain, but Eric didn't have time for gentleness.

As he stood and turned, he found Ghost had moved to stand directly behind him. Eric froze as he stared at the Wrethe.

It wore a combat rated environmental suit. It wore an open faced helmet, with what looked like a memory plastic visor ready to extend, and its jackal head peered at Eric. It stood short for a Wrethe, shorter than Eric, but squat with muscle and the bulk of its armored suit. Unlike most Wrethe, it had pure white fur, and its dark eyes had a red tint that stood out starkly against its snowy pelt. Eric glanced down at it's hands, and saw that the Wrethe wore armored gloves, tipped with metal claws.

"You show much concern for your engineer," Ghost said. The Wrethe's high pitched rasp sounded almost like a pair of steel files rubbed together. "Perhaps he is more valuable than you suggested."

"He is my friend you piece of shit alien scum," Eric said. "And for hurting him, I promise you I'll kill you."

Ghost stepped closer, so close that Eric could feel its hot breath on his face, "Then perhaps I should kill you, now, and finish your friend. I haven't had a fresh meal in some time."

"Then my other friends will storm the engine room," Eric snapped. "And they'll kill you. So stop the bluster and get the fuck out of my way shorty."

Ghost drew itself up and one claw came up. Eric tensed as the claw stopped only inches from Eric's face. "I will not kill you, but I'll make you a bargain."

Eric didn't trust himself to speak. He wanted to scream obscenities at the damned Wrethe.

"I will let you and your *friend*," Ghost fairly spat the word, "leave, but I will mark you, so that I may recognize you when the time comes. Otherwise, because all of you humans look too similar, I may end you quickly rather than properly break you." Ghost cocked its head, "Or, you could set your friend down and leave him to die. Your choice."

Eric stared at the Wrethe, "Do it, you waste of oxygen.

I'm getting bored."

The Wrethe extended its thumb and Eric bit back a grunt of pain as it gauged a line across his cheek, and then cut another line to bisect it. The Wrethe made two more cuts on his other cheek and then stepped back. "When we meet again, I will savor your death human. I will feel your terror and despair as I break your spirit."

"The name is Eric," he replied, "When we meet again, the only thing you'll feel is the bullet I put through your brain." Eric stepped around the Wrethe and walked out of the engine room without a glance back.

***

Run had set up one of the metal tables in the galley as an operating table. He also had a pair of men standing by, one of them held Run's bag of tools. Eric recognized the two space hands, Matvei and Anastasei, though he couldn't remember which was which. Eric lay Pixel down on it and stepped back. Run glanced up at Eric, "You have a wound on your face. I would recommend you allow me to treat you."

"No," Eric said. "Take care of Pixel. He looks pretty bad." Eric tried not to think of how many of his teammates he had seen die, and how some of them had seemed in better shape than Pixel did now. The engineer's face had gone pale and his cheeks seemed sunken. His normally expressive face was slack.

"He will live," Run said. He pulled out a set of what looked like torture equipment to Eric. "I will need someone to hold him still, however."

"Why not just sew him up?" Eric asked, uneasy with that idea.

"He has taken internal damage. I will need to make repairs to his organs. If I had my full lab--"

"Right, well, what about painkillers?" Eric asked. "Surely you have something, hell, you have the darts that knock someone unconscious, that would work, right?"

The little Chxor shook his head, "That would prove suboptimal. I find that the administration of pain after an injury

419

encourages my test subjects to avoid such injuries in the future."

Eric cocked his head, "That' actually makes a certain level of sense."

"Of course," Run said. He pulled out a scalpel and what looked suspiciously like a glue gun to Eric. "Now hold him still."

Eric cringed, but he waved forward the other two. "I've got some other stuff I need to take care of..." He trailed off as Pixel started to moan, then shout. Eric felt his stomach turn over. This reminded him far too much of his own memories at Blackthorn. He backed out of the galley, and blindly felt for the hatch controls. The door opened behind him and he stumbled out into the corridor. If only he could have escaped from that damned Blackthorn mission so easily.

***

"I have a ready courier ship at the spaceport," Lieutenant Colonel Andreysiak said as they broke into a run. Two of his men carried the woman between them, while the others formed a perimeter around their primary and the prisoner.

They had secured a panel truck for the final movement and moved to an otherwise empty warehouse. "They'll have biometrics scanners in place, and my people don't have appropriate identification," Eric said. "And I don't think security will let your... package through."

"They might have obtained genetic material from myself or some of my team," Andreysiak said. "So we'll have to hit them and push through. Get to my ship and launch."

"They'll lock down the entire spaceport and shoot down any ships..."

"Not if they're under a bomb threat," Andreysiak said. "Blackthorn has set up a contingency for this, their radiological alarms will go off in approximately thirty minutes. We'll hit their security right after that, slip through in the confusion of evacuation and complete extraction. After we reach Blackthorn Base, we'll transfer your personnel to a ready ship and your mission is complete."

"How'd you rig the radiological alarms?" Sergeant Schill asked. "Those are almost foolproof."

"We have some small quantities of radiological built into a weapons casing that we obtained on the planet," one of the security escort said. "Totally safe, but they won't know that without taking it apart."

"Which hangar? And I need the best map you can provide to brief my people," Eric said. He had a headache and he realized that this all had gone far beyond the original scope of his mission. Evacuation to an alternate LZ he could understand. A staged nuclear threat to cause a mass evacuation of a major spaceport... *Who the hell* are *these people,* he wondered, *none of them bat an eyelash at the attention this will draw, it's almost like they don't care.*

Blackthorn Five passed over a datacard, "It's all on there. Blueprints as well as patrol schedules."

Eric brought it up and skimmed it in only a few moments. Whoever or whatever Blackthorn was, they laid out the information in a fashion that let Eric see the overall picture in only a moment. That meant they had lots of experience with this sort of thing and very good intelligence and data miners. "We will go in through Delta Five delivery gate. Push to the hangar and extract." He frowned as he considered the defenses on the gate, as well as the location of nearby hostiles. Further losses would happen and Eric felt a special sort of horror as he realized he might well lose his entire squad if things went completely wrong.

He turned on his squad radio net and spoke, "Alright boys and girls, this is where it gets interesting..." He laid out his plan to them. Their total silence afterward showed their discipline, but it also told him what he already knew. They realized just how deep in the shit they already dug themselves. Even Jenkins seemed sober and quiet.

The drive to the spaceport seemed worse, for the tension seemed to ratchet as they made their approach. Eric felt the additional weight of his team's losses. He found it impossible to focus on the current mission with almost half of his squad down as killed in action. This mission had gone worse than any since his time as a private in the Grantville mission. *At least it is damned near impossible for anything to be worse than Grantville,* he thought.

As they drew near the security gate, Eric raised the back gate of the truck and Wranski and Lobochev rolled out. The pair had the call-signs Alpha and Omega, mostly due to their constant competition as sharpshooters, they began and ended every combat. A few seconds later, the shrill wail started that Eric hoped signaled the spaceport evacuation. "Alright boys, that's our signal. Cowboy, take down the guards, Alpha and Omega provide over-watch."

He heard their acknowledgments and then the truck pulled to a stop at the gate. Over the rumble of the truck's engine, he barely heard the cough of Jenkins's CKY pistol. A moment later, he heard a groan as the gate began to open.

"Cowboy, Omega, you've got a roving guard approaching from your three, I can't get a shot, he's behind armored glass," Eric heard over the net.

"Omega, Cowboy, I can't get into that corridor, door's locked with a biometrics keypad," Jenkins drawl sounded terse. Eric understood why. That corridor led straight back to a nearby guard post, where the local quick reaction team stood on standby. If they couldn't take down the guard...

"Shit," Omega said. "He spotted something wrong, he's on the radio."

Eric closed his eyes, *so much for that.* "Go to plan Bravo Two. Cowboy take down that guard and secure the corridor."

Krensk and Halsh opened the back of the truck and dove out, and Eric turned to Andreysiak, "We'll hold their reserve team in place, your people should have time to get the ship up and operational. We'll come in hot, sir, so keep the ramp down for us but be ready to go."

"Good hunting," Andreysiak's smile sent a chill down Eric's spine. Not because it was the grin of a fellow killer, but because the bastard seemed to find their predicament amusing for some reason. *I'm going to lose my squad and all this bastard will do smile.*

Eric followed his men out the back. A dull crump signaled that Jenkins had opened the door with a shaped charge. A moment later he opened up with his FAMAR PN2-11. The roar of the eleven millimeter machine gun signaled he had engaged the guard. By the time Eric reached him he had started to lay suppressive fire down the corridor. "Yee-haw!" Jenkins shouted.

The panel truck rolled away, even as Lobochev ran past, his rifle at the low ready. Eric tagged Halsh on the shoulder, "Jam their wireless."

"I am," Halsh shouted over Jenkins's fire. "But they have to have a hardwired backup. I can't access that--"

A rattle of fire from a doorway to their rear sent both of them to cover. Eric saw a five man team of spaceport security had emerged from the terminal building.

Eric returned fire, even as he heard Lobochev call out on the net, "This is Omega, I'm hit, armor blunted it but my leg's down."

Eric swore when he saw where the sharpshooter had fallen. He had some cover from their current attackers, but once the QRT moved around to their right he'd be exposed without cover. Worse, a ten meter gap lay between him and any other cover.

"Alpha, this is Mongoose, lay suppressive fire, Commo, you're in position for retrieval," Eric snapped out the order, even as he sprinted out of cover and then rolled into a drainage ditch. His new position gave him the opportunity to lay suppressive fire at the alternate exit of the QRT.

"Commo, got him," Halsh said. "Mongoose, tell Omega he's put on a few extra pounds." Eric gave a grim chuckle at that, Lobochev stood well over two meters tall, and massed a hundred and twenty kilos without his gear and weapons.

"Doc," Eric called to Krensk, "Take Omega. Alpha, move up to your next position."

Eric heard no response for what seemed like an eternity,

"Negative Mongoose. I've got a police team that has moved to block the gate. I've also got eyes on a SWAT armored vehicle headed towards your location, they just passed my firing point. I'll have to hold position. I will provide suppressive fire and draw their attention. Will try to withdraw without becoming decisively engaged."

Eric closed his eyes, "Roger, good hunting." Alpha might manage to withdraw, but the odds were against him, and with how the police force cut him off, he had nowhere to go.

"Cowboy here, they're bringing up--"

A ear-shattering explosion whipped Eric's head around. Even over the sound damper in his helmet his ears rung. A cloud of dust and debris marked the guard shack and Jenkins former position. A glance at his wrist-comp showed Cowboy's icon as red. "All personnel, withdraw. Commo bound with me once Doc and Omega make cover. You have first bound." That would leave Eric with the trail position, but he refused to expose his remaining personnel to risks he wouldn't take.

He saw Krensk drag Lobochev around the next corner. Eric popped up and gave a short burst of suppressive fire at the security team. Halsh took off in a sprint, and then took a knee at the corner and lay suppressive fire.

Eric broke into a sprint. His body armor seemed to drag at him. He felt an impact between his shoulder blades, but the liquid steel armor stopped the bullet without a problem. Eric slid behind the corner, and lay prone, "Alright Commo, move to your next position."

"Acknowledged," Halsh said and bounded back.

"Mongoose, Alpha here, I've got eyes on QRT Two, they're mounted up and headed towards your position," The sharpshooter sounded winded, and he bit his words off as if in pain. Eric glanced as his wrist-comp, and saw that Wranski's icon had gone amber and flashed orange. Eric felt tears well up in his eyes. Even as they bled out his men did a damned fine job. "I'm pinned down on this floor, but I'll attempt to--"

His voice cut out with a squeal of static. Eric bit back a curse as the enemy jammed their frequency. *At least I know they couldn't crack our encryption,* he thought grimly.

Eric saw the security team sprint into the open, he felt a grim smile draw his lips back as he let them get out into the open and then put a three round burst into each of them. The QRT had finally got out of their building and began to lay suppressive fire on him.

Eric crawled back as rounds peppered the area around him and blew holes through the cinder block wall. He rolled to his feet and loped after Halsh. He found Halsh at the next intersection, and he remembered then that the other QRT would use this road. Even as the thought that, he saw Halsh bring up his Hammer. The TRA Hammer fired twenty five millimeter sabot rounds. It should blast through the QRT's lightly armored trucks. It also had a mean kick and a visual and audible signature that hit almost as hard as the round.

At thirty meters distance, even with the sound dampers, the sharp crack of the first shot assaulted Eric's ears. His helmet visor darkened against the bright flash. Eric sprinted forward across the street, even as the QRT returned fire. Out of the corner of his eye, he saw the lead truck swerve out of control. The truck struck a parked vehicle and rolled. The truck behind it skidded to a stop, but the gunner stitched the air with fire from his crew served weapon.

Eric staggered and his world went white as one of the rounds passed close enough that the supersonic passage twisted his head around. He stumbled and fell just past Halsh as his commo specialist fired again.

Eric thought he'd gone blind until he realized his helmet had completely died. He wrenched it off, and grimaced at the crack that went along the visor. He glanced back at Halsh, and then felt a wrench of pain as he saw what remained of the man. At least two of the heavy rounds from the crew served weapon had struck him, and they had mangled the man almost beyond recognition.

Eric swore and staggered to his feet. He shook his head as the world spun, and felt at his ears. His fingers came away bloody, either Halsh's Hammer or the enemy fire had ruptured his eardrums.

Another burst of weapons fire chewed up the corner. Eric shook his head again and broke into the fastest pace he could manage. He stumbled around the next corner before anyone could put a bullet in his back. *Maybe we showed the bastards some caution,* he thought.

He staggered down the next two blocks and then turned into the hangar where Andreysiak's ship lay. He saw the panel truck first, pulled up almost at the ramp of the sleek ship that sat ready. Eric could hear the whine of the ship's machinery. He hoped that meant they had made the ship ready. He found Krensk and Lobochev just inside the doors. The squad medic had Lobochev' laid out and parts of his aid bag lay strewn around. "Get him aboard," Eric rasped and pointed at the ramp.

"Can't move him, yet. I got to stabilize him, he dead-lined outside, I just got him breathing again," the female medic said. "I need thirty seconds, and then I need three people to help me move him."

"Roger, I'll get some people down here," Eric said.

He jogged up the ramp and almost ran into one of Andreysiak's security men at the top. Beyond him, he saw the Lieutenant Colonel and another pair of security men. "Good, glad you're here, I need three of you to come with me, I've got a wounded man I need to get aboard and we can go."

"Negative, sergeant," Andreysiak said. "Mission is complete, we're out."

"They're just down the ramp, it will take ten seconds-"

"We can't risk it," Andreysiak said. "Wrobochesky, close the hatch."

Eric had his SKL-15 leveled on Wrobochesky's forehead before Andreysiak he even consciously heard Blackthorn Five's words. "Do it and you're dead. Walk down the damned ramp and help my people."

"I expected better of you, Sergeant," Andreysiak said, and Eric heard the smile on the other man's voice. Eric realized he had pointed his weapon at the wrong man. *I screwed up again,* he thought, *and again my people will pay the price.*

426

He spun, but not before Andreysiak fired. The TRA Wasp fired twin lasers which cut ionized channels through the air. A millisecond later the Wasp pulsed ten thousand volts at a modulated amperage designed to incapacitate.

Eric let out an involuntary scream as he lost control of his body. The physical pain was raw and intense as his muscles spasmed. It felt like barbed wire being dragged across his entire body. The emotional pain from the knowledge that he had sacrificed his entire team for nothing hurt far worse. He lay on the deck and could do nothing but watch as the hatch closed behind him.

"Should we finish him, sir?" One of the security team asked.

He heard Andreysiak chuckle, "Bag him, waste not, want not, as they say."

He felt a pair of arms grasp his trembling hands and jerk him up to his knees. Even as he heard the ship's thrusters fire, he saw Wrobochesky draw a black bag from a pocket. Eric felt a cold sweat break out on his forehead, his childhood memories welled to the front of his mind.

I deserved this, he thought, *I failed my squad, I got* all *of them killed.*

***

Crowe still waited in the lounge with Elena. "Alright, we've delayed long enough," Eric said as he walked up to the other man. Eric could almost hear the approval of his team as he confronted the other man face to face. Eric had retrieved his TEK-15 and the laser rifle, and had both slung, with the submachine gun on a single point sling from his right shoulder.

"Holy shit, what happened to your face?" Crowe asked.

"Had a meet and greet with Ghost," Eric said. "I'm pretty sure that whether or not you're right, Ghost has to be dealt with, which means we need control of the bridge. The damned Wrethe has locked down the other two access hatches, and can do the same with the aft one if it wants. So we need the bridge to override those controls. Which means I need you to hack the bridge controls."

"Look, Eric," Crowe said, "I know that this Wrethe may seem like a bad ass..."

"This Wrethe seems like a psycho who will kill us all for kicks," Eric said. "And you seem way too relaxed for this situation, so I'm going to give you a bit of taste of what *my* day has felt like." Eric brought up his TEK-15 with a single smooth motion and aligned the sights with Crowe's forehead at a range of less than a meter. He saw the other man's eyes go wide as he thumbed off the electronic safety. "Now, this is how it's going to go. You are going to come with me to the bridge access stairs. You'll override the lock-down and get us on the bridge. Since you're so concerned about Ariadne you can watch her. She's going in with Rastar, Anubus and I."

"Eric, put the gun away," Elena said sharply.

"If you go for your pistol, I'll put a burst through Crowe's forehead and then we can see which of us moves faster," Eric said. "I don't want to kill either of you. I need him, dammit, we all do." Eric realized that aiming his weapon had not been the smartest thing to do. But still, he had got his point across at least.

"Eric, you don't want to do this," Crowe said. "We are so close to getting the proof that Ariadne is the rogue psychic and finding out why she has manipulated--"

"I don't care," Eric said. "Psychic or not, we need the bridge. We've delayed that long enough. Your argument would hold a lot more weight if I had not just come from where Run has Pixel on a makeshift surgery table." Eric pursed his lips. "Do you realize how it feels to see everyone else fully engaged, even the damned Chxor, and here you are relaxed in the lounge? I'm a bit angry, right now, Crowe. And you know I'm impulsive, especially when I'm angry. No where near as bad as Rastar, but do you trust your life to my temper right now, Crowe? Do you?"

Crowe's face drained of color. "I'll do it. But I'll remember this."

"Please," Eric said. "Please do, because next time I might just pull the trigger anyway. Remember that you signed

Mike's contract, and that you joined this team. And if you don't pull your weight, well, then I'll make sure your dead weight doesn't drag me down. Now let's go."

***

"How is Pixel... oh, what happened to your face?" Ariadne asked.

Eric reached up and wiped at the blood. He winced in pain as his fingers brushed wound on his cheek. "Ghost is a real nice fellow. Run has Pixel, he says he'll be fine." Eric decided not to mention that Run had two men to hold Pixel down while he worked. "I convinced Crowe to come try a hack on the door controls."

"Good," Ariadne shot both Elena and Crowe a glance. "Elena, I'd like you to back up Simon, Mandy and Miranda. They're at the forward access hatch for engineering."

"You do not want me to help with the bridge?"

"No," Ariadne said. "We've got Rastar, Eric and Anubus for that, and I would rather less gunfire that might damage anything essential on the bridge."

"Very well," Elena and Crowe shared a glance, "I will assist the others."

Crowe pulled out his computer and ran a connection cable to the door control. He frowned, "I can do this, but are we sure..."

Eric leaned over Crowe's shoulder, "Are you dead weight?"

"I said I can do it." Crowe snapped. "Get out of my personal space."

"Sure," Eric turned away. "So what's the plan?" He asked.

"I will kill Krann," Rastar said. "She deserves to die for what she has done, both to my people and to us, if she is the rogue psychic," his hide had gone a deep red color. "I hope you do not feel offended that I wish to take this kill."

Eric shrugged, "Honestly, no. I said before we should have a one Chxor limit."

429

"Right," Anubus growled. "And we've exceeded our one Wrethe aboard policy. Which means I get to kill Ghost. In return for that, I will restrain Mike."

"Just restrain?" Eric asked.

"If he is mentally controlled, then I will limit myself to restraint. If he has betrayed us, then he deserves to die for his failure," Anubus growled. "But I will allow Ariadne to judge that."

"I think he's under control. I couldn't feel his mind. I'm not certain it is Krann who is the psychic, but someone has shielded that area. There may be someone else on the bridge, perhaps out of view of the camera," Ariadne said. "For that matter, without Pixel to access the camera feed, we don't know what's going on."

"Wait, they can shield an area from you?" Eric asked.

"Yes, at least it appears so," Ariadne shrugged. I can only barely sense around the edges of that barrier, and even that drains me more than it should."

"We really need a manual on this stuff," Simon said.

"Yeah," Eric nodded. They at least need some way to tell when she might be lying in order to manipulate them into... something.

"Maybe when we get time," Ariadne said.

"I've got the hatch controls on this door and the upper one overridden," Crowe said as he looked up. For a second, he had a look on his face that made Eric want to aim his TEK-15 at him, but the look disappeared before Eric could react. He half thought he might have imagined it.

Or has Ariadne messed with my head, he thought, *to put doubts about Crowe in there?*

"Open the lower one," Rastar said as he drew his pair of Ragers and the two riot guns. "Wait for us to get into position before you open the upper hatch."

"Of course," Crowe said. The other man stepped out of the way. Rastar led the way up the stairs, followed by Anubus and then Ariadne and Eric. Rastar paused at the upper hatch, and the big Ghornath seemed to gather himself. "Ready?" he asked.

430

"Ready," Anubus growled.

"Ready," Ariadne said.

"Let's kill this bitch," Eric said.

"Do it Crowe!" Rastar bellowed. A moment later the hatch drew open and Rastar charged forward.

He froze a few steps in the doorway. Eric could see him completely freeze, one leg raised to run forward, arms poised to sweep the room for a target. He heard Ariadne gasp then. "It's Krann, she's dominated his mind! I'll try to free him..."

The air temperature secmed to drop ten degrees in a heartbeat. The lights seemed to dim, then, and Eric felt goosebumps rise on his arms. The very air seemed to hum with energy in a way that just felt alien and *wrong.*

Eric heard a gunshot then, and saw a splatter of red Ghornath blood spatter Anubus. *Shit, Mike has fired, we have to stop him or he will kill Rastar,* Eric thought.

Anubus dove under Rastar's legs and out of sight. Eric ran up the stairs. He saw Anubus tackle Mike. Then Krann stepped out from the side and raised a hand.

Eric brought his submachine gun up, but a wave of force slammed him backwards. He struck the bulkhead hard enough that stars exploded in his vision. At the same time, for a moment, he felt as if someone had pumped ice water directly into his heart.

He heard Ariadne shout something, and the force went away. Eric dropped to his knees, and he shook his head to clear his vision. He felt his heart tremor in shock. He looked over to see Ariadne clutch at her head. "She's too strong, God, how is she so strong..." Her voice trailed off as she seemed overwhelmed by some sort of mental attack. Eric looked up. Between Rastar's legs he saw Krann draw her pistol.

Crowe had come up the stairs behind Ariadne. Crowe's words went through his head, and he wondered at the entire series of events. Had Ariadne controlled Krann all along? Had this all been some elaborate ruse to put her in command? He stared at where Ariadne stood, her face contorted in concentration and pain.

431

He saw Crowe shake his head, yet then he saw Krann draw her pistol. If Ariadne controlled her, then the way to stop the Chxor from taking shots at Rastar would to kill or injure Ariadne. If Krann were the rogue psychic, then he needed to injure her.

"Eric, please, help me!" Ariadne said.

Her words and tone perfectly matched that of Ivanna. A brief vision of her as she died flashed through his mind. He felt his tension ease as he made the decision, for better or worse.

Eric rolled over to his side and brought his submachine gun up again. He triggered a single burst, afraid he might hit Rastar as he fired between his friend's four legs. He saw green blood explode out of Krann's left leg.

Rastar stumbled forward, and brought all four of his weapons to bear on Krann.

The two Rager Twelves fired on full automatic even as Rastar fired the riot guns. Krann's head and upper torso seemed to explode. Eric glanced back to see Ariadne slump and then catch herself on the stairs. Behind her, Crowe frowned and shook his head.

"I have Mike," Anubus growled. "I will put him in the closet for the moment."

"Sounds good, we need to search the bridge, make sure that the threat is over." Eric said. He frowned then. "Hey, this doesn't count as mutiny, does it?"

***

Ariadne went straight to the navigation console. After a minute's work, she looked up, "Krann programmed a shadow space jump back to Logan. I don't know what she intended to do when we got there, but that was the course she had plotted."

"Guys... you want to see this," Rastar said from where he stood over Krann's body.

Eric turned. He stared at the body with a puzzled expression. At first, he just saw green Chxor blood and bloody meat. Then he saw the spreading pool of purple slime that seemed to come from inside. Rastar rolled the body over with

432

his riot guns, and the pool became a tide.

Eric gagged as he saw that most of the Chxor's head and torso had become an empty cavity, and the lumpy purple ooze seemed to have replaced Krann's internal organs... to include her brain, or whatever the Chxor equivalent. "What the fuck is this?"

"I have no idea," Ariadne said. "We need Run up here."

"I did not think that was normal," Rastar said. "Normally when I kill Chxor they're green on the inside. This kind of thing really isn't right." Eric saw the Ghornath go to the intercom, "Run, report to the bridge and bring your tools."

Eric put a hand over his mouth, partially to contain anything that might spew out. "No one touch it, it could be contagious." He looked up, "Maybe Krann had some kind of disease..."

"One that liquified her internal organs without any outward signs?" Anubus shook his big jackal head. "No. This is something else," he growled. "Something wore her body like a suit... something psychic."

"Something much stronger than me," Ariadne said. "She-- it, held Rastar even as it overpowered me *and* attacked Eric. That takes a serious kind of talent."

Run hurried up the stairs. "Who is hurt? I have brought my tools, I will need someone to hold down my patients so they can not escape."

"Krann is dead," Eric said. "So we don't need to hold her down. But we need you to tell us what the hell this shit is coming out of her."

Run walked forward. He stared down at Krann's corpse. Run immediately pulled his helmet out of his tool bag and sealed it. When he spoke, his voice came muffled, "I recommend we don environmental suits and remove the body from the ship."

"You know what she is?" Ariadne asked.

"No," Run said. "However, anything capable of maintaining a living host while replacing brain material is very dangerous. I will take samples, but unless anyone intends to purposely seek infection, I would recommend touching the remains as suboptimal."

"How do we get it off the bridge?" Eric asked. He gestured at the broad puddle of purple slime. He thought he saw chunks, perhaps organs or something else, within the slime. "For that matter, Rastar's shots splattered a lot of it across the bulkheads."

"I will perform complete decontamination," Run said. "I do not trust humans to be as thorough as you should to remove contagions. This will require approximately twelve hours."

"We need access to the ship's systems," Ariadne said. "And for that matter, this thing only affected a Chxor, so aren't you at the greatest risk?"

"This is true," Run moved well back. "I will supervise removal. I require ten personnel--"

Eric rubbed at his face. "Alright, so one threat solved to leave us with, well, whatever the heck this is." He looked over at Ariadne, "Can you see what that bitch did to Mike?"

Ariadne looked down, "I can, but I'm not very good with this sort of thing. Even if I can figure out what she did, I'm not sure I can undo it, not without doing some damage." She looked tired and worried, and almost as if she'd aged ten years in the past few minutes. *This whole psychic battle thing really took it out of her,* Eric realized.

"We need to see the extent of his damage," Anubus growled. "If he will be permanently damaged from what Krann did, we should kill him."

"Hey man, I think that might be harsh," Rastar said. "But we do need to know how bad she messed with Mike. If only to determine if we need to select a new Captain."

"Because that went just *swell* before," Crowe said.

Ariadne gave a sigh, "Rastar, I'll need you to hold him still."

"Not me?" Anubus growled, but Eric thought he heard a note of humor in the Wrethe's voice.

"He'll fight," Ariadne said. "I can feel that from here. I don't trust you not to lose your temper and... hurt him."

"Ripping his arms off would probably hurt," Anubus

nodded. "I'll get the hatch. Rastar, you grab him."

Eric saw Crowe signal him to watch Ariadne, but Eric shook his head. The other man's suspicions seemed too far-fetched now, after what they had discovered about Krann. Something had *replaced* the Chxor's insides. Who knew what capabilities a creature like that might have?

Anubus activated the closet hatch and Mike leapt out with a shout. He had a knife in hand, though Eric had no idea where it had come from. Rastar stepped forward into the attack and swept the man up in a four-armed bear hug. Mike struggled, but he almost disappeared in Rastar's arms.

Rastar turned to face Ariadne, "Alright, Ariadne." Eric saw that Mike's knife had stuck in Rastar's side, but the Ghornath didn't seem to react to the wound.

"Let go of me, you traitor!" Mike shouted. "I'm the Captain! You all betrayed me!"

Eric shook his head at those words. Yet even as he did, Crowe's warning came back to mind.

Ariadne walked forward and rested her hands on either side of Mike's head. "Shhhh, it'll be alright Mike, just let me see what that bitch did to you."

"She didn't do anything!" Mike shouted. "She warned me before Anubus led this mutiny," Mike growled. "What did he offer you to betray me, Ariadne? Did..." Mike's voice trailed off.

Ariadne closed her eyes, and Eric watched with unease as Mike's eyes rolled back in his head. After a long moment, Ariadne spoke, "I found it, she's put a series of suggestions in his head. The main one is that Anubus allied with this other Wrethe and that they turned the rest of us to seize the ship. She played off his fears and doubts..." Ariadne opened her eyes, "I'm not sure I can undo all of it."

"Clever plan," Anubus growled. "Make it seem we betrayed him. I'll have to remember that."

Eric chewed at his lip, "What if we leave him be, will it fade?"

"I don't know," Ariadne said. "He's firmly tied everything that happened in with what Krann, or whatever pretended to be Krann, planted in his mind. He might pull himself out, but he might not."

Eric looked at the others. No matter what, he could not see a right answer. Worse, the one person in charge, the person *Mike* had selected, seemed unable to make a decision about what to do. For that matter, everything Ariadne had said sounded far too close to what Crowe had suggested. Could *they* be the ones who had their minds messed with? What if Mike lay in the right, what if Anubus had made his bid for control, and somehow turned Ariadne?

"Guys, we can't leave him like this," Rastar said. "What happens if you try to undo what she did?"

"I don't know," Ariadne said, her voice nervous. "I've... had bad things happen before when I tried to modify memories in someone. It could unbalance him or even shatter his mind."

"Let's try to avoid that," Simon said from the hatch.

"Aren't you supposed to be watching the engine room hatches?" Eric asked.

"I will be very... unhappy with you if Ghost has escaped," Anubus growled.

"I've put some of the others around the engine access hatches. They probably can't take down the Wrethe, but they can warn us if Ghost makes an escape attempt. I also locked down the Armory, just to make sure that Ghost doesn't access our weapons."

"Hey man," Rastar said, "Good idea."

"Unless we need more weapons," Eric said.

Simon looked around the room, particularly at the splattered remains of Krann. "I think we have enough guns."

"You can never have enough weapons," Eric answered.

"Enough!" Ariadne said. "We need to work together, not fight one another." She looked away from Mike, "Excellent job to lock down the Armory, in the future, please let us know beforehand. I assume that Rastar as the Master of Arms can access it?"

"Yeah, should be him and no one else," Simon responded. "I tried to get you, but there was no response on the bridge intercom."

"I observed the panel indicating an attempt to reach us," Run said. He pointed at the panel, and Eric noticed the splatter of green and purple fluids across it. "However, due to the risk of contamination, I suggest we leave it alone until I have performed full decontamination. I cannot take this action while you remain on the bridge."

"Run, we've got a lot of things to do," Eric said, "It's not like-"

"I see I must use my command voice," Run said. "ALL PERSONNEL EVACUATE THE BRIDGE WHILE I PERFORM DECONTAMINATION PROCEEDURES!" His shrill voice cut through Eric's head like a drill.

"Run, that is *not* a command voice, you sound like a blender full of marbles," Ariadne said.

"YOU WILL LEAVE IMMEDIATELY OR I WILL BE FORCED TO PACIFY YOU!" Run shouted. Eric rubbed at his temples, as he fought the onset of a headache. He could feel his left eye twitch. "I MUST PREVENT INFECTION-"

"All right!" Ariadne shouted. "We're going!" She looked at Rastar, "Bring Mike, the rest of you, come with me."

"Thank you for your cooperation," Run said calmly. He glanced over at a flashing light. "What is that light?"

"That is a repeater display for the engineering computer," Rastar said. "The light indicates that there is an issue with the generator coils..."

"Now we deal with Ghost," Eric said. "Plans, anyone?"

Rastar nodded as he walked Mike over to the stairs. "I have thought about it for some time. I believe that our best option..."

***

"You have not bargained in good faith with me," Ghost's high pitched rasp spoke as Eric drew near to the Ambassador. "So I have initiated my program. You have thirty minutes before the ship's reactor detonates."

"Look," Alara said. "We have started to move the gold

437

up, but it's a lot of mass to move. We haven't pushed it out the airlock yet to get it to your ship because-"

"I will no longer tolerate your lies," Ghost said. "I gave you your engineer. Clearly you did not reciprocate."

Eric gave Alara a nod, "We've got this." He walked up to the intercom, "Ghost buddy, this is Eric, you remember me, right?" Eric asked.

"You are the irritating human, yes?"

Eric heard the Ambassador snort behind him, he studiously ignored that. She thought *Eric* irritating, did she? Eric smiled slightly, eager to deal with this last threat, and pay Ghost back for how he had injured Pixel, "Yes, that one. Now, we appreciate the effort you've gone through, so I'll give you this one opportunity to get off the ship alive. My buddy Rastar wants to just kill you and he's the Master of Arms, so normally I'd be good with that. But I figure I'd give you the opportunity to go. Leave the engine room now and I'll make sure you get off this ship alive."

"I am confused... is this some sort of human humor?" Ghost asked.

"Nope, me being a nice guy, giving peace a chance and all that," Eric said. "Now what do you say?"

"I say, human, that for your insolence, I will torture you for weeks. I will feed you your own eyes, after I force you to watch me kill your companions..."

Eric flipped off the intercom. "Well, that went well."

"What did you just do?" Alara asked. "We almost had him-"

"He's going to try to kill us anyway, he's already activated his sabotage program. So best if we get him angry and possibly too angry to think," Eric said. "Rastar and Anubus have already gone to the aft hatch. The straightest shot to an airlock goes through there, and we locked down the other two manually. I want that bastard to come out here where we can shoot it. Now I suggest that you and your Marines go aft, out of the line of fire."

"Why did you even have me speak with the Wrethe if you intended to anger it into combat all along?" the Nova Roma

438

Ambassador demanded.

Eric shrugged, "You bought us some time, and jabbering at him seemed to calm you down a bit." Eric smiled as she glared at him. "You're pretty sexy when you're angry, you know? Anyway, the crew cabins should be safe enough. I would recommend your helmets though, just in case things go bad. Granted you might prefer to just vent yourselves rather than die waiting for rescue, but I'll leave that to you."

Eric turned away and pulled his rifle off his back. "Alright, time for me to get into position." He listened to the Ambassador's choked sounds of anger as she tried to restrain herself. Some days he loved his job.

***

Eric glanced over his shoulder as he heard a hatch open. He frowned as Simon stepped out of the galley. Pixel had an arm draped over his shoulder, and took slow, cautious steps. "Pixel, you should not be up and around," Eric said.

"I know," Pixel said. "But Simon needs my help to do his job."

"You think it will work?" Eric asked.

"I looked at the bit of code that Crowe pulled from then engineering repeater console," Pixel said, his voice strained as he took several more steps. "I think that Ghost's talents are more exclusive to computers. It has, well a feel, to it, I guess."

"Can you override it?" Eric asked.

"I will need direct access and some time," Pixel said.

"We're working on both of those, and Simon's part should get us the time you need," Eric hesitated. "Be careful, both of you."

"You too," Simon answered and Pixel just managed a nod.

Eric continued down the corridor until he came to where Rastar stood. The big Ghornath had a set to his shoulders that seemed more serious than usual. His hide had turned an odd, orange color, which Eric had not seen before. "You ready, big guy?"

"Yes," Rastar nodded. "I hope this works."

"It's a good plan, Rastar," Eric said. He tapped his fingers on his jaw impatiently as they waited. Simon would need several minutes to do his part, and they could not take any actions without that. He frowned a moment later, "But if anything goes wrong..."

"You wish to tell me what a great friend I have been?" Rastar asked.

"Well, that," Eric nodded. "But mostly, I got to ask, what's with the stack of cokes in the cabin?" He personally tried to avoid caffeine and energy drinks in general, but he understood why some humans liked them, but he had no idea why his Ghornath friend seemed so fond of them, especially coca cola.

Rastar looked down at him and a slight green shade came over his hide. He opened his mouth to speak.

"Rastar, this is Simon, we're ready here," Simon's voice interrupted from the station nearby.

"Good," Rastar's hide flushed a brighter orange. "Come on up and take position at the airlock. Eric, since Ghost seems to like you so much, would you do the honors?"

"Sure," Eric smiled as he toggled the intercom switch. "Hey there Ghost, Eric here, just letting you know that we've come to a decision."

"You surrender?" Ghost asked.

"Funny you should say that," Eric smiled. "You a fan of history? I like military history. The battles and everything are nice, but the heroics are what I like. You know, the stories about a single unit or sometimes individual who changed the course of events."

"Your words waste time," Ghost growled in its high pitched voice.

"We've got enough time for this," Eric said. He added that extra tone of boredom to his voice that he knew drove people nuts. "See, human history has all kinds of last stands, ones where a few brave men and sometimes women held off their enemies until the last breath. The Alamo, Iwo Jima, Acturus Three, Patrol Base Tripoli... well there's a few. Hell, back in some of those wars, men and women, sometimes even children strapped bombs to themselves and ran at the enemy, just to kill a few more of them before they died."

Eric waited for a response, but Ghost did not speak.

Eric smiled a bit as he thought about how the wheels must begin to turn in the alien's head. "Something you might have forgotten is that Wrethe do not have a monopoly on spite. We've realized that you intend to kill us, regardless of what we do. So we put it to a vote, and you know what, Ghost? We decided that if we can't save ourselves... well we can damned sure take you out."

"You are bluffing," Ghost said.

"Check the reactor feeds, you dumb dog," Eric snapped. "Right now you should see a sharp spike in feed to the fusion reactor. It should have jumped from standby status to almost full load, right?" Eric felt his smile grow wider as he waited. Perhaps it was a flaw, but he loved to anger his enemies. *Come to think of it, I just like to piss people off in general,* he thought. "We've turned on every system on the ship. The reactor has reacted to that. In addition we've increased the feed, so even if you manage to shut those systems off, you'll need to cut the flow to the reactor to bring it back down."

Ghost spoke a moment later, "This is foolish. Give me what I want and I will leave-"

"No," Eric said. "And in the words of William Barrett Travis, 'Victory or Death.' We can't trust you, Ghost. So we'll do what we know will work. When your little trap goes off, the fusion reactor will detonate, our engineer estimates almost a fifty megaton release."

"You are insane. Clearly this is some sort of bluff," Ghost snarled.

"Try me, Ghost," Eric said. He flipped the intercom off. "Well, that went about as I expected. How long do you think?"

Ariadne spoke from behind him, which startled Eric, he hadn't heard her come up behind him, "We've fifteen minutes before the reactor detonates. Ghost's ship probably takes at least ten minutes to do a full start up. It needs to clear the blast radius... so pretty soon."

"Dude, you sounded pretty scary there," Rastar said.

Eric gave a thin smile. He felt it best not to mention to the others that he had meant exactly what he said. When it came down to it, he would accept his own death if it meant he killed his enemy in the process. For that matter, he could remember a few times he had nearly died for that very reason.

"Well--" Ariadne broke off, "He's coming!"

Eric spun around and brought up his laser rifle. He hoped that the weapon would penetrate Ghost's armor better than his TEK-15. Ahead of him, Rastar spun around and sprouted weapons from each of his four arms. The big Ghornath advanced towards the hatch, ready to pour fire from the four TEK-15's he had. They all figured those would have better penetration than the Ragers or the Chxor riot guns.

Down the corridor, he saw Simon draw his pistol and duck around the corner, headed for the airlock and the most direct route for Ghost to escape the ship.

A moment later the engine room hatch opened and a blur of motion exploded out.

The thunder of Rastar's four SMGs signaled the start of the ambush. Eric brought up the rifle and his holographic sights centered on Ghost as the murderous Wrethe charged into Rastar's fire.

Eric got off one shot before the Wrethe closed with Rastar. Eric heard his friend grunt in pain and stagger to the side as Ghost slammed into him. The armored Wrethe swept past a moment later. It paused for just a heartbeat and Eric thought for certain that Ghost would come back down the corridor at him and Ariadne. Eric saw Rastar stumble and fall to his side.

The moment passed, and Ghost ran for the airlock.

Anubus dropped from the ceiling. The two Wrethe grappled with one another. Eric heard a screech as Anubus's claws raked across Ghost's armor. Ghost gave a shout and threw Anubus up against the bulkhead. The big Wrethe hit hard enough that Eric felt the vibration through his feet.

Eric squeezed off another shot and saw Ghost stagger

from the hit on the torso. Suddenly the air seemed to grow cold and Ariadne stepped up next to Eric, her hand extended. A moment later, Ghost let out a howl of pain as smoke emanated from its open helmet. Eric fired off another shot as Ghost staggered.

Simon came around the corner and fired his ancient relic of a gun. The loud concussion of his shots assaulted Eric's ears, even as Ghost let out another banshee shriek. Eric advanced on the Wrethe, and fired the laser rifle twice more as he did so. He saw Ghost drop to the ground, battered by the weapons fire.

The Wrethe writhed on the ground and as Eric drew close he saw flames crawl out of Ghost's flesh. He brought up his rifle from a distance of two meters. He knew one of the others might have paused to make some snappy comment. Instead, he just leveled the sights on Ghost's head and triggered a final shot.

Ghost lay still.

Eric stepped back and lowered his rifle. "Well, that went well." He looked over at Anubus, "You okay?" The Wrethe stood to his feet, and Eric saw that its arm hung dead at its side. Black blood dribbled on the deck.

"I will live," Anubus growled.

"Rastar, you alright, bud?" Eric asked.

Rastar groaned, "Dude, I need a coke." The big Ghornath lay where he had fallen, but he raised one arm and gave a thumbs up.

Crowe leaned out from behind the corner, "That's all?"

The harsh buzz of an alarm startled Eric enough that he brought his weapon up, "What's that?" A moment later, a deep Ghornath voice snarled from the intercom.

Rastar grunted something that sounded almost angry. Eric looked over at his friend. Rastar pushed himself back up to his feet. Eric saw blood pumped from three deep gashes in his side. "It is an automated warning," Rastar said. "The main reactor has become critical."

"Oh," Ariadne said. "Where's Pixel?"

"I dropped him off at the lounge..." Simon said. "I'll go get him."

"Crowe can get him," Eric said, just as he remembered that he hadn't seen the other man involved in the fight. Red lights started to flash from the ceiling. The alarm grew more shrill. "Probably better run, Crowe," Eric said. He tried not to think of the threats he had made to Ghost. He really did not want to face death by fusion reaction.

"We should check out the engine room," Ariadne said. "See if there's anything we can do and if Ghost left any traps behind."

Simon holstered his pistol and stepped forward, "Right, another one of those explosive locks could give us a lot of problems."

Eric stepped away from the Ghost's body, even as he wondered if he should check the Wrethe to ensure it no longer posed a threat. He followed Ariadne and Simon as they entered the engine room.

As he passed Rastar, Eric paused. His friend had managed to stand, yet he still looked to be in pain. "Do you want me to send Run down?" Eric asked.

"No," Rastar said, "I'm good, man. Got a solid constitution, but you might want to have him check Anubus, he doesn't look so good."

"Not a problem," Eric said, even as he made a mental note to have Run check with Rastar. The wound looked serious. He stepped up to the intercom, "Run, this is Eric, if you're done on the bridge, we have wounded down on second deck main corridor." Eric didn't wait for a response.

Simon and Ariadne stood near the main console. Lights and alien text scrolled across the screen and holograms flashed above the console. "So, you guys know what to do, right?"

"I don't really know anything about engineering," Ariadne said. "Pixel planned to show me, but he never got around to it."

"I'll see what I can do," Simon said. "I think this should bring up the main menu." The former cop tapped several controls and a moment later a shrill siren started up. "Or maybe not."

"Whatever you did, I think you made it worse," Eric said. "Great job, moron."

"Says the guy who blew up the main weapon mount and burned out all the capacitors?" Simon snapped. "I don't see you making things better."

Eric opened his mouth to retort, but Ariadne cut them both off, "Shut up, I'm trying to contract Pixel or to read his mind and find out what we need to do."

"Hey, that's a good idea," Eric said. Only after she shot him a sour glance did he recognize his own tone of condescension. *Well,* he admitted, *she does surprise me when she has a good idea.* It wasn't that he didn't trust or respect her abilities, he just felt surprised when she used them in a way that he would not have thought to try. Eric made a mental note that if they survived this, he would work on expressing himself a little better.

"God, this is no good, he needs to be here," Ariadne growled. "He can't see what's on the console and the text is in a language neither of us speak..."

Eric's eyes focused on a flashing indicator which materialized above the console. A moment later, a deep Ghornath voice began to speak over the intercom. Eric only recognized one word, "Evacuate."

Come to think of it, he thought, *if we live, I'm definitely going to ask for some engineering tips from Pixel.* Eric remembered their last conversation on the subject, and Pixel's sarcastic comment about his own inability to stop Eric from his own inadvertent act of sabotage.

Eric froze. His gaze snapped over to the main reactor, and he saw a small terminal set into the side. Inset at the center of the terminal sat a large red button inside a clear cover to prevent casual access.

"It's too late!" Ariadne shouted suddenly. "Pixel says the reactor coils have gone critical, and Ghost must have put some kind of lockouts into the system. We have to try to get to Ghost's ship-"

"No!" Eric shouted. He vaulted over the railing. The

strange gravity of the engine room threw him in a spin. He landed hard on his knee and swore. Eric pushed himself to his feet and limped to the console.

"What are you doing?" Simon shouted. "You heard her, we need to get out of here!"

"The engineer's override," Eric shouted back. He reached the terminal and pried at the button's cover. He saw a pin at the side, just as the terminal lit up with flashing red and purple lights. Eric pulled the pin and the cover snapped back with a sharp crack.

He hoped that he was right. "I really hope he wasn't joking with me about this..." Eric muttered, even as he mashed the button.

The world went dark.

***

Eric hung suspended in the pitch black darkness for what seemed like eternity. He heard no sounds, and at full extension he could find nothing to hold onto.

"Are we still alive?" Simon asked.

Eric answered, "If I have to listen to you in the afterlife, I'd be disappointed." Come to think of it, he somehow doubted that Simon shared his belief structure and he didn't know if this counted towards death by combat. *Sabotage, that's a tough one... or would this be considered suicide?*

He heard a snick, and a moment later a pinprick of orange fire appeared off to his right. Eric looked over and could barely make out Ariadne as she clung to a railing. She held held up her lighter but the oppressive darkness seemed to swallow the light. "We're alive. Pixel says you must have scrammed the reactor."

"Yeah," Eric nodded.

"He says it was either a totally brilliant move or sheer stupidity," Ariadne said. "But he won't be able to say until after he looks the reactor over."

"We're still alive, right?" Eric asked. He rolled his eyes, didn't anyone appreciate what he had accomplished? He gave her the bird too, for good measure. *At least I can be as rude as I want when it doesn't matter,* he thought.

"I'll let him explain," Ariadne said. "And just because it's dark, it doesn't mean I can't sense what you do."

Right, he thought, *psychic.* He cleared his throat, "So...what now?"

"I NEED LIGHT IN ORDER TO OPERATE ON MY SUBJECTS," Run called out, his shrill voice loud enough to carry down the corridor and into the engine room. The pitch still retained the ability to penetrate straight into Eric's brain like a drill. "ANUBUS, I DEMAND THAT YOU-" Run's voice cut off, though Eric thought he heard muffled shouts. He wondered if it made him a bad person that he hoped someone had stapled Run's lips together with his own stapler.

"Dude, you guys alright in here?" Rastar asked. "Also, I think Annie might be more hurt than he said, he tried to claw Run when he tried to help him."

"That little moron is lucky you pulled him off me," Anubus growled. "He comes near me with that staple gun again and I'll use it to staple his mouth shut."

"Hey man, that's not nice, he's just trying to help," Rastar said. A moment later, light blossomed in the doorway as he held up a lantern in one hand. "Hey guys, need some help getting out of there?" Eric saw the big alien held Run with his two left hands while he clung to the hatch frame with his lower right hand.

"You look kind of occupied, and you're wounded, stay there, we'll get out on our own," Eric said. Actually, now that he thought about it, he saw that Rastar's wound did not appear as bad as earlier. Certainly his friend showed no signs of undue pain as he held Run.

"Oh, hey, Pixel's here, with Crowe," Rastar said. He moved out the hatchway and a moment later Pixel swam through the hatch.

The engineer had a flashlight out and swept the engine room. Eric noted that the light pointed at his face for longer than strictly necessary. "You're either smarter than I thought or really lucky," Pixel said. "I'm betting on the lucky part."

Eric shook his head, "Why? I saved us all."

"Do you know what happens when you scram a fusion reactor?" Pixel asked as he pulled himself along a railing towards the main console. Crowe floundered along behind him.

"Uh," Eric frowned. "I imagine it cuts fuel and stops the reaction?"

"I could have done that from the fuel valves," Pixel said. "But between Ghost's program and the damage from before we took the ship, that might have caused the reactor coils to lose containment as they lost power. I didn't want to risk it, not when it might vent the plasma through the ship and roast us alive."

"Oh." Eric said. "So what did I do?"

"That button you pressed vented the plasma and cut fuel to the reactor. It also directed all of our emergency power into the coils, which probably burned some more of them out," Pixel said. "What we don't know yet is where that superheated gas vented. Probably vented to the exterior, as we're still alive. But there's a good chance it could have struck the ship we're docked with, which created debris, and possibly damaged Ghost's ship."

Eric frowned, "But we survived, so that doesn't matter. You get the engine back up and--"

"And like I said, the scram process used our emergency power to maintain the coils. Which is why we're setting in the dark, because there isn't enough power for the emergency lighting system. Which means we don't have enough power to start the fusion reactor up again. Especially not this Ghornath style gravity pumped reactor."

"Oh." Eric said. "Well, I'm sure you can figure it out."

"Thanks for the vote of confidence," Pixel said. He swept his flashlight around the engine room. "But everything tied into the grid will be drained."

"Hey, uh, Pixel," Rastar said. "I hate to bring this up, I'm not real savvy on engine stuff, and all. But what about the main weapon capacitors? Those were all disconnected already right?"

Pixel froze, "You know that just might work..."

Eric gave a smile, "See, even when I screw up, I still manage to save us all."

Mike rubbed at his forehead. "So power's up, and Rastar and Eric have supervised salvage of the other ship. What else did I miss?" He'd called the meeting ten or twelve hours after they finished salvage operations, and only five hours after Pixel managed to get the reactor up. Ariadne had spent over an hour with him already, and though she hadn't said anything afterward, Eric could tell that she seemed worried about how Krann's tampering might have affected Mike.

Even so, Eric thought, *he seems back to normal now.*

Ariadne cleared her throat, "Whatever 'lived' inside of Krann, it mimicked Chxor behavior, even their thought patterns and it possessed significant psychic abilities."

Eric met Crowe's eyes across the bridge. The other man had insisted that they still did not know for certain that Ariadne had not been the source of the psychic attacks. Eric disagreed, which was why he had refused to back Crowe's request that they corner Mike before the meeting. Even so, he wondered how the other man had spent the past two days. Certainly from his scatter of tools and the way he slumped near the communications station, he had stayed occupied somehow.

"I have disposed of the remains so as to prevent the risk of infection. However, I will need to take blood and tissue samples from all personnel who have come into contact with the possible source of infection," Run said. The little Chxor looked around at the others, and gray skin and oversized hairless head seemed a sinister reminder to Eric of the danger of the Chxor. They had thought they had Krann a prisoner, yet she had still nearly captured the ship.

"That would be all of us," Ariadne said.

"More than us," Pixel said.

"Engineer Pixel is correct. Because we do not know the vector, be it contact, fluid transfer, airborne or some other means, I must inspect all personnel aboard the ship to insure no further contagion has spread," Run said. "This will require a deep tissue sample, to insure that the contagion--"

"You're assuming it's a disease," Mike said. "What if this was just some lab experiment by the Chxor, or some parasite that Krann picked up in her travels? For that matter, it infected a Chxor, with completely different physiology than Humans, Ghornath and Wrethe. I'm not going to force everyone on the ship to participate. If people are worried about it or if they show signs of infection, then you can test them."

"Your argument is illogical," Run said. "We do not know enough as of yet to determine the risk. Should this be a viral outbreak and also species compatible-"

"No," Eric said, "He's right. It just infected a Chxor." He would not let the little bastard get near him with needles. He might learn more than that Eric didn't carry some strange parasite. *He might see some of what they did to me at Blackthorn's labs.*

"As much as I hate to say it," Anubus growled, "Run is correct. We can't be certain who is affected. Something like that could control one of you now." He glanced over at Rastar. "For that matter, weren't you hurt before?"

"What?" Rastar looked around. He turned a white color, though Eric found it hard to see against the purple and white Hawaiian shirt. Rastar held his hand to his side, "Oh yes, a nasty set of scratches, and some grazing shots from when Mike... was confused. I bandaged them myself. They still pain me, but I cope with it well. And I have a good constitution so I will heal well enough without attention."

"Really..." Anubus growled. "For all we know, you're infected and this parasite heals you more rapidly. Perhaps it operates to protect its host somehow?"

Rastar gave a laugh, "Annie, you say the silliest things. I mean, come on, man, Ghornath have a great constitution, we heal pretty quickly." Rastar raised the bottle of coke he held in one hand, "Especially when we have such excellent brew."

"That's what you say, but we can't know without a test of some kind," Anubus growled. "And I think we can agree that if you're--"

"Enough," Eric snapped. "Rastar is not infected. And

Run will not test anyone against their will or without some reasonable suspicion. For that matter, Rastar killed Krann, so I think we can safely say that he's above suspicion."

"And he has healed from serious wounds before we ran into Krann," Pixel said. "So really, I don't see any case for Rastar getting checked out for that." He looked at Mike, "I do think that we all need to get checked, though, just in case."

"Me too," Ariadne said. "None of you felt the mind of this... thing. It perfectly emulated a Chxor, right up until it acted, and then it was like... like someone pulled off a scary mask and revealed something far worse underneath. Something malevolent. It *hated* us, it wanted to play with us, which is the only reason I think we survived."

"It underestimated us?" Eric asked. That bothered him. He didn't like to be underestimated. He had talents, and while he might not be a psychic, he felt certain enough of his talents that anything which disregarded him as a real threat...

"Yes," Ariadne said.

"Either way, you killed it," Mike said. "And that's what matters." He rubbed at his head, "So, where does that leave us?"

"We're down to about thirty percent power output on the reactor," Pixel said. "Its enough to make the drive function along with secondary systems. Not enough to fight or even defend ourselves really."

"What do you suggest?" Mike asked.

"Replacement of the coils. They took some additional damage from Ghost's sabotage, but they already had significant damage. I've spent the past week trying to think of a source of conductive material, but there's only one that will prevent us from having to salvage systems from our ship or remain here in this system longer than we really want." Pixel shot a glance over at Anubus. "If we utilize a hundred kilograms of the gold-"

"No way," Anubus growled.

"We're sitting ducks without full power output," Pixel said. "No defenses, no weapons, we can run away but we can't even power up our shadow space drive at the same time as we power our standard drives."

Everyone on the bridge looked at Anubus. The big Wrethe stood still, but Eric saw his claws extend from his sheaths. "You want to take this away from me?"

"A trade," Mike said. "I'm sure you have something you'd be willing to accept as equal value-"

"I have Ghost's ship," Anubus growled. "What more can I want?"

Eric tensed and his hand went down to the grip for his TEK-15.

"What about Ghost's armor?" Pixel asked. "It's damaged, but I could repair it. Also, that ship's seen some rough use. I bet it needs an overhaul, probably has parts scavenged from a dozen ships, and that kind of thing doesn't come with a manual. I can figure that out for you."

Anubus cocked his jackal head, "That... might be acceptable."

"Think about this," Mike said. "Ghost's ship has no shadow drive. Our former friend might have some kind of larger ship in the system, but we've no way to find it. You need to get your ship out of the system, and *our* ship is the only way to do it."

"You're charging me docking fees?" Anubus growled.

"No, I'm saying either you're a part of this team or you're not, you can't have it both ways," Mike said. "And I say that we live by the charter that you all signed." He swept his gaze around the room, "And while I'm willing to throw a pass on the *Red Hunter*, that gold is something our entire team worked for, along with the salvage from the *Sao Martino*. So you can keep your ship and 'your' gold and stay here and try to find someone willing to put up with you, or you can come with us and be a part of a team."

Anubus rolled his shoulders, "You know I could force you to do what I want?"

"You could try," Mike said.

"Didn't work out so well for Ghost," Eric muttered loud enough for everyone to hear. Ariadne and Mike both shot him a glare, and he shrugged. *What, like they didn't think the same thing*, he thought.

"You had a well thought out campaign, Mike," Anubus growled. "Very good preparations, clearly I underestimated your cunning. I will not forget this in the future." He gave a nod, "I will abide by the terms of our 'charter.' However, should anyone else violate it, I will *insist* they receive the same treatment, agreed?"

"Of course," Mike said. He looked a bit surprised, Eric thought. Probably at Anubus' assumption of a cunning plan. Eric kept any comments to himself, in that regard. It made Mike look like a better Captain. Besides, if Anubus thought Mike so calculating, then maybe he would downgrade his suspicion of the others.

One more reason it sucks to be in command, Eric thought, *the big scary alien plans to kill you.*

"Right," Mike said. "Crowe pulled the data from the *Sao Martino's* logs, as well as the navigation charts for both shadow space and normal space. It doesn't give us a lot more than we had, the ship ran mostly aid missions to Saragossa. But it does have coordinates for human systems, mostly Nova Roma occupied systems."

"So we head that way," Eric shrugged.

"From what we can tell from this ship's logs," Crowe said. "The Ghornath aboard acted as privateers against both the Chxor and the Nova Romans."

"So they might shoot us first and ask questions later," Pixel said. "I see the problem."

"I find a course that ends in our demise suboptimal," Run said.

"Right," Mike nodded, "Crowe suggested a route back through Chxor space, towards the Centauri Confederation, or possibly Tannis. The thing is, both of those routes will take us right back through the Logan system, and one will take over ninety days." Mike brought up the map on a holographic display. A number of the systems had the symbol that noted Chxor occupation. Many of the others plotted the fringe of human space, or simple alphanumeric codes that meant they had nothing worth a name.

"We don't have that much food," Eric said. "Even with the ration bars we found aboard the *Sao Martino*. For that matter, I'm not sure how our environmental systems would hold up."

"We may find other ships, maybe we could trade," Ariadne said.

"We may find pirates who will kill us for our ship and supplies," Eric said.

"The other route will take over eighty days to get to the Vega system," Pixel said after a moment. "I think there's some stations there, but we'd be hurting on the environmental side. Tannis we could make too, but that will cut our environmental systems to the bone. The biggest issue will be water, the recyclers work only so well." The engineer frowned. "Worse, I think we're too low on spare parts, if we suffer one failure... well, we might have to wait for someone to show up and save us, and there's not a lot of friendly traffic out on the fringe."

"Ghost should remind you of that," Anubus growled. "Anyone we encounter will be a threat."

Eric glanced at Mike and saw the Captain had nodded, and wore a small smile. "You've already thought through all of that. So I'd assume you prefer Nova Roma space. Which leaves us three possible destinations: Tibur, Malta, and Danar. According to the Chxor as well as the *Sao Martino*'s logs, Danar fell to the Chxor. But the system is vital to the Nova Romans defense, so I think we can safely assume they'll have forces there to try and recapture the system. We might be able to link up with them, prove our story, and maybe get an escort back."

"What about Tibur?" Rastar asked. "That is near to Ghornath Prime, we might even stop by, perhaps pick up some of my people?"

"Captain Santiago mentioned heavy military patrols from the Nova Romans at Tibur. I imagine with the Chxor attack on Danar they will stand to high alert. Worse, we could jump right in the middle of a battle," Mike said.

"And the same goes for Malta," Ariadne said. "And for

454

both we'd need to go back through a number of Chxor systems."

"Whereas if we go on to 567X43, it'll take thirty six days and then we'll have two options, continue to Danar or go up to the independent colony in the Crow system."

"No relation," Crowe drawled.

Mike ignored the interruption. "We don't know what we might find at Crow, or even if the colony is still there. The *Sao Martino* never went up that way, and none of the records show much more than the fact that there was a colony there. From 567X43, it's eleven more days to Danar. We can make the Nova Roma system in four days after that."

"So we go to Nova Roma, then?" Simon asked.

"That looks to be the best option," Mike answered. "So unless any of you have any big reasons to avoid it, I think that our best option is there."

"Well, other than one glaring fact," Eric said. He gave a sigh, "You do realize that we may actually need that Ambassador now, right?"

"Huh, I'd forgotten about her," Mike said. "Well, if she becomes an issue, we can always vent her out the airlock."

Eric snorted, "Don't worry about her, I'll manage her." Everyone stared at him. "What, you don't think I have people skills?" He smiled as he thought of how he had managed her so far. Perhaps more time with her would give him the perfect opportunity. *I bet she's all pent up inside...*

"Eric..." Ariadne spoke slowly, as if she had to choose her words carefully. "We know you try, but sometimes..."

"Look, I said I can handle her," Eric snapped. "And if I need any help, I'll let you know, right?"

"Okay..." Ariadne shook her head.

"I have a question," Anubus growled, "Since we are, as you all say, partners. What happened with Ghost's corpse?"

"I saw the Wrethe's armor and weapons in the armory," Eric answered after a moment. "I'm not sure who put it there."

"Oh, I stripped its gear and armor," Simon said. "I wasn't sure what to do with it after that."

"What about the body?" Anubus growled. "I worked up

something of an appetite."

"Ew," Ariadne said. "Don't Wrethe have some kind of funeral practice or something?"

"We do, we eat our vanquished foes," Anubus growled.

"Right," Mike said. "Uh, what did you do with the body Simon?"

"I didn't touch it after that, I just left it there," Simon answered, "It's not like I wanted to mess with the corpse or anything."

Eric glanced at Run, "You doing some experimentation you need to tell us about?"

"I have no need to tell you about any of my experiments. Your lack of understanding would make that a pointless endeavor," Run said. He took a step back as Anubus advanced. "I will however, state that I did not touch the Wrethe corpse."

"That's not the same as saying you didn't have someone else drag it off." Pixel noted.

"Do you have any Wrethe corpses stashed away aboard the ship?" Mike asked with a tone that suggested his patience had expired. Well, Eric had to admit that the way Mike's hand had dropped to his pistol suggested that as well. *Of course,* Eric thought, *he's got his damned finger in the trigger well,* again. It would be a terrible shame if their captain managed to shoot his foot off.

Run paused in thought for a moment, "No, I do not."

Mike sighed and rubbed at his forehead. "Right, someone find out where our dead Ghost went." He lowered his hand, "Ariadne, start a plot for our jump. Pixel, start preparations for your repairs... how long will you need?"

"I can use the time on route to the next system to make the preparations. After that..." Pixel frowned, "Maybe fourteen hours to repair the coils. I would suggest we go to the outer system, where we can conduct repairs with less of a chance of discovery."

"Alright," Mike said. "Sounds like a plan. Anyone else got anything?"

"Guys, are we sure we want to go back?" Rastar asked.

"I mean, we're doing alright without civilization. Why not stay out here longer?"

Eric frowned, "Buddy, we're barely on the edge of survival. We all nearly died because of this pirate and we have limited supplies."

"But we've had so much fun, I would hate to see that come to an end," Rastar said.

Eric frowned. He remembered how many Chxor they'd killed, and to tell the truth, he *had* found their fight with Ghost full of excitement. *Other than the whole thing with Pixel's injury,* he amended. "Well, even so, we need supplies. Don't worry about the whole Ghornath thing, I'm sure the Nova Romans won't hold it against you."

"I might hold it against some of them," Rastar growled and his hide flushed deep red.

"We don't have a whole lot of options, it's there or the Centauri Confederation or Tannis," Mike said.

"Nova Roma is better than those," Rastar said. "I just fear that our group will go its separate ways once we arrive, you know?"

Eric patted Rastar on the shoulder, "Don't worry, big guy, wherever you go, I'll stick with you."

The big Ghornath looked down at him, and for a moment, Eric remembered his last team. The men who had stood with him on his final mission as a Commando. The men that Andreysiak had killed to keep Blackthorn's secrets safe. He had viewed them as brothers, despite their flaws. The Centauri Confederation had betrayed their loyalty, but Eric still felt he had failed them. If only he had figured things out then, instead of later. If only he had made one right decision in that series of wrong ones...

He would not make the same mistakes, not again. As he looked around at the mixed group, he realized that these people had become his new team, and for better or worse, he possessed that rarest of things: a second chance.

For just a moment, the ghosts of his past went quiet.

###

Fool's Gold
The Renegades
by Kal Spriggs

Anubus figured his safest long term option lay in the murder of the entire crew.

Unfortunately, in the short term, he required them alive. He knew little enough in regards to navigation much less engineering or half the other flight systems. Anubus figured the others realized that which explained why they disregarded his threats so far.

As he sat with his back secured in the corner he did another quick threat analysis of the crew lounge. Mike stood with his back to the tank of water with the eel. Anubus had observed the human's poorly hidden fear of either the water or eel or both. He thought the ploy too obvious to consider a true weakness, which made him wonder why the Captain bothered. Anubus also found the tank a source of annoyance, mostly at the others insistence that 'Rainbow' vanished when motionless.

He could not understand how the others might not sense the Arcavian Fighting Eel. Even if Anubus couldn't see the eel, he could smell the creature's scent on the water from across the room. More than that, he could hear its heartbeat, a slow, rhythmic pump that could have almost lulled him into a relaxed state.

Fortunately, the incessant chatter of his companions countered that hypnotic beat. Their scents assaulted his nostrils even as their rapid movements drew his gaze. They smelled like food, and they acted like it too, and it took considerable self control for him not to indulge in the buffet that they presented.

Instead, Anubus forced himself to take shallow breaths and walk slowly towards Eric's buffet. The scents there did not smell nearly as delectable, for he could not sense the blood just under the skin, ready for his jaws to plunge into the hot flesh...

I need to work on my self control, he thought, *or just kill someone, either would do.*

That reminded him that he had not finished off Ghost,

458

Eric had taken that prize. Worse, the others insisted that they did not know what had happened to the corpse. Simon had gone as far as to accuse Anubus of the body's theft and consumption. Anubus thought it a ruse of some sort, perhaps designed to frustrate him. He had prowled the entire ship, but though he caught traces of Ghost's scent, they seemed faint, and grew fainter as time passed.

"Anubus," Crowe gave him a nod from the buffet table. The human had a substantial mix of greens and some other, non-meat, items. Anubus couldn't help but wrinkle his muzzle at that.

"What do you want?" Anubus growled. He realized that the distraction of the prey-scents and prey-movements of the crew had pulled him away from his measure of threats. A clever action, on their parts, he thought, for it kept him on edge and made it difficult to focus.

He forced himself to look Crowe over as another predator, despite the obvious herbivore choices of meal. The human stood taller than most of the others, all except Eric. Yet Crowe seemed the least physical of the others, and Anubus had seen him engage in their hunt only once. This would have made Anubus downgrade him as a threat, yet the other man seemed to have a remarkable survival instinct. More, he moved with far greater stealth than the other humans, and seemed to view the others as expendable, which made for the possibility that he would bait a trap with one of the others should he and Anubus square off.

Not that it would save him, Anubus thought. He had hid enough of his own abilities that he felt confident he could kill Crowe should it become either necessary or simply opportune.

"Just saying hello," Crowe said lightly. "I heard that Pixel plans to start his work prepping for the reactor coil rebuild tomorrow, I guess you must be pretty unhappy over that, huh?"

Anubus cocked his head, the other man's attempt to provoke him seemed to obvious for it to be anything but a ruse, but Anubus couldn't see where the human's line of questions would lead, so he decided to play along. "Whatever it makes me, I have agreed," he growled.

459

"You have, but I can tell you, it doesn't seem right, you know?" Crowe said, his voice low. "I mean, you worked hard for that gold, you've protected it, hell, you moved most of it throughout our trip. It should be your choice, not Mike's."

Anubus drew his lips back in what a charitable human might have called a smile. Anyone else would have seen it his bare fangs as the threat it truly meant, "If you seek to play me against the Captain in some game, you're painfully obvious. I do not appreciate your assumption that I am so easily manipulated."

Crowe took a step back. Anubus could taste the sweat that beaded the man's skin, and scent the metallic taste of fear in the air. "Sorry, I didn't mean to come across that way at all."

"I'm sure," Anubus growled. He realized that he had dropped into hunting mode, and forced himself to sheath his claws. *The others would react poorly if I disemboweled him at dinner,* Anubus thought, *and then I might not restrain myself from further...excitement.*

He stalked past Crowe and went to where the meats lay out. Eric had called them something fancy, but he viewed them as burned food. He didn't mind scorched prey, but only when he killed it himself. Anubus particularly liked the taste that plasma weapons left on the meat, the crispy on the outside still moist on the inside texture just completed the taste experience.

As he selected the least burned items and put them on a plate, he unfocused his eyes and studied the others. The smell of the meat calmed him, and overpowered the other scents in the room, which made it easier to focus on the others as threats rather than just prey.

The Ghornath Rastar made the most obvious threat. He stood over three meters in height, and massed over three hundred kilograms, Anubus estimated. Further, his four arms had bulky muscle and he had already shown his fighting prowess and an explosive temper. *His simpleton charade at friendship to all irritates me though*, Anubus thought, *I know it's a ruse, but I'm not sure what he hides under that act.* Worst of all, the horrid Hawaiian shirts that Rastar had found among the former Ghornath crew's possessions assaulted his eyes, the bright patterns clashed so perfectly as to cause Anubus physical pain if he focused on him. Also, the Ghornath had showed an as yet unknown ability to heal from his wounds. *I'll figure it out soon enough, and take it for myself.* Any fair fight with Rastar would pose a substantial risk, Rastar certainly did not seem prey, but another hunter. Except that Rastar acted like prey, which gave Anubus a headache as if he'd looked at the shirt too long.

Anubus thought he could handle Rastar, if only through an ambush attack.

His focus ranged from the former policeman Simon to the mercenary Eric and then to some of the passengers and those not yet fully admitted to the crew, such as the two females Mandy and Miranda. Both had combat experience, though he suspected they would find him a greater threat than the Chxor they had fought before. The dark haired Micheal Santangel from Saragossa seemed cunning, and he stalked with a certain poise that suggested a fellow hunter, yet his attention seemed focused too much on the Nova Roman female Ambassador, which meant that Anubus could probably use her as a distraction to make the kill.

Some of the others, particularly the two Nova Roma marines might pose a threat, though Mike's insistence that they have access only to whatever weapons they had taken in their escape meant that most lacked weapons. Even as he thought that, he heard a scrap of conversation between Mike and Ariadne, "...Illario and Duello both want to join. Duello's a merc, Illario's a former ganger, both from Nova Roma, I've already interviewed them, but I'd like you to check them out."

Anubus nodded at that, it only made sense that the psychic would read their minds. He raised his expectation of the Captain yet again at the man's forethought. He planned to use Ariadne as his secret enforcer, someone who could bend minds and ferret out their secrets would make any move against Mike almost impossible.

Of the others in the room, Illario and Eric seemed the most dangerous at first glance. He had seen the scars that covered the former ganger. The stocky, heavily muscled, human also seemed very proficient with the knives he wore, which varied from the paring knife he ate with to the machete he had strapped to his side. Still, Anubus felt the other human would stand little chance if Anubus chose to hunt him.

Eric, on the other hand, seemed focused on ranged weapons and under other circumstances, Anubus might have killed the human at the first opportunity. Yet the narrow confines of the ship eliminated his advantage in the ranged hunt. Anubus felt that Eric would require a careful stalk, but success would follow.

Of them all he viewed the small blonde female human Ariadne as the greatest threat. He had already seen what one psychic could do when their Chxor prisoner Krann revealed her abilities. It had held Rastar, Eric and Ariadne at bay while it controlled Mike. While Ariadne might have such proficiency, she had already shown herself extremely dangerous. Her ability with telepathy and her pyrokenetics combined, as well has her odd precognitive flashes made her a difficult threat to quantify. His own abilities to heal himself were at a disadvantage against her abilities.

Anubus felt certain that if he could get her within arms reach that he could kill her. She massed only fifty kilograms at most. Yet he wondered if he *could* get her within arms reach. Worse, she acted as prey might and seemed to show what Anubus could only consider actual care and affection to others. In anyone else, he would have considered that a weakness, yet when she viewed someone or something a threat to those she cared about...she unleashed her inner hunter.

Ariadne the hunter scared Anubus.

***

The edge taken off his hunger if not entirely satisfied, Anubus returned to his normal post. The others might have expected him to return to the cabin and sleep, and at times he did so, if only to maintain that cover. In truth, like most Wrethe, Anubus did not need sleep. He could put himself into a semi-trance state while he put portions of his brain to sleep.

Which meant he could stand watch indefinitely, other than the need to eat or relieve himself. *And of course the paramount need to hunt.* Which he somewhat satisfied with his post.

The stack of gold bars appeared untouched since he left his vigil earlier. Even so, Anubus cautiously scented the air outside the door. He fully opened his senses as he stepped into the narrow room which housed the treasure.

The others might have found it odd to see his 'fur' stand on end, and then to shift, as if in a breeze. They could not have known that each follicle sensed vibrations in the air, which allowed him to hear the heartbeats of the passengers down the corridor and the thrum of the reactor deeper in the ship. He sensed no sign of movement nearby, so Anubus did what he knew any individual might do. He seared the immediate area for traps and the likely ambush that awaited.

That took ten or fifteen minutes.

Once Anubus felt certain that the others had not initiated their move against him, he did his final check. He counted each of the three hundred bars that made up the stack. This required him to move the entire stack, but he had already moved them all to verify no concealed bomb or bug lay within the pile of gold. It took Anubus an hour to replace all of the bars in proper order and to verify their weight and heft and to examine them to ensure no one had removed portions.

His examination of his position complete, Anubus settled down to his stalk of prey. He crouched, ready, in the shadows of the corner near the door. With a slight effort, his 'fur' changed colors to match the shadowed gray bulkhead behind him. He thought that he had managed to keep this a secret from his companions. They knew of his stealth and speed, but he did not think any had caught him when he allowed himself to alter his pattern.

Anubus knew that the wealth would draw someone eventually. Wealth, as he knew, represented strength. Strength in turn represented security. All creatures needed security in order to survive, and as Anubus knew all too well, all creatures, both prey and predators wanted to survive.

So someone would risk themselves, sooner or later, for the gold, if only for the security that it would bring them later.

And then, Anubus would make his kill.

Anubus let his conscious mind drift to sleep with that pleasant thought.

***

"You'll never survive if you remain prey," October growled. The big Wrethe loomed over Anubus. The golden brown pelt showed October's age, for a lattice of scars showed October's battle experience with dark streaks that gave the big Wrethe a tiger striped appearance.

"I'm not prey," Anubus snarled back. "I killed you, didn't I?"

"You're weak, not fit for the meat I give you," October's deep growl continued. "Soon enough I'll make you meat for your replacement."

"I made sure he died before he was ready," Anubus snarled. "And then I killed you, remember? You're dead, you're a ghost."

October vanished and in his place stood Ghost. The short, snow white Wrethe's high pitched keen almost put Anubus into a killing frenzy, "No... I'm Ghost. And you only thought you killed us. You never finished us, you never fed. How does that feel, to know you failed, and that your survival is a risk?"

"You're dead," Anubus growled. "What happened to your corpse doesn't change that."

"But it does," Ghost said. "What hunter fails to complete his kill, Anubus? Or should I call you what October named you?"

"You wouldn't know that," Anubus growled. "This is a dream, one I can wake up from when I want." Even as he said the words, Ghost faded out.

"You always run from what you fear, don't you Runtling," October's bass growl caused Anubus to spin. "Always so quick to run, to hide. You do that now, even from yourself. So afraid, aren't you? That's why you're weak, you know, your fear. A true Wrethe fears nothing."

"You could have used some fear, meat, I killed you, didn't I?" Anubus felt his lips draw back in a snarl. The dream version of his sire seemed to draw taller at his show of rage.

"You tried, but you failed, you never made certain, you never claimed your kill, Runtling," October chuckled. "And you tried like a coward, in a fashion that would have killed you if not for luck. You know what's worse than your failures, Runtling?"

"Stop calling me that," Anubus growled.

October leaned close enough that in his dream, Anubus could feel the massive Wrethe's hot breath on his muzzle, and he could smell the sharp musk of the ancient Wrethe. "The worst thing about you is that you don't want to survive, you know you don't deserve it, but you're too much of a coward to die."

Anubus shouted, "All creatures want to survive, October, you taught me that. It's what we do, and it's what Wrethe do best."

October's features melted back, and the hulking Wrethe shrank into the familiar form of Mike. "Survival requires we work together, that we have rules that govern us, Anubus. Why do you work against us so much?"

"Because you'll turn on me, as I will, as soon as it works in my favor," Anubus growled, caught off guard by the sudden change. "It is the only way for a hunter to win, to strike when his prey is most vulnerable. It is the way of survival."

"That's why you killed me, Runtling?" A sibilant lisp spoke from behind. Anubus turned to find that Kull squatted nearby. The tan colored Wrethe seemed tiny, still in youth, not yet grown. "We had a deal, and you turned on me rather than face October. We could have taken him together."

"He would have killed you both," Ghost's whine spoke. "Together you are weak. Your friendship made you weaker."

"He's right," Anubus snarled. "There is no other way."

"Too bad it failed," October's voice spoke from behind him. Anubus felt the massive jaws of his sire lock around the back of his neck. "You die now. Because you are *weak*."

465

*** *

Anubus snapped out of his nightmare. He could sense that many hours had passed, and a moment later he heard what had penetrated his dreams. The scuffle of footsteps in the hallway.

Had the time come? Had someone finally given into their desire for his gold?

"Hey, Anubus, are you here?" Pixel's voice came from the corridor. A moment later, Anubus caught his scent, and that of the others with him. "We're here to get the gold for the reactor project."

Anubus gave a snort of disgust. He shifted his color back to midnight black and growled, "Yes. I know, come in."

Pixel and five others stepped into the narrow compartment. He could taste their fear at how they shared the close confines with him. Anubus fed off that fear, used it to restore his confidence after the nightmare. *Stupid dreams,* he thought, *October's dead, and the rest comes of eating scorched meat.*

He would have to find something raw... and soon, he decided.

"Yeah, um, we need a hundred kilograms," Pixel said.

"You've said that before," Anubus growled. He saw no need to make it easier on the engineer. The human served his purpose, but Anubus found him an annoyance, he held power and security through his knowledge, which seemed an alien thought to the Wrethe. Knowledge could serve as a strength, of sorts, yet knowledge shared dissipated that strength.

"Well, we'll start counting them out..." Pixel said. Anubus felt his lips draw back in a snarl as the engineer rested a hand on the stack of bars. He forced himself to look away, he had grown too possessive of the gold, he figured, yet it hurt to see that much wealth slip away.

Pixel directed the others to start taking bars even as he annotated their removal on his datapad.

"What progress have you made on my ship?" Anubus

growled.

"Oh, well, not much, as yet," Pixel answered. "I did crawl out and do a quick rundown of the systems. The ammo for the weapons is at around twenty seven thousand rounds. You've got a bomb bay, with two fission warheads, I'm not sure of the yield on those, but they're ship-killers for sure. It's got a fission reactor and..." the human frowned and checked at notes on his datapad. Anubus swallowed a snarl of frustration. The monkey faces the human made as he checked his notes only increased Anubus's urge to make an example of him.

I would never have tolerated such weakness in my presence before, not when he doesn't show me proper respect as a hunter of men, Anubus thought. How far he had fallen, all due to a simple miscalculation.

"Oh, here we go, fission plant with a reaction-less drive, looks scavenged from a Centauri Confederation ship, pretty diffcrent from ours," Pixel said. "The whole thing needs a lot of attention, but nothing seems mission critical. You'll need to wear a suit, though, the environmental pack expired, I wouldn't trust it."

"How long to conduct repairs?" Anubus growled.

"Depends on the parts," Pixel said. "Honestly, I would recommend we wait until I can put new stuff in, especially to replace some of the older systems. It'll cost more, but I think you'll see a payout in improved performance."

"Very well," Anubus growled. He glanced impatiently at the steadily decreasing stack of gold bars. As he watched, another of the passengers took a pair of bars out. *I can't watch this much longer without killing one of them,* he thought. The repercussions would probably not work out favorably, he reluctantly decided.

"I will leave you to finish," Anubus growled. He stalked out of the room, and tried to console himself that he had invested in a ship, rather than lost the gold entirely.

Somehow, that made him want to kill something even more.

***

Anubus returned after he prowled the ship for what felt like forever.

He performed his routine search of the compartment upon his return. He settled into his inventory of the gold, yet he felt his rage return as he contemplated the significantly reduced stack of bars. The count took him over an hour and thirty minutes, because he counted it three times.

The stack held one hundred and ninety eight gold bars.

He would have to kill Pixel.

Anubus spent two hours in consideration. He spent another hour searching for scents and clues of who might have stolen it, but he caught scents of almost all the crew, before he finally left his reduced fortune and located the engineer in the lounge. "You stole two bars from me, why?" He had crept to within centimeters of the human.

The engineer looked up, and Anubus could scent the surprise and fear even as he read those same emotions on the human's stupid monkey face. Anubus could understand the fear, but the surprise puzzled him. Surely he must know that Anubus would notice the two additional missing bars.

"Uh, no, we took one hundred bars, exactly," Pixel said. He held up his datapad, "I took notes."

"I counted the bars, one hundred and two have gone missing," Anubus growled.

"I didn't steal your stupid gold," Pixel snapped, and Anubus cocked his head at the show of anger. He couldn't tell if it were genuine, however unlikely, or a show.

"You took responsibility for it when I left," Anubus growled. "So you are responsible for it's theft. Therefore it is you that will have to die for it unless I locate the thief."

"I don't have time to watch over that gold, I have work to do," Pixel answered. "And if you'd stop with your paranoia, you'd realize that I don't care about your damned gold. This ship has a dozen problems more important to me than something we can't eat or use to defend ourselves. Thanks for ruining my appetite, and please kill me after I finish all my work for the week."

Anubus watched the engineer walk off. He felt too shocked by the human's behavior to act. The Wrethe felt a mix of rage, frustration, and oddly enough fear. Did not the human realize what Anubus could do to him? *If he doesn't fear me,* Anubus wondered, *then do I need to fear him?*

Anubus considered a dozen schemes which might show why the human showed such a total disregard for the danger Anubus presented, yet none of them seemed to fit with the engineer's previous actions. Anubus became so focused on those myriad thoughts that he never heard Rastar come up behind him.

"Annie!" Rastar pounded him on the back, "Pixel said someone raided our gold, what can I do to help?"

Anubus's claws extended and every muscle in his body tensed at the impact. He barely fought down an urge to lash out at the big Ghornath. "You can stay out of my business. I'll settle this myself."

"Dude, this is all our business. Someone stole from the crew, they stole from us all," Rastar's hide remained a mellow brown, which made it difficult for Anubus to read him. "Besides, I'm the Master of Arms, shipboard matters like this are my job, man."

Anubus forced himself to sheath his claws and focused on the steady heartbeat of the Arcavian Fighting Eel. "Then when I find the thief, you may remove the remains. But I will find the person responsible, and I will kill them."

"No," Mike said, "You won't."

"What did you say?" Anubus felt his lips draw back in a snarl.

"We have rules here, Anubus. This person violated those rules, but that doesn't justify you doing the same," Mike said. The human's calm words seemed a strange echo of his troubled dreams.

Anubus didn't respond for a moment, half afraid that Mike would morph into October or that Ghost would appear as in his nightmares. A part of him worried most that he would see Kull. Finally he spoke, "Very well, we shall see about your rules, but I will find the one responsible."

"I'll help, Annie," Rastar said. The misuse of his name brought back Anubus's rage.

"I have a name, one that I chose for myself, I will not tolerate your butchery of it," Anubus growled.

"Hey, dude, no need to get hostile, I know you're not real comfortable with open friendship, the whole tough guy thing," Rastar had gone a green shade, which either meant he found the situation humorous or had tried to make some sort of joke. Either way, Anubus decided he hated the oaf that much more.

Anubus looked over at Mike, "I will find the thief, but I demand that when I do, he receive full punishment for his betrayal."

"We'll see," Mike said. "And trust me, I'm not real happy with someone who provoked you."

"I don't trust anyone," Anubus growled.

"Really?" Mike asked, "I hadn't noticed."

***

Anubus prowled the ship, his senses alert. He did not expect to actually find his gold, too many locations existed where a cunning opponent might hide it. He did, however, expect to provoke the thief into a panic, or if the theft lay as part of some greater conspiracy as he suspected, then his actions would cause one of the members to act without the support of the others.

Anubus heard snippets of conversation as he prowled the ship, whispers from those who had some idea of what had angered him. The heady stink of fear clung to those he came across, while most of the rest of the passengers and crew seemed to avoid him when possible.

He took note of those who either showed no fear or showed other emotions. The Nova Roma Ambassador was one such, along with her escort of marines. The Ambassador seemed either unaware of his potential threat or thought herself protected by her escort. She smelled of musk and a scent that Anubus associated with confidence, and as Anubus swept past her, he smelled Eric's scent on her, as if they had recently been in contact. Her marines just seemed resigned, as if they feared nothing more than their current assignment. Anubus did not understand human's association of authority and position, for he doubted that the Ambassador had earned her position, yet the Marines gave her loyalty all the same.

As the day wore on, Anubus found more and more time to think. After due consideration, he came to realize that the theft could not be the product of a lone thief. The timing and events that surrounded it suggested, instead, that the others had conspired to provoke him. They wanted him to act out of proportion. The only reason Anubus could decipher lay in that they wanted him to make the first move, or seem to, in order to eliminate him without alarm from the other passengers.

If he estimated the purpose of the theft correctly, then Mike must surely serve as the source of the theft. As Captain, he would see Anubus as a threat, therefore, with the further evidence of Ghost as to the danger of Wrethe, he would seek to remove that threat.

The thought of dragging Mike down, of tasting his warm salty blood made Anubus's heart race. He felt his body start to release some of the chemicals which normally preceded a hunt. *Yes,* Anubus thought, *a hunt of Mike would satisfy my urges, and show that I am not to be trifled with.*

Anubus's obvious counter would be to eliminate Mike. However, he felt that the others would oppose that move, especially Ariadne and Eric, both of whom seemed to owe him some loyalty. While he did not understand Eric's loyalty to the Captain, Ariadne had as much as admitted to how easily a psychic might control him. Anubus could well understand why she would want a malleable tool in overall command, to take the fall for any failures if nothing else.

While Eric remained largely replaceable, he needed Ariadne's services, and he did not know for certain if he could manage to hunt her successfully. That meant he must make some less obvious move against Mike and whatever other tools he had in play.

Anubus considered a subversion of Mike's plan and the

thought pleased him. To turn one of Mike's tools against him, to corner the thief and force him to reveal Mike's role would both counter the threat and show Anubus as the true hunter. Better than that, he would have the opportunity to break the thief, and to make him reviled not only for his crime but also for his betrayal of Mike.

The only thing I have to do now is find the thief, Anubus thought. That led him full circle however. He didn't know who had stolen the bars. Which meant he didn't know where to start.

Anubus returned to the storage compartment that held the remainder of his gold. He stared at the stack for a long while. He knew that if he could not find the thief, then he had only one option. He could not let the theft go unpunished or he would appear weak. If he appeared weak, other hunters would seek to make him prey. Again he came back to the simple brilliance of Mike's plan, which put Anubus in jeopardy no matter which way he went.

Which brought him back to his original solution. Kill Mike and any one who supported him. Start off with the most dangerous and pick them off while before they knew what happened. He'd have to try for Ariadne tonight, when she slept, he figured. It seemed the only time she might not sense his attack before he had her within his jaws.

Unless, of course, someone else wanted him to make such a strike. Someone who wanted him to act against the Captain might have set the conditions to make it appear as if Mike planned to eliminate him. *That would be the best strategy by a weak hunter, to play the strong against one another,* Anubus thought. They might eliminate the most dangerous and capable of the crew, and therefore take over, all for the risk of the theft. He caressed the gold bars and he savored the smooth cold feel of them, even as he felt rage boil up inside. The perfection of the gold calmed that rage, even as the two missing bars marred that perfection and incited it further.

And what if that hunter expected him to figure it out? With his sudden suspicion, Anubus almost turned and headed to find Mike. If someone had played them against each other, then the best option was to team up, to hunt their opponent... No, a true hunter needed no allies, he thought.

Besides that, Mike must have figured out that possibility if he did mastermind the operation. Which meant he realized the opportunity when offered. *But does he know, that I know,* he thought, *and does the lesser hunter know that we both know?*

The more he thought on it, the more he realized just how dangerous his opponents were, and how crafty they must be to hide their schemes behind their stupid monkey faces and their prey-like movements. He should have known better than to trust humans, especially after what happened at Garris Major. The trap there, so perfectly timed to intercept his forces...

He knew his executive officer had betrayed him, then, even if the coward pleaded for his life and that of the rest of the crew after Anubus cornered him on the bridge. How else could the Colonial Republic force have emerged from shadow space on top of his own element just as they broke their attack formation?

The betrayal had sealed his fate though, and his pleas for the others had only meant Anubus destroyed the ship with all aboard to prevent the escape of the man's accomplices. *Of course, after the blind jump that took us out of the trap and into Chxor space, that left me adrift in a shuttle for capture,* he acknowledged. Still, things had worked out well enough, until now. He had a prowler, he had three hundred kilograms of gold, and he had a pack.

That thought broke his concentration. *Wrethe do not have packs, we do not form friendships, I hunt alone*, he thought. The very idea that he needed the crew appalled him, the fact that he found some form of security in their presence... *I sound like some kind of tame dog.*

No, best to follow through with the simple option. Kill the Captain and any crew that would support him. Once they arrived at 567X43... no, Ariadne had already plotted the course, Anubus did not need her anymore. The system lay only one system away from Danar, sooner or later Anubus would find passage aboard a ship he could bribe or hijack. He could afford to wait, he could not afford weakness. For some reason he

473

remembered Kull and the words from the dream. "I am the lone hunter," Anubus growled, "And I don't believe in ghosts."

"Hey man, I'm right with you there," Rastar's deep voice spoke from behind him.

Anubus spun, his claws extended, ready for the attack, prepared to rend and tear. Rastar stood calmly in the hatch. He didn't even have his weapons in hand and his relaxed pose shocked Anubus enough that he managed to rein in on his instincts. "What... why are you here?" Anubus snarled. The Ghornath had one of his more hideous shirts, one that gave Anubus and immediate headache as he tried to watch Rastar for any sign of threat without actually having to look at the shirt.

"I found your gold," Rastar tossed the two bars from hand to hand, "Sorry it took so long. I had Eric do a shakedown of the crew and passengers while I watched for suspicious activity, as it was, I nearly didn't catch the thief. He slipped up though, tried to ditch the bars and I spotted him."

"*You* caught him?" Anubus demanded. He did not bother to hide his incredulity. The idea that he could have so underestimated the other's capabilities... he had known that the Ghornath hidden something underneath his moronic exterior, but he must have genius level skills to maintain his buffoon act and still locate the thief. What surprised him more was the pack mentality, Eric acted to flush the game while Rastar closed the trap. That kind of move required trust, something that seemed absurd in the face of it. How had Rastar known he could trust Eric?

"Yeah, and I'm afraid I lost my temper with him when I found where he tried to hide them," Rastar shook his head. "Crowe tried to slip them in my drawer in the cabins, right underneath my Hawaiian shirts, can you believe that?"

Anubus felt his lips draw back in a snarl, "Crowe is the thief?" The news did not surprise him, the other man's hacking skills and his stealth made more sense. Which brought to question how Mike had learned of the man's past and who had put Crowe up to it.

"Yeah, he was..." Rastar sighed. "It won't happen again, I

promise you that."

"You killed him?" Anubus felt a surge of surprise, he had not thought Mike so ruthless as to exterminate one of his own tools.

"No way, man! I just beat him to a pulp," Rastar said. "Trust me, he won't forget the consequences of stealing and he admitted it to the others too, I made sure of that." The big Ghornath turned blue, an emotion which Anubus thought meant regret, though he could not think of why Rastar might regret his actions. *Perhaps he regrets that he gave me so much information with which to figure out his hunting pattern?*

"No, but he's terrified of me now, dude," Rastar sighed, "And since I lost my temper, some of the others seem pretty unhappy too. But you probably know how that goes, what with the whole big alien thing. Pretty rough to be so misunderstood, right?"

Anubus could think of no response to that. Did Rastar toy with him, did he view this as some sort of game... or had he simply had luck and stumbled across Crowe's plan? The combination of the shirt and the thought that of all things *Rastar* might be exactly what he seemed proved too much. Anubus sank back on his haunches and looked away.

"Yeah, man, you don't need to say anything, I get ya," Rastar said. He tossed the two bars to Anubus, who caught them out of the air with little of his usual grace. The world seemed too shaken up, especially with how many curves that the Ghornath had thrown him. "Well, anyway, I'll see you at dinner, Eric's doing Mongolian barbeque. You'll love it, they're race of humans that ran the open steppes, nomads who believed in peace and spreading their brotherly love. I watched in a holo where they incorporated everyone they came across into their empire, they didn't care what race or religion, they just let everyone in, isn't that cool?"

"I have read of these Mongolians," Anubus growled, "Ruthless killers who butchered entire nations." He had nearly selected Khan as his name, from his research, but had settled on Anubus after reading of the Egyptian God of Death.

"I think you got that part a little off, man," Rastar laughed. "Don't believe everything you read, right? It's alright though, let's go get some food, hey?"

Anubus gave the alien a slight nod. "I will join you in a moment."

He waited until the scent and sound of Rastar vanished before he turned and carefully placed the two gold bars back where they belonged. He had much to think about, much to ponder. Anubus felt some urge to continue with his original plan, yet his survival instincts cautioned him against it. He was the lone hunter, yes, but he moved in the shadows of a pack. He held no loyalty to them, yet they seemed to feel some for him. That made them vulnerable and gave him greater strength. He would just have to ensure he never let his guard down.

Yet as he peered at the gold stack, he felt dissatisfaction boil up at the sight of the perfect stack. He had played into someone's plan. He had not looked deeply enough into the situation to see the goals behind the thief, and he had underestimated Mike, Crowe, and certainly Rastar.

At least, I hope I underestimated him, Anubus thought darkly*, otherwise I know that the universe is a hunter with a perverse sense of humor that merely toys with me.*

***

Anubus sat secure in the darkest corner of the lounge. The loud sounds of the crew around him no longer seemed like a herd of clueless prey. Instead, he saw the deeper meanings behind the loud noises and the brash scents. They were a pack, one that somehow shared trust, and that, he realized, made them far more dangerous than the individuals he had first appraised them as.

Anubus began his new threat assessment, and this time he began to match individuals into groups, packs that would fight together, not out of mere opportunity, but out of...*friendship.*

I almost feel sick at that thought , Anubus realized. Yet he had to consider it, if only to fully appreciate the threats he faced for when they inevitably turned on him, just as everyone

476

did... eventually. However deluded their trust and friendships and however they might turn on one another later, for now, they believed themselves a true pack and Anubus would have to view them in that fashion.

Even if it caused a new emotion to burn inside him, one he refused to admit as anything other than ridiculous. *I will* not *envy them their self-delusion,* Anubus thought.

Yet some part of him wondered if friendship, however fragile, might be possible for a Wrethe, or if like everything else about him, his animosity came from his very genetics.

###

Systems Failure
The Renegades
Kal Spriggs

"I'm bringing us thirty degrees down, prepare to fire on my mark," Mike said. He matched action to words as he adjusted the controls at the pilot station. On his sensor repeater he saw the enemy ship exposed to the fire of the five turrets. "Mark!"

A moment later, the five turrets opened up. The light particle pulse guns sent a wave of energy at the enemy ship. The lower angle allowed the ship to fire all five of the turrets at the same target and dropped them below the middle band of the enemy ship's defense screen. If their main gun were operational, Mike would have swung the bow upwards and fired that instead

"Multiple hits," Simon said. The somewhat dour former cop seemed bound to keep his voice steady, despite the hour of maneuvers that had required the well-positioned shot. "I'm reading power levels dropping on their defense screen and their reactor signature dropped." The enemy corvette looked to be a Barracuda class, from its maneuvers and reactor signature. It mounted a pair of external missile racks and two light laser turrets. Mike's earlier maneuvers had already coaxed the missile launch, which had allowed Eric to pick them off at long range. The two laser turrets were heavier than their own, but also fired slower and took longer to recharge.

Mike nodded, even as he spun their ship around to put the thicker waist band of their defense screen in between their ship and any return fire. The charged plasma would deflect energy weapons and projectiles while the magnetic field shielded them from radiation. "Any transmission from the enemy ship?" Mike asked.

"Nope," Crowe said. The communications officer had a bored look on his face. "I'll tell you if they start talking."

Mike grimaced, but let Crowe's insolence slide, for the moment, "Navigation, good work with the maneuvers, get us a course that uses our acceleration, I want to get in behind them and-"

"Missile launch!" Simon's level tone disappeared. "I have sixteen missiles on the way. Intercept time thirty seconds!"

"What!?" Mike asked. "They already volleyed their external racks!"

"Looks like they kept something in reserve," Eric said. "Switching fire, Simon, get me a target solution, I'm firing blind!"

Mike shifted the ship into an evasive maneuver and tried to gain some distance even as he watched Eric shift fire. It didn't look good. The missiles were fast, not Nova Roma quality, but certainly military grade from the Colonial Republic. They were fast and agile, and at such close range, the missiles had every advantage.

Eric was good, Mike had to acknowledge. Even with the unfamiliar Ghornath systems and almost no warning he managed to pick off six of the sixteen missiles before they reached attack range. That meant ten of them got through. They swept over the corvette in a wave of destruction, each with a kiloton yield of plasma. Most detonated almost in contact with the hull. The bridge shuddered and shook as missile after missile pounded into them.

Crowe let out a shout of surprise as one of the hits threw him out of his couch. *That'll teach the bastard to strap down*, Mike thought with sullen satisfaction. One missile detonated directly outside the forward view-port and dazzling light filled the bridge. When then wave of plasma cleared, the displays were dark and only the emergency lighting lit the room.

Mike blinked at the dim lighting, still dazed from the forward screen. He gave a sigh, "Terminate simulation."

"You sure?" Pixel's voice came over the intercom. "I could have my assistants do some simulated damage repairs on the actual damage we have."

"Yes, I'm sure." Mike said. A moment later the view screen cleared and showed the gray emptiness of shadow space once more. "Everyone assemble up here and we'll do an after action review."

Crowe stood from the deck, "That was a little too fancy with the simulated gravity, Pixel."

"You are welcome, my friend," Rastar said. "I'm the one that found the simulation files in the officer quarters. Good thing the Ghornath crew had backups. I think it added much realism to the simulation."

"Yeah," Crowe said sourly. "Great."

"I thought we were sticking to standard ship classes?" Mike grunted.

"We did," Rastar said. "Simon incorrectly identified it as a Barracuda class corvette. However, Pixel and I selected a Hammerhead class corvette for the simulation, based off of its common use as a privateer or raider. A Hammerhead corvette has four missile racks versus two."

Mike grimaced. The big alien had done exactly as he'd asked… and it was Mike's fault that he accepted Simon's identification without confirmation. "Right." Mike heard Simon swear. Out of the corner of his eye, he saw Simon pull up the sensor logs again. "Hey, no worries, brother, that's my fault as much as yours."

"Still, I should have caught it," Simon said. "I wish we had more complete sensor logs for identification."

"I'd kill for a set of Jaynes Ships," Mike said. Even that kind of off the shelf software would be better than the kludge of salvaged Ghornath and Chxor data. He glanced over at Crowe, "Any luck recovering more of the ship's logs or data?" The stale smell of his own sweat reminded him that it had been a long day, even before the other man spoke.

Crowe frowned, "I'd have more time to work on it… except we've been drilling for the past twelve hours. And we've died… seventeen times."

"Eighteen," Simon said. "Don't forget the one where we struck that derelict ship in the first fifteen seconds of the simulation."

"Right… how could I forget that one?" Crowe said, his voice filled with mock puzzlement. "After all, it was such a combination of excellent piloting, marvelous navigation, and breathtaking sensor readings." The tall man looked down at Mike, "So... are we done here?"

"We're done," Mike said. "Rastar has some crew drills he wants to do for fire, boarding, and abandon ship, but we'll implement those later." He had grown *very* tired of Crowe's attitude. The man seemed to have two settings: sullen and sarcastic.

"Oh, great," Crowe said.

"Listen, you'll do the drills and you'll work hard at them," Mike snapped.

"Or what?" Eric grimaced. Mike looked up with surprise and saw a mixture of frustration and irritation on the other man's face. "Look, Mike, we've been at this for *twelve* hours. We're all exhausted..."

"And in a real emergency, something like we already had, you'll be tired then too," Mike snapped. "And we'll need to do our jobs regardless."

"Whatever," Crowe snorted. "I'm done here."

"Don't walk away from me, Crowe." Mike said. He could feel his pulse pound at his temples.

Ariadne stood and stepped between them. "Look, why don't we all just calm down..."

"I don't have time to listen to Mike *and* her," Eric snapped. "I'm out too."

Mike bit back a snarl and turned back to his console. He wanted to scream and yell, but he knew that, as the Captain, such displays would be... counterproductive at best. He felt overwhelmed and exhausted. Part of him wanted nothing more than to sleep. The rest of him was terrified of what he would find in his dreams.

He glanced around at the others, who remained on the bridge, their faces tight with tension. "Take a break. We'll discuss this tomorrow."

He sat down as they shuffled out. His eyes went to the gray nothingness of Shadow Space. Part of the tension came from their circumstances, he knew. They'd been forced together: companions of necessity. *How can I expect them to work together when even I don't want to anymore,* he wondered.

He had heard of crews going mad, on long jumps through Shadow Space, driven insane by the emptiness and isolation. Even the best crews sometimes let it get to them and became surly and depressed. Mike didn't want to see what Anubus would be like if he became even more surly.

He sighed, and for just a moment, he let his eyes go closed.

***

"Mike," Kran said, her voice soft. "They've betrayed you. Just like your other companions have before. You can't trust them, you can't trust anyone." She spoke softly, her ugly Chxor face calm and emotionless. And then she stepped forward and kissed him. Her lips were warm and rubbery, and felt as sensual as kissing a water balloon.

She stepped back. "They're coming to kill you. You can trust me. We have to stop them."

Mike turned to face the door as his former companions attacked. Only this time, they didn't win. Kran caught Anubus as he came through the door, held him up and ripped his arms out of the sockets with her mental abilities. Ariadne tried to stop her, but Mike fired and struck her in the chest. She fell to the deck in a spreading pool of her own blood. Eric lined his sights up on Mike, but Kran caught him with her psychic powers and wrenched his head around backwards.

Rastar gave a shout of anguish as all four of his limbs twisted around to aim his guns at his own head. The four guns fired at once and his headless corpse toppled to the deck.

"Now, it's just you and me, Mike... just you and me," Krann's voice said from inside of Mike's mind...

***

Mike woke with a shrill yell. He realized he'd nodded off, in his seat on the bridge. He felt sweat bead his brow and he wiped it away even as he fought to control his ragged breathing. A glance over showed that Simon was still present, though the other man at least pretended to be too engrossed in manning his watch to notice Mike's nightmares.

Again with the nightmares, he thought. He hadn't been able to sleep since the *Sao Martino* and Krann the Chxor... or whatever had worn the outside of Krann the Chxor. Every time he closed his eyes he heard her voice and he went through another iteration of the events on the bridge. In some, his companions took him alive and tortured him. In others, he killed or helped to kill them. Always there was Krann's voice, never ceasing.

He'd told Ariadne, and she'd tried to help. She said she thought the mental effects would ease, over time. That gave him little comfort. He couldn't sleep, he felt exhausted. Mike wanted it to end... and he wanted to do his job, not to be plagued by nightmares.

He stood up from the chair and groaned. His body ached and his brain felt sluggish. A glance at the chrono showed it was early morning. Most would be asleep. He spoke loud enough for Simon to hear, "I'll be down at the lounge."

Mike took the elevator down. He paused outside the door and took a calming breath before he walked through. As always, the large aquarium lurked to the side, the water and the Arcavian Fighting Eel that lurked inside it made the hair on the back of Mike's neck rise. He headed for the far side of the room and stood at the bar. Eric tended to leave food out for those who had the night shift, and Mike slowly made himself a sandwich and tried to think.

The arguments of the day lay heavy on his mind. His nightmares only seemed to give more weight to his worries. Did he push the others too hard? Was it his own uncertainty about them as companions that made him so hard on them... or it was it their lack of training and preparation that made him uncertain?

Eric walked through the back door from the galley. "Oh, hey Mike." The mercenary looked as if he hadn't slept at all and he blinked at Mike with bloodshot eyes. He carried a tray filled with pastries.

"A little early for breakfast," Mike said. He kept his

voice neutral.

"Huh?" Eric asked. He glanced down at the tray, "Oh, right. Pastries will keep just fine." He set the tray down and then let out a sigh. "I couldn't sleep."

"Me too," Mike said. "I..."

Alarms wailed and the ship shuddered. There was a surge of acceleration that threw them both into the food bar. Mike pushed himself upright even as he heard Simon's strained voice over the ship's intercom. "Captain to the bridge, all crew to the bridge."

Mike rushed out the door and up the ladder well. *Simon's got watch on the bridge,* he thought, *and Matvei has the engine watch.* It felt like an unguided transition,which would be very, very bad, he knew. Once they'd plotted their course, they shouldn't emerge from Shadow Space early, not unless Ariadne had plotted their course incorrectly... or they'd suffered a failure to their Shadow Space drive. Due to the non-euclidean geometry of Shadow Space, they could be far off course. They could be back in the Chxor Empire or halfway across the Colonial Republic or even deep in the depths of uncharted space. The drive should only shut down if it had failed or if someone had shut it down.

All that went through his head as he stepped through the final hatch and onto the bridge. The forward view ports showed a baleful green star clouded in a nebulous gas cloud. Simon was at his console, "The shadow space drive went down, I'm getting no response from engineering. I'm trying to bring up the sensors now."

Mike moved to the command console. "Bring up the sensor plot," he said. He could tell at a glance that their unguided transition had given them a huge velocity differential with the system. Their defense screen could take a few hits but a large enough object would kill them at that speed. Far out on their plotted course, at least a half hour away, he noticed a large asteroid or planetoid.

Mike heard the hatch open behind him, but he was already bringing the engines online. They had time to alter course, but he didn't want to wait. That was when he noticed the error code on his console. He bit off a curse and said, "The maneuvering thrusters are locked out."

Pixel answered him, "Yeah, the engine room is on lock down. From what I can tell, the shadow space drive failed catastrophically." He paused and Mike could hear regret in his voice when he spoke, "The engine room is showing lethal levels of radiation." That meant that Matvei was dead, Mike knew. "I'll try to bring the thrusters online remotely..."

There was a thunderous detonation and the entire ship rocked. The lights went out and then began to flicker. The flickering finally died, but the sullen red emergency lights came on a moment later, followed by a chorus of alarms.

Mike brought up a damage report even as he heard a litany of damage from Ariadne, who had slipped into her position without him noticing. "Impact near the bow," she said, her voice tight. "Thirty degrees off axis, forward compartments are open. Looks like we have a fire in section three and four."

"Yeah," Pixel said, "Also severe structural damage. We're in danger of catastrophic failure. Pressure is dropping in all forward compartments."

Mike winced. The cargo bay was in section five. All their passengers were closest to the danger. Mike turned and found Rastar had just stepped onto the bridge, "Rastar, take Anubus and Eric. Move the passengers out of the cargo hold, past..." he paused and glanced at his display. "Past bulkhead fifteen, at least." Rastar gave him two thumbs up and ran off the bridge, Eric and Anubus followed behind him.

Mike glanced over at Simon, "Get sensors online and find out where the hell we are." He looked over at Crowe, "Get on the comms, try to find if anyone is out there, we need help."

Crowe grimaced, "That hit took out our radio and laser transceivers. I have nothing to work with."

"Then cobble something together," Mike snapped. "We need help, that's your department." He looked over at Ariadne, "I think you need to go down and manage damage control."

She nodded and when she spoke, her voice was level.

"I'll take Mindy and Miranda," she said, "And gather others on the way." There was a look of confusion on her face, almost as if something bothered her. She paused again, a question in her blue eyes.

"Get on it," Mike said, "We don't have time to talk." He locked over at Pixel, "What can you tell me about our systems?"

"The fusion reactor went into emergency shutdown," Pixel said. "Looks like it took damage to the control system. The thrusters are offline and the engines are out until I can get power online." Pixel looked over at Mike. When he spoke, his voice was tight with tension, "I *might* be able to access the truck compartment and bring the reactor online from there."

Mike glanced around the mostly empty bridge, he was running out of bodies. "Do it"

Mike keyed through his console. Without primary power, he had limited options from the bridge. He watched on the sensor relay as the planetoid approached. *Surely Pixel can get something online in the next twenty minutes,* he thought.

Rastars voice came from the console, "Hey Mike, we're moving the passengers now. We're putting them in the lounge, for now."

"Any issues?" Mike asked.

"Nope," Rastar said. "Anubus reasoned with a couple stragglers, I guess he was pretty persuasive, they just ran past me."

Mike snorted, "Possibly a discussion of his food options for the evening. Keep me posted." He toggled another switch and activated the intercom, "Ariadne, what's your status?"

"We are at the damaged area, Mike." Her voice was loud and there was a chorus of rushing wind and the noise of fire in the background. "It's not-" Her voice cut out in a burst of static, followed by a chorus of new alarms on his console. Mike frowned and glanced at his overlay. The section she and her damage control crew had occupied flashed red and then went black. A message displayed structural failure of the compartments in that section.

Mike felt his heart go cold. "Ariadne?" he asked, on the

486

open channel. He received no response. He let out a shaky breath and then opened a channel to where Pixel should be, at the console in the trunk compartment. "Pixel, I'm showing section four just suffered structural failure. We have people in there, what can we do?"

Pixel grunted and he sounded distracted. "Yeah, if section four failed, it would be explosive decompression. We can't do anything."

"Ariadne was in there," Mike said. He kept his voice low, "She was trying to tell me something."

Pixel took several long seconds to answer. When he spoke, his voice was sad, "I'm sorry Mike, but if section four went, she probably was blown out of the ship. She might have suited up in time." Pixel gave a harsh grunt. "But you and I both know that without suit radios, we'd never find her." Pixel was silent for a long while. "Look, Mike, I think I can get the reactor back online, but it will be risky."

"Define risky," Mike said. He felt like he had too many shocks already, but this was his job, and he would be *damned* if he didn't do his best.

"Well, if something goes wrong, I'll almost certainly die," Pixel said matter-of-factly. "But it will probably bring up the reactor and should unlock the thrusters and engines." He paused. "If it doesn't work, it will almost certainly wipe out our emergency power."

Mike frowned. A glance at the display showed the impact with the planetoid was in only ten minutes. "Can you get clear?"

"Not in time, I'll have to basically trigger a manual restart from here. If there's any kind of plasma surge, it will vent through the trunk compartment." Pixel said.

Mike closed his eyes. "Okay, do it." He looked over at Crowe, "Any progress?"

Crowe grimaced again. He had no sneer in his voice when he spoke, but he still seemed sullen, "I have a transponder from what looks like a Ghornath battlecruiser. I can't understand a word they said, but they're talking with us."

Mike blinked at that. The Ghornath had never had a huge

fleet, their battlecruisers were their largest ships. From what he'd heard, most of them had been destroyed when the Nova Roma Empire attacked their world, only a decade back. "Very well..." he said, "Keep talking to them, I'll get someone up here."

He opened a channel to the lounge, "Rastar, you there?"

"Yes, Mike, we're monitoring from here." Rastar answered. "Mike are you aware--"

"Get up here," Mike interrupted. He didn't have time for questions, not when every second mattered. "I need you to talk with some folks."

The emergency lighting flickered and died. Mike's breath sounded suddenly loud in the darkness as the secondary systems shut down. *Come on Pixel,* Mike thought.

The bridge came alight. All the consoles powered up, many with flashing damage icons. Mike gave a whoop as his controls went live again. He spun the ship on it's axis and brought the engines online with gentle force. "Great job, Pixel, system are online. Get back up here," he waited a moment for a response. "Pixel?" A glance at his display showed a new red icon of damage near the engine room.

Mike bit off another curse. He hoped that the engineer had made it clear, yet after the other shocks of the past few minutes, he felt far from certain of that. "Simon I'm bringing us stable relative to the rest of the star system. Make sure we don't have anything else out here to collide with--"

The screen cleared to show a Ghornath in military uniform. The Ghornath barked harsh words in his native tongue. The voice blared from all the speakers. At the same time, Mike's console locked out again. "What the hell?!" Mike demanded.

Crowe swore, "Some kind of override." He pounded at his console. "I'm locked out of everything." He looked at the Ghornath and then back at Mike, "Well, this is your department, right?"

Mike stood up. "Hello, I'm Mike Smith, we captured this vessel from the Chxor Empire..."

"He can't hear you," Rastar said. The Ghornath on the screen continued to speak.

"What is he saying, then?" Mike demanded. "Why did he take over our systems... who the hell *is* he?" He felt exhausted and angry, especially at this Ghornath windbag who wouldn't shut up.

"*She* is Fleet Consul Malika," Rastar said. "She is congratulating us on our training and effort. She also is informing us that we are a compliment to our instructors."

"What?" Mike raised both eyebrows in shock. "We almost died, half our crew *did* die."

"She also informs us that this is the third tier of difficulty and the most hazardous of the surprise drills, which are part of the training package we activated. She congratulates us on our success and requests that we send any comments to Ghornath Fleet Training Command, attention Fleet Consul Malika."

"A drill?" Mike said. Even as the screen cleared to show shadow space once again. A moment later, his console cleared as well to show all systems back at standby and all damage cleared.

"I sure have a comment for them," Crowe snarled. "They can take their rutting sims and--"

"Mike," Pixel's voice came from the console, "I'm on my way up."

Mike couldn't force himself to speak for a moment, but he finally leaned forward and responded, "Acknowledged." He opened up another channel, "Ariadne, you there?"

"We're here," Ariadne said. "The console locked out on us and notified us that we were casualties for the exercise. I was trying to let you know that there is no damage."

Mike let out a breath of relief. He opened up the ship's intercom. "All crew report to the bridge."

He waited as they assembled. He felt both humbled by their actions and relieved that they had survived, after all. "First of all, I want you to know that I had no idea. I'm so sorry--"

"No worries," Rastar said. "We all figured that out. And it was a good drill."

"I wouldn't say *that*," Crowe muttered.

"I haven't sweat that much since rookie week," Simon said. "But we did learn a lot and we worked well together."

489

"I for one am *very* glad it was a drill," Ariadne said. "But I agree, we worked well together. It just goes to show you who great a team we make."

"When trapped like rats with our lives at stake," Eric amended.

"You're just unhappy you didn't get to die gloriously," Simon said. "You should have seen it, Mike got all misty over Pixel and Ariadne. Makes me wish I got the chance to do the same. Next time it's our turn, guys," Simon said with a smirk.

"Yeah," Pixel said, "Uh, next time you can go through that. I, for one, thought I was going to die." The engineer still looked shaky. "It even showed the plasma surge on the console."

"Mike, you did great," Ariadne said. "I think we can all agree that without you this would have ended in failure." Her face showed total sincerity and she met his gaze with her level blue eyes.

"Thanks," Mike said. He looked around at them all. "I think we all deserve a break. Eric, perhaps you could arrange something for us in the lounge. Since Matvei sat this one out, he can take the rest of Simon's watch."

As he watched them file out, Mike felt some of his worry ease. Yet at the same time, the weight of responsibility felt heavier on his shoulders. No matter what they said, he *had* failed them. Too many would have died. The so-called 'level three' difficulty or not, his crew had died and he had been unable to save them.

He would not let that happen again.

###

Part Five

A Murder of Crowes
The Renegades, Book Five
by Kal Spriggs

Simon sat back in the couch and stared at the fish tank and sipped at his water. He reached up and adjusted the tie he wore and hid a small smile. They all had received some new clothing from the salvage of the *Sao Martino*. While some of the others, particularly the longer term escaped prisoners, wore a mix of whatever eclectic wear they could put together, Simon had rather different taste.

Fortunately, he had found a business suit that fit him almost as well as if made for him. He had also managed to trim his dark hair and he almost felt human again. Something about how they had looted the ship still left him with an uncomfortable feeling, as if he had directly robbed the dead. He knew that legally their actions were considered salvage, but emotionally it still felt wrong. Still... he had to admit that the change of clothes and the additional stores had changed them from what felt like a band of vagrants to something a little less unsavory.

Well, he admitted, *changed some of us, anyway.* He caught a reflection of Illario Urbano in the glass of the aquarium. The former gang member had changed out his ragged prison environmental suit for a set of skin-tight bright orange pants and a flamboyant sleeveless green shirt which hung to just above his ribs. Simon thought the man would have looked ridiculous but for the gang brands and multitude of knife scars and needle punctures that stippled his exposed skin. While the gang fashion might differ from what he would see in the Confederation, the obvious signs of a hardcore criminal showed clearly enough.

Had Simon still carried his badge he would have called for a backup before he frisked Illario and booked him for whatever illegal items he possessed. Instead, when Illario caught his gaze in the reflected glass, Simon forced himself to give the other man a polite smile. *Ah,* Simon thought a moment later, *apparently Illario wants to have that conversation we've put off so far.* A moment later the ganger swaggered over and sat down next to Simon.

"You busy?" Illario asked.

Simon maintained a polite smile. He tried not to think about how the other man's cheap cologne burned his nose. Simon ignored every police instinct he had that wanted him to back out of knife range and go for his pistol. He knew exactly what a thug like Illario could do at such close range with even a toothpick, much less the small arsenal of knives he no doubt wore.

"Nope, just searching for Rainbow," Simon said politely. It wasn't entirely true, though he did spend at least a few minutes each day locating the chameleon-like eel, he mostly selected the spot because it gave him some time to muse and reflect. He didn't think that Illario would understand that need, though.

"Rain what?" Illario asked as his scarred face pulled back in a grimace of confusion.

"Rainbow... you know, the unfortunately named Arcavian Fighting Eel?" Simon said.

"Oh, right." Illario nodded. "The fish that the mind-freak named." He gave Simon a leer, "You like to watch it, eh?" Somehow Simon doubted that Illario meant the fish.

"She has a name," Simon said, "And looking for the fish is a good exercise in observation."

"Right," Illario's smile seemed greasy somehow. "Anyway, bro, I just wanted to chat, you know, get to know you and let you get to know me."

Here it comes, Simon thought, *now to see how low he thinks he can buy me for.*

"Of course," Simon said. He kept his voice bland, and remembered his grandfather Montogmery's advice. *Never give them a sign, don't look nervous, but don't look interested either. They don't know what to make of you then, and they'll overplay their hand. A big offer, right up front, that means they're in over their head, and that means you can turn them.*

"So, I interviewed with Mike, earlier. He said that there might be a permanent place here, working the ship, security, maybe helping to find things we can't get normally," Illario gave

Simon a wink. "You know."

"Oh?" Simon asked.

"Yeah..." Illario peered at Simon for a long moment. "Uh, *pula*, has he talked with you about it?"

Simon just cocked his head, "Should he have?"

"Well, you see, he said he wanted your advice. And I know you used to be a..." Illario caught himself and gave a fake smile, "... well, a cop."

"I did law enforcement, yes," Simon corrected.

"Yeah, well, I wanted to clear the air between us," Illario said. "You know, make sure we don't misunderstand each other."

And here we go, Simon thought.

"So, since Mike really trusts you, I wonder what it might take to get in good with you." The offer seemed so openly spoken that it assaulted Simon's sense of self worth. *Why not just slap me on the ass and call me a whore,* Simon thought.

"Excuse me?" Simon asked

He saw sweat bead up on Illario's forehead. This would be the moment of truth, it would show how much a threat Simon should rate the former, or not so former, criminal. *What tactic will the man choose*, Simon wondered.

Illario went with one Simon would never have suspected: he went with the truth. "Look, *pula*, this is the best offer I could ever get for honest work. I got a place here, one where I can make good money, one where I got safety. All I need to keep it is to get you to tell Mike I'm good. I want to know what that will take, and anything that won't jeopardize this will be worth it."

Simon stared at him. "You want to prove you're trustworthy by bribing me?"

Illario shrugged, "Call it a bribe, call it a tax, call it a gift, or just call it a favor, it's all the same. I can get things, that's my skill, that's what I can bring to this crew besides muscle, and the dog and the cat bring more of that than any one human can provide." It took Simon a moment to catch the slang about Rastar and Anubus. *That's right, Cats and Dogs, Ghornath and Wrethe.* "You wear that cheap suit you got off the wreck like you think you're special, but I know how all you cops have your needs, just like other people. Me, I bet you'll want me to get you some women when we hit port."

"No," Simon snapped.

Illario smiled, "Ah, *sbirro*, I see, you watch the fish here while the 'fish' you want is just out of reach. You need a little help reeling her in? I can help you there, too. She's a good looking piece, I admit, but not all up there," Illario waved his hand around his head, "Just like most mind-freaks."

Simon leaned close, "Just a suggestion, you want me to tell Mike to trust you, you shouldn't try to piss me off."

Illario's smile vanished, "Now I see what you got in you *sbirro*, and I see you think you're an honest *pula*, and that just means you're the worst kind. All full of yourself and how important you are, too afraid to go out and get the things you want, do the things you want... so you take your fear out on the people brave enough to do it." Illario cracked his neck, "Cops like you, they burn out or they go bad worse than the rest. You won't take a gift, and a friendly warning wouldn't work, someone would get hurt."

"Is that a threat?" Simon asked.

"No, sbirro. I wouldn't threaten you anyway, too obvious," Illario said. "I might go after that pretty little blonde mind-freak, but not you, you probably got a martyr complex like my mother."

"Her name is Ariadne," Simon snarled, "And if you touch her–"

"Hey bro, I got nothing against her," Illario said. "Besides, I'd sooner stick my *cazzo* in a recycler than get her pissed at me. Got a cousin who messed with one of Shadow Lord Imperious's drug shipments. I ain't getting no mind-freaks cross with me after what they did to him, not over a *sbirro* like you, anyhow."

"So why are you still talking?" Simon asked. *I should have kept my cool,* Simon thought, *I tipped my hand and Grandpa Montgomery would kick my ass for letting so much slip.*

"*Pula*, I'm just passing the time," Illario shrugged. "I bet you'll tell Mike to ditch me at the first port we make. You'll tell him I'm a druggy, a convict, and probably a killer. You'll tell him I'd kill my own brother over a whore and pimp my sister for drug money."

"Would you?" Simon asked, his voice level. "I see the needle marks on your arms. I can see the green tint on your iris, you probably did Morphate, maybe Dreamweed or even some real hard stuff like Primus. Some of those you would sell your soul for a second hit."

"*Sbirro...*" Illario looked almost sad for a moment, "I done worse than that. But I'm clean now, not a damned thing in my system. What you don't realize is that even if Mike doesn't trust me, he can use me. Someone like me brings something that even a sbirro like you can appreciate." Illario smiled, "I'm disposable. It's not something I might be proud of, but it's true. Got a job so dirty or dangerous that not even a martyr like you wants to do... well, send me instead. I get caught, well, just a bad seed, nothing to tie it to Mike or anyone else. You *pula* use people like me all the time. You just don't want to associate with me because I'm the mirror on all the shit you hide in the bottom of your soul."

"I don't like you because you're weak," Simon growled. "You're an addict. You might claim to have it together, but that first port we hit, you'll have all those drugs right at your fingertips. And someone out there will want information on us. You're weak, and your weakness will make us vulnerable."

"Fuck you, *sbirro*," Illario said. "Not all of us grew up with money. Your daddy may have sent you to a nice school and given you money for your birthdays, my dad died working the hard labor mines at Volaterra. My stepfather beat the shit out of me and kicked me out of his apartment for my thirteenth birthday. I earned everything I've ever had with blood... mine and the people in the way." Illario stood up, "You go ahead and tell Mike that I ain't worth shit, but you wait and see, he'll see my value." The ganger turned away and swaggered off.

Simon took another sip of water. For just a moment he wished for a good beer. *Well, that went well,* Simon thought with sarcasm.

***

Simon found Mike up on the bridge. "Captain, got a moment?" He saw Mike had pulled up the flight simulator on the captain's terminal. With the Ghornath-sized terminal, he looked almost like a kid at play on his father's computer.

The ship's captain glanced up, "Ah, what's up, brother?"

"I just talked with Illario," Simon said.

"Let me guess. He's a danger, probably turn on us for drug money, and you want me to ditch him first chance we get?" Mike asked. He didn't look up from the flight simulator.

Simon paused, his eyes narrowed, "You already knew what I'd say. Why'd you tell him to talk to me?"

"I figured it best to get that out in the open, and I held out some hope he might convince you," Mike said. "But really, I decided to hire him on regardless."

Simon gritted his teeth, "Mike, scum like Illario are-"

"Dangerous, I know. Worse, he'd probably pimp out his sister for drug money and shank his own brother over a whore," Mike smiled slightly, "But that's beside the point."

Simon waited patiently.

"The point is, Simon, that regardless of that, we can use him. Illario, like told me and he probably told you, is both expendable and deniable. Better than all that, he's loyal, as far as it goes. He'll do a job that even Anubus might hesitate over."

"I hadn't realized we might take *that* kind of job," Simon said.

Mike sighed, and paused his simulation. He turned to face Simon. "Look, brother, would you torture someone for information? Would you slap around the Nova Roma Ambassador if we needed it to happen? Would you know where to sell an illegal cargo if we picked one up?"

Simon looked away.

"And yeah, we might come to that," Mike said. He reached out a hand and rested it on Simon's shoulder. "The way I see it, we got three options when we get back. We go our

498

separate ways, we try to take some mercenary work... or we try our hand at privateering for whoever will take us."

"Piracy?" Simon asked, he couldn't keep the shock out of his voice. He stepped away from Mike, "You're thinking of going pirate?"

"No." Mike shook his head, "Privateering for a government, probably going after the Chxor, so I'd say Nova Roma or the Colonial Republic," Mike shrugged. "It pays better than straight up mercenary work, and we can run cargoes along the way to earn some spending money."

"With this ship?" Simon asked.

Mike shot a glance at the open bridge hatch and then at the camera that Pixel had installed. He pitched his voice low, so as not to carry, "Look, brother, this ship is Ghornath military, high tech, rare, probably worth a lot... but there's not one government in human space that would let a bunch of nobodies like us keep her."

Simon frowned, "Why not?"

"It's well armed, for one thing. Most governments get nervous with well-armed civilians. Makes them worry about revolutions and such," Mike shrugged. "Worse than that, it's well-armed, alien-built, and irreplaceable. Plus Nova Roma went to war with the Ghornath and it has served as a privateer against them. They'll want her as a trophy if nothing else. On top of that, the Chxor went full out against Nova Roma. They captured Danar... well, that's what Crowe found on the *Sao Martino*'s log, anyway. So the Nova Romans will want every warship they can get. A small fast ship like this is perfect for a scout or escort."

"Danar?" Simon asked. He remembered the system had been mentioned before, but he hadn't paid much attention, to be honest. Everything outside the Confederation had seemed so distant and of little importance before he went on the run from his own nation. In the time since his escape from the Chxor, he hadn't paid much attention to where they were headed, so long as it was away from the murderous alien empire.

"A major military hub, only one jump away from the Nova Roma system itself. They've got the second largest shipyard outside of Confederation space there and the only big yards besides Nova Roma. That means the Chxor can threaten the Empire's capital. I would bet the Nova Roma Fleet will throw a hell of a lot of ships at Danar soon enough in an attempt to take it back, but that kind of battle will mean they'll be low on ships like this, especially if they lose."

"So we lose this ship," Simon shrugged. "We could hire on with..."

"Screw that. I worked as a crewman for a dozen crappy tramp freighters. We got a good team here and I'm not going to let us get broken up in a big crew, as assistants and hired help," Mike grimaced. Besides that, I've got a few other ideas... some info I picked up before the Chxor captured me. There's some very valuable things on some of the planets the Chxor overran. We could do some recovery. I mean, half those places probably aren't even considered worth guarding by the Chxor. There's museums, art galleries, alien archeology sites..."

Simon stared at the other man, "You've clearly been thinking this through."

"We've had plenty of time... and I try not to sleep too much anymore," Mike grimaced. "And truth to tell, getting some back on the Chxor... that seems like damned fine thing to me right now."

Simon winced at the reminder of what Krann the Chxor had done to Mike. Or the creature that had worn Krann's body like a suit had done, in any case. *I wonder if he still suffers from nightmares over the experience,* Simon thought, *at least he doesn't wake up screaming anymore.* They still didn't know what the purple slime inside the female Chxor might be, but Run had locked the remaining samples in his improvised lab and labeled them with all manner of hazardous symbols.

"All right, brother, now that I've given you plenty to think about, I've got to get back to this simulation. Damned Ghornath systems are designed for four arms... takes a lot of getting used to for battle maneuvers."

Simon winced at the reminder of the hours and hours of simulations they'd run. "I thought we wouldn't keep the ship?"

Simon asked. He understood the importance of rehearsals, and to be honest, as the main person on sensors, he should probably work at that task as much as possible. But he hated the odd Ghornath displays and he'd become increasingly frustrated at how complex the simulations had become. Mike seemed determined to work them hard.

"That doesn't mean we won't have to fight while we're aboard," Mike said as he turned back to his console. "I'd like to be able to at least dodge well if it comes down to it. Besides, there's always a chance we can keep her. With our luck, who knows?"

***

Simon watched the rest of his companions assemble with a suspicious gaze. Mike's earlier words, especially about privateering, lingered in his mind. Though Mike had made it out to be some kind of service, Simon saw it as something less than that. *Privateers are little better than pirates with a piece of paper and mercenary work can be less legitimate and* far *riskier,* he thought with a grimace. Mike's words and his position on Illario rubbed Simon the wrong way... and made him reconsider his decision to stay with the others.

Run interrupted his train of thought, "You did not show up for today's inventory of ship resources. As a result, I noticed a thirty percent decrease in my overall efficiency. This is unacceptable."

Simon looked down at the little alien. "My apologies, I had to discuss some crew issues with the Captain." Oddly enough, Simon found he got along with the diminutive Chxor better than he did with most of the others. For all his weirdness, at least Run liked things orderly.

"I will accept this, but only so long as my schedule is not disturbed in this manner again," Run said. "We must keep to the schedule, so that I have sufficient time to conduct my experiments."

Simon gave him a nod in reply. As the Chxor walked away, Simon returned to his study of the others. Run, he guessed, would not care whether they went privateer or even outright pirate. For that matter, Simon somewhat doubted the diminutive alien would even care if they attacked more of his people. He certainly showed no remorse for those they had already killed.

At that thought, his gaze went to Eric Striker. The former commando and mercenary would probably accept any decision that led to more combat. If his previous behavior showed any sign of his future actions, Eric would probably initiate hostilities just for the opportunity to fight. When combined with his 'hobby' of improvised explosives, Simon wondered how much longer the other man would survive, especially given the temperament of others aboard the crew.

That thought, in turn, brought Simon's gaze to Rastar. The Ghornath's temper had already put them in one brawl. Yet he seemed to possess a honor code, of sorts. He had already mentioned that he took mercenary work before. Simon wondered how the alien's ethics would hold up, particularly given the chance to fight the Chxor. Then again, Simon didn't know how the alien might handle work with the Nova Romans or if he might already have fought them.

Pixel, the ship's engineer, might go either way, Simon would guess. Despite himself, Simon had taken a liking to Pixel. His obvious pseudonym irritated Simon, yet whatever secrets he might hide, the engineer showed a level of honesty and hard work that Simon could appreciate. Even so, Pixel seemed willing to do things that set Simon's teeth on edge. Particularly his fascination with explosives, which he and Eric indulged when they thought he wouldn't notice. *As if I wouldn't notice the mess the two of them make and the burns and scorch marks from their failures,* he thought.

Simon didn't really have to even think about Anubus. The cannibalistic Wrethe would welcome any potential fight and gladly steal and murder. Simon still marveled that the violent sociopath hadn't tried to kill them all and take the ship for himself. Really, Simon hoped that Mike would send him on his way once they made port. *Preferably after he tips off the authorities,* Simon amended.

And that left Ariadne. Simon didn't want to think that she'd go for the privateer or mercenary work. Yet... she seemed hooked on the idea of the group as some kind of surrogate family. If Mike pitched it to her right, she might be convinced to look after the others and stay on. The thought of just how badly things might go for her afterward made Simon wince. He stared at her for a moment as she talked with Pixel. Her easy smile and open face made him worry even more. *There's a thousand ways that mercenary work can go bad,* he thought, *and most of them lead to bounties, courtrooms, and either executions or long prison stints.*

When privateering went bad, the subjects normally just wound up vented out an airlock.

Simon shook his head. Better that someone with some knowledge of the law stuck around. If nothing else, he might be able to nip some of the more harebrained ideas in the bud. Failing that, he could at least point out the guilty parties to the authorities.

"Alright," Mike said. "We'll reach 567X43 in a couple days." Simon nodded at that, he had been aboard the bridge when Ariadne plotted the course, some of the others, such as Rastar, had not though. A brief like this, Simon felt, was essential to operation of the ship. Standards and procedures like that would make sure that they overlooked nothing. "When we get there, it's likely that we'll encounter someone, possibly someone friendly enough to help us out."

"If not, we can find someplace quiet there and shut down," Pixel said. "Then I can finish up the repairs to the fusion reactor." Simon caught the engineer's glare at Eric. He wondered if it would be enough to break up their love affair with scratch-built explosives.

"Using up more of my gold?" Anubus snarled. His gravelly voice made goosebumps rise on the back of Simon's neck. Anubus was flat out terrifying in a lot of ways. Useful in a fight, Simon had to admit, but terrifying.

"Using our gold to improve our ship," Mike answered.

"Unless you want to be aboard a defenseless vessel? We need full power from the reactor to power weapons and the defense screen at the same time."

"I've got my prowler," Anubus growled.

"Right, in case you *want* to be stranded aboard a ship without Shadow Space capabilities," Mike said. "Be my guest. We could have left you back there where you found your little toy... I'm sure given enough time you might have found where Ghost dropped the Shadow Space module."

The two meter tall alien turned his jackal head towards Mike, "Do not provoke me."

"Okay, guys, how about we just move on," Ariadne said, her voice cheerful. "We need each other, which is important to remember. Also important to remember is how great a team we make!"

Simon saw Eric roll his eyes and heard him mutter, "That has to be the stupidest way to change the subject I've ever heard." His words made Simon clench his fists. What was the other man's issue with Ariadne? *Yeah, she's a bit more... upbeat than most bosses,* he admitted, *but her heart is in the right place and she's capable enough.*

"As I was saying," Mike interrupted. "We've got just a short distance to go and then we'll be back in civilization. Even if we don't find anyone there, we can take some time to do repairs and such. You've elected me as Captain, but I still would like to discuss my plans a bit. Now we have two options, either we head towards our galactic north—"

A shrill scream cut him off. Everyone's attention went to Elena, the bounty hunter stood near Mike's shoulder. Simon had mostly ignored her for the past weeks. She seemed capable enough, but he felt more than a trace of unease at dealing with someone of her profession. Besides, the way she fawned on Mike made Simon rather annoyed. The other man either enjoyed it or tolerated it, so Simon just ignored it. She normally wore her red hair tied back and a smug expression on her face.

Right now her expression was one of fear. She had her hand extended to the forward view-port of the bridge. "I just saw

Ghost!"

As one, their attention went to the transparent view port. It seemed to show little besides the gray emptiness of shadow space. "You saw a ghost or you saw *Ghost?*" Mike demanded. The short man's tone was sharp and his dark eyes suddenly looked intense.

"I saw the damned Wrethe's armored suit and then Ghost's muzzle through the visor," Elena snapped. Her accent had grown noticeably thicker, a sure sign of stress, Simon noted.

"Look, the whole incident with Ghost was stressful, you might have been mistaken..." Ariadne began. Her tone sounded more hopeful than confident, Simon noted.

"No," Anubus growled. "We never found Ghost's body... and I have caught scents of the other Wrethe aboard the ship." He swung his jackal head around, "It seems likely that one of you has betrayed us and nursed our enemy back to health."

"Uh... I blasted Ghost's skull all over the deck," Eric said. "So I think you might just be smelling residue from that." He had a confident smirk on his face and his tone suggested they were worried over nothing.

"These are fresh scents," Anubus growled, "Pheromones, not blood or tissue. Ghost must still live." His statement met with silence on the bridge.

"Right," Mike said. "Pixel, lock down the ship. We'll search the entire vessel, level by level. We lock down the airlocks first and if Ghost is outside, we'll find some way to kill it out there."

Pixel went to the engineering console and started his work without a word. "Eric, I want you and Rastar to organize the search teams. Crowe-- " Mike broke off. "Wait, where the hell is Crowe?"

Simon glanced around, now that he thought of it, he hadn't seen the other man at all. *And he's a sneaky sort too, if Ghost does have some kind of helper in our crew, then I couldn't think of a more likely traitor,* Simon thought darkly, *Illario doesn't have the brains for it.* "Kind of suspicious that he's not here, isn't it?" Simon asked. The others looked at him, "Look, he's already proven to have... questionable ethics. Plus he's got a number of illicit skills. He's a hacker, he's a liar, and we've already seen evidence that he knows how to use that knife of his." During the break out from the station, Crowe had killed at least two Chxor.

"Well, Elena, you and he got friendly not too long ago," Eric said in a snide tone of voice. "Maybe you could shed some light on that."

"Yes..." Elena spoke. She either didn't catch or chose to ignore his insinuation. "I remember, he disappeared right after the fight with Ghost. But why would he work with the Wrethe?"

"Clearly some plot to get my gold," Anubus growled. "You already caught him once when he stole two of the bars. This must be some plot on his part to take what remains."

Despite himself, Simon found he agreed with the Wrethe. They had drawn close enough to human space that the riches might have tempted the other man to betray them. Simon felt certain that the way Rastar had flipped out on the man over the earlier theft would not have improved his opinion of the crew. *Not that I can blame Rastar,* he acknowledged, *I'd probably have lost my temper if I found him trying to place the bars in my gear as well.* Still, he wouldn't have beaten the other man. Turned him over to Mike for punishment, yes, but the beating Rastar had administered hadn't been right under their charter. That sat wrong with Simon, they had rules for a reason.

"Okay, first order of business," Mike said. "Lock down the ship. Since Crowe is involved, lock down all the terminals too, until we know more." He looked over at Rastar and Eric. "You two do manual locks on the airlocks. Mandy and Miranda, you'll secure the bridge with Ariadne and Pixel. Simon, Anubus, Elena, Run, Illario, and I will start the search, Rastar and Eric join us after you've secured the airlocks. Run, be sure you bring your medical equipment."

Simon nodded. The search party and security elements all contained technical and combat elements, which he approved of. Granted, Simon hoped that *he* wouldn't need Run's medical attention. The Chxor's cache of power tools, straps, and staple guns made him more than a little uneasy.

"No," Anubus growled. "If Ghost is on the hull, it is after my Prowler. We need to go out there and kill it before it steals my ship."

Simon had forgotten that the Wrethe had clamped the small vessel on the hull of the *Gebnar.*

"Yeah... with how poorly you docked it, no one is getting it off the hull any time soon," Pixel said. The engineer didn't look up from where he worked on the console. "You managed to lock onto an unarmored section of hull over our port sensors. At least one of your clamps punched through the hull. You couldn't get off with your maneuver thrusters, and you can't safely engage the main drive this close to the ship. The *Red Hunter* is stuck."

Anubus's lips drew back over his teeth in a snarl, "Why didn't you tell me this earlier?"

Pixel looked up after he hit a last button, "Something of an insurance policy, in case *you* betrayed *us*. Besides, we can't do anything about it without a lot of work. And we have bigger priorities just now." His comment met with total silence. Simon quietly upped his estimation of the engineer. *Apparently he's not as unaware of some things as I thought,* Simon realized. A moment later, Pixel gave a smile, then opened up the ship's intercom, "Attention all passengers of the *Gebnar.* We have a possible security situation, the Captain will brief you."

"Okay," Mike said with a nod. "All personnel, move to your quarters and take up defensive positions. We may have an uninvited guest. Crowe, if you're near an intercom switch, please contact us immediately." They waited a long moment in silence. Mike clenched his jaw, and Simon saw the muscles stand out on the short Asian's jaw. Mike switched off the intercom and when he spoke, Simon could hear the anger in his voice, "Now that that is settled, get moving people. Whatever Ghost and Crowe are up to, we need to find out and put a stop to it." Even as he spoke, Rastar opened the storage closet and swept his guns across the entrance. The big alien gave Eric a nod and the two entered the lift. From their drills, Simon knew that the two would secure the rear airlock first, then the port and starboard ones located further forward.

Simon followed the others as they started down the stairs to the next level down from the bridge. The first compartment was one of the sets of crew quarters they shared. Mike activated the automated door while Elena and Simon took up ready positions with pistols. Despite his dislike of the bounty hunter, Simon admired her professionalism. She stood in a balanced position, pistol drawn, finger out of the trigger well, but ready to fire at any threat. Not so much with Mike, who held a Chxor submachine gun casually in one hand, finger on the trigger. *We really need to do more of those training classes,* Simon thought.

The hatch swept open. The oversized crew quarters sat empty, other than some litter and trash from where some of Simon's less tidy companions had eaten their lunch. Once again, the scale of the ship gave Simon a weird feeling of juxtaposition. Even Anubus looked dwarfed by the oversized room as he swept into it. The Ghornath-sized nests that lined the walls were not designed for humans or even the larger Wrethe. The *Gebnar* was a captured Ghornath ship, after all. The large furniture and lockers, like most of the rest of the ship, were designed for the three meter tall, eight-limbed aliens. Only Rastar felt truly at home with the ship.

The Wrethe paused and sniffed the air. "I don't smell Wrethe... but I smell blood. A lot of it."

"Shit," Mike said. He glanced in the room, "Where? I don't see any."

Anubus slowly spun in a circle. Finally he turned and walked back through the hatch. He paused outside the door for the other set of quarters across the corridor. "Here."

Simon trained his pistol on the hatch. The archaic 1911 forty-five felt cool in his hands as he took up a two handed stance. It was pure muscle memory as he readied himself to fire. The world seemed to slow down as Mike moved up next to him and leveled his submachine gun at the hatch. Illario moved to one side of the hatch, a drawn knife in his hand. Mike nodded at Run to trigger the switch to the side of the automatic door

The hatch swept open without a sound.

508

The quarters looked much like the ones they had just searched. They held the same oversized nests and the same clutter of human trash... with one addition.

Crowe lay sprawled across the floor, head thrown back and eyes wide in a crimson pool of blood. Three parallel gashes ran across his torso from his right hip to his left shoulder. Bits of bone shone white against all the blood while his intestines glistened where they had bulged up out of the wound. Scrawled across the bulkhead behind the body in Crowe's blood was the words: *Ghost Lives.*

"Well, I guess that rules out Crowe as a suspect," Simon said.

***

Rastar and Eric joined them a few minutes later. Simon had entered the room and studied the crime scene for a moment. "A lot of blood spatter. Someone was seriously angry at him."

"Someone... *really?*" Eric asked. "Look at those claw marks. Milla here saw Ghost already and now there's Wrethe claw marks on him. Plus I can read the writing on the wall. I think we know who did this."

"Not necessarily," Simon said. He ignored Eric's unintentional pun, even as he made note to use it later. "We know what it looks like... but appearances can be deceiving." He frowned, "Look, didn't you say you killed Ghost?"

Eric nodded.

"Well then, a more likely culprit right off hand, rather than a magically regenerating Wrethe is the one who already hated Crowe for stealing from him," Simon said. "One who already mentioned that he prefers to kill from stealth."

"He does have a point," Anubus growled. "It would be clever of me to somehow frame Ghost for killing him. But I did not. And there is no scent of Wrethe in the compartment. Ghost was not here."

Eric shifted his stance and his rifle lay pointed in the general direction of Anubus, "You would say something like that, if you'd killed him, wouldn't you? And it's not like we can smell

509

pheromones."

"He didn't do it," Simon said. He knelt closer and wished he had a rubber glove. He *really* didn't want any diseases the deceased hacker might have had. He pointed at the wound, "Look at the wound, it's too deep to be his claws. For that matter, I'm pretty sure if he cut that deep he'd have blood all over himself... and I'd imagine it takes him some time to get blood out of his fur."

"That much arterial spray would take me at least an hour to lick off of me," Anubus nodded. "And I'm sure any lesser beings such as yourself would run screaming at the sight of a real hunter fresh from a kill such as this." The Wrethe ran his tongue over his teeth and lips in a fashion that suggested how tasty he considered *that* idea.

Mike turned to Run, "Can you take a look at him, find out what killed him and get us some clues?"

"Normally I perform vivisection on live subjects," Run said. "However, I think a dissection of the corpse and the wounds will provide useful knowledge on internal human workings." He frowned, "It is too bad the corpse is past revival, this would provide greater research potential."

"Uh, yuck," Eric said. He glanced at Mike, "Look, Crowe was a jerk, but are we sure we want to let the little Chxor bastard cut his corpse up?"

Mike shrugged, "We need information. It's not like he'll care." He pointed at the corpse. "Alright, Run, I'll have Ariadne send someone to help you move the body."

"I should search the area first, and we need pictures of the crime scene for any later investigation," Simon said. "Which there *will* be once we get to human space."

"Well, as long as it's not your average Colonial Republic hellhole," Eric said.

"Good thinking, Simon," Mike said. He apparently ignored Eric's comment on the Colonial Republic. Then again, the smaller man had seemed rather ambivalent about the Colonial Republic before. *And he seems to be in favor of privateering, I wonder if he's done a bit of it before... or worse,* Simon thought.

"Best to be as above-board as possible." The smaller man frowned down at the corpse for a long moment. "The rest of you, we need to search the rest of the ship." He backed out and Simon saw him pause, "Illario and Elena, let's go."

The ganger started. He had a look of shock on his face, "Sorry, yes Captain, I'm ready."

"I will stay," Elena said. Her eastern European accented English was even thicker. From her pale face, Simon guessed the blood bothered her more than she liked. "I have some experience in criminal behavior and I've searched crime scenes before." She held up a hand, and Simon saw she had a small recorder in it, "Also, I found this in crew quarters, it will work to record the scene."

Mike seemed torn. "That's half the search party." Still he gave a sharp nod and spoke, "Very well, Simon, you and Elena work this. Let me know if you find anything."

Simon nodded, "Okay, I could use the help." He hadn't worked a lot of murder scenes before, mostly he worked protection or corruption investigations. He didn't trust himself to not miss the essential clue, not if an extra set of eyes might help.

He squatted just outside the sticky pool and looked at the body. "Something hit him, knocked him back, I think." He looked over at the splatter of blood on the wall. "Look, it looks like it sprayed up, a bit. Whoever killed him knocked him down first, so he couldn't fight back."

"Not easy with how big he was," Elena said as she began to record the crime scene. "Almost two meters tall and strong. Someone big, da?" She pointed at the splayed hands, "He must have fought back."

Simon frowned, "Maybe. Or maybe someone tranquilized him somehow."

"Drugs?" Elena dropped her voice. She lowered the recorder and glanced over her shoulder at where Run had begun to take samples from the blood pool. "You think the Chxor was involved?"

Simon shrugged, "I'm not discounting it. I want to get a handle on what happened, and the worst thing to do in any investigation is to decide how it happened early on. Got to stay open for the possibilities."

"You have worked this kind of thing before, da?" Elena asked. She looked uncommonly serious. "I have not much experience in this kind of thing, murder. Larceny and that kind of thing, I've investigated some between bounties, even some cheating cases when work was slow."

"Most murder cases are open and shut," Simon said. "You find the murderer near the victim, usually in shock. Most people can't handle the emotional toll of a murder. The ones that can, they're harder to find." Sociopaths or just people who could kill. Simon had kept up on his professional reading. Modern society ran around ten percent of people who could kill without some kind of emotional repercussions. Some of the frontier worlds ran higher, but not much. "Since we found him like this and in what looks like a frame of either Anubus or Ghost, well, I'm leaning towards someone like that."

"Do you think there is danger to crew?" Elena asked.

"Yes," Simon said. "Anyone who resolves their problems with murder is a threat to the crew. He, she, or it is also a threat to us from the perspective of the law. We're already on shaky ground showing up in a former Ghornath pirate vessel, having stolen it from the Chxor and escaped from a Chxor prison. If we show up and some of our crew has murdered each other, well, I wouldn't be surprised if they threw the lot of us in jail again."

Elena cocked her head. "This makes sense." She stepped away from the body. "Perhaps we should think about... contingencies?"

Simon glanced back at Run, but he saw the little alien had withdrawn to the hallway with his samples. "Contingencies?"

"If it is some of our companions, perhaps even a conspiracy, you and I might become liabilities, da?" Elena said, her voice pitched low. "You, a policeman and me a bounty-hunter, they would know that we would enforce the law."

Simon felt a lump of ice materialize in his stomach. *That is a particularly nasty thought,* he realized, *and one altogether too likely for me to discount.* Even so, he shook his head, "No, I

512

think it's too soon to get worked up over *that.*" He took a deep breath, "But I'll keep your offer in mind."

She gave him a single nod. Then her eyes widened. "Look, there, isn't that Crowe's computer?"

Simon turned. He hadn't noticed the small device in his initial search, which surprised him. The round, black metal cylinder held the scavenged components which Pixel had put together into a computer for Crowe. It had obviously rolled away from Crowe's body and somehow lodged under one of the sleeping nests. "Good eyes," Simon said as he knelt down and retrieved it. "It doesn't look damaged, either. Maybe we can get something off of it."

"Perhaps," Elena frowned. She looked around again, "I think that is all. I have the entire scene recorded, you are done, no?"

"Yes, I am done," Simon said. He stood up and backed out, careful not to step in the blood.

Run looked up at him, "May I recover the corpse for my research?"

Simon grimaced in distaste. He somehow doubted that the little Chxor would stop at merely finding out what had killed the man. On the other hand, they needed to know. *Why does every decision I make here seem loaded with moral implications,* he wondered to himself. Still, he answered the Chxor without hesitation, "Yes, you may take the body."

Elena gave a grimace, "I will assist you." The look she gave Simon suggested she didn't trust the little Chxor as far as she could throw him.

Simon turned away and walked towards the stairs. He toggled the automated doors without much thought as he balanced the computer in one hand. Could they get information from the device, and if they did, would it tell them anything about why persons unknown murdered Crowe? *If Elena is right...* he thought, *can I trust any of my companions to try?*

He almost walked into the aimed weapons of Mandy and Miranda. Simon froze, but the two lowered their weapons after a moment, "You scared the crap out of us," Mandy said. "Weren't you supposed to help Mike search the rest of the ship?"

He glanced behind them and found Pixel and Ariadne also ready for combat. Though with Pixel, the engineer looked rather comical with the pistol in his hand.

"Sorry," Simon said. "Elena and I were searching the crime scene."

"We heard about Crowe..." Ariadne said. She shook her head, "I'll admit, it's awful that Ghost killed him. I guess we know that he wasn't working with the Wrethe then."

Simon shrugged, "The two aren't mutually exclusive."

"We've been working with Anubus and he hasn't killed us," Ariadne said.

"Yet," Pixel muttered. The engineer echoed Simon's own thoughts.

"But I don't think it was Ghost," Simon said. "Anubus says he didn't smell Wrethe pheromones in the compartment. For that matter, someone knocked him down before it cut him up and the wounds are too deep for claws."

"You think one of our passengers?" Mandy asked. "I *told* Mike we can't trust those Nova Roma--"

"Or crew," Simon said calmly. "You and Miranda didn't get along with Crowe, as I remember. One of you could have held him down while the other cut him open."

"He was a selfish pig, but I wouldn't murder him!" Mandy snapped.

Her response seemed truthful enough, Simon figured. It was hard to fake that kind of instant revulsion. Then again, women tended to be better actors than men, Simon knew.

Pixel interrupted, "Hey, is that his computer?"

Simon nodded, "You think you could crack it, find out what information he might have on it?"

"Maybe..." Pixel frowned. "He loaded his own software on it from his implant. I'm not sure what information would be on this one as opposed to the other."

Simon frowned, "I forgot about his implant. I need to tell Run to try and recover that..."

He trailed off at the looks of shock on the others faces.

"What?" Mandy and Miranda both shifted away from him and moved back towards the doors to the bridge.

"He would have to open his head to get it out... and pull it out of his *brain*," Ariadne looked very pale. "You're going to not only let Run play inside Crowe's head, you're going to *tell* him to do it."

Simon thought about it for a moment. "Yeah, it's a little gruesome, I'll admit. But maybe we can get some information off of it. And lets be honest... Run probably had his head opened up already. And if he gets to play with Crowe's brains, maybe he'll be less likely to try to open up *your* head, Ariadne."

She shivered at that. "Promise me, none of you will let *that* happen if I die."

"Of course not," Simon answered instantly. "The little weirdo won't get anywhere near you, alive or dead, with his 'medical' tools." Pixel grunted noncommittally as he plugged in the computer to a console. "I like you with your brains inside your head, thank you."

Ariadne gave him a weak smile, "Thanks, you say the sweetest things."

***

Mike and the others arrived on the bridge a few minutes later. "Ship is secure, no sign of Ghost on-board, so we probably have the damned thing somewhere out on the hull. The armored suit is missing from the armory, probably Crowe's work. But we can figure that out later." He looked around at the others, "In the meantime, we need to figure out what happened to Crowe and how it is related to Ghost."

"What about our other passengers?" Ariadne asked.

"As victims... or accomplices?" Simon responded.

"For now, we release the lock-down," Mike said. "And I'll want to do an interview of everyone aboard, to include all of us."

Eric grew red, "You think one of us–"

"I don't know what to think," Mike said. "But for someone who swears they're a great shot, I'm not sure how you

515

missed a Wrethe's head from point blank!"

"At least I wasn't a psychic's meat puppet at the time, huh?" Eric responded with a snarl.

"We don't solve anything by bickering!" Ariadne said. She looked back and forth between the two, "I think we need to focus on finding out what happened before we move onto accusations, agreed?" Her smile disappeared as she looked at the sullen and angry faces. For a moment, a flicker of something like fire glinted in her eyes. "Agreed?" She asked, her voice sharp.

"Yeah," Eric said and Simon felt a spurt of humor at the surprise and fear on the mercenary's face. *Serves him right for pushing her so far,* Simon thought wryly, *maybe he'll learn a lesson.*

"Of course," Mike answered a moment later. Simon saw the elected Captain rub a hand over his close cropped black hair. Perhaps it was the light, but it almost looked like the smaller man had added some gray hairs to his head. He looked over at Simon and met his gaze, "Okay, we need information."

"I'm working on Crowe's computer," Pixel said. He still hadn't looked up from the console, "Simon found it. It has lots of interesting code. Crowe was much better at this than me."

"I'm sure he'd love to hear it," Simon said with a snort.

"Humility was his middle name," Eric said with a smirk. *Like he's one to talk,* Simon thought. The big mercenary looked around at the others and passed a hand through his blonde hair, "Okay, so... what next?" He looked far too cheerful for Simon's peace of mind.

"I am disturbed by the likelihood that we have a murderer and possibly a traitor among our group," Rastar said. The big Ghornath had an odd shade of orange to his hide. "Ghost was bad enough, but that someone could have helped it... and that someone murdered Crowe..." The alien paused, and his hide went white. "Could they be the same person? Perhaps Crowe found out about it and was killed for it?"

"Or someone found out Crowe helped Ghost," Mike said, "And they killed him for it."

"Or the two things are unrelated," Simon said. His head hurt and the constant accusations made it worse. "Look, I say leave this to the professionals. Pixel works the computer, Run works the body, and Elena and I do some interrogations."

"What about the murderous Wrethe on the hull?" Eric asked. He hefted his rifle and gave a smirk, "Maybe someone should do something about that."

"No." Mike said. "We tackle our problems one at a time, and Ghost can't get inside or kill any of us--"

"Any more of us," Ariadne said.

"-- if we're inside and it is outside," Mike finished. "So stay inside and maintain security of the airlocks. You emplaced the telltales in case someone tries to open a hatch, right?"

"Yes," Rastar said, but Simon caught a strange glance between him, Pixel, and Eric. *Why do I have the feeling,* Simon thought, *that these telltales involved Pixel's help too?*

"Good," Mike frowned. "I feel like I'm forgetting something..."

The lift door opened. Mandy gave a shriek.

Simon drew his pistol and saw that at least half of the others in the compartment had done the same. Most of the weapons were aimed at the open lift doors.

A moment later, Run stepped out. Red blood had splattered across his face and tunic. His arms were red all the way up to his shoulders. His shoes, as well, seemed sodden with blood and he had left bloody footsteps in the elevator. His shoes made squish sounds as he walked forward. He had a completely bland expression on his face. "I have completed the initial autopsy," Run said. "I have determined that Crowe was terminated by a large bladed knife, approximately twenty centimeters in length. In addition, the fatal attack was the central wound. The others were done afterward to give the appearance of Wrethe claws."

"Uh..." Mike gulped as he stared at the Chxor. "You could have cleaned up and *then* told us."

"I find that making a report while the material is still fresh facilitates greater insights," Run answered. "I also projected that you would wish to know this information as soon as possible."

"The answer is both yes..." Simon said, "...and also a resounding no." He closed his eyes, "Next time, Run, please take the time to clean yourself before you tell us the results. If nothing else, it is more sanitary."

"True, I would not wish to contaminate my control population," Run nodded. "Very well, I will clean myself." He turned around and squished back into the lift. "I will decontaminate the area after I decontaminate myself."

"The little Chxor scares me," Miranda said.

"Yeah..." Pixel still hadn't looked up from his console. "Oh, hey, I think I'm making progress here." The engineer appeared oblivious to the stares of disbelief of the others, Simon noticed.

"So, we know I didn't kill Crowe," Anubus growled.

"Unless you figured a clumsy frame would exonerate you," Simon said. "So you used a knife and made it obvious that it wasn't you, to throw us off. And you could have worn your ship's suit and hosed it off afterward."

"That is..." Anubus cocked his head, "Remarkably astute. Actually, I wish I had considered that. I like how you think, human. You are more dangerous than I thought you." *Great,* Simon thought, *I just made myself more of a threat to our paranoid homicidal alien.*

"Come on, guys," Rastar said. "We know Annie didn't do it, he wouldn't just murder someone in cold blood like that." Rastar, like Pixel, seemed immune to stares of disbelief. "He just does the whole dangerous personality thing to keep people at arms length." The Ghornath slapped Anubus on the back.

"Touch me again and I will rip your throat out with my teeth," Anubus growled.

Simon saw Mike bury his head in his hands. *Yeah, he's definitely getting some gray hairs up top,* Simon thought, *thank god no one tried to give* me *that job.* Simon looked around at the others. Part of him wondered if this murder was some part of a conspiracy as Elena had suggested. Most of him wondered if the murder was the thing that would finally shatter their little alliance.

If that happened, he just hoped it didn't turn into a complete bloodbath.

***

"Well, that's interesting," Pixel said.

"What is interesting?" Simon asked. He walked up to stare over the engineer's shoulder. Lines of code filled the displays. "It looks like gibberish."

"It is gibberish," Pixel said. "Crowe had an extremely complicated encryption algorithm to protect his data. Worse, apparently if you attempted to hack it and failed, his software triggered a virus that would scramble everything. Then the virus would have the computer overwrite all of its data storage a couple thousand times with random code."

Simon frowned, "So, you can't crack it?"

"Oh, maybe... if I hadn't already triggered the virus," Pixel said.

Simon sighed, "Damn, that could have been the break we needed. So I take it there's no way to get the information, then?"

Pixel pulled the connection from the console to Crowe's computer. The tall engineer looked at Simon with surprise, "Oh, I didn't say that." He slid the casing off of the computer and exposed the guts of the machine. Pixel set it down on top of the console and pulled out his multi-tool. The engineer carefully pried a small cooling fan out of the way and then pulled a tiny data crystal out of a hidden slot underneath it. "We've got this."

Simon quirked an eyebrow, "What exactly is this?"

Pixel gave him a half smile, "Yeah... so Crowe had me build this computer for him, right?"

Simon nodded. "So he could reprogram some of the systems on the ship."

"Well, I didn't exactly trust him," Pixel said. "But I knew he could program better than me, so I couldn't expect to ever hack his equipment." He pushed the data crystal into a slot on the console. A moment later, a new folder came up. Pixel browsed through it for a moment. "So, when I made the computer, I added this, a backup drive that was hardwired in so that it copied all of his files. Even stuff he deleted. It has limited storage, but I made it so that when the storage got full, it would cause an internal switch to kill power to the unit. Crowe would probably come to me to fix it."

Simon shook his head, "That's…"

"Smart?" Pixel asked

"Devious," Simon said. *Remind me* again *not to underestimate Pixel,* he thought. He also made a mental note to check anything the engineer did for him, just in case. Now that he thought of it, Pixel's services included life support and the fusion reactor. That thought, in turn, reminded Simon of the two Chxor ships that Pixel had destroyed; one through the reactor overload and the other he'd programmed to ram into the Chxor orbital ring. *So the engineer might be one of the more destructive people aboard,* Simon thought. That led to a thought that made him go cold: what if the laid back and friendly engineer were some sort of high-tech serial killer?

Pixel sorted through the files, "Okay, let me read through these and I'll see if anything applies."

"I could do that, you know," Simon said.

"You could," Pixel said. "Then again, it would take you hours. You could use that time doing something useful, like, oh, I don't know, maybe finding the psycho killer?"

"Right," Simon grunted. He really needed someone else to help out, someone he could trust. Mike had taken Elena for his interviews with the passengers.

On cue, Pixel spoke up, "Oh, did you ever talk with Santangel? He said he did some police training, maybe he could help."

"Assuming he's not our deranged killer, of course," Simon said. Even so, he kicked himself for forgetting about the Saragossan. The other man had been useful a few times to keep the other escaped prisoners in line. He seemed smart, highly educated and Simon could use someone with police or investigative training.

Especially since Mike had absconded with Elena. As Captain, Simon couldn't really complain, and he would agree that the bounty hunter would be a net asset in interviewing the passengers. Even so, that left Simon by himself to search down other clues.

"Alright, let me know as soon as you have something," Simon said.

Pixel looked up, his blue eyes innocent, "Of course."

***

Simon found Michael Santangel in the cargo bay they had converted into quarters. The olive-skinned man sat at a table by himself with a small notebook. His dark hair was meticulously groomed and his dark green eyes were focused entirely on his work. He didn't look up when Simon cleared his throat. "Yes?"

"You probably heard," Simon said. "There's been a murder. The Captain appointed me to investigate it." It wasn't, technically, a lie, but it did take liberties with what Mike had told him to do. Still, without some authority, he couldn't expect the crew to listen to him.

"Yes, of course. You have a background in law, this is fortunate, no? I assume you have come to me, my friend, to provide assistance?" His accent, whether an affection or not, made him seem cultured and educated. The way he said it all, without the need to look up from his notes, made it clear that he considered his assistance a favor… one he would expect to be repaid.

Simon could deal with that. He recognized the type: Santangel was well-born, and probably had expected to become a police chief or senior investigator within five years due to his family connections. He had the skills, Simon would guess, but he also had the connections. He clearly saw this as his opportunity to make new connections. The other man probably had aspired to politics eventually. Instead his planet was conquered by the Chxor and he was stuck aboard a vessel full of fugitives.

"Yes, I need your assistance," Simon said. "Crowe was

521

killed with a knife of some kind, but the cuts were made to look like a Wrethe's claws..." He filled him in on the details. The other man jotted down some additional notes as he spoke.

"I have made observations on who among the crew and passengers that Crowe spoke with and was known to deal with," Micheal said. "It is a long list. Although Crowe might have thought himself quite adept at interaction, he was also disliked by most aboard because of his arrogance and untrustworthiness." He turned the notebook so Simon could look at the list. As he had expected, it included most of the people aboard. Simon noticed stars next to several names, to include his own.

"And these marks?" Simon asked.

"They are to note people that Crowe either angered or that viewed him with suspicion," Santangel smiled. "I've also annotated who I know had business arrangements or agreements with him, to include the details, when I knew them. I've also asked around among the other passengers down here to fill in additional details."

"You're very thorough," Simon said with approval.

"I don't always have the opportunity to make a good impression," Michael said. "But when I do, I choose to be very thorough."

***

"Crowe has been a very busy little beaver," Simon said.

"Yes, this is something I noticed, as well," Michael Santangel said. His accent seemed to add extra weight to everything he said. Simon found it almost hypnotic how the Saragossan seemed to choose every word with thought beforehand. "It seems to me that he had a number of schemes going on at once, with a large number of the passengers and some of the crew."

That seemed something of an understatement. Simon had seen the other man interact with a number of personnel on the station, before they made their escape. Since then, he had noticed, but not really put any thought into Crowe's many interactions. It seemed like he should have paid more attention.

"His dealings seemed mostly restricted, so that he didn't associate with some people while he worked with others," Simon looked again at the notes from Michael. He had added times and dates and people to it, so that the mess of notes was nearly incomprehensible. They had then moved it to a console, where they'd projected a timeline and interaction chain into a three dimensional map. It looked like the diagrams that he'd seen from the Confederation Security Bureau when they fought organized crime or when the Centauri Military fought Separatist insurgents. "So, from what I can tell, he interacted with four distinct groups. First, there was our crew: Mike, Ariadne, Eric, Pixel, Elena, Rastar, Anubus, Run, Mandy, Miranda and myself. Most of that looks like it was mission related."

"Some, but not all," Michael said. "He introduced Elena to Mike. He avoided Ariadne whenever possible after he learned of her telepathic abilities. He also did not work with Mandy or Miranda whenever possible." Santangel's disagreement seemed strongly presented, but Simon wasn't sure if that was disagreement or some effort to swing the conversation in some different path.

"That's true," Simon nodded. "But I think Elena used him as an entry point, more than anything else." He chose to ignore the overly forceful attitude and focus on the words.

"Which doesn't explain some of their later encounters, I believe," Michael said. "I think we really need to look into why they spent so much time together later." Simon heard something ugly in the man's tone, almost as if he had some personal grudge.

Simon shrugged, "Well, no, but some of it was work related and she seems to fall into the next group that he associated with," Simon took a deep breath and pulled up the next network. *Best to change the subject,* he thought. "This seems to be the people that he tried to either suborn or manipulate because he saw them as threats." It was a long list, and a dangerous one. High on the list were Rastar and Anubus. Crowe had tried to set the two at odds with one another, either to eliminate them both... or just for kicks.

Also on the list was himself, Eric, Elena, the Nova Roma

Ambassador, and Michael Santangel. Michael had pointed out several encounters where Crowe had seemingly tried to instigate violence between him and the Nova Romans aboard the vessel. The list also included Illario, who, Michael had confirmed, had been seen with the man in deep conversation a number of times.

"Then there's the third group, the people he had business dealings with: Pixel, Bastien Jascinthe, Mike, Illario Urbano, and the Ambassador." Simon highlighted those names. "These people either worked with him on some project or traded services or help with him." Simon had added Pixel to the list because of the computer he'd built, though Michael had discounted the importance of that. Michael had pointed out that Bastien had gone to Crowe for certain luxury items, which apparently Crowe had obtained both on the station and aboard the ship, to include perfumed soap, candy, and computer software. It looked as if Illario had obtained goods as well and his appearance on two lists made him stand out to Simon.

"Yes, this group I find troublesome," Michael said softly. "They are people who Crowe might have some leverage over, either for goods or for his knowledge of their needs or addictions. It is not a great leap in logic to assume he might have sought to pressure them... and one of them might have snapped in return."

Simon frowned, "Doesn't fit the profile," he said. "None of them would brutally murder someone over a trade for some simple luxury items." *Well,* he privately admitted, *Illario might.* "Which leaves the last group: the people we saw him with that doesn't have an explanation."

Michael shook his head, "These are probably linked in with the last group, only single dealings rather than a common occurrence..."

"No," Simon interrupted, "That might make sense for one or two, but we've got Crowe meeting with several of these people on multiple occasions. The lawyer from Tau Ceti, Wendel Henrike, for instance. Seven times. The guy is a slime-ball, what did Crowe want with him? The reporter, Valeria Zita, three times. She's been awful quiet for a war correspondent, don't you think? Then there's Ilario Urbano again, big surprise there, they met six times in the past week alone, far more than necessary for some minor business in Crowe's black market goods. Last, the Nova Roma mercenary, Donato Duilio, he met twice the day before he was killed." Simon had little dealings with any of them. The reporter he had avoided for much the same reason as he had avoided the lawyer. He didn't trust members of either profession. They both told stories for a living, which was a polite way to say they lied for money.

"Perhaps," Michael gave a shrug, "But, as you said, Crowe was involved in a number of schemes, these could be efforts to confuse anyone who watched his movements?"

"No," Simon shook his head, "Because that suggests that he thought his movements were being watched... but if he thought that, why meet someone alone in the crew quarters? What does Ghost have to do with all of this?" Simon threw up his hands, "Where the hell is Ghost, anyway?"

"Not inside the ship," Mike answered from the doorway. "But Ghost's suit is missing from the armory. I'd guess our murderer used it to give us a good scare. Or Ghost is out on the hull, in which case we're going to have to kill it somehow."

Simon looked up, "Finished your search?"

"Security sweep, yeah," Mike moved forward to stare at the network maps. "Huh, busy at work, eh?" His eyes flicked from image to image. The short Asian seemed to have little issue in following the diagrams.

"Yes," Simon rubbed at his temples, "When it comes down to it, it's easier to list who couldn't have killed Crowe than who might have done so." He sighed, "Really, I've only got three of the passengers who I can honestly say had nothing to do with this."

"Well," Mike said, "Brief Ariadne and I. We're going to start interviewing the crew and passengers. This will help a lot, especially if they have something they can't explain. We'll start with the crew, so you and Michael here can brief me up, and then we start with you two."

"Us?" Michael asked, "That hardly seems necessary..."

Simon found himself in agreement. For one thing, Michael had provided extensive help. For another, Mike's words almost suggested that *Simon* was as much a suspect.

"Necessary or not," Mike said, "I'm doing it. We need to cover all the bases. Hell, Simon was on the bridge with me when it happened, but I'm still going to interview him."

Simon pursed his lips, but he didn't argue. Logically, Simon knew that they had to give the appearance of impartiality. It rubbed him raw that anyone might even think he would have done the crime. Even so he gave a firm nod, "Absolutely, we have to explore every option."

***

Simon sat on the couch and stared at the glass wall of the aquarium. The crew that had finished with the interviews had moved into the lounge at Mike's suggestion. Eric had begun his work on dinner. For all of the other man's faults, Simon had to admit that he had real talent when it came to food. The Hungarian Goulash he made was quite simply the tastiest thing Simon had ever eaten. His mouth watered at the memory. *It would be a shame if he used one of the kitchen knives to murder Crowe*, Simon thought.

Ariadne sat down next to him. She looked tired, Simon noticed. He wondered if she used her psychic powers during the interviews. He wasn't sure how he felt about that. *Invasion of privacy versus making sure justice is done,* he thought. It wasn't a moral argument he wanted to have with himself at the moment. If she saw any sign of his internal moral dilemma, she didn't show it when she spoke, "So, I was thinking."

"Oh?" Simon asked. "I thought you were interviewing passengers?"

"I'm on break, Mike wanted to take a break before the passengers," She said. She shook her head tiredly, "Anyway, back on the first ship we hijacked, Crowe showed me an object." Ariadne frowned, "It was what triggered my... vision and caused me to pass out."

"Yeah, I remember you said something about that, but

526

Crowe wasn't there," Simon said.

"What if he was or if the vision was accurate? What if he had something... something alien... something valuable? Might he have been killed over it?"

Simon looked over at her. Ariadne brushed some of her blonde hair out of her blue eyes as she stared at him. "That's not a bad suggestion, actually. And he already showed he had an ability to hide stuff. What did it look like?"

"It was angular, like a... rectangle, kind of squashed," Ariadne frowned. "Black and... green, I think, and glossy," She frowned, "There might have been words or glyphs on it, I'm not sure."

"Okay, that's something that would stand out. Small, angular, black and green, alien-looking," Simon jotted down some notes.

Elena spoke up from behind them, "What is this?"

"A possible lead, Ariadne was wondering if Crowe was killed over an object he carried."

"As if anyone needed a reason," Elena said. She shook her head, "Mike and I opened his locker, after everyone came to the lounge, there was no object like that there. We did find a stash of valuables, to include the identity cards of the dead crew of the derelict ship. I think he planned to hack them to create false papers for himself."

"That's... pretty low," Simon said. "Smart, but nasty. I almost think someone did us a favor when they killed him." He sighed a bit, "Nothing else, no sign that he might have had something particularly valuable?"

Elena frowned, "Now that you mention it, we did find a case, small, about the size of a cigarette box. Lined with foam. It was empty, though."

Simon and Ariadne exchanged a glance, "That is very interesting." Simon stood, "Where did Mike go?"

"He was checking with Eric about something, I think he mentioned the passengers," Elena said. The bounty hunter looked confused. "Why?"

"Well, I think we need to search the ship... again," Simon

said. He didn't want to think how hard it would be to find the small object in question. Particularly if someone hid it ahead of time.

"You have new theory?" Elena asked.

"I think Ghost and our late friend Crowe might be unrelated, after all." Simon said. "I think that Crowe had something valuable, and someone else figured out. Something small, easy to hide, easy to take. Either they killed Crowe to take it or Crowe discovered it was missing so they killed him to hide the theft. Everyone heard that Crowe had stolen from Anubus, so they made it look like Wrethe claws did the deed."

"So we find this item and we find the murderer?"

Simon nodded. "Yeah..." He frowned. Something bothered him. Alien technology, possibly alien artifacts, valuable and hidden. *What am I missing...* Mike's arrival interrupted that chain of thought. The short man walked up to the group. His face seemed tight with either tension or anger, though Simon couldn't guess which, though he did see lines of worry around the other man's eyes.

"Ariadne, we're going to start with the passengers," Mike said.

"Captain, we had a thought," Simon began. "Crowe might have been killed for something he was carrying. It's something to add to the questions you ask. Ariadne can describe it."

Mike just nodded. He rubbed at his eyes. "Something needs to break our way on this, and soon. We've got a back-from-the-dead Wrethe out on the hull, a murderer on board, and it looks more and more like Crowe was just using us for his benefit." He paused, "Oh, and we're on the run from the entire Chxor Empire. Did I miss anything else?"

Run spoke up, "The vessel has damage and is unable to fight, our crew possesses limited training in their duties, no discipline, and are highly inefficient with much energy wasted in emotion, and I think the Wrethe plans to kill you and take your place."

"Right, thanks Run," Mike said, his voice even more

tired. *Yep, he's definitely got some more gray hairs,* Simon thought, *they couldn't* pay *me to take his job.*

***

Simon paced the lounge in thought. Passengers had begun to trickle in as they were cleared by Mike. He knew that Mike had Elena, Mandy, and Miranda move the passengers to the bridge to be interviewed and then to the lounge afterward. He wondered if the Captain had thought to put them in some kind of holding area before he interviewed them as well. *That would help tremendously,* he thought, *if nothing else, they can watch one another and prevent further criminal activities.*

That thought, in turn led him to the nagging idea that hovered just out of reach. Something about the alien item bothered him. He stared at the empty buffet table for a long moment and then things clicked. "How did I miss *that*... Bastien Jascinthe, the xenoarcheologist! If you've got something like that, you're going to try to find out what it does, right? And we've got Bastien, a self-proclaimed expert on it right here aboard ship!"

"What?" Santangel asked. Behind him, Simon saw Elena herd a few more of the passengers into the lounge. She gave Simon a nod.

"Hold down the fort, I've got to run up to the bridge," Simon said

Michael Santangel frowned, "What did you say about this Jascinthe fellow?"

"I'll tell you later, but this might seriously help," Simon said. He rushed out of the lounge and and almost ran into Eric as the other man came down the corridor bearing a tray of food. Eric gave him a narrow-eyed look, almost as if he suspected Simon were off to a fight without him.

Simon just gave him a nod and continued past. He hurried up to the bridge, and opened the door into a shouting match.

The Nova Roma Ambassador and her two Marines occupied the rear of the bridge. The tall, dark haired woman was

529

red in the face, and her diatribe continued unabated from Simon's appearance. "...insist that you treat me with the dignity and respect that my rank and position commands!"

Ariadne stood between her and the door, an angry look on her face. Mike stood near the door itself, one hand on his forehead. From his pinched expression, he clearly had a headache. From the high pitched voice of Ambassador Alara Vibius, Simon could understand why.

"Hey Mike," Simon said.

"What now?" Mike snarled.

"I was going to say that we should interview Bastien Jascinthe, he might have spoken with Crowe," Simon said. "But something suggests we have other problems."

"Someone, and I'll not go into who, just now, has insisted that my 'imprudent' and 'lustful' handling of her personage has offended not only her, but the nation of which she represents," Mike snapped. "And she refuses to be 'interrogated.' So I'll get to the historian when I get to him."

"He's a xenoarcheologist," Pixel corrected helpfully. The engineer still stood at the console, sorting files. He didn't look up from his notes, "He studies alien artifacts."

"Whatever." Mike grunted. "When I get to him, I'll ask him."

"How about I go get him?"

***

Simon hurried through the passages until he almost bowled over Mandy and Miranda. "Bastien Jascinthe," he said.

"What?" Mandy asked.

"The xenoarcheologist, from... Loire, maybe? One of the french colonies. He may know something about the object that Crowe had... that Crowe was killed over," Simon said. "Mike wants to interview him next."

"Oh, right, *that* one," Mandy grimaced. "The old guy who doesn't keep his hands to himself and thinks gray hair and his lip ferret makes him look distinguished rather than like a molester."

Simon stared at her in shock for a moment. Then again, her description of the man seemed rather apt. "Yeah, that one."

"He's claimed one of the empty storage lockers, forward," Miranda said. "Said he wanted the privacy. The others didn't really mind a bit more space in the cargo hold and I think Mike just didn't care too much, since he hasn't made much of a stink."

"He does stink," Mandy said with a snarl, "And he's slimy, with his superior tone and his grasping hands...." She paused, "Hey, if he knows something about Crowe, maybe he helped kill him? That would be great." She cracked her knuckles.

Simon got the feeling that she was more interested in retribution and the chance to beat the other man down than any real desire for justice. Still, she might be useful to intimidate the other man into telling them what he knew. "Okay, lead the way."

They led him forward and just as they passed the cargo bay where the other passengers lived, they came across Elena. "What are you doing here?" She asked.

"Retrieving Bastien," Miranda said.

"Ah, I was just looking for him, Mike said he wanted to interview him next," She answered. She quirked an eyebrow at the group, "Three to retrieve an elderly professor?"

"He might know something about why Crowe was murdered," Mandy volunteered. "Or he might be involved, in which case I'm going to work out some of my latent anger issues on him."

Elena snorted, "He might deserve that, anyway. He should learn to... ah, what is the term..."

"Keep his hands to himself?" Miranda asked.

"No... think before he speaks," Elena said. "He propositioned me, in his words, because he thought he knew another use for the term for 'head hunter.' Perhaps you need help?"

***

Simon paused outside the hatch to the supply closet which Bastien had claimed as his quarters. He frowned though, to see the hatch open. "Bastien Jascinthe?" He asked.

"Come out here you prick, we have some questions for you," Mandy shouted.

Simon sighed, "Less confrontational please." He glanced in the hatch. The old man sat with his back to the hatch at a makeshift table, made up of several empty boxes with a metal plate over the top. Papers, many covered in scribbles, lay scattered across the desktop. "Look, Bastien, we just have a couple questions for you." Simon's frown grew at the lack of response. The old man sat in a relaxed fashion, one arm propped on the back of his chair, the other lay atop a stack of papers. *Perhaps he's fallen asleep,* Simon thought.

He walked up and put his hand on the other man's shoulder, "Bastien?"

The old man's head lolled back, his eyes wide and an expression of shock frozen on his face. A broad slash crossed his throat, and his front was covered in blood. Simon jumped back with a curse.

"Huh," Mandy said, "I guess someone else didn't like him."

"Or someone else thought he should watch what he said," Elena said. She stepped into the compartment, and then came around the corpse's other side. She looked down at the desk, "This is odd."

Simon shook his head, "This is more than odd, this is damned weird." He looked over at Mandy and Miranda, "Find a console, let Mike know what happened... and I guess we better call Run down here as well." He looked back down at the desk and the scattered papers. One paper caught his eyes though. At the top and bottom were a set of symbols of some kind, sketched by hand. At the center was a sketch of a flattened rectangular box, with more symbols drawn on the surface. He picked it up, "Well, I think this settles whether or not Ariadne imagined it."

Elena looked at some of the other papers, "This one here looks like a map and this one has coordinates. There's a lot of other notes here, though some of it looks incomplete."

Simon looked at the scattered papers, some spattered with

droplets of blood. "A lot of it looks like gibberish to me, but I don't know anything about this stuff." He sighed. "This case just keeps getting worse."

"Worse... or more complicated?" Elena asked. "If this were part of a conspiracy... perhaps they are tying off loose ends, nyet?"

Miranda came back before Simon could think up a response. She spoke from the corridor, her voice subdued. "Mike says he's on his way, with Rastar and Anubus. Once they get here, he wants all the passengers moved from the cargo bay to the lounge, for now."

Simon nodded. Still, it seemed like too little, too late. The look on Elena's face suggested she saw it as further proof that someone had orchestrated the murder, most likely with the help of the Captain. *And a good part of me is starting to agree with her,* Simon thought grimly.

***

With nothing much else to do, Simon stared at the fish tank and thought. The cool blue water seemed to settle him in a way that he couldn't describe. The search for the Arcavian Fighting Eel kept his eyes occupied while his brain wandered. Unlike the others, he'd noticed Mike's uncertainty when near the tank and he wondered, absently, where the other man's fear of water came from. That thought, in turn, led to the question of what secrets the others hid.

Not for the first time, Simon wondered if some other members of their crew might have the same purple insides as the Chxor Admiral. He shivered a bit at the thought, some strange alien creature that wore the outside of a person like anyone might wear clothes. He self-consciously adjusted the fit of his suit. He knew that most of the crew had avoided talking about it, partly out of fear, partly because it just seemed too bizarre. *Our murderer could be one of them... which means we might never even guess at the motive,* he thought.

"We're going about this all wrong," Michael Santangel said, his voice low.

"Oh?" Simon asked.

"The Captain has questioned people and he plans to look for this tiny object hidden aboard the ship… yes?" Michael said. "So, even if we find the object, we have no way to link it to the murderer. Perhaps, one of our searchers might well be the murderer so he'll 'miss' it. We need to look at who could *use* this item, whatever it is."

"Valuable," Simon grunted. "We can guess at that. Also…" He paused in thought, "You know, you're right. When I first started out with the CSB, I was partnered to a customs investigation involving the smuggling of xenoartifacts. When we finally wrapped up the case, it wasn't common scum, it was major corporations that were involved and the people we took down were just the middle men. Your average criminal doesn't really have access to the money or equipment to make this stuff work."

"Resources like that require money and power," Michael nodded. "So we're looking for someone with connections to money and power… and someone who can have not just one, but two men killed."

Simon felt his heart sink… because when phrased like that, the suspect pool dropped drastically. As in, only one person worth consideration. "The Nova Roma Ambassador?"

"She has two Marines to do her work for her, she has ties to their government, and her nation has a history of seizing alien tech that they feel might help them, even if it means invasion of other nations," Michael snarled. "Or for that matter, invading *allied* nations to meet their political and strategic goals."

"Are you talking about Saragossa or this case," Simon said, cautiously. While the other man had made a valid point, and one that might help them to solve the investigation, he wondered if Santangel was… *compromised* when it came to the Nova Romans.

"Does it matter?" Santangel asked, and his accent grew more pronounced as he grew angry. "You see them as two separate incidents, I see both as an extension of their foreign policy and their expansionist and imperialist methods."

Simon raised one hand, "Hold on… now let us take a pause here, we don't know that she was behind it."

"*Yet*," Michael snarled.

"Before we start flinging accusations about, how would we go about proving it?" Simon said. He hoped to push the other man away from his anger by forcing him to think.

Michael took a breath. He frowned, but it was a look of concentration rather than anger. "That's the hard part, I'm not sure we could. The three of them can alibi one another… and for that matter, all anyone sees most of the time is that one guard is outside her quarters. We can't know if she's in there without access."

"There's a way to check, though," Simon's eyes narrowed.

"Oh?"

"Look, if she or one of her Marines killed Crowe, they had time to get cleaned up… but they couldn't have done that in one of the crew quarters restrooms, right?"

"You are correct, my friend," Michael Santangel nodded. "They would have risked discovery, and not being crew, they could not lock the quarters, correct?"

"Right. But they couldn't do it in the lounge bathroom, either," Simon said. "Because there's too many people coming in and out."

"…again, you are correct."

"But, and you don't know this because you weren't provisionally part of the crew yet, the Ambassador requested the passenger quarters for herself… and she put up enough stink that Mike agreed. The passenger quarters has its own bathroom."

"I think they are called heads, aboard ship, my friend" Michael said with a frown.

"Whatever… anyway, if she has her own, then they might have cleaned themselves up… but how likely, do you think, is it that they cleaned up that area?"

Michael Santangel snorted, "Her, not likely. The Marines are a tidy people, but they might not have had time to do so."

"Especially if they needed to arrange for a fake Wrethe

sighting on the bridge to throw us off the trail," Simon said. Honestly, he still didn't understand why anyone had gone through that effort. While it had some ingenuity in that they looked for Ghost, it hadn't kept the crew fooled for very long. Simon was hoping that Mike's search for where the murderer had hidden the Wrethe vac-suit would bear fruit.

"So... we search their bathroom for blood?"

"And question the Ambassador as to her whereabouts during Crowe's murder," Simon nodded. "I'll get Ariadne down there for that."

"You trust this woman?" Michael asked.

Simon nodded, "She's the one person I think we can trust."

***

Both Marines stood outside the passenger quarters hatch. Simon took a moment to study them as he, Ariadne, and Michael Santangel walked up. They both wore their uniforms, stained, torn and bloodied as they were. Neither man had exchanged them for the salvaged clothing. That spoke of dedication and loyalty.

Would that loyalty lead them to murder? Simon wondered. For the Centauri military, he would have given that a qualified yes, dependent upon the bribery or threats involved. He had no real first-hand knowledge of the Nova Romans, nothing beyond reputation.

"We need to speak to the Ambassador," Simon said as he and the others stopped in front of the two Marines.

They glanced at one another. The older one, Sergeant Carmine Santander, finally spoke, "That's... not possible right now." He was stocky, with salt and pepper hair and a lined face.

"Why not?" Ariadne asked.

"She's... occupied," the first man said. Both had looks of total discomfort on their faces.

Simon saw a look of anger flash over Ariadne's face. Clearly she'd had enough of the Ambassador's behavior. "Well, be better get unoccupied. Go and get her, *now*."

The younger man flushed, "We *can't*."

Simon stepped forward, "Listen, we are investigating the murder of a member of our crew. If you don't get her, she'll be guilty of obstruction in a murder investigation. Do you know what that means?"

"We do," Sergeant Santander said, his voice tight. "And I can confirm that the Ambassador and ourselves have nothing to do with the murder of Crowe."

"Excuse me if I don't take a Nova Roman at his word," Michael Santangel snapped.

"And excuse me if I don't act surprised that an aristocratic prick from Saragossa has accused us based on his own bitterness and anger," Sergeant Santander said, his voice cold.

"You think that you will get away with this, as you did your other crimes, I know that her father was the Admiral who led the attack on Saragossa!" Michael's voice had raised to a shout. Simon opened his mouth to try to interrupt, but before he could, the door snapped open.

Simon's jaw dropped as Eric Striker stood in the doorway. The man wore only a towel. "Hey, guys, what's all the noise about?" His tall, lean body was covered in a sheen of sweat and an aroma of musk filled the hallway almost immediately.

Ariadne spoke, "Eric? What are you doing here? We came to question the Ambassador…" Her voice trailed off as she finally made the connection between his lack of clothing and the location. Simon saw a flush climb up her face as she realized exactly what had kept the Ambassador so occupied. When she finally spoke, her voice was a mix of embarrassment and surprise, "*Seriously?!?* You're screwing the Nova Roman *Ambassador?*"

Eric gave a cocky grin, "Well… a gentleman doesn't kiss and tell, right?" He winked and held up his hand for a high-five from Simon… who just stared at him awkwardly. Unfortunately, the towel started to slip from his waist, but fortunately Eric managed to catch it.

Simon tried not to think through the implications. He switched his gaze from Eric to what he could see of the passenger quarters. The front room was a small dining room, as he remembered. Both couches had folded blankets on them, evidently the Marines slept there. The door to the bedroom was wide open, as well and Simon averted his eyes as he saw a flash of feminine flesh in motion there.

He glanced over at Michael, who had flushed a deeper shade of crimson than Ariadne. He looked as if he couldn't breathe and Simon hoped the man wouldn't suffer an aneurism. "Look," Simon finally said, "We think the Nova Roman Ambassador and her Marine escort were involved in the murder of Crowe. We need to search her quarters and Ariadne has some questions for her."

Erik snorted. "That's pointless and trust me, I know what I'm talking about. Sergeant Santander and Private Mui almost never leave her side and besides, I know exactly where she was when Crowe bit it," he winked again at Simon, "If you know what I mean."

Simon put a hand over his eyes. He suddenly had a headache. "You realize that it implicates you if we find any sign that she *was* involved, right? For that matter, she might have engineered it so that *you* are her alibi."

"But she wasn't involved," Erik said with a smile. "I bet you're here to search the head for bloodstains and all that, right?" He didn't wait for them to speak before he went on. "Well, that's attached to the sleeping quarters, I'd have seen either of these folks come back through if they needed to clean up after that. Unless they stood out in the hallway dripping blood and drawing attention to themselves until I went up to the bridge."

Simon gritted his teeth, but he didn't have an answer.

"Erik, how could you sleep with that detestable woman?" Ariadne asked.

"Well, she's good looking and she really has this thing about my scars…" Erik smirked. "And man is she *good* in the sack." His voice held such smugness that Simon once again lowered his expectations of the man.

"You can leave now," Ambassador Vibius said, her voice carried a level of disdain and arrogance that told Simon just what she thought of all of them.

Simon glanced over at Michael, who had a mixed look of chagrin and confusion. "Thank you for your time, Ambassador," Simon said dryly.

Erik turned around, "Hey, I need to get my clothing–"

The hatch closed in his face.

The two Marines, Simon noted, had very stoic expressions, almost as if they'd seen worse. Simon was certain that he didn't want to know.

"Aw, that's great..." Erik growled. He glanced over at Ariadne, "Now you've gone and done it, way to ruin my good time."

Simon closed his eyes and massaged his forehead. He wasn't sure if they'd proved anything from the entire encounter... save one fact.

He knew for a fact that Erik was an idiot.

***

Simon stepped onto the bridge. Most of the lighting elsewhere aboard the ship was somewhat dimmed because of the late hour. Simon had agreed with Mike's reasoning that they should do a day/night cycle to prevent a host of psychological and neurological issues that cropped up when people didn't follow those patterns. Still, walking through the quiet, dim corridors had made the hair on the back of his neck rise, especially when he considered that there was a murderer on the loose.

One look at Pixel's pale face was enough to tell Simon that he wouldn't feel any better about those corridors... and that he probably wouldn't get any sleep either.

"You've found something?"

"Yeah..." Pixel sighed. "Look, there's a lot here, and Crowe didn't index it very well. Really, it looks like he just created random links to some of it." He took a deep breath, "But I found a *very* detailed roll up of information on us... all of us."

Simon frowned, "So? Crowe was a bit of a snoop, why would this matter."

Pixel frowned, "Look, there's some stuff on there that I wish I didn't know. There's some stuff on there that I really wanted to erase, stuff that I hoped no one else knew about me. It's biased, what he's got on me, where it's not outright false." He met Simon's gaze with a level one of his own, "I promise you I didn't edit any of these files… I'm trusting you. But if you're looking for reasons that someone may have killed Crowe… well you've found them." He held out the data chip, "Frankly, I'm a little afraid for my own life after reading some of this."

Simon felt his heart sink. He already had a building distrust for some of the crew… what secrets had Pixel uncovered that he feared for his own life? For that matter, was this just an act? Had the engineer arranged the evidence to implicate someone else, and to make himself less of a threat? Still, Simon gave him a nod, "Thanks, Pixel. And while I can't promise I'll discount you as a suspect, I'll try to stay impartial." Simon held out his hand.

Pixel nodded, "Thanks." He let the chip fall. It seemed abnormally heavy to Simon. *How does such a small thing carry so much weight?* Pixel met his gaze, "Mike asked me to read through the dead professor's notes, to see if I can figure anything out. If you need me… well, I'll be in the lounge working on that."

Simon took a deep breath. Something told him that he didn't want to read through what Pixel had uncovered. Part of him knew that once secrets were revealed, there would be no going back.

Simon walked over to his console and plugged the chip into the slot. He saw Pixel give him one last look before the engineer walked to the stairs. Something of the set of his shoulders told Simon that the other man truly dreaded what Simon might think… and that he would face it nonetheless.

***

Simon knew that Mike would assemble the others for a

crew brief first thing in the morning. That was the forum he chose to address them… to make his accusations and to reveal the murderer. Simon would rather have done it with a full nights sleep and more time to prepare… but he didn't know for sure who was involved and how far the conspiracy might extend. His information still didn't quite match up… and with what he knew now, he knew that he had to act soon.

He cornered Mike just before the meeting. Simon gave the other man a smile, "Mike, before we start your brief, could I take a moment to brief the crew on what I've found?"

The short Asian cocked his head, "Sure, bro. Though I'd appreciate you brief me first. Then *I* could brief the crew. Sort of goes with being Captain, you know?"

Simon's smile grew tight, "I appreciate that." He'd expected that, and he'd already thought of an excuse, "But it is a lot of information to cover, and it would be easier to have me brief it all."

Mike frowned and Simon could tell the other man didn't quite buy it. *Well, it's not like I can tell him that I don't trust him, not with this,* Simon thought. "Look, it's either that or we push the briefing back."

Mike grimaced, "No, rounding everyone up short of an emergency is hard enough. Hell, I swear Run must disappear into a hidey hole or something half the time."

Simon shrugged. Despite Run's disregard for human life, the little alien now looked like one of the less likely suspects. "Maybe," Simon said noncommittally.

Mike frowned and Simon could see the suspicion in the other man's dark eyes. Still, he finally gave a nod, "Very well, your show." He turned to the others, who had all filed on the bridge while Simon and Mike talked. "Thanks for coming, everyone. I'll cover what our plan for the day is here in a moment. First, though, Simon has apparently uncovered some information that he feels we all need to hear."

Simon searched the faces of his companions as Mike made that announcement. He half hoped to see guilt, suspicion, or even panic. Instead, he saw boredom and mild interest. *So*

either the killers are better actors than I could have guessed or
they think they've covered their trail so well that they're safe.
The only exceptions were Pixel, Michael, and Elena. Pixel had
a pinched look on his face, as if he expected a blow. Michael
and Elena both stood near the door, as Simon had asked. He
hadn't fully briefed them, but he had needed to verify some of
the information, so both could guess where this would go.

Plus she has access to the armory, so I had someone to
lock it down, just in case this really *goes bad,* Simon thought.
She was, other than Run, the only member of the crew that he
felt he could trust. Her earlier warning of a conspiracy seemed
more and more likely.

"Alright, everyone," Simon said. "I wanted all of you to
hear this, and it needs to be said openly." He scanned the others
even as he activated his console. It brought up the files that Pixel
had given him the night before. The same files that he'd spent
the entire night pouring over. "Crowe, among his other talents,
was an accomplished hacker. He's assembled quite a bit more
than we thought from the files of Fontaine, this ship, and even
from the Chxor vessels and station. He used those files to
assemble a *very* complete dossier on all of us… to include things
that I'm sure most of you thought were safely in your past."

Simon saw many of the others go still. Ariadne looked
puzzled, which made Simon's heart sink, if she could put up such
a deceptive face under these circumstances, then it meant that
Simon had to reevaluate his perception of her. Combined with
her abilities, her pretense of confusion made her far more likely a
suspect. Mike looked angry, which Simon could guess meant
that he either was irritated that Simon went for a confrontation or
that he was angry that his past was about to be revealed. Eric
looked tense, but the twitchy mercenary always looked poised
for combat. Pixel looked grim, but he already knew what Simon
knew… did that mean that he feared what Simon was about to
reveal or that he feared that his edited data hadn't succeeded? *I*
wish I knew enough about computers to tell if he gave me the real
data, Simon thought, not for the first time. He had spent hours
agonizing over what to do, and no little amount of that time in

consideration of just how dangerous the engineer could be.

Of the aliens, Run merely looked bored, though Simon couldn't guess if the alien really felt an emotion such as that. Or perhaps the little alien simply didn't care what Simon had uncovered because he knew it wouldn't implicate him. Rastar had turned a pale shade of tan, but Simon noted the big alien's four arms all had shifted closer to his weapons. Anubus had cocked his jackal-like head, as if to study Simon more carefully. His claws were still sheathed, but Simon knew that could change in a heart beat… or mid swing.

Simon activated the simple program he had enabled and all the screens aboard the bridge came to life. He watched each face as their eyes searched the screens, each one with a different dossier. "So let's start this off," Simon said, his voice level. *Best to start with the most likely suspects,* he thought. "Anubus: wanted in the Colonial Republic system of Anvil for charges of piracy, murder, sabotage, kidnapping, and extortion. You were captain of a frigate which you stole and a crew of thirty other pirates. Among your many crimes, you apparently massacred your entire crew when you suspected they attempted to betray you to the authorities."

Simon had his hand behind his back, tucked under his suit jacket where he'd holstered his pistol. The ivory grip felt warm and comfortable in his hand as he waited for the Wrethe's reaction. Simon expected anything from a berserk homicidal rage to a seething condemnation. He did not expect the dry chuckle and the wolf-like grin, "Yes, so?"

The others had shifted away from the Wrethe, who seemed to take the cleared space around him as his due. "You killed your own crew?"

"They betrayed me and they paid the price… a fact which you all should remember," Anubus growled. The temperature on the bridge seemed to drop at his base voice. His jackal grin lent extra credence to his threat.

Simon could see that his reveal had not had the desired effect. If anything, Anubus seemed to wear his crimes like a badge of honor. *My god,* he thought, *what kind of savages have I fallen in with?* He pointed at the next screen, "Eric Striker, wanted for desertion from the Centauri Military Forces. Wanted in questioning for the murder of a senior officer. In addition, there's a significant bounty placed on the Tanis Classifieds with a note that you've killed the last police team that tried to apprehend you and bring you to justice."

Eric glowered at Simon, "The first two 'crimes' are bullshit. I served with honor, right up until-" He broke off. A rush of emotions flitted across the other man's face. "And that 'police team' I killed weren't cops, they were a hired bag team that someone deputized."

"Nonetheless, Crowe knew you were wanted, knew about your bounty, did you kill him because of that?" Simon demanded.

Eric looked at him in consternation. "Are you kidding? How was I supposed to know he had this? The bastard never said a thing."

Simon ground his teeth. "You'd be likely to say that if he confronted you and tried to compel you to work for him." He paused, "Crowe's notes say that he blackmailed someone on the team into being his partner… was it you? You could have provided him the combat power he might have wanted. Plus, you dealt the final blow to Ghost, maybe you stole the Wrethe's environmental suit after that."

"That's absurd," Eric said. "First off, if Crowe had tried to blackmail me, I'd probably have killed him then and there. I wouldn't simmer about it or hatch some weird cover up. And I'd tell you all. I'm not afraid of any of that coming up. I can explain it all and I've got records to back me."

"What about the bounty?" Mike asked.

Eric looked over at Mike with a hurt expression, "Really Mike? You think I'm stupid enough to trust Crowe in regards to that? He might not tell the rest of you, but he'd sure as hell try to turn me in to get it himself."

Simon shook his head, "None of that clears you."

"No, but none of it proves I did anything, either," Eric snapped.

Simon glanced around at the others, but their faces still showed confusion more than anything. Guilty people panicked when their motives were revealed… unless they were psychopaths or sociopaths. Finally Simon decided to move on.

"Pixel… or should we call you Kevin Lynch?" Simon asked. He brought up the Engineer's dossier on the main screen. "Wanted for questioning in the Lithia system in relation to the terrorist attack on New Glasglow's capital city of Origin. Authorities linked you to the computer that was used to reprogram the city reactor, and to the people believed to have conducted the terrorist attack." Looks of horror met his announcement, and Simon felt a sick twist in his stomach at the look of pain on the engineers face.

"I can't…" Pixel looked away. "I was involved… but I was deceived. I trusted a friend, and I never questioned his motives. I should have, but I didn't. I swear to you all, I was *not* a part of his team and I had no idea what he planned to do." He took a deep breath, "It was supposed to be a *prank!*"

Ariadne walked over to the console, "Now, look, the charges were dropped, anyway, almost a year ago. Clearly the authorities don't hold him responsible anymore."

Simon grimaced, "It doesn't matter, he was involved. He said it himself, just now. That makes him an accessory to an attack that killed millions." Some of the others looked conflicted. But Simon could tell that his aggressive stance had put them all on the defensive. He had painted all of them as possible suspects, so none of them were likely to pass judgment on their fellows.

"Mike, there's precious little on you, besides the fact that you're wanted for questioning in a smuggling operation with ties to the pirate Tommy King," Simon said to the Captain, who just gave him a shrug in return. "Ariadne, you're wanted for the murder on Cetus, Qiang, and Faraday."

The psychic went a bit pale at that, but she nodded, "I… was involved on Cetus, but it was an accident. It was self defense, on Qiang." She frowned, "Honestly, I've never been to Faraday, so I'm not sure what that's about." She said it all with a calm tone, as if being wanted for three separate sets of murders were something that could easily be explained away.

"Rastar…" Simon brought up the alien's file, "You're wanted in Centauri space for a laundry list of crimes ranging from assault and battery to murder. You also have not just one, but two bounty listings, one for thirty two million Confederation Dollars and the other for forty million Tau Ceti Separatist Dollars. One contract lists you as wanted alive, the other just requests your head."

The entire bridge went silent. They all realized, just as Simon did, that someone could buy a star ship or live a life of luxury for that kind of money.

The big alien shrugged, "Well, sometimes people have misunderstandings like this." His mirrored eyes gave no sign of his emotions, though his hide had gone a lighter tan color. Simon guessed that meant surprise or worry, though he wasn't sure.

Mike gave the big alien with a look of consternation, "A thirty million dollar misunderstanding?" His tone suggested that he didn't accept that response any more than Simon did.

Rastar shrugged, "These things happen." His brown hide took on a shade of muted green, which, if Simon remembered right, meant he found the situation amusing.

Ariadne spoke up, "He did say that Chxor space was safer for him."

Mike seemed flabbergasted by the payday. "Thirty two million??"

Rastar looked relaxed, but Simon noted how tense the big alien had gone. He could see the muscles under the big alien's hide grow taut. Simon also saw shades of red darken his brown hide. Simon decided to press harder and asked, "Did you kill Crowe because you found out that he knew?"

Rastar looked over at Simon, "I very much doubt that Crowe could collect on his own. Even if I did know, I wouldn't see him as a threat."

"But maybe you killed him to keep him silent, da?" Elena snapped.

Rastar's hide turned pink... but he didn't look over at the bounty hunter. He kept silent for a long moment, but when he spoke, Simon could hear an edge of anger in his deep voice, "I did not kill him. I didn't know that anyone else knew. I give you my word of honor."

"Someone held him down while someone else cut on him, this would take two people with two sets of hands... or one alien with the same, da?" Elena asked.

The bridge had gone totally silent. Simon saw Anubus shift, and an appraising look came to his dark eyes. "She's right."

Rastar looked around at the others. "This is absurd, Annie, I know you don't believe that I'd do that to Crowe!"

"You beat him up when you found he'd stolen gold," Mike said, his voice calm.

"But only because he tried to frame me!" Rastar shouted. His hide had turned a deeper shade of red. "And accusations such as this are wrong. I would not kill a helpless man!"

Ariadne moved forward to stand between Rastar and Anubus. She stood with a stance of determination to her slender frame and a frown on her face. The stance would have seemed absurd, except that her hair had begun to stir in a breeze which touched no one else and the air temperature in the bridge dropped sharply enough that Simon heard the environmental systems kick on. "We know he didn't do it," Ariadne said sharply. "It's greed or worse that would make anyone think that Rastar would hurt someone like that." Her voice seemed more powerful than her thin frame should produce. "He's lost his temper before, but he's never been cruel... and someone would have to be absolutely vicious to do that to him."

Despite himself, Simon nodded. He somehow doubted that the big alien had it in him to do something that nasty. Simon took a deep breath, "But you could have held him down with your abilities, or had someone else do it by controlling them."

"What?" Ariadne's look of determination was replaced by hurt and shock on her face.

"Yes..." Anubus growled. "You hated Crowe and

suspected him of being a rogue psychic. If he thought to gain leverage over you with your past, you might have used any one of us as your tools to silence him." The Wrethe cocked his head, "And indeed, even Simon here could have been your tool."

Simon felt his heart go cold at *that* thought.

"No," Pixel said. "That's not possible."

"Why?" Anubus growled.

"Because Ariadne couldn't hurt a fly, not unless she was protecting us," Pixel said.

"That's not true, she's killed before," Simon said.

"Only in self defense!" Ariadne said.

"This is going nowhere," Mike growled. "Move on with the brief, I'm sure you've got some more skeletons to drag out of the closet."

Simon grimaced, "Mandy and Miranda…" He pulled up their combined dossier which included a variety of pictures of them. "Clearly Crowe was fixated on both of you. Some of his photos are very compromising." Simon pulled up a picture that showed Mandy using the shower. The short redhead's blush went up into her scalp. "He also had a list of your previous convictions as well as systems and planets you're wanted in. Your apparent crimes included inciting riots, assault on political figures, even inciting insurrection. He also, apparently, learned that you were both psychics."

Miranda stepped forward, "So?"

"So you may have killed him to keep that quiet or because you caught him at his snooping. Or because he tried to blackmail one or both of you into, ah, sexual favors." Simon said. The last seemed the most likely, Simon had earlier decided.

"I wouldn't put it past him, the pervert!" Mandy shouted.

Miranda shook her head at her friend and turned her gaze on the others, "We've made no attempt to hide our past. He's got a lot more detail than we've told you, but not that much more that we'd be concerned about it being revealed."

"And if I caught him snooping, I'd beat his ass and cut off his balls," Mandy snapped, "Not hold him down and cut his chest."

548

"Noted," Mike said dryly. He looked at Simon, "Anything else?"

Simon took a deep breath, "This could be a conspiracy. All of you have sordid pasts, what if you learned that he knew this, what if you all worked together to silence him?" As he asked the words, he prepared himself for a violent response.

"That's absurd," Mike said. "All of us have shown that we didn't fear what he knew. For that matter, half of what he 'knew' is only half-right... or dead wrong." The derision in his voice made Simon grit his teeth.

"The fact remains that none of you have come forward with this information!" Simon snapped. "Half of you are wanted criminals, the other half are suspected of piracy, terrorism or murder!"

"And so are you," Mike said, his voice cold. "How are you any different?"

"I told you that from the beginning. I was framed for the murder of my partner," Simon said. Even so, he flushed at the reminder.

"Pull up his dossier," Mike said.

Pixel stepped over and pulled up Simon's file. Simon grimaced as the others read through it. It did not flatter, him, he knew. A series of poor evaluations. An investigation into his financial records. The case against him for the murder of his partner and the evidence that the CSB and Ministry of Justice had assembled. Simon couldn't guess how Crowe had gained that level of access. Perhaps he'd found it in the Chxor files. It didn't make much sense, but it was all he could come up with.

"Looks like a pretty solid case," Mike said, finally. "Sudden influx of cash, right after the assassination, your partner was investigating a money trail from the same account that sent you the money. He winds up dead from a bomb, they find traces of explosives in your apartment..."

"I didn't kill him!" Simon snapped.

"That's what they all say, right?" Mike drawled. "No, I'm ending this witch hunt. You've dragged us all through enough muck for the day. This is a ship full of people who saved

549

your life time and again, who got you out of that hellhole of a prison station where you would have died, otherwise."

"This is a ship full of secrets and lies!" Simon shouted. The others stared at him in shock.

Mike let out a deep sigh. "How long have you been up, Simon? How hard have you been working this investigation over the past three days?"

Simon shook his head, "Now you're trying to discredit —"

"I'm trying to say that you're under stress and make sure that the rest of the crew doesn't hold this against you," Mike said. "That's the job of the Captain, to manage the crew and ship. Clearly, I've fucked up." The smaller man gave a sigh. "I should have realized that you got too close. You're chasing shadows, and you're paranoid and frustrated."

Simon shook his head, "That's just what you would say if you were involved–"

"I'm *not* involved. This has gone from an investigation to a witch hunt. What do we gain by digging up people's pasts? Nothing... this information should have died with Crowe, as far as I'm concerned," Mike said. "We all have our pasts and as far as I'm concerned, our past is just that: the past. It's what we do from now on that matters."

Simon shook his head, "Crowe is dead, dead because either he knew something about someone here or he did something to threaten someone aboard this ship. Whoever killed him has concealed that fact, that makes them a danger to us all!"

"Unfortunately, I am required to interrupt this fascinating display of human research techniques," Run stated. "I must correct you on one fact which I have confirmed this morning."

Simon sighed, "What fact would that be, that Crowe somehow cut himself open and it wasn't murder?"

"That would be very unlikely," Run stated, his voice flat.

"Oh really?" Mike growled.

"Yes," Run said, oblivious to the sarcasm. He looked around the room with his pale yellow, alien eyes, almost as if he wanted to predict their reactions to his next statement. "Crowe is not dead."

***

"Huh, he could have fooled me," Eric said with a grunt. "He did," Run said. "He fooled all of us. But when I compared the corpse to Crowe's genetic material I had already procured, I learned that the body we found is not Crowe."

"Wait, you already had some of Crowe's genetic material?" Mike asked sharply. "I thought I told you that you weren't allowed to take genetic samples from the crew."

"Uh, bigger issue here," Ariadne said. "Someone else who looked like Crowe was on-board the ship and murdered." She frowned, and Simon could see something like panic go across her face, "We could have something like that purple ooze that was in Krann, some kind of doppelganger or... something."

"Oh," Rastar said eagerly, "Like in Space Doppelgangers, when the entire crew is killed and eaten. That was a great holovid."

"That's ridiculous," Eric said. "The whole space doppelganger thing was a bad movie. Clearly Run just got his info wrong. I mean, how would he do a genetic test? He doesn't even have any lab equipment. Besides, I think we would have noticed if he went around taking samples from us, right?"

"I am not mistaken," Run said. "In theory, if I took the genetic samples from you as you slept, you would not have noticed when I swabbed each of you, especially with sedatives added to your evening meals." The Chxor looked around at the suddenly quiet room. "My genetic research is highly advanced, I assure you, and I am not mistaken. I used what humans call DNA Fingerprinting and the Northern Blot methodologies, in order to be doubly certain. Clearly, I can see that you are emotionally impacted by my thoroughness."

"There's no way you drugged my food, I was there the whole time, I cooked it. You..." Eric broke off. When he spoke again, his voice was shocked. "I *have* been sleeping very well," Eric noted. Simon saw a look of anger flash over the soldier's face. Something else lurked in his eyes, though,

551

something almost like fear. For that matter, Simon felt extremely uneasy at how the Chxor had violated all of them. *Though, if it helps the case, I suppose I can't complain,* he thought.

"This Chxor, he scares me," Elena said, her accent thick. She had moved away from the door, Simon noticed, to take a seat in one of the oversized Ghornath couches. Then again, with how his confrontation had gone, he didn't think he needed her to watch the door anymore.

"Fear is a primitive emotion often invoked in inferior species who do not understand scientific thought," Run said, his flat voice calm. Run continued, "Once I had realized through genetic comparison that the corpse was not Crowe, I postulated that he would be someone else. A detailed examination of the blood allowed me to discover tiny nanomachines, which had already begun to decay. The machines, I theorize, were injected into the subject in order to alter the facial features and some higher level brain functions."

"Wait, brain functions?" Pixel asked, "The facial features reconstruction I can guess at, but how would you guess at the brain alterations?"

"I located remnants of the nanomachines in the subject's brain tissue along with a sedative which would have been injected with the nanomachines." Run answered. "It is an interesting application of nanotechnology, to rewrite the subjects higher level thought functions. Of course, the long term effect would be quite debilitating with these machines, they made only superficial changes to the brain chemistry and the subject would probably suffer mental regression, followed by dementia, insanity, and loss of higher cognitive functions. I would have enjoyed the opportunity to observe these effects. Unfortunately, someone terminated him before this onset."

"Wait, so this poor bastard would have thought he *was* Crowe right up until he went insane?" Mike asked. He frowned, "That's really cold."

"I think I'm going to be sick," Illario said. The ganger had moved to the back of the room, a look of unease on his face.

"Yeah," Simon said, "And there's only one person I can

552

think of who would have that kind of tech... and would need someone to look like Crowe."

"And now he's our missing person," Mike nodded. "So, if Crowe did this, who is the body?"

"I had not yet begun my genetic sampling of the passengers," Run said. "Therefore I could not determine that with any significant reliability." Run shrugged, "The subject was male and of approximately equal height and body structure to Crowe. The nanomachines altered facial structure, skin tone and distinguishing features, hair and eye color, and brain functions."

Ariadne spoke, "So why wouldn't we notice Crowe walking around still alive?"

There was a long silence. None of them could imagine Crowe injecting himself with nanomachines that might drive him insane. Eric finally spoke, his voice reluctant, "There's a body modification, a particular type of cybernetics. It alters facial features, changes them so that the person can pass as someone else. It's used by some assassins back in the Centauri Confederation."

Simon nodded slowly, "And our friend here seems to have a lot of skills and equipment that an assassin or professional thief might have... or might have stolen."

"This changes everything," Mike put his head in his hands. "Why does Crowe always make things so difficult?"

"This doesn't change *one* thing," Simon said. "We know that Crowe is still alive and that he effectively put this other poor man in position to be murdered... but we don't know who murdered him. This is *still* a murder investigation."

"Perhaps it was Crowe?" Elena asked.

Mike snorted, "That's a pretty nasty thing for him to do, I'd agree. 'Kill' himself and make us chase his killer around in circles..."

Simon shook his head, "No, that would imply that he needed to disappear... but none of us knew he was up to this. Besides, he can't have too many supplies of his nanomachines, they must have been smuggled with him somewhere. And then there's Jascinthe's murder. Someone killed him for what he had, but that doesn't fit Crowe's profile. He likes to steal, I mean, he stole from Anubus and nearly didn't get caught. No, I think this was Crowe faking his own death with the intention of avoiding whoever is after him."

"This partner of his that you made up?" Eric asked. "I don't believe it. And lets not forget that you painted all of us to look like the murderer, so that would put you in a great position to be Crowe."

"Okay, *enough*," Mike said and rubbed at his forehead. From his expression, he had a terrible headache. Simon could empathize. "Let's look at this logically. He looked over at Run, "How can we identify Crowe, if he's using some kind of implant to alter his appearance?"

"Genetic sampling would be ideal," Run said.

"No," Eric, Mike, Ariadne, Elena, Anubus, and Rastar all said at the same time.

"I can conduct a sample of all the likely candidates in only a few days..."

"No," Mike said. He gave a sigh, "What are our other options?"

Run stared at him with calm eyes, "This is an illogical fear, you should allow me to..."

Pixel spoke up, "Run, from a scientific perspective, what would our other options be if genetic sampling would not work?"

Run looked over at Pixel, "This is an odd query, but if the subject could somehow alter or conceal his genetic code, then we would have to go off of body structure, height, mass, and general body shape configuration. I have already done a preliminary analysis in order to lower the candidate field and have selected five possibilities."

"Thank you, Pixel," Mike said as he massaged his forehead, "Who would those five candidates be?"

Run pulled out his datapad, "Based off of height and features those candidates are: Eric Striker, Simon, Michael Santangel, Illario Urbano, and Matvei Singolav. Of course, this is subject to some variance, due to limited observation and study."

"Okay," Mike said, "Michael, Simon, Eric and Illario, you all will stay here. Matvei is one of the space hands we've already interviewed, we'll get him up here. Until we identify the killer, you all are at risk..." He trailed off. "Where is Illario?"

Simon turned around. "He was just here."

Elena jumped up from where she'd sat, "Crowe. The bastard played us... it must be him."

Michael Santangel toggled open the hatch to the stairs and glanced down, "No sign of him." His accent made the declaration sound that much more impressive.

"He said he felt sick," Ariadne said, "Maybe he just..."

"Ran downstairs to hide?" Eric asked. His tone of sarcasm made it abundantly clear what he thought of that.

"No," Simon shook his head, "He played us... he left before we thought through the implications, before we could tag him. That makes too much sense." *How could I have missed this,* he wondered. He had assumed that Illario had avoided him because of their earlier conversation. But what if he'd avoided Simon because he *wasn't* Illario, he was Crowe?

"Or before his would-be murderer could finish him off," Rastar said. "We have to protect him."

"Protect him?" Eric said. "He basically killed someone else."

"Yes..." Rastar nodded. "And he should pay for that. But someone else did kill this other person." The big, eight-limbed alien's hide held tones of red and orange.

"Come to think of it," Anubus grinned, "Why don't we let Crowe and his partner settle their differences and just kill the victor?"

"That's kind of cold," Simon said.

"One or both of them tried to frame *me* for this..." Anubus growled. "That does not enamor me of them. This is why I don't like *partners,* sooner or later you must fight for dominance." His deep voice held both sarcasm and anger. Still, Simon had to wonder if the alien felt at least some regret about how lonely an existence he lived. *Then again,* Simon thought, *he killed his* entire *crew.*

"No, we need to find both of them. The best way to do that is to have one of them and force the other to come to us and expose him or herself," Mike said. "Then we can talk about killing, imprisoning or whatever."

"They both need to be turned over to the authorities when we hit human space," Simon said. He felt slightly nauseated at the thought of what Crowe had done to Illario. While he hadn't liked the ganger, to erase the other man's memories and replace them with a crude version of someone else seemed horrific. *If I have my way, Crowe will go to jail for a very long time,* he thought.

Mike turned to Rastar, "First, we get to the arms room. Crowe had access, so we have to secure it, then–"

"Uh, we locked it down," Simon said. "No one is getting in there without the pass-code."

"What?" Mike said.

Simon cleared his throat and glanced over at Elena, "We thought some of the crew were part of the conspiracy to kill Crowe... so we locked it down."

"We'll discuss this later," Mike said. "When I have a chance to get over the fact that you didn't ask me." Mike grimaced, "*Much* later."

"This actually worked out well, you know," Simon said. "He can't get access to any guns."

"He has a point," Rastar said. "Though I wish he had asked me."

"You were a suspect," Simon said. He frowned, "Technically, you still are."

Mike closed his eyes, "While you two are talking this over, you might want to realize two things. One: Crowe is a hacker and you are giving him more time to get access to the armory and then lock us out. Two: usurping control over the armory on any vessel is a specific qualification for mutiny, which is punishable in most star systems by death."

Simon felt his jaw drop, "You know, I hadn't thought of that."

***

The panel to the armory was open and wires dangled from it, but Simon saw the telltales still showed it as locked down. Pixel grimaced at the mess. "He couldn't get in so he trashed the panel, none of us can get in." He peered at it, "This will take hours to fix."

Mike grimaced, "Fix it. Mandy, Miranda, stay with him, you too Ariadne. Crowe might come back."

"My friends, we have an unknown killer aboard, do not forget," Michael Santangel said. "For that matter, it could be any one of us."

Mike massaged his forehead, "A fact I'm well aware of, which is why there are three of them and one is a powerful psychic."

"What if it's *her*?" Elena asked, her voice harsh. "She could control them all and then take over the vessel."

"If it's her, then we're screwed anyway," Mike said. "Elena, you, Eric, and Anubus return to the bridge and make sure it is secure. Pixel, you locked down the computers so he cant get access?"

"I cut power to all the consoles," Pixel said. "He'd need to be on the bridge."

"Simon, Santangel, you're with me," Mike said. His eyes narrowed, "I would assume that since you planned that confrontation that you're armed?"

Simon drew his pistol. "Yeah."

Mike grunted, "So, Rastar, Anubus, and you are the only ones armed while we have not just one but two dangerous killers on the loose."

"Elena has a weapon, as well," Simon said. "And I believe that Eric sleeps with a weapon."

"You and I really need to have a talk after all of this is over..." Mike said. He closed his eyes in thought for a moment. "Crowe is a sneaky type... but when he's confronted he tends to panic. Where do you think he'll go?"

"He will need to either change his appearance once again or find some kind of leverage which will force us to work with him, at least until he can gain the upper hand and betray us," Michael Santangel answered.

"Good points," Mike nodded. "Did Simon offer you a position on the crew?"

"No, just to vouch for me," Michael said.

"Well, I like the way you think," Mike said. "So you're hired."

Santangel gave him a polite smile. Simon could almost hear the other man's thoughts. *He's thinking 'excellent, this common born criminal wants to hire me as crew, what a splendid compliment.'*

"Well, all the other likely candidates are here," Mike said, "That leaves Matvei, who would be in the lounge, with the other passengers." He shook his head, "Too difficult for him to get him out of there and we know his playbook. He'll need leverage..."

"Perhaps a hostage?" Michael asked.

"One of the crew or passengers, it would have to be someone off on their own," Simon said.

"The only passenger that valuable would be the ambassador," Mike swore. "We'd better hurry." They arrived outside the passenger quarters to find both Nova Roma Marines out in the hallway with raised arms. *This is not good,* Simon thought.

Mike led the way, "What's happening?"

Sergeant Santander answered, his voice thick with anger, "Bastard showed up and said he had important information for the Ambassador. Then he drew a knife. He said we wait out here or he kills her."

Mike grimaced. He looked over at Simon, "You'll have to take the shot, you know?"

Simon frowned, "Maybe we can talk him down."

"This seems unlikely, my friend," Michael said.

"If he kills the Ambassador... we're screwed," Mike said softly. "And worse, her blood will be on *your* hands." The other man's dark eyes met Simon's and Simon felt a surge of ice go through his veins. He had never had to take another human's life

558

before.

Mike keyed the hatch to open. Illario or Crowe or whoever he was stood only a few meters away, behind Ambassador Vibius. He had a long knife pressed into her side. He gave a smile as they stepped into the room. "Look who it is, the good policeman, the man with no past, and a man with no future." His voice was that of Crowe, from the smirk on his face to his tone of condescension. It gave Simon an odd feeling, the juxtaposition of Illario with Crowe's mannerisms. He absently wondered how long it took Crowe's implants to alter his appearance.

"*Please*," Ambassador Vibius said, her voice faint, "Don't let him hurt me!"

"Crowe, let her go," Mike said. His voice sounded calm, but Simon could see the smaller man was coiled like a spring.

"No... I don't think so," Crowe said. His smirk turned into something uglier, "This is, unfortunately, the only bargaining chip I have left."

"You have no bargaining chip," Mike said with a flat voice.

Crowe gave a giggle, "How do you think the Nova Roma Empire would react when some escaped fugitives show up in an enemy ship, with a dead ambassador, and murdered crew?"

"It doesn't matter," Simon said. He kept his voice calm and met the other man's gaze levelly. He knew that most hostage situations ended best when both sides stayed calm. If Crowe got angry, if he stopped thinking... He had to get the other man to think. "You won't kill her because if you do, you know we won't protect you."

"Protect me?" Crowe gave a manic laugh, "*Right*, I really want your protection. I've seen the company you keep and I know every cop has his price." Crowe met Simon's eyes, "You are the *last* person I want protection from."

Mike took a step forward, his arms raised, "Look, Crowe, we can resolve this."

"No," Crowe said. The Ambassador gave a whimper as he pressed the knife into her side. "We can't. We really can't.

People on this ship want me dead. I don't want to *be* dead. So you will back out... *now.* I want this door locked down and when that happens, I tell you my other demands." Crowe's voice sounded unsteady, a mix of anger, frustration, and terror lay just under his arrogant voice. He could see the man's hands tremble.

Simon felt an icy lump settle in his guts. Crowe was not thinking rationally... he was past that point. The likelihood that he would panic and murder the Ambassador grew larger with every second that Crowe held her. *Then her blood will be on* my *hands, just as much as if I stabbed her myself,* he thought.

Simon glanced over at Mike and he could see the determination on the other man's face. Mike gave him a slight nod. They would not leave here without the Ambassador. "Okay, Crowe, we're backing out. Just relax, take it easy." Mike backed a couple slow steps backwards. Simon could see the tense muscles in Crowe's arm relax and the slight motion as the knife dropped slightly."

Simon reached back and drew his pistol in a smooth, practiced movement. The archaic iron sights leveled on Crowe's chest. Simon fired once. The old pistol gave a deafening roar in the confined space. The other man stumbled back, an expression of shock on his face, and his knife fell from limp fingers. The Ambassador screamed and rushed away even as Mike and Simon ran forward.

Crowe fell back on the deck. Mike kicked the knife out of reach and knelt at the man's side along with Simon. "Get Run in here, now!" Mike shouted.

Crowe lay on his back, eyes wide. His skin had gone pale with shock and blood spurted from the big wound that Simon's forty-five pistol had made. "Talk to me Crowe," Mike said, his voice harsh. "Who was your partner, who tried to kill you?"

Crowe coughed and bright blood splashed on Mike's clothing. Crowe's voice gurgled a bit as he gasped, "You... you killed me." His last breath went out and Crowe lay still. Mike gave a curse and began CPR, but Simon sat back on his heels. He'd aimed that shot well... too well. He'd put it right in the dense bundle of arteries near the other man's heart and lungs.

Mike continued to try for a few minutes, until Simon put a hand on the other man's shoulder. "Mike." He saw the Captain's head droop. "Mike, it's my fault."

The short Asian gave a snort, "I'm, the Captain, what happens aboard this ship is always my fault. That's why I didn't want the job." He looked up, his dark eyes serious. "You did what you had to do. At least we saved the Ambassador."

Behind him, he could hear her rant at her two Marines, her voice once more the arrogant and outraged woman that they all found so insufferable. "Right." Simon gave a ragged sigh, "It doesn't make me feel any better." He had taken another man's life, deserving or not, it was a burden that he would have to carry.

Run's flat voice spoke from behind them, "I was not in need of an additional subject for dissection so soon. However, I will increase my lab space to accommodate."

"It was Crowe," Mike said. "Simon shot him because he was about to kill the Ambassador."

Run walked up and stared down at the body. "Well, this would conclude the inquiry in regards to the termination of Crowe."

Simon gave a snort at that. *Well, when there's nothing else left to laugh about, there's always dark humor,* he thought. Memories of a childhood game came back to him as he holstered his pistol, "Yes. I did, in the Ambassador's quarters, with the nineteen-eleven."

***

"What happened?" Elena asked, as they stepped back onto the bridge. "We heard that you confronted him and Run said that he needs a body moved to his 'lab' from the Ambassador's quarters. Do we know more, did Crowe talk?" She looked at the blood that spattered Mike, "Are you alright?"

Mike looked down at himself and grimaced. "Dammit, that was the only decent ship's uniform I could find in my size from the *Sao Martino*." He looked up at Eric's snort. "Laugh it

561

up. You try finding stuff my size." He sighed and went to lean on a console, an expression of exhaustion and frustration on his face. "I'm fine, but Crowe is dead and we still don't know anything concrete."

Simon shook his head, "This whole thing has us spinning in circles."

Eric nodded, "Yeah, like some stray dog trying to chase down rats in an alley." The others stared at him without comprehension. Simon saw that Anubus's lips had drawn back in a slight snarl. Eric coughed, "Uh, you know, it chases one. Then another cuts across its trail, so it goes after that one. Then a third pulls it in another direction. This goes on four or five times and the stray dog ends up at the entrance to the alley, exhausted, hungry, and confused... Come on, haven't any of you lived in an inner city?"

"I haven't exactly spent time staring at rats," Simon said.

"Nor I," Elena said.

"Your description is apt enough," Anubus growled. "And I agree. We keep reacting, instead of taking the initiative. If I start killing passengers, I can flush our murderer out."

Run spoke up from the hatch. "This seems like a viable plan. Surely with how emotional humans are, the perpetrator would feel compelled to flee."

"That plan is so far off the table, that you'd need to plot a shadow space jump to find it," Mike said, his voice tired. He looked back at Run, "Weren't you overseeing the body?"

"One human corpse is much the same as another. I shall conduct my research soon enough," Run answered. "I wish to conduct decontamination procedures on you. You have been contaminated with blood which might have contained unknown nanotechnology. It is best to maintain the health of my control subjects," Run said.

Mike looked down at himself again. "Oh, right."

"What now?" Elena asked.

Mike held out his hand, "Simon said you were packing?" Elena grimaced, but she pulled one of the small Chxor pistols out of her coat pocket. "That's it?"

562

She gave a shrug, "Is small, easy to conceal, da?"

"Right," Mike said as he tucked it into his waist band. Simon, Elena, and Eric all winced. "Eric, when you get the armory open, I want you to do a full inventory, after that you're with me as backup. Until then, Elena, you're with me. We're going through the passengers again, full interviews." He paused and looked over at Santangel, "Oh, Michael, good work, you're part of the crew now. You can move your kit into the crew quarters."

Simon gave the Captain a nod. "I'll show him where to put his things."

Run walked forward to Mike, "You will follow me to my lab now or I will be forced to use my command voice. I will not allow unidentified nanotech to infect my control population."

Simon really didn't want to listen to the Chxor's shrill, shrieking 'command voice' after everything else he had been through. Exhaustion had put a haze over everything and he had almost hit the point where he no longer cared that there was an as yet unidentified killer aboard. He looked over at Santangel and gave a nod towards the hatch.

He almost made it before Run's voice kicked in, "I INSIST YOU MUST IMMEDIATELY PROCEED TO MY LAB–" The hatch closed on the rest. *Thank god the Ghornath build good soundproofing,* he thought, *and I'm not the Captain and don't have to put up with that crap.*

***

"It is strange," Michael said as he put away his things in a crew locker.

"What?" Simon asked, from flat on his back. He had offered to help the other man move his things, but Michael had politely declined. Simon had laid down. He had stared at the bulkhead, in an attempt to will himself to sleep, but his mind seemed unable to rest. *Nothing like a complex puzzle to keep me awake,* he thought.

Michael shrugged, "On my way back up here with my things, I spoke with Eric and Rastar." Simon looked over at the tone of confusion in the other man. "Pixel has opened the armory and they already completed the inventory, but there is a weapon missing, a submachine gun."

Simon sat up, "What?" He frowned, "That doesn't make sense. I took my pistol, Elena took that Chxor pistol. You didn't even go inside. Hell, did an inventory before we took our weapons, just to see if anyone else was armed... all the submachine guns were there." It wasn't hard to miss those, they only had three, he knew.

"Yes, my friend, a fact of which I am well aware," Michael said. "For that matter, no one else could get in, not until Pixel unlocked it, and Eric, Rastar, and Ariadne were there. As I said... strange."

Simon felt a sudden dark suspicion. "At the lounge... when I mentioned Bastien. Where did Elena go?"

Michael looked up, "She said that Mike had asked her to get the next person for his interviews."

"Yes, but he was arguing with the Ambassador, at the time. He all but told me that he'd be at it for a while, why would he send her for someone else?" Simon asked. He pursed his lips, "And then there's the bounties... she's a bounty hunter, but she didn't say a word about those bounties when I read them off. No shock, no surprise..."

Michael nodded slowly, "She did seem very calm."

"That's a *lot* of money, even I might find myself daydreaming about that kind of payoff... if I let myself," Simon said. "So our resident bounty hunter, who might well have been carrying a chip with a bounty list just like we found on Crowe's computer..."

"Or might have given it to him?" Michael suggested.

"...or might have given it to him," Simon said. "She was near Bastien when he was killed." He felt his body go cold. "She was the *only* one who saw Ghost." He turned to the console and toggled up the intercom. "The Captain is doing the interviews in the lounge, this time, right?"

"I believe so," Michael said.

"Captain, this is Simon, I need to talk to you, right now,"

Simon said over the intercom.

"Can it wait?" Mike sounded distracted.

"No, I think I know who our murderer is," Simon said. He wished he had some way to know if Elena was in the compartment with Mike. *I should contact Eric and Rastar as well,* he thought. The lounge was close, maybe he should have gone there in person.

"Ah, that would be why Elena has a gun pointed at me." Mike said.

Simon felt his blood go cold. His hands activated a relay to the armory and he hoped that it would override whatever entertainment that Rastar and Eric had on. "Elena..."

"What, you wish to ask why?" She laughed. "Because they deserve it, because they are criminals, people that deserve death... and because the pay is very good."

"Let's talk about this," Simon said.

"Please don't waste my time, da?" Her voice was cold. "I know the one hostage didn't work well for Crowe and the whole ship didn't work well for Ghost. I won't try a losing tactic. Any last words, Mike?"

There was a shout, and then the sound of gunfire.

***

Simon raced down the corridor. He skidded to a halt outside the lounge. He still heard the muted sound of gunfire from within. He saw the hatch to the ladder well open only a few meters away, Eric and Rastar, both with drawn weapons, came out at a run. Clearly they'd received the message.

Simon ducked low and opened the hatch and then rolled inside. He put his back to the buffet table and heaved. Plastic cups and dishes flew and the metal trays rattled as it toppled over on its side.

A rattle of gunfire and the sharp whine of ricochets signaled that someone didn't like his intrusion. A glance to the side showed Mike, huddled behind the bullet-torn couch. Water leaked from a few stray bullet holes in the huge aquarium behind him. Simon put his head around the table. He saw a hint of motion at the back of the room, near the door. "Elena, surrender. Everyone else knows it was you. Eric and Rastar are already here, you can't take the whole ship by yourself."

"Nyet, but I can go down fighting, da?" She let loose a roar of gunfire into the bulkhead behind Simon and Mike, too keep their heads low, he guessed. As water splashed his back from the holes, Simon bit back a curse. *No,* he realized, *not the bulkhead, the* aquarium.

Simon leapt over the table and landed atop another. A glance behind him showed that Rastar and Eric had just begun to come through the hatch. Behind them, dozens of holes leaked water, and the entire crystoplass wall was stared and cracked. The aquarium wall shattered. A wall of water -- filled with one very irate Arcavian Fighting Eel -- washed across the lounge. Much of it went right out the door and carried Rastar and Eric with it. Mike gave a shriek as the water dragged him away as well. Simon clung to the top of the table as the water lifted it up and then slammed it down again. He almost managed to surf the wave, but the table rolled and Simon lost his grip. The water slammed him into the bar, where he clung desperately as the water surged through the room.

Simon bounced to his feet as soon as the water began to recede. He waded through the water to the back door and palmed it open. The surge of dirty water spilled into the corridor beyond, but no gunfire came to meet him. The back door led directly to a set of corridors that connected with the bridge lift, the rear airlock, and the passenger quarters. She could reach the rest of the ship, through going up or down, as well, but Simon felt that she wouldn't. She'd chosen this exit for a reason... just as she'd chosen her other actions with caution and care. *She even got close to me to find out what I knew,* he thought, *and to turn me against the rest of the crew.*

That thought galled him and as he drew his pistol from his back holster, his knuckles were white from the clench. He had trusted her... and she'd manipulated that trust to endanger people who had deserved better from him. She had manipulated him into the position where he had no choice but to kill Crowe.

Simon stalked forward, pistol at the low ready. Some part of him wanted nothing more than to shoot Elena down like the murderess deserved. *This is not me,* he thought, *I care about law and order, right and wrong,* Justice, *not vengeance.*

He forced himself to take calm breaths. Memories of his training at the Confederation Security Bureau's Academy on Greenfall came back to him. Oaths, which had seemed so important then, seemed so abstract and distant now. Elena was a killer, worse, she was one who had the law on her side, she *had* killed criminals. That didn't make it right, but it made it legal, if she could prove that she had done so in the performance of her bounty contracts. But now, with the whole ship against her, what would she do?

Hide, Simon thought, *that's what the guilty always try to do...* hide. He gave a quick nod, if she'd chosen this exit for a reason, it was because it was the shortest route to the rear airlock. From there, she could work her way along the outside of the ship to the Wrethe Prowler. She could secure the small craft and hold it against attacks until they reached civilized space. With a radio, she could make her case to whatever authorities they met. *An outsider, who didn't know the exact circumstances... they might rule in her favor or at least give her a chance to escape,* he thought.

He hurried along the corridor to the rear airlock, pistol held low. He stopped outside. The inner hatch still lay open, she hadn't yet cycled it. Simon brought his pistol up, no longer filled with rage, but willing to use lethal force to stop her. He felt his heart beat faster, he had already taken one person's life today... would he add another to that tally?

A cold prick of metal against his throat made him freeze. "Simon," Elena purred, "A shame you got caught up in all this, you're the only one who doesn't deserve to die." She pressed against him, hard and angular in an armored vacuum suit as she reached around him and pulled the gun from his fingers.

Simon felt sweat bead his forehead. "If you planned to kill me, you would have done it already."

She gave a slight chuckle as she backed away. A glance

over his shoulder showed she had his pistol aimed at him. She also wore Ghost's armor. "I didn't plan any of this last part... well, not except as an emergency contingency. My plan was to get the others to turn on one another, let the criminals do the work, da? You all surprised me, really, both with how thoroughly you searched, and at how you refused to fight among yourselves."

"What can I say, honor among thieves?"

"Ha, very amusing," Elena said. "Into the airlock." He walked forward. As he did, he saw a device, with a number of wires and plastic containers, all lashed together with tape, was attached to the outer airlock door. *Great,* he thought, *Eric and Pixel have been at it again.* She saw the expression on his face. "Da, it seems that Mike's telltales were a bit more... thorough than I'd like. But you have explosives knowledge, so you will fix it." She sighed, "Really, I wish I could have brought you in on this..."

"Murder, mayhem, extortion?"

"No." She toggled the inner airlock door closed. "A big payday for making the universe a better place, erasing scum that don't deserve to live. You read those bounties... Anubus alone is a threat that shouldn't be allowed to live. He has killed hundreds, Simon, *hundreds.* Eric is a killer, he's killed cops, bounty-hunters, mercs... you don't get a bounty like his from being a mall cop, either, whatever 'private security' stuff he did, it was dirty." She locked the inner hatch.

Simon's stomach roiled, yet some part of him understood her. Anubus was a threat, he would agree, and Eric's shady past bothered him too... but not enough to murder them, not in cold blood. "What about Crowe, why kill him?"

She chuckled, "I didn't kill Crowe, remember? That was all you."

"Answer the question," Simon growled.

"Get to work on your friends' toy first," she said. She tossed him a multi-tool.

Simon knelt down and began his examination. Pixel and Eric were what he would term 'talented amateurs' which meant, in reality, that they were more dangerous to experts than other experts. Expert explosives handlers did things carefully, by the book, and they basically put things together to a standard, every time. This thing looked like Pixel and Eric had cobbled it together from whatever scraps they found lying around. "I'm not sure that I *can* disarm this," Simon said.

"Stop stalling, da?" Elena said. Simon slowly began to trace wires through the mess. She seemed to take that for a sign of effort. "Crowe was special. You think the bounty on your friend Rastar is high? The various bounties on Crowe tally far more. And for the item he stole... priceless, you said earlier. An apt description, especially when you consider who he stole it from."

"The alien device?" Simon asked absently.

"Key," Elena answered, "Which is all *he* told me. But that's enough, I think, to know that the powerful man he stole it from wants it back."

"There wasn't anything about a bounty on Crowe," Simon said. He traced another wire and he suddenly felt sick to his stomach. *That's just the kind of harebrained idea that Pixel would come up with,* he thought. He rubbed some residue on his fingers and then sniffed at it.

"Da, I delete it before I copy chip to him," Elena responded. "He suspected, anyway, but that is only to be expected. And before you get all weepy over him, he worked deal with Ghost, back aboard the *Sao Martino*. Planned to sell all of us out, tried to have me convince Eric to kill Ariadne before they stormed the bridge."

Simon paused, multi-tool out, ready to crimp a wire. "Really?" He looked over his shoulder at her, "He wanted to kill Ariadne?" He didn't feel so bad about killing the other man suddenly.

Elena gave him a shrug, "Truthfully, I went along with this too, she's a threat, dangerous, violent. Her attitude is a sham, she's as dangerous as the rest. But yes, Crowe wanted her dead and he sought to use Eric to do it."

Simon turned back to the device. He thought he had it

569

figured out. Though, to be honest, he wasn't certain if he *really* wanted to do what he was about to do. Then again, the woman was a killer. "Clever of you to take Ghost's suit, you must have stashed it down here before you killed Illario, probably hidden in one of the rooms you helped to search. You seem pretty certain about getting out there. You heard Pixel though, the Prowler is jammed into the hull, you can't escape that way. Hell, you're not even a pilot, are you?"

"Lets just say I kept some secrets to myself, da?" Elena smirked. "Besides, Pixel doesn't know military tech. Most military light craft have explosive charges to sever their docking clamps in case of emergency. It'll make landing a bit difficult, but it gives me an out... and I can always leave a little present. Pixel may not have mentioned the two pocket nukes in its bomb racks, but I saw them as well."

"You'd destroy the ship?" Simon asked.

"Only if you force me. There's little profit in it," Elena said. "I can't collect on any of the others if you're all vaporized, after all."

"Right, that would put a damper on your bank account," Simon said dryly. His fingers found what he sought and he began to work. "We can't have that."

"Simon, I don't want to have to kill anyone else, I didn't intend to kill Illario, though I can't say I regret it. Your companions... well, any that get in my way at this point become a threat and I'll deal with them as such," Elena said coldly.

"Like Bastien?" Simon asked. She didn't answer. "You know, I think a bounty hunter can get away with killing a criminal like Illario on accident... but what about killing a well known xenoarcheologist? I mean, I understand *why* you had to do it. Clearly you and Crowe needed someone to find out what they could about the artifact. He knew too much about your involvement with Crowe, so he had to die."

"You assume it wasn't Crowe who killed him," Elena hedged.

"No. We already knew they had dealings," Simon said. He had almost completed the connections and he really hoped that he wasn't wrong with his guess. "Hell, half the ship knew we were searching for that artifact, which I'm sure you have tucked away in your suit there. Crowe wouldn't care what the doctor could tell us. *You* on the other hand, didn't want the doctor mentioning your partnership. You murdered an innocent man... how will that go down back at Tannis?"

"In some circles, it would heighten my reputation," She said.

"I imagine that's true, in some circles. Especially if you're the type who takes shady contracts. I'm thinking that your shiny little bounty-hunter badge wouldn't protect you from murder charges, though," Simon said. He turned away from the hatch and faced her. "How would that work out for you? I know cops don't fare well in prison, bounty-hunters must have an even worse time."

"Is this supposed to scare me? If so, you failed. Now stop wasting my time and disable the bomb," Elena said.

"Too late for that," Simon said, then ducked to the side and crouched, with his hands over his ears, his eyes closed, and his mouth open to equalize pressure.

He had timed it just perfectly. The detonation of the device was a solid blow that punted him against the wall like an angry Ghornath. Simon shook his head against the dizziness and disorientation, and crawled towards where Elena lay. The ringing in his ears meant he couldn't hear whatever she shouted as she flailed around on the deck. She tried to squint and aim through dazzled eyes, luckily she aimed in the wrong direction.

Simon managed to grab her gun hand as she flailed and pry the gun out of her fingers. She tried to punch at him, so he put that arm in a wrist lock and rolled her onto her stomach. He pulled her other arm up behind her and sat on her back. She thrashed under him, until he levered both arms up. She lay still then, though from the movement of her mouth she was either cursing him or trying to bribe him.

A few minutes later, Pixel managed to open the hatch. Simon stared at the array of weapons aimed in their direction. "Investigation's complete," he said. "You can take her away."

***

Several hours later, Simon sat on the ruined couch in front of the gaping aquarium wall. He held a cloth with ice cubes to his forehead and hoped that the headache would ease. The damp air still carried the strong smell of fish and he could hear people's feet squish in the sodden carpet of the lounge.

"Simon," Mike said. His voice seemed at once both distant and far too loud for the throbbing in Simon's head.

"Captain," Simon said. He looked over to see Anubus and Eric flanked the short Captain. He rose to unsteadily to his feet, "Anubus, Eric." Eric gave him a nod, Anubus just stared at him with dark, unfathomable eyes

"I figured we needed to discuss what to do with the prisoner... and that you might have some thoughts on that," Mike said. "We've got Rastar with her for now."

"Why not just lock her up?" Simon asked. He felt far too tired to have this discussion. What he really wanted was to sleep, but the headache had made that impossible. Run had also mentioned a concussion and that sleep would likely lead to "involuntary self termination."

"Pixel can rig up one of the supply closets to keep her contained," Mike said. "The issue is," Mike glanced around to make sure that no one had come close enough to overhear, "she's dangerous, especially after we hit civilized space."

"She's a murderer, probably a sociopath, too," Simon said. "Of course she's dangerous. That's what prison is for."

"She knows too much about us," Mike said. "Particularly those bounties. There are military ships that would go rogue for the chance to cash in on those. Plus, there's whatever bounty that was on Crowe and *this*." Mike held up the small black and green alien artifact. "For that matter, she can spin the story her way and she's got a bit of authority behind her words, especially against a bunch of fugitives."

Simon realized that Eric and Anubus were here because they had, potentially, the most to lose, as well as the least moral compunction about murdering to keep their secrets. *I guess I wasn't far off in my estimates after all,* he thought, *at least Mike is just here thinking about his crew.* Simon shrugged, "Well, at least we're headed for the Nova Roma Empire."

"Why does that matter?" Anubus snarled.

Simon looked between him and Eric, "For one thing, they don't accept bounty-hunters. For another, they have self defense laws which allow people there to protect themselves. For a third, they're enemies of most of the Colonial Republic, so your own wanted nature wouldn't matter to them." He met Eric's eyes, "And last, they don't extradite anyone. They also have various disagreements with the Centauri Confederation and the Tau Ceti Separatists. So you needn't worry about their government taking an interest in your bounty. For that matter, *Rastar's* insanely large bounty."

"That doesn't settle the issue," Eric said. "If she talks as smoothly to them as she did to us..."

"Then it will be her story against the crew, the passengers, and even your squeeze, the Nova Roma Ambassador," Simon said, tiredly. "But let me put it this way. If she dies, even 'attempting escape' then it looks like we had some kind of conspiracy going on to silence witnesses. Most customs officials will have all those same bounties in their logs. You murder her to keep that information quiet and you'll buy yourself only a few days or hours of silence. You turn her over to the authorities for murder... well, then you might get some good will instead."

Mike gave him a nod, "True enough." Eric looked conflicted, but he gave a nod as well. Anubus just seemed angry and sullen. *Then again,* Simon thought, *Anubus is always angry and sullen, unless he's killing someone.* "Right, well, we'll let you rest."

Simon eased back down to the couch. A moment later, Pixel came over, "So, good work on the bomb, by the way. I'm surprised you managed to turn it into a concussion grenade so easily. How'd you recognize the magnesium phosphate?"

"I recognized the smell. Using it as an accelerator for the other stuff is dangerous, you know." Simon didn't look up.

"Why did you have a bomb on the outer airlock door?"

"So that if anyone tried to open it..."

"I realize that," Simon said, his voice tired. "But if some well intentioned fellow left the inner door open, as say, a means to prevent the outer door from opening and someone outside triggered that, you could have vented the entire ship."

Pixel said, "Well, there are pressure doors that would have sealed it all off."

"Which would have, quite literally, sucked for anyone on the wrong side of the pressure door," Simon said. "Which would have included anyone sent down there to check." Pixel didn't answer. "Oh, by the way, the Prowler has some kind of emergency detach points on the docking clamps, so it's not as secure as you thought."

"Oh, I know," Pixel said. "I wasn't going to tell Anubus that, though."

"Probably a good idea," Simon said. He frowned again. "What about the two nukes on it?"

"Oh, I pulled some components, those are safely disarmed. You can't leave them together too long anyway. They're fission warheads, and some components deteriorate on long term exposure to radiation," Pixel said. "Mike has the key parts on lock-down."

Simon wasn't certain he trusted even Mike with those, but he felt better knowing that the engineer didn't have direct access. Simon sat in silence for a bit longer, until Pixel spoke again. "So, I was wondering..."

"Yes?" Simon asked.

"Why didn't you take Elena's offer?" Pixel asked. "I mean, she said that box was worth over a hundred million. Even split two ways, that's a considerable chunk of change. All you would have had to do was... let her go."

Simon frowned, "I would say that it's the principle of the thing, that she's a murderer and she deserves punishment for it. I would say that I couldn't trust her to keep her word. I would even say that I signed that charter and I'm part of this crew now." He paused, "But honestly, I couldn't hear a damned thing until

574

long after you guys dragged her off." He frowned, "I like to think I wouldn't have taken the offer for those other reasons, but who knows?" A part of him thought of another reason, the woman that he'd started to dream about... even if she, too, might be a murderer.

"Huh," Pixel said. "Okay, I've got one last question for you... and since you're the man that shot Crowe, I'd figure you would have the best opinion." Pixel took a deep breath. "So I was thinking about that nanotechnology. And I wondered... what if Crowe had more than one dose?"

"What?" Simon asked.

"Well, if the nanotechnology had some kind of controls that he could interface with... well, then he could really get creative with it. He could have dosed his decoy with one injection, to change his appearance and make him think he was Crowe... but then he could have injected someone else with it so that they thought they were Crowe. From what Run said, it would only last a short time, maybe a few days, but that would be long enough to act as a second decoy."

"Or to fake his death... *again.*" Simon said. He shook his head, "That's a very disturbing idea."

"Yeah," Pixel said. He glanced at the shattered aquarium. "Well, I just wanted to make sure that our lead investigator was on it."

He left before Simon could think up a proper response.

###

Crossed Stars
The Renegades
by Kal Spriggs

Ariadne walked down the corridor and then paused at the hatch for the ladder well that led up towards the second deck and the lounge. She frowned at the red indicator lights for a long moment. *Why,* she thought, *is this ladder locked down?*

Realization struck her as she heard the slosh of water on the other side of the hatch. "Right," she muttered, "Rainbow, how could I forget?" The shootout in the lounge had flooded the chamber. Most of the water had gone out the door and down the open hatch across from it, where Eric and Rastar had just come from. The wall of water had washed Mike, Eric, Rastar, and Rainbow, the Arcavian Fighting Eel, down the ladder. Fortunately, the lower hatch door was closed and the water hadn't spread over the next floor down. Most of second deck was still damp and since they had nowhere else to put the eel, Rainbow stayed in that ladder well.

Ariadne shook her head. She really didn't know how she could have forgotten. Still, at least she had remembered to have Pixel lock down the hatch, just in case. Ariadne turned away from the hatch and walked down the corridor, head down, as she mentally cataloged all her duties as the ship's executive officer.

Mike meant well, when he took her aside and gave her the list, she knew. Even so, the fact that he had needed to meant that she had failed... and that *Mike,* as Captain, thought she had failed. That last part hurt, especially in conjunction with the fact that they had yet to figure out the myriad arrangements, deals, and agreements which Crowe seemed to have created. In some cases, such as the war journalist Valeria Zita, he had apparently promised full crew interviews in Mike's name. In others, such as the Nova Roma Ambassador, he had traded information, goods, and favors. All of this had gone on under her nose, a fact which, if Crowe were around, she was certain he would have found hilarious.

Worse, in some ways, was how embarrassed she felt in front of some of the other crew. How could they trust her after such a series of complete failures?

She literally ran into someone just outside the ship's lift. She stumbled back a bit but his arm caught her before she could fall. Ariadne met the calm brown eyes of Simon and she felt a flush rise on her cheeks. *Great,* she thought, *not only do I look incompetent but I also look like I'm too overwhelmed to even walk around by myself.*

She could feel his emotions, too, because he stood so close and his emotions were so strong: irritation, anger, and frustration. She didn't need to be a mind-reader to realize that she *must* be the target of those emotions. He'd had them ever since the business with Crowe and Elena. She realized that he still held onto her, even after she had regained her balance. "Uh, hi Simon," Ariadne said, even as she cursed the awkward tone in her voice.

He seemed to notice that he still held her arm and he let go suddenly, "Hello, Ariadne." This was the closest they'd been in the past week. She had wondered if he'd been avoiding her and now she knew.

"Going up to the bridge?" Ariadne asked. She resisted the urge to violate his privacy and read his thoughts, to see exactly what he thought of her. In part, because it would have been wrong, but also because she wasn't sure she could take that.

"Yes," he nodded. He seemed unable to say anything else, though he finally opened his mouth as the lift doors opened. Whatever he was about to say, he changed his mind and waved her forward. Ariadne restrained a sigh as she stepped into the lift and pushed the button for the bridge. He followed her and a moment later the lift doors slid closed behind him. They stood in awkward silence for a long moment. She could smell his scent, a combination of gun oil and gunpowder from his archaic pistol. Finally, however, Simon gave a snort of laughter. Ariadne couldn't help but frown. *He finds me funny, does he?*

He caught the look on her face, "I'm not laughing at you, Ariadne. Just the situation." He turned and met her gaze with his chocolate brown eyes. She deliberately tightened down her psychic abilities, she didn't want to feel those emotions directed at her. For that matter she didn't want to feel her own emotions at the moment. He took a deep breath, "Look, there's something I need to say..."

The lift doors opened and Rastar and Eric stepped in, "Hey guys!" Rastar said. He had large wooden crate under each of his four arms, "How goes?"

"Fine," Ariadne said sharply. She was partially thankful for the interruption. In all likelihood, given Simon's apparent feelings about her, it was best that she have some time to compose herself fully before he spoke. Assuming, of course, that he refrained from speaking in front of the others.

Really, she shouldn't be so affected by his opinion of her, she knew. The problem was, she had begun to see him differently, right up until he went into attack mode back on the bridge.

Eric gave both of them a nod and then continued with his conversation with Rastar, "So as I see it, really, the Mod Twelve is the best design. It incorporates more capabilities and situational awareness, you literally can't miss—"

"My god, is everyone talking about how I missed Elena and Crowe?!" Ariadne snapped. "I messed up, I'm sorry, okay?" She heard her voice climb at the end and realized that she'd let her temper fray dangerously. As if on cue, she smelled burning hair.

"What?" Eric asked. His voice was filled with confusion. "I was just talking about sniper scopes…"

The lift doors opened and Ariadne stormed past him. Her eyes filled with tears and she barely heard Rastar's confused voice behind her, "I guess she's not a fan of Centauri Arms either, Eric."

"Ariadne, wait," Simon said. She glanced over her shoulder to see him try to push through Eric and Rastar, but the doors closed before he could.

"Ariadne, are you okay?" a voice asked from nearby.

She turned and found Mandy and Miranda. The two women had just come out of the crew quarters. "I'm *fine*," Ariadne said. She took a deep breath, and forced her anger aside, "Just a little stressed, but thank you for asking."

Mandy opened her mouth, a look of confusion on her face, but Miranda nudged her, "Right, well, if you want to talk, you know where to find us." The slight smirk on her face forced Ariadne to step on her anger again. "We'll be up on the bridge, not long until we get to 567X43, right?"

Her anger drained away like the water from Rainbow's tank. "Right, not long at all now," Ariadne said, and managed to return something like a smile. No wonder they were happy. The entire ship was happy. The system they would reach, 567X43, was practically civilized space. She'd even managed to cut a few days off the travel time so they would arrive earlier than expected. In all likelihood their isolation and exile was finally at an end.

I must be the only one aboard who feels this alone, she thought. But how was that new? She had been alone since Victor betrayed her, an orphan, adrift. Why would coming back to human space change any of that for her? "Well, I'll see you later, I just remembered I needed to check something up forward," Ariadne said. She turned away from them and strode off. She needed time to collect herself, to focus, and to get her emotions under control.

She strode the mostly-empty corridors and slowly picked away at her emotions. She had to get to the root of what bothered her, she knew. It was a combination of Mike's instruction and everyone else's perception of her as a failure, she thought. She had failed, she should have spotted Crowe's behavior, should have been more suspicious of Elena. For that matter, she should keep a sharper eye on all the crew, she knew.

A hatch opened to her left and Pixel stepped out. "Hey, Ariadne," Pixel said, "You looking for me?" He had smudges of dirt and grease on his face and he wiped his hands with a dirty rag before stuffing it into a pocket.

Ariadne gave him a polite smile, "No, just doing the rounds. We'll be emerging in 567X43 in just a little while, I'm just letting everyone know."

"Yeah, that's good to know," Pixel said. "I just finished calibrating the sensors. Simon said he was getting an odd flicker when he rand diagnostics, so that should be fixed, if you could let him and Mike know."

"Yeah, sure," Ariadne said weakly. The last person she wanted to talk to was Simon.

"Oh and I think I saw Run up forward a bit," Pixel yawned. "I think I'm actually going to go get some sleep. See you later, Ariadne."

She gave him a wave and continued down the corridor. She continued to pick at the complex tangle of her emotions. Pixel at least, didn't show any signs that he didn't trust her. For that matter, Eric and Rastar hadn't, she realized. So why did she feel the crew hated her?

Not the crew, she realized, *just one person... Simon.* Ariadne reached the end of the corridor and toggled open the hatch. She didn't close it behind her as she stepped into the dark storage space. She leaned against the cool metal bulkhead and struggled through her emotions. Ariadne felt like she'd let the crew down, true enough, but none of them seemed too angry about it, no one besides Simon. Simon had avoided her since he revealed the wanted notices he found on Crowe's computer. Simon had fairly blazed with frustration and irritation when she ran into him. Simon was the one person who she wanted to like her, to *respect* her.

As if on cue, a figure stood silhouetted in the open hatch. "Ariadne?" Simon asked.

Why couldn't she get away from him? "What?" She asked, her voice flat.

She heard him sigh, "Look, Ariadne, I need to talk to you. Pixel said he saw you headed down this way, so..."

"Oh, he says he re-calibrated the forward sensors," Ariadne said woodenly. She gave him the obvious out to avoid the coming confrontation. Of course, she didn't need to be a psychic to know he wouldn't take it, not after following her the length of the ship.

"Yes, he told me that as well," Simon said. "But, look, I've needed to say this for the past week. I don't know how you're going to react to it, so I'm just going to talk, okay?"

"Go ahead," Ariadne said and choked down her own emotions.

"Look, Ariadne," Simon sighed. "I know that you must be angry with me, about what I accused you of on the bridge. I know we've all been under a lot of stress." He paused and Ariadne braced herself for his next words. "So... I want to apologize," Simon said, his voice level.

"What?" Ariadne asked in surprise.

"It was rude of me to drag everyone's pasts up in that fashion. I need to apologize to everyone, really, but I wanted to apologize to you first," Simon let out a deep breath and then snorted, "You haven't made this easy, you know?"

"Me?" Ariadne demanded. "*You* are the one walking around as a tangled ball of negative emotions and avoiding me for the last week. I thought *you* were angry with *me*." She felt a surge of irritation. What was it with men?

Simon looked surprised, "Oh. Honestly, I just figured you knew what I wanted to say and you were making me sweat." He took a deep breath, "Then again, you've respected our mental privacy, so I shouldn't have made that assumption." Simon snorted, "Well, now I doubly feel like an idiot."

Ariadne felt her irritation drain away. "You aren't an idiot," she said.

"Well, anyway, I wanted to apologize," Simon said, and his chocolate brown eyes met her gaze levelly. "Because you have been honest with me from the beginning and because I *should* have trusted you. And part of the reason I've found it so hard to apologize is... well, I respect you. More than that... I really care what you think about me."

"You do?" Ariadne felt a loose, fluttery feeling in her stomach.

"Yeah," Simon looked away and in the dim lighting of the compartment, she could barely see the flush climb his cheeks. "I'd say it was friendship, but it's something more than that for me." He paused and she could see him fumble for words. He stepped closer, within arms reach, and he spoke softly and slowly, "I'm interested in you, Ariadne, and I wanted to see if you feel the same."

"Oh," Ariadne said. She felt completely blindsided. "Here, I thought you hated me…" She let out a snort of laughter herself. "Well, now I feel like an idiot."

"So is that a 'yes' or a 'no' or something else altogether?" Simon asked.

"That's a 'let's get to know one another better and see where it goes,'" Ariadne answered. "But, there is one thing I want to do…" She leaned forward. Her lips found his just as the ship made its transition from shadow space. The world seemed to lurch for a moment and both of them stumbled back.

The intercom crackled to life. "All crew report to the bridge," Mike said.

Ariadne saw a look of frustration flash across Simon's face. "That's terrible timing," he said.

"The worst," Ariadne said, just before alarms began to wail.

The End
The Renegades continues with Renegades: Out of the Cold

About the Author

Kal Spriggs started reading science fiction and fantasy in elementary school. Eventually he was the only eight year old with permission from the local public library to check out books from the adult section because he'd read everything else. He's written ever since he started running out of 'good' stuff to read when he was twelve, although he likes to think his writing has improved, if only slightly. His range of interests has since expanded to include computer and console games, tabletop RPGs, and strategy games.

An Army brat born overseas, Kal was born with a wanderlust to see what lies over the next horizon. Kal visited 22 countries on five continents before he turned 25, and hopes to add many more to the list, as well as revisit some of his favorite places. Spriggs loves to ski, hike, fish, and camp, especially in the Rocky Mountains where he spent much of his childhood.

Kal Spriggs is a graduate of the United States Merchant Marine Academy with an engineering degree. He followed in his parents' footsteps and joined the US Army after graduation and currently serves as an active duty Engineer captain. As well as earning a masters degree in environmental engineering, he's been deployed to both Afghanistan and Iraq.

Made in the USA
San Bernardino, CA
24 July 2014